LEGACY OF THE SHADOW'S BLOOD

LEGACY OF THE SHADOW'S BLOOD

LEGACY OF THE SHADOW'S BLOOD™ BOOK 1

E.G. BATEMAN

MICHAEL ANDERLE

LMBPN Publishing
PMB 196, 2540 South Maryland Pkwy
Las Vegas, NV 89109

First US edition, April 2020
Version 1.02, June 2020
eBook ISBN: 978-1-64202-866-9
Print ISBN: 978-1-64202-867-6

THE LEGACY OF THE SHADOW'S BLOOD TEAM

Thanks to our Beta Readers:

Erika Everest, Nicole Emens, Jim Caplan, Mary Morris, John Ashmore, Kelly O'Donnell, Larry Omans, Michael Baumann

Thanks to our JIT Team:

Dave Hicks
Deb Mader
Debi Sateren
Diane L. Smith
Dorothy Lloyd
Erika Everest
Jackey Hankard-Brodie
James Caplan
Jeff Eaton
Jeff Goode
John Ashmore
Lori Hendricks
Micky Cocker

Misty Roa
Paul Westman
Peter Manis
Rachel Beckford
Veronica Stephan-Miller

Editor
SkyHunter Editing Team

CHAPTER ONE

"Two Eighteen… Two Nineteen…"

Lexi walked along the balcony of the seedy Palm Springs motel and spun the room key around her finger as she counted off room numbers. She stopped, turned, and looked over the balcony and down toward the office.

Yep, the twerpy admin guy was checking out her leather-clad ass.

She gave him her best I-will-cut-you stare. He did a one-eighty and walked away from the window.

Smart man.

As she continued past the rooms, a car moved along slowly below her and matched her speed. She stopped at a door and raised her hand without bothering to look down, and the vehicle pulled into a parking space directly beneath the room.

When she'd opened the door, Lexi assessed the space. They usually stayed in shitty hotels but Dolores had outdone herself booking this one. It was super-shitty.

"Wow! This one's super-shitty." Scott materialized at her shoulder and voiced her thoughts.

Lexi jerked to the side and her head snapped toward him.

"Holy crap, can you *not* do that?"

He raised his arms. "What? You want me to walk up the stairs with these bags?" His wavy blond hair flopped into his eyes and he blew it away.

"Just…" She drew in a measured breath before she puffed it out. "Announce yourself." Her glance swept around. "And be more careful in public."

She could feel his shrug. "I *was* being careful. I waited until you scared the office guy away with your…you know, *face*."

He tried to shuffle past her to enter the room, but she blocked his path with an upraised arm.

"I have to check it's safe first." Lexi pulled a blade from…well, no one was ever quite sure where they came from, and that was how she liked it.

"Oh, right, of course." He vanished from beside her and appeared inside the room. He dropped the bags and reappeared beside her again, dusted his right sleeve, and picked distractedly at a thread. He looked up and made a shooing motion with his left hand. "Okay, go ahead." He returned his attention to the errant thread.

She stared at him, then closed her eyes. A succession of tiny jerks of her head coincided with the multitude of responses her brain flicked through and discarded. Most of them involved breaking bones. She opened her eyes, sighed, and moved inside.

Lexi walked through the room. There wasn't much to search. Two single beds stood on the left, a dresser and mirror on the right, and a door directly ahead. She opened it and stuck her head into the bathroom but pulled it back sharply and wondered, based on the overpowering smell of bleach, if she'd found a murder room.

Quickly closing the bathroom door, she turned to the motel room doorway to find it empty. A further turn revealed Scott lying on one of the beds and her eyes narrowed.

"It's safe, you can come in," she snarked.

His green eyes looked left, then right as if searching for a successful excuse, and he finally looked at her with a small grin. "Oh, sorry."

As he shifted, a spring pinged loudly. They looked at each other and simultaneously rolled their eyes. He opened the top drawer in the bedside table, pulled out a Gideon Bible, and felt around it. Finding nothing else, he returned the book and closed the drawer. "It smells funny in here. Kind of like vomit—if a dead person threw up."

"If we're lucky, we will get the job finished today and we won't have to be the main course in this revolting bugfest of a room tonight." Lexi lifted the rest of the bags onto the other bed.

"How do you want to handle it?" Scott swung his feet onto the floor and stood his duffel between his knees.

"Dolores is still gathering info, but the businesswoman being harassed for protection money wants it dealt with rapidly and quietly. I think this will be a quick in-and-out."

"She's a shifter, though, right? I don't understand why she doesn't get the pack to deal with it." Scott pulled underpants from his bag and sniffed them.

Lexi looked away with a shudder. "According to Dolores, the client doesn't want to involve the pack."

Scott raised an eyebrow. "In my experience, involving you won't necessarily make things any quieter."

"This is only our third job together. You don't have enough experience to make a judgment. Anyhow, this might simply require subtle negotiation." She pulled her cosmetics bag out and dropped it on the bed. Even with her back to him, she could still feel him staring at her. "What?" She turned to scowl at him. "I can be subtle."

He nodded as though he agreed. "So that's what you think will happen?"

"No. I'll find the gang, smack them around for a while, break some stuff, and make an example out of one or two of them, then get the hell out of this shithole." She snatched her cosmetics bag up and took a step toward the bathroom.

"What about the local resource?" he asked.

She halted and turned. "What local resource?"

"Oh, I might have forgotten to mention we got an update." He grinned awkwardly.

Lexi stared at him while she counted in her head. "Perhaps you should fill me in." She could feel her eyebrow twitching.

"What would you like to know?" he asked, picked his cell phone up, and tapped in a code.

Rather than respond immediately, she gritted her teeth, then forced her jaw to relax. "You can start by telling me *who* our local resource is."

Scott scrolled through his phone. "I'm checking. It's a private investigator. Oh!"

She sent a prayer up. *Lord, give me patience, and I want it now.* "What?"

His mouth opened once, shut again, then opened a second time. "Well, you've worked with him before. He has a *great* track record."

Lexi took the few steps necessary to close the motel room's door. "I'm not playing Twenty Questions, Scott," she stated as she turned the paltry lock. "Who is it?"

"William Levin." He swallowed.

She spun to face him, a question written on her face. "William? I haven't worked with—" Her face lost the question. "Levin? *Dick* Levin?"

He ignored her as he read the file on the phone. "It says here he gets results."

"What else does it say?" She leaned against the dresser and folded her arms, waiting while he read.

"It says you tried to kill him six…" He looked up. "You tried to kill him six times? *How* is he not dead?"

"He is." She sighed and pushed away from the dresser. "What are Dolores's other notes?"

"She wrote that one at the top of the file. I think it was supposed to remind her to keep the two of you away from each other."

"Get her on the phone." Lexi shook her head.

Scott put a hand up. "I can't. There's no signal. Hang on, I'm still reading." He paused for a moment to decipher the hen scratches. "There's a note at the bottom. It says, 'Alexa, there's no one else. Suck it up, and don't try to kill him again.'" His gaze darted to her. "Hey, your name's Alexa? Like the music thing?"

She pointed at him. "You are never to call me that. I'll be talking to Dolores about this."

He continued reading as he asked his questions. "So, what's wrong with this Dick guy—and if his name's William, why do you call him 'Dick?'"

"It would be faster to ask what's right with him. He's rude, arrogant, dishonest, a monumental pain in the ass, and I'm sure you'll get the name eventually."

His finger pushed the display up to see more of the file information. "Yeah, but you can't kill a guy for that. And how come you keep *failing* to kill him?"

"He's a vamp. They're hard to kill." Lexi shook her head in disgust.

Scott sat up. "He is? I love vamps. They're so interesting. They know stuff from, like, the past." He could see she wasn't feeling the love, so he returned his focus to his cell.

"How many vamps have you met?" she asked as she sat on the corner of her bed.

"A few." He waved his hand in a vague manner.

She stared at him and held it relentlessly.

"Okay, one. I've met one vampire. But he was one of the old ones, hundreds of years old and really interesting. Anyway, I still don't understand why Dick's not dead. I haven't seen you fail to kill anything yet."

Lexi looked around and located a new remote that apparently went with the old-as-hell tv. She picked it up. It was light—no batteries, obviously. She returned it to the dresser and turned her attention to Scott again. "Well, this vamp doesn't know when to keep his mouth shut. At least you two will have that in common."

"It'll be fine. We probably won't even see much of him."

"I wonder what he's doing here? I thought he was based in Chicago." She spoke more to herself than to Scott.

"So, tell me more. You don't talk about yourself much."

She sighed. "My last partner died under horrible circumstances. I try not to get too close."

"Really? Wow! Because Dolores told me you didn't work with a partner before me." He smirked.

Thanks, Dolores.

"Well? What happened between the two of you?" Scott put his cell phone down, which signaled that he now gave her his undivided attention.

Lexi deliberated on how much to tell him and decided a fairly short version would be for the best. "After I left Kindred, they hired him to find me, which he did. At the time, I was beating the snot out of a nasty little witch. She'd cursed a girl with the misfortune of liking the same guy that she did. Then he—"

"What kind of curse?" he interrupted.

"The girl's hair and teeth had fallen out." She took a silver-tipped shuriken out and began to rotate the little four-bladed throwing star between her fingers like a fidget spinner.

"Gross." He screwed his face up in disgust.

"It wasn't only her looks. The curse had aged her from the inside out and her heart was failing. It was a death sentence."

"Did you make her reverse the spell?"

"She said it wasn't possible. Shouldn't you already know this stuff?" Lexi stopped spinning. She was genuinely surprised by Scott's question.

"You know witchcraft is different than the sorcery I practice. There are all kinds of magic and I don't know them all intimately. That's why I'm asking. If I had cast a spell to do that, I could undo it. I've no idea how she did it. It probably involved chicken guts and dirt or something." He shuddered.

"I told her to find a way to stop it or I'd come back and kill her. As I walked away, she threw something at me. I'd sensed something was coming and ducked out of the way, just as Dick appeared from nowhere and pulled me in the opposite direction. I almost took his head off, I was so pissed." She shook her head at the memory.

"What did she throw? Did it hit you?"

"It was a spell pouch. It hit Dick and burst on him with a poof." Her hands sprang open.

"Gross! What was in it? Did it do anything?" He took a book from his bag and put it on the dresser.

"It smelled like mouse droppings and it really messed his Gucci suit up. Otherwise, it did nothing. God knows what it would have done to me." She shuddered.

"What did you do to the witch?"

"I took her head off and dropped her into the river. Dick bitched about his suit all the way to the nearest bar. We sat, and he told me he'd been hired by Kindred to track me. I told him why I left them, and he agreed to give me a head start. Then he went straight back to them and told them where I was. It was close. They almost caught me, but that was the day I met Dolores. I still can't believe my luck. She got me out and I've worked for her ever since."

"What about Dick? You tried *six* times?" Scott leaned forward, engrossed in the story.

"After the dust settled, I spent a few days tracking him. I threw silver knives and tried to drop a silver net on him, but he's a slippery fucker, so I kept losing him. I finally managed to surprise him coming out of a jazz club, and I broke his neck and dragged him into an alley. I intended to finish him off, but I decided it would be worse for him to wake up in a dumpster."

"Worse than death?" He looked doubtful.

"You'll get it when you meet him. He's a real snob. I'm kind of surprised he's prepared to work with me. And I'm damned unhappy about working with him."

He picked the phone up and scrolled further. "Well, Dolores trusts him and I trust Dolores. It says here he'll meet us at sundown."

"What's the update on the job? Why do we need Dick the Douche?"

Scott read the details to her. "Kate. Shifter female. Owns a bar down the street from here. It says, 'further information is now being sought from a local contact.' We need to speak to Dick before we see the client. Then it confirms what Dolores already told us—that her business is being targeted by local thugs. That's funny, I thought shifters *were* the local thugs."

"Don't be a bigot. I've met some good shifters this last year." She turned her attention to his phone and raised an eyebrow. "How are you reading that if there's no signal?"

"I downloaded the file from the server, duh!" He spoke slowly as though it should have been apparent.

"You keep operational data on your cell phone? What if someone gets hold of that thing?"

He snickered. "No one will ever get hold of my cell phone," he assured her and tossed it on the bed. "I'll get the rest of the gear." He vanished.

Lexi walked to the bed and was tempted to pick the device up. As she closed her hand around it, though, it vanished. She strode to the window and stared at him as he waved it at her.

She rolled her eyes and turned to the room.

Her first decision was to claim the bed closest to the entrance. When she looked at the distance between the door and Scott's bed, she confirmed that the only way someone would get to him while he slept would be through her. No one would complete that journey.

That settled, she looked around the room for the AC control and concluded that the hole in the wall near the door was where the switch should be. This would be an uncomfortable night.

Standing in front of the mirror, Lexi flicked her gaze to the door but there was no sign of Scott. She slipped a small glass vial from her pocket and placed it on the dresser before she turned her attention to the mirror. Quickly, she drew loose hairs back into her long, brown ponytail, which revealed a shaved undercut. Then, allowing her face to screw up in discomfort, she shuffled the girls around in her leather vest.

"If Dick won't appear before sundown, let's get something to eat," Scott said from his bed.

Lexi jerked from the mirror, turned, and gave him the evil eye, wondering how long he'd been there.

"Sorry." He blushed.

"We passed a barbecue place down the street. Let's hit that." Lexi swept the vial deftly into her pocket and headed to the door. "Can you sort the bags out?" she asked and turned to see there were no bags in the room and no Scott.

"Done. Let's eat," he called from beside the car.

She stepped to the empty bed and swept her fingers over the cover. While she knew the bags were there, she couldn't see or feel them.

"That will always be trippy," she murmured.

CHAPTER TWO

S till a little disbelieving, Lexi stared at the mountain of rib bones on the table in front of Scott.

While he gazed around the room, she looked at his torso. There didn't seem to be an ounce of extra fat on him. When she raised her gaze to his face, he was watching her with disturbingly green eyes.

"I can't work out where you put it all." She was embarrassed that she'd been caught staring but not sure why.

"I have a fast metabolism." He gave her a dimple-popping grin and leaned forward. "I messaged Dolores, asking her to let this Dick guy know where we are."

She looked at him with her eyebrows raised.

He gave a thumbs-up. "It's okay. No one can hear us."

"I wonder what Dick can provide that we can't get ourselves?" she mused aloud. She dipped the corner of a sugar cube into her coffee, and they both watched as the coffee rose and changed the color of the sugar. After a moment, she dropped the cube into the liquid and returned her gaze to her companion.

"I guess there's no other way to get the information Dolores mentioned. Maybe *the family* is involved."

"The what?" she asked pointedly. Her teaspoon had frozen in the air above her drink.

"Sorry. I mean Kindred—maybe *Kindred* is involved"

"And why don't we refer to them as 'family?'"

Scott rolled his eyes. "Because they're not family. Not anymore."

"They never were." Lexi stirred her coffee.

He leaned back and sighed. "Don't you miss it? Being part of an organization and fighting for justice?"

"No. You know why? Because it was all lies and now, working for Dolores, I *do* fight for justice. We rescued *you*, didn't we? From Kindred, as I recall."

"Don't you think it's weird that we're more like Kindred now than when we were with them?" He smiled. "Neither of us were blood-matched before we left, and now you've got access to my magic."

Lexi shrugged. "Your only choice for matching was a psycho, and I was considered a dud as a legacy. I feel bad that you're stuck with me. If we hadn't been in a bad situation, I wouldn't have done it. At the rate you keep having to top the magic up, we'll run into problems with that."

"You're not a dud. You're faster and stronger than any regular human and I've never seen fighting skills like yours. I think we're well matched."

"Yes, but for someone with the blood of the ancient supernaturals running through my veins, I'm somewhat of a disappointment, aren't I? I don't show a clear connection to any supe. I'm not as fast as a vamp, or as strong as a shifter, nothing. I don't think they'd ever have wasted a mage on a match with me. I suppose that's why I found it so easy to leave and not look back after I discovered the truth about them."

Scott leaned forward again and investigated the ribs for meat he might have missed. "I don't believe every individual cell can be bad. Why would the whole supernatural world agree to be policed by them if the entire organization was rotten?"

"That's the problem, isn't it? We all operated in little family units with no idea what was happening in the rest of the organization. We don't even know who the Kindred council are."

"Well, my family was definitely a problem, but I never really felt I was working on the Death Star."

"I'll tell you what is a problem. Your ability to turn every conversation around to Star Wars disturbs me."

"Yeah, I know." He laughed.

Scott looked at his watch. "I wonder when he'll turn up. If this guy's local, he might have a contact who can help." He shrugged.

"Then why can't he give us the name of the contact so I can throttle them until they tell me what I want to know?" Lexi gave him a tight smile.

"Which is precisely why you don't have my contact's name. Scoot over." When she looked up, it was into Dick Levin's smug, chiseled, irritatingly handsome face.

She didn't move and made her face as impassive as possible.

The newcomer turned his face to Scott. "You'll scoot over for a weary but stunningly attractive vampire, won't you, handsome?"

"Sure." Scott moved across the bench seat to make space.

Dick unfastened the buttons on his expensive-looking suit jacket, slid into the booth, and dropped his newspaper onto the seat next to him. He looked around. "I couldn't hear you as I entered. You must be shielded."

Lexi nodded.

"How's your earlobe, Dick?" she asked, with a staccato k at the end of his name.

"I should ask you that question since you were the one who ate it, dear," he replied with a smile as his hand moved involuntarily toward his left ear.

"I didn't keep it. I try to be discerning about what goes into my mouth."

"I suppose one of us should be," he replied with an infinitesimal twitch of one eyebrow.

"You look different." He glanced at her arm and his eyes widened. "You have the unhealing scar." He leaned forward for a better look.

She pulled the sleeve of her jacket down. Of course, a supernatural creature like him would be able to see the scar in its metaphysical form—a deep, angry red crevice the length of her forearm with white, shining energy running through it. To those with no magic, it merely looked like a healed pink-silver scar, but it would never truly close. It would always be raw and painful.

"It's a paper cut," she lied pointlessly.

Dick leaned back and gave her a perfunctory smile.

"Let's get down to it. Will you try to kill me again?" he asked, all business.

"I have to decide *now?*"

"If you want my help, yes."

"Will you crawl back to Kindred and tell them where I am again?"

He leaned forward and lowered his voice. "Last year, they hired me to find you and to be perfectly honest, I didn't put all that much effort into it. I don't like Kindred. No one likes them. They're the self-imposed bully boys of the supernatural world. So, I was trying *not* to find you. Hell, I was rooting for you. But you did a shitty job of running away. I simply followed the trail of dead supernatural bodies. Without those, I probably wouldn't have found you at all. That was on you."

"I didn't run away. I left. I chose to leave."

"No one leaves Kindred."

"Yeah, thanks. I'm getting that now. It's a shame that witch's pouch didn't give you eternally bushy eyebrows."

Dick recoiled in horror and automatically smoothed an eyebrow. "Anyway, I don't accept jobs from them anymore."

"Don't tell me you've suddenly grown a conscience?"

"Don't be ridiculous. They've adopted a ninety-day payment schedule. I can't wait that long for my invoices to be paid."

"There's the Dick I know and love." Lexi sneered.

"You got away—" he protested.

"No thanks to you," she cut in.

"*All* thanks to me. Who do you think sent Dolores your way?"

She froze. Dolores had never told her but at that moment, she knew it was true.

Dick continued, "I gave my word that I'd buy you time, so I called in a favor and asked her to get you out. I'll admit I was motivated. Kindred did something to me I considered inappropriate. I was ready to lie and tell them I hadn't seen you, but that mage girl picked the information out of my head. I tried to tell you at the time but you were hell-bent on trying to kill me." He pointed his finger at her but, she noticed, not so close that she could bite it off.

"If I had been trying to kill you, you'd be deader." She leaned forward as well. The two were now almost nose-to-nose across the table.

"Really? Because you seemed extremely bloodthirsty at the time."

Lexi looked away and straightened in her seat. His eyes narrowed and he seemed to sense he'd somehow struck a nerve. He leaned against the backrest.

"I tried to find a witch who could protect my mind, but no one would do it. Everyone's too scared of Kindred."

Lexi looked at him. She believed him and they had to work together. This hadn't gotten off well. She thought for a few moments. "I might have someone who can help you with that if you're serious."

Dick stared at her in surprise for a long moment. "Really? Sister, I am *so* serious."

"Then I won't kill you...for now."

"For now? If that changes, can you give a handsome vampire a head start?" He placed his elbows on the table, put his chin in his hands, and batted his annoyingly long eyelashes at her.

After a short silence, they smiled tentatively at each other.

Lexi chuffed a laugh and shook her head. "How've you been, you old bastard?" It was the closest she would get to making an apology and the atmosphere grew congenial.

"Bored. You?" He raised an eyebrow and smirked.

"Life's not boring,"

Dick swiveled toward Scott. "Which brings us to you, muscles. What glorious stone did she find you under?"

"Oh, I'm only—" her partner started.

"He's my traveling companion. A lady shouldn't travel alone these days."

Lexi could see that the vampire had recognized the opening for a cutting response. He opened his mouth but seemed to think better of it.

"Good for you. It's nice to travel with a friend." He sighed.

She was genuinely surprised by the apparent kindness in his voice.

"Excuse me?" A waitress appeared at the table.

The three of them turned to her as she bent much lower than she needed to place a tall drink in front of Dick, and she delivered a dazzling smile to go with the view of her cleavage.

"I didn't order this."

Lexi could see his gaze dipped no lower than her carotid.

"This is from the gentleman at the end of the bar." As she moved away, she nodded in the direction of a handsome, muscular young man with a square jaw and a varsity jacket. He smiled at Dick, stood, and headed to the bathroom. At the door, he turned and winked.

Scott looked from the man to her companion. "Do you know him?"

"Let's simply say my reputation precedes me. I don't come here anymore." The vampire raised the glass and smiled broadly at the young man while he muttered under his breath, "Not in a million years, jailbait."

"Why do they call you 'Dick?'" the other man asked. Lexi's lips twitched. He'd chosen that moment to voice the question.

"*They* don't. *She* does." Dick rolled his eyes. He turned to Lexi. "So, you need a document from my friend Leonard."

"Dolores told us you'd explain about that." She felt like she was a little behind the curve.

"There was a robbery at a bar a few days ago. The safe wasn't touched but the contents of the filing cabinet were all over the floor. It took a while for your client to discover important documents were missing."

"What documents?" Scott had his notes app open again.

"The whole block used to belong to Kate's father. He divided the land when she finished business school, and she opened the bar and sub-let the flower shop next door to a friend. The land ownership papers are missing," Dick explained.

"I thought she was being harassed for protection money." The other man used his cell phone to start making notes.

The vampire nodded. "Well, things are escalating."

"Shit! I hoped this would be a quick job. It looks like we'll have to stay longer than I had hoped." Lexi sighed. "So, how can your friend help?"

"Leonard is an investigator. We worked together for a while. He has a contact at the County Clerk's Office who can check the records and find the city's copy, if it's still there. If it's missing, you have a bigger problem than you thought."

"Have you already spoken to him?" she asked.

"I haven't discussed the particulars of the case but I've asked for his help. He might, he might not. He's probably angry with me."

Scott stopped typing. "I thought he was your friend?"

"He is, but he's so last-year. Or was it the year before that? One of those years that isn't this year." Dick waved his hand nonchalantly. "I'm meeting him for a date tonight, so I guess we'll find out. He was supposed to help me with...another job, but he's avoided me for months."

He noticed the plate of rib bones and looked at Scott.

"Did you eat *all* those?" He moved his gaze unnecessarily slowly down the other man's torso.

Scott moved his hands self-consciously into his lap.

Dick swiveled to Lexi. "Where does he put it all?"

"Excuse me?" The waitress had returned, this time with a low-ball glass containing amber liquid.

Dick stared at her with his bright topaz-blue eyes.

"This...er..." She faltered, and color bloomed in her cheeks.

"This?" he responded helpfully and gestured at the drink.

"Sorry, yes. This one's from the gentleman at the table in the corner." She indicated an impeccably dressed bald black gentleman who rose, winked at him, and headed through the door to the bathroom.

"Well, I'm sure they'll find each other," he muttered.

Another man walked past and smiled at him. "It looks like everyone around here knows you." Scott shook his head and smirked.

"Intimately." The vampire sighed.

"How about we go back to the room and talk business more privately?" Lexi signaled the waitress for the check

She brought over a folded piece of paper on a little plate and placed it in front of Dick with a smile before she turned away with a flick of her hair.

"Boy, is she barking up the wrong tree." He pushed the check across to her.

She read it, threw cash down to cover it, and passed the check to him. "I think that's for you."

He glanced at the waitress's number scribbled across the bill but made no move to pick it up.

Scott leaned closer and snagged it. Lexi looked at him with her eyebrows raised. "What? It's for our expenses." He pocketed the receipt.

Dick's gaze once again swiveled to the other man.

"Let's go then. Muscles and I can get better acquainted." He placed a hand on Scott's thigh and blue sparks erupted from the young man's skin to hurl the vampire out of the booth.

The bar went silent as people watched him skid across the floor.

Lexi smiled at Dick, who was on his butt several feet away.

He stood and dusted himself off. "I'm not averse to a little rough play but not when I'm wearing Versace."

"Sorry. It's kind of automatic." Scott didn't look even remotely sorry as he stood from the booth.

She did her best to hide a smile. "Don't take offense, Scott. He was only checking your credentials."

"Yeah, that was what it felt like he was doing." The man's face was aflame.

"So, you *are* her blood-match. Interesting. Sorry, handsome. You're cute but the surfer-dude thing really isn't my type. I'd rather take you for a good haircut." Dick picked his newspaper up and headed to the door.

They drove back to the motel and the vampire followed in his own car.

"You're quiet." Lexi glanced at her companion, who had sat with his head down.

"I revealed my ability. I shouldn't have done that. He knows you get magic from me now."

"He'd already guessed and was testing a hypothesis. Don't let it eat at you."

Scott pulled the visor down and looked at himself in the mirror.

"Seriously? You're offended because he said you're not his type?"

"No. Well, what's wrong with my hair?"

"Nothing. If you have what every other man has inside his pants, you're his type. He's merely trying to undermine your self-confidence. I told you, he's an absolute son-of-a-bitch."

"Do you call him 'Dick' because he likes—"

"No. That's purely a coincidence."

They pulled up and got out of the car.

Dick climbed out of his vehicle and walked toward them. "I couldn't believe it when you pulled into this shithole. This is the worst place in town. Even the guy with the meth lab in room twelve complained about the smell and moved out. Is Dolores punishing you for something?"

The three of them headed up the steps and entered the room.

The vampire appeared to try not to touch anything. "I heard about a man who woke up in one of the rooms here. He'd paced around it for two days before housekeeping came in and he finally realized he wasn't in the county lock-up." He gave Lexi a conspiratorial wink.

Scott looked at him. "That's not true." He didn't look completely convinced that it wasn't, though.

"No, but it could be," the vampire admitted as he looked around in disgust.

"I need to use the bathroom. I hope it's not too gross." Scott walked toward the door with obvious reluctance.

"It's really clean. This place isn't so bad," Lexi called as he entered. She sat on her bed and stared at the bathroom door while she waited.

Scott stepped out again and his face was white.

Lexi felt his sadness through their empathetic link. "Look, people get murdered every day. At least they scrubbed the tub with bleach after."

"It wasn't a murder."

"How does he—" Dick began.

Lexi shook her head to silence him.

"There's no fear, only sadness." Scott sat on the end of the bed in front of the mirror.

"Don't do this, Scott." Lexi knew what was coming.

"I'm curious." He muttered the words so softly that even Dick with his vampire hearing probably couldn't hear them.

The mirror reflecting the young man wavered and reversed everything that had happened in the room. It went back a few hours and revealed Lexi, her face twisted in obvious pain as she adjusted her breasts in the leather vest. The older man laughed and she face-palmed.

The image reversed faster. It showed a maid, the crime scene cleaners, the CSIs, the police, and the same maid backing away from the bathroom with horror on her face. Finally, a gaunt woman appeared surrounded by drug paraphernalia and looked like she'd simply had enough. He whispered a final word and the mirror returned to its natural state.

The three of them were silent. Scott stood, moved to sit at the top of the bed, and opened his new book—a sorcery tome Lexi assumed he'd probably picked up from a Seven-Eleven.

Dick went to the mirror and poked it with his index finger, and his manicured fingernail tapped the glass. "The moment I get home, I will smash every mirror in my house. Then I'll have them ground to dust."

He paused, spun on his heel, and faced the others. "But she's in a better place now. Let's talk about me."

"I can see now why she calls you Dick. It's because you're a total dick, isn't it?"

"Good guess, but no." Lexi shook her head.

"It's not?" The vampire was clearly surprised by this revelation.

Scott looked from the mirror to her. "If that leather vest is so uncomfortable, why don't you wear a different one? You must have at least twenty of them."

"They're all uncomfortable. I hate them all."

"You hate leathers? But that's all you wear." His face was a mask of puzzlement.

Lexi stood before the mirror. "Hell, yes! They're tough, flexible, and they accentuate the curves. For the purpose of gathering information, there's nothing better." She slid her hand over the tight leather jeans and looked at him in the mirror. "But they make me sweat horribly since they don't breathe." She turned to Dick. "You don't breathe. I bet this would look good on you."

He glanced at her with one perfectly annoying—because it was perfect—eyebrow raised. "Why would you think I don't breathe? How do I speak?"

With a casual gesture, he flicked off some lint she couldn't see—and her eyesight was good enough to have seen it, she thought.

"Besides," he finished as he preened like a cat, "I make *everything* look good."

"Have you been told you can be an arrogant ass?" She pulled at her leather vest. The girls needed air. He raised that annoying eyebrow, so she clarified, "I mean, lately?"

Dick sighed and moved to stand at the door and waved his face with the newspaper. "I hate this town in the summer. It's too hot."

"It's Palm Springs. It's always hot." Silently, though, she agreed. "Why do you care? You're dead."

"Maintaining an undead body as good as mine requires careful balance. Too many degrees in the wrong direction and I could be standing in a puddle of fat bigger than your thighs." He cast an unimpressed glance at her legs.

"There's nothing wrong with my thighs." She smoothed the leather over her muscular legs.

His lip lifted into a smirk. "Do you ever see the skinny girls complain about sweat rash?"

"I've never seen a skinny girl clinically decapitate a smartass vamp with her thighs."

Dick cracked his neck and stepped into the room. "So, when do you plan to leave town?"

"Don't worry, we'll be gone as soon as the job's done. Aren't you late for your date?" she asked.

"You mean the date where I have dinner with Leonard? Where he'll be pissed at me at first, then hang on my every word? Then we go back to his house, screw each other's brains out for hours, and he'll profess his undying love for me...*again.* That date?"

"I guess." She wondered why he had a problem with that scenario.

"What's the point? As far as I'm concerned, it's done. We just did it, right there in my mind where it was probably better than, as I recall, it is in reality. Nauseatingly predictable." He rolled his eyes.

"I see. So, in this scenario in your mind, did he give you the information we need?"

"Oops. I forgot that part. I should probably get ready. I don't want to be late for my date. When did you last go on a date, Alexa?" He smirked when he looked at her.

Scott glanced up from his book at the mention of her full name. A flicker of a smile betrayed his intentions.

"Alexa, play 'All by Myself' by—" He stopped speaking as a spinning metal object shredded his book but was halted by the blue aura around his body.

"That joke got old already." She stood in a relaxed pose where she leaned against the dresser and enjoyed the confused look on his face. He hadn't even seen her move and she knew it.

He snatched the throwing star from the air and placed it on the bedside table. "This book was new."

"Where did it come from?" She tried to see the cover but he put it into his bag.

"Target."

"Do you think you should try to use a book of spells from Target? You know that shit will backfire, don't you?"

"It's not about the spell. It's the magic behind it." Scott's tone was prickly.

"If you want to make yourself useful, help me get out of these leathers." Lexi headed to the bathroom.

He bolted to his feet and took a step toward her.

"From out there." She closed the bathroom door. "I only need a second to…"

Scott muttered an incantation under his breath and moved his fingers as though to snap them, although they never met.

Metal clanged on tiles and reverberated around the walls as throwing stars, knives, and other trade tools fell to the bathroom floor. Lexi stood naked except for one gold ring on her hand and gazed at the weapons around her, then looked at her leathers, which were hung neatly over the chair.

"Sorry," Scott shouted. "But you know you shouldn't keep all that stuff in your pocket, right?"

Lexi, although naked, slipped her hand in and out of the magical pocket at her hip that appeared and disappeared at her command. He was right. This job could not be over fast enough.

She shook the thought off and stood at the mirror while she delved into her cosmetic bag. After a moment, she retrieved the dental floss and pulled off a length while shouting out to him. "I'll take the first opportunity to assassinate the person who decided 'Alexa' could be a name to call their artificial assistant. Hell, it doesn't even have to be for much money. Maybe like…five dollars and a burger." She thought for a moment. "I'll accept an IOU on the burger."

"That's a good life choice for those thighs, dear," Dick shouted through the door.

"Are you still here?" She toyed with the idea of trying to kill him again.

"I'm going, I'm going," he responded. "You kids have a great time and don't stay out too late." She gave him the finger through the closed bathroom door.

He laughed. "I saw that."

Five minutes later, Lexi emerged from the bathroom in gray sweatpants and a t-shirt. She crossed to the small round trash can and opened its swing lid to toss the used floss into it. With a startled exclamation, she leapt back as light burst from the can and a 3D projection beamed into the center of the room. The figure of a crouched woman stood before her. "Help me, Obi-Wan Kenobi. You're my only hope."

"Motherfucker! Scott, if you do that one more time..." She walked through the projection, which instantly disappeared.

Scott rolled on his bed, clutching his stomach as he laughed. "That was so funny."

Lexi glanced at her scar. The magic had almost dissipated again. She walked to him and held her hand out. He took it and transferred magic to her. As she walked to the door, she stretched her arm to reveal the raw, magical wound and hesitated. Because she hadn't been born with magic like Scott, they called Lexi's magic "borrowed." It was a curious term because she had paid dearly for it. She touched the scar.

This wasn't borrowed. It was bought.

Her companion had stopped laughing and now looked nervously at her.

All matched legacies had finite magic, hers more than most. She only used it in dire situations.

Oh, what the hell.

"You should shut up now, smart ass." She stroked the length of the scar and looked directly at him with a little smile.

Scott pawed at his mouth in horror as his top and bottom lips merged to form a seal.

"I'm going for a run." Lexi headed out with a broad grin.

She felt the sense of panic from him through their empathetic link and slowed on the stairs. On the bottom step, she waited for a few moments and had begun to return to the room when the feeling subsided. He had removed the spell. She set off at a leisurely pace.

Lexi ran in the direction of the client's bar, interested to see what kind of establishment it was. When she approached the corner and saw it was dark, she decided to do a lap of the block. She passed the bar, then a flower shop. Every other business was boarded up, seemingly closed forever. At the next turn, more buildings stood with boards covered in graffiti over the windows. The next street was bordered with a fence that warned of armed patrols. When she reached the entrance, a message read *Twenty-Four Hour Storage: Closed for remodel.*

She slowed as she reached the side of the bar and narrowed her eyes as a flashlight played along the wall behind the fence. She stopped and listened to men's whispered voices.

"Shh! I heard something."

"What was it?"

"It sounded like someone running."

"If someone in this neighborhood is running, they're running for their life. They've got their own shit going on."

"Hurry. Let's get this done. Throw it everywhere."

Something splashed, followed by the smell of gasoline. That was all she needed.

She retrieved a glass vial of vampire blood from her pocket, unstoppered it, and tipped it onto her finger. Quickly, she ran the finger down her tongue and felt the thrill as adrenaline flooded her system. Her senses went into overdrive. The darkness of the night lifted, and she heard two people breathing and smelled body odor, cheap deodorant, and gun oil. She knew she already had an edge, being faster and stronger than normal humans, but the extra boost helped enormously.

This is what it would be like if my abilities were as strong as they should be.

Unfortunately, the only sense that wasn't improved by the vamp blood was her sense of self-preservation.

She hopped the fence.

"Hi. I'm not interrupting anything, am I?" She gave them her best disarming smile. It was perhaps ambitious for the situation but sometimes, it worked. On the street, they would probably have been confident and at ease in her presence. These two were in the act of carrying out a crime so they were jumpy, a common failing.

The one with the gas can spun and spilled the contents on his friend. He dropped the container on the ground and immediately tripped over it. The other was faster, reached into the back of his jeans for his gun, and aimed it at her. She wondered if she should have taken a few moments to plan before she leapt in.

The die was cast, though, so she shrugged and ignored the weapon. "I only wondered what you were doing."

He looked at the building and then at the can of gasoline. "You need this explained to you?"

Lexi glanced at the gun and then at the man who held it. She needed to get him farther away from the building. "Don't shoot me or we'll all go up in flames."

His eyes narrowed and he sneered. "Statistically unlikely."

Not today, fuckwit.

"Good, then." She turned away and walked toward the fence while she activated the magic in her scar.

The men ran after her and, as expected, the gunman didn't shoot.

The first to reach her was the unarmed man and he grasped her hair and yanked her back. She felt and heard hair rip from her scalp as she fell and noticed that the other put his gun away. Rather than struggle, she allowed her weight to take her completely to the ground before she rolled onto her shoulders and kicked upward with her heel under her captor's chin. His head snapped back and he fell. She flipped onto her feet, her focus on the second man. He drew the gun again, raised it, fired, and screamed when her magic caused the weapon to erupt in his hand.

Lexi was tempted to leave him burning but couldn't risk the building igniting. She attempted to douse the flame with magic but her scar was empty.

"Shit. It looks like we have to do this the old-fashioned way," she said to the shrieking, flailing man.

She kicked, felled him, and rolled him across the ground with her foot until the flames were out.

"I don't suppose you'd consider telling me who sent you?" she asked as she crouched beside his now unmoving form.

He sucked in a single breath, then died.

"I'll take that as a no." She stood and checked the vitals on the other man, who was also dead. Lexi hopped the fence and finished her run.

CHAPTER THREE

"Do you have to do that when I'm trying to sleep?" Scott turned his pillow over, punched it, and yanked the covers over his head to escape the morning sunlight flooding through the gossamer-thin curtains.

Lexi looked up from the whetstone she used to sharpen her katana, one eyebrow raised. "So you're speaking to me now?"

Her friend sat and pointed at her. "You left me in a vulnerable situation last night. What if someone had attacked me while you were on your run and I couldn't speak my protection spells?"

She rolled her eyes. "We both know you'd reversed the spell seconds after I left the room." With that, she lowered her head and her focus returned to the whetstone.

Unfortunately, he wasn't finished. "You used my own magic against me. Where did you even learn something like that?" He touched his mouth again and felt around his cheeks. "It was hideous."

"A great mage once said, 'It's not the spells, it's the magic behind them.'" She didn't look up.

His stuttering as he ranted threatened to crack her stoic façade. "What a pile of crap!" His eyes narrowed a moment. "Who said that?"

Lexi focused on him with a gleam in her eye. "You—*yesterday*. You muppet." She smiled.

Satisfied with the sharpness of the blade, she stood and slid the katana into the magical dimensional pocket hidden within her tight leather pants.

When she drew her hand away, the sword had completely vanished. A moment later, she withdrew a shorter blade.

It came out with several candy wrappers stuck to it.

Scott looked at the sticky mess in disgust, his mouth open. "That's revolting."

"What?" she asked defensively as though she didn't know what his problem was.

"That!" He shook his head. "I give you access to a dimensional pocket for storing your weapons and you use it for candy. I use my magical energy to keep it accessible, so if you could not fill it with shit, that would be great." He laid down again. "And you smell like you've been in a fire." He covered his head once more.

Lexi wiped the sword clean, dried her whetstone, and slipped them both into the dimensional pocket. "Come on. It's six anyway. Let's get breakfast before we see the client."

He turned onto his side and away from her.

She eyed the ceiling as if asking the gods for patience. "If you stop sulking, I'll let you change the *Gideon Bible* into the *Ferrengi Rules of Acquisition* again."

No answer was forthcoming. Damn.

Resigned, she walked around and rested her chin on the edge of the bed to give him the best puppy face she could muster.

"What are you doing?" he asked and opened one eye.

Lexi smiled. "Thinking about steak, eggs, and hash, bacon, pancakes, maple syrup, and coffee. Why? What are you doing?"

A short pause followed before he sighed. "Well, now I'm thinking about food. All right, I'll get up."

Scott pushed off the bed and walked across the room in shorts and a t-shirt, yawning and scratching his back.

Dick had been right. With his tanned body and shoulder-length blond hair, he definitely rocked the surfer look. If he ever stopped behaving like a twelve-year-old, he'd be quite a catch for some girl one day. For now, he was infuriating.

Perhaps the Good Book will teach me patience, she thought. She opened the drawer and pulled out...*The Rules of Quidditch.* She laughed.

They parked across the street from the bar and walked toward it, but when she reached the other side, Lexi was alone. She turned to where Scott stood in the middle of the street with a faraway look on his face. The lights had changed but he didn't seem to be in any hurry to move. She stepped into the street, grasped his arm, and yanked him onto the sidewalk as a horn blasted.

Reflexively, she shook his shoulder. "What was that?"

He stared at her for a moment, his expression bewildered. "I'm sorry. Wow! I caught a really weird vibe."

"You almost caught the fender of that truck, dipshit. Wake up." She turned and strode toward the bar. Absently, she touched the unhealing scar, which had itched for a moment.

They found the business locked.

"Well, this is interesting." Scott held his hands cupped over his eyes against the glass.

Lexi looked in. "What?"

"You see that? Hanging from the ceiling?" He guided her by pointing.

Lexi noticed a rustic design of sticks bound together into a familiar shape. "Is that a rune?"

"Yes, it's Eolh. For protection from bad spirits."

"Or it's a decoration left from Halloween."

"Eight months ago?"

"Let's look around." She headed around the corner. They stopped at the side of the building.

"That must be from the robbery." Scott pointed to a boarded-up window.

They continued toward the rear and found the fenced area. Lexi sniffed. The smell of gasoline was still in the air and a pile of sand lay on the ground where the burned man had landed.

"Interesting. It smells like there's been a fire here." His gaze slid to her. She said nothing.

A man walked through a gate with a beer barrel on a dolly while another man stood at the back of a truck with a clipboard. He scribbled on the clipboard and clambered into the cab of the truck.

"Can I help you?" asked a voice from behind them.

They turned to see a young woman in the doorway of the flower shop, surrounded by tubs of blossoms.

"We're looking for Kate, the owner of the bar." Scott began to walk toward her.

"That's me." She looked at them suspiciously.

Lexi held her hand out. "Hi, Lexi and Scott. Dolores asked us to drop in."

The woman glanced quickly in the direction of the man moving the beer barrels. At that moment, he returned towing the empty dolly and looked at the two of them with a puzzled expression. He approached slowly.

"Shit," Kate muttered.

When he arrived, Scott looked at him and muttered a word, then touched his arm. "You know what? I have a mad craving for a McRib."

"Aww, man! McRibs are so good." The man dropped the dolly where he stood.

"I know, right?"

"What?" Kate, clearly confused, looked at her watch.

"I'll see you soon, sweetheart." He kissed her head and began to walk down the street.

"Tommy?" she called after him. "He'll be disappointed. They'll be on the breakfast menu for the next two hours." She stared at his back. "Did you do something to him?" she asked Scott.

"I made him think he had somewhere else to be. I'm sorry. It seemed you didn't want to speak with him here, and we were told you'd asked for discretion. We might need to be quick, though. How long it lasts depends entirely on how much he actually wants a McRib."

"He lives on that shit." The woman turned and picked up a tub of red roses.

"So, you work here too?" she looked at the front of the flower shop.

"No. I own the property but my friend Daisy runs this place. I haven't seen her for a couple of days. Her delivery arrived and I'm the emergency contact."

Lexi was immediately alert. "Is it unusual for her to go off like this?"

"She's somewhat flaky. Every now and then she disappears to LA to party or heads to the woods with her coven to do whatever they do there." Kate shrugged.

Scott began to move the tubs in.

The woman stepped out of the way, her expression surprised. "Thanks."

The two entered the building behind him.

"Can you tell us what's been happening?" Lexi asked.

"When I first called Dolores, I was being harassed by a local gang. They want me to pay protection money I can't afford. Then a couple of days ago, someone broke into the office. They smashed open the filing cabinet and scattered papers everywhere. It took me a day to realize important paperwork was missing. I called my lawyer to ask him if he could send a copy, but there was no response. I learned he's gone—left town. I think there's more going on than merely harassment from a group of thugs."

Lexi looked around the room. "Did the police get any prints from the robbery?"

"I didn't report it," the woman admitted and blushed.

"Why not?" Lexi asked.

"Tommy's uncle is the police chief and the alpha of his pack. I can't let this get back to our families." As Kate spoke, she moved pots from the front of the store to the back.

"I don't understand. If you're a shifter, why doesn't the local pack protect you?" Scott asked as he entered, having moved the last of the tubs.

"If they found out about this, there would be blood on my hands. I don't want that."

"How long have you been in business here?" Lexi asked.

"Seven years. I've never been bothered like this before. A businessman has been buying up the stores and properties on this block. He already owns most of them and closed them down. After the break-in, I can't help wondering if he might be behind the harassment. And something else happened last night. I came back to find the place stinking of gasoline and two dead guys out back. They must have intended to incinerate the bar. One looked like he had a broken neck and the other was badly burned. I think maybe one killed the other, then somehow set himself on fire instead of burning the building down."

"Yes, that must have been what happened." Scott looked directly at Lexi.

She turned to Kate. "So, where are the dead guys now?"

"I had to…uh, you know, dispose of them." She averted her eyes.

Lexi looked at the boarded window. "What did you tell your boyfriend about all this?"

"I said drunken college kids had smashed the window. I told him they apologized and left money to fix it. This morning, I told him I'd reversed over a can of gasoline."

"Who's the businessman?" Scott asked.

"Caleb Linden. He was my dad's business partner and already owns the storage facility at the back of this building. When my dad died, the whole thing went to him. He wasn't very happy when he learned Dad had divided the property and given this part to me." Kate wiped her hands and passed the cloth to him.

"We'll ask Dolores to see what she can find out about him." He dried his hands and pulled his phone out to type.

"I can tell you exactly where he'll be tonight. He's holding a fundraiser for the mayor in Rancho Mirage. Everyone with money to throw at his campaign will be there."

Scott made notes.

Kate fidgeted and seemed to weigh the two of them. "Listen, there's something else—something I haven't told anyone. Walking home a couple of weeks ago through the park, I was attacked." She hugged herself as she spoke. "I've never seen the guy before. He dragged me into the bushes and I swear I thought he would kill me."

"Why didn't you shift?" Lexi asked. "You could have finished the guy."

She sighed. "I did shift. I bit him but the gun went off. It scared me, and I ran away." The woman shrugged.

"Are you saying there's a new shifter out there with no sire or alpha to control him?" Lexi asked.

"Not quite." Kate lowered her gaze and looked embarrassed. "Can I show you something?"

She locked the flower shop and they followed her to the bar. As they headed in through the rear door, they passed barrels piled up to virtually fill the back room. It was a tight squeeze. "Tommy thinks the storeroom downstairs is flooded. I told him the plumber's waiting for a part." She unlocked a door and they descended the stairway through a room filled with barrels attached to pipes. They stopped at a padlocked door. The three of them stood in silence as she unlocked it and led them along a hallway. She opened another locked door and they peered in to see a man chained at the far end of the room.

"He turned up a few days ago in wolf form, followed me down here, and simply sat there while I chained him."

Lexi walked halfway into the room for a closer look.

The young man woke up. "You bitch. Let me out of here." He ran at her. When he was about a foot away, she realized there were still a few feet on the chain so she punched him in the face. He dropped like a rock.

She looked around the room. In the other corner was a pile of bones.

Ahh! That's what happened to Crispy and Clumsy.

Lexi stepped out of the room. "I take it that's last night's visitors. What are you planning to do with this guy?

Kate sighed. "I don't know. I turned him so he's my responsibility. But he's a murdering thug."

"I suppose we could—" Scott started.

"I told you, Scott. No pets until you've proven you can be responsible."

"I didn't mean—"

"Do you want me to finish him?" Lexi began to withdraw a blade from her pocket.

"No, no. I need to think about it." The woman closed the door and locked it again.

"Well, the offer's there, but you'd have to clean up yourself. I don't do that."

The two friends looked at each other. This small job was getting bigger by the minute.

"Your boyfriend doesn't know about him?" Scott asked.

"No. He doesn't usually hang around here. He's angry about the window and is looking for any evidence that I can't handle this situation. That's mainly because he thinks I should sell to Caleb. Tommy's usually a nice guy but he's been on edge lately. His whole pack has. Their latest gripe is that I should be popping baby wolves out instead of owning a business. We're supposed to be getting married soon, but I keep putting it off. His pack makes me nervous."

"Okay, you've given us a fair amount to go on. We'll keep in touch." Lexi turned to the cell. "It's good to see you're feeding him."

"I take care of that when I close the bar. As his sire, I can command him to turn and he's as pliant as a puppy. I feed and water him, and he goes on newspaper." Kate shrugged.

She simply stared at the woman. "That is too much information."

They stood on the sidewalk. Lexi glanced at a limousine with blackened windows parked at the curbside. She sensed that someone was watching from behind the wheel but couldn't see who it was.

"Where to now?" Scott asked.

"I could devour a McRib," she admitted.

"My God! Appalling! Those things are an absolute assault on the senses," said Dick's familiar voice.

"Oh! it's you." Lexi walked toward the car.

"Climb aboard and let's talk." The vampire released the locks on the rear doors.

They slid into the back seat and closed the doors. The locks clicked, and a dark glass partition between the front and back seats slid down.

As they pulled away, Lexi looked at her car, which was parked across the street. "What about my car?"

"Maybe you'll get lucky and someone will set fire to it." Dick smirked.

She let that slide. There was no denying it was a piece of shit.

"I assume you listened to our conversation with Kate?" she asked him.

"I didn't pull up close enough until the wolf left. Where did he go? He was in a hell of a hurry."

"He wanted a McRib too." The friends exchanged grins.

"This town is going to shit." Dick shook his head.

She leaned forward. "We need to crash a party tonight."

The vampire looked at her in the rearview mirror. "You don't need to crash it. I could use a date, though."

"You're invited?" Lexi couldn't keep the surprise out of her voice.

"I'm a fine, upstanding citizen. Of course, I'm invited. But Caleb Linden isn't someone to mess with. He's not a nice man."

Scott poked at the window control.

Dick flashed him a stern look. "What are you doing?"

"I'm trying to open the window but the button doesn't work." He continued to poke at it.

Lexi stared at him until he realized he was being watched.

"That's intentional. I have a mild sun allergy." The vampire regarded him calmly with one of his perfect eyebrows raised.

The penny dropped. "Oh, God, sorry." Scott yanked his finger away from the button and sat on his hands.

"I'm not taking this car to that shithole of a motel. We'll have to go to my place so I can actually get out of the car."

"Oh, great, a morning graveyard visit." Lexi's mouth twitched.

"You live in a—" Scott started.

"I do not live in a fucking graveyard. Seriously, where do you think I hang my designer clothes—in a crypt?"

The car slowed on an affluent-looking road and stopped in front of a gate. A gaunt man stood beside the barrier and stared at the vehicle as it slid through. Dick clicked his tongue.

"Who's that?" She stared at the man through the darkened glass.

The driver's shoulders drooped. "My fan club."

He idled on the other side of the gate and watched it close in the mirror.

"I love you," the man shouted as the gate closed in front of him.

"Don't ask." He continued up the drive and into one of three garages. They waited until the garage door had closed before the locks clicked to indicate they could climb out. An internal door took them into the hallway of a spacious home.

"*Mi casa es su casa.*" Dick dropped his keys into a little dish on a stand in the hallway. Lexi looked around and noted the retro decor. The huge windows and the glass doors leading to the garden and pool were darkened almost to complete blackness, but the lighting in the room was adequate.

"You live here?" Scott asked and gazed around the extravagant room.

"Darling, I don't *live* anywhere. But yes, it's mine. I stay here occasionally." Dick headed to the bar and poured himself a drink.

She peered around the room. "The furniture's quite retro." She wanted to say, "dated," but decided not to.

"Retro? Yes, you could say that. You could also say it's the original furniture that was present when Marilyn Monroe, Cary Grant, Frank Sinatra, and Marlon Brando attended parties here. I share this with the ghosts of the past." Dick spread his arms as though introducing them to those ghosts.

"I've heard of Marilyn Monroe but I'm not sure who the others were," Scott admitted.

"Philistine." The vampire turned away and gave his head a little shake.

"Hey, here's a picture of you with some dude." The other man pointed at the wall and looked at the picture.

Dick turned. "That 'dude' is Errol Flynn."

"Should I know who that is?" Scott squinted at the writing on the picture.

"Give me strength." The vampire pinched the bridge of his nose.

"It says November 1935. You're really *old*." The younger man was clearly impressed.

"I should have dropped you at that shitty motel," Dick muttered as he walked to where Lexi poured coffee for herself from a carafe.

Scott wandered the spacious living area and peered at the photographs on the walls. He looked from one picture to the corner of the room several times.

"James Dean sat on your thing?" he asked.

Lexi spat out a mouthful of coffee and coughed.

Dick smoothed his eyebrow. "I will neither confirm nor deny that James Dean sat on my thing."

"But there's a picture of it." The other man pointed at the wall again.

The vampire glanced at Lexi.

"Well, anything's possible," he admitted before he went to see what Scott was talking about. He looked at the picture and sighed.

"It's called a 'chaise lounge.'" Dick shook his head and returned to Lexi, who was spinning a shuriken again. He opened his mouth to speak to her but she tilted her head in the other man's direction and he followed her gaze.

They watched Scott as he walked around the chaise and attempted to sit on it. First, he sat on its edge, then he tried leaning to the side on one elbow, and finally, he reclined fully on his back.

"Comfortable?" Dick asked.

"I'm not sure." Scott wiggled around. "Do you find it comfortable?"

"I don't sit in it. It's a 1930 cowhide Le Corbusier, and it's insured for half a million dollars."

The man darted off it and stood nervously in the middle of the room, looking suspiciously at the furniture around him as though trying to work out where it might be safe to sit.

Lexi returned her focus to Dick. "So, what happened with your date last night?"

He rested his face in his hands and groaned. "He was still quite bitter that I'd stopped returning his calls when I got bored the first time. Although he didn't actually admit that, he ordered the Kobe steak and two bottles of the 1961 Haut-Brion at nine hundred dollars a bottle and drank all of it. I was quite tipsy by the end of the night."

"How did you get tipsy if he drank all—" Scott began.

Dick smiled at Scott and allowed his vampire teeth to descend while his eyes glittered.

"Okey-dokey. Forget I asked." The man made his way carefully to the kitchen counter and sat on a barstool next to Lexi.

"Did you remember to ask him about the case?" she asked pointedly.

"Oh, that. Yes. He'll find out what he can and try to get a copy of the documents from City Hall. I'm waiting for him to call back."

Scott leaned forward. "I didn't mean to insult you before—about your age. It's really cool that you've met interesting people and lived through those times. I think vampires are an important link to our history. I only ever met one vampire, but he told me stories from hundreds of years ago."

"Oh? Anyone I know?" Dick sounded more polite than interested.

"His name's Dimitri. I met him in Dallas."

"With long black hair, dresses like something from *Interview with a Vampire*?"

He nodded.

Dick and Lexi looked at each other and both rolled their eyes.

"What?" The young man looked from one to the other.

The vampire shook his head. "His name wasn't Dimitri, it was *Barry*, and he wasn't hundreds of years old, he was turned in the bathroom at a New Kids on The Block concert in 1989."

"Was? What happened to him?" Scott asked.

Lexi gave him a little finger wave. "Me. I happened to him. I killed him about a year ago. Just before I met you."

"You killed him? But he seemed like a nice enough guy." He looked disappointed.

"He developed a taste for toddlers that was unacceptable to my former employers."

"I thought you said vampires were 'hard to kill.'" He made air-quotes.

"I guess that depends on how hard you're trying. His predilections were also unacceptable to me. I took it personally."

"You take everything personally," Scott muttered.

Dick loosened his tie. "Barry's behavior was bad news for all of us. It brought unwanted attention."

"You have to be careful with vamps. No offense, Dick," Lexi added. "Whatever they were like in life is intensified."

"Take me, for example," Dick interrupted and spoke over his shoulder as he refreshed the water in a vase of flowers. "In life, I was fabulous and handsome, so I became even more fabulous and hand-some." He appeared to be completely sincere.

She watched him as he pottered about the kitchen and smiled briefly at seeing him in a domestic setting before she continued her explanation. "Barry was an addict, always looking for his next hit. When you become a vampire, well, you know what the next hit is. Blood bags would never be enough," she finished.

"What happened?" Scott asked.

"The Kindred hierarchy put out a call for support. A kid had been found dead and it was a vamp kill. A five-year-old boy was still miss-ing. To be honest, no one expected to find him alive but in the end, he turned up in Austin with the kid. We were asked to help. I found them and I killed Barry."

Dick looked at her. "You get around, don't you? Which reminds me, when was the last time you went to New Orleans?"

"I've never been." She shook her head.

"That's interesting. I suppose you should know that the other job Leonard was supposed to be working on is you."

"Me? I don't understand."

"He was trying to find out where you originally came from. Dolores asked me to find out. Obviously, I wasn't really feeling the love, so I passed the work on to Leonard because I know he has a contact in Kindred. Last night, he said he'd found evidence you'd spent some time in New Orleans."

"I don't remember it, but that doesn't mean it didn't happen. What was this evidence?"

"I guess we'll see when we meet up next. He'll leave a message for me today. I'll pick it up tonight and we'll catch up with him tonight or tomorrow night."

He rearranged the flowers in the vase, then yawned. "And that's the end of story time for me, kiddies. I need to get some sleep, and you need to go shopping."

"We do?" Lexi frowned in surprise.

"I'm not taking you to the fundraiser dressed like that. I have standards to maintain. My man will take you. I'll pick you up from the fleapit tonight."

"What about me?" Scott asked.

"You have homework." Dick went to a cabinet and selected several DVDs. He handed them to Scott one by one, reading the names as he did so. "*The Wild One* with Marlon Brando, *Suspicion* with Cary Grant and *Robin Hood* with the *dude* in the photograph. Pay attention. I'll be asking questions."

"Jesús!" he shouted. A handsome young Mexican man appeared almost instantly. He was an interesting sight in a pair of tight short-shorts, a cropped t-shirt, a green scarf, no shoes, and a scrubbing brush.

"Yes, Mr. Levin?"

"Are we interrupting something?" Dick stared at the man.

Jesús waved the brush. "I was about to clean the pool."

"Wearing my Givenchy scarf?" he asked with a raised eyebrow.

"You have guests." He gestured awkwardly at the side of his neck, which was covered by the scarf.

Lexi assumed Dick had snacked on him for breakfast, something that would have been unacceptable to her when she was a member of Kindred. Now? Well, a guy had to eat and his friend didn't seem to mind.

The vampire picked the mail up from the end of the counter and leafed through it before he replaced the pile. "Any visitors or messages today?"

"Geoffrey's back." Jesús nodded in the direction of the front gate.

"Yes, I noticed that. Call the hospital and let them know they have one missing." He turned to Lexi, who was listening to the exchange with a smirk. "It's not funny. That man is the bane of my existence. Well, one of them."

His focus on Jesús again, he added, "You can do the pool later. Take my acquaintances shopping for an evening dress—you know the stores to go to—and drop them at their shitty car."

"Yes, Mr. Levin." He walked to the dish on the end of the counter and picked the car keys up.

"And put some shoes on."

"Yes, my flip-flops are there." Jesús pointed and rolled his eyes.

Dick shuddered. "I despise flip-flops. Those little toe posts are so invasive." Lexi grinned as his toes moved inside his deck shoes and she guessed he was curling them.

"Dude, you drink blood. That's way more gross." Scott screwed his face up.

"No, I'm very sure it's not." The vampire shuddered again.

"I'll pick you up later, Lexi. Please don't be dressed like Calamity Jane."

"I won't if you won't," she replied, her expression deadpan.

He stopped and scrutinized her for a moment. "My reputation will already be in tatters after I arrive with a woman. Let's not make it any worse."

His employee returned wearing sparkly flip-flops.

"Jesús, use my credit card. Is the gun in the car?" Dick asked.

"Yes, Mr. Levin."

"Good. If she tries to go to Walmart, shoot her in the face."

With that, he turned and left the room.

CHAPTER FOUR

"S ay something. If you don't open your mouth and say something, I'll gut you." Lexi looked from the mirror to Jesús and back. She turned this way and that in *another* little black dress.

He sighed and looked up from his fingernails. "Too slutty."

She turned to face him fully. "You do understand I'm not kidding about gutting you? It's kind of my job."

"You asked me to say something, so I said something." He was unfazed.

"All you've said up to now is, too slutty, too slutty, too *Amish*, and too slutty." She twisted the ring around her middle finger, a nervous habit.

"They're all too short except the Amish one, and that was as ugly as sin." He screwed his face up and pointed. "This dress is nasty. You look like you'll start twerking like a girl from a rap video." He began to twerk in the middle of the Alexander McQueen store, while the younger store assistants giggled and the older ones looked horrified.

"The dress has to be short. I might need to fight."

Jesús narrowed his eyes. "You don't go to many parties, do you?"

Scott wandered over to join them. "How's it going here?"

"Horribly." Lexi sighed inwardly at the defeat in her voice. Her mind wandered to the little glass vial, which she'd stupidly left in the motel room. She frowned at the material slung over his arm. "What have you got there?"

"Another one for you to try. I think it might work." He handed it to her.

"It's long." She held the dress up.

"Give it a go anyway. I have a good feeling about it."

"If someone attacks me in this, I'll trip over my—" Her jaw dropped when she flipped the tag in her hand. "Have you seen the price of this?"

"Dick's credit card." Scott wiggled his eyebrows.

"Okay, I'll try it. I've never even had a car that cost this much." Lexi returned to the changing room.

She stepped out five minutes later, and Jesús whistled. "Holy shit! Tell my mama I'm going straight."

The assistants moved closer, oohing and ahhing.

In front of the mirror, Lexi admired the navy dress. Tied with spaghetti straps at the shoulders, it had a daring neckline. The garment hugged her curves all the way to her thighs, where a slit from there to the bottom of her right leg provided ample room for a face-high reverse roundhouse kick if required.

"Scott, my man, you have the eye. Hello?" Jesús waved his hand in front of the other man's face as he stared at Lexi with his mouth open.

"What's wrong?" She noticed him gaping.

"Erm…erm…gloves. You need to cover your arm." He walked away to speak to a sales assistant.

"What's wrong with your arm?" Jesús leaned in to stare at both her arms.

"I'm sensitive about this scar." She held her inner forearm out to him.

"But you can barely see it." He shrugged. "You need a clutch." He picked up a matching navy purse and passed it to her.

"What will I do with this?" She turned the small, sparkly purse over in her hands.

"I don't know. Maybe you could fill it with quarters and hit someone with it," he suggested with an exaggerated eye-roll.

Lexi tested the weight of it and nodded her approval.

Jesús touched the back of his hand to his forehead. "I'm getting a migraine."

By the time they reached the register, she had a dress, a purse, gloves, and shoes and Dick's credit card was over eight thousand dollars lighter.

It had been a good day, but she had begun to feel like she needed a little glass-vial-pick-me-up. Jesús dropped them at their car and drove away without a backward glance and they headed to the motel.

"Are you okay?" Scott asked as she drove. "You're feeling a little off."

"I think I need to eat." The one thing she hated most about their empathetic connection was that he could sense her emotional state.

"We can stop for something to eat on the way to the motel."

She cursed silently. Now, it would be even longer before she returned to the glass vial.

Lexi swung the car into the drive-thru and Scott looked at her. "We're not going in?"

"I won't leave those shopping bags in the car and I won't take them out in this neighborhood." She drew up to the window.

"Two McRibs, fries, and a Coke, please. What are you having, Scott?"

"Three Big Macs, large fries, and a vanilla shake,"

They parked with the food.

"You looked really nice in that dress." He stared at his food.

"I imagine anyone would look nice in a five-thousand-dollar dress." She shook her head. "I don't get it, you know? Dick owns that amazing place, so he's clearly rich. Why does he keep doing that shitty PI job?"

"Maybe he likes it. Eternity's a long time, so he might as well keep busy."

Lexi gazed out of the window. "I've never met a vamp who lived for eternity."

"I guess if *you're* rocking up at their front door, eternity probably won't happen for them."

"I have nothing against vamps, but if they hurt people…" She didn't need to finish the sentence.

"Like Dimitri? I mean, Barry," he asked through a mouthful of fries.

"Yes, like him."

"What happened to him?"

"When I found him with one of the kids, he tried to turn me so I killed him." She shrugged and bit into her burger.

"He tried to— Oh, yuk!" Scott pulled the slice of dill pickle from the bun and held it out of the window at arm's length.

She gulped her food. "Now, I *know* you're not about to drop that on the ground."

"The birds will eat it."

"The birds won't get a chance because you'll put it in the trash. It's roasting in here anyway." She pointed to a trash can ten feet ahead of the car. They both climbed out.

Lexi looked at the slice of pickle in his fingertips. "Why don't you ask them to hold the pickle?"

"I don't like the pickle itself but I like the taste of the burger where it *was*."

"You are too fucking weird." She sipped her Coke.

She leaned on the hood with her drink as Scott walked to the trash can and dropped the little slice of pickle in.

When he turned toward the car, his eyes widened and he dropped his burger. "Motherfucker!"

Lexi whirled to see that someone had crept to the back of the car and was taking the bags from the back seat. The kid looked up, realized he'd been seen, and bolted with their purchases. She put her cup carefully on the hood and stroked her finger down her scar.

Nothing.

Scott's magic had dissipated and she shrugged and ran after the thief.

She was fast, fortunately—unusually fast for a dud legacy.

"Lexi, just—" Scott started, but she had already set off in pursuit.

In five strides, she caught up with the thief and launched herself at his back in the same moment that she sensed a release of power from Scott. The boy tripped over his own feet and fell. Unable to stop herself, she sailed over him and met the asphalt face and arms first. She could hear her friend's sharp intake of breath from across the parking lot and raised her head as he winced at her hard fall.

Lexi staggered to her feet and walked to the young thief, who stared in disbelief at his feet. His laces were tied together. She picked the bags up and kicked him in the balls before she caught the young man by the back of his t-shirt and hauled him to the car.

Scott looked concerned. "What are you doing?"

"I'll tie him to the back of the car and drag him around the parking lot a few times. Maybe up and down the street." She passed the bags to her friend, who put them into the rear footwell.

"You can't do that. He's only a stupid kid." He didn't seem to know whether or not she was kidding.

"Hey!" the thief protested.

She flicked the wrist of her hand that held his collar, and his head bounced off the car's bumper.

"Ow!"

"I could get Dick to turn him. Then I could legitimately kill him."

"I thought we were trying to stay off Kindred's radar."

Lexi released a frustrated breath. She threw the thief down and kicked him in the balls again. The kid cried.

Scott walked around the car and made to open the door, but she had locked it. He looked at her.

"Where do you think you're going?" She pointed. "Your burger is lying on the ground."

He stamped to the front of the car, huffing like a grumpy teen, picked the burger up, and shoved it into the trash.

"I don't think I'd have liked explaining to Dick that we lost all that stuff he just paid for," he muttered as he climbed into the car.

Lexi assessed the damage to her face in the vanity mirror. She had grazes on her cheek, her elbows, and on the palms of her hands.

"Let's get back," he told her. "I can heal those for you but I want to clean them first."

She put the car into drive and they glided past the thief, who tried to undo his laces with one hand while he cradled his balls with the other.

For a while, they drove in silence. She was angry that she couldn't seem to maintain a hold on the magic and that he had interfered.

"So, what exactly happened then, with Barry?" Scott asked.

Lexi was glad of the opportunity to talk about something to distract her from the rage she felt. "We traced him to an old factory. I separated from my group and he jumped me and knocked me out. When I came to, he was dripping blood into my mouth. I realized the fucker was planning to turn me. Seconds after the blood went in, it was like someone had switched on a light and I could see the whole place like it was daylight. It was useful in that moment but not a good sign for going back to Kindred, even though I experienced for the first time what those enhanced senses were like for the other legacies. I had a shuriken in my sleeve. I slid it up his middle and ran while he tried to stop his guts from falling out."

"Was the kid okay? Or did you have to..." He left the sentence hanging.

"I ran to the next floor and toward the sound of crying. I heard the others coming in the front. If they had seen me then, they would have known I'd been exposed to vamp blood. I'd heard what happened to people who were contaminated. I had to get into the light, but the windows on that level were completely bricked up. I found the boy tied up and he looked unharmed. I was relieved that I might not have to kill him.

"I slapped an explosive charge on the bricks where the window had been, grabbed the kid, and ran into the hallway.

"After a hole was blown in the wall, I took him into the room. First, I forced my eyes open to the daylight. It was the hardest thing I've ever done and I wanted to scream. Inside, I *was* screaming. At first, it was like my eyes were on fire. After a few seconds, I blinked and the worst was over."

Scott stared out of the window. "So that's how it happened. I was taught tasting vampire blood meant you were lost forever. I thought that was true until I met you."

"That was what they told me too but I didn't feel lost. I merely felt like me."

He turned to her. "Did you get away with it? Or was that when you left?"

"When they came in, I held the boy's face to the hole in the wall and pretended to check *his* eyes. I felt them watching me as I turned the crying kid's face to me. His eyes were watering from the dust in the air after the explosion. I hoped mine looked the same—only irritated. I checked his neck, then cut the cable ties on his hands and feet. I took the kid to the doorway, passed him to my sister Maggie, and asked if anyone wanted to check me, but they said I looked okay. God, my heart was in my mouth." Lexi shook her head at the memory.

"So, they let you walk away?"

"Braxton, the father of the unit, wasn't convinced. My senses were heightened, remember. Honestly, I expected a silver dagger in my back as I walked down the hallway. As I reached the stairs, he spoke my name. I almost stopped before I realized he'd whispered. There was no way I'd have been able to hear that with human hearing. I kept walking and waited for it to wear off. So, any more questions?"

"Are you going to eat that last McRib?"

They parked at the motel and Scott stretched into the back to retrieve the bags.

"It's probably best no one sees those labels." He vanished.

Lexi sighed and trudged up the stairs, trying to keep her scraped palms from touching the rusty metal railing.

He was on the balcony and his cell was ringing when she reached the room.

"If I step in there, I'll lose the signal." He put it on speaker and placed it on the metal railing, then twirled his finger in a circle. Lexi knew by now that this meant no one else could hear them. She stood near the phone while he went into the room to pull his first aid kit from his bag.

"How's it going?" Dolores asked.

She conveyed her irritation in three words. "Well, hello, Dolores."

"Oh, dear. You didn't kill him, did you?"

Lexi paused long enough that she was certain Dolores would be perspiring. "No. We talked. He's still an asshole but we can work together."

"He's forgiven you? Just like that?" The woman sounded surprised.

"Excuse me? *He's* forgiven *me?*" Her voice was so high at the end, she squeaked.

"You did leave him with a broken neck, dear," Dolores admonished.

"He told me it was he who called you that night to get me out of Chicago."

"That's right. Did I never mention that?" She knew damn well she'd never mentioned it. Lexi remained silent.

"Did you know he's rich?" Scott jumped into the gap in the conversation.

"Well, he *was* one of the most famous movie actors in the forties. By *he*, I mean his grandfather, obviously!" The older woman chuckled.

"Did you know James Dean sat on his—" Scott began.

"We're not going through that again," Lexi interjected and held a hand up to silence him.

"Have you made contact with the client?" Dolores asked.

"Yes. She thinks a local businessman is behind all this."

The other end of the phone was silent.

"Dolores?" Scott checked the cell to see if they'd lost the connection.

"Yes, I'm here. Sorry. I was looking out of the window." She sounded distracted.

Lexi was immediately on the alert. "What's wrong?"

"It's probably nothing."

"But?" She drummed her fingers on the rail.

"You know when you see the same car too many times in too many different places?"

"That fucking cult. Why can't Kindred let it go?" She banged the metal rail with her fist.

Scott brought out the gauze and sterile water. "They could be looking for me."

She shooed him away.

"They think I'm stepping on their toes, dear, but yes, Kindred might have discovered one or both of you are with me." That the woman sounded so calm irked her even more.

"Is there anything we can do?" Scott leaned in the doorway.

"It sounds like it's time to move your office," Lexi suggested.

"I have a potential client coming in to speak to me about a job later. But yes, my Spidey sense is tingling. I'll pack after this appointment."

"Do me a favor, Dolores. Pack first." She was getting bad vibes about the situation.

"And if you need us, call," Scott added.

"I will, dear. Look after each other and Scott, make sure Lexi doesn't kill William."

"I'm right here," she retorted, but the woman had disconnected.

Scott took his cell and they entered the room. Lexi sat on her bed and he cleaned the scratches on her face.

"I don't like the sound of that." She bounced her leg up and down, a recent nervous trait.

"I hope she's careful," he muttered as he turned his attention to her palms.

"I could do this myself, you know." She didn't mean to sound sharp but being in close proximity to other people when she was injured made her nervous. Irritated with both herself and everything in general, she put her hand on her knee to force her leg to rest.

"I'd rather do it myself. I want to be sure I've removed all the dirt before I close the wounds. Plus, you're really jittery." He stood and threw the gauze into the R2D2-shaped can. "I'm sorry I interfered back there. I was anxious to show you that you have other methods at your disposal now that you have magic." He returned, placed a hand on the top of her head, and whispered something she didn't catch.

Lexi wondered, not for the first time, if he used real words or merely muttered nonsense to annoy her.

"Your way would have been more discreet, but I'd already committed to my action. That's not the time to butt in with a different plan." She looked at her hands and elbows and realized there were no scrapes. When she checked the mirror, her face was blemish-free. "Nice job. Thanks." She headed into the bathroom.

CHAPTER FIVE

Lexi didn't often feel like she was outside her comfort zone. Tonight, she thought she might need a map to find her way back. She jumped at a knock on the door. Scott stood to answer it while she tried to tuck a two-inch switchblade into her purse. It wouldn't fit with all the quarters.

Dick stepped in, wearing a dinner jacket and a bow tie. He stopped in his tracks. "Well, don't you scrub up nice!"

She smiled.

"Did you actually smile? Who are you, and what have you done with Lexi Braxton?"

"So, what's our story?" she asked. "Because no one will believe I'm your date."

"You're Bianca, an old friend from Chicago. We've known each other for years and you rarely try to murder me. Do you think you can follow the brief?"

"I don't know. That last part sounds tricky." She stuck her tongue out.

"Just a second." Scott took her hand and closed his own around it.

"Erm…" She glanced quickly at him.

He took his hand away, and in her palm was a shiny silver teardrop pendant on a silver chain.

"Scott, this is lovely. Can you put it on for me?" Lexi asked. She lifted her hair and he fastened it at the back of her neck as he muttered softly.

"This will cloak your magical ability from anyone who gets too curious." He stepped back and looked at her. "Okay, knock 'em dead."

"But please don't take that literally," Dick added. They left the room.

"Don't forget these." Scott passed the purse and gloves to Dick.

The vampire handed the purse to her. "What the hell's in this thing?" he asked as they reached the vehicle.

"Put it this way." She slid into the passenger seat. "If we stumble across a pinball machine, I got us covered." She winked.

He glanced sideways at the dress as he drove away. "I must say I'm surprised. You have exceptional taste."

Lexi smiled. "What's even more surprising is that Scott selected it."

"He's quite a dark horse." Dick laughed. "He seems like a good guy. How did you meet him?"

"Through Dolores. He went to her for help when his Kindred cell was forcing him to match with someone he didn't trust."

The vampire looked surprised. "It was my understanding that mages and legacies had the autonomy to choose who they were matched with."

"They usually do, but Kindred cells essentially run independently. Scott had watched this guy grow up and he was the kind of kid who tortured little animals. He hoped he'd grow out of it, but the guy only grew nastier. In the end, Scott flat-out refused to give him access to his powers. The head of the family was a bastard too. He tried to force him to comply. He didn't feel safe there."

"Couldn't they have matched the psycho with someone else?"

"He insisted on Scott. It's unsurprising. While we don't get to meet many other units, I have met other mages and Scott's abilities are beyond anything I've seen before."

"But he wound up matched with you."

"That was his idea and the situation we were in. Actually, I think it saved us both, but he wouldn't have been wasted on someone like me if we were still in Kindred." Lexi was ready to leave this conversation behind. "Have you heard from Leonard?"

"I haven't and I'm concerned. If I don't hear anything in the next couple of hours, I'll have to drop past his place tonight."

"I'll back you up, just in case."

"In that?" He indicated the dress.

"It's surprisingly versatile." She grinned.

They pulled up at the entrance and two valets opened the doors. Lexi took Dick's arm and they entered the grand foyer, where they were offered champagne. Both declined. Somewhere farther into the building, a soulful woman's voice sang "Summertime," accompanied by a live band.

"William, it's delightful to see you." An elderly woman in a long, beaded cream dress with an organza wrap approached him and air-kissed him with a *mwah*.

"Betsy, you look younger every time I see you." He kissed the woman's hand.

"Thank you, William. I've been bathing in the blood of virgins." Betsy winked.

"Good grief, the import fees must be exorbitant." He returned the wink.

"William!" The woman feigned shock. "Are you suggesting Palm Springs is completely without home-grown virgins?" She laughed and whispered conspiratorially, "Thank goodness you're here. We simply don't see enough of you. I thought I was in for another boring evening of trying to wrangle money out of my *frenemies*, as the kids say."

"So, is there any gossip?" he asked as they walked through the entrance hall.

"Well, the town's most handsome and eligible bachelor has arrived with a mysterious, stunning beauty. Let's start with that."

"Where are my manners? Betsy O'Donnell, this is Bianca Maybury, an old friend from Chicago."

Lexi shook the woman's hand.

"Are you by chance related to the New England Mayburys?" Betsy asked.

"Oh, we don't talk about the New England Mayburys," she replied smoothly.

"Really? How perfectly delicious. I look forward to hearing you not talk about them later after you've visited the gin bar." The woman grinned at her.

She grinned in response and decided she liked her irreverence.

"Save a dance for me, muffin. I'm still holding out hope." She patted Dick's behind and moved on to greet more guests.

"Let's mingle." He led them through the rooms and pointed out various paintings and pieces of furniture.

They stood before a huge painting depicting a War of Independence battle scene. He looked at her. "You're not very talkative."

"I thought you'd use your vamp hearing to listen in on the conversations around us."

"I can do both. Anyway, I have a question. If you weren't trying to kill me in Chicago, what *were* you trying to do?" They both continued to gaze at the painting.

He'd probably mulled over her reaction to him calling her "bloodthirsty" in the restaurant the night before. More than likely, he'd already guessed correctly.

"Can we not get into this now?" Lexi asked.

"As you wish, but it's something we need to talk about, isn't it?" Dick turned to look at her face as she stared resolutely at the painting. She nodded as though she agreed.

Not if I can avoid it.

As they wandered past a group of men talking about local business, she slowed to listen. "This is a beautiful"—she looked around for an excuse to have slowed—"vase."

The vampire glanced quickly at it. "I'd guess 1899."

"As old as that?" She was surprised and leaned in to look closer.

"Not the age, the price. It looks like it came from Home Depot." He sneered.

"Well, there's William," a raised voice said from the group of men, clearly intended to get his attention. "If you're looking for property, Caleb, you could see if he wants to sell."

"Stanley, how are you?" Dick asked and maneuvered them toward the group.

"I'm very well, William." A man in his fifties stuck his hand out, and they shook.

"This is Bianca, an old family friend. Bianca, this is Stanley Horton. He's the chief of police so you be good now." Lexi shook the man's hand.

"What are—" Another man stared wide-eyed at her. He turned to Dick. "You're in...surprising company this evening." Turning his attention to Lexi, he continued with an oily smile. "Well, you look too young to be anyone's *old* friend." He licked his lips.

"And this is Caleb Linden. He's in property and virtually every-thing else. Be careful of him. He's a rascal." Dick chuckled.

"William, my reputation—" Caleb started.

"Precedes you." The vampire laughed and the men all joined in.

Lexi understood exactly what he was saying and shook the man's hand as he continued to stare lasciviously down her neckline.

She smiled and giggled as she imagined thunking the Home Depot vase into his face.

"What's this about buying my property?" Dick asked.

"Don't worry, William. I know what the answer would be." Caleb sighed.

A handsome, slick-looking man with gray at his temples smiled to reveal perfect teeth. "Will, I absolutely forbid you to sell that beautiful piece of history to Caleb. If it became a ninety-nine-cent store, the voters would blame me and this election's already giving me an ulcer."

"Bianca, this is Todd O'Donnell, the current and future mayor," Dick told her.

Lexi shook hands dutifully. *This is useful. All the players together.*

"Are you local, Bianca?" asked Todd.

"He means, are you a voter?" Caleb Linden guffawed.

"I'm visiting with my fiancé, John. We're here looking at wedding venues, as recommended by Uncle William, and to get the paperwork arranged for our wedding."

"Oh, did you hear from the records office, dear?" the vampire asked.

"No, not a thing." She shrugged.

"Not to worry. We'll call again tomorrow." He patted her shoulder.

Lexi saw a brief flicker of a look pass between Caleb and Stanley.

"How do you pass your time when you're not at parties with gentlemen of questionable character, Bianca?" Caleb asked.

Dick put his hand over his heart as though wounded, then chuckled.

She smiled, but the man wasn't looking at her face.

My eyes are up here, douchebag.

"I'm a dental hygienist, and my fiancé John is a systems design consultant." She often used the dental hygienist line as no one ever wanted to know more. People usually glazed over at John's systems job too, but not today.

"Really? If you're looking to put roots down here, he should come see me. Where is he currently?" Caleb handed her a card. She took it, smiled, and handed it to Dick. Not even a sliver of card would fit into the tiny purse with all those quarters.

"He's been working with a small tech start-up. He'd be able to tell you more about it than I could." She shrugged and gave a vacuous giggle.

"Well, I'm always happy to help a friend of a friend." The man's eyes were still glued to her breasts.

"So, you're *Uncle Will* now," Todd said, and the men laughed.

"It's a term of endearment. I've been friends with Bianca's parents for years."

Betsy approached. "Darling."

"Hello, Mother." Todd put an arm around her. "You've done a wonderful job with the party, as always." He kissed her cheek.

The woman pouted. "I have a complaint for the mayor."

"Oh, dear. Never mind the voters. Now you're in trouble with your mother, Todd," Stanley added. The men laughed raucously again.

"I hear there's *another* Mexican restaurant opening in the area. Can't we have a French restaurant? Who even eats Mexican?" Betsy asked.

"I'm sure Uncle William had Mexican only this morning." Lexi smiled sweetly at Dick.

He returned it with a kind-uncle-like smile of his own and patted the back of her hand affectionately, but his eyes quite clearly said, "Do not fucking start."

"Mother, I thought you loved *huevos rancheros*," Todd replied.

"I do, but I love French food, too," Betsy assured him.

A loud laugh roared from behind Lexi, and she turned to see a group of young men around a billiard table in the room next door. She recognized Tommy, Kate's boyfriend, from their morning visit to the bar. He was horsing around with the group. She turned away before he saw her.

"Stanley, dear, your…friends are quite exuberant." Betsy was clearly unhappy that the young men were getting rowdy.

"Of course, Betsy. I'll send them home. It's my fault they've been here all day. I thought they might be able to help," Stanley said and looked not at Betsy but at Caleb.

"They've been here all day?" The woman looked puzzled.

"They brought the produce this morning, remember? You haven't been at the gin, have you?" Caleb laughed.

"Of course I have. I paid for it. Well, they've been very well-behaved for most of the day. I haven't heard a peep." Betsy smiled and turned to her son. "People have given me envelopes all evening. It's going very well."

"That reminds me." Dick took an envelope from his breast pocket and handed it to her. "Here's another one for your collection."

"William, you are quite simply the most charming man alive." She took the envelope and it disappeared into her large purse.

"I'm sure nothing could be further from the truth," the vampire replied honestly.

"Please excuse me one moment." Stanley headed toward the billiards room.

"Your mayor thanks you for your support, Mr. Levin." Todd held his hand out.

Dick took the proffered hand. "The mayor can always count on my support."

Todd pointed an accusing finger at him. "Except on the golf course."

"Hey, I'm always there for bowling night."

The man looked at Lexi. "He's always late for bowling night."

"Fashionably so." The vampire glanced quickly at her.

"Do you wear the shirt? And holy sh…moke, the *shoes*?" She tried to picture it.

"His grandfather was an exceptional bowler, golfer, and tennis player." Betsy's eyes glittered at the memory.

Lexi heard the men leave the room behind her. They were laughing and chatting but suddenly stopped. She could feel their eyes on her back but realized their main attention was on Dick. She knew that being shifters, they would have smelled the vampire. If they had been in wolf form, their hackles would be raised at the sense of danger. In their human form, they might not have hackles but the atmosphere had definitely tensed. Lexi grasped the weighted little purse as her companion turned slowly and deliberately to face them.

"Gentlemen." He tilted his head.

She made to turn but he held her arm subtly. As this meant she would have to struggle to turn and that would draw attention, she remained as she was, facing away from the men.

"Move it," Stanley instructed quietly. They continued toward the exit.

"Have you done something to upset the locals, William?" Betsy asked in surprise.

"I believe my houseboy might have dinged someone's motorbike recently. I was under the impression the situation had been resolved."

"I'd guess from the looks those men gave you that the situation has not been resolved to their satisfaction. I will ask Stanley to ensure they don't return to the club any time soon." The woman looked suspiciously at the retreating men.

"Todd, may I borrow you for a moment?" Caleb asked with his hand on Todd's shoulder.

"Sure, Caleb." They walked away together.

"You boys promised no business tonight. You have five minutes," Betsy called after them before she returned her attention to the others.

"Uncle William, would you mind awfully if we head back soon? John will work all night if I don't wrestle that computer away from him." Lexi wanted to follow the shifters.

"You promised me a dance, young lady, and a dance I shall have." Dick took her hand and wrapped it expertly around his arm.

"I did?" She was startled. "Are you sure I promised that? Because that doesn't sound like a thing I'd promise."

He led her through the room next door toward the ballroom.

"What are you doing?" she asked.

"Giving them a few minutes to leave. I'll be able to follow the smell of a wolfpack as well in ten minutes as I can now with the added advantage of not running into them. I don't think they like me."

"Have you had trouble with them before?" Lexi took a glass of champagne from a passing waiter as they moved through the rooms.

"No. I thought I had a good relationship with the Palm Springs pack. I mean, sure, some of the younger ones can be boisterous, but I can't remember the last time I met with such hostility." He seemed nonplussed.

"Stanley's the alpha, right? Can you talk to him?" She sipped the champagne.

"It seems I will have to. Are you sure you should drink that? We might need you to fire on all cylinders later."

"This is only to get me through the dancing." She knocked the drink back and handed the glass to a different waiter on the way to the dance floor.

The band played "Blue Moon," and the two glided across the floor.

She caught bemused stares from many young men in the room. "I'm guessing you've pretty much done this town."

"Repeatedly, over the years. To the point where it's beginning to feel a little uncomfortable. It's déjà vu all over again," Dick admitted with a twitch of his lip.

"Have you never considered settling down with one person?" she asked, genuinely curious.

"Attachments bring vulnerability. I've lived a long time, Lexi, and I've gained many enemies. Some come and go but some have long memories." He twirled her. "You dance surprisingly well."

"Kindred taught me to slip seamlessly into any situation. It's funny since I was clumsy as a child."

He stopped dancing and stared at her. "You recall your life before Kindred?" He remembered where they were and their purpose and continued to dance.

"Flashes." She knew she had confirmed what he already suspected.

"So, I wasn't wrong when I accused you of being bloodthirsty. You were literally after my blood. You should have merely asked. My prices are very competitive."

"I'm not a blood whore." Lexi felt her face flame. "When Barry tried to turn me, the enhanced speed, strength, and senses were all great, although I was already very strong and fast for a human. That night, however, memories began to surface. I thought I'd never been counseled before—that's what they call it when they wipe your memories after a particularly difficult mission—but I realized they'd done it to me many times and the memories were surfacing. That was why I left. I knew I couldn't trust them and I knew that as soon as they discovered my memories were returning, they'd kill me."

"I assume the blood-hit didn't take your memories back as far as you needed?"

"Not nearly. So far, I've remembered to my late teens and the occasional flash of life before."

Dick stopped again but she forced him to continue. "How many times have you done it?"

Lexi paused, then decided she'd told him enough of the truth so might as well finish it. "Only three times. Barry, then you, then a blood den in Portland."

"You know you can't keep doing it, don't you?"

"I'm careful. Look, I'm sorry about the whole neck-breaking thing. Don't get me wrong. I still think you're an arrogant jerk." She smiled and he laughed.

"Well, you'll have to go to the back of an extraordinarily long line of people who think that." Dick glanced at the pendant Scott had given her. "What's happened to your pendant?"

She looked down and realized that the shiny silver had turned black. "I don't know. How strange." The song finished and they started to leave the dance floor. He glanced across the room at Betsy, who had watched him dance but turned quickly to speak to a group of women. He hesitated.

"Go on." Lexi gestured toward the dance floor.

"I'm sorry?" He looked blankly at her.

"She wants to dance with you." She shooed him away.

The band was playing "Unforgettable." "How apt," he said. He walked across the floor and offered his arm to Betsy, who took it with a dazzling smile on her face. They danced and spoke but Lexi couldn't hear the conversation. At the end of the song, the woman delivered him to her side.

"You dance beautifully, exactly as your grandfather did. It's like being transported back and I could turn and find Harvey standing right there with a grin on his face. Do you remember how he hated to dance, William?" Betsy looked into the distance and into another time.

Dick smiled warmly, no doubt remembering too. "You've told me."

"The fun we all had." She grasped the younger woman's arm exuberantly.

"They must be wonderful memories," Lexi said politely.

"I'm a silly old woman." Betsy wiped a tear from the corner of her eye. "You look so much like him. It's the eyes, I suppose."

He kissed the back of her hand. "Everyone says that, so it must be true."

"Harvey spoke of him often. When he never returned from Europe, it broke his heart. We never forgot our William. Well, off you go, then. Don't let it be so long next time. It was lovely to meet you, dear." She turned to the party.

The vampire watched her walk away. "Let's get out of here."

While they stood outside and waited for the valet to arrive with the car, a voice spoke from directly behind them.

"It was good to see you again, William. Perhaps we'll run into each other again soon." Lexi jumped slightly at Caleb's voice. No one approached her from behind without her being aware of them. No one.

The vampire paused for a moment. "I'm sure we shall." He sounded absolutely certain of it.

They headed down the drive in silence and didn't speak again until they had left the property.

"He gives me the willies," Lexi admitted the moment they were through the gate.

"Yes. I've felt uncomfortable around him for as long as I've known him. And when a vampire says that, it shouldn't be ignored."

She stared into the darkness. "I have the feeling we didn't pull the wool over his eyes at all."

Dick glanced at her as he drove. "What do you think about tonight?"

"I think Kate's problem is coming from much closer than she thinks it is. You?"

He nodded. "I agree. Also, I'm concerned it's only the tip of the iceberg. Something bad happened today. I think those young shifters did it and Caleb gave them an alibi."

"Telling Betsy they were hanging around at the club all day." She nodded.

"I think we need to drop in on Leonard. I shouldn't have involved him and have a very bad feeling about this."

"Agreed. We can find the shifters later."

"I don't think that's an option. We have a bogey on our six." Dick frowned into his rearview mirror.

"A what on our what?"

"Someone's tailing us. I thought all you Kindred types spoke like the military."

"No. What on earth gave you that idea? Can you lose them?"

"I'll give it a try." He accelerated and the vehicle behind matched their speed.

They rounded a bend to find a truck parked across the street. Dick skidded the car onto a side road.

"What's up here?" she asked, then twisted sideways in her seat to look out of the back and front.

"It's residential. We might be able to lose them on one of these roads."

A truck suddenly hurtled from a side road. He was able to speed up to avoid a T-bone, but it impacted with the rear of the car, which fishtailed. Dick pressed the accelerator to the floor.

"These guys aren't messing around." Lexi turned to kneel on her seat. She dug in her pocket and drew a rifle. Dick looked at her as she adjusted the scope.

"Where the actual fuck did that come from?"

"A lady never tells." She slipped a magazine into the weapon and slid into the back seat, banging her head as the car went through a pothole. "Ow!"

He made eye contact through the rearview mirror. "Complain to the mayor."

She turned to steady the rifle on the back of the seat. "I'm afraid you'll lose your back window."

"Just do it."

With a nod, she leveled the rifle as best she could. "Do we have a straight road?"

"We're coming up on a bend now. I think they'll attempt to herd us over the canyon wall. There aren't many places where that's possible, but we're heading toward one."

"Shit."

He skidded around the bend. "Okay, straight for twenty seconds,"

Lexi leveled the rifle again and took two shots in quick succession. The first was intended to shatter the window and the second the driver of the truck, but the first one took the driver and the second simply compounded the damage. The truck went out of control and off the road.

It was replaced by the two others. The one closest turned on a row of four spotlights above its cabin, intending to blind them. The large vehicle behind also had its high beams on and created a silhouette of a man who stood out of the sunroof in the first truck and tried to aim a rifle.

"Amateurs," she muttered, aimed at the man, and fired a single round as Dick swerved. With a grimace, she returned her aim to the gunman and killed him.

"I'm turning," the vampire told her. "This road leads to a hiking-trail parking lot. The moment I stop, find somewhere to hide."

He skidded into the parking lot and vanished. Lexi had a moment of indecision. She didn't need to look at the scar to know the magic had completely dissipated. Her first instinct was to retrieve the vial from her pocket, knowing it would help her in the fight to come. The moment she'd used to think was all the time she had. Before she could get out of the car, one of the trucks plowed into it and shoved Dick's vehicle several feet.

It's a good thing I wasn't hiding behind this fucking car.

A man jumped out of the other vehicle and walked closer. She put the rifle into her pocket and climbed out with her hands up. The guy she'd shot still dangled from the sunroof. He'd been a little too round in the middle for that maneuver.

"Where's your friend?" The man walked toward her with his weapon raised.

"He ran off." She tried to sound pissed about it.

When he pushed her back with the end of his rifle, she complied and noticed that these were not shifters. He ducked his head quickly into the car and returned his attention to her.

"Where's the gun?" He poked her again with his rifle.

"He took it." She maintained a blank expression as he shifted his gaze around the darkness.

"The guy's armed," he shouted to his friends. Two of them had joined him and now stood a few feet behind, which left two more near the back truck. "What's your friend's name?"

"Dick."

As she faced them, she saw the one at the very back disappear quickly and silently in the dark.

The guy before her lifted his semi-automatic weapon and called to the others. "Get the lights on and shine them around the area. We're looking for Dick."

"Aren't we all?" Lexi agreed to the men's amusement.

The next man vanished.

"To be honest, he's not usually this hard to get," she added. "If you simply stay in one place for any length of time, he'll probably get around to you." The remaining men all laughed now except the one who returned the aim of his gun to her.

"Come on, smart mouth. You can come with me." They walked to the edge of the trail and a spotlight followed them.

"Oh, good. With all this light, he's unlikely to hit me," she commented.

"Don't point it at us, you idiot. Point it ahead of us." The dark settled around them when the light was redirected.

She spun, disarmed him in three seconds, and swept her leg out to drop him while she twisted the gun out of his hold. He had other ideas and head-butted her in the face, and she stumbled back. In the darkness, she hadn't seen it coming.

Lexi struck him on the ear with her quarter-filled purse, and he fell to his knees.

I'll have to thank Jesús for that idea.

As she delivered a kick to his head with her right foot, he lashed out, and she stumbled and toppled. He was on top of her immediately with his rifle across her throat.

She had stretched her hands closer to pop his eyeballs with her thumbs when Dick's face appeared from the darkness behind him, barely visible except for his teeth. It was a truly terrifying sight—the stuff of nightmares, but not hers. The man made a choking sound, and the vampire whisked him away. She scrambled to her feet, sprinted through the darkness, and settled behind the car with the rifle.

"Should we keep moving the light?" asked a voice from the truck.

Receiving no reply, the light moved in the opposite direction until it illuminated the man lying on the ground.

"He's down! Go get him," a voice shouted. There was no response. "Chad? Mike?"

"I'm afraid they're rather indisposed," said Dick's chillingly cold voice from the darkness.

The man scrambled from the vehicle and ran directly into his adversary.

Lexi stood. In the light from the truck, she saw the trail of blood from the vampire's mouth to his white shirt. With none of their attackers remaining, they climbed into his car and drove away past the two trucks. The third vehicle, which had left the road and should have had a dead driver, had disappeared.

He leaned out and sniffed as he went past. "That one had shifters in it. I'll want to speak to them after we've been to see Leonard."

"Let's pick Scott up first," Lexi suggested.

She felt his eyes on her. "You should have sensed that head-butt coming. The more you rely on that stuff, the less you can depend on your natural ability."

"I don't rely on it," she snapped, knowing she hadn't fooled him.

"Of course not." He returned his gaze to the road.

CHAPTER SIX

Dolores checked the time. As promised, she'd packed everything in her Denver, Colorado office. The only things visible were the desk, two chairs, the filing cabinet, and the clock she now watched.

The client was expected to arrive on the hour. He had sounded desperate on the phone and in her experience, the more desperate a client was, the earlier they arrived. She considered the possibility that he might not be as desperate as he had intimated.

To distract herself from the wait, she stood and went to the window. The car was there again. A coincidence? Probably not.

When she glanced at the clock, she saw a fly walking across its face. She approached it slowly and smacked it with her yellow legal pad, then took it down and wiped the brown stain from its face with a tissue. As she polished the glass front, she considered returning it to its place, but the sound of footsteps on the stairs made her lean it against the wall on top of the filing cabinet. She returned to her chair.

The man knocked and opened the door. Three deep, angry scratches raked his face. One went through his left eye, which was half brown and half milky-white. He looked nervously around the office.

"Are you Dolores? I'm Eric. We spoke on the phone."

"Come in, Eric." She looked at the clock. "You're exactly on time."

He glanced at the clock as well and smiled nervously at her.

"Take a seat. Tell me how we can help."

"You deal with unusual situations involving unusual…people, yes?"

"That's correct." She leaned forward.

The man looked around the room. "I'm sorry, but have you just arrived or are you moving out?"

"We're preparing to decorate. So, your problem?"

"I'm sorry, I didn't mean to be intrusive but I don't want to hire you and have you disappear on me."

"Eric. I'd like to save you the effort of bullshitting me. Why don't you tell me what Kindred wants?" Dolores asked.

Eric ceased wringing his hands and straightened in his chair.

"Thank you, Dolores. I respect expediency." As he spoke, the scratches vanished from his face but the half-white eye remained. "You were involved in taking something of ours."

"As you can see, Eric, I don't have much." She gestured to the sparse room. "Do you see your property in here?"

"I thought we weren't going to bullshit." He was unsmiling.

"Under US law, it's no longer legal to keep people as property."

"*People*, quite," he agreed as though she had proven his point for him.

The door opened to admit an angry-looking young man and a pale, thin girl. She remained at the back of the room and leaned against the wall, while her companion walked to Dolores's side of the desk and sat on it to stare belligerently at her. The older woman glanced at Eric with a raised eyebrow that asked why he hadn't taught the boy any manners. His eyes flicked in irritation at the young man.

"Our asset's disappearance has caused friction for his family. They merely want him back. We know you were hired to assist with his removal. I'd like to hire you to find him again—unless you still know where he is?"

"I'm afraid I don't have your…asset." She would never think of Scott as her or anyone else's property.

The young man jumped from the desk and back-handed her across the face. She saw it coming and winced as she tried to turn her face away.

The room wavered and flickered slightly and they all saw it.

"Lucy, what was that?" Eric turned in his chair to face the girl.

"There's a glamor on the room." The girl closed her eyes, held a hand up, and muttered.

Dolores turned to the young man. "I see you favor the fae. Personally, I never approved of the unseelie fae blood being used in the legacy ritual. They are too...unpredictable, or perhaps I mean predictable." She wiped blood from the corner of her mouth.

Lucy's face tensed and eventually, she sighed. "I can't get through the glamor."

"I can." The young man drew his hand back.

"Warren!" Eric snapped.

Warren glanced briefly at the man and curled his hand into a fist. Dolores tried to get out of the chair but he struck her on the side of the head and she fell beside the filing cabinet. The room wobbled, and a door appeared in the rear wall. The three of them turned to face it while she lay unmoving on the floor.

"It's a portal." The girl walked toward it.

"Let's see what the bitch was hiding." Her assailant barged past the others, caught hold of the handle, and opened the door.

CHAPTER SEVEN

ick and Lexi reached the motel and she ran up to the room with her stilettos in her hand. Scott was watching the Cary Grant movie while playing cat's cradle absently with a luminescent blue-white light. She observed that he was fully dressed and had his sneakers on.

"Were you planning to go somewhere?" she asked.

"Only staying ready. It felt like you would need me." He dissolved the ethereal string instantly.

She snatched her leathers up and hurried into the bathroom.

"Dick's waiting in the car." She closed the door.

Seated on the end of the tub, she retrieved the vial, pulled the stopper, and shook it with her finger over the end. She stroked her fingertip over her tongue and sighed as the strength returned to her extremities and her mind cleared. These things were great and she told herself that wasn't why she took the vamp blood but sometimes, she wondered if she was simply fooling herself. She stood quickly. No, it was to help her find the memories buried by Kindred. With her eyes closed, she sought those memories and returned to her oldest ones— brief flashes of a stolen childhood—but nothing new surfaced. She replaced the stopper and put the vial into her pocket.

Within three minutes, she was in her familiar leathers. Removing the black pendant, she slipped it into her pocket. Scott still stood in the room. "I thought you'd be in the car."

"I won't leave you alone. Dolores told us to look after each other. Let me fix you."

He put his hand on her head. The pain in her nose and throat disappeared and her depleted magic re-energized.

Scott pulled his beanie on and waited at the door for her to walk through.

"What the hell happened to your car?" he asked as he stared at the dents in the bodywork, the bullet holes, and the missing back window.

"It drives okay. It's a little wobbly at the back, but otherwise fine." Dick sighed.

The young man looked around before he placed his hand on the vehicle. He closed his eyes and whispered. Dick gaped in surprise as the dents in the back buckled into their correct shape and the wheel straightened. When the process finished, the bullet holes weren't perfect but at least they wouldn't draw attention. He couldn't put the window back so he created a glamor of one instead.

The vampire gazed from the car to him several times. "If you'd consider a change in employment, I'm wondering if I could keep you on retainer."

"If this is a service you need regularly, I'd suggest *you* need a change of career." Scott opened the back door of the car, swept the glass off the seat with his beanie, and climbed in. As they drove to their next destination, they filled him in.

The neighborhood in Cathedral City was dark and quiet. Scott cloaked them when they parked a block from Leonard's house and prepared to walk to it. Lexi detected a curious odor but before she could step onto the street to follow it, Dick pulled her back. "This whole area smells of shifters. I'm sure they're still around."

"Ah, yes. That's what it is. So if we'd followed the shifters from the party, we'd have wound up here anyway." She looked into the darkness and although her senses were temporarily improved, she could neither see nor hear them.

"Why would they hang around if they've already—" Scott searched for the right words. "Uh, done something to your friend?"

"I don't like this. Simply walking in there could be a bad idea." She continued to scan the area all around them.

"I have to know if he's okay. I'll go alone." The vampire prepared to step onto the street.

"Wait, let me." She touched his arm. "Scott can keep me cloaked from a distance through our link."

"Are you sure?" He sounded doubtful.

"Yes. I…feel better now." She averted her face to avoid his stare.

Scott glanced at the other man. "Let's get to the car. It'll take a fair amount of energy. I should sit for this."

Lexi hopped the gate of the property that backed onto Leonard's house with ease. She walked through the garden to the wall at the rear and came face to face with a shifter in human form who hid in the bushes. She assumed a defensive posture and prepared to fight. He looked up, sniffed the air, then settled into his hiding place.

Well, I know the spell works.

She jumped the wall and hurried to Leonard's house. The patio door hung open on a single hinge, and the home had been ransacked.

When she entered, someone she assumed was Leonard lay dead on the tiled floor. She studied the body and suspected she knew why the pack was still in the area. Her phone buzzed in her pocket. When she glanced at the caller ID, it was Dick.

"This isn't the best time."

"Is he?"

"Someone is. I'm sorry. The place is a mess. It appears they were looking for something."

"Are there a couple of silver birch logs in the fireplace?" he asked.

"Yes, but I need to get out of here." She glanced at the logs.

"One of them is hollow. The end pops out. If he found anything, it'll be in there."

"Surely he'd have told them." Lexi didn't want Dick to know the condition of the body.

If he knew anything, she was *sure* he'd have told them.

"Dear God. I was there last night so my prints will be all over that place," he whispered as she disconnected.

Lexi stepped over the body to the fireplace. The second log she lifted was as heavy as the first, but when she moved it, she heard something shift inside. She puzzled for a few moments about how to open it and finally pushed the end. It clicked and came away to reveal a metallic lining, which explained the weight of the hollow log. She shook it until an envelope fell out, followed by a wad of cash. Hastily, she pocketed both items, stood, and returned to the door. She looked into the room and stroked the length of the scar.

Ablaze.

Little flames ignited all over the room. She started to leave, then turned again and stroked the scar again, "Oh, jeez, and definitely the bedroom." A loud whoosh sounded farther inside the house. It was time to go. She was about to turn away again when a high-pitched squeal issued from inside the house. Uncertain, she stood still and listened. It came again. She looked at the flames that now rose quickly, turned away, then spun back again.

"Shit," she muttered and raced into the house and through to the hallway. She stopped and listened but heard nothing. There were several doors, but only one was closed. Cautiously, she placed her right hand on it and pulled it away quickly. It was already hot. That would be the bedroom. She ran up the hall and glanced into the other rooms, but they were all empty.

Of course, It would have to be this room.

Reluctantly, she returned to the hot door and moved her hand over the surface. It was still cool at the bottom, so she crouched and pulled the handle down quickly as she shoved the door. Flames surged across the ceiling of the hallway in a whoosh. The room was black with toxic smoke but luckily, she didn't have to look far. A little ball of fur lay curled and still near the entrance.

Lexi picked it up and ran. The fire in the living room was well underway now. While she needed to conserve the little magic she had remaining, she would have to create a path to protect her from the flames. She used the magic, held the unresponsive creature to her, and bolted along the edge of the room to the exit. In the last moments, the flames licked at her left side, and the sharp smell of burning hair caught her nose.

She sprinted through the garden, hopped the wall as best she could with her bundle, and hurried through the neighbor's yard. Halfway across the lawn, she became aware of a snorting sound behind her. She turned to where the shifter sniffed the air where she had come over the wall. The spell was wearing off. She wasn't sure if he'd be susceptible to a spell in his wolf form, but she stroked the unhealing scar and whispered, "Sleep."

Instead of falling asleep as had happened when she'd used this spell previously, the young man staggered and shook his head as though trying to shake off a dizzy spell. Protecting herself from the flames had used the magic reserves. When she realized this moment of distraction was all she would get, she ran to the shifter, who was still unaware of her, and launched a kick to the side of his head. He dropped like a stone. She hopped over the gate and ran to the car.

"Move it." She leapt in.

Dick complied and they accelerated away. His face was like thunder.

"Maybe that wasn't him." Lexi patted the face of what appeared to be a French bulldog puppy.

"A mole on his face here?" Dick asked and pointed to the lower jaw on the right side of his face. She looked at him and nodded.

His gaze moved to the dog. "Marcel doesn't look good."

She fixed him with a horrified look. "Tell me he didn't have any more pets."

"No, Marcel's the only one."

"Why didn't the shifters leave after they killed him?" His gaze moved from her to the rearview mirror.

"It wasn't shifters who killed him. He was murdered by a vampire," she told him.

"He was *what?*" He almost lost control of the car in his surprise but regained it quickly.

"That's why they were there. The guys in the trucks were simply to delay us so they could get into position around the house and catch *you.* I think it was a trap."

"The deeper into this mess we get, the less sense it makes." Dick glanced at the puppy.

"That means Kindred either is or will soon be in town. Scott, I'm out. Can you help me?" She looked into the back of the car and frowned when she realized her friend was sprawled unconscious across the back seat.

"He's okay, isn't he? He only slumped a minute or so before you appeared."

"He'll be fine. What he did takes a ton of energy. He needs to recoup but I need help." Lexi stretched awkwardly and touched Scott's knee for a few moments.

She put her hand on the little dog's chest and whispered, "Breathe."

The animal lay still for another two seconds before he coughed and barked feebly several times. He whimpered, wobbled to his feet, turned in her lap, and flopped again.

"Oh." She wasn't sure what to do and shook him gently.

"He's okay. His heart's beating stronger now." Dick stroked the dog briefly. "Poor little guy."

They reached the vampire's house and Lexi shook Scott awake. "Are you okay?"

"I'm fine." He yawned and climbed out of the car, although he wobbled slightly and leaned against the car. "Mostly."

"Great. Hold this." She thrust the puppy at him and his face lit up.

"Can we—" he began.

"No, we can't keep it." She shook her head as they walked into the house.

The three of them gathered in the hallway and watched Jesús, who had his back to them and was mopping the floor. He had EarPods in and danced as he worked, singing "The Girl From Ipanema."

"Jesús," Dick shouted.

The man uttered a little scream and spun as he yanked his earplugs out. "Oh, my God! What happened to your dress?"

"It's fine. A little dusty but it lived. I changed after we left the party."

He walked toward them. "You smell of smoke. Please tell me you didn't burn the clubhouse down." He looked at Marcel in Scott's arms. "You got a puppy." He squealed.

Scott handed the animal to Lexi, and Jesús stepped closer to stroke the sleeping puppy. Scott moved behind him and whispered, "Sleep." The Mexican man slumped where he stood, and Scott caught him and carried him to a sofa.

Dick's jaw dropped. "That was amazing. If you could put that into an app, you'd be a billionaire."

She headed to the coffee pot and Dick followed, picking up a throw pillow on the way. They congregated around the breakfast bar. He placed the large pillow on the countertop and she placed the sleeping puppy on it.

"Right! What do we know?" she asked.

"I got Leonard killed." The vampire poured himself a large Jack Daniels. He offered the bottle to Lexi, who pushed her black coffee toward him. Once he'd topped it up, he offered the bottle to Scott, who shook his head.

"*We* got him killed." The young man took a glass and held it to the water dispenser on the refrigerator.

"Oh, I wouldn't—" Dick' protest cut off abruptly.

Thick red liquid ran into Scott's glass.

"What the fuck?" He put it on the counter.

"Waste not want not." Dick tipped his bourbon into the blood and swirled the glass. He knocked the drink back and looked at the horrified Scott. "You seem a little naive for a Kindred mage."

"They don't let mages go out on the dangerous jobs until they're matched with a legacy," Lexi explained.

"Surely they're more than capable of handling themselves." The vampire waved his fingers in a pseudo-magical fashion.

"It's complicated." She didn't want to discuss it any further.

The vampire opened the refrigerator and passed a bottle of water to the other man, who took it, nodded his thanks, and sat at the counter.

"How are your reserves?" she asked her friend as she stared at the gaping indent on her arm.

He paused to assess how he felt. "Building up. I feel like I'm at about twenty percent. I'll be fully restored in an hour."

"Halfsies?" She placed her open hand onto the counter.

He put his hand into hers, and all three of them stared at the unhealing scar as light surged into it.

Dick shook his head as if to clear it. "That's quite mesmerizing."

Lexi retrieved the envelope and the wad of money, which she passed to the vampire. "That was in the log. I don't know if he supported any charities."

"You're the worst charity case I know. Get a decent hotel." He pushed the money to her.

"I'll drop it at a dog shelter." Scott put it in his pocket and looked at Marcel. "What about him?"

"He's not going to a shelter. He'll be torn to shreds by a rottweiler." Dick was horrified. He folded his arms on the counter and rested his chin on them to stare at Marcel's sleeping face.

"You want to keep him?" The young man looked astonished.

"It's the least I can do." He stroked the puppy's silky ear gently.

She looked around the room. "What about your expensive furniture?"

Dick waved a hand. "It can go into storage." He didn't look away from the animal.

Scott removed his hand from hers. "What's in the envelope?"

Lexi removed two sheets of paper and a flash drive slid out with them. "Looking at the date in the corner, this is a copy of a page from an old desk diary. It's mostly full of meetings. Do you recognize any names?" She passed it to Dick.

He scanned the sheet. "I don't think it's the names. Look at this entry—it's the registration of a property transfer. The address is where the bar and flower shop are."

The other man read the second sheet. "This is interesting. He emailed someone at an offsite data storage facility asking for all the files from an industrial scanner created the same week as that diary page. It looks like they used a scanner with its own backup drive. That must mean the documentation was removed from everywhere else. Most people wouldn't know about this process. It's lucky for us that Leonard's contact did."

"Not so lucky for Leonard." Dick walked to a cupboard, pulled out a notebook computer, and activated it.

"Okay, what do we know?" Lexi asked.

Scott stepped into the middle of the kitchen like a teacher at the front of the classroom. "They knew about Leonard."

"But *how* could they have known?" she asked.

"Perhaps he—or most likely his contact—did something to draw attention to himself," he suggested. He wrote fiery words in the air.

Leonard, discovered how?

"When you received a call from Dolores, were you alone? How did the conversation go?" she asked Dick.

"I was alone. She told me she'd been asked to help with a situation in town. Then she said she was sending you, and I said, 'no fucking way.' She told me the situation had gotten complicated and suggested that if I could help, you'd be out of town faster. Obviously, I was *all* for that."

"No offense."

"She asked if I knew someone who could help us to get information from the clerk's office. I told her I'd call her back. I called ten minutes later and asked if she was absolutely positive you wouldn't try to kill me or break my neck again because that shit hurts. And as an aside, Lexi, we haven't even begun to visit the issue of the dumpster." He refilled his glass before he spoke again.

"I said I had a friend with a contact in the clerk's office and I'd try to contact him. We talked about the documents being stolen from the flower shop, and that was what I asked Leonard to look for—discreetly, obviously."

"I don't understand this case." Lexi scratched her head. "First, it was a gang bothering a business-owning shifter. Then–"

Scott put up his hand to interrupt. "Could this be connected to her being a shifter?"

"What?" She stared at him, puzzled.

"We've assumed Kate's being bothered because she's a business owner, not because she's a shifter. Tommy and his family clearly don't want her running a business, and now you've seen that Tommy is somehow connected to Caleb and possibly involved in Leonard's death," he explained.

"But what does that have to do with Leonard? Why was that worth murdering him?" Dick asked.

"Do you have the pendant?" Scott asked.

"That's weird too. It went black. Why would it do that?" She pulled it out of her pocket and placed it on the counter.

"It's tarnished." He stretched to pick it up and a spark spat from it onto his hand. "Fucker!"

Lexi moved quickly to stand between him and the pendant, but nothing else happened.

"Someone else's magic has touched that." He shook his hand out. "Dick, do you have any silver cleaner?"

"Silver cleaner? Sure, I use it to clean my silver daggers. It's in the solarium with the wooden stakes and everything else that can kill me." The vampire shook his head.

Scott tried again. "Baking soda and aluminum foil?"

"That I can do." Dick headed to the utility room.

Twenty minutes later, the young man had polished the silver pendant.

He cast a spell looking for magical or cursed objects and the pendant glowed green. Lexi looked around the room to see if anything else glowed. Fortunately, it didn't, and as Scott continued his work, the green glow around the pendant subsided.

"Will this be your mirror trick again? Isn't the pendant a little small for that?" Dick stared at the little piece of jewelry.

"Is it safe to ask if you have a mirror?" the other man asked.

"I moved them all to the spare room after seeing what you did with the one in your motel room yesterday. I planned to have them ground to dust." The vampire headed down the hall.

He returned with a framed wall mirror and propped it against the wall next to the countertop. Scott held the pendant before it and rolled his finger in the air. The reflection changed from the three of them to black. He continued to roll his finger until they saw the group of men around her at the party.

"There's Caleb staring at my breasts again. What a creep." She sneered.

Scott set it back a few minutes and let it play forward. "He's not looking at your breasts, he's looking at the pendant."

Lexi realized he was right. He was looking directly at it and seemingly at them through the mirror, which was even more creepy.

In the replay, Dick leaned forward on her right side to pass the envelope to Betsy. She remembered seeing that at the time. What she hadn't seen was Caleb using that moment's distraction to mutter a word. She watched his lips move, and the picture turned black.

"Caleb's a sorcerer? *Shut the front door!*" Dick's mouth was agape.

He picked the photocopy up and gazed at it with a sigh. Under it was the envelope. Scott took it, looked inside, and shook a photograph out.

The young man raised his eyebrows. "Of course, we could be jumping the gun assuming Leonard was murdered over Kate's case." He put the picture in front of Lexi, who glanced at it. To her surprise, she saw herself.

"I don't understand. I don't recognize this picture." She frowned as she stared at it.

Dick peered over her shoulder. "That's Jackson Square in New Orleans. You must have been there."

"It's not only that. I assumed this evidence would prove I'd been there when I was a child. This picture isn't that old."

The vampire tapped the photograph. "And you don't recognize the man you're with?"

"I have no idea who he is." She tried to force a memory—anything —but nothing came.

"What age would you say you are in that picture?" Scott looked from the image to her.

"Maybe fifteen or sixteen." She pinched the bridge of her nose and turned to Dick. "You asked Leonard to look into this months ago, right?"

"Yes."

"So why would it all blow up now?"

The vampire stood and tapped his chin in thought. "I think you're right. This is a distraction. Whatever happened to Leonard must have been related to the case."

"It's clear what we need to do next." Lexi finished her coffee and put the empty mug down.

"It is?" He swiveled to face her.

She smiled. "Whenever I have a question I can't answer, I find someone to help me think it through."

"Isn't that what we're doing here?" he asked.

"My method involves knuckle-dusters." She stretched and then curled her fingers.

He nodded. "I like it. It's expedient. Perhaps we should borrow one of those shifters."

"Yes. We need to find Tommy or one of his little friends." She cracked her knuckles.

"Preferably not Tommy. I don't think our client will be happy if we knock her boyfriend senseless," Scott added. He had his phone to his ear.

"By the time all this is over, she might pay us to do that." Lexi smirked.

I might do it for free.

"The pack tends to congregate at a bar off the highway." Dick picked his dinner jacket up and draped it across his arm.

"Not Kate's place?" She was surprised.

"Not for their pack meetings and until Kate's married, she's not part of Stan's pack. Also, the other place is out of the way. Jesús will take you to your motel. I'll meet you there." He untied his bow tie.

She looked at Scott, whose face was creased with worry. "What's up?"

"Dolores isn't picking up."

"Keep trying." The other two exchanged looks of concern.

Scott put his hand on the countertop while he redialed with the other, and she slipped hers into it. He flooded her with as much magic energy as she could tolerate and only stopped when her hair began to rise with static electricity.

The vampire waited until they had finished, then called Jesús' name.

"Huh? What?" The confused young man scrambled to his feet.

"Why are you sleeping on the job?" Dick frowned.

"I don't know. I'm so sorry, Mr. Levin." He looked mortified.

"Has everything been quiet here this evening? No guests or calls?"

"Nothing, sir."

"Drive my friends to their motel. Take the Jaguar and stop on the way back and pick up whatever the dog needs. Food, bed, bowls— whatever you think is appropriate." Dick looked at his watch and turned to Lexi. "It's midnight. I have about five hours."

CHAPTER EIGHT

"How are you?" Lexi asked Scott as they watched the shifter bar from their car at the back of the parking lot.

He stared ahead. "I'm fully recharged."

She repeated the question, demanding a better answer. "How are *you?*"

"I'm okay. You don't have to worry about me."

"If we were still in the cult, you might not even be active yet."

"I'm twenty-eight. I'd have been active long ago if I'd been able to match with someone I could trust." He sighed. "Well, I'm getting a crash course now. I'm not a liability, Lexi. Anyway, what happened to *you* out there earlier? I picked up some disturbing emotions." He turned in his seat to face her.

"Don't divert the issue. You can't ignore the possibility that your empathy might slow you in a confrontation."

"You mean, I might slow *you.*" Color rose in his cheeks.

"Yes, that's what I mean." She smiled. "If you feel like you're losing it, cloak yourself. Give me one less thing to worry about. Promise?"

"I promise I won't get you killed." He looked at his hands in his lap and drew a deep breath. "I would never—"

The back door opened, and Dick hopped in. "Would it kill you to clean this thing?" He shoved takeout boxes across the back seat.

"What did you hear?" She knew he would have been hiding in the shadows before they arrived.

"Apart from you two bickering? There's something going on. I think there are two shifter packs in there. One group seems quite vexed with the other."

A window shattered at the front of the bar as a man careened through it. He landed, turned into a wolf before their eyes, and howled with rage.

Scott opened his mouth to say something and Lexi snapped her hand to his lips but Dick had beaten her to it. She looked her friend in the eyes and shook her head once. He nodded and removed Dick's hand. In wolf form, their hearing was exceptional. They'd hear a whisper in a car less than a hundred feet away.

The wolf shook his head and bounded in through the window.

More howls filled the air as shifters turned inside the bar.

"This—" Scott started before he paused and removed Dick's hand again. "I've cloaked us. They can't see, hear, or smell us. As I was saying, this doesn't look good."

The vampire nodded. "I agree. I'm really not feeling this. Walking into the middle of that would be suicide. No good joke ever started with 'a vampire walks into a shifter bar.' I think we need another plan."

The young man straightened and grinned. "I've got one. A vampire walks into a shifter bar and asks for a steak. Wait, no, you won't like that one."

Lexi tightened her lips, then sighed. "We'll meet you at your place."

Dick exited the vehicle and looked at the seat again. "Seriously, this makes your motel look like the Ritz." He disappeared into the night.

"Maybe we should go back to Kate. She might be able to suggest someone who can talk to us." Scott took the keys but was stopped by her upraised hand. A side door had opened, and a tall, dark-haired man with a walking stick stepped out, holding a cellphone to his ear.

She stared at him. "Wow! They don't make them small, do they?"

"This isn't going well. They insist it wasn't them and it's getting quite heated," the man said into the phone. "Something's going on. When we got here, they were already fairly somber. It sounds like a couple of their pack members are missing or dead. Stan's not here, but they're all very evasive about where he might be."

"Maybe we should borrow this guy?" Scott suggested. Lexi nodded her agreement.

The man listened to his caller for a few more seconds. "Okay, I'll go in to see if I can make any sense out of this." He disconnected, turned to step through the door, and instantly fell asleep.

Dick carried a chair into the garage. "What were you thinking? It was ill-advised to move one dog into the house. Now, I have two. Where is he?"

"He's in the trunk." Scott walked to the back of the car.

"Bad Marcel!" Jesús said from within.

The vampire's head spun to the open door. "What now?" He strode into the house and closed the door behind him.

Lexi and Scott puffed and groaned as they pulled the man out of the trunk and sat him in the chair.

"Hello. Come on, wake up." She tapped their guest's cheek.

His eyes snapped open and alarm filled his face when he realized he was unable to move.

"Don't panic. I have some questions and I don't want you to shift and rip me to pieces before I get the answers." She tried to sound more reasonable than she felt but itched to get the knuckle-dusters out.

He stared at her.

"Oh! Scott, he can't speak." She looked at her teammate, who waved his fingers in the air.

"My bad, sorry." She gave the man an apologetic grin.

Their captive sniffed. "This place smells of vampire."

"Well, we're in a vampire's garage and this is the vampire's fucked-up car. We were attacked by shifters and clueless human thugs tonight. We're trying to work out what the hell's going on. I'm guessing from the phone call we overheard it wasn't your pack, but you might be able to help us." She removed her jacket and the shifter's face went expressionless at the sight of her scar.

He glared at her. "You're Kindred? I don't smell much shifter *or* vampire in you."

"I'm ex-Kindred," Lexi explained.

"I've never heard of anyone being *ex*-Kindred."

"We're a dying breed. Literally." She leaned on a workbench.

"May I move my head?" he asked. His voice was slow and measured. He was well-spoken and didn't seem as hostile as she had expected.

She flicked a glance at her friend, who stood behind the man. Scott complied.

The man looked around. "This is William's place."

"What makes you think that?" This wasn't going at all as she had hoped.

"I'm sitting in an original 1956 Eames Lounger. That's his car, which appears to have been shot up. And hanging over there near the washer? Well, those are definitely his Burberry boxers. I hope he's okay."

"You have to be kidding me. Is there anyone he hasn't—" Lexi pinched the bridge of her nose.

Scott sighed. "We're like the world's worst kidnappers."

She caught the man's mouth twitching and rolled her eyes. "Dick," she shouted.

The vampire walked in wearing pink rubber gloves and carrying a pooper-scooper. "This dog's shitting every— Edward? Oh, dear God, Edward, I'm so sorry." He turned to her. "You kidnapped Edward? What's wrong with you?" He dropped the scooper and pulled off the gloves.

"It was your idea to kidnap a shifter," she replied.

"I didn't mean Edward. He's the Alpha of the San Bernardino pack and a very close friend. Edward, this is awful. Come into the house."

Dick marched to the door and glanced back, confused that the man wasn't following.

"If I might move now?" Edward looked at Lexi.

Scott released him.

The shifter rose from the chair and turned to face Scott, who held the walking stick out. "Thank you." He followed the vampire into the house.

"Nothing seems to be going to plan." Her friend headed to the door.

"You are not wrong." Lexi slammed the trunk closed and, shaking her head, walked into the house behind him.

The other two men were talking as the friends stepped into the kitchen.

Edward chuckled. "It's okay, don't keep apologizing. To be honest, I'm kind of amused and I've been meaning to drop by anyway."

"Well, that's embarrassing." She flopped onto a bar stool.

The shifter took his cell phone out and held it to his ear. "It's me. I got a call and had to run. I'm dealing with something. How did the meeting turn out?"

She stood, went to the coffee machine, and pulled a mug out to pour herself one.

The man continued his phone conversation. "Oh. Well, that's not surprising, is it? Okay, head back. I might have answers in the morning." He disconnected.

"Would you like coffee, Edward?" Dick asked.

"Thanks, Will."

The vampire snatched Lexi's filled mug as she returned the carafe to the machine and put it in front of Edward. She sighed and took down another.

"Who's the female shifter you mentioned, Will?" Edward asked.

"Her name's Kate. She owns a bar here in town."

"Dick. Client confidentiality." She rolled her eyes.

"Kate is from our pack. She agreed to mate with Tommy to end hostilities between our packs. Why hasn't she gone to Stanley about this? The Palm Springs pack is the largest in Riverside County and he's the alpha. They could resolve this mess in no time."

"She wanted to keep the pack out of it. When she first contacted us, she was being harassed for protection money by a gang of thugs in town." Lexi took a sip of her coffee and screwed her face up at the bitterness.

"But this kind of situation is what the pack's for." Edward shook his head.

"Well, there's another problem now. It looks like this whole thing might have been orchestrated by a local businessman—a nasty piece of work named Caleb Linden. Do you know him?" Dick asked.

"I know of Mr. Linden." The shifter took a sip of his coffee.

"Did you know he's a sorcerer?" Dick asked.

"Actually, that would explain a few things." The other man walked to the refrigerator and retrieved the cream for his coffee, then went to a cupboard on the wall, opened it, and withdrew a bowl of sugar. It wasn't lost on Lexi how familiar he was with the house.

He put the bowl in front of her, and she spooned sugar into her mug. "Thank you."

Edward turned to Scott. "A sorcerer and a mage are the same thing, right?"

The young man nodded. "Yes. Mage is a Kindred term to distinguish between a sorcerer who's part of Kindred and one who isn't."

The shifter sat on a stool and turned it to face Lexi. "So, what has Caleb been up to?"

"He's buying up the whole block where Kate's bar is. We think he's trying to get rid of the evidence of her ownership. Dick's friend got murdered for looking into it." She stirred her coffee. Her next sip was much more enjoyable.

"Was that the records clerk they fished out of the lake today?" Edward asked.

Dick's shoulders slumped. "I didn't even think for a moment about Leonard's source."

"Doesn't Kate have her own copy?" Edward nodded when Lexi passed the sugar.

"She had a break-in. Someone stole it from her office," Scott explained. "It's possibly connected to the person who tried to attack her on the street a couple of weeks ago."

He paused for a moment and light dawned in his face. "Did she by any chance bite the guy?"

"She…might have." Dick swiveled his gaze to Lexi, then shrugged.

Edward nodded. "Which answers our question. We have a new shifter running around out there who's killed a couple of transients. He hasn't been seen for a few days but it can only be a matter of time before he strikes again. That was why we were at the bar tonight—trying to find out who it is and who's responsible for turning them. Kate should have come to us or gone to Tommy's pack."

The vampire raised an eyebrow. "Apparently, they're quite provincial. Her mate and his family aren't happy with her being a business owner. They're looking for an excuse to force her to give it up."

"Or creating an excuse," Lexi added.

"What? They never used to be like that. Tommy's uncle is the police chief and his mother was an attorney. She ran her own firm." Edward was clearly confused.

"I think Stanley has something to do with all this," Dick explained. "He and Caleb are close buddies."

Scott wandered around the room. "Dick, where's Marcel?"

"Jesús is walking him."

"William, why do they call you 'Dick?' Is it because they've seen your magnificent—"

"No," the two friends said together.

"Thank God," Lexi added under her breath.

"Come to think of it, Edward, it's been a while since—" Dick started but didn't manage to finish the sentence.

"Seriously? Someone should put a muzzle on you." She was exasperated.

"Now *that* brings back memories." The shifter's eyebrows raised speculatively at Dick.

"Oh, my God!" She put her palms up and stepped back.

"It's perfectly natural to want to have a life-affirming experience after having been in mortal danger. It wouldn't kill the two of you to —" The vampire swiveled his finger between Lexi and Scott.

"I think we should head to the motel," she interrupted.

"That's the spirit," he added.

"Not to— Oh, never mind. Come on, Scott." Lexi picked her jacket up, and they headed toward the garage door. She stopped and turned.

"Are you safe here?" she asked.

"You're asking a vampire and a shifter if they're safe?" Dick raised an eyebrow, and Edward's jaw dropped.

"Okay, but Caleb knows you're involved and he knows where you live. *And* he has his own packs of shifters and goons. Are you prepared to move quickly? Do you have a go-bag?" she asked.

"You don't live as long as I have without picking up a few tricks. Of course I have a go-bag. I'm not an amateur." The vampire turned away dramatically.

She nodded and they left.

<hr>

They parked in their spot under the room and headed up the steps. Scott put his hand out to the door and Lexi shooed him away.

"What did I tell you? Me first." She walked into the room and was met by a punch in the forehead with a knuckle-duster.

When she roused, she realized that she was sprawled on the floor and slouched against the side of Scott's bed with her hands tied behind her back. She glanced to where her friend stood at the end of the bed, his face a mask of abject fear. When she attempted to move, the thug who lay on the bed slapped the back of her head with his gun. She grunted and glared at him.

"Thank God you're awake. Your stupid friend here is playing statues. He's very good at it but I was about to shoot him. We know you have the file. Our boss wants it back." He stroked the back of her head with the gun. "Your hair's pretty."

She struggled to respond. Her head was fuzzy from the punch, and her emotions were all over the place. That was probably because something was going on with Scott on an emotional level and it flooded her through their link. She looked at him and noted the bruises on his face. He did seem physically frozen like a statue.

"What have you done to him?" She tried to twist her hand to touch her scar but the ties bit into her too tightly.

"Not a thing. Well, barely a thing. But back to the question at hand."

"Maybe Mr. Linden should come and get it himself." She looked at her friend and then at the door, trying to somehow signal to him to get the hell out.

"I've never heard that name." The man conveyed with every word that he knew exactly who she was talking about. "And my colleague is outside, so I wouldn't try that."

"He doesn't know anything. Look at him—he's damaged. Let him go." Lexi indicated Scott with her head.

The man smacked her with the gun again. "We're reasonable people. If you hand it over, you can leave. We won't lay a finger on your pretty..." He stroked her neck slowly.

"You'll let us leave?" She tried to sound like she believed the lie. Of course, she knew the moment she produced what the thug was looking for, they'd be dead.

"Sure. Tell us where it is."

She paused and tried again to make eye contact with Scott. "It's in one of the bags." Against her instincts, she did her best to look defeated.

"And they are where?"

"He hid them." She indicated her teammate with her head.

The man sat at the headboard of the bed, crossed his legs, and pointed the gun at Scott. "Where are the bags?"

The young man merely stood motionless and stared into the middle distance.

"Scott! Snap out of it." Lexi knew they'd both be dead if he couldn't pull himself together.

He blinked and looked at her. "But–"

"He wants the bags." She said it very slowly and deliberately.

Scott muttered under his breath, and the bags appeared on the bed —exactly where they had always been and precisely where the thug lay. The young man spun instantly to face the wall, not wanting to see the result.

She shuffled out of the way as the man's right arm slid to the floor and heard its opposite drop on the other side. For a long moment, she stared at the thug on the bed. His body lay in several pieces between and around the bags. Scott's backpack was in the middle of his chest. His head had fallen forward against the side of the bag.

Lexi looked away from the gruesome scene. "Can you untie me? We still have to deal with the goon outside."

For a moment, the beginnings of a scream came from outside, followed by silence. The door opened and the bloody thug fell halfway into the room.

Dick appeared in the entrance. "Did someone call for a rescue? What the fuck happened to him?"

"I'll stand outside for a minute." Scott moved carefully toward the door without looking around. He met Edward, who moved back to let him step over the second dead thug and out.

"Are you okay?" The shifter crouched to cut Lexi's ties.

"They were after the evidence." She rubbed her wrists but didn't think she could trust her legs to support her.

"I assume they didn't get the USB." Dick stared in fascination at the body mostly on the bed. The legs had rolled so the feet now pointed out, which looked grotesquely comical.

"They wouldn't have found the flash drive. It's a good thing we didn't have the paper files on us." She touched her forehead gingerly.

"I have the papers here." He held them out. "I didn't want to leave them at the house."

She attempted to stand but swayed and sat heavily on the other bed. "Can you put them in the case, please? I'll get them to Kate."

He nodded and she stumbled to her feet and grasped the legs of the second thug to help Edward drag him fully into the room.

"I don't need the help, but thanks." The shifter took hold of the shoulders and pulled.

Lexi heard Dick unzip the small carry-on case. "What's this? Woah! Your case is full of junk."

"Seriously? You choose now to start critiquing my stuff?"

"No. It's junk," he repeated.

"Well, I highly doubt those shoes are really Versace but sometimes, we have to make do," she snipped in response.

"Okay. I'm going to give this another try. Lexi, I'm sorry about this, but this guy's junk is in your bag."

"What?" Lexi and Edward moved to stand beside the vampire, who held some gray pinstripe material in one hand and the bag's lid in the other. They stared at the place the thug's lower mid-section had been lying before the bag materialized.

"Poor guy. He wasn't blessed, was he?" Dick said and shook his head. "Hey, what do you mean about my shoes?"

He started to put the papers into the bag.

"What are you doing?" she asked.

"You said you wanted the papers in here." He sounded annoyed.

"Close the lid. I don't want anything in that bag. I don't want anything *from* that bag." She stepped back.

"Are you sure? I know someone who could fashion you a great pair of earrings from his—"

"I'm sure."

Dick dropped the trouser material into the case and flipped it closed, then looked at the man again with a grimace. "We need to get rid of this."

"Don't worry, I have friends who will be only too happy to help." Edward took his cell out.

Dick and Edward shared a look. "The twins," they agreed.

The shifter stepped out to make a call.

"You have your own cleaners?" Lexi asked when he returned.

"Something like that." Dick wiggled his hand in a way that gave her an uneasy feeling.

"How did you know to come?" she asked.

"Seconds after you left, a car started and followed you. I threw my stuff in the car and drove out to follow them, and *another* car followed me. It was like the Palm Springs Pride parade all over again."

"They didn't know I was there, so they were very surprised when I mauled their faces at the traffic light. They're in the trunk," Edward explained as he entered the room.

"If we can get them up here, could your twins deal with them too?" Lexi asked.

"Maybe we'll get a quantity discount." Dick looked around. "Where's Scott?"

"I'm here." His voice came quietly from just outside the room.

"Can you help us get the other two up here?" the vampire asked.

Edward stuck his head out the room. "He's gone. Oh, he's down at the trunk. I should help. Wait, he's gone again."

"He'll be fine. Let him do it." Lexi knew there would be emotional fallout from this. She wondered if he'd be able to continue working with her.

"He should have been able to handle a couple of human thugs." Dick seemed to know what she was thinking.

"He's learning on the job." She hoped that was all it was—a blip.

Moments later, Scott reappeared on the balcony. "They're in the bath." He walked in and lifted his bag from the bed without looking at the carnage.

"You might want to check that. His lungs are probably in there," the vampire warned.

"It'll be okay. There's a protection spell on it." The young man held the bag up. It was completely clean.

"Maybe consider putting one of those on my bag in the future." Lexi glanced at her little case. She didn't really need it. It was mostly for show, but still.

Edward looked around the room. "I think this will be okay. The mess is limited to one bed and the bathroom. They should be able to clean it fairly quickly."

"Well, well," a voice said from behind them. A third armed goon stood in the doorway. He saw his colleague on the bed. "What the fuck did you do to Tony?"

Scott held his arm out with the hand raised and muttered a single word. The man was obliterated and a fine spray of red drenched the door, the wall next to it, and the ceiling.

Dick, who had stood closest, looked at himself. "My…everything."

"Sorry." The young man waved his hand and drew the blood spray from the vampire to the floor.

"I'm glad you got that out of your system." Edward's eyes were wide.

Lexi looked at the carnage. "I'll pay for another night."

A car pulled up below and three doors slammed.

The shifter glanced over the balcony. "Collect whatever gear you're taking. It's time to move."

"Where to?" she asked.

Edward shrugged. "My place for now? We need to plan."

She went into the bathroom and came out with her cosmetic kit. They stepped out of the room as the strangers appeared. A man stepped to the side to allow two others into the room.

"Wow! So fresh. I could smell it from the car." The boy's white eyes glittered.

"So hungry." The girl stepped forward and licked the door.

Scott put his hand over his mouth, clearly trying not to gag.

Edward introduced the twins politely. "This is Adele and this is Sam."

Lexi's jaw dropped in shock. She looked at him. "Are they zombies?"

"Kind of." He seemed to sense where this might go.

"Kind of?" Her eyebrows raised.

"As in, yes." He indicated the room as if to say, "Well, what else could we do?"

Dick placed his hand on her shoulder. "You're not with Kindred now, Lexi. Remember that."

Lexi took a step back. Kindred's rule was that zombies were "kill on sight." No ifs, no buts, kill immediately. She was conflicted and she guessed it must have shown on her face because the two flaky white dead people in front of her looked terrified.

"Kindred?" Adele squeaked. Her eyes widened so the entire white irises showed.

Everyone was silent and all gazes settled on Lexi.

"*Bon appetit.*" She walked away without a backward glance.

Lexi and Scott followed Dick and Edward onto the road and toward San Bernardino. Before they reached the edge of town, they turned into the hills.

The vehicles stopped at a gate and they waited in their car while Edward slid out and opened it. She continued behind the other vehicle down a long driveway through the woods that ended at a two-story home nestled among the trees.

Dick walked around to the back of the Jaguar and opened it while Edward took Marcel into the house. He was followed by Scott, who hadn't spoken a word on the journey.

Lexi waited while Dick pulled luggage out of the trunk. "Your go-bag looks suspiciously like a garment bag."

"That's not my go-bag, silly. *This* is my go-bag." He removed a huge old trunk.

Her eyes bulged at the size of it. She guessed she wouldn't have been able to lift it an inch off the ground, but his vamp strength made it appear as light as a feather.

"I don't think you quite have the concept. It's supposed to be small and light with money and identification, a change of underwear, and something to hit bad people with."

"But I don't travel anywhere without my trunk. It's French, and an antique. I've had this for almost a hundred years." He patted the trunk before he headed inside with it. "And this *is* something to hit bad people with."

Once she was settled in her room, Lexi walked through the house and found Dick deliberating between two shirts in front of his open trunk.

It stood on end and contained drawers and hanging space. She'd never seen anything like it except in movies.

"Hello, Lexi. How can I help?"

"I'm worried about Kate…and Dolores, and Scott,"

"Edward has put some of his boys onto protecting Kate. I've tried Dolores a dozen times, so I'm concerned too. And Scott—I know what you mean. He's barely spoken since the motel. You suspect he's not ready for all this?"

"I more than suspect it. I can sense his feelings through our bond. I don't know how to help him."

"I think I do." He put the shirts down.

"Is everything okay in here?" Edward asked and popped his head around the door.

"Edward," the vampire said seriously, "we need to get Scott drunk."

Lexi rolled her eyes.

Later, she lay in bed, thinking back to her life with Kindred. She remembered the lessons about werewolves and other shifters. They were dangerous, they weren't to be trusted, and they only looked after their own pack. Nowhere in her studies did it say they were big fans of karaoke. Yet there she was, listening to a werewolf, a vampire, and a mage drunkenly belting out "Delilah." It was a good sign that Scott was singing along. She smiled.

Annoying, but good.

CHAPTER NINE

Lexi wandered through the house in search of coffee.

She found Scott unconscious on the sofa with a throw covering him. He hadn't even made it to bed.

Still yawning, she entered the kitchen and set about making coffee. As she sat at the old wooden table, she watched the beverage drip into the pot.

I wonder if I could magic it to go faster?

Looking at the almost empty scar, she decided it was still worth a try and was about to attempt it when Edward walked in, wearing tight hipster jeans and no shirt.

"Morning," he whispered.

After a moment, she shook her head and realized that she'd stared at his abs. "Good morning-almost-afternoon. How's your head?"

He raised his eyebrows. "It's been better."

In silence, he made his way around the kitchen and dropped suspicious leafy green items into a plastic beaker. She watched as he went through the process.

Outstanding pecs, and you could bounce a quarter off those abs.

When he'd finally blended his green concoction, he stood and drank it with his back to her. She took the opportunity to stare openly at the well-defined lats on his back and almost called Scott in to point the muscle groups out to him. The dedication it took to gain that level of physical fitness was itself impressive, and she couldn't fault Dick's taste in men, not at all.

Lexi's gaze wandered around the room and stopped on the refrigerator. There were kids' drawings on it. "You have kids?"

"These were painted by my granddaughter. They visit over the holidays." He opened the refrigerator and removed eggs, bacon, and steaks.

"Oh, I see. You don't look old enough to have a grandchild." She tried not to sound too appraising.

"She's five. I'm forty-five. They live in Monterey with my ex-wife."

"Nice part of the world." She watched as he took bowls and knives from cupboards. "Can I help?"

"Sure. Crack and whisk?" He handed her a carton of eggs, a bowl, and a whisk. "How's Scott looking?"

"He's on the sofa, dead to the world, figuratively speaking. Where's Dick?" She cracked eggs into the bowl and looked around the kitchen for condiments.

"In the basement, dead to the world. Literally speaking." He smiled, opened a cupboard, and passed her the salt and pepper.

After a few minutes, he placed a mug of coffee on the table in front of her and removed the bowl of whisked eggs.

"Thanks." She stretched for the sugar.

"Scott talked some last night. He's embarrassed about what happened." He took a frying pan out.

"I know. I feel it through the empathic link. I felt what he was going through at the motel last night too. He was paralyzed by fear, and it's possible that when I was knocked unconscious, part of his mind lost consciousness too. He has so much to learn but not much time to learn it in. I think he's done well until now." She stood and took her coffee to the counter. He passed her a chopping board and a large steak. When he began to dice small cubes of potato, she realized he was making hash. She chopped the steak into small pieces, followed by the bacon.

"How do you know he won't freeze up like that again?" Edward asked as he scraped the potatoes into the pan to sauté them.

"He won't. It was my fault. I've been a little off my game lately." She stopped speaking when she heard Scott walking up the hallway. "Afternoon, sleepyhead. Edward's frying up something good and greasy." She took a mug down.

"Ugh! Don't." He groaned, flopped into a chair, and buried his face in his arms on the table.

"Tell me about it," the shifter agreed with a sigh.

"Not hungry?" Lexi passed the coffee to him.

"I want food but I don't think I can talk about it."

The other man's cell rang. "Yeah? Just, erm…" He started to walk out of the room, then looked at the pan. Lexi took the spatula out of his hand and he continued down the hall.

"I'm so sorry. I don't know what happened." Scott's voice was muffled, given that his face was still hidden by his arms.

"You don't have to explain anything to me. I know, remember?" She pointed to her scar even though his face remained hidden.

"I know too. I felt your disappointment when you woke up on the floor. I couldn't think or move." He sounded choked.

"I was disappointed in myself. Let's go for a walk after breakfast." She moved the pan from the heat and put the food onto plates. "Food's up," she called.

Scott raised his head as Edward walked in. She was disappointed to note he now wore a t-shirt.

"So, how do you feel about tequila this afternoon?" The shifter grinned. Lexi assumed this was an inside joke.

"I never want to look at it, hear about it, taste it, and most definitely, smell it again." The young man dropped his head again, and Edward chuckled.

"Did you want this food on the back of your head?" She stood over him with a plate.

After a few moments, he raised his head. He accepted the plate and attempted a smile, although he was wan and bleary-eyed.

The shifter took a seat at the table. "That was my beta. I've asked her to come over."

"Her? How progressive of you," Scott said.

"That position wasn't given. It was earned. She's strong enough to go for Alpha. I don't think she will yet, but that's not a fight I look forward to."

Edward talked about his pack as they ate.

"I'm worried about a friend of ours," Lexi began after they had finished.

"Dolores, I know. Will gave me the number last night. I've tried it a few times this morning, but it goes straight to voicemail. Can you track her?" the shifter asked Scott.

"I'll give it a try but I can't do it with this hangover." He pushed his half-eaten breakfast away and leaned back.

"I'm sorry. We shouldn't have let you drink so much last night. When do you think you'll feel well enough?" The older man stood and took his and Lexi's empty plates to the sink.

Scott sat with his eyes closed and breathed deeply. She felt the surge of magic and he opened his eyes. They were bright and clear. "I'll finish this and get started." He pulled the plate closer and snarfed the rest of his breakfast.

Edward looked from one to the other and shook his head. "Well, that's not fair."

"Do you have a map of Colorado? Her office is in Denver. That's where she was yesterday," Scott told him.

"I have Satnav or a tablet with Google maps on it."

"I've tried that before. It doesn't work." He stood quickly. "Where can I buy a map around here?"

"We're a ways out. Any nearby place would only sell local maps. I'll ask Jess to pick one up." The shifter retrieved his cell and texted.

Lexi waited for him to finish. "How are things with Kate?"

"All quiet. She's at the bar, and the Palm Springs pack is keeping an eye on her too. At least, I assume that's why Tommy's there again. She's concerned about her friend—the girl from the flower shop,

Daisy. Kate called another friend from the coven, and she hasn't been with them."

"Is Kate safe with Tommy? If he's under Caleb's influence too, could he harm her and be completely unaware of it?"

"We have someone in there too. She's safe."

"In the bar? Who?"

"Her mother. She could rip Tommy to pieces. He's a little soft around the middle."

"Must be all those McRibs." Scott smiled.

"Right. Jess will be here after work, and speaking of that, I'll wash the dishes, then I need to get some work done." Edward picked up a briefcase from the hallway.

"What do you do?" the other man asked.

"I'm a financial auditor. You can hate me now." He grinned.

"We'll get the dishes. You do whatever you need to do." The young man stood from the table and carried his empty plate to the sink.

"Are we okay to go for a walk, Edward?"

"Sure. I have a few acres of woods and chaparral here. It's relatively safe. I don't get bears or cougars anymore. They know better." He disappeared into his study.

Scott washed a plate and passed it to Lexi. "What are you thinking?"

"He does not look like an auditor." She dried the plate and put it on the shelf.

"No. I suppose he doesn't."

They finished the dishes and cleaned the kitchen.

She knew he wanted to talk so the moment they were done, she turned to him. "Do you want to go for that walk now?"

They headed past the stairs to the basement where Dick was passing the daytime hours and left through the back door. Within a few minutes, they could no longer see the house.

"I feel sick waiting like this. We should be out there looking for Dolores," Scott said as he scanned the ground ahead of them.

"It's two-thirty now. The maps will be here soon. We also need to work out what we'll do about Kate and Caleb. He needs to pay for what he did to Leonard."

Her companion stopped and she didn't notice until she'd taken a couple more steps. When she turned to face him, it was obvious he was ready to talk.

He looked down but after a moment, looked her in the eyes. "There's something you need to know. When—God, *if* we find Dolores, I'll ask her to get you another partner. Someone more reliable than me."

'What? But that's—"

"The right thing to do. We're not safe out there if I can't be relied upon. We'll still be matched and soon, you won't need to have a physical connection with me for the energy transfer. It means you'll be able to draw on my magic when you need it without me being a liability at your side."

Lexi picked a stick up and began to strip the bark from it. "You've really thought this through, haven't you?"

"Yes, and you can't talk me out of it, although I don't see why you'd want to. I almost got us killed last night."

"There's something I need to tell you that might change your perspective." She walked to a fallen tree and sat. "You didn't put us in that situation. I did. When we got into that room, there were two guys inside. I know, because it was the last thing I registered before I had my lights punched out. That means the third guy was out there watching us, and I didn't have a clue."

"He could have been—"

"I wasn't prepared for what might have been behind the door when we entered. I've been off my game and making excuses. I even struggled to catch that thief. I should have been able to react faster rather than leaving you to save my ass by using magic on him, and Dick had to rescue me when we were attacked. The fact is, I can't even rely on myself anymore."

"But you're the most lethal human I've ever met, and—"

"We both know that's not true."

"But your skills—"

"Don't make me as fast as a vamp or as strong as a shifter. I've never displayed fae or witch abilities or any other kind of supe."

Scott attempted to interrupt again but she silenced him. "Let me say this or I'll never get it out. I've been using vamp blood." She said it fast because admitting it to him was the single most humiliating thing she'd ever done. Her face flushed.

"I know. It helped you get your memories back. You've done it three times—you already told me that."

"It's been much more than three times. At first, it was about the memories. Then, it was because my speed and strength increased and it made me feel more like I'm supposed to be. Like I could be effective in my work like the others are." She stared at the ground. "I can barely function without it now and even with it, something's not right. I don't know what to do, and I honestly don't think I can deal with this without you." The last word was a whisper.

Scott joined her on the tree trunk. "I thought you might be happier working with someone else. Maybe Edward. Your heart rate elevates when you look at him."

Lexi looked at him like he was speaking a foreign language. "I'm jealous of his muscles. His lats are really well defined. I was going to ask him how he isolates them."

He laughed. "Oh, I can tell you that. It's the shifting. It impacts muscle groups other exercises can't touch."

She sighed. "Well, shit!"

As he slid his arm around her, he chuckled. "What a fucking pair we are—an incompetent and a junkie. I guess we're stuck with each other."

Lexi snorted a laugh.

"There's something else." She stood, walked a few steps away, and held her arm out. They both watched as the white energy filled the scar. "I've been able to do this without physical contact for a few weeks. I liked the hand-holding part. It's kind of comforting. Of course, I still can't keep the magic from dissipating." She opened her hand and stepped closer. He took it and stood.

Scott picked a long stick up and glamored it to look like a wizard's staff with a crystal ball at the top. He passed it to her. "I'll help you with the vamp blood issue."

"I won't need help. I can do this. I *won't* use it anymore and I'll flush it when we get back." Lexi was determined. She made sure he recognized the strength in her voice, and he nodded.

They continued to walk and talk for another few hours. When they returned, Edward was seated in the kitchen with an attractive woman who looked to be in her thirties. She glanced from Scott to Lexi, to her scar and back to Scott, then studied the young man from head to toe. He swallowed and Lexi wasn't surprised. She'd seen women stare at him like that before. Surprisingly, the woman then proceeded to examine her from her feet upward.

Okay, that's new.

Edward opened the map, a pair of glasses balanced on his head. He glanced up and said, "Jess, Lexi, Scott," by way of introduction, then lowered the glasses onto his nose.

"Hi." Scott proffered his hand and Jess looked at it with an eyebrow raised. Lexi thought she might turn away, but she tilted her head, grinned, and took it. After a moment's shaking, it became apparent that she had turned Scott's friendly gesture into a pissing contest and grasped his hand tightly.

He smiled, and Lexi felt the familiar surge of his magic.

The grin faded from the woman's lips, the first indication that she knew something was wrong. She looked down to see that rather than a hand, she now shook the head of an octopus and its tentacles had wound themselves around her arm.

With a scream, she yanked her arm back, ran behind Edward, shook her hand as though it were covered in slime.

The shifter looked over his glasses at her. "I think you might have deserved that. What do you think?"

"He did that to me the day we met. He thinks it's funny." Lexi fixed her gaze on the back of Scott's head.

"He's lucky I didn't shift and rip his head off."

"I don't think that would have ended well for anyone." She made eye contact with Jess to ensure that the threat had been received and understood.

Edward ignored the women. "Do you need anything else to do this, Scott?"

"I need something that belongs to Dolores. I have something in my bag." Scott headed to his room.

"How's Kate?" Lexi retrieved a mug and filled it from the coffee pot. "Anyone?"

"No, thanks." Jess shook her head.

"I'm good." Edward pointed to his full cup.

She pulled a second mug from the shelf for Scott. When she held the pot close to the mug, it made a rat-tat-tat noise as they jostled together. She didn't look up and merely drew them apart and poured.

Shit. I have the shakes. I've only been off the stuff for a day.

"Stanley called the pack in, so Tommy had to leave." Edward took a gulp of his drink.

"Isn't that Kate's pack too?" Scott entered the room.

"Not until they marry and something's come up about that too." Jess looked at Edward. She hadn't told him this yet.

Lexi made her way around the table and sat.

"Stanley insists the two of them get married, like, now." Her eyebrows had raised.

"That's unconventional, but as pack leader, he has the right to insist. But why?"

"I might know the answer to that." Scott took the coffee Lexi proffered. "We know Caleb's a sorcerer. If he has Stanley enthralled, that could extend to the whole pack. He wouldn't need to control them individually."

"So, once they're married, Kate will be in the pack and Caleb only has to say, 'Give me your land,' and she'll hand it over. We need to get her away from him." Lexi was outraged.

"Her mom's bringing her home for now, but this could cause a great deal of trouble between the packs." Jess looked deeply concerned.

"Perhaps they should come here," Edward suggested.

"We don't know if they're being followed or tracked. I don't think you want to lead them to your friends. Let's send them to Carl's place."

"That makes sense. Thanks, Jess."

The woman gave her a curt nod, then eyed Scott suspiciously before she turned to leave.

The young man took a teardrop pendant from his pocket and held it in his hands.

"Wait, is that mine?" Lexi asked.

"You'll get it back." He smiled and looked pleased that she liked it so much.

When he opened his hands, the pendant had changed shape. It was no longer a teardrop but was five-sided, wide at the top and narrowed into a point at the bottom.

She studied it and tried to decide if she liked this shape more.

Edward stood, looked at his watch, and moved to the windows to pull the shades down. He left the room and returned a few minutes later, having closed the blinds throughout the ground floor of the house. The sun was low in the sky at the front of the house and the back, where they were, was in shadow. Lexi glanced at the time. It seemed a little early for a vampire to wake.

Scott dug into his pocket and retrieved a purple crystal. "Dolores loaned this to me to help with meditation."

Fascinated, she gazed at it. "I've never seen a stone so dazzling."

He held it up between finger and thumb to give her a better look. "It's a fae amethyst."

She had to blink to force herself to look away.

His expression focused, he dropped the stone into his left hand and swung the chain over the map with his right. It moved freely in all directions. "I don't pick her up anywhere."

Edward stepped back. "This side is Denver, but the other side is all of Colorado."

They turned the map over, and Scott moved the pendant over it from north to south. "Where could she be?"

The shifter sighed. "Give me a moment." He disappeared into his study and returned moments later with a large globe. "Would this work?"

Scott moved it in the center of the table and tried again. "Nothing."

Lexi put her hand on his arm. "So she's not on Earth? That doesn't mean she's—"

"No. I won't accept that." He rested the pendant on top of the globe and sat, his shoulders hunched.

She rubbed her face and and her leg began to bounce again. "I can't think straight."

He glanced up. "Sharpen something. That usually calms you."

"Good idea. I'll sharpen everything I've got." She slid her hand into her pocket, removed her whetstone, and was embarrassed to see the wrapping from a Hershey Kiss stuck to it. With a sigh, she was about to sweep it away when she noticed something small wriggling on it. She dropped it onto the table.

"Eww, gross." She drew her hand back to squash the bug, but on its downward journey, it came to an abrupt halt in mid-air. She turned to Dick, who stood beside her with his hand around her wrist. "Where did you come from?"

"I wouldn't do that if I were you." He released her hand.

Lexi looked at the wriggling black thing in disgust. "What is it?"

The four of them leaned closer. She squinted to see more clearly.

Edward straightened a moment. "I'd say that's a tiny, tiny woman."

"It's Dolores!" Scott's voice was full of joy.

"I think you're right." Lexi frowned at the miniscule being. "Oh, yes. She's wearing her black skirt suit and covering her tiny ears with her tiny hands."

"You're probably deafening her." Dick's voice had softened.

As they watched, the tiny creature leaned on the edge of the whetstone, and a miniscule spray of brown vomit issued from her onto the table.

"I'll get that," the vampire said and wiped the table with a kitchen towel. There was barely a visible spec on it and he threw it in the garbage.

"At least she did it when she was miniaturized," Edward whispered.

The woman began to grow. The larger she got, the more evident it was that she was in distress. She was perspiring, and her hair had come out of its bun and stuck out wildly. The four of them stepped back but continued to stare in fascination as she continued to expand. She seemed to stop, finally, and lay groaning on the dining table.

"Has she stopped?" Edward asked.

Scott looked at him, puzzled.

The shifter shrugged. "Well, I don't know how big she's meant to be."

Dolores rolled over and vomited brown liquid all over the floor.

"Jeez." Lexi jumped out of the way.

Dick walked around it. "I got the last one."

Edward lifted the woman and carried her into the living room, where he placed her on the couch with cushions to prop her back.

"The monsters. Have the monsters gone?" Her eyes were wild.

Dick brought her a glass of water.

She took the glass and gulped thirstily. "Did anything follow me out? How long have I been in there?"

Lexi crouched beside her. "We spoke yesterday."

"What? It's been a week, at least. Hiding from those…things. I thought I was going to die. I've survived on Hershey's chocolate. I hate that stuff. It smells like vomit."

"I agree." Scott's face appeared around the doorway. He was cleaning the floor.

Lexi took the glass into the kitchen to refill it but stopped on her way to the refrigerator when she heard a noise. She looked at the table to where the pendant vibrated on the globe over where California would be. "Oh, look. Your spell found her."

His face appeared above the counter. "I've still got it." He grinned and she smiled in response. They were relieved to have found Dolores alive.

He put the paper towels in the trash, and Edward ran a mop over the area.

They moved into the living room.

Scott placed his hand onto Dolores's head and spoke a word.

The woman blinked and seemed to have recovered, although her pupils were huge.

Dick sat on the edge of the sofa and held Dolores's hand. "Can you tell us what happened? How did you wind up in Lexi's dirty magic pocket?"

Lexi rolled her eyes.

"Was that where I was? There were things in there." She shuddered. "Do you remember when I was in my office?"

She decided not to remind her again since that had only been yesterday and merely nodded.

Dolores continued. "I had visitors. Eric, from Kindred." She looked from Scott to Lexi.

"Eric? The Grandfather of Colorado?" Lexi's mouth hung open.

The woman nodded. "He had two others with him. Warren and Lucy." She looked at Scott now.

"Warren. That explains the bruises on your face. So, they were there for me. I don't know who Lucy is, though." His mouth set into a grim line.

"She's your replacement—a slip of a girl with a haunted look in her eyes. I don't think she'll last long. They know I was involved in your escape but I don't believe they know you're working with me. We only spoke briefly. I realized I needed to get out of there. When he hit me, I created the illusion of a glamor breaking but I actually created the glamor. I distracted them by making a door appear at the back of the room. As soon as their attention was diverted, I shrank the files. Oh, Lexi, dear. My filing cabinet is in your pocket. Could you retrieve it, please? Be careful putting your hand in there—there's something..."

Lexi was beginning to wonder what the hell was in there to have terrified Dolores so much. She dug tentatively in her pocket, thought about the item she sought, and pulled out the minuscule filing cabinet. Carefully, she put it on the floor and it began to grow.

"I made a fae door in the bottom of the wall and slipped the cabinet through, then shrank myself and got the hell out."

"Couldn't you think of somewhere nicer to go than Lexi's nasty pocket?" Dick shuddered. "I can't imagine what it must have been like." He crouched and embraced Dolores as though she'd spent five years in a Japanese prisoner of war camp. Lexi tried to ignore it.

"The trick to traveling through a fae door is to know exactly where you want to come out. Unfortunately, I wasn't thinking straight, having just had the snot knocked out of me."

Lexi felt in her pocket again and thought *monster*, but nothing came out.

The woman looked at her. "I could see weapons but they were so large, I thought I might have stumbled into a giant's closet. I couldn't get out, so I suppose the pocket has a restriction spell on it. I thought about getting a message to you. I tried to write *help* on a candy wrapper. It took me hours to get the stopper out of your giant bottle of ink.

"Ink?" She drew her brows together in puzzlement.

"Yes, dear. The red ink."

Lexi and Scott shared a look over Dolores's head before she closed her eyes and mouthed, "Oh, shit!"

"But that was when the monsters came and I had to hide. Why do you have monsters in your dimensional pocket?"

"I don't know but I'll deal with that immediately," she promised.

Dolores's eyes grew heavy, and she slumped and drifted into sleep.

Dick turned to Lexi. "That wasn't red ink, was it? She's as high as a kite."

Scott placed a throw pillow under the woman's head and glanced at his friend. "I thought you were going to flush that stuff."

"I haven't had time. We've been busy."

"We have to figure out what to do about Caleb and we can't have you shaking and jittering everywhere." Dick gestured at her.

"Hey, leave her alone. Lexi knows she has a problem and she's trying to deal with it the best way she can. She's the strongest person I know, and if she says she can do this the hard way, that's what she'll do."

The vampire startled. "Scott, I didn't mean to—"

"If it was me, I'd simply get rid of the problem with magic, but Lexi has integrity and stamina and—"

"Wait, what?" She stood with her mouth hanging open.

"I said you have integrity and—"

"Not that, you muppet. I can get rid of this with magic? Just like that?" She clicked her fingers.

"Yes. I offered to help."

"I thought you were offering to drive me to meetings." Lexi took his collar and marched him toward her room.

"You kids have fun," Dick called after them and repeated her words to her.

She didn't even turn as she frog-marched Scott down the hall, but her arm came up with the middle finger extended. The two men chuckled behind her.

"Laugh all you like. You two will get your brains gagged. There will be no more secrets dribbling out of your mouth, Dick," Lexi called before she closed the door.

CHAPTER TEN

"Good evening, Betsy." Caleb stepped into the mansion Betsy shared with her son.

"Why, Caleb, what a surprise. Todd's in his study. I'll tell him you're here." She closed the door behind him.

He stared at her and narrowed his eyes. "What the hell is that on your head?"

"It's my golfing sun visor. But this isn't my hair, it's fake. It merely looks like it's coming out of the hole on top." She shook her head and the beaded blonde dreadlocks danced with the movement. "It's fun."

"I see." He shook his head. "I think I can find the study myself." He stepped past Betsy and marched down the hallway.

You should kill her, purred a voice inside his mind.

Stop that. I can brainwash her if I need to, he replied to the relentless entity.

It would be a waste of time to brainwash that crazy old bat. There's not enough brain to wash. Azatoth laughed and the man shivered inwardly.

We're too close to screw this up. Stop it. He paused outside Todd's study door and patted his brow with his handkerchief. The voice was almost unending these days. He would be glad to get it out of his head. Soon, he promised himself.

"I'm making fresh lemonade, sourpuss," Betsy called after him.

"No need." He entered the study without knocking.

Todd was reaching for the phone when he entered. "Caleb. I'm due on a call in a few minutes. Would you like a drink while you wait? You could take it into the den."

Caleb looked from the partly open door to the little ante-room, which Todd referred to as "the den," to the bottle of whiskey on the side table.

Bushmills? If I'd wanted cough syrup, I'd have asked for it.

He muttered a word and the mayor's face became slack. "How's everything going with my construction license?"

The man leaned back, the phone forgotten. "The paperwork is ready to go but the final property is still a problem. The girl has refused to sell again, even after the attack and the robbery."

For a brief moment, he stood with his hands on the back of the chair on the other side of the desk and stared at Todd. "It won't be a problem for long. William's friend has been dealt with. Did you take care of William?"

"Stanley sent some of his boys out and I contacted the man you suggested. Stanley lost two of his and your man called me earlier today, complaining that none of his boys had returned, but…I didn't understand what he was talking about at the time." The man spoke like he was half-asleep.

"I don't know why William has involved himself in my business, but I need him taken care of. Don't let me down again. You don't want to lose your mother the same way you lost your father, do you?" Caleb's eyes were pinpricks as he focused on him.

"Of course not. I love my mother. What happened to my father?" Todd was confused.

The sorcerer walked around the desk, stopped behind the chair, and leaned closer to his ear. "I told you, remember? I asked his heart to stop and it stopped."

"That's right. You told me that." He sounded distantly sad.

"Did you find out why the girl is here?" Caleb straightened and continued his walk around the desk.

"No, but she's not who she claims."

"I know that. She lied to us." He stood in front of the man again.

"That's bad," Todd said slowly.

"Send more men to William's place."

"William's not there. They've been watching all day."

His hands curled into fists before he stretched them again. "William's a vampire, remember? He won't be out in the daylight."

"William's a vampire?" Todd's eyebrows rose in surprise.

The problem with making people's minds malleable was that it also made their brains soft.

"Send them around when it gets dark."

He should burn. He's a loose end.

Briefly, he considered that. The demon might have a point. "Actually, no. Go yourself. When you're sure he's in there, burn it down. But before you leave, send the approvals for the construction work on the last property through. Then, when you burn the house, stay inside it. Sit on that garish cowhide chaise he loves so much and watch it all burn. It'll be like watching a movie."

Azatoth laughed again.

"A movie. Burn. Okay. What if he isn't there?" Todd's face looked like he had battled sleep to ask the question.

"Burn it anyway. You'll forget our chat now." He muttered a few words and life returned to the other man's face.

Caleb gave Todd an open, friendly smile. "No, no. I don't want to interrupt. I was merely passing and wondered how you were fixed for eighteen holes on the weekend."

"I think I can schedule that in." The mayor beamed. He looked at his clock. "Good Lord! My conference call should have started five minutes ago."

"I'll leave you to it, then. I'll say goodbye to Betsy before I leave."

He found her chopping lemons in the kitchen. At the sight of him, she put the knife and the lemon down and walked around the island toward him.

"Caleb, dear. That was a short visit." She wiped her hands on her apron.

Pick the knife up and gut her, Azatoth suggested with glee.

Caleb ignored it. "Sadly, the business doesn't run itself."

"I know. You should think about retiring. Don't make the same mistake Harv made and work yourself to death." She sighed.

"Perhaps you're right. I think of him every day. The business has never felt the same without him. Not one day of the last five years."

Tears came to her eyes. "That's very touching, Caleb. There you go, making an old woman cry."

"Never my intention, Betsy. Take care. I'll show myself out." He put his hand on her shoulder.

Snap her neck.

He kissed the side of her head and left.

You're getting quite persistent, Azatoth. You seem to forget who's in charge here.

Forgive me, lord. You will gain powers beyond your wildest dreams for freeing me. The sorcerer imagined Azatoth cowering at his feet, which he would be…soon.

He climbed into his Porsche. The engine gave a throaty roar before he pulled away down the drive and onto the street. He was pleased with himself. The girl would soon be beyond the protection of her pack and the meddling witches. The moment she married into Stanley's pack, she would sign the property over to him. He wondered about telling her new husband to throttle her.

After. The place of ritual must belong to you.

"I know that, Azatoth." He spoke aloud to the demon. "I'm merely planning ahead. She's been a nuisance."

I agree. Azatoth assaulted his mind with visions of Kate being hung from a roof by her entrails.

He shook his head. "Well, that's a little exotic for me."

You could give her to me as a little gift. But you will learn to take great pleasure in these things, his inner companion whispered seductively.

Caleb doubted it. He could be vicious but the demon was…well, *demonic.*

CHAPTER ELEVEN

Lexi lay in the dark and wondered what had woken her barely after midnight.

She thought about the day. They'd gotten Dolores back and she'd lost her craving for vampire blood. She couldn't believe how healthy she felt, but she knew she'd miss the benefits of it.

Only until I've built up my natural strength and speed again.

All of that was encouraging, yet she was wide awake. Why? Irritated, she sat and pulled clothes on before she wandered down the hall to the kitchen. She stuck her head into the living room as she passed and saw the still-sleeping figure of Dolores on the couch. As her eyes grew accustomed to the dark, she realized Dick was seated in the armchair watching over her, as still as a dead guy.

"How is she?" she whispered.

"We talked for a while. She's sleeping now. I don't think she'll suffer any long-term ill effects." He tilted his head. "Maybe the munchies."

She face-palmed and shook her head. Choosing not to respond, she wandered to the refrigerator and took out a carton of milk.

"Can't sleep?" he asked from the doorway.

After a quick shake of her head, she found a glass and poured the milk into it. She swallowed half before she turned to him. "I didn't know what woke me up at first."

"Something's coming." He nodded. "I feel it too."

Lexi looked at him in surprise.

"I feel things. I'm undead, not dead." Dick went to the blinds and lifted one to peer out into the darkness.

"Sorry." She shrugged but he didn't see it.

He turned to her. "Think of it like an electric car. It runs on a different fuel but it's not any less of a car than a Trans Am."

She choked on her milk and placed her glass on the counter. "Yeah, it kinda is."

"You're right. That was a terrible analogy." He laughed.

"Could you pour one of those for me?" Edward sat at the table while she took another glass from the shelf and filled it with milk.

The shifter looked at her. "The calm before the storm?"

Rather than answer, she nodded.

"I've been watching wolves in the tree line. I hope they're yours." Dick indicated the window with his head.

"Yes. It's only a few of the pack."

Edward took the glass from her and nodded his thanks. "How's Dolores?"

"She seems okay." She moved to return the milk to the refrigerator.

He turned to Dick. "What exactly is she? The shrinking thing—I've never seen that before."

The vampire walked away from the window. "She's a sylph. It's an air sprite—fae."

"How did you meet her?" Lexi had been about to ask but Edward had beaten her to it.

"I've known Dolores for ninety years. She arranges my papers when it's time for a new ID."

"You must be coming to that time soon."

"Yes. I'll have to discover I have a son somewhere in Europe, rent the house out, and go live out the remainder of my days with my son and grandson William...again."

"Why not choose a different name?" She had wondered about this for the last couple of days.

Dick shrugged. "I don't want to."

"I'll be sorry to see you go." Edward turned from him to Lexi. "What's your story?"

"I don't know what you know about Kindred, but most of us don't really have stories. Some are born into the organization but mostly, we're runaways. Apparently, I was in the system—a foster kid. I ran away and met a kid from Kindred who introduced me and I joined."

"What could they possibly have said to you to make you join an organization like that?" He shook his head.

"My mind was wiped so I guess we'll never know."

"Oh, right. That's what the vamp blood was for. How do you feel about never knowing?"

"I'm already thinking about doing it maybe once a year. Not enough to get into the mess I was in but I still want to know."

"What if you find out something you wish you hadn't?" Dick asked.

"I'll ask Scott to melt my brain again." Lexi smiled.

Edward studied her curiously. "What made you leave them?"

"A vamp tried to turn me and that night, memories started coming back to me—missions I didn't remember being on. I realized they'd regularly hidden my memories. By the morning, I'd remembered too much for me to be safe." She stood and walked to the sink.

I'd remembered Bryan.

"You know they put us into family units, right? We live in regular homes in neighborhoods all over the world.

"I had a kind of brother called Bryan—a mage. He wasn't my real brother, but when we were kids, he looked after me like one. Then, when we were about sixteen, he was bitten by a shifter. He shouldn't have even been there, but he was with us when we were called in on an emergency mission and wasn't supposed to get out of the car. Because he didn't want to get into trouble, he hid it from us. A couple of days later, he got ill and became delirious. He started talking about missions no one remembered. Then, people came from another Kindred unit.

"I wasn't supposed to go near him, but he was my favorite brother. I know you're not supposed to have favorites, but he was much like Scott. We did everything together. He gave me this." She indicated the gold ring she always wore. "I was in the room reading to him, trying to calm him as he thrashed around. They walked in, Braxton dragged me out, and they shot him. Then, they counseled me and I forgot he ever existed. So they took him away twice. For years, I had no idea where this ring even came from."

"'Counseled?'" Edward sounded puzzled.

"Counselling is what they call hiding our memories." Lexi stared into the middle distance. "Anyway, when I was given vampire blood and the memories started to come back, I realized that it must have been the same as him being bitten by a shifter. I knew I wasn't safe so I ran."

He shrugged. "But aren't all you legacies enhanced with blood from all the supe species anyway?"

"Yes, but that happens once, in the ritual." She didn't feel like dealing with where this conversation was heading—back to the fact she was a dud. "I think I'll see if I can get some sleep now."

Dick stood. "I'll go to check the house. I'll call if I can't get back."

"Are you sure it's safe?" she asked as she stood.

He put his hand on his heart. "Well, Lexi Braxton. You care."

"Let's not get ahead of ourselves. I merely don't want to be the one chasing that dog around with a pooper scooper." She shuddered.

"You care," he accused her retreating back.

"I'm going to bed. Don't get yourself killed...again."

CHAPTER TWELVE

Todd drew up outside the house. He couldn't remember why he had come to see his friend William, only that it was imperative he find him. It seemed impolite to ring someone's doorbell at one-thirty in the morning, yet he was doing it.

"Hello?" said an accented voice.

"I need to see William," was all he could think to say.

"Listen, you. I've called the hospital, so they'll come and drag you back, you crazy motherfucker. Leave Mr. Levin alone.

"I'm sorry? I don't quite understand."

A light came on over the gate.

"Oh. Who is it?" Jesús asked in a sing-song voice.

"Can you tell him it's Todd O'Donnell?"

"Mayor O'Donnell? Of course. Please come in." The man buzzed the gate and Todd drove up to the house.

He climbed out of the car and retrieved the tote bag from the trunk. While he couldn't remember why he'd brought a tote bag with him, he felt it was important.

A man opened the front door. He recognized him as William's houseboy, Jesús.

"Please come in, Mayor O'Donnell. Mr. Levin isn't home yet, but he texted earlier to let me know he's on his way."

"Thank you." He entered and walked straight to the cowhide chaise longue.

He was vaguely aware of Jesús staring in horror as he sat on the antique.

"I'm sure this is more comfortable." The man indicated the couch.

"This is perfect." Todd sat, straight-backed, on the seat's edge.

Jesús finally shrugged. "Well, you're the mayor, so I'm sure it's okay." Then, he said something else.

"What?" Todd shook his head to clear it. In the space of a few moments, he'd actually forgotten he was seated there.

"Can I offer you a drink while you wait?"

"No. Thank you."

He realized the man was staring at his tote bag and placed his hand on it. "Why are you staring at my bag?"

"Your— No reason. Would you like me to keep it for you?" Jesús spoke slowly. Perhaps the boy was dim.

"No, it's fine." He moved it closer.

He watched absently as Jesús went to the bar, poured a scotch, returned, and handed it to him.

Did I say yes? I must have.

He took it. "Thank you."

For some reason, he felt nervous, but he had no idea why he would feel that way. He'd been in this house several times. He knocked the whiskey back and coughed. "Would it trouble you to pour me another?"

As Jesús turned to refill the glass, Todd fidgeted with the lighter in his pocket.

CHAPTER THIRTEEN

It was nearly two am when Dick arrived at his home. He parked in a cul de sac leading to the property behind his own, moved quickly across their tennis court, and hopped the wall. He walked silently around his pool, slid the patio door open with almost no sound, and entered.

He was hyper-alert as he walked past the back of the couch toward the kitchen. He smelled sweat in the air. Not Jesús' but a familiar scent he couldn't place. He also detected the smell of whiskey—his Scottish Glenfiddich single malt—and gasoline. He froze and sensed the air move near him before the light went on.

In the two seconds between registering the smells and sensing movement, he moved to the middle of the room. When the light came on, he stood in front of Betsy.

The woman appeared confused for a moment and looked where she thought he had been and then where he now was. She climbed off the couch.

"I didn't know what else to do," she mumbled and burst into tears.

Dick hugged her. "It's all right, Betsy, dear, but first things first. Why is Todd passed out on my chaise?"

They moved to the dinner table.

She sat. "He's all right. Jesús roofied him."

"I didn't roofie him. I merely crushed a few Xanaxes and Ambiens." Jesús entered with a throw, which he draped around Betsy. She patted his hand as he continued, "Betsy brought the pills with her."

He raised an eyebrow.

"I'm sorry, William. Todd came here to kill you." She began to cry again.

"Todd? Are you sure?" He looked at the unconscious man. The mayor didn't have a mean bone in his body. Dick had always thought he was too nice for politics.

"I didn't believe it myself until he turned up a half-hour after his mamma with a gas can. It's in the garage. He kept calling it his 'tote bag.'" Jesús shook his head.

"I don't think he knows what he's doing. Caleb…did something to him when he came to the house this evening. I was taking lemonade to them through that little side room to the study. You remember? Where Harv used to keep that couch he called his daybed?"

Dick nodded.

"They were talking about you and Bianca, except they said she wasn't really Bianca. I didn't understand that but then he told Todd to come here and set fire to your home. He also told him to let himself die in the fire and Todd agreed, just like that."

The vampire tried to sound calm, but he needed to know what she knew. "Do you have any idea why he would suggest such a thing?"

"He asked Todd to send paperwork through about a property deal. Are you in business with him?" She took a handkerchief from her purse.

He shook his head. "You were very brave to not give yourself away."

"I wanted to kill him." Her hand scrunched the handkerchief. "When he came to see me in the kitchen, I had to put the knife down. I couldn't trust myself."

"He must have used some kind of hypnosis on Todd." Dick tried to think of an explanation Betsy would believe.

"I always knew." She placed a hand on his arm.

Dick looked at her and opened his mouth to ask what she meant.

"I always knew that somehow, you were our William. I always felt silly for believing it, but it was my secret belief that I never shared with anyone." New tears appeared in her eyes. "He said you're a vampire. It's strange but it makes perfect sense."

This was the moment when he could have denied it. He should have denied it. Kindred could end him for telling the truth but he couldn't bring himself to open his mouth and deliver another lie to this woman. "You're not afraid?"

"Of you? Never. But William, I'm terribly afraid of Caleb." She pulled the throw around her as though she had suddenly felt cold.

"I intended to return. I wanted to be his best man, but this happened." He gestured vaguely at himself. "And I wasn't...civil at first. I couldn't be near people for a long time. I had to be sure I wouldn't hurt the people I loved. Can you understand that, Betsy?"

The woman stood and embraced him. "Welcome home, William."

Dick sobbed once, then sniffed and pulled away. "Did they say anything else?"

Betsy paused. He could see from the look on her face that he wouldn't like it.

She returned to her seat and he returned to his as though he knew he should be seated for this. Betsy leaned forward and placed her hand on his. "He told Todd that he murdered Harv."

He felt as though she had delivered a blow to his gut and froze.

"William, William." Harvey ran toward him. They had been playing tennis and stopped for martinis. He turned to watch his approach, thinking he was beautiful in his tennis whites. Not for the first time, he thought the man should have been the movie star, not him. Harv knew William was in love with him but he loved him like a brother so he accepted that was all they could ever be.

"What's up, pal? You look like you'll have a heart attack." William held a martini out.

His friend took the drink and knocked it back in one. "She said yes. I popped the question and Betsy said yes. I want you to be my best man."

"That's great news. Harv. I'm thrilled for you both." He shook the man's hand enthusiastically and smiled until his face hurt.

But it was too much for him. He needed time and distance so he went overseas a week later and never returned, not as himself. The next time he saw Harv and Betsy, it was as his grandson. They were elderly but he still loved Harv and he loved Betsy for the years of happiness she'd given the man he loved.

***

"William, William." Betsy's hand was on his arm and she shook him out of his reverie.

"I will destroy him." His voice was strangled with rage.

He left at vamp speed.

CHAPTER FOURTEEN

"Lexi." Edward spoke as he knocked on the door.

Her eyes snapped open. She felt like she had barely closed them, but a knife was already in her hand.

She yawned. "Edward?"

He stood on the other side of the door. "I think we have a problem."

Lexi opened the door quickly enough to make him jump. She stood in a t-shirt and panties and carried a knife and a gun as she looked left and right down the hallway.

He turned and hurried down the hall. "Get dressed. William's missing."

Sixty seconds later, she was in her leathers and on her way to the kitchen. As she walked past Scott's room, she looked in to see him hopping around as he tried to get into his jeans. She knew they'd probably been inside-out on the floor and rolled her eyes as she continued up the hall.

Edward looked up from his cell phone as she entered. "Jesús called. Dick's gone after Caleb."

"On his own? What's gotten into him?" She pulled her jacket on.

"I'll call someone in to watch Dolores." He stood at the window and stared out into the darkness. All she could see was his reflection in the glass.

"And why do I need to be watched?" The fae stood in the doorway with Marcel in her arms.

"Because you look awful. You're pale and weak and no one wants to die protecting you in a fight," Scott said from the hallway.

Everyone turned to stare at him.

"I see. You're learning." The woman turned to Lexi and nodded her approval. "Take care." She returned to the couch.

A knock at the back door drew their attention and a denim-clad man walked in and sat at the kitchen table. He'd clearly already received his instructions from Edward, because other than a brief nod, there was no communication between them.

Lexi looked at the clock. It was 3:15. "We don't have long."

They climbed into Edward's SUV and headed out. Along the road, she tried Dick's cell repeatedly. Finally, she sighed. "If he could answer, he would."

"There's something up ahead." The shifter slowed the car.

She stared at the flashing lights. "Is it an accident?"

"Roadblock." Edward shook his head. "Shit. I should have expected this. Stan will have his officers looking for you. I'll try telling them we're heading to Brawley."

He came to a halt and Lexi moved her hand to her pocket. Scott leaned forward and put his hand on her shoulder and she relaxed her arm.

The driver rolled his window down and an officer shone his flashlight around the inside of the car, back and front, then asked for ID. He took it slowly from where it was tucked under the visor. The officer pointed the light at it, then asked, "May I ask what you're doing out so late?"

Edward opened his mouth to tell his lie. "Of course you may, young man. It *is* rather late, isn't it? I've been to Riverside to play bingo with June and Margo. We've played bingo together for forty years." His mouth snapped shut. That was not his voice.

"Your bingo goes on a little late, doesn't it, ma'am?"

He opened his mouth again. "Well, now that I think about it, there were a few years we didn't play when June and Margo weren't speaking. Now, why was that? You know, I can't remember. Oh, of course. How could I have forgotten? Margo caught her husband in the pool house with June. Of course, he's been dead these past twenty years."

"Who did it? Margo or June?" the officer asked.

"I believe it was Mr. Jack Daniels. Don't tell Margo I said that. She tells everyone he was raptured."

The officer laughed. "Drive carefully, ma'am." He waved his flashlight and indicated that the other officers should move the barrier.

"Thank you, young man," Edward called.

After they had driven through, he turned in his seat. "What did he see?"

"A little old lady in a 1971 Austin America." Scott sounded exhausted.

Lexi twisted to look at her friend and noticed he was perspiring. "Are you okay?"

"I'll be fine in a minute. I had to do the voice, the face, the car, make the rest of us invisible, and try to think of things to say. It was like juggling fire."

They travelled on in silence.

"Scott, we're near Dick's." She stretched between the seats and shook his knee.

"Right." He muttered some words. "We're shielded."

She was about to touch her scar and open the gate when it opened before them. Startled, she glanced at him. "Was that you?"

Scott shook his head.

The gate closed behind them. They drove around an unfamiliar vehicle and directly into the garage. Lexi heard shouting the moment she climbed out of the car, and she drew her katana.

"I have to do it." The mayor was red-faced and yelled from the corner of the room.

"But William's not here, darling. Aren't you supposed to wait for William?" Betsy said, the stress in her voice palpable.

"I think we need more duct tape," Jesús said from one of the barstools. He glowered at Todd, who was secured to Dick's half-million-dollar chaise with an already sizeable amount of tape.

"Hello, Bianca dear." Betsy saw Lexi enter, and her shoulders sagged with relief. She looked at Scott. "And you must be John."

"I'm Scott."

Edward walked in behind them. The woman smiled. "I'm sorry, then *you* must be John."

"Edward."

Lexi put her katana on the counter. "There is no John. What the hell is going on, and where is Dick?"

"Who's Dick?" Betsy asked.

Jesús stood and moved to the center of the room. "Someone called Caleb messed with the mayor's head and now, he wants to kill Mr. Levin. The mayor's mamma came to warn Mr. Levin but he wasn't here, so we drugged him. His mamma says I won't go to jail for that. Then she told Mr. Levin that Caleb killed someone called Harv. I don't know who that is, but Mr. Levin got super-mad and disappeared real fast. I tried to call him, but there was no answer, so I called Mr. Edward." He turned to Betsy. "And Mr. Levin is Dick, but I don't know why that is."

Edward's jaw dropped. "I'm so sorry. I know your husband was a good friend of William's grandfather."

"Oh. She knows about the *thing* too." Jesús made pointy teeth with his fingers and held them up to his mouth.

"He has to die," Todd yelled from the corner.

Jesús screamed and ran to his barstool.

Scott walked to the chaise and extended a hand toward the air around the man.

Betsy took a few steps toward them, worry on her face. "What's he doing?"

Lexi went to stand beside her. "He's going to try to help Todd." She looked at Edward. "Can you find some items belonging to Dick? Things he has a good connection with?"

The shifter nodded. "I brought something from his trunk. It's in the car."

She sat beside Betsy. "Hi, I'm Lexi. I was asked to help a young woman in town with a gang problem. Things have escalated."

"I heard Caleb say you weren't really Bianca. So no gossip about the New England Mayburys, then?" Betsy asked while she watched Scott and Todd anxiously.

"I could make something up." She also watched them and picked her lip nervously.

The older woman put her hand on her arm. "Don't do that, dear." She left her hand there. "How could Caleb do this?"

"Caleb's a sorcerer. The bad kind." Lexi patted the woman's hand.

"And him?" Betsy turned to face her. "The good kind?"

"You're getting it." She smiled. They both turned to the men.

As Scott muttered something, a dark cloud drifted from Todd and spread across the floor.

"Whatever it is, it seems to be coming out of him," Lexi said.

"I've got this." Edward held a small leather-covered box out. They stood around it and peered in as he opened it.

"Does anything stand out to you?" Lexi asked Edward as he pushed gold jewelry around the box.

Edward pursed his lips. "Not really. He—"

"This." Betsy darted her fingers into the little box and pulled out a silver pin in the shape of a lion's head. She held it up. "It was a gift from Harv. What's that sticking to it?"

Lexi peered closely at the flaky substance and shook her head.

Edward squinted. "Skin. Vampires can't touch silver."

'Well, he's touched that," she stated.

Betsy turned to her son. "Is that normal?"

She frowned at the black smoke that built behind Scott as he stood with his eyes closed, concentrating on Todd. She opened her mouth to ask what it was when it coalesced into the vague shape of a man. Its ethereal arms slid around her friend's throat.

Scott's eyes flew open and bulged, and his face turned red. He clawed at his throat, but his hands merely went through the smoke.

Lexi threw a shuriken at the shape, but it glided through and stuck into the wall.

Edward shifted instantly, attempted to jump at the entity, but powered through it instead.

As they watched, the center of it became darker until it was almost black. Lexi felt strongly that something worse was about to happen.

She held her arm out and stroked the scar. "Freeze!" she shouted.

The black shape solidified. She grasped her katana and slashed through its arms. No longer attached to the rest of the body, they transformed to pieces of black glass and shattered on the floor, and Scott moved away.

Edward shifted to human form.

Betsy's hand was clutched to her chest. "Jesús, dear, I think I need a drink."

Jesús brought her a bottle of gin and a glass. As he turned to walk away, she caught his arm. "His clothes are still on. How strange."

"You think that's the strange thing?" The man shook his head. "Actually, I know this one. Shifters were made from a spell or a curse or something, so it's magic. It's best not to think about it. I don't have enough migraine pills for both of us."

Scott dropped to his knees, where he gasped and drew in deep gulps of air. Lexi put her hand under his arm and dragged him away while Edward picked up Todd and the chair in one and moved them away from the ugly frozen shape.

"I need to carry on. I was almost there." The young man tried to stand but there was no strength in him.

A bottle of water appeared between them. She glanced at Betsy who regarded her with a worried face. "I'm sorry, Jesús says the water cooler isn't working."

Lexi flicked a look at the man and took the bottle. "Thank you."

She passed it to Scott and he downed it.

"Do you have anything left?" he asked.

"Yes, do you need it?" She held her hand out, and the energy trickled away to leave only a drop at the bottom of her scar.

"Can you help me up?" he asked.

Edward stepped forward and lifted him easily to his feet. The young sorcerer returned to his position behind Todd, closed his eyes, and extended his arms once more.

Lexi and Edward walked carefully to the frozen black smoke-man and circled him.

"What's this?" The shifter pointed at its center.

She walked closer and crouched. Staring into the deep, inky blackness, the only light she saw was a reflection of the light in the room. "It's a knife. Why would there be a knife inside it? And it's tiny. Should I break it?" She raised her sword again.

"Not yet. I want to look at it." Scott leaned on the end of the chaise and looked like he might faint.

Betsy stepped beside him, took his arm, and put it around her to give him stability.

"I've broken Caleb's hold on Todd. He won't be able to control him with sorcery again." He wavered, and Edward tried to guide him to the couch. "No. I need to see that."

The two men moved to the black shape. Scott looked into its center.

"That's not a tiny knife. It's far away. This is a portal. If you hadn't frozen it when you did, that knife would be somewhere in me by now." He wobbled on his feet and lurched to the couch.

"Are you spent?" Lexi asked.

"I should have enough for a location spell for Dick. Jesús, do you have a local map?" The man walked away as Scott extended his hand for the pin, and she dropped it in his hand.

His eyes widened. "Wow! Yes. This is good. He's connected to this by love, loss, and grief." He blinked away the tears that had appeared in response to the emotions tied to the little pin, held it in the palm of his hand, and spoke to it like it was a pet. "Come on, little guy. Lead us to your master." He passed it to Lexi. "I need to text Dolores."

The moment the pin dropped into her hand, she felt it tug. Jesús hadn't returned with the map, so she began to walk through the room with her hand held in front of her. She asked the others, "What is this, east? He's east of us? She side-stepped the frozen black mass and continued walking.

"Oh!" Her arm was pulled sideways. "North. Could he be on the move?" Her arm jerked again. She once again stood in front of the smoke-man. Lexi circled the portal with her hand out in front of her. It pulled her from every angle.

Edward stood beside her. "It's the portal. Wherever they sent that knife from, that's where William is."

"I'm sorry. I need to recharge or I might not be much help when we arrive." Scott sighed.

"Mom?"

They all turned to look at Todd.

"Why am I taped to a chair?"

"Jesús," Edward called.

Jesús walked in with a sheet to cover the frozen portal before the mayor could see it. "Yes, Mr. Edward?"

"We need a box-cutter."

The man looked at Todd and tutted as though in disappointment. "Yes, we sure do." He walked away, shaking his head.

Edward set about releasing Todd while Betsy stumbled to find a rational explanation for his situation. "Well, goodness. Such a...a thing."

Jesús sat on the floor next to the chaise, picked at the tape, and rolled his eyes. "We think someone roofied you." He shared a quick glance with Betsy.

"What? Where?" Todd brought his freed hand to his mouth.

"At the party," Jesús said as he peeled the tape gently from Dick's prized chaise.

"What party?" Todd looked at the people around him.

Edward released him from the chair.

"Oh, my God. He doesn't even remember the party," Betsy said and walked toward her son. "Okay, dear. Let's get you home."

He pointed at the covered object. "What's that?"

"It's a statue of me naked. You want to see?" Jesús took hold of the sheet as though to sweep it away.

Todd looked at him. "No." He turned his face away. "Mother, let's go."

Edward helped him to his feet while Betsy crossed to Lexi.

She took her hand. "Call me as soon as you know anything, please."

They left and Lexi, Scott, and Edward stood around the frozen portal.

The shifter stood and waved his hand slowly through the air.

Lexi turned and stared at him. "What are you doing?"

"I'm trying to determine where that reflection's coming from." He tried to put his arm between one of the spotlights and the reflection.

Scott looked into it. "It's not a reflection. That is what they call 'the light at the end of the tunnel.'"

Edward lowered his arm. "I never thought of that."

"So, what? You unfreeze it and we simply walk in?" Lexi tapped on it.

"Honestly, I don't know. It could only be one way." The young man paused to think. "If we *can* get into it, I don't think we'll be able to use it to come back. Jesús? Do you have a hammer?"

Jesús went to a kitchen drawer and pulled out a heavy-looking meat tenderizer mallet. "Will this do?"

"Possibly. This is kind of a doorway. We'll go through it, and when we've gone, it will freeze again. I want you to count to ten, then smash the shit out of it."

"I can do that." The man tested the weight of the implement in his hand. "Hmm… Can't I just shoot it?

Scott smiled. "That'll work, but seriously, wait until it's frozen."

"Then you need to get into Mr. Levin's day car and wait for a call. He might need safe transport." Edward cracked his neck. He seemed to be getting ready to turn.

"Wait." Lexi squinted at the far-away knife frozen in the portal. "What's that on the hilt?"

They all looked closer. "Oh!" Jesús exclaimed. She jumped. "It's like a hand. See the black shape behind it? That's a man—kind of, maybe." His finger drew the outline of the shadowy figure onto the blackened glass. It was indeed a man or something resembling a man, trapped within the frozen portal.

"What'll happen when you reactivate this?"

"I expect he'll continue his attempt to kill me." Scott sounded so detached and clinical that she blinked in surprise.

"I'll go first, then—" she said quickly.

He interrupted her and held his hand up. "If he's traveling through it, we can't enter it until he breaks the surface at this end. We need to be sure he keeps coming. The moment he leaves it, the portal could vanish, so we have to remain in contact with it when he's out to keep it active."

Lexi stepped back. "You're right. He won't come out with us waiting for him. Can he see us?"

Scott thought for a moment. "He's frozen in there and probably unaware of the passage of time. He'll still see what he saw before it froze."

Edward looked at him. "Which is you, waiting to be stabbed in the back."

"Then that's what he needs to see when I reactivate it. I'll take a step farther away. He looks to be deep in there, but portals can be visually distorted. He could be much closer." The sorcerer took a step away from the portal and turned his back.

"I don't like this." Lexi stood at the side and sweat prickled her scalp. She heard the bone-cracking sounds of Edward shifting and watched as the wolf stretched his injured leg, then padded around the back of the portal to the other side.

Scott gave a quick nod before the portal shimmered and became almost solid smoke once more.

No sooner had the surface lost its rigidity than the blade appeared from its murky depths. Lexi swung her katana onto it and Edward leapt at the arm to clamp his jaws over it.

A hideous, inhuman screech issued as the assassin was dragged out.

They had expected a man, a sorcerer, a wolf, or a vampire. What they were faced with was none of those. It was vaguely bipedal in shape, but its skin was black and oily. The mouth was huge and fanged, and the top half of its face was full of black eyes. Its second arm emerged and tried to swipe at Lexi, followed by four more arms. Each had a pincer on the end.

Edward whimpered and retched, his mouth black as he pulled away from the creature and collapsed, writhing, on the floor. Her sword was dragged from her grasp by one of the pincers.

It still seemed determined to attack Scott and thrust with four of its arms to grasp his shoulders. He pulled away and fell forward, which made the creature fall with him. Once on the floor, it climbed onto his back, drew its head back, and opened its mouth. Yellow fangs glistened from black gums and began their descent to his exposed neck when it was halted by the sudden appearance of Lexi's knife protruding from its mouth.

It gurgled and burst into a huge splash of slime that caught her and totally covered her friend.

She realized they were farther from the mouth of the portal than she had intended.

"No," she cried and spun to see that the portal was still open. Standing beside it, his face turned away and eyes screwed shut, was Jesús. He had poked one finger into the swirling surface and waved the meat mallet in the air in front of him.

Lexi slid closer and stuck her foot into it. "You can stop that now, Jesús. You did great. Scott, are you okay?" She was concerned that he hadn't moved.

He didn't respond immediately, but after a few breaths, he said, "What the fuck is all over me?"

"Some kind of demon gunk. I think it must have liked you. How do you feel?"

"Pregnant." He shuddered.

"Not up for a second date, then?" She looked at Edward. He had shifted but lay unconscious on the floor. "Edward? Scott, can you help him? I don't want to take my foot out of the portal."

He placed a hand on the shifter and black slimy liquid ran from his mouth. There was a surprising amount of it. He coughed and brought up the last of it, then sat and leaned against the wall. "What the hell was that?"

"Precisely. That was a demon," Scott said.

Edward rubbed his face. "I might have nightmares for the rest of my life." He stood and looked into the portal. "That tunnel looks long. Will there be any more of those in there?"

"I hope not. Are we ready to go? It's nearly sunrise." Lexi asked, her foot still in place and her katana raised.

"I need a minute. I asked Dolores to send stuff through to your pocket. Is it there?" She began to retrieve various items from her dimensional pocket, including several crystals and a couple of cell phone power packs. As they appeared, she passed them to Scott. He held each crystal for a few seconds to draw the stored magical energy from them and discarded them in turn. Finally, he picked up a power pack that had four blue lights along its edge.

"Ha! Dolores is a genius." As he held it, the lights blinked out one at a time. He held his hand out to Lexi and transferred energy to her, then picked up the second and half-drained it, leaving two blue lights. He picked his bag up and threw the power pack into it.

They looked at each other and nodded. She turned to Jesús. "Start counting."

In silence, they stepped through.

CHAPTER FIFTEEN

In the space of two steps, they were in a room that stank of abandonment and urine. Someone screamed, and they all looked up. The shriek had come from an upper floor.

Scott twirled his finger. "We're shielded, but I'll have to drop the shield when we get moving or I won't have the strength to fight whatever's coming. Was that Dick screaming?"

"I hope so. That means he's still alive." Lexi withdrew her flashlight from her pocket and played it around the room. A set of shuttered doors with small windows at the top stretched the full length of one side.

"Is this a garage?" he asked.

She shrugged. "I'll take point," she stated and took a step toward the door.

"Wait. Take this." He fumbled in his bag, brought out two earpieces, and passed one to her.

Lexi smiled. It was Kindred protocol to wear the communicators on a mission. "You can take the boy out of Kindred…" She placed it in her ear.

"We don't know what might be up there or how many. Be careful." Edward shifted and padded through the room, sniffing. She followed him with the light while he examined dark corners and shook his head at the disgusting smells.

They moved carefully to the hallway. She gestured that the shifter should go left and scout the rest of the ground floor and he nodded and turned away. Lexi smiled briefly at the absurdity of a nodding wolf, then climbed the stairs a few steps ahead of Scott. She reached the door to the second floor and extended her hand toward the handle when a garbled message came through her communicator. The sound confused her and she couldn't understand why it only came only through the earpiece and not from directly behind her. She turned and gasped when she realized a black cloud was enveloping her and there was no sign of Scott. Lexi froze and waited for him to appear or to repeat what he'd said over the comm.

"For fuck's sake, Lexi. Move your ass *now!*" His voice came loud and clear and she guessed he must have boosted the signal with magic.

"Forward or backward?" She hesitated and waited for the response. Finally, she panicked and turned to retreat down steps she couldn't even see. Her assumption was if something was going wrong, it was probably behind her.

The door flew open and before she could turn again, she was yanked inside by the back of her jacket. It immediately slammed shut.

She found her feet in a second, slightly dizzy and with her blade out, but couldn't identify anyone to aim it at. The room was in complete darkness.

Whatever it is, it's really fast.

Lexi fumbled for her flashlight but she had lost it, probably on the stairs. A muffled yell issued from farther inside the building.

Her mind began to play tricks. She imagined being surrounded by demons with their teeth bared an arm's length away, and a cold drop of sweat trickled down her back. Cautiously, her senses alert, she drew her second blade. The long, metallic ring seemed twice as loud in the dark.

She tried to breathe slowly to quiet the sound of blood rushing in her ears. It occurred to her that if she could hear her blood, so could a roomful of demons or vamps. Her heart pumped faster.

As she strained into the silent blackness, she realized she could still hear Scott and that his tiny, tinny voice came from somewhere ahead of her. She'd also lost her earpiece, obviously.

Knowing she had to move, her first instinct was to go toward the device, but she feared they'd be expecting that and block her exit. Instead, she backed up to the door. It had been reinforced and she couldn't feel a handle.

Well, shit!

From there, she inched along the wall to where the window should be. Wooden boards covered it, and she didn't dare to turn her back to the room to try to pry them loose. She continued around the room and kept the wall at her back while she waved her blades ahead and to the sides. As she moved, she tried to calculate the best use of the magic she had.

I could use it to fill the room with light. But if I do that and there are fifty demons in here, I'll need the magic to deal with them. What if I use it on whatever's in here but Scott's injured and I need it to heal him? What if I need it for Dick or Edward?

Life was so much easier with Scott beside her.

Lexi tried to recall if she'd seen any of the room before the door slammed but remembered nothing of any value. She'd heard something fall and roll when she landed and realized that would have been the flashlight. It could have rolled anywhere, though, so wasn't of much use to her.

The pained howl of a wolf broke the silence. Was that Edward? Where was Scott?

She wanted to use magic but because it was finite, it was the last option.

Her next step was taken with the thought that she hoped the floor was intact and that she wouldn't step into thin air. Scott's tinny voice hissed from the earwig again a second before a crunch cut it short, followed by silence.

The sound had pinpointed the location of something, though. She flung a silver-tipped star and was rewarded with a screech.

"You bitch! You'll die for that," said a voice from the darkness. It wasn't one of the demons, then, so probably a vampire. Maybe the one who killed Leonard. She now had the sense it was only the two of them in this room.

"I'll die for *that?* Surely you planned to kill me anyway." She hoped he might respond so she could throw another star.

A second later, he surged into an attack that hurled her face-first to the floor.

His knees dug into her back, and the swords were ripped from her hands. She lay helpless and grimaced as they clattered across the room. Instinctively, she stretched her hand forward in an effort to activate the magic in her unhealing scar, but her arms were wrenched apart.

I should have used the magic earlier.

Drips of liquid landed on her ear, and the metallic tang of blood filled her nostrils. She must have caught him in the face with her shuriken. The thought gave her some satisfaction, but she wasn't strong enough to struggle against him. She had run out of options.

Here we go again, she thought and twisted her head to let the blood drip onto her face. It ran in rivulets down to her nose, chin, and as anticipated, to the edge of her mouth. She licked her lips.

It has been zero days since I last took vamp blood.

Instantly, the darkness was gone and her attacker's face appeared in the corner of her vision. She flashed her gaze around the room. It was empty and dirty with graffiti on the walls and a perfectly round hole in the center of the floor.

Another scream from above dragged her attention away from the odd aperture.

"Poor William isn't faring too well. Caleb asked me to drag it out. It's been fun, but nature will take over shortly. My friends will take him to the east side of the building to meet the sun. Perhaps he's already there. I'm afraid you'll miss that part."

His face descended and she jerked her head back and drove it into his nose.

"*Bitch!*" He pulled away.

Lexi used his momentary withdrawal to shove him off and turn onto her back, but the vamp attacked again. She tried to push him away with her feet but he resisted her effort to force him back. When that failed, she hooked him around the neck with her thighs. He tried to twist his head, no doubt to sink his teeth into her femoral artery. Thanks to his blood coursing through her body, her hold was strong enough that he couldn't immediately extricate himself. By the time he realized his predicament, it was too late.

She flipped to the side and smirked at the satisfying crunch when his neck severed from his spine. He slumped and she rolled free and raced to the window. She jammed the blade of her knife into the corner of the wood and twisted to lever a nail out enough to squeeze her fingers into the gap. Hastily, she wrenched one of the boards off. The vampire, paralyzed on the floor, was unable to move out of the morning sunlight from the east-facing window and burst into flames.

While she was now able to see, she still couldn't work out how to get the door open. She knew she could accomplish it with magic, but it might bring more of them. Frustrated, she sheathed her weapons, turned into the room, and looked through the hole in the floor. Her gaze moved above her and she located the place where bolts had been set in the ceiling. They were in an abandoned fire station.

This was where the pole had stood.

Before she could change her mind, she sat on the edge and dropped to hang by her fingertips. It was a fair distance but she let go, landed with a jarring pain in her ankle, and drew her katana before she'd even caught her breath. She didn't think her ankle was broken, which was good. Her first choice was not to use magic on herself and she preferred to keep it for one of the others, if needed.

She hobbled across the floor and into the hallway. To the left was what had probably been a small kitchenette. A wolf lay dead on the floor. She staggered momentarily in shock until she saw it was brown. Edward's wolf form was white and gray. Its throat had been ripped out, so her teammate had been there. Quickly, she found the way to the stairs. The black smoke was gone and as she started her ascent, a string of expletives came from the hallway to the right. She knew the voice and hobbled around the corner to find Scott once again covered in slime.

"Is this becoming some kind of fetish?" She was relieved, and tight knots of muscle relaxed that she hadn't realized were tense.

"Just don't." He looked furious and she helped him up.

"Why didn't you fix that?" he asked and looked at her foot in the beam of a flashlight.

"Is that my flashlight?" She blinked in recognition.

"It's mine. It fell through a hole in the ceiling and hit me on the head so it's mine now."

He took her hand and whispered something that sounded like "heal."

The pain in her ankle disappeared.

When they reached the foot of the stairs, he shone the light ahead of her and up.

"It's okay, I can see. I've been at the hard stuff again." Lexi strode upward.

"I thought you threw that shit out." Scott sounded disappointed.

She stopped. "I did. I got it from the source this time. It was a situational requirement."

"That's disgusting."

"Yes. Yes, it is. Look." Edward, in human form, peered down at them from two floors above. He appeared to be in pain.

They hurried to where he was crouched and clinging to the railing.

Scott stooped to assess him. He had a bite on his shoulder and a hideous rake across his face and Lexi assumed the blood around his mouth wasn't his.

"Don't waste it on me. I'll heal. See to him." The shifter pointed through a doorway.

The sorcerer placed a hand on his head. "I'll hurry your healing along a little."

She entered the room, where a ripped white shirt lay on the floor with a pair of black pants next to it. At the other side, Dick sprawled in only his boxers and covered by a net of silver. The restraint became more difficult to see when it sank farther into him and hissed and sizzled. It was already deep in his flesh from his head to his feet. He shook violently as though in shock.

"Hey, Dick. Smoldering hot as always." She swallowed. He was difficult to look at but she did it. "There's a vamp downstairs who tried the Lexi Thigh-Ride. I'm afraid he didn't come out of it as well as you did."

He tried and failed to laugh. "I've met him. He doesn't have my sympathy." As he spoke, blood dribbled from his lips. She tried to move the netting from his side and a chunk of flesh lifted with it. He screamed and her stomach churned. Instinctively, she dropped the mesh and it hissed alarmingly.

"How do I look?" he asked through chattering teeth.

"Honestly? Like Pinhead, minus the pins. What happened?"

"I raced out of my front gate at vamp speed, straight through a fucking portal, and into a brick wall."

Scott entered the room and turned immediately to hold onto the door frame. "Jesus, fuck!"

"What can we do?" Lexi asked the vampire.

"Well, it's been on for a while and you can see how deep it is. I think this might be it," Dick said and gritted his teeth to stop them chattering.

"Scott?" Lexi turned to him for guidance.

The young man rubbed at his face. "I'm not sure. On a vamp, silver clings to the skin around it. Taking that off will tear him apart. I can't see how he'd survive it."

"Could you translocate it?"

"Translocation causes friction in the air around the object. It wouldn't be a…helpful result."

"What if we tarnish the silver like Caleb did?"

"That won't work. Tarnish is silver sulfide and water. It would like bathing him in liquid silver." Scott looked away again.

Dick dragged in a strangled breath as the net sank even deeper.

"There's something you can do." He followed his statement with a low keen from the back of his throat.

"What? Anything." Lexi felt defeated.

"You can tell me why you call me Dick. I might not get another chance to find out."

She barked a laugh and choked back tears simultaneously.

"This will be so disappointing," she warned him. "It's because you're a detective. A private dick."

"Are you shitting me?" He raised his head a little, then screamed. After a moment, he continued, "That is so anti-fucking-climactic."

Edward entered the room. The bite marks and scratches were gone. "Can you at least make it so he can't feel it?" His voice broke. He sat beside his friend and slipped his hand under the edge of the net to cover Dick's hand, so far untouched by the net.

"I...uh, I might be able to try something else. I can't tarnish the silver but maybe I could gild it if we had something gold." He pulled his bag from his back, crouched, and began to yank everything out of it. "There must be something. I have to have something gold."

Lexi tapped his shoulder and when he turned, offered him her ring. "Is this enough?"

"The ring Bryan gave you?"

She could see he didn't want to take it. "I've got a new family now and I don't want to lose any of you."

Scott took the ring and turned it over in his fingers. He seemed to be planning how he should approach it. After a long moment, he drew in a deep breath and exhaled slowly. "All right."

He closed his eyes and muttered while sweat gathered on his face. Lexi studied him quickly, a little concerned as he seemed unusually pale. The three of them turned to the vampire and noticed that the visible parts of the silver net began to take on a golden hue from the head downward. The hissing sound it emitted reduced as it changed and finally stopped. When Scott had finished, the ring was completely gone and the net was gold.

"It's not over yet. We still need to get it off him, but it should come easier and his own healing should kick in." He sat on the floor, breathing like he'd run a marathon.

With the net now covered in gold, it slipped more easily out of the flesh but it was still a slow and tense process. It took Scott and

Edward about twenty minutes to peel it slowly from Dick, inch by agonizing inch, while Lexi found flattened cardboard and covered the gaps in the windows.

Finally, footfalls on the stairs drew Edward to the door. "In here."

Jesús entered, carrying a length of rolled black plastic, which he dropped at the sight of Dick who was still covered in a bloody pattern. "Santa Maria!"

"He should be healing by now. Why isn't he healing?" Lexi asked.

The Mexican clicked his tongue and shook his head. He turned to the three of them. "Out, you get out now." He herded them out of the room.

"What was that about?" Scott asked.

"He'll feed Will. It will help him heal. I'm embarrassed that I didn't think of it," Edward explained as they sat on the floor in the hallway.

After a few minutes, Jesús appeared at the door. "We can move him now."

They walked in to find Dick zipped into a body bag.

Scott looked at it and tilted his head with a small smile. "I'm surprised he doesn't have a diamond-encrusted body bag."

"I'm right here," the vampire said from inside and his voice sounded like it had gained strength.

"Oh. Where's your earpiece?" Scott asked Lexi as he picked the net up.

She slung his bag over her shoulder. "The vamp stamped on it."

"He busted your communicator? What a bastard." He shook his head.

Startled, she stared at him with her mouth agape. "He also killed Leonard and tortured Dick. I know you like your tech but get some fucking perspective." She slapped him upside the head and walked out.

CHAPTER SIXTEEN

Caleb sat in his office the next morning and waited to receive the call informing him of Todd's death. He wondered if he should have called off his request to burn William's home after he'd set up the portal trap, but what was the point? The mayor had to be dealt with sooner or later and sooner was better.

For a few moments, he fantasized about the call. Would it come from Stanley? Betsy? He imagined feigning shock and horror, then he imagined telling Betsy the truth and watching her little old face crumble. The mental image made him chuckle. It no longer mattered, though. Tonight was the night. It had to be. He'd clear Kate out of that store, pull its magical wards down, and tear it to pieces.

He was distracted by visions of Todd burning, his hair aflame and face crackling. Irritated, he shook his head. *Not now.*

Hahahahaha. Azatoth laughed in his mind.

The telephone in the outer office rang, then his personal line. "Yes,"

His secretary spoke. "It's Mr. Hughes."

His lawyer would no doubt have called to confirm that everything was ready to go ahead. "Put him through... Donald. How are things?"

"Hello, Caleb. I haven't received the paperwork from the mayor's office."

"You haven't? That's strange. Todd was going to send it last night." He hung up.

Caleb tried to recall if he had told Todd to send it or bring it. Conflicting orders—such as "Bring this to me after you've killed yourself"—didn't always raise the flags it should. He was sure he'd told him to send it. If the news of his death had reached his staff, they might have failed to forward it. He'd have to find out. The next mayor might not be as malleable as Todd had proven to be. He picked the phone up. "Get me the mayor's office."

The call was answered without delay. "Mayor's office."

"It's Caleb Linden. Put me through to the mayor."

"I'm sorry, Mr. Linden. The office is in disarray at the moment. We don't currently have a mayor."

"My condolences." He stifled a giggle that wasn't his own.

"I'm sorry?" The voice sounded puzzled.

"I…sorry, I automatically assumed…" He left the sentence incomplete and experienced a niggling feeling of doubt.

"The mayor has taken an extended break."

"He's…are you sure?"

"Yes. He called this morning and he's had a sudden family emergency. But he did ask me to send a package to you. It should be in your hands within the hour."

"I see. Thank you for your assistance."

Caleb disconnected and leaned back to consider what could have happened. Perhaps his brain had finally scrambled and he had been committed? It didn't matter. The paperwork was on its way.

He walked to the wall of bookcases, opened a drinks cabinet, and poured himself a whiskey.

Ten minutes later, the delivery arrived. His secretary placed it on his desk and left, and he smiled. Everything was turning out fine. A little last-minute, maybe, but that was okay. He opened the envelope and slid the documents out, and the smile froze on his face and slowly faded. The envelope contained several blank sheets, although the one on the front presented a clear message. It was a photocopy of two hands flipping the bird. He recognized Todd's class ring and Betsy's engagement ring.

How uncouth.

William was behind this. He knew it. Reluctantly, he came to the conclusion that things hadn't gone according to plan at the abandoned fire station either.

Caleb rocked thoughtfully in his chair. *I don't like this. There's too much interference. I think it's time to put my contingency plan into place.*

Azatoth spoke. *Dismember them.*

He rolled his eyes. *That might be overkill.* He looked at the telephone. *They won't like this.*

Azatoth hissed. *They don't have to like it. They serve...you.*

The man smiled again. William and his friends would have a nasty surprise if they interfered. He wadded the paper, dropped it into the trash, and snatched the phone.

CHAPTER SEVENTEEN

Lexi was awoken by the sound of Edward's telephone ringing. Having lost her favorite sweats in the junk-filled suitcase, she slipped quickly into shorts and a t-shirt. She headed past Scott's empty room and continued to the kitchen. Edward stood beside the kitchen door, speaking on the phone.

"I'm very well, Stanley. How are you? I hear we've got a wedding to attend."

He listened.

"Why would Tommy be worried? Marcia told me they were going to some spa or whatever it is women do these days."

The shifter glanced at her and raised an eyebrow. "Yes, I heard you'd requested that they hold the wedding immediately and it's about time, in my opinion. Those two have been pussyfooting around long enough. Marcia said that was why they were going to the spa—to get away from the menfolk and plan a wedd— You wanted it today? Is she pregnant? Well, I'll be honest, Stan. She's got a lot of family around here. I'm sure they'd be put out to miss Kate's wedding. Why not make it a month from now? Give me a chance to fit into my suit."

Edward held the phone away from his ear and Stan's tinny voice could be heard screeching through it. He rolled his eyes.

"You seem a little on edge there, Stanley. Is everything okay? Stanley? Stanley?" He hung up and smiled. "I think we were disconnected."

Lexi sat, picked up her low-tops, and slipped them on. "He sounded hysterical. Is he normally like that?"

"No." He tilted his head and drew his brows together in thought. "He sounds like the mayor did last night when he couldn't burn Dick like he was supposed to."

Lexi instinctively tried to twist her ring. When she realized her finger was empty, she placed her hands on the table in front of her. "So, the need to get them married is definitely part of the compulsion."

"I don't get it. Why now and why so fast? Caleb's been here for years. If he always planned to force this wedding through, he could have told Stan to demand it before now." Edward shook his head.

She stood and looked along the hall to the basement door. "How's Dick?"

"He's sleeping and healing. He'll be okay." Edward sat at the table and shuffled paper as she wandered away to locate the others.

Dolores sat at a table in the garden, watching as Scott threw a ball for Marcel. The puppy chased it and when it stopped rolling, he stood and barked at it.

"You're supposed to bring it back." The sorcerer explained Fetch to Marcel as though he were speaking to a human, then gave it another try with—unsurprisingly—the same result.

Lexi took a seat next to the woman. "How are you feeling?"

"I believe the kids would say I'm 'coming down.'"

She face-palmed. "I am so sorry."

"Well, I'm happy you don't actually have monsters living in your dimensional pocket. It needs a damn good cleaning in there, though, and I don't think I'll ever be able to look at chocolate again."

"It won't happen again—" she began.

Dolores leaned forward. "You need to train so you don't have to resort to such things."

Lexi spread her arms. "Well...you know, as soon as I can get to the gym."

"You don't need to wait for that." The woman turned toward the house. "Edward, dear?"

He came out through the patio doors. "Yes, Dolores?"

"Are you busy right now?"

"I've got my beta coming over in an hour. What do you need?"

"Lexi needs a little workout. If you manage to bite her, I'll give you this shiny dollar." She held a dollar coin out and put it on the table in front of her.

"What?" Lexi's jaw dropped.

The shifter grinned and flexed his leg.

"She's kidding." She turned to Dolores. "You're kidding, right?"

"I'll give you a three-minute head-start." Edward started to shift.

Lexi bolted into the woods. Knowing she couldn't outrun him, she tried to think strategically. Her performance was still enhanced a little from the diminishing vampire blood in her system, which was as well because she was now too far away from Scott to draw magic. She found a small grove of trees and ran around it. When she reached her starting place, she bounded as far as she could in another direction. She gauged that the jump took her almost thirty feet before she vaulted into the branches of a tree, hid behind the trunk, and peeked out.

As expected, she didn't have long to wait. A few seconds later, Edward appeared, padding along at a leisurely pace. He followed her scent around the grove and returned to the starting place. After a moment, he made another circuit, this time at a trot.

She watched from the tree with a smile.

When he reached the beginning again, he sat on his haunches and tilted his head but soon set off again at a run. She shuffled to turn and sit with her back against the tree while she held her hand over her mouth to silence her laugh. When she looked again, there was no sign of her pursuer.

Damn. I should have paid attention.

The grove was empty and she waited a few seconds to see if he would repeat his search, but he made no appearance. She climbed silently from the tree and she decided it was time to move on. Uncertain which direction to choose, she stood motionless behind the trunk and tried to make a decision when a long, wet, warm tongue licked the back of her leg from her ankle to the edge of her shorts.

Lexi shrieked. "Dude, that's gross."

Edward shifted. "That was for tricking me. First one back gets that shiny dollar." He began to shift again and she ran.

When she came out of the tree line, Edward was seated with Dolores, spinning the dollar, and looked like he hadn't even broken a sweat. He smirked and she stuck her tongue out at him as she strode past.

She showered, donned her familiar leathers, and joined the others again.

"Betsy called." Scott passed her a glass of juice. "Todd remembers everything."

"Everything? He knows what he tried to do?" She raised her eyebrows.

The shifter followed her into the house and stood for a moment while he tested the temperature of a bowlful of scrambled eggs. "He wants to know what Scott did to his mother." He put the bowl on the floor and scratched Marcel's neck as he descended on it. "Todd's upset because Betsy seems perfectly at ease with William being a vampire." The others joined them in the kitchen.

"What'll he do? Will he tell anyone?" For some reason, everyone absently watched Marcel snarf the food as if it were the most fascinating thing in the world.

Edward straightened. "You can ask him yourself. They're coming over."

Lexi looked at the others, who didn't seem concerned. "Is that safe? They might be followed."

"A few of the pack are waiting on the highway to deter anyone following."

An hour later, Betsy, Todd, and Jess joined them in Edward's kitchen.

"Is William here?" Betsy was fidgeting.

"William's catching up on his sleep. He's more of a night owl." Edward smiled.

"Oh, of course." The woman giggled. "Does he sleep in a coffin?"

The shifter laughed. "This is Will we're talking about. He sleeps in Ralph Lauren sheets and won't let anything with a thread count lower than six hundred touch his skin."

Betsy smiled. "Our William always did like to have the best."

Todd shook his head. "Well, we can't stay. We're on our way to the airport. I'm getting Mother the hell out of here. We're going to Europe."

"Oh, the vampire capital of the world." Dolores smiled.

The man froze.

She laughed. "Kidding."

Betsy joined her laughter and patted Todd's arm while he shook his head.

He held an envelope up. "I wanted to drop this off. Caleb asked me to post it last night. It was still in the outbound mail tray this morning." He put the envelope on the table. "It's my approval for further construction work to go ahead at various properties Caleb's been buying up on Palm Canyon Drive. I've voided it and requested a full investigation into his proposal."

Lexi turned to face his mother. "Can you tell me what you know about Caleb?"

The woman frowned. "He appeared nearly six years ago and came to the house a few times to meet with Harv. He seemed very pleasant. Then, out of nowhere, Harv announced he was taking Caleb on as a partner so he could expand the business. I was shocked. We'd been talking about selling the business. Within a year, Harvey died of what we thought was a heart attack and Caleb bought out Harv's half of the company."

"This sounds familiar. It's almost exactly what happened with Kate's father."

"The bastard." Todd clenched his jaw and fists simultaneously as though they were one muscle. "I still can't believe he killed Dad. What the hell is he? Mom says he's a sorcerer. Things like that don't even exist. And what did he want with our family business?"

"You were never interested in the company, Todd. I'd have sold it anyway."

"How are you taking this shit so well?" He looked exasperated but realized he'd cursed in his mother's presence. "Sorry, Mom."

"When you've lived as long as I have, you're never really surprised by anything. The good *or* the bad." Betsy stood, collected her bag, and took both of Lexi's hands. "Give William my love and tell him to be careful. You too, dear. I'll call William tomorrow. Oh! Tomorrow night."

The visitors left, followed by their wolfen motorcade.

"I've been looking into Caleb Linden too," Dolores announced. "I've only been able to trace that name back about ten years. He didn't exist before then."

Lexi "So who the hell is he?"

"He bought a mining operation in South Africa. There was some kind of investigation because employees stopped going home after a while. Then, he simply abandoned it, sold up, and moved here. There was another purchase of land in England, but there doesn't seem to have been any activity at the site. So, what do we think?" Dolores asked.

The younger woman leaned against the counter and folded her arms. "I think I want to know what's so special about Kate's land."

"And why now?" Edward added. "We can assume the demand for Kate and Tommy to marry immediately has come from Caleb. What's so special about now?"

"Some supernatural group you are," Jess said from the doorway.

They looked up to where she stood at the patio doors.

Edward shrugged. "What are we missing?"

"It's the solstice." She entered and took an apple from a bowl on the countertop. Her movements casual, she pulled a chair out and turned it before she sat on it backward and took a bite from the fruit.

Dolores rolled her eyes. "I feel stupid for missing that."

The shifter's phone rang again, and he moved away to answer it.

"So, we've got a working theory for why now, but we still don't know what's at the heart of this." Lexi frowned in thought.

Scott turned to her. "Do you remember that weird vibe I got at the bar?"

"The one that nearly got you flattened by a truck? Yes, I remember it. And those Norse protection runes hanging from the ceiling."

Jess straightened. "Kira makes those. She and Daisy belong to the local coven."

The young man picked Marcel up and allowed the puppy to lick his nose. He turned to Jess. "Does Daisy sell them in her flower shop?"

"I don't think so. I don't remember them having price tags." The woman bit a piece of apple off and offered it to Marcel, who snapped it out of her fingers and dropped it immediately on the table and shook his head.

Dolores picked up the discarded fruit and placed it on the edge of her plate. "Jess, can you find out why Kate wanted the runes? She might simply have liked the look of them."

"I'll see what I can do." She stood and headed outside with her cell in her hand.

The woman sighed and her brow wrinkled as she thought. "Tell me about the demons."

Scott leaned forward. "Size of a man, black, jello-like skin, except for the pincers and claws on their arms and legs which were gray, huge mouths, and too many teeth."

"Poisonous skin," interrupted Edward with his hand over the mouthpiece of the phone.

"Way too many eyes. Like, all over its freaking head," Lexi added.

"They burst into goop when they die. It's gross." The young man shuddered.

Dolores nodded. "I know what you're describing. Did you notice its weaknesses?"

Lexi folded her arms. "My katana."

The other woman rolled her eyes. "Anything else?"

"Like what?" Now, she leaned forward too.

"These creatures don't have noses. They smell through their

mouths and they don't have ears. They hear through soundwaves bouncing off their eyes. Loud noises can effectively blind them. They are vile lower-level creatures, have a hive mentality, and communicate by clicking their pincers. If they can't communicate, they can freak out but twice, you've met them acting alone, which is unusual."

"Good to know, but I hope to never see one of those things again." Scott shook his head in disgust.

"She what?" Edward pinched the bridge of his nose as he listened. "Okay. It looks like we've got a wedding to attend. Gather here as soon as you can and we'll travel together." He disconnected and turned to face them.

"That was Marcia, Kate's mom. Tommy turned up and spoke to Kate, and she went off on the back of his bike."

"Can we head them off?" Scott made to stand but stopped when Edward shook his head and spoke quickly into his cell phone.

"You think the wedding's going ahead today?" Lexi noted three of the wolf pack from the perimeter were walking out of the tree line.

Jess entered quickly. "It's definitely going ahead today. Kate took her wedding dress."

Edward moved the cell away from his ear. "How do you know?"

"Kira was squeezing into her bridesmaid dress when I called. She wasn't happy."

Edward returned to his call.

Scott looked up from Marcel. "Why?"

"She thought she had longer to lose weight and bought it a size too small." She rolled her eyes.

The shifter returned. "I hope you asked where the ceremony's taking place."

"It's at a private club—the same place the mayor's fundraiser was. I hear you're familiar with it." Jess had walked around the table and now put her hand on Scott's shoulder and leaned down to stroke Marcel, who dozed in his arms.

Lexi felt irked by the move and deliberately looked away. "We're dressing for a wedding, then."

Edward moved coffee mugs into the sink. "I am, you're not."

"Excuse me?" She raised her eyebrows.

"While Caleb's distracted by the wedding, you need to get to the bar and find out what's going on there. Jess, you go with them. Caleb's already got the rest of that block, which includes the storage warehouse at the back. I'd guess whatever's going on started there."

"Good call." She nodded her agreement and could see why this man was the pack leader.

"Dolores, you'll be safe here—" the shifter started.

"I'm coming to the wedding. I'd like to get a look at this Caleb Linden." She stood, headed to the family room, and returned seconds later dressed for a wedding.

Within five minutes, the two friends were in Jess's car and on the way to Palm Springs.

Scott leaned forward between the seats. "Did you learn anything more about the runes?"

Jess flicked her gaze to him in the rearview mirror. "The coven sells them at a farmer's market, along with other Wicca and witchcraft paraphernalia. She gave those particular ones to Daisy when she first moved into the store. Apparently, the flower shop is on a site that was owned or rented by a palm reader in the thirties—Princess Zoraida. She already had a good reputation when she arrived from doing a couple years at the World's Fair in New York, but when she moved into the store, her 'connection to the other side' became much stronger." She took her hands off the wheel to make air quotes, and he wriggled uncomfortably in the back.

"Scott, can you text Dick to see if he remembers this Princess Palm-Reader?"

"Zoraida," the other woman corrected.

"Yes, that. He'll get it when he wakes up. It shouldn't be long," she confirmed with a nod.

"I'll park near the entrance to the storage place." Jess glanced at Lexi, who nodded again.

They stood in front of the gate and studied the *Closed for remodel* sign.

"I thought these places were supposed to be accessible twenty-four seven?" Lexi raised her leg to kick the gate.

"Wait." Scott muttered a few words, and the barrier glowed. "Don't touch it. There's a protection spell on it. The rest of the fence looks okay." He walked along it and waggled a finger between the metal bars. The posts bent as though he'd hit them with a truck.

Jess clapped him on the shoulder and whistled. "Magneto!"

They jogged across the parking lot to the building's entrance.

With one last furtive look around them, they stepped inside. No one sat at the reception desk. Jess headed toward a set of double doors in a hallway behind the desk that led farther into the building. She pulled on the handles but they were locked and she scowled at the security pad beside the door. Lexi, who had come up beside her, glanced around and noticed there were several such doors.

The shifter turned to Scott. "Can you do your thing?" She wiggled her fingers.

"We need to be careful about using magic in here. Caleb's probably left a few surprises for intruders. Magic could set them off."

"We could take a door each and kick it in," Jess suggested.

Lexi shook her head. "We're not splitting up, not until we know what's going on in here." She looked at a map on the wall beside the door that showed the layout of the facility. Removing a shuriken from her pocket, she popped it onto the front of her leather vest. It stayed there, thanks to the magnet in the lining of the vest

A door down the hall opened.

They froze.

A man walked toward them but he didn't seem particularly concerned about them. He wore a dirty shirt that had at some point been white, a lanyard, and a *My Name's Clyde, I'm happy to serve you* badge from a local pizzeria.

As he approached, Scott stepped into his path and he stopped.

"Hi, we're looking for a staff member. Can you—"

The newcomer walked around him without acknowledging him or even focusing on him, turned to the double doors, swiped the card, and walked through. Jess slipped her foot into the crack before it could close.

They followed My-Name's-Clyde-I'm-happy-to-serve-you down the hallway and past roller shutters on either side to another set of double doors. When he opened them, Lexi drew the shuriken, used it to slice through the sleepwalking man's lanyard, and caught the pass with her other hand as it fell. He turned unexpectedly, and the shuriken bit into his neck.

"Oops!" She stepped back to give herself clear fighting space, but he made no sound. He trailed blood as he continued to walk down the hallway. She popped the shuriken onto her vest and turned to the others to show them she had the lanyard. They stared beyond her with shock on their faces. When she spun again, her jaw dropped.

"What the fuck?" she whispered and drew her katana.

The hallway ended abruptly ahead of them at what, according to the map, would have been a junction with hallways leading forward, left, and right, each lined with storage units.

The roller-shuttered doors of the units were still present on one side of the hallway, but everything ahead of them was gone. The units and the rest of the facility had been replaced by a huge pit about two hundred feet across and God only knew how deep. It curved in sections toward the southeast and a mechanical grumbling came from its depths.

Scott appeared at her shoulder. "That's moving toward where the flower shop would be, isn't it?"

Lexi nodded. She looked to her left and where Clyde, with blood dribbling freely down his dirty shirt, descended a ladder at the end of the hallway and vanished from sight.

Her eyes narrowed in focus, she peered across the chasm and located many such ladders between levels descending into the pit. She counted them. "This is insane. I see at least ten stories." As she stared in disbelief, the workers at the bottom smoothed the dirt into curved sections like spirals.

People traveled up and down ladders as though asleep. They wore work clothes, uniforms, and pajamas, and a woman in a wedding dress stumbled along in one high-heeled shoe as she dragged a length of wood.

"There! It's Daisy." Jess pointed across the chasm. Lexi tried to identify her but there were too many people. Having never seen her, she couldn't guess which one was the flower-seller.

"You see those curves? It's kind of a shell pattern. What is it?" she tilted her head in various different angles as she tried to make it out.

Scott peered at it, his expression focused. "It's a nautilus shell. We need to get out of here."

"Just a second." She stepped to the top of the ladder. Clyde, who was on the next level down, walked toward the top of the next ladder. The sudden movement of dark shapes against the dirt walls alerted her to the presence of something she really didn't want to see again, and she stepped back.

Several demons with their many eyes and arms scuttled along the wall toward the man and descended upon him.

It must have been the smell of blood. Sorry, Clyde.

She retreated out of the sight of the slaughter. "You're right. We need to go."

They turned quickly but found their retreat blocked by three demons that had crept up behind them. The closest was a few feet away from Jess. Scott jerked his arm toward it with a word. The beast glowed for a moment, then scuttled sideways onto a unit door between them and the exit and moved toward them. It used its legs and two arms to hold it securely in place and held four more arms and their talons poised to strike.

Scott shook. "It's shielded against magic."

"I bet the door isn't." Lexi drew her finger down the unhealing scar and the door burst and catapulted the creature out and over the pit, and it plummeted.

The other demons crept closer but seemed more hesitant now.

A low growl issued from Jess, who had shifted.

"Don't bite them, they're poisonous," she warned the woman.

The shifter moved forward and back several times, and Lexi realized she was distracting them.

Scott extended his open hand to her. She passed him the katana and he vanished.

When he reappeared behind the second of the remaining demons, he positioned himself to strike but saw too late that its black eyes also continued to the back of its head. The creature's six arms—which had been poised to strike forward—flicked toward him.

At the same moment, he disappeared again and appeared between the two demons with his back to one of them.

He delivered a mighty slash immediately to behead the creature and reappeared beside Lexi seconds before its body burst into slime.

The remaining demon had flipped its talons toward where he had stood a moment before.

Before it could right itself, she threw a shuriken into one of its eyes, and the creature uttered a high-pitched squeal.

She realized there was no hope of blinding it, though. "This thing must have fifty eyes. Screw this."

Jess darted forward, and she used the distraction provided by the shifter to plunge her *wakizashi* into its brain, then danced away to avoid its flailing talons. It fell and curled. She stepped forward to retrieve the blade and shuriken, but Scott held her back. A second later, it burst. She snatched her blade by the handle as it began to fall into the ooze. After a horrified moment in which she stared at the shuriken covered by the goop, she sighed and put her hands into the mess to retrieve it.

They stood in silence to regroup and something scuttled closer. The demon's squeal had drawn attention.

"Move." Lexi pushed Scott and Jess toward the entrance and ran behind them, looking over her shoulder every two seconds the whole way.

The sorcerer smacked the green buttons to release the doors but the scuttling sounds of the demons in pursuit grew louder.

CHAPTER EIGHTEEN

As Edward and Dolores approached the club, they were almost run off the driveway by a bus full of wedding guests coming in the opposite direction.

She clutched the door when he swerved to avoid them. "I hope we haven't missed the wedding."

They turned onto a side road leading to the parking lot and delivery entrance at the back of the building.

The woman withdrew a gift-wrapped box from her purse.

His eyes bulged. "A wedding gift? You like to be prepared."

"I was a Girl Scout." She rearranged the glittery bow.

Edward's brow creased. "In Fae?"

"In Wisconsin." Dolores released her seatbelt as the car drew to a halt.

They climbed out of the car and started to walk toward the entrance. He looked across to the playground, shouted, "Oh, my God!" and bolted.

When she caught up, he was crouched over two young children. They had been playing with nerf guns and the ground was littered with foam projectiles.

"Are they..." She didn't dare say it.

"No, they're only asleep but I can't wake them." He felt hurriedly for a pulse.

Dolores put her hand on his shoulder. "I guess he's keeping them out of the way. Leave them. They're probably safer asleep."

Edward stood and strode away from the children.

They passed through the kitchen, and no one batted an eyelid at their presence.

"The security in this place is shocking," she observed. "I mean, I'm not complaining or anything."

He approached a cook. "Excuse me, we seem to be—"

The man looked straight through him as he stirred a bowl.

She peered into the bowl. It was empty. "Caleb has enthralled them all."

The shifter looked more closely at the staff. "You're right." He studied a young man with a cheese grater. The cheese was long gone and he now grated his hand and seemed to have done so for some time. Edward winced and looked away.

"That's horrific." Dolores spun away.

He shook his head. "Do you have any fae magic that can make him stop?"

"Yes, I do." She looked around, found a rolling pin, and cracked the man on the back of the head. He fell into an ungainly heap.

Edward crouched to check the man's vitals. "If you ever feel inclined to work fae magic on me, don't bother."

"You wanted him to stop and he stopped." Dolores passed him a tea towel.

He bound the mangled hand, his expression both angry and a little confused. "Why would Caleb do this?"

"I don't think he'd do it intentionally. There's no point. I think he's merely stretched too thin. He's trying to control too much. It's easier for him if he simply puts them into a loop."

The shifter looked around the kitchen. "Well, I'm relieved to find he has limits."

They stood next to a cart with a wedding cake on it. Written in icing was *Chester and Jeanette.*

"I don't understand it. All this over a strip of land. He's hijacked someone else's wedding to force Kate and Tommy to marry so he can gain access to the bar? Why? Why didn't he simply walk in there and brainwash her months ago? We're missing something."

Dolores found a white apron and tied it around her waist, then gave the gift to him. "I need to get to work. You find Kate and see if we can get her out of here." She picked up a tray of champagne glasses and headed through a swinging door to the party.

Edward gave her thirty seconds before he followed her through the door. He walked along a hallway that opened into a large ballroom. A man stood on the stage in the corner of the room and held a microphone, and although his lips were moving, no sound came from his mouth. He'd probably been singing for hours. The shifter continued to the next room, which had been set up for the ceremony. People were seated in the chairs and simply stared ahead. He worked his way around to the foyer and headed up the stairs, then crept along the hallway and listened at doors as he passed. About halfway along the hall, he heard crying from a room near the end. He knocked quietly and walked in.

Kate was seated in her wedding dress with mascara running down her face.

"Kate?" He didn't know if she might be in the hypnotic cycle too.

"Edward!" She stared at him. "Are you...normal?"

"Not if you ask my ex-wife."

She bounded up and wrapped her arms around him. "I'm sorry. I know I shouldn't have left. Tommy told me Caleb would massacre my family if I didn't come and get married. I didn't know what else to do. But I got here and I don't know these people. There's something wrong with them. I think this has something to do with the bar, because last night—"

"Okay, calm down. I'm here to get you out. Less talking, more moving." He ushered her toward the door.

Edward opened the bedroom door a crack and peeked out.

He whispered, "Surely there are back stairs in a place this size. They must be at the other end of the hall. We need to move quickly."

They hurried down the hallway and reached an open landing leading to the stairs to the foyer. Edward saw the fire exit sign at the other end.

"We'll have to move quickly to that exit."

He took her hand, looked her in the eye, and nodded once. She nodded in response.

They stepped out and prepared to move when the band struck up. Both of them startled, paused, and gazed down the steps. The guests stood at the bottom and stared at them with huge, empty smiles and weariness behind their eyes. The Palm Springs pack were gathered—about thirty men and women and all unsmiling. He looked at the fire exit and considered their chances of sprinting to it when he felt a hand on his shoulder and turned.

"Stanley, good to see you." Edward noted that the man appeared to have stepped out of a room behind them. "I was worried I'd missed the main event. I've come to give the bride away on behalf of her mother." He offered his hand to Stan, who merely stared at it.

"That's awfully kind of you, Edward."

He jumped at the new voice. Caleb stood on the other side of Kate, sweating profusely. There was no room he could have hidden in. He had appeared as though from thin air.

The mental weight of the man immediately seemed to thrust down on him. He was confident that he wouldn't be able to pick any thoughts from his head, but he knew that was the least of his worries.

"Now that you're here, let's get started." The man's smile was cold.

They descended the stairs. Kate held onto him tightly and he felt her shaking.

The moment they reached the bottom of the staircase, several of Stan's pack launched at Edward. He managed a couple of good swings before they surrounded him. It took several men to hold his arms back and force him to his knees.

"Now, let's see what you're hiding." Caleb placed his hand on the shifter's head.

As the man strained, Edward saw Dolores in his peripheral vision. He dared not turn toward her.

Caleb removed his hand, having been unable to access the shifter's thoughts. "Unfortunate. No matter. I can still manipulate you and through you, your pack as well as Kate. As soon as Kate is under my control, I can get what I want from her."

"Not likely," the woman retorted before Stanley smacked her across the mouth.

Edward growled. Caleb looked at Kate and smiled, and the shifter took the chance to glance at Dolores. He could see she wanted to help him but knew that would destroy any chance of stopping their quarry in the long run.

"This might hurt a little." His captor placed his hand on his head again.

The shifter looked directly at him. "Don't mind me. You do what you've got to do." He wasn't speaking to him, though. Dolores stepped into the crowd.

Edward closed his eyes and released Jess and Kate from the pack, which was his right as alpha.

It's up to you now, Jess.

CHAPTER NINETEEN

The three teammates didn't stop running. Jess didn't shift into human form until they were on the other side of the fence at the car. They scrambled into the little vehicle.

"Fucking go in!" she shouted at her key as she tried to jam it into the ignition with a shaking hand.

Lexi leaned closer, placed a hand on top of the woman's, and made eye contact. The shifter's eyes were golden, an indication that she might turn again. "Breathe."

Jess leaned back, put her hands in her lap, and breathed slowly in and out. After a few seconds, she opened her brown eyes and nodded at her, then slid the key in and started the engine.

They rounded the corner and Scott shouted from the back of the car, "Wait. The door of the flower shop is ajar."

"Are you sure?" The shifter tried to glance at it as they passed.

"He's right." Lexi pulled a shuriken out and placed it on her vest. "Scott, can you shield us?"

"Done." He nodded once.

She looked up and down the road but didn't see anyone watching. Of course, they were dealing with a sorcerer so that didn't mean they weren't being watched by a dozen of Stanley's brainwashed wolves.

"Oh!" Jess stopped outside the store with her hand on her chest. Lexi glanced at her.

Scott turned to face her. "That's being caused by whatever's going on underground. It got me the first time. Try to ignore it."

"I'm not usually sensitive to this kind of thing. It's weird, I feel… kind of lonely." Tears welled in her eyes and she blinked them away and looked embarrassed.

Lexi glanced at her. "Magic hits people in different ways, especially bad magic."

They crept into the store and found a young woman removing flowers from buckets. She stopped what she was doing and turned slowly. Her eyes and nose were red, and she appeared to have been crying. Looking around, she narrowed her swollen eyes and frowned.

She removed a short, nasty-looking knife from her pocket. "You seem to be trying quite hard to remain unseen. Should I start waving this around indiscriminately?"

"Would you unshield me, please, Scott?" Jess asked.

He did as he was asked.

"Hi, Kira." The shifter gave her a little finger wave.

"Holy shit, Jess!" The tension dropped from the other woman's shoulders.

"Sorry. We didn't know who was in here. Are you okay?"

"My allergies are playing merry hell in here. Speaking of 'we,' I know you didn't do that yourself. Perhaps I could meet your friend?"

Scott took the rest of the shield down.

"This is Scott and Lexi. Kate called them to help with the problems she's been having."

He peered at Kira in her bridesmaid's dress and glanced into the box she was filling with flowers. "I guess you're picking a bridal bouquet."

She nodded, then looked at Jess. "What's going on? I got a five-second call from Kate, then you called about my protection runes. It's all a little sudden." She pulled out the bodice of her dress and took a deep breath, then sneezed.

Lexi glanced at one of the runes, which seemed to move slightly as though there was a breeze. There was none, however, and she returned her gaze to the young woman.

Kira focused on it too. "Something bad's going on here. Those have been vibrating since I walked in."

"Yes, you might want to get out of here. A sorcerer is up to something awful underground. Do you know Caleb Linden?"

The girl shuddered. "I've met him. I knew he was something, but I get that vibe quite often from people who don't know they have latent abilities. I tend to ignore it. It's none of my business." She continued to pull flowers from buckets.

Scott rubbed the back of his neck. "The vibes here are incredibly strong."

"I know! I almost didn't come in. There's always been something here. Previously, it was residual and connected to Zoraida, but it's stronger today than I've ever felt it. There's supposed to be work going on at the storage place in back of here, but it feels as though it's right beneath my feet. I thought they might have disturbed something." Kira turned to her task.

Lexi walked around to face her. "Caleb has a group of brainwashed people there, and they're digging a giant pit. Daisy's there and some nasty lower-level demons. The pit's almost the size of the block."

The woman dropped the flowers in her hand. "Demons? What's he doing?"

Scott shrugged when his teammate looked at him. "He's opening a portal to hell."

Jess rubbed her forehead. "Hell isn't below us. That's bullshit. I've seen subways deeper than that."

He turned to her to explain. "There are different dimensions and certainly more than one hell dimension. They move in their own orbits and occasionally move through the earth, but it's very rare that one coincides with when the veil between the dimensions is thin."

"Like now, on the solstice." Kira nodded as the significance came to her.

"So Caleb has decided this is the best time and place for a breach." Lexi glanced at the runes again.

Scott turned to Kira. "Do you have much more to do? You shouldn't hang around. They're making a nautilus portal. That means something's coming through—something very bad.

The woman nodded. "Okay, I need a length of white ribbon, then I'm done. I'll have to contact the coven."

She yanked flowers out of various buckets while he walked to a reel of ribbon on the wall and tugged it. The ribbon cascaded from the reel, and he gathered it quickly. He looked on the surface of the desk, tried a drawer and found it locked, then stretched to the shuriken on Lexi's vest. He picked it off and sliced cleanly through the ribbon. It left a fine line of red blood on the fabric. "Oops." He turned it to a different blade and cut again.

Noticing Lexi's raised eyebrow, he said, "Thanks." He moved to replace the shuriken onto the vest, then seemed to think better of it and handed it to her.

"You're welcome." She rolled her eyes, took it, and returned it to its position.

With another smirk at her friend, she turned to thank Kira and leave when a loud crack drew everyone's attention.

One of the willow-twig runes had split down the middle. They remained silent and watched as half of it fell to the floor.

"I'm getting out of here." Kira picked her box of flowers up and headed to the door with Scott and Jess directly behind.

Lexi looked from the half-rune swinging in the air to the other one, which was also swaying. She followed the others through the door.

Kira looked into the box of flowers. "I hope these are okay. I can tell you the magical and healing properties of any herb but I don't know a thing about flowers. I have no interest, not with my allergies."

Jess stared at the store. "What happened to the rune?"

"A portal to hell would require very strong magic. It's encroaching on the store. I think it would be best if I forget the wedding and call the head of my coven." The woman shook her head and turned to the others.

She put the box on the ground, then found a tissue and blew her nose before she retrieved her cell phone.

Lexi touched Scott's arm. "Can you do anything to bolster the protection in the remaining rune?"

He shook his head. "I don't think that's a good idea. It would interfere with what's already active. The rune could end up useless."

"Have a look through the window at the bar. How do they look?"

In response, he jogged to the front of the bar and looked through the window. He gave a thumbs-up and ran back. "They're fine. Still hanging and not moving."

She looked at the flower shop again. "So, it looks like the portal will be directly under the flower shop. This might explain why it's all so last-minute with Kate's property. It's merely Caleb's bad luck. He dug up the rest of the block and the thinnest point is under the one piece of land he doesn't own."

Jess took her keys out. "You think ownership's a factor?"

"It's all guesswork, but yes." She nodded. "Did Edward get back to you yet?"

"Not yet." The shifter shook her head.

"Can you contact the pack and let them know what's happening?"

The beta gave a curt nod and stepped away.

"Shit!" Lexi rubbed her face.

"What?" Scott looked worried. He could probably sense her conflict.

"This is huge. Are we even equipped to deal with this? We might need to call Kindred."

His jaw dropped.

"We've got a low-level demonic invasion going on down there. Something must have already aligned enough to let them through, and it looks like these are nothing compared to what's coming."

Jess began to cross to the other side of the street.

Kira put her cell away and turned to her. "The coven is coming here. We'll shore up the defenses in the store. They'll start getting here within ten minutes. The farthest is half an hour away. I assume you'll go to the wedding." She picked the box of flowers up. "Here's your invitation."

Scott opened the trunk and moved aside for her to put the box into it.

"Thanks." The woman smiled at him but looked away when his teammate closed the trunk much louder than necessary.

The two women glared at each other.

Lexi rolled her eyes. "Portal to hell?" she reminded them and headed to the front of Jess's car.

Scott followed her, completely oblivious to the interaction.

Jess joined them again. "I can't reach Edward or anyone through the pack link."

He thought for a moment. "Caleb might be blocking your communication with magic."

Kira was standing across the street from the flower shop when Ulla, a coven member, arrived. She parked and joined her on the pavement.

"I'm here. I had to lie to get out of work. If this is some kind of joke, I'll sue you for an hour's pay."

"Let's cross. I didn't want to go back alone." She led the newcomer across the street but Ulla froze halfway, obviously feeling it.

The woman took a step backward. "What *is* that?"

"It's why we're here. Come on, we need to get started." She tried to encourage her to move forward but she wouldn't budge.

Ulla shook her head. "I'm not going there, just the two of us. What the hell is it?"

"We need to strengthen the protections to counteract some very dark magic."

The woman's eyebrows raised in alarm. "No shit, there's dark magic."

Kira nodded. "Okay, let's wait for the others."

"Are you two trying to get yourselves killed? Get out of the street," called a voice from the sidewalk.

They looked up as Demeter, the leader of their coven, locked her car door and began to walk toward them. She stopped abruptly. "Oh!"

Standing in the middle of the street, she yanked her cell phone out and typed. Kira felt her phone vibrate and heard Ulla's do the same.

"Come on, girls, we've got work to do." Demeter ushered them to the sidewalk outside the flower shop.

Kira retrieved her cell to find a WhatsApp from their leader to the coven. *THIS IS NOT A DRILL.*

Ulla scratched her arms as though the creepy feeling could be removed.

The three of them were silent for a few moments, then Demeter took their hands and began to sing.

"The earth, the air, the fire, the water,

Return, return, return, return,

The earth, the air, the fire, the water,

Return, return, return, return."

Over and over, they sang the chant. Three voices, then four, then seven, then ten crowded into the little store and everyone held hands in a circle.

The door opened and another witch entered. Gaia had a five-pound bag of salt and began to pour a circle around them on the floor.

Kira stared at her and decided the woman had watched way too much *Supernatural.*

She noticed a tub containing willow branches intended for floral displays. Quickly, she grasped it and a reel of twine and moved to the center of the circle. As the women continued to chant, she fashioned a new protection rune.

CHAPTER TWENTY

Dolores moved out of sight but continued to watch.

"Edward, call your pack in. I want them here." Caleb sounded tired and she wondered what was keeping him going.

"I've called them." The shifter sounded like he was in a dream state.

"Finally! Edward, tell Kate to sign her land over to me."

Obediently, he turned to the woman. "Kate, sign your land over to Caleb."

"Screw you!" she shouted.

The sorcerer was furious. "Hit her."

She tried to duck out of the way of Stan's hand but the slap came from Edward.

"That should have worked." Caleb's eyes were wild. He stepped forward, grasped her head, and muttered a few words. His face was strained as if he tried to break through a psychic wall.

"Those witches! I'll kill the lot of them." He paused as though listening to something. "Yes, if you like. Entrails, the works." He stepped back and took a breath to compose himself.

Dolores wondered who he had been talking to.

"Edward, since I can't read your memories, we'll have to go the long way around. Where's William?"

The shifter responded with no emotion in his voice. "He's at my house."

Caleb's eyes lit up. "Splendid! Are any of your pack members with him?"

"Yes."

"Tell them to kill him."

Edward paused for a moment, then nodded. The command had been sent.

"Okay, boys and girls. On with this charade, then. Edward, you wanted to walk the bride down the aisle. Go ahead."

He took Kate's arm and pulled her roughly into the room set up for the wedding. The minister stood at the end of the aisle with Tommy. The shifter dragged her down the aisle and stood behind her.

The minister began, "Dearly Beloved—"

"I don't think so. Skip to the necessary parts," Caleb snapped.

Dolores ducked out and walked into the foyer. She stood for a moment before she felt eyes on her and knew instantly who it was. She strode to the nearest table, picked up champagne glasses, and placed them on her tray.

"I haven't seen you before," the sorcerer said to her back and his voice dripped with suspicion. She ignored him and moved to another table and more glasses.

Suddenly the pull on her mind was strong and the glasses fell, rolled from the tray, and shattered on the floor. He turned her without laying a finger on her.

"I was talking to *you*. What's your name?"

The compulsion to tell the truth was so strong, there was nothing else she could do. "My name is Dolores, sir. May I get you a drink?" She managed to recover a little and smiled in the same vacuous way the hypnotized people had.

"What are you doing here?"

"I'm doing my job, sir. May I get you a drink?"

"Why haven't I seen you before?"

"I'm from the agency, sir. May I get you a drink?

He turned to the other room. "Are they married yet?"

Dolores took the opportunity to sidle away and pick glasses up until she was sure he was no longer watching her. She sighed. All her answers had been truthful. He'd merely asked the wrong questions. She headed down the hallway and darted into the billiard room, then closed the door behind her and tried not to hyperventilate. When she turned her back to the door, her gaze was met by a scene of pure horror.

Todd was seated in an armchair in the corner of the room, covered with blood. He inflicted tiny cuts all over his body with a razor. Betsy stood in front of the chair between her son and one of the demon creatures and brandished a billiard cue menacingly. To her credit, a pile of goop with another cue laid in the middle of the table. She'd already eliminated one of the beasts.

This woman is in her eighties.

The fae was impressed but noted that the old woman had cuts on her face and arms and looked like she was on her last legs.

"That's enough of that." She approached the demon from behind. With its many eyes, it saw her coming and flipped one of its arms toward her. She put her hand up. The moment its claw touched her palm, the creature shrank to the size of a bug and she stamped on it and ground the goop into the carpet.

Betsy darted instantly to Todd and wrestled the razor from his hand.

Dolores rushed to help her. "What happened? I thought you had left."

"Edward's friends escorted us all the way to Ontario airport. We parked the car, and I don't remember anything after that." The woman broke down. "They said Caleb wouldn't be able to do this again."

"Scott protected him from sorcery but I don't think that's all Caleb is using." She thought for a moment. "I need to get the two of you out of here." She gestured with her arm and a door appeared in the wall.

Betsy hesitated. "Those monsters came out of a door like this."

"This is a fae door. It will take us to safety."

They each took one of Todd's arms and walked him slowly toward the portal.

The handle on the door to the hallway turned.

CHAPTER TWENTY-ONE

Dick's eyes sprang open. He wasn't usually a late sleeper, but he was still recovering from the silver attack.

He listened for the sound again—a wolf padded along the base-ment hallway and he knew immediately it wasn't Edward. He knew his gait as man and wolf. The door opened and the wolf entered, its hackles raised. Although he recognized it, he could see this was no friend.

Instantly, he knew something had gone horribly wrong.

The wolf didn't rely on sight and instead, sniffed the air. Instinc-tively knowing where the threat would come from, it looked up a fraction of a second too late. Dick descended from the corner of the room above the door and bit into its neck. The wolf threw him off and he pounded into the bedside table. The creature tore at him. A fraction of an inch from his throat, it yelped and spun to where Marcel had sunk his teeth into its tail.

The second's distraction was all the vampire needed. Before his assailant could attack the puppy, he yanked its head back and sank his teeth into its throat. The wolf whined and sagged.

Dick pulled his clothes on at lightning speed and reached for his cell when he heard several growls. He managed to read one word on the screen before Marcel rocketed under the bed. When he turned, three more wolves snarled in the doorway.

CHAPTER TWENTY-TWO

Scott touched Lexi's shoulder from the back seat in the car. "What are you thinking?"

She put her hand over his and drew energy. They'd only done it a few minutes previously so she didn't need to do it again, but she wanted Jess to witness the intimacy.

What am I doing?

Hastily, she removed her hand. "Honestly? I'm wondering what the collective noun is for demons because I've got one. *Fuck No!* A 'fuckno' of demons."

The shifter slid her gaze to her. "Works for me."

Scott laughed. "I think 'legion' is the name for a group of demons."

"Not anymore. It's a fuckno. What is it?"

"A fuckno." Scott saluted. "I meant, though, what do you think we should do now?"

"Oh, that. Find Caleb, decapitate him, go back and destroy the fuckno of demons, then try that Korean place we just drove past."

Jess's gaze slid back to the road. "Their barbecue is amazing, but we've got a better place in San Bernardino. If we're still alive by the end of the day, I'll treat you both." After a moment, she added, "Would you really do that? Chop the guy's head off in front of a roomful of ordinaries?"

"Yes. They can be made to forget." Lexi shrugged and focused on the road ahead.

Anyone can be made to forget.

They headed up the drive to the clubhouse.

She turned to the back seat of the car. "We're not exactly dressed for a wedding."

"Are you sure?" Scott smiled.

A glance at Jess revealed that she wore her Alexander McQueen dress. When she opened her mouth to complain, she realized she wore one too. Startled, she gaped as both turned dark burgundy, the same color as Kira's bridesmaid's dress.

Lexi turned to Scott, who was now in a dark gray suit with a burgundy tie.

"What the…" The shifter darted confused glances at her attire.

"They're waiting." Lexi indicated the valets, and the car inched forward.

One of the men approached the window. "Invitation?"

"We're bridesmaids. Do we need one?" She indicated her dress.

"I've got it." Scott leaned forward and muttered a word as he held out a supermarket receipt for tampons he'd found in the back of the car.

Jess's eyes bulged and her cheeks flushed. She beamed a rictus grin at the valet as he nodded and opened the door.

Lexi approached the man. "Isn't it quite late for a wedding? It's nearly seven."

He smiled in an unfocused way and climbed into the car.

The shifter frowned. "I'm not thrilled about a sleepwalker driving my car."

Lexi shrugged as he moved the car around to the back of the building, apparently without problems. "Is Edward here?"

"No, and neither is the rest of the pack. If they were, I'd sense it." Jess seemed troubled.

They entered the foyer, and the shifter looked around. "Oh! The pack *is* here." They approached a group of people who stood with glasses of champagne in their hands.

"Rose. Where's Edward?"

"The bride looks beautiful," Rose said with a vacuous smile.

Jess's eyes narrowed. "Caleb must have brainwashed Edward."

"How do you know he's not..." Lexi didn't finish the sentence.

"Because I'd be the alpha."

Lexi took a glass from the waiter and sniffed it. "But you're still you." She passed the glass to Scott.

He muttered a word over it and nothing happened, so he knocked the drink back. "I wonder whose wedding this was supposed to be?" He snagged the invitation from a guest's hand. "Chester and Jeanette were supposed to be getting married at 3pm this afternoon. I'm guessing most of these guests were here to attend that wedding."

"I think we know where Chester and Jeanette are." Lexi thought of the bride working in the pit.

The three of them went into a side room and closed the door.

"We need to find Edward and Dolores," Scott said. "Caleb must have gotten to Edward when I had you shielded at the flower shop, although I'd have expected you to fall under his control as soon as you were unshielded."

Jess sighed. "I know what it is—why I couldn't sense the pack. What I felt back at the flower shop. Edward kicked me out of the pack."

Lexi nodded. "Of course. It was the only way he could stop you from being taken over by the man."

The door to the study opened and Caleb walked in, followed by Edward and a couple of his pack.

"Ahh! Miss Braxton—or do you prefer 'Bianca' these days? I'm afraid you've missed a splendid wedding."

Lexi moved her hand to her unhealing scar.

"Edward, would you mind placing your knife at your throat? If I am harmed, please cut your own throat."

The shifter did as he was told, and she lowered her hand slowly.

The man walked closer to her and extended his hand—not touching, but close. Her gaze flicked to Edward and she ground her teeth. "I don't sense an affinity for any of the lower supernaturals. All I sense is your mage. My, you did get the short end of the stick, didn't you?" He looked at Scott. "My talented young nemesis. You've caused some inconvenience to me today." He touched the young man in the center of the forehead and he fell heavily to the floor. "I bet you don't know that one." Caleb chuckled as he made his way to a desk and picked some papers up.

"Come along, new Mrs. Ellis. Be a dear and sign your name on these papers."

Lexi watched as Kate entered the room. She leaned over the desk and signed where she was told to.

"There we are. Now, you've been a lot of trouble, haven't you, Mrs. Ellis? I think you should come with me. I have a friend who has…let's say, taken a shine to you and would very much like to meet you in the flesh."

Lexi shook with fury and wanted nothing more than to separate him from his head, but when she glanced at Edward, the blade bit into his skin.

Caleb laughed at her predicament. "Gentlemen, take care of our unwanted guests, please."

He laughed again, gestured with his arm, and created a whorl of black smoke—a portal. He took Kate by the arm, stepped through, and vanished.

Lexi stood protectively over Scott and prepared to face Edward and his two pack members. She tried to estimate their chances when the door opened and another twenty shifters streamed in.

Hastily, she glanced at Scott and wondered if she could simply catch hold of him and get enough magic to send them all to sleep at once. Her thought was interrupted by Jess.

"I challenge you as pack leader and alpha of the San Bernardino pack."

Edward blinked.

The conflict was very evident in his eyes. He'd been told to kill them but this was a challenge for alpha. It was in his DNA to not deny this.

The pack retreated and left the two challengers facing each other. She knew she could go for her katana now, but if Jess could win this fight, she might not have to kill Edward—and she really, *really* didn't want to kill him.

The pack began to file out of the study, and she was dragged along with them. The guests were all still in the ceremony room but most of them had collapsed.

Lexi caught up with Jess. "Can you win this? And can you do it without killing him?"

Edward glanced at the two of them. His eyes were like granite.

"I don't know." The woman looked at her and she saw the emotions that had been missing from Edward's eyes—regret, fear, and determination. Lexi dropped back as the current alpha and the contender led the group into the ballroom. Suddenly, she wasn't sure who would be alive at the end of this. She smoothed her hand over her dimensional pocket.

The pack surrounded the alpha and the beta, and they both shifted.

Edward snarled and snapped at the air immediately. He was a huge wolf, and Lexi knew he was fast and strong. Jess, small and wiry though her wolf-form was, had fought her way to beta, however. She imagined that had required prowess and guile on her part. The opponents stalked each other in circles, bared their teeth, and snarled continually.

Jess danced in and away, always angling toward Edward's injured leg, but he wouldn't let her near it. His hackles were raised and it was clear that even though he was under the sorcerer's influence, he wouldn't hold back. He had been given the order to kill them. Jess might actually be forced to kill him to stop him. Equally, if he came out of this mind-control to find he'd killed Jess, he would be heartbroken.

This might end badly.

The shifters surrounding the challengers were eerily quiet.

Jess was on her third taunt when Edward snapped. He gave a

guttural snarl and surged into an attack, only to find her gone. Lexi had never seen a creature other than a vampire move that fast. The beta had flipped onto the larger wolf's back and she bit once into his shoulder.

He squealed and twisted toward her throat, but she evaded the attempt, leapt clear of him, and darted away. Once again, they circled each other. Edward shook out the pain from the bite and blood flew from his fur. Jess's ears drooped and she looked momentarily sad. He snarled wildly at her, and her ears pricked up again.

The beta attempted another feint, but he had expected it. He ran her down and bit savagely into her rump and she squealed.

Lexi turned cold, slid her hand into her pocket, and took hold of her katana.

It looked like Jess had made a costly mistake. Edward was on top of her, ready to rip into her again, until she took careful aim at his left back leg—his injured one. She realized that the smaller wolf hadn't made a mistake at all. She'd deliberately given him the opening to allow her to reach his injured knee. Her jaws closed on it, and his howl filled the air. Jess used his distraction and pain to put some distance between the two of them.

Edward tried to drag himself after her, but it was useless. She shifted again and the pack bowed to her as the new alpha. He shifted too, knowing he had lost and that the shifters were no longer his pack. Jess was their alpha, and Caleb did not control them.

Lexi raced to the study to find Scott still unconscious. She stroked her hand down the scar and said, "Awake."

He sat up, confused and alarmed.

"Morning, sleeping beauty."

"What happened?"

"Caleb."

He lay still for a moment to allow it all to come back to him.

"Come on. Edward's injured."

Scott stood and wobbled, so she put his arm around her shoulder and led him to the other room.

Edward was still on the floor when they returned to the ballroom.

Jess was in the hall, leaning against the wall to try to compensate for her injuries. "I never wanted to do that to him."

"Let me see what I can do." The young man put his hand on Jess and healed her.

"You won't be able to heal what I took away from him." The woman looked at the floor.

He walked to Edward. As the shifter opened his eyes, he stopped cautiously. "Do you still want to kill us?"

"No. I'm controlled by Jess now." He didn't sound defeated.

Scott put his hand on the other man and muttered a few words.

Edward stood and flexed his knee. "Holy shit! It's better than it's been for years. I could go another round with Jess."

Lexi looked at him

"Kidding. She's earned her place."

"But I didn't want it. I'm not ready for that kind of responsibility. I'm so sorry." Jess stood in the doorway.

"What do you think my intention was when I released you from the pack? This was the best outcome I could hope for. And I'm not going anywhere. I'll be here to help you…boss." He smirked.

Lexi walked up to the two of them. "We need to get to that pit and stop Caleb."

"I don't think you'll do that." Stan entered with his much larger pack. There were at least thirty of them, and they began to shift.

"We don't have time for this shit." She yanked her katana out.

"You're right," the shifter agreed and strode past her toward Stanley.

"Stanley, I challenge you as alpha and leader of the Palm Springs pack."

His adversary shifted and leapt at him in wolf form in one fluid motion. Edward didn't even bother to shift. He delivered a mighty right hook to the side of his adversary's head and completely changed his trajectory. The wolf landed awkwardly and lay still.

His pack stood and shook their heads as though coming out of a deep sleep. They bent the knee to Edward.

Jess stared at Stanley's unconscious form as he shifted, then glanced at Edward. "So, what happened to 'I'm not going anywhere?'"

He shrugged. "I'll still be on the other end of the phone."

Scott looked around and moved to the door. "Where's Dolores?"

"I haven't seen her since Caleb—" The shifter stopped and realization dawned on his face.

"What?" Lexi felt Scott's heart hammering through their link, or maybe it was hers.

"I set the pack on Dick." Edward turned to his new pack while he retrieved his cell. "We're looking for a short woman with her hair up, dressed as a maid."

They began to flood out of the door, but one man turned. "How short?"

He shrugged. "Anywhere between half an inch and five feet." He turned to Lexi, and they brought each other up to date.

She didn't put her weapon away. "Right. We need to get after Caleb. By the time we get there, he'll have had nearly an hour's head start."

The shifter placed his hand on Scott's shoulder. "Can't you take us through a portal? Like Caleb's?"

The sorcerer shook his head. "His portals go through a low-level hell dimension. It's where those demons come from. I don't know how to make one safely. If I get it wrong, we'll be lost in there."

Edward shook his head. "Whatever's coming through that portal he's creating in the pit could well be through by the time we get there."

"Then it's a good thing you've got a short-cut," said Dolores from the doorway. "Sorry I had to step out. Betsy and Todd didn't get away as we'd hoped. I've left them getting medical attention in Fae."

"Are they okay?" Lexi gripped her blade tightly, expecting awful news.

"I doubt it. I think Betsy will have them all guzzling gin by the time I get back."

"I meant Betsy and Todd."

The woman patted her arm. "They will be. They're being helped."

Lexi turned to Edward and Jess. "Get your people together. We're going after him."

Dolores took Scott's hand. "Show me where we need to go."

Jess held her cell out. "Someone needs to help the witches in the flower shop. Now!"

CHAPTER TWENTY-THREE

Kira placed the new runes around the space while she chanted with the witches. Suddenly, the atmosphere in the room changed. She likened the feeling to a vacation she had taken when she had dived to the ocean floor. One by one, as they felt it, the witches stopped chanting.

Seconds later, the new rune splintered. She considered skipping out of the ritual ring to pick it up.

Demeter caught her hand tightly. "Something's changed. Don't break the circle."

As they waited in trepidation, the flowers in the tubs around them blackened and crumbled. A loud rumble issued and the floor in the back room buckled and began to fall away. The witches stared in horror at the creature that clambered out with its black eyes and many arms. It stood motionless as though assessing them.

Demeter faced it as it moved closer with an unnerving clicking sound. "Don't break the circle." She began to chant again, and the creature lunged forward with one of its sharp-taloned fingers. One of the witches wrenched her hands free and ran. The creature caught Demeter around the throat.

Kira was in shock and couldn't make her body move.

The door's right there. We should run.

The monster took a step closer, then froze and tilted its head downward. Her eyes followed its gaze. One of its feet was planted in the salt. It vibrated and a moment later, it burst and covered Demeter in ooze.

She caught Gaia's arm. "It's the salt."

They looked at the protective ring of salt. It was too close to afford them any protection, though, as the creatures could still reach them with swipes of their talons.

Kira took her cell out and sent a message to Jess.

A clicking sound drew their attention to the rear of the store, where more creatures now climbed out of the hole.

She stooped, snatched a handful of salt, and threw it at the nearest monster. The grains caught it squarely in the face and it exploded.

"Hey, it's better than slugs." She heard herself laugh with a little too much hilarity.

"Is this right? Aren't they the goddess' creatures too?" Freya asked. Everyone suspected she was still a Christian. She'd only joined the coven to embarrass her husband, a pastor who was screwing his secretary.

Demeter faced her. "Oh, fuck off, Carole."

Freya looked at her feet. "I see. Well. I mean, I thought we don't use our mundane names."

"I'm sorry, Freya." Their leader sighed. They were all terrified.

One woman raised a hand. "Couldn't we simply step out and lock the door?"

"Maybe there were only a couple of them," one of the ladies squeaked.

The clicking resumed, and a scramble for the salt on the floor ensued.

Kira put a pile of salt into Freya's hand. "Think of your husband and throw this."

The creatures retreated as the women scooped handfuls of salt from Gaia's bag and the poured circle. They scattered it across the floor to stop the creatures from creeping forward.

One of the witches laughed. "Ha! Now you're stuck."

The creatures stepped onto the wall, then the ceiling.

"Well, shit!" Kira looked hastily around her for a weapon, but all she could see were dead flowers.

The women were being herded against a side wall.

Her cell rang and she risked a glance at it.

Either get out or stand against the wall.

One of the creatures stood between them and the exit, and they were already pressed against the wall. She shrugged.

A hazy, swirling light appeared in the middle of the room and turned into an arched doorway.

"Holy Mary, Mother of God." Freya crossed herself.

Demeter pursed her lips and her gaze slid to the woman. "I knew it."

An object appeared out of the haze, landed, and rolled across the floor.

"Grenade!" Demeter dived on top of as many of her coven as she could.

No explosion followed, but Lexi burst through the fae door with her katana in one hand and a nerf gun in the other.

Scott appeared at her side. He turned to her and smiled. "Alexa, play 'Mr. Brightside' by The Killers.

A voice came from the object on the floor. "Here's 'Mr. Brightside' by The Killers." An incredibly loud noise issued from the speaker, and Demeter covered her ears "What the hell is that?"

They watched as the creatures covered their eyes, shook their heads, and stumbled into each other. One plummeted from the ceiling, landed on its back, and exploded in the salt.

Kira stood again. "I believe that's Mr. Brightside."

Lexi aimed the nerf gun and fired at a demon on the wall. Several salt-covered sponge balls bounced off it, and a moment later, it popped in a spray of goop. Scott began to bring salt rocks into existence and slung them at the enemy. His partner moved to the back room and fired as she moved. After shooting a few more salted sponge bullets, she was out. She dropped the nerf gun and put her katana to use to skewer the creatures that writhed on the floor, incapacitated by the music.

She turned to Scott and grinned. "I like your music."

Dolores came through with bags of salt and passed them to the women. They dove into them without hesitation and hurled the contents everywhere.

When Lexi glanced over her shoulder, a demon dropped from the ceiling between the fae door and the witches. Demeter threw herself in front of the other witches as it lunged. A sharp pincer pierced her in the chest and she slid off it and fell, lifeless. The creature moved in to attack another witch. Opening its huge maw, it revealed row upon row of pointed teeth.

Freya snatched the salt lamp in Daisy's window display, stepped in front of it, and wedged the huge salt rock into the creature's mouth. "Take that, you cheating bastard."

It exploded, and the woman, now covered in goop, shouted, "Yes!"

Lexi refocused. The creatures continued to emerge from the hole. She picked up the Bluetooth speaker, held it out as she fought her way closer to the hole, and thrust her katana into their skulls when they appeared.

As she perched over the aperture, more of the floor fell away. She jumped back, but the chasm now separated her from the others. Pots of flowers slid along the floor as the back of the building lurched. More of the creatures spilled out.

"Lexi," Scott shouted.

She turned as a twenty-pound bag of salt appeared in the air over the breach in the floor. Reflexively and with no thought at all, she met it with her katana and sliced the bag open.

It released its contents and the majority of the salt went into the unnatural entrance. The top three demons burst, followed by a loud rumble.

Demon goop surged out like a geyser.

When it died down, she peered in to see that most of the demons had been destroyed. She put the speaker into her pocket, looked at Scott, shrugged, and jumped in.

"No!" he cried, but it was too late. She slid down the goop-filled tunnel.

It was about twenty feet long. Lexi glided through the foul-smelling gunk and killed the creatures methodically along the route. She emerged covered in slime, but it had been worth it for the fast descent. Scott's state when he climbed out of that tunnel would be a real reason to laugh in all this.

She now stood in what appeared to be a natural hollow in the wall of the pit. Her unhealing scar itched so badly, she wanted to rip her arm off. One wall of the little cave was covered in iridescent, undulating light. The dimensions were aligning, and she stood exactly where the demon would appear.

When she looked across the pit, the first person she saw was Scott. He and the witches had come through the fae door. Lexi looked at herself—she was covered in slime and he was not—and rolled her eyes.

The clicking in the cave was deafening. Demons scuttled frantically in every direction as shifters poured out of the fae door with axes and salt. Both packs fought the creatures with weapons. Some had shifted to distract the demons, but none of them dared bite them.

The brainwashed citizens in the pit attacked the shifters with shovels and picks. Scott had already begun to put them to sleep in an effort to keep them safe and out of the way. Dolores shrank any monster she could get close to and stamped on them.

Lexi didn't have to search to find Caleb. He stood facing her with Kate at his side. With the witches' protection broken, she was merely another victim of hypnosis and stared into space.

The air crackled, and a slow, nasty smile spread across the sorcerer's face.

She looked at the sea of demons between her and her enemy. A reckless voice in her head told her to simply attack and start slashing.

A sudden pain through the empathetic link made her look back quickly. The bride in her dirty wedding dress had struck Scott across the head with a shovel. He sent her to sleep but stumbled, his hand on the back of his head.

Lexi leaped to a ledge running along the side of the pit. She had to jump down a short distance later and plow through a few demons before she could climb again and finally return to her friend. When she reached him, she healed his head, then pulled the speaker out of her pocket. "What happened to the music?"

He held his phone up. "We're too far underground and my sounds are in the cloud."

"Can't you boost it with magic?"

"I don't think so." He tried to take the speaker from her hand.

"It's worth a try." She touched her hand to her scar and the device began to play the next song on his playlist.

The demons began to show signs of confusion again, but both wolf packs turned to Lexi as "Barbie Girl" rang out. She passed the speaker to Scott and disassociated herself from it. He face-palmed.

"Look at that. Even Caleb's horrified. You've embarrassed us in front of the bad guy." She shook her head.

"Well, it's doing the job and I like it." The words were barely out of his mouth when a man who had crept up behind them pushed him into the sea of demons below. While she knew he was most likely hypnotized, she punched him in the face. The speaker was crushed under the panicking demons and she honestly couldn't say she was disappointed. She moved to vault after Scott, but Dolores held her back. The creatures weren't hurting him. They were ferrying him to Caleb.

"Enough!" The sorcerer's voice echoed around the huge chamber and distressed the demons again.

Scott was dropped in front of him, and a monster placed its pincers around his neck.

Everything stopped.

The creatures had the shifters surrounded. Lexi realized that all the humans Scott had put to sleep were back on their feet and now stared disconcertingly at her.

Caleb gestured arrogantly, and Dolores's portal vanished. He turned his face to the cave. Lexi ran along the ledge, stopped when she was about level with him, and glanced at the hollow area. It was almost completely filled with iridescent light, and a figure moved slowly toward the front. The man grasped Kate by the back of her neck and shoved her to her knees. "A fitting welcome gift for my new friend."

The beast couldn't be seen clearly through the veil of the worlds, but Lexi could make out that it was at least ten feet tall. Its body glistened red as though it was covered in blood. It roared, and the black creatures throughout the cavern shrank away. Earth began to slide down the wall to the left. She wondered if the whole place might be about to collapse and her gaze returned to the demon.

As it moved closer to the front of the cave, she again tore her gaze away and looked at Scott. Since he lay face-down, she couldn't see him clearly but she saw Caleb. His face was a mask of terror. She smirked. It was small consolation that he'd clearly bitten off more than he could chew.

The demon reached the front and began to enter the human world.

CHAPTER TWENTY-FOUR

A guttural voice boomed, *"Why can I not enter?"*

Caleb looked at the creature in horror. "I don't understand. She signed the property over to me. You should be able to step through."

After a moment's silence, he clutched his head and screamed. "Azatoth—my Lord, please."

He twined his fingers in Kate's hair and pulled her up. "You signed the papers. It's mine."

She was unfocused but she answered truthfully. "It wasn't my property. I already sold it."

"What?" Caleb screeched. He looked from her to Azatoth and back again. He slapped her and screamed in her face, "To whom? Who owns it?"

More earth sifted beside the wall of the large area.

"Ah! That would be me."

Lexi spun to where Dick stood at the entrance to the pit with three shifters. Her jaw dropped.

"Close your mouth, dear. The wind might change and you'll be stuck like that." He winked at her, then looked at Caleb. "I swore I'd ruin you when I discovered what you did to Harv. I meant it."

"Get him," the sorcerer screamed, and a sea of black demons moved as one toward him.

The side of the cave that had first shown signs of the veil now looked like a normal cave wall. The dimensions were beginning to move out of alignment. Azatoth noticed too and howled in frustration.

"My Lord, I can still bring you over," Caleb assured him hurriedly. "I'll use my power—our power—to draw the edge of the veil out. It would only be a few feet."

Lexi felt the power of his magic. Fully unleashed, it was so much more than mere sorcery. The veil shifted and undulated, then began to move.

Azatoth took a step.

The earth sifted down the side of the underground space again.

She glanced at Scott again and knew she had to get him out of there. Perhaps she could drop while the monsters pursued Dick, who raced at vamp speed around the cave and dismembered the creatures around the shifters.

The huge demon took another step. She tried to gauge how far he was from the land owned by Caleb. It could be mere inches now.

Something touched her shoulder and she turned, ready to behead whatever it was. She gaped when she focused on Scott's face. She peered at the version who was on the ground in front of Caleb and in the grip of a demon, then back at the one who stood before her.

"Yeah, that won't last for long." He grinned.

Sure enough, the other Scott faded, and the demon holding him skittered around in search of him.

Lexi wanted to hug her friend. Instead, she clutched his arm. "I think we'll need a miracle."

He smiled and pointed upward. She grinned when she realized that the roof was covered in bags of salt. "Shall we make it rain?"

"Going somewhere?" Caleb asked. Scott and Lexi turned toward him.

Dick had been racing past the sorcerer, probably to free Kate, and his feet seemed frozen to the floor.

The sorcerer grinned, although his face was red and sweaty. "What do your friends call you? Dick? Well, I'm afraid your luck's run out, *Dick*."

The vampire punched him hard. The sound of his nose breaking echoed through the pit.

He took a handkerchief out and wiped his hand. "Only my friends call me Dick."

Lexi drew her hand down her scar. "Burst."

Salt rained on the creatures, and they began to explode randomly on every side.

Caleb jumped at the chaos, then sneered at Lexi. "No matter. You're too late." His breathing was labored and sweat ran down his temples. His gaze slid to the cave.

Azatoth had begun to emerge from the portal.

The points of two huge horns appeared, followed by a hooved foot covered in red slime. Its veiled doorway was narrow now, but it looked like the beast would make it through.

The sorcerer pulled Kate to her feet. "I think you should be awake to meet your new friend."

The woman shook her head, saw the creature standing before the ritual entrance, and screamed.

The side of the cave finally gave and a wolf with a metal collar around its neck burst through, howling and snarling. It collided with Azatoth, and both wolf and beast tumbled through the entrance of the portal. Everyone's eyes were glued to the shrinking veil, waiting to see if anything would emerge again. The length of chain from the wolf's collar which had dangled out of the mouth of the cave was cut off, and it dropped heavily to the ground.

"No!" Caleb screamed.

A new noise started to fill the space—the sound of chatter as people awoke from their state of hypnosis.

Dolores shouted, "Gas leak, this way to the exit," to anyone who would listen. Her new fae door looked like a set of double doors with an exit sign above it. Beyond it was the storage company's parking lot.

Lexi drew her katana and turned to finish Caleb but he had vanished.

Scott cast a spell on the room but there was no sign of residual magic. He wandered to the little cave, climbed up, looked around, and dropped again. "There's no sign of the demon or the shifter."

She looked at Dick. "You bought Kate's land?"

"When Betsy told me what Caleb had done, I wanted to kill him. Then I decided it might be better to stop him from getting what he seemed to want more than anything. I went to Kate, and she signed it over then and there. Of course, when I returned home, they caught me with one of those portals."

She raised her eyebrows. "Are shifters usually so trusting of vamps?"

Kate joined them. "We are when the vamp uses his own home as collateral."

The vampire chuckled. "Of course, we promised to swap again if we were still alive at the end of this. We're still doing that, right?"

The woman smiled. "I hear your place is really fancy." She shook her head. "Is it over?"

"By my calculations, it will be at least another thousand years before that dimension aligns with any location on Earth again," Dolores interjected.

"What about Caleb? Won't he be angry?" Kate looked nervous.

Scott looked around. "I'm surprised he had the energy to get himself out of here. He'll probably be depleted for months. Still, I'd rather know where he is."

"I'll work on that tomorrow. Let's get the hell out of here." Dolores looked at Lexi. "And you need a bath."

***

Lexi stood outside with Scott and Dick. "What's next for you?" she asked the vampire as he retrieved his cellphone.

"I need to make sure Betsy and Todd are all right when they return from Fae and sort out the paperwork with Kate to ensure I get my home back."

"Well, I guess it's goodbye, then." She extended her hand to him.

He stepped back. "I'd hug you but you don't smell very nice." He turned to Scott. "Did you show her yet?"

"Not yet, but I've got it here." Scott grinned. He took her hand and covered it with his own and she expected to see the little teardrop pendant appear. When he removed his hand, she gazed into her palm at the gold ring.

Her face lit up. "Is it mine?" She drew him into a hug and whispered, "Thank you." When she released him, her eyes glittered.

He blushed. "Look on the inside."

She turned it to the streetlight. Inside were two dates, May 16th, 1980, and September 23rd, 1990, and interlocking hearts.

Lexi looked at Scott. "I don't understand. The September date is my birthday, but what's the other date?"

"Those were there when I drew the gold from the net. I suspect they were always there but hidden by magic."

She gazed at the ring. "Bryan found it in Braxton's safe. It was in an envelope with my name on it."

"I'd guess it's probably your mother's wedding ring," Dick said and slid his cell phone into his pocket. "Well, Jesús isn't picking up. I'd better see what he's up to. Lexi, it's been…well, I'm not sure what it's been, but you saved my life and for that, I'm grateful."

"You're all right, Dick."

He turned to Scott. "You're a fine young man, Scott. I hope we meet again."

CHAPTER TWENTY-FIVE

The vampire entered the house and called, "Jesús."

He dropped his keys in the dish and was immediately aware that something wasn't right.

When he entered the living area, he found Jesús gagged and bound in the Eames lounger with a box-cutter held at his throat.

"Hello, sir." The man with the blade was reverential.

He turned his back on the scene and walked to the kitchen where he took a glass and filled it from the refrigerator's blood cooler. He nodded and looked up. "Hello, Geoffrey."

The man watched him drink the blood. "What are you doing, drinking that stuff? You don't need that. You've got me. You don't need him, either."

Dick glanced at Jesús. His eyes were red and his breathing was labored. He'd probably cried so much his nose was blocked and he looked terrified.

The vampire returned his gaze to his unwanted visitor. "Really? My Givenchy scarf?"

"I'm sorry, sir. He wouldn't shut up."

For now, he needed the knife to move away from Jesús. "Geoffrey, what are you doing? I said you would be welcome here when you were healed, but you keep running away from the hospital."

"I couldn't bear to be away from you and they'll never let me leave. Not now."

He narrowed his eyes. "What have you done?"

"She was giving me pills—pills that would turn my blood bad. I had to make her stop."

A muffled squeak issued from Jesús.

Dick glanced at the trickle of blood on his houseboy's neck. "I see. And you thought getting blood all over my Eames lounger would encourage me to welcome you home?"

"I didn't think—"

"No, you didn't. Well, if you're back, you're back. I'll get changed. You would absolutely not believe what these stains are. I don't know if they'll ever come out." He washed the glass out and turned it upside-down on the drainer.

The two men both watched as he walked to the little bowl and lifted the keys out.

"You'll have to get yourself a key made." He threw the keys across the room to Geoffrey, who instinctively moved his hand to catch them. By the time they were in his hand, Dick was at his throat.

The vampire pulled the scarf from Jesús's mouth, used the box-cutter on the ties, and walked to the bar and poured them both a large drink.

CHAPTER TWENTY-SIX

Lexi and Scott were very pleased to be back in their piece-of-shit car and headed out of Palm Springs.

She looked at her companion, who grinned broadly as he drove. This was a real treat for him as she rarely let him take the wheel.

In all honesty, she didn't have the energy. Edward had invited them to stay the night and she'd been tempted. If they'd stayed, though, they'd have to get involved in the clean-up and that really wasn't her thing.

Relieved that she'd at least avoided that, she took the opportunity to close her eyes.

"Holy shit!" Scott swerved and the car spun, left the road, plowed through a fence, and impacted with a billboard.

Lexi put out her arms and was hauled against the seat by her seat-belt. "What the fuck? Are you okay?"

"I'm fine. I only—" He looked at the road over his shoulder, his expression dazed.

"Then what the fuck?" She leapt out of the car and walked to the front. "Well, this is going nowhere."

"I'm sorry. There was someone on the road."

"Really? Or did you nod off, you jackass?" She punched him in the arm.

"Could I offer you a ride somewhere?"

She turned to the familiar voice. "Dick?"

"Dude, was that you? Why were you standing in the middle of the road?" Scott leaned heavily on the hood and dragged his fingers over his scalp.

"I was worried you'd miss me." The vampire walked around the car.

Lexi folded her arms. "You're *lucky* we missed you. What are you doing here?"

He released a huge, dramatic sigh. "I am so over Palm Springs."

She raised an eyebrow. "What's up? Wouldn't Kate give you back your house?"

"Oh, we resolved that. Jesús will look after it for a while."

"I thought you were going to check on Betsy." Scott pulled his duffel out of the trunk.

"I'll write." Dick turned to Lexi. "Can I come along for the ride?"

Lexi narrowed her eyes. "You've already agreed on this with Dolores, haven't you?"

"Well…" He spread his arms and shrugged.

"We seem to be shit-out-of-luck in the engine department, anyway." She began to walk toward his day car.

The three of them climbed in and the vampire locked the doors. "So, where are we heading?"

"New Orleans." She smirked.

He looked in the rearview mirror. "Wait, what? No. It's too humid. I'll die."

Scott raised a brow and smirked. "You're already dead."

"You know what I mean." He rolled his eyes.

"It's your own fault. You gave me the clue." Lexi held the photograph up.

"Well, shit. Buckle up. Do you want the radio on, or should I simply ask Alexa to play something?"

CHAPTER TWENTY-SEVEN

S cott lay across the back seat with his hands over his ears. "We've been driving for days. I can't listen to this noise anymore."

Dick glanced into the rearview mirror. "It's been three hours, you insufferable child. My car, my rules—and take your feet off the window. People will think there's a monkey in the car."

Lexi snorted and turned to face the young sorceror. "I quite like it. I've never really listened to old music before."

The vampire slid his gaze to her. "It's not old, it's classic."

Scott moved his feet, sat, and rested his chin on the back of her seat. "It's so disturbing I can't even meditate." He slumped in his seat. "I'll go into my dimensional pocket to—"

Dick's cellphone rang. He passed it to Lexi and she answered it. "Hi, Dolores, how's it going?"

"It's going remarkably well." The fae sounded pleased. "Caleb has surfaced. He's in Mexico."

"You're kidding!" Lexi had thought he would never be seen again.

"Right, where can I turn?" Dick had heard Dolores clearly.

"What? What's happening?" Scott straightened again.

The vampire glanced at him. "Caleb's in Mexico." He raised his voice and added, "Where in Mexico, Dolores?"

"Cabo San Lucas," she continued. "He appears to be on vacation. I have to say I'm a little surprised. There's a large community of duende in the area. How he thought he'd fly under the radar there is beyond me. He checked into the resort this morning."

Dick's face lit up. "Cabo? I adore Cabo. And I don't need to turn around. It occurs to me that I have an old friend with a private plane based in Phoenix."

Two days later, Lexi gazed out of the window of their suite onto the pool area in the resort hotel.

Upon their arrival, Dick had connected with the duende who had first seen Caleb and recognized him from pictures Dolores had distributed through her large network. Once in their room, they didn't risk leaving it and monitored his movements through the strange young duende.

They waited for their opportunity to eliminate him.

Lexi spoke to Dick as she watched the people at the poolside. "I still can't believe you called Betsy."

Scott nodded. "I can't believe she hopped on a plane and flew down here."

The vampire's voice came from the body bag. "She has as much if not more right to be here as the rest of us. Although I'd have preferred it if she watched from the window. I had forgotten how strong-willed she can be." He paused. "What are you doing?"

"Nothing." Scott continued to point his finger at the bag and he smiled as little diamantes appeared where he indicated.

"I don't see why we couldn't do this at night so I could do it. I should be the one doing this—to his face." The vampire sounded sullen.

She watched Caleb through the scope as she spoke. "You know why. He comes out to sunbathe at the pool for an hour a day. It's the only time he's accessible. Anyway, you *will* be doing it."

He ignored that and continued to complain. "I can't believe I'm back in Cabo. I haven't been here since I was alive. This whole burning-in-the-sun thing is such an inconvenience."

Scott looked astonished. "Really? I think I could fix that."

"I doubt it." Dick sighed. "I think I'd have heard about that by now."

Lexi glanced at her friend. They both shrugged. *Why not?*

"It's kind of against the rules to even try something like that," the young man continued, "but since we're fugitives, I'll see what I can do."

"Are you shitting me?" The vampire sounded indignant.

"Shh! It's going down." Caleb sat in his usual lounger, reading his newspaper. Lexi's gaze followed a beautiful young server who carried a tray. She approached from behind and to his side, put the drink down, and turned to walk away.

Unfortunately, she turned at the sound of a click.

Caleb, still reading his newspaper, had produced a fifty-peso note and held it up between two fingers. The young woman's gaze shifted uncertainly to Lexi's window.

"Shit!" She shook her head to indicate that the woman should get out of there.

Dick half-sat in the bag. "What's going on?"

"He's trying to tip her." She couldn't keep the disappointment out of her voice.

Scott stood to look out of the window. "If she takes that note, he'll sense the magic."

Her gaze remained focused on the scene through the scope. "If she doesn't take the tip, he'll know something's wrong."

The server looked at the other guests around the pool, then glanced at the window. She raised her hand to a thin chain around her neck and pulled.

As it broke, so did the spell. Had anyone been looking, they would have seen the beautiful young woman instantly turn into a little old lady.

Betsy leaned forward and snagged the note from Caleb's fingers. "*Gracias.*"

She walked as far as the bar, then turned to watch.

"Is she inside?" Dick asked.

Lexi shook her head. "No, she's at the bar, ordering a drink."

"What if he sees her? We shouldn't have involved her." The vampire wriggled so much inside the bag that she was tempted to tell Scott to sit on him.

"It was your idea." She rolled her eyes.

Caleb put his newspaper down and picked the glass up. She focused on his lips as he muttered a word. He seemed satisfied that the drink was safe, glanced at the little pot of olives and cocktail sticks, and smiled. With a practiced movement, he snagged an olive and dropped it into the drink before he knocked it back.

"I'm glad she's here. I'd never have thought to put it in the olives." She shrugged.

The sorcerer sat bolt upright, instantly aware that something wasn't right. He looked around and his jaw dropped at the sight of Betsy seated at the poolside bar with a glass of gin. She toasted him with a broad smile.

He muttered a word at the woman, then muttered again. He seemed to have discovered that his magic wasn't working.

"What's happening?" Dick punched the bag from the inside.

Lexi took the shot. The gun was shielded by magic so no one heard it. The bullet was a Scott special, a combination of tech and magic, and it found Caleb's heart without breaking his skin.

She addressed the body bag. "It's done. Over to you."

The sorcerer clutched his chest. It was clear he knew something was coming.

Dick paused for a moment before he said, "Stop."

His heart stopped and he sagged onto the lounger, dead.

Lexi stared at the ocean from a little table on the promenade.

Betsy placed a hand on her arm. "Where will you go now?"

"We only got as far as Phoenix when the call came. I guess we'll go back to pick up the car and continue to New Orleans. How about you?"

"I'll return to the house. Dolores will contact me about visiting Todd in Fae. It'll take some time for him to heal."

Dick turned to the older woman. "What's the point in knocking around that big place alone? Why don't you come to New Orleans with us?"

"Dick, I'm eighty years old. I'm too old to be gallivanting around the country fighting monsters."

Scott stood, removed the chain from his pocket, and placed it on the table in front of Betsy. "You don't have to be too old to do anything."

She picked it up with two fingers and dangled it in the air in front of her face. "I'll admit it was good to move around without arthritis pain."

"Here it comes." Lexi sat up excitedly.

The vampire passed Marcel to Betsy. "If this doesn't work—"

"Dude, have some faith." Scott clapped him on the back and sat.

He turned to the young man. "I'm sitting here about to face the sun. I think I'm showing an extraordinary level of faith in you, Scott."

Dick faced the ocean and saw his first sunrise in over seventy years. A tear rolled down his face in a moment so magical that nothing could spoil it.

"Okay, I got one," Scott began. "A vampire walks into a shifter bar..."

CHAPTER TWENTY-EIGHT

Amy lay motionless in the coffin and remained as quiet as she could. She was fairly sure the museum would be empty by now, but there was another reason to not move. The padding beneath her was hard and uncomfortable and every time she shifted even slightly, her nose was assaulted by a musty smell.

It had never occurred to her before that coffins didn't need to be as comfortable as they looked. The user wouldn't ever leave a one-star review on TripAdvisor. She might, though. *Museum of Death. One-night stay. Coffin extremely uncomfortable, no breakfast.* She stifled a giggle, then sighed. She wondered—and not for the first time—why on earth she'd said yes to this ridiculous plan.

As Jamal had explained it, she had to be the one to do it because the coffin was so stupidly small that only she would fit. She could have argued or flat-out refused. There were probably a few places he could have hidden. But, of course, she had relented. She always did with him. One look into those dark-brown eyes and her bones simply melted, along with any semblance of common sense.

She wondered what might happen if she were caught there. If she finally sat up to find herself surrounded by police officers. She could be kicked out of medical school, for one thing. And what might possibly be worse, her parents would discover she wasn't spending summer break with Julie's family in the Hamptons. She was in fact, shacked up with her boyfriend in New Orleans. She had to stop herself from giggling again. Her dad would have a stroke.

Jamal had been desperate to come. He was obsessed with the place —and with voodoo—and told her he wanted to "find his people."

So much for that idea. She frowned in the darkness.

The locals treated him like a tourist wannabe and didn't understand how serious he was about it. If she was honest, she didn't get it herself. She didn't know whether she believed or not, but she didn't like to see her boyfriend dismissed so casually. They'd both eaten nothing but ramen and worked extra shifts for months to afford this break. But at the end of the day, their response didn't matter. This would show everyone.

He was about to get a top-level recommendation—one they couldn't ignore. *The* top-level, if what Jamal said was true.

A bead of sweat trickled down the side of her face and entered her ear. At least she hoped it was sweat.

Fuck this. I'm getting out.

She pushed the lid up and moved it to the side. When she sat, it slid off. Too slowly, she lurched out to catch it and missed. She hunched her shoulders and gritted her teeth as it fell to the floor with a bang. The sound was like an explosion in the stillness of the room.

If anyone was in the building, that noise would definitely bring them running. She waited.

After a few moments of silence, Amy drew the cellphone from her purse and clicked its flashlight on to find her bearings inside the Museum of Death. Carefully, she climbed from the coffin and dusted herself off with her hands. She played the light around the room and caught dust motes from the disturbed coffin in the beam.

Instruments of torture, autopsy photos, and newspaper headlines with pictures of serial killers were illuminated. As she flicked the light around, a death mask loomed out of the darkness. She stumbled back against the coffin. It wobbled on the stand and for a breath-holding moment, she thought it might collapse, but it settled. She blew stray bangs away from her face.

As a med student, she had seen corpses and witnessed a couple of autopsies. Death didn't frighten her, but still.

This place is creepy as hell.

She crept through the rooms and finally located a glass cabinet. A photograph above it was easily identifiable as the much-adored voodoo queen, Marie Laveau. With a slow and cautious motion, she stroked the face in the picture. In front of that and beneath the glass were several pieces of her jewelry. There were other trinkets and pictures, but they didn't interest her. She pulled at the frame, but nothing budged. Irritated, she cast the light over the cabinet and found a keyhole. It was locked.

"Shit!" She glanced around the room. Jamal was relying on her. She'd come this far and wouldn't go home empty-handed.

Amy approached a wall display and lifted a heavy metal surgical implement from its bracket. As a medical student, she should know what it was called. Jamal would know. She tested the weight in her hand and decided it would do.

Resolute, she returned to the cabinet, swung the instrument at the glass, and turned her face away at the last moment. She was rewarded by an almighty crash. Most of the top shelf disintegrated and the jewelry and pictures fell to the shelf below.

Hastily, she picked through the glass but withdrew her hand quickly. "Son of a bitch!" She had cut her fingers and looked at the incisions in the light from her cell. They were minor but stung a little, which merely increased her irritation. She played the light over the tiny shards again until she saw the glint from a ring. That was it. She was done. Without care for any further possible injury, she brushed the glass aside, snatched the ring, and ran to the door.

The apartment, fortunately, was only a couple of blocks away and a few minutes later, she burst through the door, closed it with her butt, and leaned against it. She had run all the way and heaved breaths with her hand on her chest.

Jamal walked through from the living room. "Did you get it?"

Instantly, she was annoyed. "Yes, Jamal, this *is* blood and it *does* hurt."

He walked to her and cupped her hand tenderly in his. His gaze settled on the ring which glinted in the light while a trail of blood dribbled into her palm from her fingers.

Amy looked at him and realized he wore only his shorts. The air-con was off and a sheen of sweat covered his body. White dots of paint trailed intricate swirling patterns around his face and chest, starkly vivid against his dark-brown skin.

"The blood will be good for the ritual." He plucked the ring from the little red puddle, turned away, and headed toward the living room.

She rolled her eyes, followed, and noted the flickering light from the many candles around the apartment. He'd already started the ritual.

Reverently, he placed the ring onto a bed of herbs and flowers in a wooden bowl and turned to her. His eyes flashed in the candlelight as he looked at her with hunger. It was almost her favorite part. This had all been totally worth it.

Jamal approached her with an intensity in his eyes that thrilled her. As he undressed her silently, her heart skipped a beat. He led her into a circle he'd marked out with chicken bones, picked up two cups, and passed one to her. She sniffed the contents. The drinks always smelled disgusting and they tasted worse, but they made her fly. She drank without hesitation.

He muttered words with a creole lilt to his voice that—being from Boston—he didn't usually have.

While she admitted to being somewhat naive regarding Jamal, she was generally cynical by nature and suspected this was all bullshit. That said, the sex was great. They'd complete his little ritual and get down to it.

Entirely focused, he dipped his fingers into a dish of oil fragranced with herbs and trailed them over her body while he muttered words she didn't understand.

Finally, he took the ring from the wooden bowl and indicated to her to kneel. Once he'd slid it on her finger, he cried, "I beg and implore to speak to the lady of New Orleans of old, the owner of this ring, and to see her made flesh again."

I hope she won't be disappointed to find herself in my skinny white body, Amy thought as she played along.

The drink began to take effect and she closed her eyes as she swished her long blonde hair around. She hoped they would get to the best part soon.

CHAPTER TWENTY-NINE

"You have to know where it is." Scott hovered in Lexi's peripheral vision, seated on his bed in their New Orleans hotel room.

Her eyes strained as she stared unblinkingly at a toothbrush, the subject of her latest lesson in magic. "I can see where it is. I'm looking directly at it."

"Not only with your eyes." His voice had taken on a Zen-like tone that made her want to smack him—or maybe worse.

"What else am I supposed to look with? My teeth?" She shifted her position on the end of her bed but kept her gaze on the toothbrush on the table.

"With every fiber of your being—you must know where the object is in the universe."

"I know where in the universe it will be." She pushed the words out and clamped her jaw again.

Scott cleared his throat. "Try not to have thoughts like that. If it ends up there, I will not be happy."

Despite the cool, air-conditioned room, prickles of sweat broke out on her forehead and neck. Her hand was clasped over the unhealing scar on her arm, the reservoir of magic she borrowed from him.

"Now, think about where you want the object to appear. Without looking at its destination, command it to be there."

Her gaze flicked involuntarily to the opposite side of the table, where the toothbrush was supposed to appear.

"Shit!" Lexi scowled as the magical connection was broken. The energy built up within the toothbrush careened it across the room and imbedded it in the wall. "There, I moved it."

"Hang on. I'll put it back and we can start again." Her friend climbed off his bed. He had almost taken hold of the toothbrush when he jumped away in alarm as it was joined in the wall by a knife. He gaped at her.

"If you take that toothbrush out of the wall, you won't wake up tomorrow morning." She bounced the tip of another blade against her fingers, ready to throw.

"Fine, it's your toothbrush." He rolled his eyes and returned to his bed to sit cross-legged. "Look, you always complain that your legacy abilities aren't as good as they should be. Building up your ability to use magic will help with that. If you're not strong enough to lift a car, you can lift it with magic. Not fast enough to save a life? Save them with magic."

She pulled her hair out of the ponytail and rubbed her scalp. "I don't understand why this is so hard. The other things I've tried to do with magic work fine."

"Some things are harder. Teleporting is hard but you'll get it. And you need to break the bad habit of touching the scar when you draw magic." He stretched his head to the side and cracked his neck.

Lexi looked at her unhealing scar. "I'm empty again. Why does it simply drain out of me like that? Even when I don't use it?"

"I don't know. But as long as we stick with each other, it'll never be a problem."

She leaned back on her bed. "Maybe *you* should spend time training. You don't practice weapons training nearly enough, or hand-to-hand combat."

"So, you can get me in a headlock and give me a wet-willy again? I don't think so." Scott poked his nose.

"Are you picking your nose?" She screwed her face up in distaste.

"I'm not picking it. Magic tickles the hairs in my nostrils. It's so annoying." He moved to sit in front of the mirror and held his hand out, and a little pair of scissors appeared. With his nose raised, he gazed up his nostrils and went to work.

"Gross!" She threw a cushion at him. "There's a mirror in the bathroom for that."

A knock at the door drew their attention. He looked at Lexi, whose bed was closest to the door. She returned the look and didn't move. Finally, he rolled his eyes dramatically, flicked his hand, and the door opened.

"Hello, boys and girls. How are you settling in?" Dick entered with Marcel in his arms and waved the puppy's little paw at them. At the sight of the sorcerer in front of the mirror, he put the dog onto Lexi's bed, walked over, and sat beside him. "What are you watching—anything good?"

"Nothing. I'm trimming my nose hair." Scott waved the scissors.

"Scott!" Dick moved away from him. "Surely there's a mirror in the bathroom for that."

"Fine!" The young man stood and retreated to the bathroom.

Dick sat before the mirror and ran a finger along his eyebrow. "Wait, can you wind this back before you go?"

Scott turned with a look of disgust. "No. I won't invade someone's privacy for your entertainment."

"You did it before." The vampire sulked. He shifted his gaze to Lexi in the mirror and raised an eyebrow at her. She shrugged.

The request made her think about the woman who had died in their Palm Springs motel room before they had arrived. Her friend had insisted on using magic to reverse what the mirror had captured to watch the woman's tragic last minutes. She glanced at Scott. He didn't meet her gaze, though. She knew that empathy and emotion played a big part in sorcery and made for a controlled, compassionate mage.

Without the empathy, he'd be a monster like Caleb was.

She still wondered if he was too tenderhearted for the job.

"That was different." Scott turned away and managed two more steps.

Dick finally dragged himself away from his reflection. "How is it different?"

"It was my way of making her last moments... I don't know...not be alone." He shrugged, walked into the bathroom, and closed the door.

The vampire turned to her. "He's annoying and adorable, all at once—" He stopped speaking when he saw her hold her sharp little knife by the tip of the blade and tap Marcel gently on the nose with the handle.

Lexi said, "Bop," when she tapped the puppy's nose, then moved the handle out of the way when he tried to bite it. "What can I say? He's a genius wrapped in a Care Bear inside a sulky teenager."

"I heard that," the sorcerer shouted through the bathroom door.

She looked up and noticed Dick staring at her hand with a frown. A little confused, she glanced at the blade in her hand. "Oh! right." She pocketed the knife and stroked the dog's head.

The vampire stood. "Well, before you slice and dice my little companion, I have to take him out for his evening constitutional. And I'll visit some old friends—if I still have any here. This hotel simply won't do."

At his dismissive tone, she glanced around the luxurious room and wondered what was wrong with it.

Scott stuck his head out of the bathroom. "Are you kidding? It's better than what we usually get by a mile. You've seen what we usually get. There's a gym downstairs and a pool on the roof. There are batteries in the TV remote, and it has air-con."

Dick flicked his hand toward him. "Oh! it'll do for you. I mean me —it won't do for me."

Lexi stopped rubbing Marcel's belly. "What's wrong with it—not enough designer furniture and half-naked young men, *Meester* Levine?"

He ignored her. "People in this town know me. I can't be seen in a hotel room with floor to ceiling windows. Exactly like I can't be seen drinking margaritas on Bourbon Street in the middle of the day."

She handed Marcel to him. "You can't spend all day hiding."

"I'll spend all day sleeping," he explained.

Scott returned to the room, "But you don't have to do that anymore." He stared from Dick to Marcel with a grin.

The vampire passed the puppy to him. "Have you ever switched shifts? It's like I've worked nights for over sixty years. It'll probably take me another sixty to get used to being awake during the day."

Lexi nodded. "The thought had never occurred to me. Although I'm surprised you don't own a place here already." She watched as he stepped to the mirror again.

He's probably checking that his face is still perfect.

"I did once, but Katrina had other ideas. I donated the land to the victims of the hurricane."

Scott put Marcel onto the floor and they watched as he padded to Dick, sat at his feet, and wagged his stumpy little tail from side to side.

He looked curiously at the vampire. "What will you do, then?"

"I have acquaintances who might be able to help. I think I'll—" He stopped speaking when he noticed the toothbrush and knife protruding from the wall. "Do you know—never mind." He shook his head. "I'll go see them now. Would you mind looking after Betsy? Maybe you could take her for something to eat? She's getting dressed." He turned to Scott. "Apparently, she's wearing a new dress. She's quite excited about it so be a decent chap and tell her she looks nice or something."

Dick opened the door and stepped into the hallway. He turned to them. "And please, make sure she doesn't get into trouble while I'm gone."

Lexi followed him to the door. "What trouble will a little old lady get into?" Dick was already heading down the hallway with Marcel doing tiny gallops next to him to keep up. She turned to Scott. "So basically, he's gone for a night out with his pals and saddled us with his eighty-year-old friend to look after. Why bring her if he intended to simply dump her on us? Dick is such a dick."

"I think it's sweet how protective he is of her." He checked the time. "It's been a long day of traveling. It's already ten pm and we don't want to tire her out. Maybe we could take her to the hotel restaurant for a little supper before bed." He retrieved his wallet from the dresser.

"Who's ready to hit the Quarter?"

The two friends looked toward the still open door and Betsy, who obviously wore her enchanted necklace. She looked like an eighteen-year-old and her dress was so short and tight that Scott's ears turned red. "You look nice," he said in a strangled tone.

Oh, dear!

"We're almost ready." Lexi's voice sounded a little strained, even to herself.

"Okay, I'll get my purse." Betsy beamed at them before she turned and headed to her room directly across the hall.

Lexi whirled to face her friend. "What have you done to her?"

"What? Why are you looking at me?" Scott shrugged as he put his wallet into his pocket.

She pointed across the hall. "She didn't look like that in Cabo."

"She wore that frumpy waitress dress in Cabo." He shrugged again. "This must be what she looked like when she was young."

"No one has ever looked like that. You have to fix it or we'll have to spend the whole night peeling douchey guys off her." She stormed past him and began to pick up various pointy objects and secrete them in the lining of her pants and vest.

The sorcerer shook his head vehemently. "I don't think she'll like that very much."

Lexi spun and punctuated her words with prods on his chest. "I don't think Mayor Todd will like that *you* made his mother look like a hooker."

"Come on. To be fair, that's the dress, not the necklace."

Betsy walked out of her room and across the hall into theirs. She sighed. "I think we might have a problem."

"Ya think? Sorry, I mean…what problem?" Lexi walked to the doorway and leaned against the open door.

"My ID says I'm eighty. Scott dear, could you rustle me up a new one?" She waved her fingers in pseudo magical waves in the air.

Scott looked at his partner.

She shook her head. "Sorry, Betsy, most of the bars in the French Quarter are run by supernaturals. A fake ID won't work on them." It wasn't true but the woman wouldn't know that. "How about Scott puts you safely into your fifties and you won't be asked?"

Betsy took a step back and covered the necklace with her hand. Her gaze slid to the side and Lexi was convinced she was about to bolt down the hallway in her five-inch heels.

Finally, the woman sighed. "Thirties. Not a day over thirty-two."

She nodded at Scott as Betsy headed into her room.

He muttered his incantation.

"Oh my!" Betsy said from across the hall a moment before she returned. Her body had lost its girlish frame and become curvier in very noticeable places. "Now you're talking. This dress will never do. I need to change."

Noticeably excited, she hurried to her room and closed the door.

The two friends stood side-by-side in the doorway of their room, their mouths in a perfect O.

Lexi recovered and punched Scott's arm before she scowled at the closed door. "You made it worse." When she received no answer, she glared at him. He blushed to the roots of his hair and she punched his arm again. "Try to remember she's old enough to be your grandma." She sighed. "This is all Dick's fault. I liked him more when I thought he was dead."

CHAPTER THIRTY

Dick sauntered through the Quarter with Marcel. They'd walked several blocks and the streets had quieted around them.

He stopped and took in the sight of the shadow of Jesus projected from the statue on to the back of St. Louis Cathedral. When he looked down, the puppy was doing his business.

"Marcel, really. In front of Jesus—have you no respect?" He pulled a little bag out of his pocket and cleaned it up.

"Good boy." He patted him on the head, tied the bag, and dropped it into a trash can.

That done, he turned his focus to a presence he'd been aware of for a few minutes. "You can come out, you know. I don't bite. Well, only recreationally."

A figure stepped from the shadows into the streetlight. "Hello, Mr. Levine. It's been a long time," said a deep creole voice.

The vampire studied the elderly African American man with grey dreadlocks who wore a monk-like cowl. He carried a staff with markings engraved on it and it was apparent that he leaned more heavily on it than he had in the past. "Hello, Joseph. It has. How are you?"

Joseph stopped at what was regarded in polite supernatural circles as a sensible distance away. "Happy and healthy and hoping to remain so."

Dick raised an eyebrow. "Then is it wise to wander alone at night?"

"I'm never alone. The spirits are always with me." The man spread his arms and a breeze swept through the street.

He sighed at the sudden cool breeze. "I don't imagine your spirits would consider following me around while I'm here?"

The man laughed. "You never did enjoy the climate of the Crescent City." His face lost its joviality. "So which faction have you come to join?"

"Faction? You're kidding me—that's still going on?" He shook his head, saddened by the revelation.

"Hostilities between the clans have simmered for years but it's blown up in the last few days. Things are changing in the shifter community too, although that's more civil. Everyone is restless. And here *you* are, coincidentally." He drew the last word out as though looking for the lie in it.

Dick tilted his head as he considered what he'd heard. "What do your spirits tell you?"

Joseph smiled. "They tell me you need another bag."

He looked down. "Marcel!" He slid his hand into his pocket again, thankful that he'd come prepared.

When he had tied the bag, the other man seemed to have made his mind up. "How about we get your dog a drink of water? He's safer off the street. We have rats bigger than him."

The vampire dropped the bag in the trash and lifted the puppy from the ground. "Don't you listen to him, Marcel. You are ferocious. I'll have you know Marcel recently saved me from a demented shifter." He stroked the animal's belly.

"Ah! A traitor to his kind." Joseph laughed.

They entered a tiny bar. From the outside, it looked like a house, but Dick had known of it for many years. He observed that it was full of humans. They stopped speaking and looked up when he entered.

"Let's go to the back." The other man led him through the building.

They entered a courtyard with greenery and flowers climbing the walls to the surrounding balconies and a trickling water-feature on the rear wall.

"This is charming." Dick took a seat in the little courtyard and sniffed the air. "Night-scented jasmine."

A woman came out and placed two whiskey glasses on the table and a water-filled bowl on the ground, which Marcel all but leapt into.

He scratched the puppy's head, then straightened to face his companion. "*Kouman timoun yo ye?*"

Joseph chuckled and he guessed his Creole was a little off. "The kids are well, thank you for asking. But not kids anymore and not interested in the old ways. Their gods are technology and money. So, if not to pledge allegiance to one of the clans, what brings you to town?" He leaned back and it was obvious that the man was more relaxed there. The vampire wondered what magic was in the walls to make him so confident but decided he didn't want to know.

"I'm visiting with a…for convenience, let's call her a friend. She's on a personal quest that has brought her to New Orleans and I offered to help." He tried not to stray anywhere in the discussion that would require him to lie.

"And your questing friend, where is she?" Joseph looked dramatically around the small courtyard as though someone might suddenly appear.

"Around. The hotel or a restaurant maybe. Detaching the fingers of a pickpocket is a distinct possibility. Who knows?"

Joseph leaned forward and shook his staff. "My spirits tell me something is different about you, William Levine."

Dick accepted the scrutiny for a few moments. Finally, he lifted his glass. "A new conditioner. I'm worth it."

His companion laughed. They clinked glasses and drank.

Marcel went to Joseph and his stumpy tail wagged. He scratched the dog's neck, then produced a treat. Dick couldn't begin to guess where from.

The vampire nodded his appreciation of his drink before he returned to the subject at hand. "Who would you say is the more accommodating faction at the moment? I need a place to stay during the day."

"Ah yes, I remember your home. It was beautiful. It is an outreach center for the homeless now. Have you seen it?"

"I'm glad they were able to put it to good use, but no. I wouldn't like to see it so changed." For a moment, he looked into the middle distance and envisioned his New Orleans home of years gone by.

"I wouldn't suggest it's safe to go to any clan right now. Almost all of them demand that visitors show fealty. They all watch too much television. If the first one you visit can't help, you won't be welcomed by the rest. They won't talk to each other and they barely talk to me. Kindred is out of town and the clans talk about making grabs for power all over the place. You should go to the sanguinaires—the living blood drinkers. They're trying to stay out of this spat."

Dick was shocked. "Kindred is out of town? But why? I've never heard of such a thing. Are they on a team-building event?" He took a gulp of his whiskey. "Although it begs the question, how many Kindreds does it take to build a raft?"

"None," Joseph supplied. "They'd make us do it."

They laughed and clinked glasses again.

The man sniffed the air. "There is powerful, dark magic in the wind tonight, here and across the country."

Dick stroked an eyebrow absently. "Are the sanguinaires still at the same place?"

"Of course. Whether living or undead, we are all creatures of habit."

"I try not to be so predictable." He was a little offended.

"Do you still have that giant trunk you always travelled with? And the silver lion's head pin? You remain the only vampire I've ever heard of who wears silver."

"I stand corrected." He raised his eyebrows. "Apparently, I am predictable."

Joseph looked at Marcel. "Not completely. I must say, I never expected to see you with a puppy."

"He belonged to a friend who passed. We've found ourselves to be a surprisingly good fit." He leaned down, picked Marcel up, and stood. "Well, I'll say good evening, Joseph. Thank you for the drink and the information. Take care of yourself."

"I don't have to." The man smiled.

The vampire laughed. "Yes, of course. You have your spirits."

A breeze stirred the air in the courtyard and he breathed in the scent of the flowers. "Quite delightful." He nodded to Joseph and left.

The two continued through the streets until finally, Marcel refused to walk. He turned to the puppy who sat immovably and yawned. "Are you tired, little guy?" He picked him up and held him close to his face. "We're almost there." Marcel licked his nose.

Dick crossed the street and entered a bar. It had been a few years since he'd been there, but he recognized a few faces. They looked wary, though, which gave him pause.

A tall man stood. "Is that you, William?" He crossed to him and unsurprisingly, stopped a short distance away. The vampire stared at him in surprise. This convention wasn't usually followed by non-supernaturals, simply because there was no point. If any supernatural had ill-intentions toward this human, those few feet wouldn't save him.

"Hello, Oberon. I've heard things are tense these days and wonder if I could have chosen a better time to visit." He thought it best to clarify immediately that he wanted nothing to do with whatever the situation was between the clans.

His friend nodded at the message. "How can I help you?"

"I need a place to stay for a couple of nights. I'm with friends, but they can stay in a hotel."

"Martine?" Oberon called to a woman who stood behind the bar and she looked at him. "Is 3b in the apartment building free?"

She lifted a large black book and dropped it onto the bar with a thud before she pulled a pair of glasses from her head and propped them on her nose. Once she'd opened the book, she ran a finger down the page, then closed it. "It's free." She put the glasses onto her head again.

The man nodded, paused, then asked, "How about 3a, on the front?"

The woman stared directly at him in evident disapproval as she opened the book again and settled the glasses onto her face. She ran her finger down the page. "Yup." She made no effort to close it and simply stood and looked at him with exaggerated patience.

He stared in response.

Finally, she frowned. "What?"

Oberon put his hand out. "The keys?"

She rolled her eyes, lifted two keys from a shelf behind the bar, and handed them over.

The man looked at Marcel and grinned. "So, who's this? May I?" He held his hand still until Dick nodded. Cautiously, he put the back of his hand out for the puppy to sniff, then stroked the animal's head.

"This is Marcel. He's one of my traveling companions." He waved the tiny paw again and simply couldn't explain why it gave him such delight to do that.

Oberon looked at him, his expression somber. "Be careful walking the streets, my friend. Kindred is out of town."

He raised his eyebrows. "I heard. I've never known them to leave New Orleans unprotected. I can't imagine what's holding it all together right now."

"It's only been a few days but it'll all hit the fan soon. We're simply trying to keep our heads down." The man shook his head.

Dick saw how worried he looked and knew he was right to be concerned. When things kicked off between supernaturals, it was often the humans who were caught in the middle. "Do you know why Kindred left? Where they've gone?"

"Apparently, some idiot opened a portal to a hell dimension in Palm Springs. Creatures have poured through for days—hundreds of them. Nasty buggers, it would seem."

"Oh, that. Yes, I'm aware." He wasn't quite sure what else to say.

Oberon's eyes narrowed. "Now that I think about it, isn't Palm Springs your neck of the woods?"

The vampire smiled. "And now you know why Marcel and I have chosen to put a healthy distance between us and home."

"It's perfectly understandable." The man handed the keys over.

Dick reached for his wallet. "How much do I owe you?"

"William, you insult me." Oberon put a hand up.

Martine picked a pen up. "Obe, what do I put in the book?"

The man looked at the vampire with his eyebrows raised.

"Dick."

The woman smirked. "Okay, and the other room?"

Oberon replied this time. "Marcel."

She wrote the names and snapped the book closed.

"Do you have time for a drink?" he asked.

"I need to get Marcel to his basket. Would you like to meet for dinner tomorrow evening?"

"I'd love to, William. But a couple of the clans—at least those who can stand to be in the same room—are meeting for a parlay tomorrow night. They've chosen my establishment to host it."

"What an honor," Dick said with an eyebrow raised to emphasize the sarcasm.

"Quite. It'll come to nothing, though. They'll bluster for a couple of hours, drink my best whiskey, and leave disgruntled." Oberon rolled his eyes. "Can I send a snack round?" He indicated two young women who donated blood to sanguinaires in the corner of the room.

"In public?" He raised a brow. Of course, he'd already been aware of the tang of blood in the air.

His friend laughed. "We're human, my friend. Kindred leaves us alone."

"Ahh. And no thank you. I'm fine. I dined early." He had brought a few blood bags in his temperature-controlled box as he preferred to be personally acquainted with the source. For now, he didn't want to risk it. The young ladies were probably in good health but one of the thugs who shot up his car in Palm Springs had given him an upset stomach for a couple of days. It wasn't worth the risk.

Outside the bar, Dick checked his cell and was rewarded with the location of the oyster bar where Lexi, Scott, and Betsy were. He attempted to put Marcel down to walk but the puppy would have none of it. With a chuckle, he conceded defeat and held the dog in his arms as he made his way through the streets.

CHAPTER THIRTY-ONE

exi sat with Scott and Betsy in the small oyster bar on Bourbon Street.

She glanced yet again at the other woman's plunging neckline. "Where did you get those dresses?"

"I've been shopping on the Internet since Cabo. Everything was waiting when I arrived in the room." Betsy looked at herself. "Although I'll have to visit the stores tomorrow. This dress is a tight squeeze."

"I noticed." She raised an eyebrow.

The older woman's gaze slid over her leathers. "How can you bear to wear all that hide? You must be melting."

She sighed. In all honesty, she didn't have an answer and she *was* melting. New Orleans was so much worse than Palm Springs had been. She gazed around the room, noted that there didn't seem to be any supernaturals in sight, and decided to risk removing her jacket. "Is there anything you'd like to do while you're here, Betsy?"

"I'm not sure. I've only been to New Orleans once, with Harv. We didn't even visit the French Quarter. I stayed around the pool at the hotel for two days while he was at a conference, then we left."

Scott sat up excitedly. "You'll want to have a good look around while you're here then. Maybe we could take a tour."

The waiter appeared at the table and took their orders.

After he left, Betsy tutted. "Oh dear! I forgot to order one of those Hurricane cocktails everyone's drinking."

"I'll get it." Lexi stood and headed to the bar. She waited patiently at the busy counter for the drink and noticed that it became steadily louder thanks to a group of young men somewhere behind her. Finally, she took the drink, turned, and as she stepped away from the bar, bumped into someone.

A young man shook about a teaspoon of beer dramatically from his hand. "Hey—careful, stupid." His friends went silent.

He looked at Lexi. "Oh, sorry. I mean, my fault." At that moment, he looked like he might pee his pants.

Shit!

She didn't respond but returned to the table as the group shuffled into the back of the bar.

Back at the table, she stood for a moment, perplexed by the two hurricane cocktails already in front of Betsy on the table.

"Oh, some kind young men at that table over there heard me mention the drink and dashed to the bar." The woman gave a little finger wave to a group of three men at a nearby table who stared at her. Their thoughts were etched on their faces and it wasn't a pretty sight.

Lexi raised an eyebrow. "Well, that's not creepy."

Scott peered into the throng of people. "What's wrong? I felt you getting irate."

She signaled to him with a little twirl of her finger and he mirrored the motion as he muttered an incantation. He nodded that it was safe to speak.

"A few shifters saw my scar," she said as she pulled her jacket on again and sat. "I should have been more careful. All they have to do is mention me to local Kindred and we're in trouble."

"We won't be here long. Don't worry about it." Scott pulled the drink she brought closer to him. "I might as well have this. Betsy will be on the floor if she has all three."

Lexi smiled. "Sure."

The sorcerer looked like all his Christmases had come at once. He picked the drink up and turned to watch the people.

While he was distracted, she slipped her thumb up her sleeve and stroked the scar to activate its power. "I think these two should stay sober tonight," she whispered.

Scott turned to her, having felt the discharge of magic. "What did—"

"Excuse me."

She looked up in response to the nervous voice. It was the shifter again and he held another hurricane. "I'm sorry about that. I wasn't sure if I'd spilled your drink too so I got you another one." He held it out to her but she didn't take it.

This guy's so nervous, he's making me nervous.

"It's okay. It was my fault."

"I thought you were all away, clearing a mess up in Palm Springs." He left it hanging as though she might respond.

She didn't and he looked even more anxious.

"Well, here you go, anyway." He put the drink onto the table and stepped back.

"Thanks for the drink," she replied dismissively.

When he'd moved away, Scott took his cellphone out.

"Are you messaging Dolores?" Lexi asked and he nodded. She took a sip of her drink, screwed her face up, and pushed it away. "That's strong."

"Do you think so? It seemed strong at first but it tastes like fruit juice now." Betsy stirred her drink with the straw.

The sorcerer's gaze slid to Lexi and he gave her a look of pure disappointment.

She focused on the shifters, who filed out of the bar with their heads low.

Betsy shook her head. "Lexi dear, you killed their buzz."

"I didn't mean to. But it explains why they were being so raucous. They thought there were no Kindred in town to keep an eye on them."

Scott's phone beeped, and he picked it up to read the screen. "Dolores got out before Kindred arrived. No one will remember us except Edward, and he's out of Palm Springs too." He continued to read. "Well, that's interesting. No one remembers Caleb either."

A dark look crossed Betsy's face. Caleb had posed as a family friend and her husband's business partner for years before he murdered her husband, then brainwashed and almost murdered her son. "He was a prominent member of Palm Springs society. How could everyone forget him? I know I never will."

The sorcerer patted her hand. "They'll remember there was someone but not the details. Dolores says she wasn't responsible for that. It must have been part of how he manipulated everyone's minds."

The woman shook her head. "It seems impossible. He was a business owner. Who did all those people think they were employed by?"

"I have no idea. I'll ask Dolores next time we speak." He shrugged.

She looked at her cocktail and put her glass down, looking guilty. "Does she have any news about Todd?"

Scott smiled. "Yes. He's getting there. The scars have all healed but they're keeping him asleep while they repair his mind."

Lexi brushed her scar discreetly. *Okay, she can get a little buzzed.*

The food came and they talked casually.

Betsy finished her drink and banged her palms on the table. "Wow! That drink really hit me. Let's dance." She stood and whirled into Dick.

"William!" She slapped her hands onto his cheeks and planted a kiss on his lips before she hugged him. "You've always been my favorite homosexual."

"Well, thank you. You're too kind." He examined her curiously. "Why Betsy, you've...grown." He smiled and gave her another hug. Then, over her shoulder, he mouthed, "what have you done?" to the two young people.

Lexi shrugged. Regulating someone's level of intoxication was harder than she thought, but she wasn't sure that was what Dick was referring to.

Betsy stepped back and patted his face again. "Dick, I'm going to the powder room. Oh…do you mind if I call you Dick?"

He shrugged and raised his palms. "Everyone else does."

"Dick, you must try the hurricane. It sneaks up on you and hits you between the eyes like a force-five." She tottered to the back of the room in her tight black satin dress.

Lexi noted that the three men who had bought her the drinks watched her progress.

The vampire shook his head and sat. "Harv would be spinning in his grave."

Scott put his arms out to Marcel and the other man passed him over for a little attention.

She turned to her friend and asked innocently, "Can you do anything to make her less drunk?"

He stared at her with his eyebrows almost at his hairline. "Gosh, what a good idea."

Before she could retort, he closed his eyes and muttered inaudibly.

"So…" Dick leaned forward. "I've got us a couple of apartments in the Quarter. We can move there tonight. And you won't believe what else I've heard—"

"That Kindred's moved en masse to Palm Springs?" Lexi winked at him.

"Oh, you know." He looked crestfallen. "How did you know?"

"I was careless and was seen by a pack of shifters. They saw the scar."

Scott finished his drink with a slurp of the straw. "I thought we'd taken care of everything in Palm Springs."

"Not quite," the vampire explained. "Those lower-level demons were still coming through a portal we didn't know about. Apparently, there are hundreds of them."

"Oops!" The younger man shrugged. "My bad."

Dick narrowed his eyes at Lexi. "What are you looking at?" He turned in his seat.

She nodded toward a table near them. "That table of three guys is now only two guys. I'm going to check on Betsy."

Before she could take a step toward the bathroom, Betsy came through the crowd with a dazzling smile. "I'm ready to go when you are."

They moved together to leave the restaurant. At the door, Lexi turned and as the crowd parted, saw the third creepy guy on the floor near the restroom, cupping his balls. She smiled.

On the street, she took the older woman's arm. "Have I told you that you are an absolute joy to be around?"

"Why Lexi, how sweet of you to say that." Betsy looked puzzled for a moment. "Where are we going now?"

"Dick has found somewhere else to stay. We have a place too if we want it. We're going to have a look," Scott explained.

As they wandered along Bourbon Street past the revelers, Lexi realized that she received a few strange stares. Not only that, people crossed the street to avoid her.

Dick had noticed it too. "Shifters are worse gossips than old ladies."

"Hey." Betsy tottered closer and thumped his bicep.

He took her arm. "I'm sorry, but I don't think a jury of your peers would find you guilty of being over twenty-five."

She smiled and raised her chin. "I'm thirty-two today."

"Hmm." He studied her for a moment. "You looked less trouble when you were eighteen."

The woman giggled.

They turned a couple of corners and stopped halfway down the street at a door beneath a gallery covered with baskets of flowers.

"This is delightful."

Lexi smiled. Betsy looked young but spoke like she was from another time, which of course, she was.

"I bet there's no gym or rooftop pool," Scott muttered.

They made their way to the third floor where the two apartments were located.

Dick produced a key and handed it to Scott. "Here's yours." He dangled another in the air. "And here's ours, Betsy dear. You'll have your own room and I'll feel better knowing where you are."

"Come on then, jailer, let me in." The woman smirked and rolled her eyes.

As always, Lexi walked into their apartment first. It was surprisingly modern, decorated in subtle grays with polished hardwood floors and modern furnishings. The only indication that the building was old was the high ceiling. The air-conditioning, along with ceiling fans, made the air crisp and cool, and she sighed.

She made her usual check of the rooms and ended in the bedrooms. One had a king-sized bed and the other held two queens. Even with two bedrooms, she knew they would bunk in one room. Some Kindred habits never left. Both rooms had floor-to-ceiling windows and doors onto the balcony at the front of the building.

Satisfied, she wandered across the hallway and into the other apartment. Being on the back of the building and closed in on both sides, it had no windows. It was perfect for a vampire.

Scott appeared in the doorway. "Do you want me to scoot back for the bags?"

Betsy shook her head. "Not for me. I'll need to pack. I'm afraid I went through the new clothes like a Tasmanian devil and they're everywhere." She headed into Lexi and Scott's apartment to have a look at it.

"I can bear witness to the fact that they are indeed everywhere." Dick rolled his eyes. "I haven't even opened the trunk yet—"

"Say no more." Scott disappeared.

Lexi returned to their apartment and stood at the doors to the balcony.

Betsy came in behind her. "What a lovely balcony." She stood beside her and stared out. "What will you do while I play the tourist?"

She retrieved the photograph she carried and stared at her young face smiling at her. "First, I'll go to where this was taken to see if it rings any bells. I'm not hopeful, though, and I suspect this memory is lost with a thousand others, wiped by Kindred." She returned the photograph to her pocket. "Then, I'll see a local witch, someone

Dolores knows. She'll give me access to records about Kindred activity here about ten years ago. We might be able to trace the man in the picture."

Scott reappeared with Dick's trunk. He set it down, vanished again, and returned two minutes later with his and Lexi's bags. With a small smile, he passed the toothbrush and knife to Lexi. "I repaired the wall. The toothbrush was really embedded."

Her face colored. "Let's head to the hotel. Betsy can gather her gear and we can check out properly." The four of them locked the apartments and wandered downstairs.

Once on the street, they began to walk in the direction of Bourbon Street and their hotel beyond it. A clatter of footsteps made them all turn. A girl of about eleven or twelve years old ran toward Lexi. "You're needed," the youngster said, a little out of breath. "I been looking for you all over."

"Excuse me?" She was perplexed.

"There's been a robbery. They said to come get you." The girl was insistent and Lexi could sense that she was a shifter, although she was probably too young to have shifted yet.

Betsy glanced up and down the street. "Honey, maybe you should call the police. Don't you have an adult with you?"

"It's a community problem. I was told to come get *you*." The girl attempted to pull her now, her expression urgent.

Dick frowned at her. "Isn't this something your pack can deal with?"

"She's supposed to come. It's her job," the girl hollered and the words seemed to echo in the street.

Lexi looked up quickly and confirmed that a few people had stopped to watch them. Her gaze scanned the buildings, where people watched from windows.

"Fine, I'll come." She turned to Dick and Betsy. "Would you mind dropping our key card at the front desk?" She slid it from her pocket and passed it to him.

The two friends followed the messenger. Within a few minutes, she'd led them to the corner of a street and pointed to a store where a small crowd had gathered. "Over there." She ran quickly down the street before they could ask any other questions.

They stopped on the corner to speak, still a short distance away from the crowd.

"What do you want to do?" Scott asked. "We could simply leave town."

"What I want to do is run in the opposite direction like she did." Lexi pointed at the girl who'd already covered considerable ground. She sighed and thought for a moment. "With Kindred out of town, we won't have a better chance to follow up on the photograph, though. Okay, they think we're Kindred so let's be Kindred until we can get out of this."

They crossed the street and approached the store. She noted its name with a small frown. The Museum of Death wasn't what she'd have chosen for a tourist outlet, but maybe her experiences left her a little cynical.

She studied the crowd and briefly caught the gaze of an old man with dreadlocks who wore a monk-like cowl and carried what looked like a wizard's staff. He narrowed his eyes as he returned her gaze, then nodded once.

Weird.

A man stood in the doorway with keys in his hand and she focused on him. "So, what happened?"

He raked his fingers through his hair. "We think there's been a robbery."

"You think?" Lexi glanced at the small crowd and confirmed that the guy with the staff had disappeared as she'd suspected he would.

The key-holder continued. "The alarm on the front door tripped. When I got here, the door was unlocked—apparently from the inside —and a glass display case inside was shattered. We're not sure if anything has been taken as the manager's on vacation. I've looked after the place but I don't know the exhibit well. I can't tell what, if anything, is gone. I was told if anything happened to not call the police but to contact the owner's friend, Alice."

A woman stepped forward, who she guessed was Alice. "I tried calling but no one picked up. In the end, I had to send the kid out." Okay, so she wasn't Alice and was most likely the mother of the young girl.

"No worries. Let's see what we have." Lexi entered the museum and turned to find Scott still standing outside. He looked like he was working himself up to enter the building. Even with her stunted legacy abilities, Lexi could feel the presence of something within and already knew he wouldn't like it at all.

Once inside, he looked around and his face darkened.

They followed the man through a curtain to a back room.

He pointed at the coffin on a stand. "This isn't usually open. I think someone sneaked into it and climbed out after we'd closed for the night."

"Are you sure it wasn't only a prank? Maybe you should have simply called the cops." She looked at a shelf that held things in jars she'd rather not have seen.

The sorcerer gazed around. "There are…things in here. Things that aren't safe to be removed."

'That's why we called you," the man agreed.

Lexi looked at a row of death masks on the wall and scratched her scar absently.

This place is as creepy as hell.

Their guide pointed to a pile of broken glass in a cabinet with a few objects protruding from it. "This is the case they broke."

She looked at the glass. "I see that. Is everything usually left in darkness at night?"

"Back here is, yes."

"And no CCTV?"

"It's being upgraded. We're kind of between systems." He shrugged apologetically.

"Okay, leave us to work." She was keen to get out of this little shop of horrors.

The man walked through the curtain without protest and left them alone.

Scott gazed around. "I can't see the reflective surfaces being of much help if it was dark." He stood in the center of the room, faced the casket, and closed his eyes. She stood out of the way as he moved his hands in circles.

A shift in the air gathered a swirl of dust before it coalesced into the shape of a young woman with long hair seated in the casket. She dropped nimbly to the floor and looked around before she approached the case. Her hand rested on a photograph at the back of it for a moment before she retrieved some kind of implement, which she used to shatter the glass. She reached down, jerked back and appeared to look at her hand, then picked something up and ran out of the room.

Lexi walked to the picture. It was the only thing still upright above the mess of glass and artifacts.

"Hi," she shouted.

The man pushed through the curtain.

She tapped the woman's face. "This picture—who is it?"

He gaped at her. "Are you kidding?"

"Listen, I've had a long day and night."

"It's Marie Laveau. The Voodoo Queen."

"Oh right, of course." Even she had heard of her. "And what was directly in front of the picture?"

The man stared at the mess. "I think it was her ring."

"Okay. Don't touch anything with your hands." She removed a sharp-tipped knife from her pocket and handed it to him. "See if it's missing."

His expression a little anxious, he stooped and poked through the glass with the blade. "There's blood here."

Scott's eyebrows raised and his mouth opened, but she shook her head discreetly.

After a few moments, the man stood and handed the knife to her. "Yes, there's a ring missing."

Lexi slid it into her pocket. "It looks like a small, slim girl hid in the coffin, broke the cabinet and took the ring, and ran. See if any staff members can remember someone fitting that description entering the museum today. In the meantime, we're done here for now."

They walked out and headed toward the apartment.

"What do you think?" Scott asked as they walked.

"I think the real Kindred can deal with it when they get back. We have our own stuff to do."

He nodded. "Is that why you didn't want me to take the blood for a locator spell?"

"Exactly! I won't reveal myself for a two-bit crime like this. Hopefully, we'll be out of town by tomorrow."

"I wish you hadn't said that." He grimaced. "It always feels like you jinx us when you say that."

They reached their building and she put her hand out to open the door when it was thrust open.

CHAPTER THIRTY-TWO

Dick stared at the katana a fraction of an inch away from Betsy's face. "Lexi, you are not to kill Betsy. She's my dearest friend."

Lexi slid the blade into her pocket. "I was preparing to defend myself."

"Against me? The most dangerous thing I'll ever approach you with will be a cupcake." The woman laughed but it was a little strained.

Scott checked his watch. "Where are you two going? It's after two am."

The vampire extended his arm to his companion. "Betsy's never seen The French Quarter so I'm giving her a tour."

Betsy took his arm but before they walked away, she turned to Lexi. "What happened with the little girl?"

"It was a break-in at a creepy death museum. Someone stole…" She looked at Scott.

Scott rolled his eyes. "Marie Laveau."

"Marie Laveau's ring," she finished. "She was some kind of—"

Dick held a hand up. "I know who Marie Laveau was. Lexi, your education is somewhat lacking."

The older woman's eyes widened. "Did you catch the perp?"

Everyone looked at her.

"The perp?" Dick asked and fought to hide a smile.

"Yes, dear. The unsub." She seemed to be warming to her subject.

The vampire put his other hand over hers and addressed Lexi. "Marcel's snoring his little head off in the apartment. We collected our bags from the hotel and settled up. Come along, Nancy Drew."

"Have fun," Scott called from behind them as they headed up the street.

Betsy rested her head on Dick's arm for a few moments, then looked at him. "How long did you live here?"

"A few years. Not long. It's good to be back, though. New Orleans has a way of getting under your skin, even if the heat is somewhat uncomfortable for someone of my disposition."

They approached a street corner and he led them purposefully straight ahead. She glanced at him. "Where are we going?"

He patted her hand. "I think my oldest friend should meet some of my oldest silent friends."

They chatted as they walked through the streets while he pointed out hotels, stores, and bars he knew, although many had changed since he'd last been there. Finally, they reached a metal gate.

"A cemetery?" Betsy stopped abruptly.

"You're safe with me, dear. I like to check up on who's no longer with us since I was here last."

He guided her through the side gate and they walked along the narrow, tomb-lined paths.

The moon was almost full, which allowed her to read the tombstones as they passed. "Were the friends you're looking for all supernaturals?"

"Heavens, no. Some are, of course." He stopped facing a small family plot. "This is Marianne. I stayed with her while I waited for my house to be renovated. I see her son has joined her. He didn't like me very much—in fact, he assaulted me."

"He what? I hope you beat him senseless." Betsy shook her fist in the air.

"I couldn't catch him. He kicked me and ran away. He was quite fast for a five-year-old." Dick touched the stone plaque. "That was forty years ago. Forty-five is very young to die, isn't it?"

Betsy looked at the stone, then at him again. "You must have died around the same age."

Dick merely nodded.

Along the next aisle, they stopped before a large, ornate tomb. "This is Stephen and many of his ancestors. He was the alpha of a local shifter pack. I had tremendous respect for Stephen. Everyone did. He was fair and forward-thinking."

"He liked you too," a voice said behind them.

They turned toward it and he narrowed his eyes to stare at a woman with long hair he thought might be equal parts of gray and brown. She looked gaunt. "Geraldine? Why, you've barely changed."

"You're kind, but I think there have been one or two changes between twenty and sixty." She walked forward but stopped a little distance from them.

The vampire didn't move but he introduced the women. Betsy stepped up to the other woman and put her hand out. "It's lovely to meet a friend of William's."

Geraldine flicked her gaze briefly to him and they shared a look that said, "Humans, they haven't a clue," and she shook the proffered hand.

Dick looked around. "This is a strange place to find the living at such an hour."

The newcomer shrugged. "I'm contemplating my mortality and visiting old friends." She broke into a wracking cough and it took her a few seconds to regain her composure. "Are you here to choose a side?"

He smelled blood on her breath, took a handkerchief out, and stepped closer to her, holding it out like a white flag. "Good heavens, no. I'm trying to avoid whatever's going on and I certainly don't want to be here when this place finally erupts. I can't get out of here fast enough."

She took the handkerchief and wiped her mouth. "Did you know Kindred left?"

"I heard they're back already." He thought it might be prudent to bolster Lexi's fake Kindred identity.

Geraldine raised her eyebrows. "Really? I'm surprised. As I understand it, something has happened to draw them across the country, but it's not entirely an accident they left no one here."

Dick stepped to Betsy's side. "Do you think they're looking the other way? Leaving the city unprotected? But why?"

She held the handkerchief up but he gestured for her to keep it. She stuffed it into her pocket. "They aren't always as impartial as we'd like them to be."

"Well no, that's true, but who do you complain to—Congress?"

The woman barked a laugh and began to cough again. She yanked the handkerchief out.

"I think, in this instance, your concerns might be unfounded. I know what's been going on across the country and Kindred weren't even aware of it until it had mostly all blown over."

"Well, I've been wrong before. Time will tell." Geraldine walked forward and touched her family tomb. "So, do you plan to spend your final moments reminiscing in front of my father's tomb?"

"My final? Oh!" In his melancholy mood, he'd failed to consider the sun's imminent rise.

Her brow furrowed. "You don't have family here, do you?"

"No. No, I don't." He knew what she was asking—"Do you have a family tomb to hop into?" Happily, the answer was no, but he didn't know what else to do. He didn't want anyone to know he could walk in the sun and hoped Betsy wouldn't say anything. A little disconcerted, he looked around. While he could reach cover at vamp speed, he wouldn't leave his friend there alone.

"I'm sure my father wouldn't forgive me if I allowed you to fry in front of him." Geraldine unscrewed a bolt and removed the front stone from her family tomb. It would have been heavy but even at sixty, her shifter strength made it appear as though it were no heavier than cardboard.

Dick looked inside the tomb with horror. His gaze darted about, looking for a reason to not have to climb in there wearing a designer suit.

"Come along dear, hop in. We can't have you flaming up, can we?" Betsy appeared to be enjoying it.

He glowered at her. "Yes, of course. Right." Reluctantly, he slid feet first onto the top shelf.

"There's a good man. I'll pop back for you at sunset, shall I?" His so-called friend could barely contain her glee.

Geraldine prepared to replace the stone. "You're lucky. They took the bricks from the front and pushed Dad down the back a few months ago when I got my diagnosis. I've had a reprieve of sorts so I won't be joining him quite yet, but it'll be soon enough."

"Geraldine, I'm sorry to hear that. Thank you so much for this. You're exactly like your father." He looked at Betsy, who still grinned unashamedly. "Betsy dear. Without the bricks on the face, the light will come in along the edges. I'll need you here to block the sun."

Her jaw dropped.

"In you hop." He patted the stone ledge.

With the shifter safely behind her, she gave him a withering look. She sighed and rolled her eyes to acknowledge that she knew she'd been caught by her smart mouth and climbed up.

Geraldine replaced the front stone. "Don't do anything in there to disgrace my father's memory."

"Geraldine!" Dick was horrified.

They listened to her laugh and cough as she walked away.

Betsy wriggled in an effort to get comfortable. Finally, she rested her head on his chest. "We won't be here until sunset, will we?"

"No. We'll give it half an hour or so, then make good our escape."

She stretched to touch the wall. "I think this would be the hardest part for me."

He looked down and spoke to the top of her head. "We don't usually sleep in tombs."

"Not that, silly." She slapped his shoulder, then sighed. "Everyone dying. Friends, family, loved ones. Making friends knowing you'll lose them. Falling in love, knowing—"

The vampire kissed the top of her head. "You've always had an incredible knack for getting to the heart of things."

She was silent for a moment before she asked, "What happened? In Europe."

"Oh, the usual story. Boy meets boy. Boy takes part in inadvisable practices and dies. Boy comes back."

"When you came back as your grandson, Harv and I used to talk about all the ways you were so similar to our William. But we'd talk about the differences too."

"I think people see what they want to see."

"No. I think in many ways, you are different. You were quite the hot-head, exuberant and excitable. When you returned as your grand-son…" Betsy straightened suddenly and hit her head. "Ouch. What was that? Your heartbeat?"

Dick chuckled and rubbed her head. "It does now and then. I like to think that vampirism isn't a true death. It's merely…very close."

She settled again. "What will happen to you, when you die?"

"Do you mean heaven or hell?"

"No, you goose. I mean your body."

"Well, I recall you once told me you and Harv held a lovely memo-rial service for me. So that's already done. I suppose I'll simply blow away in the wind one day."

"I don't think so. I'll leave instructions with Lexi and Dolores that when you go, you're to be buried with us in the family plot. I think Harv would like that."

Dick was choked up. He knew, if Betsy could see in this dark place, she'd see tears welling in his eyes and cleared his throat. "Come on, she's gone. Let's get out of here. God knows what this has done to my suit."

"And my dress." Betsy shuffled out of the way to allow him access to the front.

"I suppose, but I care less about that." He unscrewed the bolt and peered through the brickwork at the top.

Satisfied that they were unobserved, he climbed out and lifted her to the ground.

She was laughing. "Dick, you really know how to show a girl a good time."

He smiled. "In my defense, showing girls a good time has never been my forté."

"Do you not mind being called Dick?"

"I'll tell you a secret but you must never tell Lexi." He paused until she nodded. "I rather like it. It's like being a secret agent with a new identity. Dolores will make me a new passport and driving license for my Dick identity when I've decided on a surname."

They dusted their clothes off as best they could and wandered toward the exit. Betsy read names out from the tombs as they went. "What about Trudeau. Dick Trudeau."

He tried it. "Dick Trudeau. No, too many hard consonants."

"Dick Nicholas?"

"Dick Nick?" He raised an eyebrow.

"Oh, good point. Ooh, here's a good one. Grayson. Dick Grayson. That sounds—"

"Familiar? Dick Grayson is the Boy Wonder. I am no one's Robin."

"You're kind of Lexi's Robin." She smiled.

"That's Scott. He is Lexi's Robin. I'm more like—"

"Batgirl?" Betsy laughed.

"Betsy!"

The vampire stopped at a tomb covered in writing with beads and other paraphernalia scattered at its base. "This is Marie Laveau's tomb."

She put a finger out and touched a marking of XXX. "Lipstick?" She frowned at her fingertip, which was now red.

"The three Xs are voodoo prayers to Marie. This is how people usually get her attention rather than stealing her jewelry. Do you have any requests while we're here?"

The woman patted the tomb. "I think I have everything I'll ever want and more than I could ask for." She turned to him. "Let's go to the apartment. It looks like we'll both sleep through the day."

As they walked through the Quarter, he mulled over Betsy's last response.

Women really are a mystery.

CHAPTER THIRTY-THREE

Three hours later, the morning was overcast and hot as the street cleaners made their way through the Quarter. They moved down sidewalks and swept disposable cocktail cups into the street to be gathered by street cleaning vehicles that moved slowly and loudly behind them.

Lexi and Scott entered Jackson Square.

"I heard it raining in the night. It belted down for all of ten minutes. Why is there no difference to the humidity? This can't be normal." She tried to adjust her leather vest as they walked.

A man in a business suit stared as he passed. She gave him her warning look and he averted his eyes.

They stopped roughly halfway across the width of the square and stood before the doors of the cathedral. She retrieved the photograph, looked from it to their current position, and estimated that they were roughly in the same place now as she had been all those years before.

In silence, she turned in a circle and scanned the area.

Scott looked from her to the cathedral doors and back again. "Anything?"

She turned the corners of her mouth down in an exaggerated

frown and shook her head. "Not a thing." Irritated, she shoved the picture into her pocket.

They continued to wander around the square. She turned to her companion and pretended not to notice the hostile looks she received from the fortune-tellers seated at tables, where they prepared their little street businesses for the day ahead. "Did Dolores get back to you about her contact here?"

"She's setting up a meeting and she'll call later this morning," he replied absently. He wasn't looking at faces and instead, stared at the tabletops as they passed.

"What are you looking at?" Lexi focused on the tables too.

"I'm curious to see which tarot decks and other forms of divination they use." He glanced at her before he returned to his curious study. "Professional curiosity."

Lexi pulled him out of the way of an oncoming bicycle. "Professional curiosity? Since when have you ever used props like cards or tea leaves? I didn't think that was the way of a mage and his sorcery."

"It's not really. They take magic from the earth and I take it from the air. We use it differently too, but it's essentially the same magic."

Scott turned away from the tables after receiving many suspicious looks. "I'll be happy to get out of here. God knows how the local Kindreds cope. These people are so hostile it makes me uncomfortable."

"Same here." Lexi adjusted her vest again. *In so many ways.* "Kindred are probably the ones to blame. I don't know how they run this town but I can guess."

As they turned onto Decatur, two men approached. The large one smiled at her to reveal a gold tooth and the other held a bottle and a rag. She glanced at the bottle and wondered if it was chloroform. The men moved directly toward them.

"Good morning, my friend." The large man addressed Scott. "I bet I can tell you where you got your shoes."

"I'm sorry?" He frowned in confusion.

"I can tell you the city, the state, and the exact name of the place." He smiled at the sorcerer in a friendly way that put Lexi's guard up.

He looked at his low-tops. They were regular Converse.

The man continued. "I can tell you where you got them. If I'm wrong, I'm gone."

She was about to tell the guy to take a hike when Scott grinned. "Okay."

"My name is Tyrone and this here is Julian. What's your name, my man?"

"Scott."

"Well, Scott. If I'm right, you'll tell me the truth, okay? Shake my hand." The man held his hand out and he shook it.

While they were shaking hands, the other man crouched and squibbed a creamy substance from the bottle onto the front of Scott's Converse.

"Hey!" The young man was surprised.

The man leaned toward Lexi's boots and she stepped back quickly. He glanced into her eyes and returned his attention to Scott's feet, took the rag, and polished his trainers.

Tyrone continued to talk. "I said I'd tell you where you got your shoes—the city, the state, and the exact place. Well, I can tell you, my friend, you got those shoes on your feet, in the city of New Orleans, in the state of Louisiana, and the exact place is right here on Decatur. That'll be forty dollars—twenty dollars each for the shoeshine." He flashed the gold tooth again.

"I didn't do the lady," Julian told his friend. The large man glanced at her and she simply inclined her head with her brow raised. He looked at Scott with a smile. "Twenty dollars."

The sorcerer's jaw dropped. He looked at Lexi and she smirked in response. As he focused on the man again, his cheeks colored. Then, to her surprise, he grinned. "You totally got me."

"Yes, sir, we did." Tyrone smiled.

Scott withdrew a twenty from his pocket and passed it to the guy. "I've paid more for a valuable lesson. Thank you, guys." He shook both their hands and they continued.

"Considering you basically got mugged, you look remarkably happy." Lexi's eyes narrowed.

He pointed across the street to the Café Du Mondé, "Beignets! I've been dying to try them."

As they crossed the street, a scream made her glance over her shoulder. Tyrone's pants were on fire. He yanked a pile of burning dollars from his pocket and dropped them wildly. While he patted the flames on his pants out, his friend stamped on the burning money, but the blaze didn't extinguish until all the money had turned to ash.

Scott skipped ahead of her and opened the café door. She raised an eyebrow at him as he smiled and looked at the overcast sky. "It looks like a beautiful day for learning, all round."

They ordered at the counter and waited until the coffee arrived alongside beignets, barely visible under a mountain of powdered sugar. Scott took one but made the rookie error of breathing in as he went to stuff it into his mouth. The result was the inhalation of a sizable portion of sugar and a coughing fit that drew the attention of everyone in the cafe.

"Good work, slugger." Lexi grinned.

He took a long sip of his coffee, then wiped his wet eyes.

She had been looking forward to trying the square sugar-laden donuts. While she'd seen them elsewhere, she'd always felt you had to try them for the first time in New Orleans. Now, she wondered if this *was* the first time. She could have been in this cafe, even in this seat, and still have no recollection of it.

It wasn't a pleasant thought and she took a breath—well out of range of the powdered sugar—and drew the tasty-looking morsel toward her mouth. She halted her hand a few inches away, suddenly aware of a small face very close to hers. Her gaze slid to the right. It was the young girl who'd found her the night before.

Lexi sighed and turned her face fully to the girl. "Is there some kind of tracking device on me that I have yet to find?"

The youngster put her hand on her jacket. "You have to come."

She looked at her beignet and then the girl. "I'm kind of having a moment here."

In response, she tugged at her sleeve. "They said you have to come."

"Listen." She replaced the beignet and turned in her seat. "We've looked at the crime scene. We're on the case, totally all over it—"

"It's not the museum." Scott stared intently at the youngster. "Someone's died, haven't they?"

The messenger nodded.

Shit!

"Can we get these to go, please?" Lexi asked the server. She grasped Scott's hand for a quick boost of magical energy.

The two friends left the café and followed their young guide. They neared the crime scene and she was aware of Scott staring as she slid a finger down the front of her vest, then sucked powdered sugar from it. "What? I missed it."

He raised an eyebrow and shook his head. "Nothing. Are we going up?"

"I'll go first. You check the gawkers." She looked at the crowd of locals who had gathered. Once again, she met the gaze of the man in the cowl and turned to her friend. "Make sure you speak to Dreadlock Gandalf over there."

Scott looked up. "Who?"

When she turned to point at the man, there was no sign of him. "This town is so creepy." She shook her head, dusted sugar from her vest, and passed the beignet bag to him. "They were so good. I left you one." With one last swipe of her mouth, Lexi headed into the building and up to the second-floor apartment. She stared at the corpse and examined it from every angle as she tried to work out what was supposed to go where. Hands down, she would swear she'd never seen a corpse as fucked up as this one, and given the condition she'd left some creatures in, that was saying something. When someone entered the room, she ignored them.

A man spoke from behind her. "It amazes me how you people always get here before—whoa!"

She glanced at the newcomer. The tall, handsome, African American man gazed slack-jawed at the body. He pulled a Dictaphone from an inside pocket, which revealed a glimpse of his police badge. She kicked herself mentally for not preparing for this. He would ask for her name and ID. Things were about to get awkward. She allowed her thumb to stray to the scar in case she needed to send him to sleep.

He stepped beside her. In her peripheral vision, she could see him tilt his head in the same way she'd done. When he lifted the Dictaphone, he merely opened and closed his mouth as though unsure where to start. Finally, he began to speak into the device. "Male victim, late teens or early twenties, African American—"

Lexi passed him two wallets hanging side by side from the blade of her stiletto knife and he stopped speaking. He took them in a gloved hand, flipped one open, then the other.

Clicking the recorder back on, he continued "Jamal Simpson, nineteen. Torso has been completely splayed. Front and back of the body are both visible. We might be looking for a butcher."

She turned to face him. "A butcher?"

The cop nodded as he switched his recorder off. "You can't tell from this angle, but I'm willing to bet his spine's missing."

"It's not missing," she protested.

He rolled his eyes. "You know you're not supposed to disturb the scene."

"I haven't touched him. It's over there." She pointed a thumb behind her.

The man turned and grimaced at the gory display of a spine hung from a floor lamp.

"Well, I assume it's his." Lexi shrugged. "You said a butcher."

The cop turned to the body again. "Someone big and very strong, given the strength required to rip out a human spine. He's been spatchcocked, also known as butterflying. It's usually done to chickens. In fact, I do it to chickens when I'm barbecuing, but I don't think I'll do that for a while. The backbone is removed, the back ribs pulled apart, and the breastplate flattened."

"Oh yes, I see the bloody footprints." She nodded and he continued. "Then the legs and wings—or in this case, arms—are spread to allow fast, even cooking."

Lexi frowned. "How big is the oven here? And what do you think the white stuff is?" She inspected the smears of white over the boy's skin.

"It's not mixed with the blood, so I'd say that's an oil-based theatrical paint. He's clearly an amateur or he'd use flour if he was going to use anything." He looked at the floor and poked at a pair of short shorts and a spaghetti string top with the toe of his shoe. "Is there any sign of the girl?"

She shook her head. "Amy? No, but I only just got here."

He looked at the ID and confirmed the girl's name with a nod.

A cop called from outside the room. "Detective Broullard, one coming in."

Lexi felt Scott's presence. The cop turned to him. "Who are you?"

"Scott. I'm—"

"He's with me," she explained, then diverted his attention before he asked exactly who she was. "There seem to be a few ritual pieces here."

"I'm happy to leave that to you if I can. Of course, it'll have to be bagged and tagged but I'll leave it for you to work your mojo." Broullard moved across the room to get a closer look at the spine, which gave Scott a full view of the corpse.

"Oh! Oh!" He lurched out the door.

The man's gaze followed his rapid retreat. "What's with him?"

"I'm training him." Lexi studied the grisly scene, taking in the bowls, cups, beads, and bones scattered about the floor.

Broullard gestured toward the corpse. "So, is this one of yours or one of ours?"

Yours or ours. She had assumed, by this point, that he was directly connected to Kindred in some way. It seemed the police there had a working relationship with Kindred she'd not experienced elsewhere. Many of her ex-employer's organization were police officers but their Kindred affiliation was certainly not in the open and they never trusted non-Kindred officers.

"Well?" She glanced toward the door.

"Ours," Scott's muffled voice said from the hallway.

"Okay, I'll wait outside. You have about a half-hour until the uniforms get here. I'll let you do your thing." Broullard headed to the door.

"Be careful you don't step in the vomit," she called,

The cop looked around the floor. "What vomit?"

A moment later, they heard the sound of Scott throwing up in the hallway.

He tilted his head toward the door. "First day on the job?"

"Something like that." Lexi rolled her eyes and refocused on the corpse.

She waited for the cops to retreat, then stuck her head out the door. "Are you ready?"

Scott nodded. He still looked miserably green but followed her into the apartment.

The sorcerer looked around the room and his gaze traced the blood spatter trails up the walls and drapes, clearly trying to avoid the body. "Strange, there are no mirrors in this room. I don't see anything shiny enough to get a playback." He waved his hands experimentally. "And not much dust." He lowered his hands and sighed. "They don't make this easy. All right, then."

He held his arm out with his palm up and muttered a few words, and a ball of light grew in his hand. It elevated and spun above the body.

"What's it doing?" The light moved so fast, Lexi couldn't maintain her focus on it.

"It's following the path of anything magical in the room."

They watched as it bounced across the room from Jamal, over to the spine, back to the victim, through the couch and finally, it rocketed out the side of the couch, significantly smaller, and into a large cupboard at the bottom of a wooden shelving unit. It didn't come out.

She turned to her friend. "What does that mean?"

Scott put his finger to his lips and pointed at the cupboard.

Her eyes widened and she hurried to the apartment door. "Broullard?" She dug her hand into her dimensional pocket and drew the katana.

The cop entered and raised his eyebrows at the blade. He opened his mouth to speak but when she signaled silently to the cupboard, he nodded and drew his gun.

She motioned for Scott to stay back and she and the officer crept forward.

Broullard yanked the door open and she brought the katana to within an inch of the girl's face. Her eyes were wide but there was no reaction.

"Amy, I presume." She withdrew the sword.

"Is she dead?" Scott leaned around her.

"No, catatonic." She felt the girl's neck and found a pulse but couldn't see any injuries. Amy was curled in her underwear and covered in blood, but none of it seemed to be hers. Lexi looked at Scott. "Can you bring her out of it?"

"I'm not sure this is the best place for that." He indicated the mangled corpse without looking at it. "If she sees that, her mind will probably close up again."

"Okay, let's see if we can get her out of this cupboard first." She took the girl's right arm and Broullard leaned forward to take her left one but jumped back and struck his head on the top of the cupboard.

"Shit!" He gestured to Amy's other side as he rubbed his head.

When she leaned into the cupboard, she saw why he had jumped. The young woman's hand was clenched tightly around a gore-covered machete.

CHAPTER THIRTY-FOUR

L exi finished describing the scene. She'd left many of the details out in front of Betsy, who was still clearly horrified.

"That's simply awful. What happens to her now?" The older woman shuddered. She stood from her seat at the table on the balcony overlooking the street and took her coffee cup inside.

Scott put his feet onto the chair she had vacated. "They were able to walk her out of the apartment but she wasn't there mentally. She's in the hospital now, cuffed to the bed until the scene gets processed."

Betsy turned. "But I thought the detective said she wouldn't have been strong enough to do that."

He nodded. "He thinks she's a victim but with no other suspects, they have to be careful. Personally, I think it was her. There was magic all over the scene but no indication of it entering or leaving the room. The trail faded and stopped around Amy."

Dick was seated against the wall in the room and remained out of sight until the sun went down. "What will you do? I'm sure Kindred won't be gone for much longer."

Lexi slapped her friend's arm. "Feet!" He put them down hastily. "It's a murder so I can't not investigate it. If it wasn't Amy who did it, there's a psycho on the loose."

Betsy washed her cup and put it on the sink. "But isn't that the job for the police? If they have the girl and the body, surely they'll investigate it."

Scott turned in his chair to look at her. "Incredibly strong magic was present in that room. It's not a job for the regular police to investigate alone. I guess that's why this Broullard guy is on it."

The vampire spoke from behind the wall. "So, what's next?"

"I came here for a reason. Dolores has sent us the name of her contact, so I'll see her before I do anything else."

At an unexpected knock, they all looked toward the door.

"That was my door." Dick stood and moved to the peephole.

Lexi walked across to join him. She mouthed, "Who is it?"

He looked at her, shrugged, and moved aside to allow her to look. All she could see was the back of the man's head and a key in his hand. She waited until he had it in the lock before she opened her door quickly.

"Can I help you?" she snapped.

The man jumped and turned with shock on his face. "I'm… I clean these apartments."

She studied him suspiciously. "What's your name?"

The guy looked into the corner and said "Erm…Mike."

It was clear he was lying, and not very well. She looked into the hallway to check for anyone else, then stepped out. "Well, Erm-Mike, that apartment is occupied by someone who likes to sleep late."

"Oh, I see. Well, I'll come back later." He turned to walk away.

"Erm-Mike?" Lexi leaned against the wall with her arms folded.

He paused and looked over his shoulder.

She smiled sweetly. "Don't you want to clean this apartment?"

"Oh, well…"

"And where's your mop and bucket?"

The guy ran.

Lexi touched the scar briefly and a second later, Erm-Mike sprawled on his face. As she stepped toward him, she felt a breeze when Dick moved rapidly behind her before his apartment door clicked shut. *Damn, that vamp's fast.*

She held the guy by his shirt collar and sat him against the wall. Her grin widened as she glanced at his feet.

The old shoelace trick.

The handsome young man was clearly petrified and looked down, baffled by the fact that his laces were inexplicably tied together.

Scott stepped into the hallway. "He doesn't seem to have the disposition of a cat burglar, does he?"

"I'm not a thief." He blushed. "I'm a fan."

Lexi's eyebrows raised.

"I was in the bar when he arrived last night. I'm a donor there. I've heard of Mr. Levine and came to offer my services."

Dick shouted through his apartment door. "Who's out there at what-the-fuck-o'clock?"

"See, you woke him." She shook her head. "Come back at a decent time."

"Midnight," the vampire shouted quickly.

She released the man's shirt, returned her apartment, and closed the door.

Dick returned after his visitor had left. "What will you do next about the case?"

Lexi shrugged. "Broullard seemed to think we would know what the voodoo paraphernalia was for. I suppose it's the kind of thing the local Kindred see all the time, but I couldn't tell you what they were trying to do."

He frowned as he poured himself a drink. "Do you know what ingredients they used?"

When she shook her head, he added. "I'll come and take a look. I might see something helpful. If I can't help, I know a guy."

Deep in thought, he held the glass against his bottom lip before he finally took a sip.

She shook her head. "If my legacy senses were better, I could have given you ingredients and quantities."

Betsy glanced at her watch. "I must get ready. I'm going for a walk to soak up the atmosphere." The woman stepped to the mirror on the wall and began to brush her dark, shiny hair. She glanced at Lexi through the reflection a few times before she finally asked, "What exactly is a legacy?"

Her gaze darted around to avoid direct contact. "It's kind of a diplomat."

Dick spat his bourbon across the room and made choking sounds.

The older woman patted his back and turned to her. "I'm not naïve, dear. I know you killed people for Kindred. What I'm asking is how you become legacies and mages."

Lexi smiled. "For the record, I also once rescued a kitten. The job involved more than running around poking people with pointy things."

"Not much more," the vampire muttered.

She gave him a hard stare, then turned to Betsy.

"Kindred also has the ability to send people to The Hollows. It's a prison in its own dimension so they don't always kill transgressors. To answer your question, sorcerers are born. You can't acquire the ability to be one like you can with other magic. Once a sorcerer has been trained to a certain level within Kindred, they are given the title of mage. There are a couple of ways to make a legacy. We can be born directly of the bloodline from a legacy parent, or the legacy blood is introduced to our DNA in a ritual and gives us... Well, it's *supposed* to give us properties of the supernatural creatures who offered their blood for use in the ritual."

"So that's vampires and shifters and fae?" Betsy put the hairbrush down and picked up a pair of earrings.

Lexi smiled. "Yes, and dozens more that you've probably never heard of."

Scott held a finger up. "And one drop of blood from a sorcerer who disguised himself as a witch after being told sorcerers couldn't participate in the ritual because we're too awesome."

She rolled her eyes. "*Not* a single drop of sorcerer blood because legacies are already blood-bound to sorcerers. It was decided that would upset the balance."

"Okay, yes," he conceded, "that part might be a myth—"

"That sorcerers tell other sorcerers. Not one legacy has ever shown sorcerer tendencies." She shook her head at him.

"But if a legacy and a mage have a child, won't the child have sorcerer blood?" the woman asked.

"The offspring of a blood-bonded couple will either be a sorcerer or a legacy or possibly merely a regular human child—" She stopped speaking when she realized Betsy's expression had changed to one of sadness. "What?"

The woman turned to the mirror and once again looked at Lexi's reflection as she put the earrings in. "Maybe that's what happened to you. You could be the child of a mage and a legacy who was born human."

"If that were true, where are my real parents?" She sighed. "But it's not true, the part about being born fully human. I do have slightly enhanced abilities."

Betsy nodded. "So, the alternative is that the ritual didn't work as well with you. Do you know why that could have been?"

"I've never heard of it ever going wrong with anyone else. They told me I was a runaway who elected to go through the legacy ritual, but they lie so I don't know if that's even true. I've met a few other legacies. Some are so connected to the legacy blood in their veins that they can almost shift or move like vamps or sing like sirens."

The older woman turned away from the mirror and faced her, tilting her head. "Do you think the man in the photograph might be your father?"

She shrugged and turned away. Betsy was too perceptive.

The sun had finally made an appearance later in the afternoon, and Lexi fidgeted with her leather vest again as she strode along the sidewalk with Scott. "How far to this place?"

"It's on the next street, I think." Scott took his cell out, opened the maps app, and flicked the little blue cursor. It careened off the screen and hovered ahead of them with its little arrow pointing right.

"Nifty trick." She smiled. He hated it when she used the word "trick" to describe his magic.

He rolled his eyes.

They entered Thought and Memory, a dark little magic and witchcraft store. He immediately began to poke around in baskets and on shelves. A young man with a long, bushy beard shoved a box of sage sticks onto a shelf and approached them. "Can I help you?"

"Could I speak to Anne Bird, please? Tell her it's—"

"I know who she is. Back to work, James." The woman entered from the back of the store. She had long blonde hair and moved confidently toward them. James continued to stack the shelves, while Anne turned to the door she'd walked through. "Sam?"

A voice responded from the room beyond. "Yes, Mom?"

"Where's that box?"

"What bo—" A young woman stuck her head out and took one look at Lexi. Her face darkened. "Oh, *that* box. It's on the shelf behind you under the divining rods." She disappeared into the room again.

Anne went to a shelf behind the checkout and picked up a box about the size of a ream of paper. "Here it is. If you don't mind leaving, I don't want people to see you in here. You're bad for business." She glanced at Scott, her eyes narrowed. He replaced the crystals he'd intended to buy and stepped out of the store.

"Well, thanks." Lexi shrugged, turned away, and followed him.

"Honestly, I feel like I have a big sign on my back saying *Kindred scum*." Lexi glanced over her shoulder to where the proprietor stared at her through the window. "Let's get back to the others."

When they reached the third floor, Lexi darted back onto the staircase, pulling Scott with her, and mouthed, "The apartment door's open."

He whispered a reply. "I gave Betsy a key."

"Why?"

"I don't need it and she likes the balcony." He shrugged.

She rolled her eyes and continued carefully. Sure enough, the woman was on the balcony with a glass of lemonade. She'd removed the enchanted necklace and was an eighty-year-old again who gazed onto the street.

Scott stepped outside. "Hi, Betsy. How are you?"

"I'm very well. It's a little hot out here but the flowers are lovely." She touched a tendril of blooms that trailed from the basket above. "Help me in, dear."

He offered her his arm and she rose slowly, making pained noises.

She sat on a dining chair indoors and fanned herself. "I expect you're wondering why I'm fifty years older again."

As he replied, he closed the balcony door so the air-con could regulate. "I assumed you didn't want to let yourself get lost in the magic and forget who you are."

"Clever boy." Betsy smiled.

"Clever girl," he countered. "I gave it to you because I believe you are wise enough not to be taken over by the magic. The enchantment is for others, not yourself. Of course, there's the benefit of losing the aches and pains but don't overdo it."

Lexi smiled at the two of them. She plucked the shuriken from her vest and sliced through the tape on the box.

The older woman looked at the sharp, intricately designed object. "I do like your little murder brooch. It's very pretty."

She raised an eyebrow. "I think we'll have to watch you."

With a grin, she put the shuriken onto the counter and flipped the box lid open.

"I don't understand." Utterly baffled, she lifted a dark-red fabric vest out and held it up.

"That's pretty, dear." Betsy stretched to feel the fabric. "Linen, I think. It looks more comfortable than the leather one."

Lexi frowned. "I expected documents."

The other woman leaned over the box. "Is there anything else in there? Maybe the documents are hidden to mislead prying eyes."

"No." She lifted the tissue paper to make sure before she looked at Scott. "Is there an enchantment on it?"

He put a hand over the box. "Nope." He took the vest and held it up. "It seems a little heavy for linen." With a small frown, he slid two fingers into a little pocket in the front, pulled a key out, and passed it to her.

She turned it in her hand but saw no distinguishing markings on it. "I'll have to take it back. She's mixed me up with a customer. Maybe she does alterations on the side."

The sorcerer looked more closely at the fabric. "Can I see your shuriken?"

Lexi passed it to him. "Be careful. I don't want to have to pay for this."

He held it next to the vest and let go. It snapped to a hidden magnet in the garment. "There are a few magnets along the front and magnetized pockets for blades, which explains why it's heavy. I think this was definitely meant for you."

She held the key up. "But why hide the key in a vest? And how is a key without a lock supposed to help?"

Scott rolled his eyes and tutted. "I think we're being dense."

"Speak for yourself." Dick walked through the door.

Lexi held her palms up. "Does everyone have a key to this place?"

The vampire waved the key in his hand. "The young man who tried to enter my apartment had a master key. It fits both locks. So, why is everyone but me dense?"

"Dolores must have sent the vest," Scott explained. "Mrs. Bird put the key in it. Try it on. I bet it fits."

She removed six little knives and a length of garrote wire from the lining of the leather vest and tugged at the hem in preparation to lift it off.

The sorcerer spun away, and Dick rolled his eyes and turned.

"Okay, you can look. This is fantastic." Lexi turned in the linen vest.

"It's lined and feels so cool. What a revelation." She clicked the ornate shuriken into place on the front. "This material's amazing. I need to find out if they do pants in this."

"Yes, I *think* they do pants in linen." Dick drawled with sarcasm. He shook his head. "I need to dress for dinner. Then we can head to your crime scene and I can be back in time for my new little friend."

Her brow creased. "I thought you were on the blood bags."

"There's no sense in looking a gift horse in the mouth." He grinned. "He smelled very healthy."

"I'll get ready too." Betsy walked slowly to the other apartment.

Dick watched her go. "That woman is remarkable. If she were a man, I'd marry her."

Scott laughed. "Don't tell her that or she'll ask for a new necklace to help her grow things she ought not to grow."

The vampire's eyes widened. "Scott! She was married to my best friend."

"It never ceases to amaze me how the object of someone's affections can remain so oblivious." The young man shook his head. "If I were to guess, I'd say she was in love with you long before your friend."

The other man shook his head firmly. "That's positively ridiculous. Betsy and Harv are one of the greatest love stories of a generation. All the girls wanted Harv and all the boys wanted Betsy. She had the looks of Lauren Bacall, the grace of Audrey Hepburn, and the humor of Doris Day." He turned to face Scott. "And if you say, "who?" so help me I'll—"

"Calm down. I've heard of the middle one," the sorcerer assured him.

"But you always looked like you," Betsy said as she entered as a woman in her thirties in a silk dressing gown. She went to the table at the mirror and retrieved her hairbrush. "Better looking than Clark, classier than Cary, and probably more gay than Rock." She patted Dick's face before she retreated to the other apartment again.

Five minutes later, she was back. "The bathroom's all yours."

They sat at a table in the Napoleon House restaurant and looked at the menu.

"Have I turned into an eighty-year-old again?" Betsy asked.

Scott looked up. "No. Why?"

She pinched the bridge of her nose. "I can't see a word on this menu."

"It is a little dim in here." Lexi agreed and glanced at the ceiling.

"The lighting in here is more a hint of light—a suggestion for atmospheric purposes." Dick took the menu and read it to the older woman.

When he reached Jambalaya, she called a halt. "That's the one for me!"

Lexi and Scott ordered po' boys, and the vampire asked for a double Jack Daniels and "keep them coming."

Betsy put her hand on Dick's arm. "You won't be drunk at a crime scene, will you? I'm sure that's terribly bad form."

"Darling, I'm undead. It's impossible to incapacitate me."

Scott grinned. "Except that time—you know, when Caleb's vampire pal almost cubed you."

She scowled. "That monster."

"Sorry, Betsy." The young man's brow drew down in a guilty expression.

"It's all right dear." She smiled at him and turned to Dick. "Do you miss food?"

"Not really. I did for the first ten or twenty years, though."

The meal arrived and Scott picked up his po' boy. "I think I'd miss it forever." He tucked in but dropped half the contents of the sandwich down his front.

Lexi stared at him. "At least as much as you miss your mouth."

———

Scott flicked a finger at the crime scene tape across the door. A further whisper opened the lock and the door swung open.

Betsy's eyes widened. "That's awfully clever and so useful."

Lexi turned to glance at her, then at Scott.

He received the unspoken message. "You two go up. Betsy and I will keep a lookout."

The woman darted him a withering look. "I have a strong stomach."

He frowned. "I haven't. I threw up the last time I was in there. You're staying to look after me."

"Oh, you dear boy." Betsy took his arm and patted his shoulder.

Scott leaned through the door behind Lexi as she entered the building. "Take a look down the couch. The light went wherever the magic was, and it went through that couch. Something might be stashed there." She nodded and headed up the stairway with Dick.

She touched her scar. "Open." The door to the apartment flew open and banged against the wall.

"Jesus! Isn't there a dial on that thing?" The vampire put his hand over his chest. "My heart."

"Which doesn't beat." She smirked. "Drama queen!"

He turned to her. "I resent that remark."

"What would you prefer?"

"Sensitive queen."

She rolled her eyes. "Get in."

They entered the apartment and wandered through to the living room. The body was gone, thank goodness. She glanced at the lamp in the corner, relieved that the spine had also been removed.

Dick walked to the center of the room. "That's an enormous quantity of blood."

"No snacking," Lexi warned.

He screwed his face up. "Seriously, would you eat food off the floor?"

"Five-second rule." She shrugged.

"Animal." He shuddered and sniffed the air several times.

Lexi opened drawers and poked around on shelves. "What can you smell?"

"Well, I can detect at least three hallucinogens."

She held a black satin bag up and shook it next to her ear. "Anything else?"

"Blood, star anise, blood, mandrake, blood, and mugwort."

"Very good." The unexpected voice spoke from the door.

It was the disappearing Gandalf from the crime scenes. Lexi's katana was in her hand in an instant.

Dick stepped between them in a fraction of a second. "Please don't decapitate Joseph. Marcel's taken quite a shine to him."

With a dramatic sigh, she put the sword away. "This voodoo stuff makes me antsy."

The vampire smiled at her with no sincerity whatsoever. "What a charming thing to say to a voodoo priest."

She studied the new arrival suspiciously. "Joseph and I keep almost bumping into each other."

"Yes, I am quite eager to make your acquaintance." The man's voice was deep, rich, and southern. Lexi couldn't shake the feeling that something about her amused him.

Dick stepped aside. "Joseph, Lexi. Lexi, Joseph." To his friend, he said. "Lexi used to be with our Kindred friends but recently had a change of heart and decided to spread her wings."

Joseph nodded. "Ah! I'm sure that went down well. Are you planning to stay in New Orleans, Lexi?"

She answered honestly. "No, I'm planning to get the hell out of here before the local Kindred return."

He grinned. "That's a shame. It's a family get-together I'd pay money to see."

"So, what were they up to in here?" She indicated the ritual area in the room.

"Young Jamal has only been in town for a couple of weeks. He and his pretty young friend have done the rounds and tried to ingratiate themselves with the local priests and priestesses. They were tourists. I didn't detect the capacity for anything like this in either of them."

"You mean murder?" Lexi went to the couch, intending to ease her hand down the back of it, but paused and stared at it.

I've battled demons but I still don't want to stick my hand down the back of this couch in case it's icky.

Joseph shook his head. "I mean power. Something powerful and quite evil has been in this room."

"Did you hear how Jamal died?" Dick asked.

The other man nodded. "I've spoken to the detective. It seems quite…exotic."

Lexi opened a cupboard, glanced in, and closed it again. "And where might this evil something be now?"

He spread his arms. "It could be anywhere. I'm sure your mage friend could locate it."

She returned to the satin bag and upended it onto a side table. It was a pile of bones. When she moved to swipe them into the bag, a strong hand caught her wrist. Joseph studied the bones. He glanced at her, raised his eyebrows, and laughed a deep, loud belly laugh, then walked out the door.

A little startled, she narrowed her eyes. The guy was annoying. She followed him through the door to ask what was so funny, but when she turned into the hallway, he was nowhere to be seen.

"Seriously," she snapped as she entered the room again. "That is one creepy fucking dude."

Dick smiled. "He's very nice when you get used to him."

Lexi returned to the couch and lifted the cushions. "We'll have to speak to Amy, won't we?"

"It looks that way." He looked at the couch. "Is there nothing in the couch?"

"Not even a quarter." She pushed the cushion into place again.

He raised an eyebrow. "I've never heard of a couch without a quarter hiding in there somewhere."

They headed out and down the stairs.

Betsy greeted them. "Interesting. Two went in and three came out."

Their two friends stood beside Joseph.

"I was introducing myself," the man said jovially. He turned to the older woman and bowed. "Good evening, little mother, you look extraordinarily well."

Her hand went involuntarily to her necklace.

"Ah, the necklace." He turned to Scott and nodded appreciatively. "Nicely done."

Lexi felt a tug at her side. She turned to see the young girl had found her again. "You have to be kidding me. Don't you have a curfew?"

Joseph held a hand out. "Hello, Agatha."

"Hi, Joseph." The kid held his hand without hesitation.

"Suffer the little children to come unto me, and forbid them not; for theirs is the kingdom of Heaven." He patted her cheek. "You need her, don't you?"

She nodded her head and they both looked at Lexi.

"Another one." Scott's shoulders slumped. It wasn't a question.

"Do you need me?" Dick asked.

Lexi shook her head. "No, it's late and, as I recall, you have an arrangement."

Betsy touched her arm. "May I wait in your apartment, dear? I'd like to enjoy the balcony for a while."

She smiled. "Of course. And if you prefer not to room with a sleazy vampire, you could stay with us."

Her gaze drifted to Joseph and she regarded him with a questioning eyebrow.

He sniffed the air. "I'll be around."

"We'll see you later," she assured Betsy and turned to Joseph. He was gone. "How does he do that?"

Scott shrugged. "Probably the same way I do."

"Yes, but it's not creepy when you do it."

Once again, they followed the girl through the dark streets.

CHAPTER THIRTY-FIVE

Dick opened the door of the apartment, well aware that Betsy was across the hall and peered through the peephole to get a glimpse of the young man. He stood with his fingers twisting nervously and wore a Saints hoodie and jeans. The vampire studied him for a moment. "You must be Mike."

"Actually, it's Peter. Sorry. I panicked when I saw her earlier. I've seen her around but not up close and personal like that. I thought I would mess myself." He gave an apologetic shrug.

"Don't worry, Peter, she affects us all that way. Well, come on in." He stepped aside to allow him in, then winked at the spy hole before he closed the door.

He headed straight to the kitchen, opened a cupboard, and pulled out a bottle of Jack. "Would you like a drink?" he called. "I have bourbon or tea."

"No thank you," Peter responded. "I just had a couple with friends."

He's not exactly the life and soul of the party, is he?

Dick poured himself a large drink and walked in to find his visitor in exactly the same position he'd left him in. "Well, it seems I have catching up to do, chin-chin."

Peter smiled. "Penis."

He choked on his drink. "Pardon?"

"Chin-chin is Japanese for penis."

The vampire struggled to lower his eyebrows. "Well. I did not know that. In fact, it's remarkable that in all my years, that hasn't come up before. Have you eaten? I don't want you fainting on me."

"Yes, I'm fine. Thank you."

Dick led Peter through to the living room and gestured to the couch. "Great! I'm ravenous, Take a seat."

His visitor complied but he noticed the man's heart lurch when he said the word "ravenous." He decided he should probably slow things somewhat.

As non-threateningly as he could, he sat on the other side of the couch. "So, Peter. You said you were a fan. Of vampires in general?"

Suddenly, the young man perked up. "No, your movies. I think they're great."

What an astute young man. I was completely wrong about him.

"Peter, we will get on like a house on fire. Tell me, what's your favorite?"

"*A Long Dark Night in Hollywood.*"

He frowned. "But I die at the end of that one."

"I know. It always makes me cry when she holds your hand to her cheek and says, "Don't go, Johnny, don't go," and as you slip away, she doesn't see your other hand open and the diamond ring falls through the gap in the floorboards."

"I had to drop that goddam ring about a hundred times before it finally slipped through the—"

The vampire straightened quickly and Peter looked like he might have a heart attack. "Stay right where you are. I'll be back in a jiffy."

Humming "Tonight" from *West Side Story*, he hurried into the bedroom, opened a drawer in the big trunk, and flicked through a pile of DVDs before he drew one out and closed the drawer. He walked through the room and dropped a copy of *A Long Dark Night in Hollywood* onto the couch. "Be a dear and put that on. We can watch it for old times' sake." He moved to the kitchen, took a pack of Betsy's popcorn out, and threw it into the microwave. While it popped, he texted Lexi.

I have a theory.

Five minutes later, he was back on the sofa. Peter shoveled handfuls of popcorn into his mouth with one hand while he held his wrist out. Both had their gazes fixed on the movie in companionable silence.

Dick was unaware that anything was wrong until the bowl slid from the man's lap and scattered popcorn across the floor as he slumped.

"Peter?" The vampire checked his watch. They'd only been going seven minutes but he could hear the man's heart slowing.

Alarmed, he jumped to his feet to help him, but the moment he stood, he felt light-headed. He swayed and fell heavily. While not quite unconscious, he couldn't move when the door opened.

"Get Peter out. He'll be dead in an hour if he's not already. Drop him in a dumpster somewhere."

"What about the vamp?"

"I put enough roofies in Peter's drinks to fell an ox. Lorenzo wants us to take him to the roof and tie him up. He'll meet the sun in a few hours."

Dick began to lose consciousness.

"Why not chop his head off now and get it over and done with?"

Lexi stared at the body. "So where's his head?"

Broullard exhaled sharply and shrugged.

She looked around. "This is the smallest bathroom I've ever seen. How do you behead someone in such a tiny space? The logistics are a nightmare." She noticed that he stared at her from her peripheral vision. "Like you didn't think it too. So, out with it. Why am I here?"

The cop pointed at the body. "This gentleman was Ambrose Jackson. His wife, Cora, does housekeeping for an agency that services several vacation apartments in the city."

The penny dropped and she nodded. "Let me guess—Jamal's place?"

"Correct."

He handed her a framed photograph of the couple on a vacation—a happy, smiling African American man with his loving white wife. "Could it be racially motivated?"

"They've been married for thirty years. The neighbors say they haven't had that kind of trouble for at least ten."

Lexi handed him the picture. "And the wife?"

Broullard shook his head. "She hasn't been seen but she had a key to Jamal's apartment."

She immediately followed what she suspected was the detective's train of thought. "You think this housekeeper could have let herself in when the two of them baked and butchered Jamal. Then Amy woke from a drug-addled stupor and found her boyfriend scrambled?"

"Spatchcocked. It looks like the most likely scenario. Simply because they were practicing voodoo at the time doesn't mean that caused his death."

"Okay...so you think she then came home and decapitated her husband." She peered into the little vanity sink at a blood-covered steak knife. "With a steak knife? This can't possibly be the murder weapon." She glanced at the body. "I'll admit it's not the cleanest cut but I'm sure you'd have to be built like Arnie to take someone's head off with an old steak knife."

They walked down the hall past piles upon piles of boxes that lined the wall. "What's all this?" Lexi asked and gestured at them.

"Stolen goods. It appears Mr. and Mrs. Jackson had a little side business—actually, I think they had a few side businesses. This stuff is everywhere. Games consoles, iPhones, there's a foot-high pile of counterfeit currency in the bedroom, a stash of narcotics in the kitchen, and we found an undocumented illegal in the back bedroom who says she hasn't left the building for over a year. They didn't treat her very well."

Her brows drew together in puzzlement. "Why did the wife work as a cleaner? No, let me guess, it was part of their victim selection process."

"Again, correct."

"Is there any indication they practiced voodoo?" She poked around the shelves and looked at him when he didn't respond. He looked from her to the wall, his expression a little sarcastic.

She turned and noticed the large painting of Marie Laveau on the wall.

"Oh, right. Duh." She stepped to the window and looked out, then turned to the door. "Where the hell is Scott?"

"I told them not to let him in. I don't want him puking all over the crime scene again."

"Fair enough." She nodded. "Listen, we'll have to speak to Amy. We'll go in the morning if that's okay with you."

Broullard stared at her for a few seconds. "I must say I like this whole new Kindred approach. It's much easier to work with."

Don't get used to it.

He took a notepad out, scribbled a few lines, and ripped the page out to hand it to her. "That's the hospital room."

"Great, thanks. I'll head off now. I'd like to get a couple of hours of sleep." She headed down the staircase to where Scott waited for her.

He shrugged dramatically. "They wouldn't let me in."

Lexi squeezed past the cop on the door. "You don't look disappointed about that."

"I'm not. I don't like to see the evil things people do to each other."

"You and me both." She took her cell out and read the screen. "Dick has a theory."

"About what?"

She shrugged. "Who knows. I won't ask."

"Why not?"

"Because he's being intentionally vague," she snipped as she put the cellphone in her pocket again.

Betsy was asleep on the couch when they returned. Her eyes opened sleepily as Scott closed the door.

He winced. "Sorry. I tried not to disturb you."

She sat quickly. "It's all right. What time is it?"

Lexi consulted the clock. "A little after three. Don't tell me Dick's dinner is still in there."

"I have no idea. I decided to rest my eyes and dropped off immediately."

Marcel jumped off a chair, ran to the door, and sat beside it as he yipped sharply.

"I'll take him." Lexi took the lead from the table.

"I'll accept your offer of the other bed." Betsy headed to the second bedroom and the younger woman opened the front door.

When she and Marcel entered the hallway, she considered knocking on Dick's door. She was less than impressed that he'd left Betsy feeling like she couldn't go back to the apartment.

When they reached the stairway, the puppy darted up the first two steps leading to the roof access and ate something from the floor. She tried to wrestle it from his mouth and realized it was popcorn. "You don't mind floor food, do you, boy?" She turned to walk down but he whined and stared upward. "There's no more, come on." She pulled him away and he followed reluctantly.

Lexi woke to a welcome smell. She crept over Scott, leaned down beside his ear, and whispered, "Bacon."

His eyes snapped open and he sniffed before he flung the covers back. They walked out to find Betsy cooking.

"I'm sorry. I tried to be quiet. You've only had about three hours."

The sorcerer rubbed his eyes and gave her a full, dimple-popping grin. "Bacon."

Marcel ran to the door and whined.

Lexi looked at the plateful of bacon, then at the dog. "Do you think he'd go on the balcony?"

The other woman guffawed. "I'm sure the people below us would be delighted."

She crouched beside the puppy. "I'll take you after breakfast."

The two friends sat at the dining table, ready to tuck into bacon, eggs, and biscuits. Scott tore a piece of bacon in half and gave it to Marcel.

"I made some for him too. I'll get his bowl." Betsy picked her apartment key up from the counter and headed across the hall.

Thirty seconds later, she returned, her expression anxious. "I think something's wrong."

The others stood quickly and hurried across the hall. The older woman remained at the back and pulled the door almost closed to stop Marcel from following.

Lexi put her head in. "Dick?"

Betsy peeked around Scott. "He's not there. I looked in all the rooms."

She nodded acknowledgment, passed the dining table, and stood with her hands on the back of the couch as she stared at the upturned bowl and the popcorn spread across the floor. "It looks like there might have been a struggle. Even if there wasn't, Dick's a neat freak. There's no way he'd leave it like this."

They turned at a shuffling sound. Betsy hadn't closed the other apartment door properly and Marcel had managed to work it open with his nose. He raced down the hallway.

Scott ran after him. "No!" He vanished and reappeared ahead of the puppy to block his way down the stairs.

The two women raced from the apartment after them. Instead of trying to run down the stairs, however, the dog spun and moved up. Lexi found him at the door to the roof where he scratched and whined. She remembered the popcorn on the stairs and looked at Scott while she drew her short-sword. When she was armed, she nodded for her friend to release the lock.

They stepped out into the morning sunlight and stopped in shock. Dick was hogtied with heavy chains and lay on the roof between a folded sun lounger and an AC unit. Marcel bounded to him and licked his face but he was out cold. Scott spoke a word and the chains shattered. He lifted the man in his arms. "I'll take him downstairs," he said before they both disappeared.

"Oh!" Betsy jumped. Marcel ran in circles and scratched at the roof where Dick had been, then lifted his leg and peed against the door before he bolted down the stairs.

The older woman turned to Lexi. "Can you disappear like that?"

She rolled her eyes. "No, we have to go the long way."

Scott had placed Dick on the couch in his apartment when the women entered. "Where are his blood bags?"

Betsy went to the fridge, then returned to Scott's side. "He uses these tubes."

The sorcerer took the bag and tube from her. "Doesn't this gross you out?"

The woman smiled. "I prefer a good chardonnay." She stroked the vampire's hair. "Will he be all right?"

"He hasn't desiccated so he's still with us. That's all I can tell you at the moment." He pierced the opening of the bag with the tube and fed it into Dick's mouth. He gave the bag a slight squeeze. They watched anxiously and after a few moments, he swallowed.

Lexi stood behind the couch while her friend hovered and squeezed the blood patiently into his mouth until his eyes fluttered open. Betsy crouched closer to him and put her hand on Dick's shoulder. "I think he's trying to speak."

Scott pulled the tube from his lips and they both leaned closer to listen.

The vampire put his hand over Betsy's. "Could you ask Lexi to stop licking my feet?"

They looked at Marcel, who stood on his hind legs with his paws on the arm of the couch, licking his feet.

Lexi rolled her eyes and went to pick the dog up but he dodged her and started on the popcorn strewn on the floor. "What happened to Mike?"

"Mike? Oh, Peter." Dick sighed. "I think they killed him." He sat stiffly. "I intend to obliterate them."

Betsy squeezed his hand and left the room.

He checked his watch, then looked around the room. "They took my shoes but not my watch?" Baffled, he shook his head.

She walked to the couch and tapped Dick's feet. He shifted them to the floor and she sat. "Who were they?"

"They mentioned someone called Lorenzo. I don't know who that is yet. They filled Peter with drugs without him knowing. I can't believe the poor man's gone and it's my fault."

Lexi frowned. "You seem to have grown attached to him remarkably quickly. How is it your fault?"

"Do you know about the exchange?"

She raised her eyebrow. "You mean the illegal blood exchange?"

The vampire stood. "Oh, don't get your panties in a twist. Remember, you're only pretending to be Kindred. The blood exchange is considered a great honor. Offering one is tantamount to adoption. If anything—by which I mean death—happens to the donor while they have vampire blood in them, they will be reborn." He checked the time again. "I need to get changed." He walked into the bedroom.

Confused, she continued to speak to him from outside the room. "So, you did or didn't offer this to Peter?"

"I didn't. Honestly, at first, I thought he was a dud. Then it transpired he's a fan of my movies. Such a charming, well-educated young man." He returned in a dark-red velvet dressing gown.

"Which explains this." She picked the DVD case up from the table.

Betsy entered the room with a margarita. "Ah! One of my absolute favorite movies."

"But I die at the end of it. Why is it everyone's favorite?" He looked at the glass. "Isn't it a little early for that?"

"It's for you. I thought you might need it." She held the glass out.

He took it, held her hand, and kissed it. "Betsy darling, I will love you until I die...again."

She blushed.

He straightened and held a finger in the air, tilted his head, and listened. "They're back." Before anyone could ask who he meant, he was gone.

Lexi rolled her eyes and followed.

CHAPTER THIRTY-SIX

"Lorenzo told us to lock him up here and stay away."

"He doesn't need to know we came back."

"What's the point in going out there to clean the dust up? It's probably blown away."

"Vamp dust has a street value."

"People snort that shit?"

"Not like that. The voodoo stores might buy it."

"It's the big key. Do you want me to do it?"

"No, it isn't locked. Who was supposed to lock it last night?"

"Charlie." The voice responded a little too quickly and noticeably higher in pitch.

"Idiot."

"Well, the vacuum cleaner makes sense now."

"Time to suck up a nice little profit."

The two men stepped through the door onto the roof of the apartment building and looked around.

"It looks different in the day. I don't remember the sun lounger over there or the robe."

They walked across the roof.

"I don't see any dust. Maybe the wind blew it—"

The door slammed shut and the men spun to face Dick, who held a margarita and wore nothing but a tiny pair of Versace baroque briefs. "Gentlemen, let's talk."

The skinny guy dropped the vacuum cleaner, ran to the edge of the roof, and jumped. He screamed briefly.

The vampire stared after him before he turned to the remaining man. "But there are balconies at the front. Why on earth did he run to the back of the building?" He shrugged.

The stocky guy moved to draw a gun.

He closed the space between them in a second, grasped him by the throat, and held him several inches off the roof by the time the gun was in his hand and free of his pocket. "Let's talk about Lorenzo."

"He said you were a vamp. He'll kill me if I talk."

"You don't seem to have fully grasped your current situation. Let me help you with that." He lowered his captive, pulled his face close, and allowed his vampire teeth to descend inches from the man's eyes.

The gun clattered onto the rooftop.

"But it's daylight. I... What? We were only doing what we were told to." His voice had climbed several octaves as the toe of his boots scraped the surface of the roof.

Dick lifted him higher. "You poisoned Peter to poison me."

The man squeaked a terrified protest. "That's what Lorenzo told us to do."

He lowered him to stand on the roof but kept his hand about the man's throat. "And Lorenzo is?"

"He leads one of the clans."

The vampire frowned in thought. "I've never heard of him."

"He took over a few years ago from Giovanni."

"I liked Giovanni." He sighed. "Where is Peter?"

"We..." The man seemed to feel the need to rethink his answer. "Lorenzo told us to throw him in a dumpster. We... Lorenzo gave him enough of that stuff to—"

"Fell an ox. I heard." He tightened his hold on the man's windpipe. "It's very difficult, these days, to find an actual fan of my work, and you killed him. I have to say, I'm very upset. And where are my Christian Louboutins?"

"That's Lorenzo's…thing. He asks…for the…shoes." The man's face purpled slightly, and his breathing was shallow and gasping around the obstruction.

Lexi stepped out from where she had watched.

The captive beat a fist against the vampire's arm and pointed behind him.

Dick released his hold fractionally.

"He was going to kill me." The man stared beseechingly at her.

With a withering smile, he hoisted him again. "What do you mean, 'was?'"

"You can't kill me in front of Kindred," the man protested and kicked wildly. "They won't let you."

She leaned against the door. "Well…no, actually, I'm okay with it. Maybe you should tell him where his number-one fan is."

"In a dumpster on Conti Street—where they're fixing the old hotel up."

Lexi had taken a little knife out and cleaned her nails with it. "And why does Lorenzo want my friend here dead?"

"I don't know. He only told us to do it, not why." His face faded from purple hues to a bright red.

Dick dropped him on the roof and turned to her, about to speak. The guy scrambled to his feet and ran in the opposite direction to the one his friend had taken, straight off the building, and screamed.

She looked after him. "Why didn't he jump off the front where the balconies are?"

The vampire shrugged. "I think I might have somehow given him the impression the front of the building was that way. Did Scott catch the first one?"

The sorcerer came through the door. "He landed on our balcony. Betsy almost had a heart attack. I sent him to sleep. Did you get what you needed from the other one?" Scott looked around for the second man, then shrugged. "If you're done here, I'll go get rid of him." He disappeared.

"Don't you think it might be best to leave Peter where he is?" Lexi wandered to the back of the building and looked down with a grimace. "That guy won't get up again."

Dick took a sip of his cocktail. "I owe it to the young man to find him and return him to his family."

"Excuse me?"

"Also, whilst I didn't offer an exchange, if he was drinking with Lorenzo or one of his clan, it's quite possible he was given vampire blood before coming to me."

"You're telling me it's still possible that Peter could turn?"

"Honestly, I doubt it. I don't think he was lying to me and he didn't seem used to socializing with us. If he were, he wouldn't have offered himself to the sanguinaires. The clans prefer to keep their supplies to themselves. They take traceability in the supply chain very seriously. But if he did exchange with another vampire, we don't want him to wake up hungry in the middle of a populated area tonight. That could be bad."

"I can see that." Lexi looked at her watch. "It's still early. I might be able to get over there before the city gets going."

Dick marched toward the door, but she put a hand out. "Where do you think you're going?"

"I thought we—"

"There is no we. You need to keep a low profile. Walking through the French Quarter in daylight wearing nothing but..." She squinted at him and all but shuddered. "Wearing really tiny briefs won't help."

"These briefs were three hundred dollars. They should be seen." He sighed. "Fine, I'll get dressed, but I'm coming."

He vanished, and in the time it took her to descend one floor, he was waiting in jeans and a hoodie.

Lexi raised her eyebrows. "You own a hoodie?"

"It's Peter's."

As she approached the apartment door, it opened and the other thug walked out. "Morning." He smiled and nodded at her. Dick turned his back discreetly until the man had rounded the corner and was halfway down the stairs.

Scott followed him out of the apartment and stopped beside her. "He's going to visit his mother in Natchez. He hasn't been the best son, so he's going to apologize."

They arrived at the tall dumpster. Lexi looked at Dick and waited.

He gazed around the quiet streets before he fixed her with a wide-eyed look. "I'm not getting in there."

"He's your friend."

"But…you owe me a dumpster from Chicago."

She rolled her eyes and turned to Scott.

He immediately took a step back. "Don't even look at me. Turn those eyeballs away."

"Oh, for God's sake. Give me a lift up." She stepped into his interlocked hands and climbed onto the edge. "I can't see him."

"Maybe he slipped beneath the top layer of slime and filth," Dick suggested.

Unimpressed, she stared at him with distaste. "There are rats and roaches in there."

"And a potential killing machine." he reminded her.

With an exasperated sigh, she dropped in. She lifted sheets of drywall and kicked roaches off her boot. "It stinks in here." She dropped the remnants of a door. "Dick, he's not in here."

"Dick's not here," Scott called in response.

"Where is he?"

The sorcerer's voice grew quieter as he continued to speak to her with his back turned. "He's across the street with a guy—oh, wait. It's Peter."

"What?" Lexi heaved herself up and glowered at where Dick talked to a man who was crouched on a doorstep. She scrambled out, dropped to the ground, and scraped something off her boot before she marched across the street.

Peter shielded his eyes and squinted at the vampire. "Bus delit."

Dick crouched beside him. "What?"

"S'dayl–" the man slurred and lowered his head.

He slapped his cheek. "What are you trying to say, Peter?"

Peter straightened a little, stretched a trembling hand, and stroked Dick's cheek. "S'okay." He leaned forward and pulled the hood up to cover the vampire's head.

"He's protecting me from the sun." He sighed and smiled, leaned in, and spoke slowly to the other man. "I'll explain everything later, but we'll take care of you first. What on earth is that awful smell?" He turned quickly. "Ah! Lexi. You're back."

She scowled at him.

He put a hand up. "Don't act like you didn't deserve that. You were in there for less than a minute. I was in that dumpster in Chicago all night with a broken neck."

Lexi gritted her teeth and looked at Peter. "How's he doing? He doesn't look dead."

"Pie-eyed, but no, not dead."

She shook her head. "How did the drugs not kill him?"

"Pfft! Do Roofies for fuuuun." The man giggled.

Dick raised an eyebrow. "Apparently, he's built up something of a resistance." He looked at Scott. "Can you do something?"

The sorcerer shook his head. "I think we should get him to the hospital. I can heal people, but I need to know what's going on with them. I haven't a clue what those drugs might have done to him."

The vampire stooped to pick the drugged man up.

Peter caught his hand and pulled it to his cheek. "Don' go, Johnny, don' go," he mumbled and burst into tears.

"There, there." Dick patted his back and glanced at Scott.

The young man retrieved his cell. "I'll call a cab."

Dick stood with the nurse. "I don't know how many. I wasn't there. I found him on a street corner."

"But you're willing to pay for his treatment." The nurse raised an eyebrow.

He plucked the forms from her hand. "He's someone's son. Wouldn't anyone with the means do the same?"

She regarded him with suspicion. "Quite frankly, Mr. Levine, no."

"Well then, thank goodness I'm not simply anyone." He ignored the pen he was offered and instead, drew his Mont Blanc special edition pen from the shirt pocket beneath his hoodie.

Lexi rolled her eyes and turned to Scott. She took a slip of paper from her pocket. "Let's visit Amy."

They took the stairs to the next floor and found the psych ward.

The police officer outside the hospital room slipped quietly into unconsciousness, oblivious to the two friends entering the room.

Amy lay cuffed to the bed and stared at the ceiling.

Lexi spoke as she entered. "Hi, Amy, we'd like to ask you some questions if that's okay."

The girl kept her gaze fixed on the ceiling. "I heard them say they know who did it. They'll let me go after a psych evaluation."

Lexi moved to the chair beside the bed. "Can you tell me what happened?"

"I don't know. I woke up and—" Amy closed her eyes and tears ran from the corner of her eyes into her hair. "It was horrible."

She lowered her voice when she asked the next question. "When we found you, the machete was in your hand. Do you remember picking it up?"

"I woke up on the couch. I thought someone was there. It felt like someone was close by. I grabbed it and hid. I don't remember anything else. Everything was fine. We were only doing some…I don't know, ritual stuff."

Scott asked, "What was the ritual?"

"Jamal wanted to speak to Marie Laveau." The girl blinked and tears streamed from her eyes.

The two friends shared a look.

Scott leaned against the wall and folded his arms. "Using the ring you stole from the museum."

Amy blushed and she nodded.

Lexi leaned forward. "Where is it now?"

She shrugged and rattled the bracelet cuffed to the bed's railing. "When I woke up, I wasn't wearing it. They said a woman came in and killed Jamal. Maybe she stole it."

Scott muttered, "Sleep." Amy closed her eyes.

"Excuse me, what are you doing in here?"

James from Thought and Memory, the witchcraft store, stood in the doorway. He wore scrubs.

He raised an eyebrow. "Oh, it's you."

She blinked. "I thought you worked in the witchcraft store."

James continued into the room. "Sam and I help out when we can. She won't leave the place."

Lexi moved away from the bed. "Why do you want her to leave?"

The man moved to the notes and checked them. He flicked a glance at Lexi. "You haven't noticed? Everyone's getting out. With all this shit going down with the vampires. Do you honestly think we haven't seen what's been going on? You look away while your pals make moves. I'm amazed you all weren't away for longer."

She pinched the bridge of her nose. "I don't understand this."

"You need to leave. The doctor's coming to assess her." James spun on his heel and marched down the hallway.

"What the hell was that about?" she asked.

Scott shrugged.

Back in the ER, they found Dick seated in a bay next to Peter's bed.

The sorcerer took the chart from the end of the bed. "How's he looking?"

"They've pumped his stomach and he's on saline and electrolytes. They'll test his liver and kidneys."

Scott replaced the chart and placed his hand on the patient's stomach. "His kidneys are fine. His liver's not great and he needs to hold off on the booze and recreational drugs. I think he'll be out of here in twenty-four to forty-eight hours."

Lexi patted the vampire's shoulder. "Hey, the museum case is solved."

Dick held his gaze on the patient. "Oh, that's right. Amy stole the ring. I realized that last night."

She stood with her mouth agape.

"I've been a little busy." He gestured a hand in Peter's direction.

"I've just seen Anne Bird's son. He seems to think Kindred are allowing one vampire clan to dominate the city."

He straightened. "Oh, yes. Betsy and I spoke to an old shifter friend of mine yesterday morning. She thinks Kindred were behind Palm Springs and that they left to allow this little war to happen. But we know that's not true."

Lexi thought about it as she chewed the inside of her cheek. "They do seem to be taking their time to get back here."

They sat with Peter for a couple of hours until his results came back and confirmed Scott's assessment.

She rose. "I need to find Broullard. Will you stay here?"

"No." Dick smiled an unattractive smile "I need to get out of sight."

"I don't think any other vamps will see you out in the daylight."

"Oh, I'll visit them soon enough." He stood and kissed the now sleeping Peter on his forehead.

They headed out of the hospital and waited for a cab.

The vampire took sunglasses from his pocket and slid them onto his face. "What will you tell the detective?"

"He'll need to know Amy killed Jamal while she was possessed by this Marie Laveau woman."

He shook his head. "That makes no sense. I honestly can't see it. Marie Laveau was beloved and known for her kindness and deep religious convictions. What could have happened to her spirit to make her hack someone up like that?"

When the cab pulled up at the apartment block, Lexi looked up and scowled when she saw Betsy wasn't alone on the balcony. Agatha was with her. She glanced at Scott. "This can't be good."

When they entered, Agatha made eye contact with the sorcerer.

She watched the exchange. "Another one. Well, at least I won't have to hunt the detective."

They followed the girl to Decatur Street.

The two friends waited patiently with the crowd at the end of the alley beyond the cordon until Broullard noticed them. He stepped out from behind the tape and signaled them to walk with him. "You're late."

They joined a line for coffee.

"We were at the hospital." Scott pulled a ten-dollar bill from his pocket.

Broullard turned. "Did you leave with Amy?"

Lexi narrowed her eyes. "No. We spoke to her. She was waiting for a psych evaluation. Why?"

He moved to the front of the line. "Can I get three flat whites, please?" He turned to the others and motioned to Scott to put his money away. "I've just had a call from the station. The doctor discharged her to the care of her parents, but when they arrived, she'd already left. Admittedly, she's no longer a suspect and not much of a witness. They've been to the apartment and she's not there either. It looks like this one's ours after all. It seems to be a case of simply bat-shit crazy."

Her gaze flicked to the sorcerer before it returned to Broullard. "That might not be the case."

He paid for the coffee and they walked to the end of the counter. With a sigh, he glanced around to make sure they wouldn't be over-heard. "Go on."

Lexi began to pick up sachets of sugar. "Are you aware of the break-in at the Museum of Death?"

"Yes, I heard about it." He stared at her coffee. "What happened to 'pure, white and deadly?'"

Lexi looked at her drink, utterly clueless about what he meant. "It was Amy. She stole Marie Laveau's ring to try to communicate with her spirit. We think she was possessed and went to town on Jamal. Cora found the ring when she went in to clean-slash-burgle the apartment. She went home, put it on, and took her husband's head off."

They took their drinks and returned to the crime scene.

Broullard blew on his coffee. "I've seen some weird shit in my time, but from the way people speak about Marie Laveau, there's simply no way she would be that kind of spirit."

"I agree."

Lexi startled and spun quickly. "Joseph, I swear—"

Joseph traced the patterns on his staff idly with his finger and looked at her. "I think it's time for you to return to the museum."

The cop nodded. "I've never known you to be wrong, Joseph." He turned to her. "Do you want to check this one before you go?"

She turned to him. "What's missing this time?"

"Au contraire, a piece of lost property has appeared." Broullard lifted the tape for her but dropped it in front of Scott. She passed her coffee to her friend.

They walked up the narrow alley and her nose twitched at the smell of garbage and rat piss. The body of a man lay on the ground. The first thing she observed was the shiny shoes. Then she noticed a burn hole in his pants. Her gaze trailed to his face. It wasn't one she had expected to see.

Broullard lifted the blood-soaked collar to show large, industrial staples. "This is Ambrose. Well, it's his head…stapled to an unknown's body."

Lexi looked at him, a little startled. "It's the shoeshine extortion guy."

He took a notepad and pen out. "You'll have to narrow that down."

"He has a gold tooth and hangs with a shorter guy. We passed him on Decatur near Jackson Square. Scott could probably tell you his name."

"Tyrone?" he asked. She nodded. "Well, now we're looking for Tyrone's head and I'm thinking of retiring."

CHAPTER THIRTY-SEVEN

Agatha walked along the street, thinking about the Kindred lady and how she smelled strange. She couldn't put her finger on what was strange about her. And why wasn't she staying at the usual Kindred place? What was that about? It wasn't a problem, obviously. She had her weird scent and could track her with an hours' old trail.

She smiled. *If this is how good I am now, imagine how awesome I'll be when I shift. It'll be soon, I'm sure.*

As she passed a gate, she detected an unusual odor. The girl stopped, turned her head and sniffed, and peered up the narrow corridor along the side of the big house. The smell was out of place, and she'd never seen this gate open before. She crept quietly along the side of the building and tried to remember where she'd encountered the scent before. Was it food? The door of the building stood ajar and brought her closer to identifying the smell. She pressed her face to the sliver of open doorway. It swung in about a foot and stopped. She sniffed again.

What is it?

With one tentative step after another, Agatha entered the house.

She was four or five steps in when finally, it hit her what the smell was.

Blood.

Instinctively, she spun toward the door, but a woman stood in her way with a knife in one hand and a man's head in the other. Agatha whirled and ran into the mansion. She entered a large white hallway dominated by a glittering chandelier. When she reached the front doors, she twisted one handle, then the next, but it was no use. The door was locked and soft footsteps approached from behind.

She bolted to the right and flew up a wide, curved staircase as fast as her young legs would take her.

At the next level, she turned. The woman was no longer behind her. She took her shoes off to quieten the sound and ran along another hallway to the door at the end. Relieved, she reached for the handle but stopped. The smell drifted to her again. Her pursuer was on the other side of the door. She could feel it. Her mind raced and when she glanced out the window beside her, she realized she was at the back of the house. This door would lead to the back stairway used by servants or slaves. The mansion was old.

Agatha backed away quietly, returned to the curved staircase, and continued up. She tried several rooms but most of them were empty and she could find nowhere to hide. Finally, she entered what appeared to be a large sewing room with a big table in the center. A giant pair of scissors rested on top of a pile of fabric. A sewing machine stood on a smaller table near the window beside a mannequin, and rolls of fabric leaned against a wall.

She was about to pick the scissors up when something caught her eye. Her heart thudding, she ran around the table to the window and halted at the sight of a young blonde woman on the floor. Her hands were tied and although she seemed to be awake, she couldn't get any response from her. The window was locked and there weren't enough rolls of fabric to hide behind. There were closets in this room, but the woman would surely look in closets.

A little desperate now, she glanced down. Beneath the closets were small cupboards with two sliding doors—the kind you might put shoes in or that adults might overlook. She slid a door open and peered inside. It didn't appear to be in use so she scrambled into the small space and slid the door closed with her foot. She opened the door near her face the tiniest of fractions to allow her a glimpse into the room. The woman on the floor was mostly out of view. Her nose twitched.

Lord, it's dusty in here!

In the silence, she wished she could shift. If she could, she'd be able to rip the woman's throat out. She'd heard of children shifting before their time, usually brought on by a stressful situation. Maybe this situation counted as stressful.

I'd better not shift in this tiny space. I'll break my neck.

The door to the room opened. The woman entered, swinging the head in her hand. Agatha closed her eyes.

"We have a guest." The woman seemed to be speaking to the blonde. The girl looked through the sliver and willed herself to not close her eyes. "We'll have a little fun." She walked to the mannequin, pulled its head up and dropped it onto the floor, then replaced it with the head in her hand and squashed it onto the body. "There."

The youngster swallowed a sob and closed her eyes again. The woman came closer and the closet door above her opened, then closed, followed by another.

The feet turned away, walked across the room, and out. The door clicked closed and Agatha released a breath.

Then, without warning, she sneezed.

Horrified, she held her breath and waited to see if the woman had heard.

CHAPTER THIRTY-EIGHT

Lexi and Scott entered the Museum of Death. He shivered and she felt his disquiet.

The same man they'd seen on the night of the break-in was behind the cash register with his back to her.

She walked to the counter. "I heard the boss is back."

The guy turned. "You just missed him. He's freaking out about the mix-up."

"The mix-up?"

"You don't know?" He led them to the back of the building. The cabinet had been replaced and she crossed to it quickly. Marie Laveau's picture was still in place but now, beneath it, was a label stating, *Marie Laveau's ring.* Beside it rested a shiny ring with a blue stone.

Her eyes wandered to the picture of a stern-looking woman beside Marie's picture and read the label in front of the picture, *Marie Delphine LaLaurie's ring.* There was a space where the ring should be.

"Exactly." He released an exasperated breath.

Lexi raised an eyebrow. "Am I to assume she stole the wrong ring?"

"It looks that way. We need to get the other one back and without delay, obviously. Here's a picture of the ring we're looking for."

She looked at the image and the woman's photograph again. She wasn't about to admit that she didn't know who she was either. "Obviously. Well, no time like the present."

They stepped outside and Scott shook himself as if to loosen anything that might have clung to him. "I hope I never have to go back in there again."

"Stop. Please—wait," a voice called.

They turned to see a couple walking hurriedly toward them.

The woman held a toddler in her arms. "Have you seen her? We've looked everywhere."

Lexi blinked. "I'm sorry?"

"Aggie. She was supposed to find you and take you to the detective, then come straight home."

She stepped closer to respond, but the woman stepped back.

Why the hell are these people so afraid of Kindred?

"She delivered us to Broullard maybe an hour and a half ago. I didn't see her after that."

The man felt in his pocket and pulled a little doll out. "She always comes back. This is very unusual. I'm worried. Can you find her for us? We don't want to bother you—"

"It's fine. That's what we're here for." Scott attempted to take the doll, but the man jerked his arm away.

His eyes narrowed and he watched the sorcerer suspiciously. "Who are you?"

Lexi interjected before her friend could share his name. "He's with me. I'm training him." *What the hell. It worked with Broullard.*

After a moment, the man passed the doll to Scott. The sorcerer muttered a few words and began to walk.

Agatha's parents followed but remained a short distance behind as though they didn't want to be seen with them. That was fine with Lexi.

At her signal, her friend created a barrier around them.

He nodded to confirm it was safe to speak and she wasted no time. "Do you any idea who Marie Darlene—"

"Marie Delphine LaLaurie," he interrupted.

"Great, you know her."

"No, I merely have a better memory than a goldfish—or you."

Lexi sighed. "We need to know who she is. Can you look it up?"

She took the doll from him and felt its pull as it sought its owner.

Scott scrolled through his cell. "Okay, Marie Delphine LaLaurie. Born 1787, died 1849… Oh. Oh, dear. As soon as we've found Agatha, we need to make finding that ring our number one priority."

When she glanced at him, his face was pale. "You will have to give me more information than that, you know."

His gaze remained fixed ahead. "A rich lady of the city who tortured, experimented on, and butchered her slaves."

"Slaves! Jamal, Ambrose, and Tyrone were all African American."

"Exactly."

Lexi halted and turned to him. "So we have the spirit of a racist psychopath running around the city."

He sighed.

"Well, fuck!" She scratched her head and scowled.

Scott continued to read. "There's some sick stuff in here, but it says most of it is probably only urban myths."

"You saw what she did to Jamal. Do you think what she did was mythical?"

They increased their speed.

"We must have walked ten blocks. Where the hell is she?"

The doll tugged. "Okay, we're turning here." Lexi looked back. Agatha's parents were still about twenty paces behind them.

Her friend was still reading. "It says here that she's buried in St. Louis Cemetery Number One. Oh, or Paris."

They crossed Bourbon Street with its busy bars and restaurants and continued.

She tried to think what their next move should be. "Where did she live while she was here? Could the building still be standing?"

"Looking… A big mansion. The LaLaurie mansion. It's a nice-looking place. They say it's haunted."

Lexi shook the doll. "No shit. Wait, it's stopped pulling." She looked around for signs of Agatha.

Scott looked up from his screen. "Lexi?"

"What is it?"

He held the cellphone up so she could see. It showed a picture of the LaLaurie mansion. When he lowered his arm, she stared at the same building directly in front of her.

They turned to Agatha's parents. The horror on their faces confirmed that they knew exactly where they were.

As she returned the doll to the girl's stricken mother, her husband bolted across the street and through the open side gate.

"Wait." Scott ran after him.

Lexi looked at her scar, which was empty again. She turned to follow but a flicker of movement drew her attention. Joseph had appeared—from thin air, as usual—and pointed up. Her gaze followed and she muttered an expletive when a third-story window shattered and a sheet of material rolled from it. Agatha climbed out after it.

Her mother gasped. Lexi glanced at the woman, who put her hand to her mouth. Her eyes flashed from brown to gold and back to brown and she obviously fought the urge to shift. She stood on a public street and would incur a Kindred death sentence if she shifted. Fortunately, she held her son so would resist the instinct.

Agatha started to climb down the fabric but had only managed to descend about a foot from the window ledge when Cora appeared at the window. She thrust her hand out holding a knife, the ring clearly visible. With a cruel smile, she sliced the tenuous lifeline. It tore the rest of the way and the child fell.

Her mother screamed.

"No!" Lexi raced forward from the opposite corner with her arms out as though she might catch her, but she was too far away.

A moment later, she landed on her knees with the weight of the twelve-year-old girl who had translocated now in her arms. She huffed at the impact and her elbows and knees scraped painfully. The girl sat and threw her arms around her. A moment later, she saw her mother, scrambled to her feet, and ran to her.

Lexi tried to stand but fell back. The translocation had taken everything, even the strength in her muscles. But Scott had run into a building with a psychopath waiting. She wasn't about to let him die.

Joseph extended his hand to her. She initially thought he was offering to pull her up, but he slipped something into her hand.

A little bemused, she looked into her open palm at a stone with sigils painted onto it.

"This has power," he said.

She looked up to ask what kind of power but of course, he was gone.

Come on then, power stone. Help me get off my ass.

Lexi tried to stand again, and as she wobbled, arms came around her and raised her to her feet. Energy pulsed into her muscles and she turned to Anne Bird and her daughter Sam.

She nodded her thanks to them and ran through the gate and into the house. Inside, there was blood on the floor. She yanked her katana out and glanced at her scar. Scott's magic was completely drained and she couldn't understand how she had been able to use it to save Agatha. He still wasn't close enough to replenish it.

You're a disappointment, she told the stone in her left hand, shook it, and flipped it in the air.

Her senses alert, she crept through the house and her soft-soled boots made no sound on the tiled floor.

When she rounded the staircase to the second floor, she found Tyrone's head on a plinth. She paused to listen for any indication of where Scott might be. With the choice of a long hallway or the stairs to the next story, she looked from one to the other. When she returned her gaze to the hallway, a black wolf stared at her. Agatha's dad, obviously, and that made her decision easy. The wolf had cleared that level. She nodded and moved to the stairs. Before she headed up, she looked at him and whispered, "She's okay. She's out front."

Lexi reached the next level and immediately saw Scott walk out of a room ahead of her. He jumped at the sight of her and she smirked and rolled her eyes. After a less than polite hand gesture, he pointed to the opposite hallway to indicate that she should check it. He turned right and made his way to the end of the hallway. As he opened the door, Lexi stopped and turned. He entered a bright, sunny room where Amy sat in the middle of the floor.

What the hell is she doing here?

Scott hurried to the girl, crouched beside her, and checked her vitals. Even from this distance, it was obvious that she was catatonic again.

A shape broke away from the shadows and approached him from behind. It was Cora, and she held the knife. Lexi broke into a run and slid her hand into her pocket to pull out a gun or throwing knife.

Cora's brainwashed. I can't kill her for that.

She felt the weight of the stone in her other hand. *This will do.* It would distract her for the seconds she needed. She threw the stone at the woman and it was a perfect shot and caught her squarely in the temple.

What she hadn't anticipated was the explosion. It wasn't loud, but a bright flash followed immediately by a wet whoosh left Scott, Amy, the room, and part of the hallway covered in a coat of red.

Lexi, who had barely reached the entrance, skidded to a halt in the blood. Her jaw hung open in shock at the devastating transformation of the view before her. She shook her head several times while wet gore dripped from the ceiling. Cora had been completely obliterated.

"Wh…wh…wh." Scott finally gave up.

His body had protected Amy from the worst of it although, as she had suspected, the girl had zoned out again. *Small mercies.* The sorcerer stood holding his arms away from his body. "This is so bad."

Rivulets of red ran from his hair into a gap in the back of his collar. He turned slowly and stared at her.

"It's not my fault. It was the stone—I didn't know it would do that." She stopped speaking under the intensity of his withering stare.

"Why is it always me?" Scott's voice was a squeak.

Lexi giggled. It was involuntary and she clamped her jaw until the compulsion left her. "Can't you whoosh it somewhere else like you did in Palm Springs?"

He sighed. "It's different magic. I have no fucking idea what you did."

"She was coming up behind you with a blade but I was trying to avoid killing her."

"That went well," he snipped.

She stared around the red room. "Can you see the ring?"

"Are you looking at this room?" He waved his hand wildly. "She and everything on her is liquid. It must have been on her but there's no way to find it now." He sighed and looked at the catatonic girl. "Let's take Amy to the apartment. We can clean her up and try to unfuck her brain before her parents see her."

The sorcerer incanted a glamor so he and Amy could walk through New Orleans without horrifying the citizens. They stepped onto the street.

Agatha came running and put her arms around Lexi. "Are you okay?" She looked at Scott. "You smell bad."

Lexi waved her hand in front of her face. "Phew! I know—boys, right?"

The youngster laughed while she pretended to be oblivious to Scott's scowl.

The parents headed away with their daughter while the two friends made their way to the apartment with Amy.

The girl gazed fixedly ahead and required nothing more than his hand on her back to direct her. Within a few blocks, they were at the apartments, where Betsy and Lexi removed Amy's blood-soaked clothes and Scott threw them into the washer with his own. The young woman simply stood staring into who knew what while they wrapped her in Betsy's gown. The two women left her there, still in a daze, and stepped into the bathroom.

Betsy washed the blood from her hands. "Will Scott be able to bring her out of this?"

Lexi directed her to a towel before washing her hands. "Possibly. I think we should let her rest while her clothes are cleaned, then Broullard can take her. It's a good thing Scott took most of that. Otherwise, we'd be washing it out of her hair."

The other woman frowned. "How will we encourage her to rest? Could we poke her to topple her onto the bed?"

She threw the towel into the bath. "I think you've spent way too much time with Dick."

They entered the bedroom to find Amy curled in the bed with her eyes closed.

"I'll be honest, that was easier than I expected." She looked at Betsy. "I need to speak to Scott."

"That's fine. Leave her with me. I'll read my book and stay close."

They walked up the hall and the older woman settled into an armchair while she headed across to the other apartment.

Dick passed her a coffee as she entered. "All quiet?"

"Yes. Betsy's reading and Amy's sleeping. How's Scott?" She blew on her drink before she took a sip.

"I'm here and I'm fine." He walked into the room in shorts with his blond hair in damp waves.

Lexi sniffed and looked toward the kitchen. "What's that smell?"

"I incinerated my clothes." He took a mug from Dick.

"I'm sorry about the...I don't even know what to call that." She grimaced.

"Deconstruction?" the vampire suggested helpfully.

"It's as good a word as any." Scott shrugged.

She studied him anxiously. *He looks traumatized.*

The vampire sat and Marcel jumped into his lap. He looked at her. "I guess you're back on track with your investigation into the photograph. I'll pay a visit to this Lorenzo chap and see if we can have a heart-to-heart about his manners."

"I'll come and watch your back. Scott, I think you should rest."

The sorcerer nodded. He scrolled and tapped on his cell while he extended his arm across the counter to her. She slid her hand into his to refill the magical energy.

Dick smirked at them. "A picture of domestic bliss."

They both flipped him the bird.

The vampire put Marcel onto the floor and went to the door. "I'll get ready, then."

After a few minutes, she finished her coffee and thumped Scott's shoulder. "Get some rest."

Scott watched as Lexi left the apartment. He returned his gaze to his cell and typed.

I know where that is. I can meet you there in twenty minutes.

Quickly, he dressed, looked in on Betsy, and headed out of the building and down the street. Moments later, he turned left onto Bourbon street and walked several blocks until he reached a small eatery. He looked at the sign—Nola Po'boys—and entered. The unassuming establishment was rumored to sell some of the best local dishes in New Orleans. He ordered a catfish po'boy to go, put his bag down, and took a seat in a booth opposite an unhealthy looking man who fidgeted with a package. "Is this it?"

The man nodded but made no other movement.

He waited for a response before he prompted, "Can I see it?"

After a furtive glance around the room, his companion slid the package across the table. Scott looked inside and smiled. He squeezed the contents in his hand and his smile broadened. He passed some folded notes across the table. "That'll do nicely."

The stranger snaked his hand out and the money was gone. He stood and left without a backward glance.

The sorcerer glanced around, sure that no one was watching. He took the item from its packaging and pushed it into his bag—or more precisely, into a specific room in his dimensional pocket. The server brought his po'boy and he left to walk to the apartment.

CHAPTER THIRTY-NINE

The women spoke in hushed tones as they retreated along the hallway. The apartment door opened and closed.

Marie Delphine LaLaurie opened her eyes.

She raised a finger to her face and slipped it into her mouth. When she removed it, she wore the ring.

Delphine had known the importance of the ring instantly. When she gazed at it through the young girl's eyes, she knew it to be hers. She remembered scrubbing dried blood from the claws around the stones after an evening's entertainment at the mansion. Her brows lowered at the thought of what had once been her stronghold. She hadn't recognized the mansion when she returned as Cora and Amy. Everything was different—everything was different *everywhere*. The only things that hadn't changed were the toys. Their screams sounded exactly as she remembered them.

With a small smile, she rolled onto her back and stretched her arms into the air. Amy's skin was pale and young. It made her recall her life before and how her skin had begun to loosen and wrinkle with age but now, it was young again. She rose from the bed and studied the slight form in the mirror.

The girl was too skinny—was she sick? She thought about some of the games she'd played in that slender body. They should have been difficult with her scrawny little arms, but she was filled with a power she'd never experienced before. Taking the boy's spine had been easy. Cora had been even stronger but she liked Amy's delicate features more. She opened the robe. The girl wasn't perfect, though. Her breasts were too small.

She touched the face and thought about the shock on it when she approached Amy outside her apartment as Cora, held a knife to her throat, and forced her to put the ring on. For a moment, she'd considered leaving the older woman in the street with the knife in her gut, but they were so pliant after she'd taken them over that it didn't hurt to keep her around.

Cora's body had been exhausted when she'd had to pursue the little girl. It had been unfortunate that she'd had to race through the house and search all the rooms, only to lose the little shit. She'd barely managed to shove the ring into Amy's mouth seconds before the blond boy came in.

Delphine turned from the mirror. She pulled the robe around her and walked along the hallway to the living room.

Almost soundless, she crept past the sleeping Betsy, walked to the kitchen, and drew a knife from the block. A thrill ran down her spine as she tested the blade. She returned to the living room and stood over Betsy, who remained asleep with a book in her lap. Until now, she had avoided looking directly at the woman before for fear she might give away that she had been aware of her surroundings. She stared at the long, lustrous, dark hair, full lips, and rounded breasts. This would be the perfect body. She would take this new body out and find new toys to play with.

Her mind made up, she aligned her finger with the other woman's —not touching, but close. In one quick movement, as she had done as Cora with Amy, she slid the ring from her finger directly onto her new body's.

Betsy's eyes jerked open and in a moment, Delphine went from looking down at her to looking up at Amy. She smiled at the young blonde, whose face slackened as she gazed unseeingly into the distance. With a calm, unhurried motion, she stood, took the knife from the catatonic girl's hand, and led her to bed.

She left the bedroom and was walking through the apartment when the door opened.

Dick entered and greeted her with a smile. "How's Amy?"

With easy nonchalance, she picked the book up and hid the hand with the ring carefully beneath it as she settled into the chair and tucked the knife under her thigh. "I just checked on her. No change."

"I'm going to visit Lorenzo. I'll be back in time for dinner and I'll take you somewhere nice with a jazz band."

"That will be lovely." She smiled. "Have a nice time with Lorenzo."

He raised an eyebrow. "Betsy, you have a strange sense of humor."

Delphine lifted the book and felt she'd made a mistake but had gotten away with it.

Once he'd left the apartment, she headed to the bedroom to change. The tight black dress she wore was perfect and she stood before the mirror to admire it a little longer. She heard the door again.

"Betsy?" said a man's voice.

She slipped a gown on over the dress and peeked out to see the young, blond man. "Yes?"

"I'm popping out but I should only be an hour. Do you want anything?"

"No, thank you." She smiled at the sound of the door closing.

Although a little impatient, she waited ten minutes before she stepped out and closed the door quietly.

Delphine knew these streets. Things had changed, of course, but not everything.

The bar was loud and she stepped to the counter and ordered a glass of rye whiskey. While she waited, she gazed around her. She turned to the mirror behind the bar and studied Betsy's face, pleased that it showed none of the outrage she felt.

The barman poured the drink and quoted the price.

"Let me find that for you." She smiled and opened the woman's purse.

"Make that two, please, barman. I'll get these."

She turned at the sound of the deep melodious voice and looked into the eyes of the tall handsome black man. "Why, aren't you…" Her gaze took him in, and she paused deliberately before she smiled. "Simply charming." He lifted the drinks and she followed him to a table.

He smiled. "I'm Bobby. May I ask your name, beautiful woman?"

"I'm so pleased to meet you, Robert. I'm Delphine."

"To the beautiful Delphine." He held his glass up.

With a coy smile, she held her glass up. "And to the devastatingly handsome Bobby."

They clinked glasses and drank.

The man leaned forward. "So, what do you do?"

"Do?" She was puzzled. For a moment, she wondered if he referred to her little entertainments.

"For a job," he clarified.

"Oh, I see. Well, my friend Bobby, I create sculptures—of a kind."

"Ah! An artist. Might I have seen any of your work?"

"Oh, a few pieces have been on display around the Quarter, recently. Who knows?" She laughed. "What do you…do?"

"I am in the Navy, ma'am. Speaking of which, I see some of my brothers-in-arms over there. Would you mind if I invite them to join us?"

Delphine looked at the bar and noticed two more muscular black men.

Ah! My friend Bobby is playing with me. Men. Then, now…they never really change. But I like to play too.

Betsy's face split into a huge grin. "Bobby, I would be thrilled to meet your friends."

Two other men joined them at the table.

"This is Darnell and Cole. Boys, this is Delphine. She's an artist."

Darnell sat and Cole went to get drinks. When he returned, she looked at each of them in turn.

The atmosphere had become predatory. She smiled, knowing these men were unaware of who was predator and who was prey.

"How interesting." She leaned toward Bobby. "You have the finest arms I have ever seen." She turned to Cole. "And you have the most beautiful eyes." Finally, she gazed at the third man. "You have the loveliest lips. Are you gentlemen by any chance interested in sculpture? I find myself in need of new subjects."

"We would be honored." Bobby flashed quick glances at the other men.

"Let's go to my place of residence, it's rather small—embarrassingly so—but I'm sure we could continue our conversation there in private." She couldn't wait to get them home and fulfill her plan to make the perfect man.

CHAPTER FORTY

Dick showed his teeth to enter the private bar. It wasn't difficult to locate Lorenzo, who sat on a dais surrounded by half-naked women. He almost laughed. A young woman draped her arm over his and he noticed it was peppered with bite marks. He looked at the arm, then unsmilingly to her face. She stepped back.

The vampire was aware of the gazes fixed on him as he navigated the room. The small pockets of conversation around him had ceased.

He ordered a drink at the bar and turned. It wasn't necessary to shout across the room as they were vampires and his quarry would hear. He leaned lazily on the bar. "Lorenzo, can I buy you a drink?"

Lorenzo looked up as though he hadn't previously noticed him. He smiled disingenuously. "I'll have what you're having."

Dick flicked a glance at the barman. "Another, please." He smiled warmly at Lorenzo—he was an actor, after all. "Ice?"

The man flicked a hand. "As it comes."

"Rohypnol?" He raised an eyebrow.

Lorenzo smiled wider and his teeth descended. "As it comes."

The vampire took both drinks to an empty table in the middle of the room and sat. He placed the second next to the empty chair opposite him.

314

His quarry left the dais and appeared in the chair at vamp speed.

"I'm William. My friends call me—well, never mind. I don't think we've met."

The man's mask slipped briefly and his eyes flickered with annoyance.

Dick pretended surprise. "We have met? My bad."

Lorenzo flicked his hand in a dismissive gesture. "I was in the clan when Giovanni led it. You would have no reason to remember me."

He leaned forward. "Lorenzo, I feel there's an elephant in the room. A Peter-shaped elephant. Why on earth did you try to have me killed?"

"We run a tight ship here. I lead the largest and soon to be the only vampire clan in New Orleans. I expect visitors to present themselves within twenty-four hours of arrival. If they don't, I take it as a personal insult and their lives are forfeit." He threw his drink back. "Thank you for the drink. But your life is still forfeit." In an instant, he was on his throne and the table was surrounded by six vampires.

Dick sighed and finished his drink. "Are you sure I can't change your mind about this, Lorenzo?"

His quarry looked up with every appearance of having forgotten about him already. He looked at the vampires surrounding the table. "Why is he still here?"

The enforcers took a step forward but in the space of two seconds, three of them were headless. Their bodies thudded and began to desiccate.

The others turned in circles, looking for the threat, and Lorenzo stood as he shoved his naked donors aside.

A loud bang caught everyone's attention. Lexi had allowed herself to become visible. She appeared at the bar and smacked her bloody katana onto the counter. "Hello, Lorenzo. I think we need to talk about your ship."

In the moment when he saw Lexi, Lorenzo's lips began to shift into a smile. This faded, however, when his brain caught up with what she had done. His jaw dropped. "But I thought Kindred—"

"You thought what?" she asked innocently.

A vampire near her rocketed toward her but froze about a foot away, paralyzed by a magical shield around her.

"Do you see what I'm talking about, Lorenzo? How is this respect?" She flicked her katana and the dead vampire dropped.

That's the last of the magic.

"Tobey!" A young human blood donor screamed and threw herself at Lexi, who punched her in the face. The girl collapsed, unconscious, beside her desiccating friend.

"This crap will stop or we'll back another clan." She walked to the door and turned to the room to point at Dick, who followed her. "And he's off-limits. Have I made myself clear?"

The vampire turned to her as they walked through the French Quarter. "So, it's true. Kindred is backing a clan?"

She looked around as she walked. "He doesn't have much of a poker face. When he saw me, his face went from joy to confusion to annoyance in a second. He definitely has a deal going with Kindred."

Dick took a handkerchief from his pocket and blotted the bloodstains on his suit. "I haven't personally read the Kindred rulebook, but I suspect cutting deals with factions isn't in it."

"Correct. Speaking of Kindred. Surely they'll be back soon. I didn't get very far in my investigation."

"No, but you took a murderer off the streets and saved a few lives." He sighed. "But you're right. I think we've outstayed our welcome here."

Lexi grimaced. "Scott will be annoyed with me. He hates it when I put my katana in the dimensional pocket without cleaning it first. That's the problem with you vamps. I can't wipe my blade on you to get the blood off because you instantly start turning to dust, which only makes it more of a mess."

He looked at her with an eyebrow raised. "We're sorry."

She spun as a hand caught her shoulder. "Holy shit, Scott. I could have taken your head off."

The sorcerer chuckled. "Aww. It's cute you think you could do that."

"What are you doing out?" She scanned the area warily. "Did Broullard pick Amy up already?"

He made his own study of the street as they spoke. "I'm looking for Betsy. She was going to watch Amy but when I went to check on them, Amy was asleep and Betsy was nowhere in sight."

Dick looked immediately concerned. "Why didn't you do a locator spell?"

"I tried." He paused and clearly didn't want to say the next part. "She's not showing up."

"Could—" Lexi asked but couldn't complete the question.

Scott shook his head. "She's not in Fae. I called Dolores."

The vampire dragged his fingers over his scalp. "What did you use to locate her?"

The sorcerer dug in his pocket and held the object out. "Her wedding ring."

Dick took it. "She never takes it off—never."

Lexi started walking and snatched Scott's hand to refill her magic reservoir. "Okay, let's get back to the apartment. We'll see if she's returned, then we can fan out from there and cover more ground. Can Dolores join us? We shouldn't leave Amy alone."

They entered the building and found Broullard waiting outside their apartment door. "Tell me you have Amy. Her parents are going nuts."

"We have her." Scott opened the door to the front apartment and walked in. "Betsy?"

There was no response.

The cop did a double-take and stared at Dick. Clearly, he'd identified him as a vampire.

"Broullard, this is our neighbor, Dick. He's lost his friend Betsy and we're helping him locate her."

"Detective. Lexi speaks very highly of you." He shook the detective's hand, unlocked the door to his apartment, and opened it.

"She does? Well, that's great. I don't mean to be rude, but—"

"What the actual fuck?" The vampire's voice emerged as a squeak when he stepped into the apartment.

With a sigh, she waited at her door for a moment and was about to enter when Dick's raised voice made her step into the hallway again. "Young man, if you don't get out of here, I can guarantee there will be nothing left of any of you."

A man's voice responded. "I think that should be up to our lady friend."

Lexi and Broullard glanced at each other. Two men bolted from the apartment and down the hall as though the devil himself were after them. A third was shoved through the door. He turned and squared up to the vampire. The cop coughed lightly and put his hand casually on his hip to reveal the police badge. The man saw it and allowed Dick to escort him along the hall.

He turned to him. "Seriously, dude, she's kinda weird anyway."

Scott signaled to Broullard. "I'll take you to Amy." He led the detective across the hall to the other apartment where Betsy leaned on the door, twirled her hair around a finger, and winked suggestively at the young man.

She stepped aside to let them in "There's room inside for two more big ones." She smiled at the detective.

Lexi stepped into her apartment with her eyebrows almost at her hairline. *Wow!*

Dick waited at the top of the stairway for a few seconds, then returned to her apartment. He marched around the room and threw his arms up. "Sailors. Three fucking sailors. Call Dolores." He pointed toward their apartment. "She's going to Fae—tonight." He was almost hyperventilating.

She put a hand on his shoulder. "Dick, breathe. Or don't. Honestly, I don't know what's best in this situation."

Scott returned. "Betsy's helping Broullard get Amy ready. When she's dressed, I'll try to bring her out of the catatonia."

Relieved that this, at least, seemed to be close to resolution, she nodded. "When Amy and Broullard have gone, I want to do a locator spell with the key we got from Anne Bird. Let's see if I can find what it opens before Kindred gets back."

Scott inclined his head to indicate his agreement.

Dick took the ring out and put it on the table. "Why didn't the locator work with her ring?"

The young sorcerer's face went slack.

"What?" Lexi could feel a jolt of shock through their empathetic connection.

"The ring. Betsy's wearing the ring."

No one had to ask which ring. Suddenly, she was alone. Scott had disappeared and Dick had raced at vamp speed to the other apartment.

When she entered it, Scott crouched over Broullard who lay facedown with a carving knife in his back. "He'll be okay. Go." He pointed toward the bedroom.

She ran along the hallway. Dick sprawled on the floor with a silver letter opener in his chest. She couldn't imagine how Delphine could have gotten the drop on a vampire.

Amy was still oblivious in the bed and Betsy—who was obviously Delphine—stood on the other side of the bed with an open pair of scissors to her own throat.

The possessed woman snarled. "Let me go or I'll take your precious Betsy with me."

"What would be the point of that?" She shook her head and took a step forward.

"To break his heart." Her smile was malicious as she glanced at the vampire.

She could only imagine how strong and fast the woman was now —strong enough and fast enough to take down a vampire. She touched the scar and said, "Sleep."

Delphine remained standing and stared at her with a small smirk. "She's already asleep, stupid."

Shit! Where the hell is Scott?

Lexi sensed that she didn't have long to act. She could only think of one course of action and didn't like it. She took another step toward Delphine. "I can't let you do this." She put her hands up to show the woman she wasn't armed.

The madwoman surged into an attack. The scissors lowered from

Betsy's throat and pointed at the new target. Instead of pushing her attacker back, Lexi pulled the woman toward her and they landed hard. The scissors plunged into her stomach, and Delphine grinned.

She flailed and screamed as she slapped ineffectually at the woman's arms, while her assailant yanked the scissors out and held them over her.

Lexi tried to speak.

Delphine leaned closer. "What are you trying to say, honey?"

She drew in a ragged breath. "I got you…right where I want you."

Her fingers closed around the necklace and she tugged hard. It snapped and slipped from Betsy's neck.

The scissors fell when the arthritis in her eighty-year-old fingers made them too difficult to hold.

The woman screamed in horror. "No! What is this?"

Scott appeared behind her and pulled the ring from her hand.

"You took your time," Lexi whispered.

"I was healing Broullard. I can't be everywhere at once."

"I bet you could." Dick coughed and blood sprayed over his shirt. He wiped it and avoided the letter opener that still protruded from him. "Shit."

Scott crouched and faced him but the vampire pushed him away. "See to her."

The sorcerer put one hand on Lexi. A metal marble appeared in his hand but disappeared in seconds.

Broullard entered, holding towels. He passed one to Scott and moved to Dick.

"You can pull that out." The young man pointed at the letter opener.

The cop hesitated.

Dick gasped. "You're looking a little pale there, my friend."

He smirked. "We could be twins."

The vampire grasped the opener and pulled it out himself. He slumped and Broullard pressed the towel on the wound.

Lexi closed her eyes as the pain faded in her stomach.

CHAPTER FORTY-ONE

Betsy watched the young woman, who gazed at the ring. It sat under an upturned glass in the middle of the table. "Are you thinking of taking it for a spin?"

Lexi looked at her with an eyebrow raised. "Would you recommend it?"

The old woman sighed and pushed down a wave of nausea. "I don't remember a thing about it. I think I'm quite happy about that."

"I wonder if Amy will remember anything." She looked curiously at the ring once more.

Betsy thought about what Amy had done to her young beau. "I hope not. Will you take the ring to the museum?" She opened the oven, removed the cookies, and put them down beside the other piles of cookies, brownies, and cupcakes that filled almost every surface in the apartment.

"We'll get Joseph to exorcize the spirit first. That is a disaster waiting to happen—again. In the meantime, we'll see where this leads us." Lexi took the key from her vest pocket and put it on the table.

The old woman gave her a plate of cookies and patted her cheek before she walked out of the kitchen. "I hope you get your answers, dear."

The door opened to admit Scott and Dick. The young man made a beeline for the cookies on the counter with Betsy behind him. When he reached out, she smacked his hand away. "These are for the detective."

His shoulders slumped. "Again? Won't you make any for me?"

The woman stepped closer to the counter but turned to face him. "Scott dear, I promise. Whenever I stab you, you'll get cookies too."

"Well, when will that be? Because I want a cookie." He stepped closer to a tray.

"Sooner than you think if you steal one of the detective's cookies."

Scott continued to whine. "But he's not even here."

"He needed to see his wife. And maybe get away from me. But he'll be back and when he is, he'll have these waiting for him." She looked at everything she'd made. Baking relaxed her and she dearly needed something to keep her busy.

Dick gazed at the stacks of baked goods. "Nothing says 'Sorry I stabbed you' like a double chocolate chip cookie."

The sorcerer pointed at him. "You stabbed Dick. Why don't you make him cookies and I'll have them?"

The vampire pinched the bridge of his nose. "Don't get her started again. She's chased me around offering her neck for the last two hours. It's positively indecent."

Betsy twisted the corner of her apron. "I hate that you have the memory of me attacking you with a letter opener. I don't know how you can bear to look at me."

"And you think chasing me with your neck out will traumatize me less?" He rolled his eyes.

Lexi broke a cookie in half and ate it while she looked directly at Scott and made "mmmm" sounds.

A whine filled the air and the old woman looked at the puppy. "What's wrong, Marcel?"

"That was Scott." Lexi chuckled.

Betsy looked at him as he sighed pathetically over a pile of the delicious-smelling baked goods. "Fine. One. You may have one cookie because you didn't let anyone die."

He put an arm around her. "I know it's been said before, but it wasn't your fault. I healed Broullard, Lexi, and Dick within minutes and no one blames you."

She plastered a big smile onto her face. "It's kind of you to say that, Scott. Really, everyone, I'm fine." She felt every one of her eighty years.

Dick lifted her chin. "It's good to hear it. And I hope your dance card isn't full because I plan to take you out tonight."

"You're very sweet, dear, but I think I've had as much excitement as I'll ever need. I'm ready to see my son and go home."

The vampire took her hand. "How about dinner, then?"

"Yes, dinner would be lovely. Somewhere quiet."

"I want to point out that this"—Scott held the cookie up—"is the price Betsy put on me saving your lives. One cookie…between you. Remember that."

The old woman snatched the cookie away. "And that's why you can't have nice things."

Dick picked his jacket up. "Okay, we'll see where the key leads, then I'd be delighted to escort you to dinner."

Betsy waved goodbye as they left. The door closed and she allowed the smile to fade from her face. She looked around the apartment and sighed. It had been quite an adventure, except for stabbing everyone. After she checked on the tray of cookies in the oven, she walked to the balcony and looked out. It was dark, and mosquitos were becoming a pest. She drew the screen across the doors and looked at Marcel. He'd fallen asleep on the floor no more than two steps away from his dinner. She turned her head at a knock at the door, slipped the necklace below her neckline, and opened it.

The young man smiled. "Is William here?"

"I'm afraid you've just missed him. Are you Peter?"

He nodded shyly. "Yes, ma'am."

She stepped back and opened the door a little wider. "Come in. How are you feeling now?"

"I'm…much better, thank you." He took her hand quickly and

kissed it. "I didn't know William was hiding the most stunning woman in all creation here. He's full of surprises."

Betsy smiled at the pale young man, but that comment had seemed a little forward. "Well, thank you. Would you like to wait? I'm sure he'll return soon. Can I get you a drink?"

Peter scratched his little goatee beard and glanced toward the table, then narrowed his eyes at the upturned glass over the ring. His face expressed puzzlement. He dragged his gaze back to her. "That's very kind of you." His head tilted toward the glass. "Hmm!"

"Excuse me, I have to check on my cookies." She returned the oven and stooped to look through the oven door before she felt a chill as though the man stood incredibly close—directly behind her, perhaps —and her heart raced. At Marcel's growl, she straightened and began to turn. The apartment door opened and her three friends entered.

"Don't look at me. It's your key. Why didn't *you* pick it up?" Dick shook his head.

Betsy shook her head when she realized she was alone in the kitchen. "Peter?" She looked around in bewilderment. "Dick, your friend Peter is here."

The vampire smiled. "He is? Peter?" There was no answer.

She stared at the swaying screen across the balcony doors. "I don't understand. He was here. I spoke to him not three seconds before you opened that door."

Marcel continued to growl, this time near the balcony.

Lexi and Dick shared a look.

"What did he look like?" the vampire asked

Betsy shrugged. "Handsome, pale. Long dark hair and one of those tiny little beards they wear these days."

"Lorenzo," Lexi and Dick said together.

Scott stood at the table and picked the key up for the locator spell. "Betsy, where's the ring?"

They all spun to look at the glass in the middle of the table that no longer contained a possessed ring.

The young man put his hands on the back of a chair and stared at the glass. "This is bad."

Lexi looked at Dick. "I'll kill him."

CHAPTER FORTY-TWO

"How is she?" Lexi glanced at the door as Dick entered.

He closed it behind him. "Lying down."

Scott snatched a cookie. "Even with a thirty-two-year-old body, this will take its toll. I've recommended she keep the necklace on until she's home."

Dick narrowed his eyes. "I thought it was only a glamor."

He sat on the arm of the couch. "Do you know the saying, you're only as old as you feel?"

The vampire nodded. "I see. Well, we need to get her out of here. She's not safe. I won't risk her again."

"I've messaged Dolores." The sorcerer broke the cookie in half.

Lexi twirled the mystery key in her hand. "Right. We can't simply sit here. Dick, do you have any idea where Lorenzo would go?"

"A few. But is it Lorenzo? Perhaps we should ask where *Delphine* would go."

She dug her fingertips into her forehead and screwed her face up. "Shit."

"We—" A thump at the door silenced Scott. He threw the cookie into his mouth but spat it into his hand immediately. "That's horrible. It tastes like liver."

"That pile of cookies was for Marcel." She smirked.

"Marcel gets his own cookies?" He rolled his eyes.

Lexi drew her katana and went to look through the peephole. "It's Broullard." She opened the door.

The detective entered the apartment, his face rigid.

Scott's shoulders slumped. "Another one?"

Broullard shook his head. "*One?* No. Six. I came straight here. They were found about fifteen minutes ago."

The sorcerer made his way to the kitchen sink and washed his hands. "Who were the victims?"

"A group of tourists. They were in a courtyard behind a bar. The bodies are a mess." The man stopped speaking and he stared as Scott scrubbed his tongue with his fingernails, then seemed to recover. "Yes, well. Their throats were ripped out and every one of them was found with the head facing the wrong way."

Lexi decided it was time to break the news to him. "What color were they?"

He looked at her and raised an eyebrow. "What? But you have the ring. It can't be her. Anyway, it looked like a vamp attack to me."

She pushed her chair in. "It's Lorenzo. The vampire clan leader. He was here almost an hour ago and took the ring."

Broullard's jaw dropped. "Is everyone okay? Betsy?"

Dick, who stood at the window, turned to him. "She was here alone and she's shaken up but unharmed."

The detective exhaled sharply. "This is bad. But we know it's Delphine we're following, not Lorenzo. Her previous hosts seemed to mentally go to sleep. She didn't appear to have access to their minds."

"That's usually how it works, but I've never heard of a vampire being possessed before."

They turned to the door where Joseph stood. Lexi didn't jump this time as she'd half-expected him.

The vampire nodded to him. "When I told Betsy I was going to visit Lorenzo, she told me to have a nice time. I thought she was trying to be funny. As Delphine, she wouldn't have known Lorenzo had tried to have me killed."

"How would Lorenzo have learned about the possessed ring?" Broullard asked,

He put his suit jacket on. "She said he looked at it almost straight away and thought at the time that he was simply puzzled. An upturned glass covering a ring in the middle of the table must have looked like an odd sight."

Broullard nodded. "So, he was looking for it."

Dick stood in front of the mirror and straightened his tie. "No. She was clear that his face showed surprise."

Joseph leaned on his staff and nodded. "It called to him. That's probably how Cora found it inside the couch."

Lexi looked at everyone a little warily. "Has anyone else felt it call?"

"Evil calls to evil," he explained,

Lexi looked from him to Dick. "Really? You didn't feel a hankering to try it on?"

"Are you serious right now?" A slight hissing sound escaped from Dick's fingers. "Ow!" When he removed his hand from his tie, he was wearing the silver lion's head tie pin. He glanced at Joseph. "Old habits…"

Broullard looked puzzled. "If he wasn't after the ring, why was he here?"

The vampire took a handkerchief out and wiped flakes of burned skin from the pin. "I think he was probably here to kill Betsy."

Her jaw dropped. "After the warning I gave him?"

He nodded. "You told him I was off-limits. I'm sure he thinks my friends are still on the menu."

She moved to the window. "We need to get out there and start looking."

As the others readied themselves to leave, Broullard gazed around the room at all the cupcakes and cookies. "I hope they aren't for me. She's already given me three boxes full of them."

"Pfft!" Scott muttered.

"Someone tell her I forgive her. She'll give me diabetes." The detective shook his head as they moved to the door.

Scott looked at Lexi. "I've shielded the apartments. We need to let Betsy know we're going out but that she'll be safe. Dolores should be along shortly."

"I'll tell her." She went to the other apartment and immediately heard whispers. Someone was in the bedroom with their friend. Without hesitation, she ran through the apartment and burst through the bedroom door. Betsy and Dolores stared at her in surprise.

She put her hand on her chest. "God! I thought—" She blew a short burst of air out in relief. "I don't know what I thought. We're heading out after Lorenzo."

Dolores smiled. "We're good here."

"Aren't you going to Fae?" She was surprised.

"Betsy wants to be sure Dick's safe before she leaves."

Lexi nodded and headed out.

On the street, she asked, "Should we go to the mansion again?"

Joseph considered this. "There are other places she might also be drawn to. Do you know her previous home, detective? The antique store?"

Broullard nodded. "I know it. I've done the tour several times."

Dick stepped beside him. "I'll join you as you might need someone who can match Lorenzo's speed."

The cop glanced at his vehicle. "I'll leave my car here, then. It's only a couple of blocks and it'll be easier for you to pick up a trail."

The vampire stared at him. "I'm not a bloodhound."

Broullard stuttered an apology.

"I'm kidding. Jeez, tough crowd." Dick shook his head.

Lexi's gaze slid to Joseph. "What will you do?"

"I'll warn my people to stay off the streets." He turned and walked away into the night.

Lexi, Scott, Dick, and Broullard walked together as far as Royal Street, then separated and proceeded in opposite directions.

The vampire and detective walked down the quiet dark street.

They fell silent when they approached the antique store and found the glass door shattered.

After a hasty glance at each other, Broullard drew his gun and nodded his readiness. They stepped in carefully.

Strange shadows were cast through the store from the streetlights outside.

Furniture was positioned in three sections to create two paths through to the back. They each took a side and crept through. The cop seemed to be trying to hide his jitters, although he responded with tiny jerks of his head to every creak.

"Detective Broullard," Dick began in a conversational tone and made the man jump again. "I'm sorry, do you have a first name?"

"Charles."

"Lovely to meet you, Charles. Do you think there's any way you might regulate your heart rate? It's deafening me."

With a wry smile, Broullard stood and breathed with slow, measured breaths. "Can you smell anything?"

The vampire sniffed. "Beeswax, mothballs, and blood."

"I think my grandmother wore a perfume like that."

Broullard took another step and stumbled into a marble standing ashtray. He caught it quickly before it could fall, but the metal tray inside it rang loudly.

Dick looked at him and so didn't notice when a fist swung out of the shadows and caught his head. He fell, stunned.

A second later, Lorenzo's hand held the detective by the throat against an ornate cabinet. "I thought I already dealt with you." The voice was unusually effeminate.

The assailant sniffed at Broullard and his teeth descended. He bit into his neck but pulled away immediately. His breath came heavily and he drew his head back as he breathed in and lowered it forward as he breathed out.

Lorenzo vomited pints of blood over his captive in several heaves. He dropped the man, who skidded away while he spat in disgust and wiped the blood from his face. The possessed vampire retched blood over the furniture and floor.

"Problem, madame?"

The crazed gaze darted to Dick. "William. Your life is still forfeit," he said in a more masculine voice before he vanished.

Dick looked across the store. "Oh, dear God. Please, no." He stumbled across the space, still dizzy from the blow.

Broullard stood from where he had half-cowered. "I'm okay, the blood's not mine—"

"Not you, you idiot. This is a Louis XV gilt wood and Aubusson tapestry chair. That blood will never come out."

The man stared at him with his mouth open.

He huffed and shook his head. "Come on, then." When he reached the door, he turned. "On the bright side, Charles, if you die tonight, you'll wake up again tomorrow night with Lorenzo and Delphine as your parents."

Lexi and Scott entered the mansion, this time through the front door as it opened to allow a workman out. It was the middle of the night and the house was a hive of activity, mostly centered around the sewing room. They walked to the door of the room but didn't enter. The blood-soaked bolts of cloth were gone, as was the carpet. A team of white-clad people removed the wallpaper and painted the ceiling.

A man who had been scrubbing the floor looked at them with curiosity on his face before he stood.

Scott lifted his cell to his ear as though he were listening to someone. He looked at Lexi and held the cell to his chest. "How would *you* say it's coming along?"

Her gaze darted around the room. She screwed her face up like she was looking at the world's most fucked-up job. Her glance at the guy was intended to convey, "I have your balls in the palm of my hand right now, my friend. Do not fuck with me."

He quite understandably froze.

She shrugged. "It's coming along great."

The sorcerer returned to his cell. "Great."

The guy looked like he might faint with relief. Without a word, he dropped to his knees and continued to scrub.

They wandered away from ground zero.

Scott looked over his shoulder. "How is all this going on? The owner?"

Lexi considered the question for a moment. "Broullard probably contacted a clean-up crew that works for Kindred."

He dropped the cell into his pocket. "I can't see Lorenzo getting in here with all these people around."

She stopped and looked at him. "We did."

"Oh, right. Good point."

They continued to check the house room by room.

Finally, they stood at the stairs to the attic and peered into the dark. She found a light switch and the steps gleamed with red lights. "You have to be kidding me."

Scott sneered. "It's a little macabre."

They ascended cautiously and looked around. The room wasn't big, and it was clear that no one was there. They turned to the exit and stopped in surprise. Detective Broullard stood in front of them. He was a ghoulish sight, covered in blood almost from head to toe. Worse, he didn't speak and simply stood and stared at them.

Scott leaned closer and poked him hard in the chest.

"What the hell was that for?" the detective snapped.

The sorcerer exhaled sharply. "I thought you were an apparition. I see them sometimes just after they've passed, and if they've been hit by a truck or something, they kinda look like this." He waved his hand in the detective's general direction.

"Charles? Ahh…there you are. You found them. Excellent work."

"'Charles'?" Lexi looked suspiciously at them. "You two haven't been—"

"No! I'm a married man," Broullard protested.

Scott stared at the blood. "So, what happened to you? Let me guess, someone threw a magic stone." His gaze slid to his partner.

The cop looked perplexed. "What? Oh, you mean one of Joseph's stones. Only an idiot would use one of those."

Her friend smirked as his gaze slid sideways to her.

Dick patted Broullard on the shoulder. "The detective had the damnedest luck. Lorenzo knocked me for six, then went to feed on our friend here. But it appears he may have drained the people he killed earlier tonight. He'd gorged himself on blood and had a slight reaction."

"Slight. Yes, well." The detective grimaced.

Scott put his hand on his neck and healed the puncture wound.

Lexi asked, "Any idea where he or she might have gone next?"

The vampire raised an eyebrow. "That's another thing. It's not only her in there. Lorenzo is conscious and he spoke to me. Also, he is very, very strong." He rubbed the back of his head.

Scott nodded. "It makes sense when you consider what Amy was able to do to Jamal."

She sighed. "That's disappointing news. I hoped she'd wander into the sun and burst them both into flames. If Lorenzo's awake in there, he won't let her do that."

"That ring is like the gift that keeps on giving, isn't it?" Dick turned to the stairs.

Broullard looked at his watch in horror. "Dick, look at the time. You have less than fifteen minutes to get out of the sun."

Lexi rolled her eyes. *Dick keeps forgetting the time. He'll blow his cover.*

The vampire headed down the stairs. "Yes, gosh. I absolutely must run. The furniture in this place is giving me a migraine anyway." In an instant, he was gone.

The detective looked at her. "Do vamps get migraines?"

She shrugged "Hell if I know. Shall we make a move?"

Broullard bit his lip. "Hey, I have an idea. It's fifteen minutes until sunrise—"

"Twelve," Scott interjected.

"Why don't we simply wait twelve minutes." The man sounded exhausted.

Lexi knew exactly how he felt. "Okay. Let's do a last check around the house on the way down."

As they descended the stairs, they bumped into the man who had been working on the floor. He stepped away at the sight of Broullard, who flashed his badge. The man hurried around them.

The detective scowled at his clothing. "I'm running out of shirts."

They returned to the apartment building and he climbed into his car.

Scott and Lexi climbed the stairs, stumbled into the apartment, and fell onto their beds. Both were asleep in seconds.

CHAPTER FORTY-THREE

A thump at the door woke Lexi from an all too short sleep. By the time the caller knocked a second time, she was opening it.

Broullard didn't look like he'd had much sleep, but he spun fast enough and gaped at the sight of her in a vest and panties with a katana in her hand. "Sorry. Downstairs in ten. Five if you can."

She shuffled into the bedroom and poked Scott. "We're up."

He groaned. "What time is it?"

"It's best you don't know." She dragged her leathers on. "It'll only upset you."

The sorcerer looked at himself. "Eurgh! I'm still in my clothes." He stared at her as she pulled her boots on. "When did you get undressed?"

Startled, she stopped and wrinkled her brow in thought before she shook her head slowly. "I don't remember."

The two of them were at the front of the building in six minutes.

Lexi looked at the detective. "You look like you didn't get much sleep."

Broullard rubbed his face. "I didn't get any. Neither, it seems, did Lorenzo. While we were in the mansion, he was…busy."

They scrambled into his car and arrived at a bar two streets away only minutes later.

Several people had gathered outside, some with curious faces and others worried. A woman caught Lexi's arm.

"Please, is my daughter in there? I mean…she passed, we know that. But is there any way to tell if she was there?"

Someone else came forward and pulled the woman away. The witch was adorned in pentacles and goddess symbols and clearly felt she had to pull the woman away from the Kindred bitch for her safety.

Scott looked at all the worried faces. "Who are all these people?"

Broullard marched forward. "Word gets around. It's not even an official crime scene yet."

"I can see that." There was no crime scene tape and the people guarding the door looked like the clean-up crew from the mansion.

They entered the back room. The desiccated remains of at least thirty vampires lay in fragile piles around the room.

"It looks like there was a hell of a battle," Scott muttered.

The detective looked at him and shook his head. "This is all one clan."

"You're sure?" Lexi made her way around piles of ash. Some were still vaguely in the shape of a person.

Broullard nodded. "It was a massacre."

"Were there any witnesses?" She approached a table with wallets and purses piled on top and sifted through them.

"A few people from the bar out front said one man went in and came out again about twenty minutes later."

"Lorenzo? Alone? Are you sure?" Scott appeared to be struggling to believe it.

She dropped a wallet onto the pile. "How do you know which wallet came from which pile?"

Broullard shrugged. "I don't."

His answer annoyed her but she decided to leave it for now. She turned to Scott. "Find out what her name was."

She was talking about the daughter of the woman outside. He nodded once and left the room.

"I guess the war's over," the other man muttered.

Lexi turned to him. "What?"

"They've been at it for years, haven't they? I guess that's been resolved. No one will stand against his clan now."

She walked to a couple of sheets that covered human bodies. He glanced at them. "Donors."

At a loss for words, she stood, turned slowly, and took it all in. Her gaze stopped at red, floor-length drapes. "What's behind the drapes?"

Broullard glanced at them. "That's the stage area when they have live bands." He pointed in the opposite direction with his thumb. "The guys are waiting to get started."

"The guys?" She turned to see the people in white overalls. They had a large industrial vacuum and uncoiled the cables and plugged them in. She knew what this meant.

Scott was on his way in. He had also stopped to stare at them, his face horrified. He continued to walk toward Broullard and Lexi but she marched toward the men and strode straight past her friend.

She stopped in front of the white-clad men. "Unplug that and get it out of here. I want you here with a dustpan and brush. Take pictures, then bag and tag each pile separately. Where possible, I want to see each bag with some form of ID." She turned away.

One of the men called after her. "Wait. You want us to bag them separately? Why?"

Lexi halted and allowed her expression to settle into cold and inscrutable. Her companions' body language indicated that they saw the difference. She had called on her inner Kindred bitch. As she spun to the man, she heard Broullard speak to Scott. "She won't kill him here in front of everyone, will she?"

Ignoring him, she faced the man and opened her mouth to speak.

He almost stumbled over his words. "I'll do that now. Right now."

The men scrambled to remove their equipment.

Broullard exhaled a tension-filled breath. "I'm sorry. If there are new procedures we weren't aware of—"

"There are people outside—family members. We won't give them the contents of a vacuum cleaner and ask them to take a scoopful.

Where possible, we will give them the remains of their loved ones. Scott."

He jumped. "Sorry, yes?"

"I want each of those wallets and purses with the correct remains. And let that woman know if her daughter is here."

Lexi turned to the detective. "Was the clan leader here?"

Broullard shook his head. "Thomas? He wasn't identified as being among the remains."

"Are you sure? There are remains unaccounted for with no ID."

"The clothes aren't a fit." The man seemed confident.

Lexi pinched her bottom lip as she thought. "Maybe Lorenzo intentionally chose a time when Thomas wasn't here to teach him a lesson?"

He scowled but thought about it. "I doubt it. You know what he's like—he'd rather simply kill people. Although he was never really a fan of getting his own hands dirty."

"You've seen that he's being influenced by Delphine now. I think he'll be fairly hands-on from here on."

Scott moved between the various piles of dust with the personal effects and muttered his locator spells. An hour later, they had almost all the names but a few vamps hadn't carried ID.

He approached Lexi with a large clear bag filled with ashes and another clear evidence bag with clothes and a small sequined coin purse.

"Thanks. Can you take it—" She paused, looked at him, and felt him through their link. He was emotionally ragged. "I'll do it." She took the bags, went outside, and squinted in the daylight to look across the sea of faces. Her gaze finally settled on the woman, whose face crumpled when she realized instantly what this meant.

She walked to her and gave her the bags. The mother held them in her arms and leaned against a man as she sobbed. Lexi glanced up and saw the witch staring at her as she returned to the bar.

When she returned, the tagging work was almost complete. She glanced around the room to ensure nothing had been missed and narrowed her eyes at the long stage drapes.

Those drapes moved. I'm sure of it.

Lexi turned to the cleaners. "Wait outside but don't go anywhere."

As they filed out, she glanced at Broullard and Scott, who both watched her curiously.

When the door closed, she pointed to the top of the drapes. Something moved very slightly on the far side.

The detective narrowed his eyes. "That area was searched."

She drew her katana and Broullard his gun. They walked hesitantly forward.

"Wait." Scott muttered a few words and the drapes separated.

Something moved among the stage lights but was difficult to make out. Lexi focused and tilted her head in concentration.

A tangle of people tied up?

They walked forward and Scott untied a rope to lower it slowly.

Broullard stared. "I think I might throw up."

What faced them was horrific. A vampire's arms, legs, back, and head had been broken and twisted to unusual angles. Long, silver-plated pins had been driven through the joints to ensure that when they set at the unusually fast speed a vampire healed at, it would appear unnatural. He looked like a crab. His eyes were full of terror and his mouth had been stitched closed with silver wire.

The sorcerer put his hand on the victim's head and he lost consciousness.

"Can you do anything about this?" Lexi asked him.

"I'll sort the silver out, for now, then I might need someone strong to help me fix this mess." He retrieved a metal ball from his pocket. "I'll plate the silver in steel and pull it out."

She took the metal ball from his palm. "Why didn't you do that in Palm Springs instead of using my gold ring?"

"I didn't know if it would work. I've been reading up since then."

Lexi dropped the ball into Scott's hand. He flicked a finger out and the drapes began to close.

They left him on the stage behind the heavy curtains and she went to the door and called the cleaner in from the bar. He approached her nervously.

"There's a witch outside with purple hair. I'd like to speak to her." She watched him walk out through the front area.

"I think you're wrong about this war being over," she said and turned to Broullard. "I have a horrible feeling it's only just begun."

He sat on the edge of a table. "Is there any chance we could get more Kindred into town to head this off?"

She sighed. "About that—"

"Get your hands off me, you motherfuckers."

She turned as the man in white overalls and two of his cronies dragged the witch in with her arms behind her back.

Her eyes widened. "What the fuck are you doing?"

"You said—"

"I said I wanted to speak to her, not fucking interrogate her. Get out of here." She half-drew her katana and they ran.

Lexi didn't like the suspicious way people looked at her because they thought she was Kindred but she missed being able to terrify pricks like that. She turned to Broullard. "I'll drop those fuckers into the Mississippi."

That's a few too many fucks. I need to get a grip. She breathed slowly for a few moments.

A little calmer, she approached the woman. "Do you have anyone here?"

The witch rubbed her arms. "No family. Probably some friends."

"I can't stay here," she continued. "We have this sicko to catch. The remains are bagged and being labeled, along with personal effects. Can you help those people outside find their loved ones?"

A cold stare was the initial response. "I don't know what you think—"

"I can help." The girl's mother entered, still cradling the bags she had given her. She handed them to her husband and his shoulders slumped as he turned away. The woman moved to the first bag and the purple-haired witch joined her. She read the tags.

Broullard put a hand on Lexi's shoulder. "I'll see she has everything she needs." He went to her.

Scott came through the drapes and vaulted down from the stage. He approached Lexi and ensured they couldn't be overheard.

She looked at the drapes. "How is he?"

"He's at Dick's apartment."

"Good. Let's get a move on."

The detective returned. "I'll oversee the rest of this process and catch up with you later."

The woman seemed to have her task in hand and now had a notepad and pen and appeared to be writing a list of names.

With their work there complete, the two friends walked to the apartment.

CHAPTER FORTY-FOUR

Betsy greeted them with coffee as they entered.

"You won't believe how much I need this." Lexi was halfway through the drink before she pulled it away from her mouth to breathe.

Scott finished his coffee. "Are you ready?"

She sighed and nodded.

The older woman sat and picked the puppy up. "I'll stay right here with Marcel." No one could blame her.

The sorcerer scratched the dog behind the ears. He looked at Betsy. "The apartment is still shielded. You're safe, but if you need us, Dick will be listening."

They entered the vampire's apartment. He had moved the couch to the side of the room and Thomas remained in the middle of the floor, unconscious with his broken, crab-like limbs.

Lexi shuddered. "The way his head is twisted—it's grotesque."

Dick stared at her with an eyebrow raised.

She glanced at him. "What?"

"What do you think I looked like when you broke my neck? I had to have it re-set and I didn't have a mage to keep me unconscious."

Her grimace was genuine. "Oh. I feel bad about that, but it wasn't my fault. I was hyped-up on vamp blood."

"Yes. As I recall, that was *my* vamp blood."

"Yeah, I guess." Lexi shrugged. "Sorry, Dick."

Scott put a hand on both of their shoulders. "Well, we can all laugh about it now."

They both glared at him.

He looked pointedly at Thomas. "Let's get on with this, then. I'll break the bones where they were broken by Delphenzo. You two twist them into position and hold them in place until they start mending."

"Delphenzo." She rolled her eyes.

"Yes, it's a cross between—"

"I know. Stop speaking." She took one of Thomas's arms and they began to reset the joints and bones.

While they worked, Lexi looked at Dick. "I don't understand this place. Everywhere else I've been, when someone's turned, they leave and stay dead to their families. Here, the family seems to board the windows in their old bedroom and change breakfast time. So many humans are aware of the supernatural world here."

He nodded. "It gets stranger than that. Mothers sometimes allow their vampire kids to feed off them." He shuddered. "It gives me the heebie-jeebies."

Scott frowned. "Why?"

"It's like..." The vampire seemed to try to find the right words. "You know when you hear about women who breastfeed their kids until they're seven or eight?"

"Okay. I hear you." The young man signaled that he didn't need to hear any more.

They twisted the victim's head the right way. Like every other bone and joint they'd worked on, it cracked and crunched.

Lexi looked directly at Dick. "I really am sorry."

"I forgive you." He mussed her hair with his knuckles while she held Thomas's head in place.

She narrowed her eyes. "But if you ever do that again, I'll break your neck all over again."

"And just like that, our little moment's over." He poured himself a drink.

They moved Thomas onto the couch as a knock sounded at the door.

"It's Broullard."

Dick went into his bedroom as she opened the front door.

The detective stepped in. "How's Thomas?"

"Sleeping but otherwise, possibly in good shape."

"Let's be honest. I think any shape is preferable to the one we found him in." He smiled a humorless smile.

Lexi let him in, and he looked over the couch at Thomas. "Will he walk?"

"If we did it right." Scott yawned.

"Don't. Just…please don't yawn." Broullard sighed. "So, are you busy?"

Scott shook his head. "Another one? For the love of…"

Lexi stood outside Mardi Gras World and stared at a boat that had crashed into what appeared to be a short boarding dock. The vessel had been tied off and a cordon placed around the area. Scott had walked a little farther to see the front of it.

"Anything?"

He shrugged. "The boat's called *A Stone's Throw*."

Broullard held a little notepad. "Has the ring been here?"

The sorcerer nodded.

She boarded and waited while her two companions stepped behind her. "I'm not really into nautical…anything. Is this a shrimping boat?"

"Yes, although the owner appears to have been in the business of fishing for crabs. These are crab traps." The detective pointed out several net-covered tunnels on the deck.

"Do you know who the victims are?" She poked around a few boxes on the deck.

"The captain and four tourists. We have IDs for the tourists but I'm waiting for registration details to come back on the owner. Until then, he's merely Crab Boat Guy."

Lexi shrugged. "So, where are they?"

Broullard steadied himself as the boat rocked. "The tourists are below deck and he's in the pilothouse."

"The what?"

He rolled his eyes. "The front part." He extended his hand to stop Scott from following her. "Do you mind staying here?"

The young man sat on a deck bench. "No part of me minds that. I'm sorry I threw up at your other crime scene."

She expected the detective to follow her but instead, he sat as well. "I'm not much of a boat person. If I go in there, I'll seriously disturb *this* crime scene."

Lexi rolled her eyes and made her way past winches and nets to the pilothouse. She could see why he thought it was Lorenzo. The head had been turned one hundred and eighty degrees so the body lay on its back but the head was face-down. There wasn't much to look at. Peeking her head out the door, she saw her two companions in conversation, so she decided to have a look under the body. She could always blame the rocking of the boat.

She caught Crab Boat Guy and turned him onto his front. The man's lips moved.

Shit, he's alive.

Instinctively, she drew in a breath to call Broullard to get the paramedics when a horde of tiny crabs escaped between the lips of the corpse and scuttled across the deck.

The back of her hand slapped over her mouth, she straightened hastily. After a few seconds, the compulsion to vomit had mostly left her. She flipped the body back as she'd found it and returned to take her place with Team Vomit at the other end of the boat.

"Are you okay?" Scott was concerned. He'd have felt her emotional shift.

Carefully, she sat beside Broullard before she tried to speak. "Is there any point to me looking at the tourists?"

"I guess not. They're the same as those in the courtyard—heads twisted and throats ripped out."

They disembarked by silent consensus. Once on land, Scott muttered a few words. "The ring went this way." He pointed toward Mardi Gras World. "Do you want to follow it?"

Lexi chewed her lip, then shook her head. "Honestly, I think we need backup."

Broullard nodded. "Will you come to the station?"

"Not yet. We need to do a little research and will catch up with you."

"Can I drive you?"

"No, we need to see some people."

Back at the apartment, they heard Dick and Betsy from the stairs.

"Tell me what you need and I'll get it for you."

"I merely want a few things. Come in with me if you're so concerned."

"I don't think you comprehend the danger you would be in."

The two friends hesitated outside the door before Scott spoke the shared thought. "Should we simply go—"

Dick called out to them. "Come in."

Lexi opened the door. "If this is a bad time…"

Betsy stood from the couch. "Don't be silly, dear, this is your apartment. Good heavens, you look exhausted. I'll put coffee on."

The sorcerer yawned. "I'm going to lie down."

"We need to talk." Lexi pulled him back by the collar.

"Urgh!" He dropped into a chair and put his head on the table. "I'm listening."

"Where's Dick?" Betsy looked around the room. "Has he— Oh, for goodness sake!"

The younger woman looked toward the apartment door. "If you don't mind me asking, what's going on?"

Betsy rolled her eyes. "Dick won't let me go into our apartment.

He seems to think Thomas might tear my head off or something." She scooped coffee into the machine.

Scott lifted his head. "He might. He lost considerable blood. He'll want to replace that, possibly with yours."

"Oh! I thought he was being over-protective." She blushed.

Dick walked in with her belongings. "I'm being the right amount of protective. There you go—everything you could possibly need." He looked at Lexi. "What's your problem?"

She sighed. "We need backup. Kindred backup. I'll have to tell Broullard we're not Kindred."

He grimaced. "Oh dear. That'll be an awkward conversation. Can I come?"

Her death stare, unfortunately, did nothing to diminish his humor.

CHAPTER FORTY-FIVE

The two friends walked along Royal Street toward the police station.

Scott stepped behind Lexi to allow a couple to pass, then moved beside her again. "What will you say to Broullard?"

"I'll simply tell him we don't have the backing of Kindred and there is no Kindred cavalry riding toward New Orleans on shiny freaking horses."

"Can't we…uh, leave him a note? I can't see this going down very—Hey!"

She grabbed him and shoved him through the closest door and into an art gallery. Once safely inside, she yanked him against the wall between the door and the window. "Am I seeing things? I'm seeing things, aren't I?"

He peeked out and darted his head behind cover again. It must have taken a moment for him to process what he'd seen because he immediately looked out again. His jaw dropped.

Lexi took a breath and looked again. It was undoubtedly Caleb. "Who did we kill in Cabo?"

"Can I help you?" The assistant looked ready to throw the two of them out of the gallery.

"We're looking for a gift but the guy it's for is right across the street."

"Oh my, that's awkward." The man looked out. "Is it for the chief of police?"

"Yes." Scott led the man into the store.

She ignored them and peered out again. Utterly confused, she dragged her gaze from the miraculously not dead sorcerer to the man who stood with him. Even more startled, she retrieved the photograph of herself in Jackson Square.

Her friend moved beside her and she glanced at the assistant, who stood with a smile on his face and an unfocused look in his eyes and stared in the direction of a wall. She showed Scott the photo. "It's him. It's the guy from the picture."

He looked out again. The man across the street with Caleb was in uniform. "He's the chief of police? He must be Kindred. If he is, why would he talk to an evil sorcerer?"

"Caleb manipulated the whole of Palm Springs. It's not a stretch to guess he's done it here too."

She glowered through the window and grasped the hilt of the katana in her pocket. "I want to know what they are saying."

"Okay." The sorcerer muttered a few words and in a moment, they were able to hear the conversation.

"And I have a problem with my pet vampire," the chief blustered. "Lorenzo has way overstepped the mark. The agreement was that we'd let him gain a block. He was supposed to help us cull the shifters, then go after Carla's clan. There's only six of them but they style themselves after a family. Somehow, he eliminated Thomas and his entire clan, including a couple of human donors. He wasn't sanctioned for that."

"How's your girl doing with the other investigation?" Caleb's voice made her shudder.

"I spoke to her yesterday. She's wrapping things up. There was definitely magic at play. The security camera's suddenly on the fritz and no one remembers seeing it."

"It doesn't matter. I know who the culprits are, or at least know one of them." He laughed. "I still can't quite believe it. She's not quite the harmless old bird I thought she was."

"I'll rip her eyeballs out," a guttural voice exclaimed.

Visions of Betsy being tortured and screaming assaulted Lexi's mind. She held her head as the images became more obscene until suddenly, they were gone. Shaken, she stared at Scott, who had clearly seen the same and protected them from it. He leaned heavily against the wall with his eyes closed before he returned her gaze. She peeked out of the gallery window to where Caleb pinched the bridge of his nose.

She opened her mouth to speak but he shook his head quickly. Instead, she mouthed, "Azatoth?"

Scott nodded.

The conversation outside the station continued.

"Are you all right, Caleb?" The chief sounded concerned.

"I'm fine—it's a headache."

"Please, my lord, I can't think." The man's voice sounded weary.

"I am closer. Soon, I will be with you."

Caleb's voice was strained when he tried to continue his conversation. "I've been busy but I'll locate her tonight and send friends over. How is it going with the shifters?"

"Lorenzo hasn't moved on them yet. He's doing it tomorrow night."

"Good. We'll chastise him after he's taken care of the shifters and the witches. The supernatural population in New Orleans has grown out of all proportion. We need this cull."

The two friends looked at each other. She was keen to get out of there.

The chief continued, "That reminds me—Broullard has dealt with things while I've been away. I passed him in the hallway a few minutes ago. I haven't had a sit-down with him yet, but he's asking awkward questions. Should I arrange to have him counseled again?"

The Kindred term raised Lexi's eyebrow. The official was definitely Kindred, then. But why did he take orders from Caleb? Was he yet another person under the sorcerer's thrall?

"No. Find a reason to send him to the bayou with the shifters. He'll be collateral damage. Keep me informed."

He climbed into a waiting car and drove away. The chief remained outside.

Scott exhaled sharply. "That was intense."

She wiped her brow. "Those visions. How did we see them?"

"We picked up all communication from where they were standing. I didn't specify the frequency." He shuddered. "So, he still has that demon in his head. And I bet it's really pissed after not crossing over."

Lexi rubbed at the goosebumps on her arms. "What do you think he meant by 'soon, I will be with you.' I thought he wouldn't get near our dimension for hundreds of years."

"I don't know. But it's very clear what Caleb's plan for Betsy is. We should get back to the apartment. I need to protect her."

They left the gallery as the man on the steps looked up. He raised his eyebrows in surprise and stared directly at her for a moment before he raised his arm to make a come-here signal with two fingers. She looked around in the hope that he had targeted someone else.

Scott prodded her back. "We have to go over there. If it gets difficult, I'll send him to sleep."

She approached the man and opened her mouth to deliver a vague greeting.

He spoke first. "I thought you were in Cabo."

"I…I was." She wondered how he knew she had been there.

"I wasn't expecting you here yet. When did you get back?"

"Just now." She was winging it.

Who does this guy think I am?

He stretched an arm out, took hold of a railing, and looked around. She realized he was waiting for a couple to walk past. His voice lowered. "Do you have any leads on who killed the doppelgänger?"

"Nope." She saw his eyes narrow at her brief response. "I'm waiting for results from the lab."

"Make sure your paperwork's in order. When the head of the Kindred council asks specifically for you, it could mean big things for your career. You just missed him, by the way. And I'm fine, thanks for asking."

"I was about to," she told him and shrugged.

The chief continued. "Palm Springs was a shit-fest. There were hundreds of the buggers. One of them broke my glasses and I can't see for shit. I barely recognized you from across the street."

He held a hand up with a bandaged finger. It looked shorter than it should have been. She noticed one of his other fingers was also missing a tip, an older injury. "He's talking about wanting another one. Son of a bitch. The perks of the job aren't worth this."

Lexi nodded as though she had a clue about what was going on.

"Who's that?" He pointed to Scott, who remained a discreet distance away and looked around with a vaguely disinterested expression.

Despite the natural instinct to do so, she didn't look at him. "He's…going to look at my car."

"I see. You're getting straight back into things then. I only recently got back myself and it looks like shit's been going down here. You can't leave them alone for five minutes." He raised a hand and she froze while he tucked a lock of her hair behind her ear. "You look nice. Cabo must have agreed with you. I thought you weren't going to hide your scars again."

It came so suddenly that she freaked out on the inside, her mind a whirlwind. "You know what they say about Cabo."

"I better not get a bar bill. Anyway, I have stuff to do." The man headed up the steps, then turned to her again. "Stay in the apartment. It's best you're not seen on the street yet."

"Yes, sir." She waited until she was sure he had entered the station.

Lexi turned to Scott. "Let's get the hell out of here."

His face was perplexed. "Who did he think you were?"

"Message Dolores. We need to see her."

At the apartment, Dick and Betsy were waiting when they entered.

The vampire stood. "How did Charles take the news?"

Lexi marched around the room. "I need a drink. Is Dolores here yet?"

"I didn't know we were expecting her."

The older woman slid off the stool at the breakfast bar. "I'll put a pot of—"

"No thanks. Dick?"

"Coming right up." Although he looked surprised, he disappeared and returned with a bottle of Jack Daniels. He poured a large drink for her and she threw it back. She stood and breathed slowly with her eyes closed for a few moments as she tried to slow her racing heart. Wordlessly, she held the glass out to him. He raised an eyebrow but refilled it.

As she lifted the glass, she thought better of it. With a sigh, she put it down. "I need to contact Joseph. Should I simply say his name three times into the mirror?"

Dick wiggled his cell phone at her. "Or I could call him for you."

"That sounds reasonable." She turned to Scott. "What message did you send to Dolores?"

"I told her we need to speak to her."

"Send her a nine-one-one."

He took his cell again out.

Lexi turned to Betsy. "I'm sorry, but you need to get your stuff together."

The vampire gazed intently at her. "What's going on?"

"Do you know what a doppelgänger is?" she asked him.

Dick's brow furrowed. "Theoretically."

"That's what we killed in Cabo." She focused on Betsy. "Caleb's still alive and he's coming after you. He'll try to locate you but the attack could be physical or psychic. I think it's best to move you to Fae." She grinned when Betsy downed the shot on the counter.

Dick was a blur. In seconds, he had already moved two of the woman's cases into the room while messaging Joseph.

Lexi thought for a moment, then spoke to him. "There are a few other people I need here. I imagine Joseph could help us with that if he feels like it. How's Thomas?"

"It's about time for him to wake up. It might help to contain the situation if the first thing he sees is a Kindred legacy holding something long and pointy."

"Bring Betsy. I don't want her out of my sight, but I want both of you to stand between her and Thomas when he wakes up." She led the way to the other apartment and they waited for the vampire to open his eyes. After a few moments, they were joined by Dick and Betsy, who held the glass and bottle.

She expected the healed vampire to spring into action, but when his eyes opened, he merely lay there and stared at the ceiling.

Her first thought was that he might be paralyzed. "Can you move?"

He nodded slowly. "Are they all gone?"

"Everyone who was there," Scott answered. "All the vampires and a couple of donors."

Dick stood with Betsy behind him. "I have some blood bags. Is that okay for you?"

"I'm good, thanks." Thomas continued his fixed stare.

Lexi wondered if she'd misunderstood his response. "You lost considerable—"

"I lost everything. You should have let me go."

She decided she didn't have time for this. "You can meet the sun when Lorenzo's dead."

He barked a laugh, then looked at her. "I don't think you know what you're dealing with."

"We know exactly what we're dealing with, and we need all the help we can get. Dick, get the blood."

In Lexi's apartment, the fae door appeared. She leapt to her feet and walked to it. Her boss entered the room and the portal behind her vanished.

"What do you know about doppelgängers?" the girl asked immediately.

Dolores straightened her already pristine skirt suit and placed her purse on the table. "I know they're difficult to make. It takes thirteen sorcerers."

Scott looked at Lexi. "Thirteen mages. The Kindred council."

"Well, Kindred outlawed the practice but that's probably why there were originally thirteen on the council. There are several spells, all of which require thirteen." The woman looked at him. "You don't know any of this?"

He blushed. "I guess I missed that day at Mage School."

She sighed. "It's advanced and the details of the spell-work, like everything else in that ridiculous organization, is quite secretive. But I do know this—the magic requires that the sorcerers participating in a spell to create a doppelgänger each have to donate a piece of themselves. Traditionally, the tip of a finger."

Lexi nodded. "We've seen the chief of police. He's Kindred and two of his fingers were missing their tips. One recent and bandaged, and the other had long healed."

Scott shook his head. "The chief wasn't a sorcerer. I'd have known."

"Each sorcerer can use a proxy," the fae explained. "Whom do you suspect of being a doppelgänger?"

The girl sat heavily. "Caleb's not dead, he's after Betsy, and it looks like he might be the head of the Kindred council."

"At least, that's what the chief thinks," Scott added. "We know how manipulative Caleb can be."

Dolores's eyebrows raised in alarm. "The head of the Kindred council tried to release a high-level demon from a hell dimension?"

"*Is* trying. It's still in his head. We eavesdropped and heard it telling him it was getting closer." Lexi stood. "What does that mean? I thought the portal to that dimension couldn't open here for hundreds or thousands of years."

The woman thought for a moment. "He might try to make his way through other dimensions. How did Betsy take it?"

"She's through here." She led her boss to the other apartment where Dick was seated on the couch and Thomas in the chair opposite.

"Good evening, William." Dolores smiled. As she approached the couch, she noticed Betsy asleep on his shoulder, cradling the half-empty bottle of Jack Daniels.

"I see." She sighed, retrieved her cell, and typed a short message.

Lexi shook her head. "I don't understand. Okay, he looked exactly like Caleb—which is kind of the point, I suppose. But he sat up before I took the shot and looked directly at Betsy, and I would swear he recognized her. Azatoth has some revolting plans for her, by the way."

Betsy straightened suddenly. "Caleb *and* Azatoth can kiss my wrinkly old butt." She slumped against Dick's arm again. He tried to use the opportunity to maneuver the bottle out of her hold but she wouldn't release it.

Dolores pocketed her cell. "A sorcerer can maintain a psychic link with the doppelgänger. He probably watched out of the creature's eyes."

The inebriated woman began to snore and Dick slid the bottle gently out of her hand. "What exactly is a doppelgänger?" he asked softly. "I mean, what is it made from?"

"It's a human, usually chosen for their size and shape." The fae took the bottle from his hand and put it on a table. "Sometimes, but not always, they are a willing participant. The mind is wiped and replaced and the face altered by the spell."

Lexi shook her head as she mentally replayed the shot she'd taken at Caleb's heart. "Is the original always mentally linked to the copy and aware?"

"No, that would only happen if the original was a sorcerer. When the transformation is complete, the doppelgänger believes they are the original."

She drew in a deep breath. "We have another problem. I think there's another doppelgänger out there and I think it's a copy of me. Since we got here, every supernatural creature in town has known who I am. I thought it was because a group of shifters had seen my scar."

Scott's jaw dropped. "Detective Broullard. At the crime scene, you said he didn't ask your name or ask for ID. But there can't be one of me because no one seems to know who I am."

"And when I picked this vest up from Anne Bird's store..." Lexi turned to Dolores. "You didn't send this to Anne Bird for me." It wasn't a question, but the woman shook her head anyway.

"So that key we found in the pocket—" the sorcerer started.

"Must belong to the doppelgänger," she finished.

She yanked the photo from her pocket and held it up. "This isn't me."

Her boss took the photograph and studied it. "Did you find out who the man is?"

"That's the chief of police. He's older now, of course, but easily recognizable."

"The man missing the tips of his fingers." The woman exhaled, her expression grim.

Lexi nodded. "He thinks I'm the doppelgänger, who Caleb specifically requested to investigate a shooting in Cabo."

Dick twisted on the couch to face them. "But why would anyone make a doppelgänger of you? Okay, no offense, but what's the point? You've said it yourself—as far as legacies go, you're a dud."

She stared at him.

He stroked an eyebrow. "Don't give me the murder face. They were your words, not mine." He propped the still snoring woman against the backrest and stood. "I'll check the other apartment for anything belonging to Betsy."

When he opened the apartment door, he stood face to chest with a huge man. He stumbled back. "Jesus!"

"Ah! Simon, there you are. Come on in." Dolores beckoned to the man who had to stoop beneath the doorframe to enter. "This is Simon. He'll help me with Betsy."

The vampire narrowed his eyes. "I can carry her."

"Dick—" The fae raised an eyebrow.

He rolled his eyes, "Et tu, Dolores."

She smiled kindly. "I'm sure you understand that the fae don't want a vampire loose over there."

"Actually, I don't. I'm fairly sure from what I've heard I'd be the least scary thing over there. Besides, you sylphs taste of ozone. Urgh!" He shuddered.

The woman leveled her gaze at him. "I won't ask how you know that."

"Dolores! I've dated fae."

"He's dated everything," Scott muttered.

The vampire fixed him with an indignant look.

Lexi remembered that Betsy's son was still in Fae. "How's Todd?"

"Todd's awake and doing very well. The fae girls are fighting over him. It's for the best that Betsy's coming over. If he stays there unchaperoned much longer, he'll come back married."

Dick smiled widely. "But fae babies are delightful. Who wouldn't want those genes in their family? It didn't do Grace Kelly any harm."

"Or Halle Berry," said a deep rich voice.

Lexi spun. "Joseph. I'd like a word with you in a moment."

Dolores created a fae door and Scott pushed the bags through. Simon walked around the couch and lifted the sleeping Betsy gently into his arms. Dick stepped forward and kissed the young-looking woman on the head, then watched as the man stepped through the portal. On the other side, he turned and held a small, frail woman in her eighties.

The vampire smiled. "It's been wonderful seeing her young again. She's the last connection to who I was."

"She'll be safe." Dolores patted his arm, then stepped through and the doorway was gone.

Lexi turned immediately to Joseph and pointed a finger at him. "You knew!"

"I did?" The man knew he wasn't fooling anyone with his innocent face.

"About the doppelgänger here—with my face. You must have known. Why didn't you say anything?"

"It's not for the rest of us to interfere in the business of Kindred. Men have been killed for less. And how do you know that *you* are not the doppelgänger?"

That comment disturbed her more than she was willing to admit.

CHAPTER FORTY-SIX

A knock at the door delayed Lexi's response as she went to see who it was. She peered through the peephole at Agatha with her parents.

She opened the door and smiled. "Hello, Agatha."

The girl ran in, sat on the floor, and began to play with Marcel.

Her father sniffed. "I smell vamp—" He stopped when he saw the others around the room. After a wary moment of scrutiny, he nodded to Joseph and the couple sat at the table.

Lexi closed the door, looked at those gathered, and was a little surprised by the turnout. Scott, Dick, Joseph, Thomas were unsurprising, of course, but Anne was there with Sam and James as well. Geraldine had arrived soon after Broullard and now Agatha's parents, who were called George and Olivia. Everyone had fallen silent and stared at her, obviously waiting for her to speak. She took a deep breath.

"My name is Lexi. Well, it's Alexa but I go by Lexi. I used to be a Kindred legacy based in Texas, but I found myself at odds with their ethos and I left. This is Scott. He's my blood match." She paused to see the reactions. "Joseph already knows but the rest of you don't seem surprised."

Broullard raised his hand. "I'm surprised."

Sam stared intently at her face. "How can you look so much like Ali? Okay, you don't have the scars, but I assumed you used magic to hide them. Are you sisters?"

So that's what they call her. I wonder why they didn't steal my name along with my face.

"Scars?" she asked.

"Ali was mauled by a shifter about five years ago," Broullard explained.

Olivia nodded. "I knew she was too nice. I said as much, didn't I, George? And she smells different."

James leaned back and folded his arms. "I thought maybe Alice had a stroke. Sometimes, that can make people behave differently and even smell different than supernaturals."

"I thought she was a pod person," George added.

The scrutiny made Lexi uncomfortable and she pushed on. "Since you've mentioned pod people, you should know why I'm here. I've tried to find information about my past. I was given this photograph." She dropped it onto the table. "And I came to find out why I was here back then and who the man is."

Broullard tapped the picture. "That's my boss, the police chief."

"I know that now. I've just learned it's not me in the picture. It's a doppelgänger."

"You're Dolores' friend. I wondered why no one turned up for the documents." Anne pointed at the linen vest. "So that's not your vest."

Lexi put a hand on the garment. "No. I guess not. But I really, really like it."

James Bird shook his head. "How do we know Alice is the doppelgänger and not you? She's been here for years."

Joseph, who had leaned on the back of her chair, stood. "I can tell you with absolute certainty that Lexi is not a doppelgänger."

She twisted in the chair to look into his face. "That's not what you said earlier."

"I was only having some fun." He laughed and she bristled, feeling his joviality was inappropriate.

Everyone nodded and appeared to accept what she had said. She had imagined it would be a hard sell, but Joseph's word seemed to carry considerable weight.

"I need to tell you what I learned today. Why you're here." She leaned forward. "It seems your local Kindred unit had an arrangement with Lorenzo. They allowed him to make a play for an extra city block while they were out of town."

Broullard narrowed his eyes. "How could they know they'd be called away? Were they lying about the disaster in Palm Springs? Was it faked?"

Lexi shook her head. "No, it was orchestrated by a man we know as Caleb."

The detective's jaw dropped. "Caleb? The chief's friend? He said that Caleb guy is high up in Kindred. I'm sorry, but this sounds less plausible."

Thomas steepled his fingers and tapped them against his chin. "Lorenzo took far more than a city block."

Joseph leaned lazily against the wall. "Lorenzo is now possessed by the spirit of Delphine LaLaurie."

"Oh, shit." Sam Bird and Geraldine said at the same time.

"What he did to me kind of makes sense now." Thomas sounded hollow.

James straightened. "What did he do to you?"

The vampire refused to meet his gaze. "I don't want to talk about it."

Dick pulled his cell out, scrolled, and showed it to the man.

He stared bug-eyed at the phone. "Fuuuuuck!"

Thomas glared at his fellow vampire. "You took pictures?"

"It's evidence. I'm a PI."

Everyone looked at him.

"Well, I am." He smoothed an eyebrow.

Broullard frowned. "Licensed?"

"You say potato." Dick poured himself a glass of bourbon.

Anne Bird shrugged. "What does all this have to do with us?"

"They have something else planned. This time, it's something involving the shifters tomorrow night. They mentioned the bayou, but I don't know what they're planning." Lexi looked at Geraldine to see if it meant anything to her, but her gaze was drawn to Olivia who had covered her mouth with her hand.

"Tonight's the eve of the full moon," George answered. "The new shifters are out in the Bayou for their rite of passage. Their first change is at full moon tomorrow night. Some of them are already there. We were leaving to take Agatha when Joseph called."

Lexi was horrified. "They're already there?"

She patted Scott's arm. "Get Dolores here." She turned to Anne. "They have something planned for the witches too, but we don't know what or when."

"Why are they doing this?" James asked.

Her face screwed up in disgust. "Population control. It's a cull. Caleb has decided the supernatural community in New Orleans is too big to control."

Broullard frowned. "I don't know what you think I can do about this. If what you're saying is true, we won't be able to rely on any support from the department."

"You're here because we overheard a conversation between the chief and Caleb today. Apparently, you've asked questions—too many."

The detective raised his eyebrows. "I did bombard the chief with questions today. What am I supposed to do about that?"

Dick put a glass of bourbon in front of the man. "Pal, if I were you, I'd take a few sick days on the other side of the world."

Anne leaned forward. "How can we help?"

"Lorenzo and Delphine are the immediate problems. We need to get the possessed ring away from him. He'll be easier to deal with and taking him out of play will set Caleb's plans back. But I think it'll take more than the handful of people we have here."

Thomas rubbed his face, his expression grim. "I'll speak to the other clans. The situation has been hostile lately and I've mediated relations between them. I think I have the respect of the other leaders, but I don't have my clan behind me to watch my back anymore. It would help to have backup with me."

"Dick and I will come with you." Lexi turned to Scott. "I'll need you to help get the kids out of the bayou and keep them somewhere safe."

"It'll be difficult to protect that many people. I already have a permanent shield on us so Kindred can't find us." He checked his cell. "Dolores will be with us in a few minutes."

Sam looked at her mother. "We should touch base with the local covens. If something's coming, we need to protect ourselves or get out."

Her mother raised an eyebrow. "I won't go anywhere. They won't drive me out of town."

Joseph pushed away from the wall he'd leaned against. "I'll help with the children."

"What can I do?" Broullard stood.

Lexi exhaled sharply and shrugged. "Honestly? Take your wife and get the hell out of town."

He folded his arms. "I won't run away. This is my city too."

Scott thought about it. "I can shield you, but Caleb might be able to break through that. Now that I think about it, it's a wonder he hasn't broken through already. He's ahead of me in ability and he has demonic powers too."

"Demonic?" Sam asked.

Dick held a finger up. "Oh, right, we didn't share that part. Caleb's working in collusion with a high-level demon called Azatoth."

"The deceiver?" Joseph shook his head. "This is very bad."

James raised an eyebrow. "He's a demon. Aren't they all deceivers?"

Lexi shared a glance with Scott. "What do you know about him, Joseph?"

"My spirits have spoken of him. He's tried to escape from the realms of hell for eons, moving through the hell dimensions. It takes years of effort on his part. He sends his mental tendrils out, trying to ensnare a creature in another realm. Once he has them, he uses them to help build his power.

"He connected briefly with a human a hundred years ago. The man had no magic and could not call the demon forth, but he was a writer.

He attempted to make him use the name Azatoth in his work because names have power. His plan was to spread the name through the human world. It almost worked, but the writer had misheard the demon's name as Azathoth. To this day, that name is used the world over."

"Of course! *Call of Cthulhu*, the role-playing game?" Scott looked surprised by the revelation. "I knew it was familiar."

"Yes." The other man nodded. "And the writer was HP Lovecraft."

Dick steepled his fingers on his chin. "But now he has a sorcerer. It was our dumb luck that he didn't manage to come through last time in Palm Springs. I doubt we'll be that lucky again."

Scott looked at Lexi. "I don't think there's anything we can do about the demon right now. If Caleb tries to locate Broullard and he's not where he's supposed to be, they might be suspicious."

"Then let's make sure he's exactly where he should be." Joseph held a voodoo doll in his hand. "May I trouble you, my friend?" he asked the detective.

Broullard sighed, pulled a few strands of hair from his head, and passed them to him.

The man tucked the hairs into the doll's fabric vest. "I'll leave this in the bayou when we round the children up."

The other man swallowed. "Leave it somewhere safe."

Scott muttered a few words and announced that Broullard was shielded.

Lexi looked at Dick, whose eyes were sad as he watched Agatha play with Marcel. He glanced at Joseph in unspoken communication.

"Agatha. Can you do a very important job for me?" Joseph asked.

The girl looked up and nodded.

The old man crouched and scratched Marcel behind the ear. "Can you and your mom look after Marcel for a little while?"

She smiled. "Sure, until you kill the ghost lady."

Lexi shook her head. *Kids.*

By the time Lexi, Dick, and Thomas stepped onto the street, it was 2:00 am. The witches had already left, and the shifters had begun to ferry the children from the bayou.

They walked toward the vamp bar on Frenchman's Street.

Lexi slid her gaze to Thomas. There was nothing of the predator about him. He walked purposefully but without any real attention. She needed to bring him out of it. "Are you sure the other clans will help?"

He sighed. "Vampires are selfish by nature. Our decisions can be arbitrary. They might help, they might not."

She stepped around trash bags on the sidewalk. "Why would they hold you in particular regard? Why aren't you selfish?"

"They show me a semblance of respect because I was a priest. Honestly, I think it simply amuses them. All except Lorenzo. He's never liked me, clearly."

Her eyes widened as she glanced at Dick before she returned her focus to Thomas. "How does that work? An ex-priest leading a vampire clan?"

"Vampires can have a crisis of faith too. I didn't really have a clan. It was more like a congregation and I didn't sire vampires. My group was made up of people who struggled with what they were. Anyway, the clan we'll see here is the second largest after Lorenzo's. Their leader, Anna, stopped all communication with the others a year ago. I'm the only vampire not of her clan that she'll speak to. She won't even hear you out without me there."

Dick clapped him on the shoulder. "Well, it's a good job we have you with us."

The other man seemed disinclined to speak after that. He walked faster to move ahead of his companions as they made their way through the streets.

As Thomas stepped out to cross the road, a sudden surge of power stole her breath. A hooded man appeared beside her with his arms outstretched. She and Dick were bathed in a blue-white light. Lexi couldn't see the man's face and before she could react, Thomas' head was detached from his body, which fell. A bright flash illuminated the street and a moment later, a boom filled the air. It could only be the sound of something fast colliding with something impenetrable. In the next moment, Lorenzo stood in front of them. He picked himself off the ground, smiled and gave her a little salute, and was gone.

Lexi turned to the hooded figure, but he was gone too.

The two companions stared at Thomas' desiccating body.

Dick caught her arm. "We need to get to the apartment."

She created a shield around them which faded and died after a few seconds. "Shit." She didn't need to look at the scar to know that it was empty.

He lifted her unceremoniously and moved at vamp speed, only stopping when they reached the door to the building.

She wriggled out of his grasp. "Let go of me."

The vampire dropped her. "I could have simply left you."

Her face flamed with shame. "It would have been preferable. Open," she commanded and held her hand out to the door. It blew into the hallway.

Dick frowned at her. "How did that work and the shield didn't?"

"I'm closer to Scott so the magic's coming back." She stormed through the entrance.

As they made their way up the stairs, she glanced at the scar which slowly filled with light. *Better late than never.*

The vampire gestured over his shoulder at the damaged door. "Aren't you going to fix that?"

Lexi stopped and gave him *the* stare.

He rolled his eyes. "Okay. I'm sorry I threw you over my shoulder like a rag doll. I panicked. I didn't even see him move and it freaked me out."

She marched down the stairs, lifted the door, and leaned it against the frame. "There, fixed."

As they entered the apartment, Broullard jumped up. "You were qui…" His voice died in his throat and he stared at their faces.

Lexi went directly to the bourbon, stared at the bottle, then sighed. She glanced speculatively at Dick.

"Hey, I'm off the menu, remember? God, you're worse than…me."

He dropped into a chair and looked at the detective. "Lorenzo attacked us. He killed Thomas."

Broullard narrowed his eyes. "How in hell did you two survive?" He looked from one to the other. She ignored him and stared at the bourbon again.

The vampire answered. "Honestly? I don't know. A guy appeared—a sorcerer, I guess—and shielded us. Thomas was too far away. I don't know how the guy knew it was coming or who he was. He wore a Saints hoodie."

The other man shrugged and shook his head. "Him and everyone else. Why did Lorenzo wait until you were outside to attack?"

"Scott has this building shielded." Lexi rubbed her face. "Can you check that the others got home safely? Then, we need to speak to Joseph."

The door opened and Scott entered. He walked quickly to Lexi. "Are you okay?"

She looked at her feet, swamped by a feeling of failure. "Lorenzo killed Thomas."

He sighed. "I felt you were angry."

"It was nothing." She looked away and her face colored.

Dick raised an eyebrow. "I think we all felt she was angry when she blew the front door off its hinges."

"I didn't hear anything. I only just got back." Scott backed out of the room and returned a minute later. "The door's fixed."

Lexi sat heavily. "Okay, where are we?"

Broullard pocketed his cell. "Everyone made it safely home."

The vampire retrieved a glass. "What the hell are we going to do?"

She was at a loss. "We'll have to try to approach the clan without him."

"What about this other sorcerer? Are Kindred back?" the detective asked.

The question went unanswered as she thought through their options. "Okay, change of plan." She stood, took the key from her pocket, and held it up to Scott. "At first light, we go to see what this unlocks. If Kindred is back in town, I'll have to see them."

Dick poured a large drink for himself. "What if it's the other you?"

Lexi exhaled impatiently. "Honestly, I don't know. But I don't think they're all in on Caleb's plan."

He laughed without humor. "How can you be sure of that?"

She pushed her irritation aside and explained. "When the chief thought he was talking to Alice, he didn't speak to her as though she knew what was going on. He also explicitly told her to keep out of sight but wouldn't say why."

Absently, she turned the key in her hand. *Am I really about to meet my doppelgänger?*

CHAPTER FORTY-SEVEN

"Are you kidding me?" Lexi stared at Scott.

He held the key and looked at the door in front of them. "Apparently not."

"They live on the same block?" She ended the sentence on a squeak.

The two of them had set out after first light. The key had led them first to the left. Then left at the corner and left again at the next. She took it from Scott. "Is anyone in there?"

His face strained with the effort. "I can't tell. There's a strong shielding spell on the building." He thought for a moment. "You give it a try."

She barked a laugh. "If you can't get through that, what's the point in me trying?"

"Come on—reach out and see what you get."

Lexi closed her eyes and placed her hand over the scar.

"It's empty. How could you not see that?"

"I think your doppelgänger *does* live there. The protections on the house let *you* through but not me."

"Great." She sighed. "That puts you on lookout duty."

She stepped to the door with the key in hand. It swung open

before she had a chance to use it and she looked at Scott and held the key up. "So, what was the point of this?" She turned to the open door and entered.

The house was still. The first floor held a business, with its entrance from the street. This hallway led directly to a stairway and the second floor. She climbed the stairs, entered a sparsely decorated living room, and froze when she glanced at a photograph on the wall. It could have been a picture of herself if she had ever worn a police uniform. Once again, the doppelgänger stood with the same man as in the other photo. They were both in uniform. The woman's face, while identical to Lexi's, did things hers never did—smiling broadly and openly. It was disconcerting.

She glanced into the kitchen, where two cups and plates lay in the sink. Following the hallway to a bathroom, she noted men's and women's products on the shelf.

Okay, so she doesn't live alone. Does she live with her blood match? Does she even have a blood match? She made a mental note to ask Broullard.

In the bedroom, a photograph drew her eye once again. It looked exactly like she might have looked in her early twenties if she had ever worn a wedding gown. The groom's face was obscured by the veil and a thousand pieces of confetti frozen in the air.

Lexi gazed at the bride who seemed so in love and so happy. She wanted to smash her face in. She felt like this creature—this unnatural doppelgänger—had somehow stolen her life.

The front door opened and closed downstairs. Someone was home. Her gaze darted around but there was no exit.

Quickly, she moved to the doorway of the bedroom but the top of someone's head was already visible on the stairs.

She had no choice but to retreat into the bedroom and step into a cupboard with louver doors. The coat hangers were effectively stilled with an arm and she tried not to breathe. A figure moved around outside the cupboard. Through the slats on the door, she could see a pair of men's boots walking around the room. They stopped at the cupboard door and steam rose to her nose, accompanied by a smell of cinnamon. He held a cup of spiced latte and his other hand grasped the cupboard handle. She slipped her hand into her pocket to slide a blade out and her vision blurred. It took a moment to realize she was somewhere else.

Horrified, she spun and gaped at the giant creatures that surrounded and loomed over her. One was directly above. In a flash, the katana was in her hand. She lashed out at the monster closest to her. The blade burst through its skin and hit something hard—bone?

"How cool is this?"

When she whirled again at the loud voice, an avalanche of hard, white balls struck her and flung her off her feet.

"What have you done?" Scott screeched.

Lexi staggered to her feet. "What is that? Where the hell are we?"

He sighed. "We're in my dimensional pocket."

Irritated now, she kicked the balls out of her path. "And what is that?" She pointed at the oddly slumped creature and realized they were everywhere.

His face colored. "It's a Taco Bell chihuahua. I collect them. I just bought that one from a guy a couple of days ago. It was the only one missing from my collection and you killed it."

"I thought it would eat me. How are we here?" Still a little dizzy, she sat on the floor and picked up one of the white beads that was currently the size of a basketball.

The sorcerer pulled the bag from his back and sat beside her. "A guy turned up at the house. I couldn't get past the shield to get you out but your dimensional pocket is linked to mine, so I pulled you out that way."

She looked at the canvas bag. "Hey, wait. Your dimensional pocket is inside that bag."

"Yes."

"So…" She threw the ball aside and dragged the bag into her lap. "Inside this bag, in my hands, is a dimensional pocket with us inside it."

"I guess."

"And there's a bag in there, and inside *that*, is a dimensional pocket with us inside it. Man, that is so fucked up."

Scott took his bag. "It's the same dimensional pocket. There's only one of us."

Her face turned sour, having been reminded of the doppelgänger. "Speak for yourself."

He stood and held his hand out. "Let's get out of here before you have an existential crisis."

"Can we not go anywhere yet?" She placed a ball behind her neck and lay down to stare at the giant toys.

The sorcerer muttered a word and the balls rolled back to the split in the fabric. "What's up? Did the mage see you?"

Lexi felt the tug of the ball at her neck. She sat and it rolled with the others. "No. I don't think so. Uh…so it *was* a mage."

"Definitely. And fairly powerful too from what I could tell. He could sense me too, even though I was shielded. Did you learn anything?"

"She's a cop. You'd think Broullard would have mentioned that. And she's married."

Scott didn't respond. She assumed he would be navigating her conflicted emotions.

Good luck with that.

She watched as he sealed the rip she'd made in the toy. "Scott, what if I am the doppelgänger?"

He lowered his hand and turned to her. "Joseph said you're not."

"Would he even know? I have no real memories of childhood. I could quite easily have simply appeared one day. My whole life was about being a legacy and working for Kindred. Now, it's all about working for Dolores. This Alice has a career and a husband. There were two cups in the sink and two toothbrushes."

"You feel like she's stolen your life." He held his hand out.

Lexi took it and pushed to her feet. They were back on the street. She turned to the house and looked at the windows. A shadow shifted at one of them. "Let's go."

They didn't speak again until they had turned the corner.

Scott turned to her. "I feel like we're missing something. Why did they create her?"

"Maybe they fixed in her what they couldn't fix in me." She shrugged. Talking about this made her feel exposed and she didn't like it. It was time to change the subject. "I'm sorry I broke your toy."

He rolled his eyes. "They're collectibles."

"Right. I'm sorry I broke your collectible toy." She smirked.

As they entered their building, he paused and pointed up. Someone was up there. He mouthed, "Broullard." They continued to where he leaned against the wall.

Lexi nodded at him. "I thought you'd have been at the other end of the country by now."

He straightened quickly. "I sent my wife to stay at her mother's, but I have some news."

She sniffed the air and smelled cinnamon—exactly the same as in the mage's house—and was immediately on the alert.

Habit kicked in and she stepped ahead. "Me first." She moved forward to check the apartment.

Scott smiled at the other man. "Have you been waiting long?"

"Only a couple of minutes. I thought you were in. It smells like Betsy's been baking pastries. Is she back?"

"Hmm!" Lexi frowned, looked around, then glanced at Broullard "Back? Oh, Betsy, no. She's not back. You had news?"

He sat on a stool at the counter. "The shifters are gearing up to attack Lorenzo's clan."

The sorcerer gaped at him. "Do they know what Lorenzo did to Thomas and his entire clan?"

"They do, but you know what shifters are like. It's all 'I'm more alpha than you are' with them." Broullard shook his head.

Lexi's gaze studied him. He looked uncomfortable. "I feel like you haven't told us everything."

He sighed. "They're talking about taking Kindred on too."

That brought a scowl of disapproval to her face. "They'll bite off more than they can chew."

Scott exhaled a long sigh. "This is suicide."

She nodded but focused on Broullard. "We need to speak to Joseph."

The two friends sat with Joseph and Geraldine in the courtyard of the little bar.

"You'll get yourselves killed. You need to give us a chance first." Lexi pleaded with Geraldine.

"A chance to do what?" The shifter shrugged.

She rubbed her face. "Firstly, a chance to think of something."

The woman smiled a cold smile. "We've already thought of something. We'll rip Lorenzo's head off."

"I cannot even begin to explain to you how fast he is. He must be ten times faster than any vamp I've seen in my life. I looked right at Thomas when his head was taken off and I didn't even see Lorenzo. He's that fast."

"Not in the daytime, he's not." Geraldine coughed into a handkerchief and they waited.

Scott stood and walked to a wall of flowers. He leaned into them and breathed deeply. "That's amazing." He sighed, then turned to the others. "We need to get that ring back."

Lexi shook her head. "I don't think either of them is willing to let that happen."

"I might be able to assist with that." A light breeze rippled through the courtyard as Joseph spoke. "My spirits have dominion over the dead, so the dead are mine to command."

She looked at him and quirked an eyebrow. "Could you make him get up in the middle of the day and walk into the sun? Because that would really work for me."

The man drew his mouth down in thought. "Possibly."

Geraldine folded her arms. "What about Kindred? They interfered with the first night of The Shifting. Worse, they plan to murder our children and deserve to be destroyed."

"Something is bad in Kindred. We're looking into it, but we don't know who's involved and who's not." She lifted the coffee in front of her and took a sip. "If the kids have somewhere safe to go, will they still be able to continue tonight?"

"Most of the families observed the first night at home. Tonight is shifting night. How can we ensure our young are safe to shift?"

Scott sat and leaned forward. "I've spoken to Dolores. The fae are offering the Immortal Glades."

The shifter's eyes widened. "I thought the Immortal Glades was a myth. But the fae can be tricksy. How can we be sure the kids will come back?"

He smiled. "You can select a few of the elders to go with them."

"And you." She pointed at him. "I want you with them. I trust you."

The sorcerer shook his head. "But you barely know me."

Geraldine grinned. "I'm a good judge of character."

"We really need to—" he began, still shaking his head

"That's fine," his partner interrupted. "We'll make it work."

The shifter nodded her agreement.

Lexi looked around the table. "Great. So, we'll get the kids to safety and Joseph can do his thing with Lorenzo. Does anyone know where he'll be sleeping?"

Joseph nodded. "He lives at the bar."

She turned to Scott. "Can you sort out the details with Dolores and Geraldine? If this doesn't work, you'll need to get the kids to safety. I'll see you across the street from Lorenzo's bar in an hour."

He nodded. They walked away from the others and although he didn't look happy, he took her hand and transferred magic to her. "We only transferred this morning and you're almost empty again. It's getting worse. We shouldn't be apart."

The magic drained remarkably fast, something she'd noticed, and it worried her. Still, this wasn't the time to discuss it. "I'll get back to the apartment and let Broullard know what's happening." She turned at the door. "Joseph, do you know where in the bar Lorenzo sleeps?"

"He has an apartment over it but his entire clan has been there for the past few nights. He won't let any of them go home."

"Okay, I'll see you there in an hour." She walked through the bar and out onto the street.

At home again, Lexi took out the key to open the door but was immediately dragged into the opposite apartment by Dick.

She opened her mouth to speak but he made wild helicopter signals with his finger. While she wasn't happy to use the magic, she made it safe to speak. "What's wrong?"

The vampire closed the door and whispered, "You paid you a visit."

"Excuse me?" She narrowed her eyes. "And why are you whispering?"

He continued in a low tone. "Your doppelgänger was here earlier with a tall, dark-haired young man. Very handsome, actually."

"Did she see Broullard?" She glanced instinctively toward her apartment door. "Where is he?"

"He put a note under my door a while ago. He went to check on his wife and will be back soon."

Lexi sighed with relief. "Okay, so I've been to her place and she's been to mine. What did she say?"

"Do you think I'm crazy? I didn't speak to them. I peeked through the peephole in the door and didn't make a sound. She looked exactly like you…well, except for the thighs, obviously. And scars down her face. It looked like she'd been mauled by a bear or a shifter. Maybe a shifter bear." He stopped and thought for a moment. "Would that be a werebear? Anyway, he couldn't get past Scott's shielding but she did. She walked straight in."

"They were in our apartment?"

"Only her and for less than a minute. They were talking when she came out. She said 'There's no way that apartment is being used by Kindred unless Julia Child is a legacy. The place is full of cookies.' Then they walked down the hallway. Where's Scott?"

"He's making arrangements with the shifters and I'll meet him with Joseph at the bar. Hopefully, we can put an end to Lorenzo and Delphine. If that doesn't work, Scott will help to get the shifter kids to Fae tonight."

Dick walked her to the door. "It's so frustrating having to stay out of the way in daylight."

Lexi met with Scott and Joseph across the street from Lorenzo's bar.

She scanned their surroundings in all directions. "Is he in there?"

Scott nodded. "Yes. Well, the ring's in there. Assuming it's still on him, so is he."

The other man began to shake his staff. She hadn't looked properly at it before. The symbols carved into it were unfamiliar to her and bones and shells hung from a fibrous string wound around the top. They made a clattering sound when he shook it.

He stooped and dropped granules of salt or maybe light sand onto the sidewalk in an intricate design. When he spoke, it was in a language that sounded vaguely French but was possibly an African dialect. She raised her eyebrows at Scott.

"Haitian, I think," he whispered.

Joseph continued while the two friends stared at the door of the bar across the street.

The sorcerer stiffened. "The ring's coming closer. I can feel it."

After about a minute, Lexi opened her mouth to ask what was going on when she heard shouts from inside the building across the street. The door opened and several vampires massed in the doorway. The man at the front pushed back against the others and wedged an arm and leg against the frame, while he covered his face from the daylight with his other arm. After a few moments, he was shoved out into the sunlight. He emitted a short scream and burst into flames. It wasn't Lorenzo, though. Several vamps behind him edged—obviously against their will—toward the door, pushed from behind.

She turned to Joseph. "What's happening?"

"I'm pulling him to the door but he's forcing his clan to block his exit. I can continue but he'll push them all out to save himself."

Another vampire, this one a young woman, stood at the edge of the doorway with a look of terror on her face. All she could think of were the parents of the vampire girl Lorenzo had killed. "Stop. Just...stop."

The man stretched his staff out and dragged it through the symbol on the ground. The door across the street slammed.

"Shit!" She punched a wall in utter frustration. "Let's get out of here."

Broullard, Scott, Joseph, and Lexi sat around the table in the apartment.

The detective stood, walked to the window, and looked onto the street. "The only people equipped to deal with this are Kindred, and they're the ones behind it."

Scott looked at the time. "We need to start moving those kids to Fae. Hopefully, Lorenzo will spend the night running around the bayou looking for them."

Joseph shook his head. "He'll know instantly by the smell that they're not there."

The sorcerer folded his arms and pushed his bottom lip out, his expression thoughtful. "Maybe."

Broullard looked at him. "What are you thinking?"

He smiled. "I can leave a wolf-scented trail through the least populated parts of the bayou. It should keep him busy for a while."

The man looked doubtful. "But he moves so fast."

Lexi leaned forward and took one of Betsy's cookies from a tub in the middle of the table. She grinned. "He can't move faster than his boat." She pushed the bowl to Scott. "That deserves a cookie."

CHAPTER FORTY-EIGHT

Dolores, Scott, and George arrived at a small jetty in the bayou, twenty miles out from the city.

The sorcerer looked at Agatha's father. "Are you ready?"

He nodded "Ready when you are."

They climbed aboard the boat and set off. George sat at the outboard motor and steered the craft through the bayou, deserted by all life beyond gators and bugs.

Scott worked his magic as they moved through narrow channels and paused to climb onto dry land and push through tendrils of Spanish moss dangling from the limbs of trees.

They climbed aboard the boat and continued the journey.

Dolores twisted to face the shifter. "Can you tell me about the shifting ritual?"

"On the first night, the children gather with their parents, older siblings, or other elders. We spend the evening around campfires in the bayou. The older ones tell stories—old stories, the passing on of knowledge—and tell them their own stories."

The sorcerer looked curiously at him. "Their own stories?"

George nodded. "About their first shift, however many years ago that was. The second night, the kids shift. They feel the moonlight for the first time and run. After that, they can shift anytime. Those who get the curse—the ones who shift because they are bitten—can only turn on the full moon or the command of their sire. They are not shifters and are what we call werewolves."

The others already knew this but both nodded politely.

"What happens on the third night?" Dolores asked.

"The new shifters tell their story and they repeat the old stories back to us. Usually, they shift a few more times too, merely because they can. We run as a family. We'll run with Agatha tomorrow night, I hope."

For several hours, they laid a trail around the bayou over miles of wetland. Scott carefully increased the scent as they moved, giving the impression that the shifters were closer together.

"I've done everything I can. It's almost sundown. Let's get to Fae."

On land, Dolores summoned the fae door and stepped aside for them. The shifter hesitated and peered through to a forest path that opened into a grassy glade.

Scott tapped his shoulder. "Or you can stay here and wait for Lorenzo."

George turned to him. "Have you been over there?"

He grinned. "Nope. This is my first time and the anticipation is killing me." They stepped through.

When they reached the clearing, Agatha ran to her father and hugged him. "Dad, there were fae people here and some of them were flying." She caught his hand and pulled him along the edge of the glade to the base of polished wooden stairs that led to platforms in the trees. They ascended to find nine youngsters and twenty adults seated there with cups and plates, laughing and joking.

"How's Marcel, Agatha?" Scott asked.

She grinned. "He's great. I looked after him good. Mom couldn't come because she has to look after Anton, so she's watching Marcel too."

A girl of about sixteen in a pair of denim shorts and a strappy top that revealed her midriff jumped up as they approached. "You sit here,

Dad." She spoke to George but she gazed at Scott in a way that made him feel uncomfortable.

The shifter nodded to the other parents before he sat and put his arm around Agatha. The sorcerer sat on a tree branch that extended a foot higher than the platform they were on. Immediately, the young shifter woman sat beside him, closer than he felt was appropriate.

"We've learned about the first shifters, and Grandpa told me about when he shifted for the first time out in the bayou and he ate a raccoon—can you believe that?" Agatha pretended to throw up.

George laughed. "He told me that story too, Nugget." He mussed his young daughter's hair.

She straightened and finger-combed it. "Tell me about your first shift."

He flicked an uncomfortable glance at Scott and Dolores.

"I have work to do," the fae announced.

"I'll help." Scott attempted to rise but the young woman curled her arm around his.

She turned to George. "Scott doesn't need to go anywhere, does he?"

The shifter shook his head. "Of course not. Scott, you're welcome to listen. But Gretchen, don't you make a nuisance of yourself."

The girl released his arm but tutted and rolled her eyes.

He tried to concentrate on the tale but he worried about how Lexi was doing without him. They'd agreed that she and Dick would stay in the apartments unless needed. She was a world away, but he could still feel her emotional state. She was pensive. Although, he reminded himself, she was always pensive, so that was a good thing. He came out of his reverie when Gretchen put her hand on his knee.

He stared at the hand and into her face. Her lips twitched. He looked at George who was finishing his tale. "And that's what a muskrat tastes like."

"Daddy, you didn't." Agatha was horrified.

Something tickled Scott's head and he patted his hair. Finding nothing, he lowered his arm and tried to think of a way to get the girl's hand off his knee without offending her.

The shifters began to look at the moon.

"It's almost time." George looked into the sky, and the youngsters stood to make their way down the steps.

"Remember what you've been told." Dolores' voice came from below. "You mustn't travel beyond this forest. I've secured safe passage for the pack in this forest and glade only. This isn't your world and to put it bluntly, humans are not the top of the food chain here. Neither are shifters."

Scott felt another tickle and slapped the back of his neck quickly. Something crawled down the back of his t-shirt. He leapt to his feet, yanked his shirt out, and searched down his back with one hand and up with the other. Gretchen moved away from him. The remaining adult shifters stared at him as though he had gone crazy.

As the crawling sensation moved to his side, tickling him, he fought a manic giggle. He pictured a spider or scorpion and hopped frantically before he finally pulled his t-shirt off. It was on his stomach. He swept his hand to flick the tiny winged creature off as it seemed to be making its way into his pants. It spun away and landed on a branch, and he squinted to see it better from where he stood, breathing heavily.

"What the hell is that?"

Gretchen addressed his abs, "Did it bite you?"

He held his t-shirt up to cover himself in front of the girl, who looked much too appreciative.

His gaze remained fixed on the creature as it began to grow.

It slowly became larger and was clearly not an insect. A fully formed and very beautiful young fae woman sat on the branch and studied him.

Her eyes sparkled. "Well, that was quite a ride. Do you want to go again?" She tilted her head and smiled.

He stared open-mouthed at the scantily clad fairy. Her shiny auburn hair hung over her shoulder like satin, her lips were large, and her eyes smoldered with an intense dark-brown. As if that wasn't enough to befuddle his brain, her clothes were just the wrong side of decent.

"Do you like what you see?" She winked.

"Aleena!" Dolores stood on the platform. "The forest and glade are off-limits to fae tonight."

Scott jumped at the woman's voice and replaced his t-shirt quickly.

Aleena kept her gaze on him. "I'm going."

A low growl issued from beside Scott. He turned to see Gretchen's golden wolf-eyes fixed on the fae woman.

"Gretchen!" George admonished the girl. The fairy glanced at her, giggled, held her arms out to her sides, and fell back off the platform.

The sorcerer gasped and stepped to the edge, but she skimmed the long grass of the glade gracefully with almost no movement to her wings. She floated upright at the edge of the forest and gave him a little finger wave before she vanished.

Gretchen stepped beside him, her face like stone. "With a little luck, she'll hang around and Agatha will bite her wings off. That'll make a better story than a muskrat."

Scott turned to Dolores. His brows were drawn in thought. "Can you fly?"

She looked at him as though he'd lost his mind. "Of course I can." She looked into the forest where Aleena had disappeared. "I probably shouldn't have let you come. This could be a problem."

He bristled. "I'm not interested."

"It's not always optional with some of my kind. Be careful while you're here."

"I can look after myself." He knew he had begun to sound sulky.

Dolores patted his arm. "Of course you can, dear. But don't speak to anyone."

Gretchen slipped her arm through his. "I'll look after him."

"You'll do no such thing, young lady." George curled his finger to her. "You come and sit with me until they get back."

She complied and went to sit with her father but wouldn't release Scott. He was forced to sit there too and blushed furiously.

CHAPTER FORTY-NINE

Lorenzo awoke. He breathed in, assessed the taste and smell of his surroundings, and concluded that nothing was amiss.

About time. Delphine's voice sounded snippy in his mind.

He made a mental eye-roll and wondered if the enhanced abilities were worth the exhaustion from this psychopathic harridan who lived in his mind. She didn't ever seem to shut up. Worse, the compulsion to follow her every whim made it a constant battle to not give in to her desires. Her life-force was incredibly strong, more than when he first wore the ring. It had taken considerable time to control her but now, it seemed to have become harder.

Draining the tourists in the courtyard directly after he put the ring on had been the result of her inability to control the bloodlust. It was inconvenient, but they had come to an agreement. He allowed her entertainments and she gave him extraordinary speed and strength. In his quiet moments, he still couldn't believe he'd eliminated Thomas' entire coven on his own. They hadn't known what hit them. His lips twitched as he lay there and recalled what Delphine had done to Thomas. It had been a disgusting display and quite distasteful but he had been a sanctimonious prick, after all.

His thoughts turned to Joseph. Now *he* was a disappointment.

Lorenzo had always respected him and even liked him. But he couldn't go unpunished, not after he pulled his voodoo shit.

This caused a problem, though. He needed Joseph to help him get this fucking woman out of his head without losing the abilities the ring gave him.

Well? Do you intend to move?

Without thought, he stretched to touch the metal lid above him. He snatched his hand away. She'd made him reach out like that and he decided she could damn well wait.

The absolute shame and embarrassment of his present situation were that he was forced to sleep in a metal box in case Joseph tried something again. He inwardly groaned at the thought.

The box was useful for another reason, however. He was aware that Delphine had moved in his body while he was asleep. At least she couldn't get out in the daytime, but he had woken the night before with his silver-tipped dagger in hand as he stood over Darnell, one of his most trusted clan members.

Of course, he knew about Delphine LaLaurie. Almost everyone who lived in or visited the French Quarter knew about her, but he wondered why the mad bitch had such a problem with black people.

"It's time to visit the bayou. I promised to reduce the shifter numbers."

Who cares what you promised?

"I like to think of myself as a man of my word." He thumped the lid.

The box opened from the outside and Darnell waited next to it.

Lorenzo stood and stepped out of the metal box. "Any news?"

The other man closed the box once his leader had taken a couple of steps away from it. "The donors are here."

Ahh, breakfast! Delphine's desire for blood raised his anticipation. His teeth descended.

He closed his mouth and mentally reasserted control over himself. His gaze located a familiar donor, although he didn't know her name. "Well?"

She approached and held her arm out.

Lorenzo rolled his eyes. "I want information. Did you do what you were told?"

"Yes. The shifters were seen heading to the bayou a couple of hours ago. I watched Joseph. He went to one of Oberon's guest apartments but I don't know why—"

He cut her off. "That's okay. I can guess who he's with. I think I'll have to speak to Oberon about the company he keeps." He turned to Darnell. "Keep Joseph's serviteurs busy until I get back but I want Joseph alive."

The donor remained and offered her arm again.

"You can go. I'll eat out tonight." He smiled when he felt Delphine's disappointment.

A little later, Lorenzo parked his Porsche nine-eleven on the gravel beside the jetty. This was the second location he'd stopped at. The shifters didn't always use the same place for their ritual but he knew this was the right one. It stank of wolf, which was a good sign. He looked at the available craft moored along the waterside. The giant tour boat was no good as it was too large. The airboat would be too loud. That left the small boat with an outboard motor in front of him. He untied the line, dropped into it, and looked around for a potential owner. There was no doubt that he was alone so he shrugged and started the motor.

The boat moved slowly through the water and he followed the scent of the wolves and branched off into smaller, narrower water lanes. The smells intensified. Moving at this speed was frustrating, but he couldn't afford to miss a potential victim. He was supposed to kill a handful of them. That's what he'd agreed but he was powerful now. He intended to obliterate the pack's future generations and couldn't wait to find the newly turned shifter kids. Neither, he sensed, could Delphine.

After they'd returned to the boat for the third time, he began to wonder where in hell they all were. Every time he thought he was close, he would find himself on an island with nothing but cypress trees for company.

"Finally!" he muttered to himself after more than an hour. He approached a small jetty, which led to a cabin.

A fire-pit burned outside, and the windows glowed with light. The smell of wolf was heavy in the air. He cut the motor and drifted to the shore. With the motor off, he could hear low, muttered voices from inside the cabin. He deduced they'd finished their shifting and were all inside, so he tied the boat off and stepped onto land. Knowing how keen the wolves' hearing was, he guessed they would already know someone was there. In mere seconds, they would catch the scent of a vampire. Sadly for them, they didn't have seconds.

With his improved speed, he hurtled around the cabin to the door and burst through immediately, only to find it completely empty. He walked to the center of the room, a little confused as he knew he'd heard people. Suddenly, flames flared all around him and seemed to fill the cabin. Within a second, he was outside. He checked his clothes for fire damage, stepped away from the building, and scowled as the blaze incinerated it.

Oh dear. You've been tricked. Delphine laughed, but Lorenzo could tell she was angry too.

He walked around the cabin to find the little boat but it floated beyond reach and it too was engulfed in flames. "Whoever did this, I'll tear them to shreds."

Oberon huffed as he lifted the crate of empty beer bottles into the dumpster behind the bar.

"You must be Oberon." He jumped, startled. The voice was male but it sounded quite soft.

He spun, puzzled, and looked around for someone else. "Lorenzo —" The words cut off when he was held by the throat against the edge of the dumpster.

"I'd like a little chat about who you've rented your guest apartments to lately." The vampire had taken control of the conversation.

The sanguinaire tried to answer but his larynx was being crushed.

"Obe?" Martine stepped out and froze at the back door of the bar.

Before she could react, his captor had dropped him and held her by the hair in front of him.

"Your friend here would like you to answer us."

"Us?" His gaze scanned the area and returned to the vampire. "It's someone called Dick. He's here with friends."

Lorenzo remembered the apartment across from William's. When the Kindred bitch had told him William was off-limits, it hadn't taken him long to learn that the vampire had a puppy. He'd gone there to snap the scrawny little mutt's neck. As soon as he had left the staircase, he'd felt drawn to the other apartment. He could smell the dog but something seductive had drawn him to that apartment. The stunning woman who had answered the door had assumed he was Peter, a friend of someone called Dick.

Peter, of course, was the name of the guy they'd poisoned to get to William, so that couldn't be a coincidence. Was Dick a friend of William's?

He had decided in that moment to forget the dog. Instead, he'd intended to murder the woman if she had the slightest connection to his adversary.

Delphine interrupted his thoughts. *I could have told you his name is Dick. I stabbed him with a silver blade.*

Martine squealed. "He has another name—William."

"Oberon. Did you try to lie to me?" The entity within him spoke now. Lorenzo had opened his mouth to speak and her voice came out. She had become even stronger and without warning, she spun Martine and drove her head into a wall. With their combined strength, that was all it took to reduce her skull to a bloody, dripping pulp. The body fell and Delphine released the piece of hair and scalp still in his hand. "Now, what is William up to?"

The vampire forced himself to regain control of his own body. "So, William's still in town. Interesting." He was about to finish Oberon when a globe the size of a basketball floated into view. It was high and very bright.

"What the—" He stared at it as it began to pulse and glow brighter and after a few seconds, he had to avert his eyes. Suddenly, it blasted light and it was like staring at the sun. Lorenzo shrieked as the light scorched his eyes and skin. He covered his face with his arm before he disappeared in the opposite direction.

CHAPTER FIFTY

Agatha padded through the forest. She had been running and the breeze through her fur had been exhilarating. Beneath her excitement, she was aware of the edges of the mental link with her pack and knew it would strengthen over the next few hours. She stopped to sniff at the undergrowth. Every new scent was like a story in her mind, the passage of creatures, what direction they had traveled in, how many, and how long they had stayed. In some cases, she could picture the animal simply by its smell. Others were a mystery, no doubt denizens of this strange, beautiful world.

The edge of the forest opened before her. A dirt track ran along the edge and she wondered if it circled the whole woodland area. The moon reflected upon a beautiful lake before her on the other side of the track. She knew she shouldn't leave the trees, but this was a perfect opportunity to see her reflection and to look upon herself as a wolf for the very first time. She sniffed the air, listened to the silence, and looked up and down the track. Tentatively, she stepped out and made her way across it to the water.

Standing at the edge, she looked at her reflection. She had already seen that her fur was black at the roots and turned to a reddish-brown at the ends but now, she could see that around her snout and cheeks, it was white, exactly like her mother and older sister, Gretchen.

Oh, my God. I'm a white girl. It was hilarious. She laughed and it sounded unnatural coming from a wolf.

Ripples flowed through her reflection and distorted it as though something had moved in the water. Her ears pricked and she took a step back, ready to return to the forest. As she glanced across the water, she saw the reflection of another white face. She looked up at a beautiful horse that stood motionless in the reeds. When she focused on it, the animal whinnied and shook. She remembered she was a wolf.

The poor guy must be terrified.

She shifted to human form and walked around the edge of the lake to the horse.

"It's okay. See? I'm only a person." Agatha could see it wore a bridle but no saddle. She held her hand out slowly. The horse backed away from the water's edge and stepped tentatively toward her. It nuzzled her hand, then allowed her to stroke its flank.

The girl muttered softly as she stroked it. "You're the most beautiful thing I've ever seen. I wish I had an apple for you. You look as beautiful as a unicorn."

Before her eyes, a horn appeared in the middle of the creature's head. It was white and pearlescent. Her heart exploded with love. She looked around and wished one of the others could come out of the forest so she could share the experience, but she and the unicorn were alone.

"So, you shift too. Are unicorns shifters?" She wondered how many of the horses she'd seen on earth were unicorns in disguise.

The creature shook its head so its long mane fell to the side, and she stroked it. It shook its head again and this time, tilted its head toward her. Was it an invitation?

"Do you want me to ride you?" Agatha couldn't quite believe it.

When the unicorn did it a third time, she didn't need to be asked again. She wound her fingers into its mane and, using her shifter strength and agility, vaulted onto its back. It surprised her how comfortable she felt, and she looked around again, hoping one of the others might still appear and capture the moment with their cellphone.

What a profile pic this would make.

"I wonder if I could ride you into the forest. I'm sure none of my friends would eat a unicorn." She'd never ridden a horse in her life and tried leaning in the direction of the track to encourage it in that direction. It stood unmoving. "Giddy-up?" she asked hopefully.

The animal took a step forward.

"Well, that's something but not the right direction." She pointed. "We want to go that way."

Another step toward the water made her deduce that it probably wanted a drink. "Okay, you get a drink as long as I don't fall off." She looked at the ground and now realized how high she was. The shift was making her bones stronger but that fall would still hurt, and there was no Lexi to catch her with magic this time.

The creature took two more steps and its front legs were in the water, but it didn't seem to be drinking.

"I'm gonna be honest. This is turning into a disappointment." Agatha decided it was time to dismount.

She tried to lift her leg over so she could drop off, but the limb wouldn't move. It was stuck. Confused, she attempted to lift her other leg, but that was stuck too. She decided to try to pull her leg up with her hands but she couldn't shake its mane from her fingers. Alarmed now, she pressed her hands down to lever herself up, but her body was stuck solidly to the unicorn. When she tried to pull her hands free, they wouldn't move.

As she watched, the unicorn's horn blackened from its tip and dissolved into nothing. The creature's body slowly darkened to black to reveal an ugly horse-like creature. It flicked its head and looked disdainfully at her with red eyes, while its jaws snapped and showed sharp, pointed teeth.

Agatha shrieked into the forest "Help. Help me." She screamed and thrashed frantically as it stepped further into the water.

Her gaze locked on a beautiful fairy seated in a tree above her. Her head was tilted and her brow drawn with curiosity as she stared at the little girl's predicament.

"Help me, please. I can't get off."

The fairy stared a moment longer, then rolled her eyes and flew into the forest.

"Don't leave me, please," the girl cried, and the creature took another step. It seemed to delight in drawing her terror out.

***

Scott pulled a tub of cookies from his bag and passed them around the group.

Dolores looked at them. "Betsy's?"

He nodded. "Is she still here? How's Todd?"

"They're here, staying in my cottage. He's ready to go home but now we know Caleb's still alive and a threat to them, they'll stay a little longer. We really must resolve that issue."

The sorcerer nodded his agreement. "How will we find Caleb?"

"If that demon is with him, it must still be trying to escape to this earth. The hell dimension he was in when we last encountered him is of no use to him now. I have someone trying to find other possible points of intersection—" Dolores stopped speaking and stared into the distance.

Scott followed her gaze and noticed Aleena, the young fae woman, returning at speed.

She drew to a halt in the branches of the tree. "A kelpie has one of the pups."

As one, the adults stood.

"What's a kelpie?"

"Who has it got?"

"Where?"

Aleena pointed at Gretchen. "The one that smells like her."

Wings unfurled from Dolores's back. Her skirt suit was gone and so was her middle-aged visage. "You all wait here." She swooped away toward the tree line.

"The hell I will." Gretchen shifted and bounded to the ground from their platform.

Scott expected her father to call her back but they all shifted and followed. He wanted to as well but knew his boss would expect him to obey her orders.

"Alone at last." Aleena wiggled her eyebrows.

He ignored her and began to pace.

She sat on the branch, watched him, and began to sing quietly in a language he didn't understand.

Dolores burst from the forest to the edge of the lake. A moment later, she was joined by the shifters, who barked and growled at the edge of the water. They could smell the girl's trail and knew where she was.

The surface, however, was still.

The fae hovered over it before she plunged in. She found them a few feet down. Agatha was still on the creature's back but was beginning to unstick. Her hands had loosened and drifted limply in the water.

She surged out of the water. "I found them. She's still stuck to its back, though. If I try to pull her off, the kelpie will strengthen its hold on her and disappear into the depths. I have to grab the bridle. It's the only way to control the beast."

Without waiting for a response, she submerged again. The creature had begun to move. It became aware of her before she could get close and began to thrash its head in an attempt to prevent her from taking hold of the bridle. Its head met hers and shoved her back.

If this thing knocks me out, I'm no good to the girl.

She glanced to where George and Gretchen swam down. Each took one of Agatha's hands. It was now or never.

Dolores swam in quickly, aided by her wings, and ignored the creature's thrashing and attempts to bite her. She grasped the bridle and commanded her intent with her mind as she stared into the beast's eyes.

Let her go.

The kelpie had no choice but to submit. The sticky surface on its back dissolved and Agatha floated free. George and Gretchen swam with her to the surface. The fae kept hold of the bridle until they were out, then she released and rocketed to the surface. It snapped at her feet as it followed.

She hovered above the water for a moment and flapped the water out of her wings. Caution pushed through and she moved higher a second before the kelpie's head thrust from the water with a snap of its pointed teeth. It splashed into the lake and sank into the depths.

Quickly, she flew to where George blew into Agatha's lungs. There was no response.

Dolores made a fae door. "Let's get her to Scott."

The shifter sat back, exhausted. Another lifted the girl's limp, unresponsive body and a couple of the others helped her father. They walked through the door and onto the platform.

Scott sat on the branch, glassy-eyed, and smiled at them while rivulets of blood ran into his t-shirt. Aleena sat on his lap and feasted on his neck. In two seconds, all the shifters except the one holding Agatha had shifted and circled her with warning growls.

The fae stopped, looked at them, then turned her face to Scott. She fixed her gaze on them and made one long lick up the length of his neck.

Dolores was furious. "Release him."

Aleena smiled and rubbed blood from his lips, then her own. "You know that's not how it works, Dolores. He's mine now."

The wolves snarled and moved closer.

After a glance at Agatha's lifeless form, the young fae rolled her eyes and stood. "Fine. But only temporarily."

Scott shook his head in surprise at the wolves surrounding him. "What's going on?"

The man holding Agatha stepped forward. "She needs your aid."

He helped him lay her down and put a hand over her eyes.

"No." Gretchen's hand flew to her mouth. The wolves still around Aleena whined.

Dolores calmed them. "It's okay. He's only reading her."

The sorcerer nodded. He placed his hand over the bottom of her ribs and muttered.

"I don't understand. It's not working. What's happened to my magic?"

Aleena shrugged and smirked. "Oopsie."

Dolores gave her a withering look. She thrust a handful of stones into his hand and he held them in his fist and drew the magic in.

He began again and nothing happened for a few moments, then water gushed from Agatha's mouth. She gulped air, convulsed, and threw up more liquid. Her eyes fluttered open and her father pulled her into his arms and wept.

A shifter woman sighed. "Why would she go near a creature like that in the first place? Much less climb upon it's back?"

Aleena snorted. "She thought it was a unicorn. It even produced a horn to encourage her to climb up."

George stared at her. "You were there before the kelpie ensnared her. You could have stopped this."

The shifters moved toward the fae.

Scott wobbled, still drawing the last of the magic from the stones into him. He began to feel it again in the air and drew on that too. After a few moments, he sat bolt upright. "Something's wrong with Lexi."

"Okay, you go. I'll get the others home." Dolores called her fae door again as he picked his bag up."

"I don't think so." The young fae crooked her finger at him. He dropped the bag immediately and walked to her.

She looked at the shifters. "His blood is in my heart and mine is in his. If you kill me, you kill him."

Dolores looked meaningfully at Gretchen and drew the young sorcerer's attention. "Scott, you need to return to Lexi."

While his focus was diverted, Gretchen stepped beside Aleena and swung her fist so hard into her face, the fae was unconscious before she landed.

"Damn, that felt good." The shifter shook her hand out.

Scott shook his head and gaped at the unconscious fae girl. "What's going on here? What does she keep doing to me?"

His boss picked his bag up and pushed it into his hands. "She's Dearg-Due, a form of dark fae. She mesmerized you. It'll leave you feeling a little uncomfortable for a while. She won't be a problem soon as she'll be in a cell in The Hollows within the hour."

"What kind of uncomfortable?" He looked nervous.

"You'll…uh, pine for her." She stepped to Aleena, stooped, and poked her in the forehead. The unconscious fae shrank to the size of a wasp. Dolores produced a little bottle from her pocket, pulled the stopper out, and dropped the diminutive creature into it before she secured it and slipped it into her pocket.

"I need to get to Lexi." Scott moved to the door.

Half of the shifters lined up behind him. George patted him on the back. "Whatever's going on, you won't face it alone."

While the remaining shifters waited with Dolores, Gretchen, and Agatha for the rest of the kids to return, Scott and the others stepped through the doorway.

CHAPTER FIFTY-ONE

Lexi looked at the fae door and sighed with relief when Scott walked through with the shifters. Immediately, she began to draw magic from him. They were in the scented courtyard at the back of the tiny bar where they had met Joseph. She was on her knees and held her hand over a bloody, ragged tear in a man's neck. He gasped when he realized she was covered in blood.

"It's not mine. Well, most of it isn't. Can you help this guy?" She moved aside to allow him to close the wound. It had closed halfway, then stopped responding. The wound lay half-open and blood dribbled out slowly.

The sorcerer shook his head. "I'm losing him." He put his hands over the man's heart and head. "What happened?" He muttered his spells.

"It was Lorenzo's clan. They began to attack about an hour ago. I was with Joseph when he got the call." She indicated the damaged bodies lying around her. "Most of this happened before we got here. Somcone managed to keep them out at first, but no one here was as strong as Joseph. They've attacked every few minutes and it feels like they're playing with us. They seem to know exactly how long it takes

Joseph to raise his protection magic. He's exhausted and my magic disappeared in the first five minutes."

Scott looked around. "Where's Dick?"

"He went to get help." She looked soberly at him. "He's been gone a long time."

Joseph came out of the bar with towels and hurried toward the man on the ground next to Lexi. He took in the condition of the body and passed one of the towels to Scott as he gazed around the courtyard. Dried blood encrusted his head and his eyes were slightly unfocused. "They'll be back at any moment. We should—"

Vampires surged over the roof at the rear and dropped into the courtyard. Their faces filled with shock in mid-air when they noticed the pack of wolves that had apparently appeared from nowhere.

"Keep them off me," Scott yelled.

Lexi lurched into action as a man barreled into her with his teeth bared. His movements were a blur, but it was nowhere near her first fight with a vampire. She had neither the time nor the space to draw her katana, but she used his momentum against him, spun him easily, and yanked a button from her vest. It came away with a length of silver wire at the back of it which she flicked deftly around the vampire's neck. He tried to right his balance but she shoved him away with her foot and hauled hard on the wire to sever his head. As he fell, she drew her katana and finished the next one with a deft sweep.

Pain flared in her arm as glass shattered against it. She looked up and scowled when she realized it had been thrown by the female vampire who had been close to meeting the sun earlier that day in the failed plan to eliminate Lorenzo and Delphine. The others were almost all gone. She and the man beside her were the last and it was a desperate move by a vampire surrounded by wolves. They descended on her. Lexi glowered at the cut on her arm and the blood that trickled visibly.

No good deed ever goes unpunished.

The vampire woman and her friend were savaged moments later by the wolves.

She felt a wave of sadness and turned to Scott, who placed the blood-soaked towel over the face of the guy he'd tried to save.

Lexi glanced at the glass doors to the bar. "We need to get inside. Let's move the bodies in."

Joseph shook his head. He looked sad and weary. "Leave them. Their work is not done." They entered the building and the man closed the glass doors and began to pour sand on the floor.

Scott extended his arms to the doors with his palms out and muttered a few words. A bluish light flowed across the apertures, then vanished. "We're protected."

He put a hand over her cut arm. While he healed her, he looked at the worried faces in the bar. His gaze fell on two people slumped over a table in the corner. "Are they—"

She shook her head. "No, they're tourists. Joseph thought it would be better if they slept through this."

A moment later, he tapped her arm to indicate he'd finished healing her. "Why hasn't he controlled the vamps like he did before?"

Lexi looked at the healed wound and nodded her thanks. "They're starting too far away, and they're in and out before he can get a mental grip on them."

The sorcerer studied Joseph's remaining people. "Couldn't the serviteurs help?"

"They're busy keeping the vamps away from the front of the building and look at them—they're almost wiped-out."

He glanced at those who stood over sand patterns on the floor and tables along the front wall. They did look exhausted.

George left his group of shifters and joined them. "We should be out there." He pointed to the courtyard.

"We need a better plan than wasting your lives to slow them. They'll know the last three they sent didn't come back, and it'll be sun-up in a couple of hours. I think the attacks will get bigger."

The words were barely out of Lexi's mouth when a half-dozen vampires landed in the courtyard. They raced toward the doors but met Scott's shield and fell back. The glass doors vibrated for a couple of seconds, then stilled. The invaders looked at each other before they leapt away and over the low roof at the side of the courtyard.

Scott went to look through the windows on the front of the building. He returned a few minutes later. "Why are they doing this?"

She shrugged. "I'd guess Lorenzo's pissed that Joseph tried to light him up this afternoon."

He raised an eyebrow. "And he'll be very pissed if he followed the trail through the bayou to the end. Anyway, I mean why are they attacking this way? There's enough of them to have stormed in here the moment the sun went down. Is this a distraction? If so, from what?"

Lexi retrieved several shurikens and clipped them to the front of her vest. "You saw what Lorenzo and Delphine did to Thomas. Maybe the plan is to make an example out of Joseph. Or perhaps they're amusing themselves while they wait to see if any shifters return from the bayou."

The sorcerer drew his brows together in thought. "I'm surprised Lorenzo's not back already. I'm sure we led him on a merry trail, but he should have discovered the truth by now."

She looked at a map on the wall. "Could you track the ring with this?"

He seemed to consider it for a moment but finally shook his head. "I could use one that's a little more detailed. The whole of Louisiana's on that."

After a moment's thought, she seemed to have an idea. "But couldn't you see if you can feel the ring close by?"

Scott rolled his eyes. "Yes, of course. I don't know why I didn't think of it." She stared at him. He usually closed his eyes for something like this but this time, he merely stared directly ahead. "He's here."

"What, in town? Can you tell how close?"

"I'd say about twenty feet." He pointed to the courtyard. Lexi turned to see the vampire on the other side of the glass.

Lorenzo stared at her. "You're behind all this? I think you missed a memo. You need to speak to your boss." He stepped forward and swung at the glass. His hand met the shield first but the glass vibrated so much, she thought it would shatter.

Lexi smirked. "I think I'm up to date, thanks. How's your new roomie?"

His voice changed and became softer and higher. "You're looking well since I stabbed you in the gut." His face became furious, then calm.

She flicked her gaze to Joseph. He stood barely out of sight and waved his staff over a symbol on the floor. Quickly, she dragged her focus away and settled it on the vampire again. "It's obvious who wears the trousers in your relationship."

Lorenzo took a few steps back and blurred as he raced into the barrier. The sound was like a huge echoing crash and one of the panes in the glass door cracked. He smiled. "I'll tear you apart." That wasn't his voice—did that mean he and his creepy passenger shared control or was there inner conflict between them?

A little puzzled, she wondered why Joseph's work didn't seem to have any effect on the invader. Then, out of the corner of her eye, she saw the dead man with the gash in his neck rise to a seated position.

Lorenzo touched the shield softly, clearly testing it. He looked at Scott. "This is your work? You're good but it won't save you." He smiled menacingly at the young man and his fangs descended slowly.

While he spoke to her friend, she flicked a glance at the dead man. His eyes were milky white like the zombies she had seen in Palm Springs, but they'd had...personality. This one looked somehow empty and hungry. It jerked its head toward Lorenzo, who now walked backward to take another run at the shield.

The vampire hadn't noticed the dead man's action. He stopped inches from the undead's face, which jerked again in the direction of his hand.

It was covered in blood and she wondered whose but decided if Lorenzo had killed Dick, he'd have mentioned it by now.

The vampire sneered. "Even a magical shield can only take so many—"

Even through the closed door, the crunch of teeth on his hand was audible, followed by his pained howl.

He ripped his hand away and held it up. It was missing a finger but sadly, not the one the ring was on. He turned to the undead man and decapitated him with a blurring swing of his arm. A roar of pain followed and he cradled his hand. "Joseph, you're next."

Scott winced. "Did he hit that guy with the same hand?"

"He did," Lexi confirmed, knowing Lorenzo would be able to hear them without difficulty.

"He didn't think that through, did he?" Her friend smirked.

The vampire was clearly in agony and stared at his hand. In the place where he had been bitten, the skin began to turn black. Horror crept over his face as he looked at it, then at them, and suddenly vanished. Tiles slid to the ground from the low roof, the only evidence of his hasty retreat.

She spun to face Joseph. "What did you do?"

The man leaned heavily against the wall behind him. "I raised what was once my good friend to a zombie state. His bite was death."

His knees began to give way. She bolted toward him and caught him around the waist. Scott took his other side and his staff. They led him to a chair and lowered him gently. As his head drooped, the two friends shared a worried glance. Scott wrapped the man's arm around his staff and settled it against him.

Joseph looked at him and patted his hand.

Lexi pulled a chair up and sat beside him. "I'm sorry Lorenzo killed your friend…again."

The man nodded. "I would have drawn the spirit from him anyway to allow him true rest."

A dozen vampires landed in the courtyard and began to fling themselves repeatedly at the shield. It obviously hurt them, but their clan leader had told them to do it so they persisted. The cracked pane of glass shattered and others began to vibrate.

"The shield won't hold for much long—" Scott cut off as a glowing ball hovered over the courtyard. The vampires looked at it but didn't stop their assault.

The light from the ball grew in intensity, then blazed like the sun. The attackers covered their heads and curled on the ground, their screams of agony shrill and disquieting. The sorcerer looked away when they burst into flames.

The ball turned black and fell.

"What the hell was that? I've never seen anything like it."

"Is it safe to go out there now?" one of the shifters asked.

Joseph touched his head gingerly. "Let's give it a few minutes."

Scott looked at the man's wound. "Would you be offended if I treated that cut on your head?"

"I would be grateful." He smiled at him.

He took a bottle of water and cloth from his bag and set to work on the injury.

"Do you think it's over, then?" Lexi asked.

Joseph shook his head. "It's almost over for Lorenzo. His body will decay but you'll have to get to him quickly. His bite is contagious now. He could start an epidemic." He looked at her, his expression grim. "And you saw how strong Delphine is. She'll look for a new host."

She wiped her forehead. "Damn. There's no way to know where she'll go next."

The man winced as Scott dabbed at the cut. "She has a lust for blood. I think she'll choose another vampire."

The sorcerer sighed. "But how can we know which one before she kills again."

Lexi poked his arm. "He was right there. Why didn't you simply obliterate him?"

"I'd have had to bring down the shield to do it. I don't think I could have matched his speed."

The magical barrier hummed and she spun reflexively. Dick knocked a rat-tat-tat-tat on the shield. She sagged with relief, then gave him her angry face. "Where the hell have you been?"

"Lorenzo attacked Oberon's place before he came here."

Scott turned and moved to bring the shield down. As he did so, the vampire caught a glimpse of Joseph and concern flooded his face. He entered and hurried to the man.

"I'll be okay, old friend. I am merely tired."

Lexi looked out to see that Joseph's people and the shifters had begun to move the bodies into a storeroom on the other side of the courtyard.

Joseph interrupted, "Is Oberon—"

"He's fine. His friend Martine didn't fare so well. I managed to catch one of the witches and begged her to help me before she fled town. She gave me a couple of those fun balls. I could use a few more but I think all the witches have gone now."

"Perhaps they're the only ones with any sense," Lexi muttered.

Scott rubbed his face. "This is insane. Kindred has to intervene. He's killed what? Fifteen humans? That wasn't part of his deal."

Dick picked up a chair that had been toppled. "I would imagine the plan was to remove him anyway. He's a loose end and it fits the narrative. A supe goes crazy and Kindred steps in and deals with it. Everyone's happy. It makes me wonder how often this happens. This is turning into a perfect shit-storm."

"Could we go back to plan A and pull him out into the sun?" Lexi located a trashcan and held it out for the cloth and cotton wool Scott was discarding. "I feel less inclined to keep his clan alive."

The sorcerer shook his head. "Joseph won't be of any assistance for some time, I'm afraid."

She looked at the man. Her friend was right. Although the cut was healing, Joseph looked like he was probably magically spent. She peered into the courtyard at the piles of dust.

"Okay. We'll have to go after him. We'll try to get Delphine before she finds another host." She turned to Dick. "It's almost daylight. Can you get to the apartment and make sure Broullard's okay before you turn in?"

He fixed her with a disbelieving stare. "What's the plan? Is there a plan? Or will you simply run in there to kill Lorenzo with your sword out and your fingers crossed?"

"I won't target Lorenzo. I intend to kill the rest of his clan so Delphine will have nowhere to go. Then, we can wait for Lorenzo to die. Joseph, he won't turn into a vampire zombie, will he?"

"No. As he is overcome by the bite, he will simply decay."

Scott put his first-aid kit away. "Aren't you forgetting that she'll still have one place left to go? Into you."

"And that's assuming you don't get savaged by a roomful of vampires," Dick added.

Lexi looked at the two of them. "There can't be that many of them left. I'll go in like before. Invisible. It'll be fine."

The vampire looked doubtful. "They didn't know what was going on before. Even if you're invisible, it won't be so easy again."

"Fine. Do we have any other ideas?" She looked around the room.

"I have something that might help." Joseph put his hand into his pocket and withdrew a woman's ring.

She frowned at it. "That looks familiar."

"It sat for several years in a display case next to the one on Lorenzo's finger."

Lexi raised her eyebrows. "Marie Laveau's ring."

He nodded. "She won't possess you, but if she deems you worthy, she may assist you."

Without hesitation, she took the ring and slipped it onto her finger. She stared at the stone and waited to see if she felt different. Noticing the room was quiet, she glanced up. Every pair of eyes was on her. "What are you looking at? Get to work."

A collective sigh of relief filled the air.

Dick patted Joseph on the shoulder. "Right, well. I'll be off then." He walked to the door and turned to her. "Good luck, and don't get killed."

"I'll do my—" she started.

The door closed and he was gone.

"Best."

CHAPTER FIFTY-TWO

Lexi stood in the alley a few doors down from Lorenzo's bar. She looked across to the alley on the opposite side of the street where her friend stood with a handful of shifters.

Anxious to make as little noise as possible, she mouthed, "Is he there?"

He shrugged and couldn't hear her, obviously. She peeked out along the street and studied their target.

"What was that?"

She jumped and spun defensively. Scott was directly behind her. "I have a sword in my hand, you dimwit."

"Sorry. I couldn't hear you."

Her sigh revealed her irritation. "I asked if Lorenzo's in there."

"Yes, he's there. George has had someone watching the place. He turned up a few minutes before sunrise."

Satisfied, she returned her focus to the building they were watching. "That was cutting it close. Can you pinpoint where he is in there?"

The sorcerer closed his eyes. "The ring is on the second floor now. So unless he's already passed it on to someone else, he's up there too."

Lexi turned to him. "Do you think that's possible?

"Possible yes, likely…no."

"Okay. I'll go in. Give me sixty seconds, then you come in with the shifters."

He scowled. "I should go in there with you."

"You need to protect the shifters. I can shield the sound of my heartbeat but not a roomful of shifters. If that building is full of vampires, I don't want to be responsible for Agatha losing her father. And we'll be in there sixty seconds apart. I'll barely have time to use the magic before you're there again."

Scott took her hand and attempted to transfer more magic to her.

"You won't get any more into me. The tank's full, but I'll be using it fast when I go invisible, so stay close but safe inside that building."

He nodded and vanished. She looked across the road to where he stood with the shifters once more. As she put her hand on the scar, about to make herself invisible, a car roared past the alley and screeched to a halt.

She looked across at the others with a shrug she hoped asked the burning question in her mind. *What's going on?*

The sorcerer appeared next to her again. "Some idiot in a sports car parked outside the bar."

Lexi looked at George and the other shifters who seemed to have lost all sense and forgotten they were supposed to be hiding. They crowded out in front of the alley and looked at Lorenzo's bar with their jaws dropped.

"Yoo-hoo!"

Lexi's eyes widened at the sound of Dick's voice. "What's that fucking vampire up to now?" She stuck her head out and scowled. He stood in front of the bar and waved at the security camera. She pointed in his direction. "I want to know what he's saying. Now!"

CHAPTER FIFTY-THREE

Lorenzo had burst through the door of his bar with his hand wrapped in cloth. He'd avoided the gazes of his few remaining clan members as he walked through to the stairs leading to the second floor. "I'm going upstairs. I don't want to be disturbed."

Darnell had taken two steps and stopped. "Where are the others?"

He stopped, turned, and opened his mouth to speak but found himself staring speculatively at each face. After a few moments, he became aware that it wasn't he who looked at them. It was her. She was looking for her next host. He spun away and climbed the stairs.

Now, he paced the room, his mind in a fog. How could this have gone so fucking badly?

Perhaps you need blood. Delphine purring in his mind was the last thing he needed.

A huge part of him wanted to rip the ring from his hand, but he couldn't bring himself to do it. Instead, he unwound the cloth from it and stared in horror. The whole hand was black.

"I'll have to lose my hand. It's not the end of the world." He pulled his jacket off and froze at the sight of black veins climbing his arm and disappearing into his shirt sleeve. He raced into the bathroom to a mirror and yanked his shirt off. The buttons pinged in different directions but his gaze was glued to the black veins which extended beyond his shoulder and onto his chest. It was too late. "Fuck! Fuck, fuck, fuck."

Lorenzo looked at the expression of disgust on his face in the mirror. It was her again.

He punched it and glass fell into the sink below.

A sound behind him drew his attention. He looked around the door. Five of his clan had gathered in his living room. "I said I didn't want to be disturbed. What do you want?"

"I thought—" Darnell stopped speaking. He seemed confused but his gaze wasn't on his boss' face. It was on his black hand.

"Thought what?" He moved his hand behind his back.

The man shook his head in apparent confusion. "You called us. Didn't you call us?"

It wasn't the hand they were looking at, he realized. It was the ring calling to them the same way it had seduced him.

"Get out," Lorenzo shouted. Automatically, his hand came from behind to shoo them away.

They didn't move, however, and stared fixedly at the ring for a long moment before they began to edge forward. He'd had enough. Fury surged and he moved through the room faster than they could track him. When he returned to his previous position, the bodies lay on his carpet and began to desiccate.

"Is there anyone else you'd like to call out to, bitch?" he bellowed into the empty room.

The doorbell sounded and he heard someone shout, "Yoo-hoo!"

His teeth gritted in frustration, he moved to the desk and looked at the security screen. He flicked a couple of buttons until he looked through the camera at the front entrance and gaped at the screen as he tried to comprehend what he saw.

William Levine—or Dick as the idiot called himself these days—stood outside in the street during the day and leaned on a gallery post in front of his building. He didn't stand in direct sunlight but it was daytime, and this wasn't normal. On the screen, he could see the light creeping slowly down the post. He stared in fascination as it moved inexorably toward his visitor's head.

He checked the time, then looked at the screen again. At that point, he realized Dick made no effort to even cover his eyes. How could he stand it?

Agonizingly slow seconds ticked past until the sun met the vampire's hair and began to slide slowly over his face. He scrolled through a cellphone screen, seemingly oblivious to the process.

Lorenzo was transfixed and unable to drag his gaze away. He stared until Dick's face was fully bathed in light. Finally—lazily—the vampire retrieved a pair of sunglasses from his pocket and slid them on.

As frozen and shocked as her host was, Delphine was quite the opposite. She raved and screamed inside him. Her spirit threw itself at Dick in a tsunami of wanton desire. The vampire outside seemed completely oblivious to her attentions, but Lorenzo could barely hear himself think.

He finally spun away from the screen. Their visitor spoke again and she twisted him to gaze at the screen.

"This is some kind of trick. The feed's not live. It's a recording." He pressed a button and a disc ejected from the equipment, but Dick was still there. His voice was audible and he smiled cheerfully. "Good morning. It's a beautiful day." He exchanged pleasantries with people on the street below.

I want him, Delphine moaned.

No.

"What do you care? You'll be dead in a few hours. Don't you want vengeance?"

"How is this vengeance?" he asked aloud.

I'll wear him like little Amy. I'll walk him to his friends and tear them to pieces. For you. I'll do it for you.

He dropped into a chair and sat with his face in his hands, feeling wretched. After a moment, he pulled his hand away quickly. It smelled of decay.

While Dick had apparently been too far away to feel the pull of

Delphine's spirit, the clan had not. The remaining ten of them had shuffled up the stairs, filed into the room, and stared at him with hunger in their eyes. Lorenzo roared and dispatched them all—his own clan. He honestly didn't care. If he wouldn't live, neither would they. He finished and swayed dizzily.

Why did you do that? She sounded suspicious.

"I've made my decision. I want revenge. Did you want *him* as your next host or one of them? I merely removed his competition." He didn't care whether she believed him or not.

But you're weak now. One of them could have bested him.

Don't worry, Delphine. I have one last fight in me.

Perhaps revenge was all that was left. But it wouldn't be the revenge she wanted. While there was still strength in him, he'd destroy this sun-walking William Levine. He'd hold the vampire's heart in his hand and let her watch through his eyes as he crushed it.

He turned to the security equipment and reached for the microphone.

CHAPTER FIFTY-FOUR

Lexi stood with Scott in the alley, out of sight of Lorenzo's bar. Whatever stupid gambit Dick was up to, she didn't want to get him killed any faster than he was already likely to be. She watched as he stood at the door in full view of the camera and scrolled through his cellphone. Periodically, he swiped left or right with a nonchalant motion. "What the hell is he doing?"

Her companion glimpsed out. "I think he's on Tinder."

"Get him on the phone. We had a perfectly workable plan." She was furious.

Scott dialed Dick's cell and they waited while he picked invisible fluff from his jacket sleeve and ELO's "Mister Blue Sky" began to play. Finally, he held the cellphone up, rejected the call, and dropped it into his pocket. Her face fell into a grim expression. "I'll break his neck again." She could see the vampire roll his eyes so he'd clearly heard her.

The security system hissed into life. "Hello, Dick."

"Loren—no, wait. It's Delphine, isn't it?" He sounded thoroughly enchanted. "How are you, my dear? I understand I just missed you at Joseph's place. I'm simply devastated. We must catch up."

Lorenzo's voice sounded almost coquettish. "Let me see when I can…fit you in."

He grinned. "Ooh! You minx. I'm free now. How about breakfast at Brennan's? They do a wonderful dish—Eggs Hussarde, with the most divine Marchand De Vin sauce. They also have a cocktail called a Corpse Reviver. I'm sure Lorenzo might be interested in trying it. How's his hand?" Dick finally glanced in Lexi's direction with a raised eyebrow as the other vampire attempted to regain control of his vocal cords, which resulted in a strangled growl. "Delphine darling, is that your stomach growling? I'll tell you what. Since I'm here, why don't I pop in now? We can order in."

The door buzzed and he disappeared inside.

Scott turned to Lexi. "Well, now what?"

"Fuck! Get the others. We're going in." She wasn't sure who she wanted to kill first out of Lorenzo and Dick.

The sorcerer appeared across the road where he spoke to the shifters, and she stroked the scar and thought the word "hidden." Dick had shoved a piece of paper in the door on his way in to stop it from closing properly. She ran into the bar with her katana drawn and whirled in all directions, expecting an attack, but was met with silence. When she saw no other vampires, she dropped the invisibility to conserve her magic and hurried through to the back of the bar. She forced herself to move slowly and quietly as she crept up the stairs.

Lorenzo's apartment was directly in front of her. Dick stood in the doorway and the other vampire was in the room, facing them. A playful smile played on his lips but in a moment, it was gone. Lexi registered the shift from Delphine to her host. She pushed a shield around Dick as their adversary blurred toward him. The attacking vampire bounced off it but was on his feet again in an instant.

Lexi tried to push a shield around Dick again, but her magic was depleted.

There was no time to plan but Lorenzo didn't target him anyway. The ring was on her hand before she could react.

Delphine's voice began to speak to her. *Go to the daywalker. Put the ring on the day walker's hand. Why are you not moving? Do what you're told. I order you.*

She ignored it because honestly, she didn't feel controlled by the spirit. At the same time, she felt something was different.

"Lexi." Dick spoke in urgent tones. "Take it off—quickly." He approached her and tried to catch her hand, but she pushed him away. He catapulted across the room and onto his back in the blink of an eye. She looked at her hand in surprise as she hadn't meant to do that.

That's it. While he's on the floor, put the ring on him.

Delphine's voice didn't sound remotely seductive. It was whiny.

Lexi strode to Lorenzo. He sprawled on the floor and looked defeated. She caught him by the throat and lifted him. It felt remarkable like this was the kind of strength she was always meant to have. This was her birthright.

She gazed into his eyes. He looked terrified and she liked that. "What did I tell you? I said he's off-limits. Do you not remember me saying that?" She looked at his arm where it hung black and useless at his side. She grasped one of his decaying fingers and twisted. It came away easily and she dropped it as he screamed.

That's right. Give him pain.

"Stop screaming." She shook him. "I need to ask you something."

He silenced himself. She stared at him and realized that he was little more than a wreck of a man.

"Are you listening?" She felt the muscles in his neck work, which she assumed was him trying to nod.

He looked into her eyes, then away, and clearly didn't like what he saw there.

"Does she talk like this all the time?" She loosened her grip slightly to allow him to answer.

Lorenzo sniveled and choked out a, "Yes. It never stops, even when I'm trying to sleep."

She shook her head. "How annoying."

"And the compulsion to do what she says," he continued. "It's relentless."

"Compulsion?" Lexi thought for a moment and listened to

Delphine's ceaseless speech. "I don't get that. Only the irritating chatter."

Dick touched her shoulder. She turned to look at him and he stepped back with shock on his face. "Lexi, your eyes."

In that moment, she knew her eyes were black, but she couldn't say how she knew.

She drew her arm up to backhand him. But while her attention was diverted, Lorenzo ripped the ring from her finger and threw it across the room.

Lexi turned slowly to look at him. The expression on his face gave her pause. She tilted her head as though a different angle might give her a new perspective on this cockroach in her hand. Finally, she decided he looked confused. "Not what you expected?" she asked, conversationally. "But thank you. She was annoying."

Before he could answer, she snapped his neck with a twist of her wrist and let him fall.

Her eyes were still black. She looked at the scar and noticed that it was filled with what looked like shiny, wet, black tar.

Scott entered the room, paused, and stared at her in horror. She shook her head before her eyes became soft, brown, and desperate.

A voice that wasn't her own or Delphine's spoke from her mouth. "She needs your magic, boy. I can't hold her except for a few seconds."

He raced to her, grasped both her arms, and began to push his magic through the blood bond and into her.

Her eyes went black again and she snarled and fought. He tried to take her power away and she knew she had the power to strike him and kill him, but something stopped her.

"I'll kill you," Lexi screamed.

The young sorcerer gritted his teeth and hung on.

Dick scrambled to his feet behind her, wound his arms around her, and pinned the tops of her arms to her sides.

Scott looked frantically from one hand to the other. "Where's the ring?"

"It's over there on the floor." The vampire gestured with his head.

The other man's eyes widened. "How can the ring do this from over there?"

A hand settled on her head and she twisted to see that Anne had arrived with James and Sam.

The witch removed her hand abruptly. "This isn't the ring. It's something else."

"Help us, please," Scott cried.

They encircled Lexi, Scott, and Dick.

Anne began to chant. "Banish the negative harm and pain, only positive shall remain."

James and Sam took up the chant. A breeze lifted around them and grew in intensity until finally, the black-painted windows in Lorenzo's apartment exploded and the wind howled away.

Lexi felt the strength leave her body. She slumped, almost unconscious. As if from a distance, she watched as her scar filled with white energy before her eyes closed.

When she woke again, she knew they were back to normal but something was different. She looked around the room. Scott's bed was empty and she was still in her clothes.

Whispered snatches of conversation drifted to her. "But she didn't even have the ring on at that point."

Lexi felt wiped out. She sat, gave it a few seconds, then stood and walked up the hallway.

When she rounded the corner into the room, Dick held Marcel up and waved his little paw at her. "Anne's asking about the day-walking thing." He turned to the woman. "Lexi knows. She was there in Chicago when a witch threw a spell pouch that exploded all over me. I spent a night paralyzed and now, I can walk in the daylight."

Joseph nodded. "I can confirm that every word he speaks is truth."

She almost snorted at the Joseph-stamp-of-approval. Every word *was* true, but Dick had woven together three barely connected incidents. She glanced around. No one seemed inclined to call him a liar and she wouldn't say anything. If it ever got back to Kindred that Scott had done this for him, he'd be sentenced to death—or, at the very least, life in The Hollows.

Anne shuffled to the edge of her seat. "What was in the pouch?"

Lexi was surprised she hadn't taken a notepad and pen out.

The vampire opened his arms, his palms up, in an exaggerated shrug. "I have no idea. I wasn't able to get the muck out of the fabric. By the time I knew I'd be able to sunbathe in the South of France again, the suit had been discarded."

The woman sat back muttering, "I wonder what it was."

It was Geraldine's turn to lean forward. "So you didn't need to crawl into my father's tomb."

Dick winced. "Ah! No, I'm afraid not."

"Well, I hope that ruined another suit. You deserve it." She scowled at him.

The vampire put his hand over hers. "I apologize unreservedly."

Geraldine looked at his hand, then at him with an eyebrow raised. "And making poor Betsy climb in there with you. You're a very bad man."

Scott passed a cup of coffee to Lexi. She glanced quickly at him but had to look away. The desire she had felt to kill him was still fresh in her mind and she felt ashamed. The worst thing was that he would have felt her feelings through the blood bond—the murder and the shame. She focused instead on Geraldine. "You're looking well."

The shifter smiled at Scott. "Well, your man here is quite the physician. It's not a cure but I think he might have given me another year or two."

Anne stood and looked down at her. "I might have a few things to give you another year on top of that. Visit me at the shop."

Geraldine stood. "I'll walk out with you."

The two women said their goodbyes and left.

Lexi removed Marie Laveau's ring and handed it to Joseph. "Did you get the other ring?"

"Yes. I will put the spirit within it to rest."

She turned to Broullard. "Detective—"

"I think you can call me Charles." He smiled.

"You never mentioned that Alice is a police officer. Why not?"

"Ah! Well, the simple answer is that she kind of is and kind of isn't a police officer."

"That's the simple answer?" She frowned at him.

"She used to be a uniform but was posted to what most officers call the Special Ops team."

Lexi was familiar with the process of Kindred legacies joining the police force to work on supernatural cases, keeping the details off the official books.

He cleared his throat and looked uncomfortable. "Whatever you say she is, I've known her for years—not well but well enough. I felt protective of her and feared you meant to harm her. We look after our own."

She sighed. "I don't mean her any harm. What would be the point?"

Peter walked in from Dick's apartment. "The popcorn's popped and the movie's ready to go."

"Excellent." The vampire picked Marcel up and turned to the detective. "Charles, would you like to come and see one of my movies?"

"I'd love to, thank you." Broullard said good evening and followed them to the door.

"It's Peter's favorite," Dick explained. "*A Long Dark Night in Hollywood.*"

As the door closed, Lexi heard Broullard ask, "Don't you die at the end of that one?"

Joseph looked at Lexi. "Did you find your answers in the end?"

She shrugged. "I found a problem I thought I'd already solved and answers to questions I never asked. Does that count?"

He sighed. "Ah yes, your friend Caleb. What will you do about that?"

Her brain flooded with the questions and concerns she'd stored away while dealing with Lorenzo. "I don't know. It's clear now, though, that he knew we would be looking for him. He created that doppelganger out of a living person merely to make them a target so they'd die instead of him. I'm not happy about that."

"So, you simply forget him?" the man asked,

Scott answered from the kitchen. "How can we do that? He's trying to bring that demon across into our realm. If we don't do something, it'll be mayhem. But if we pursue him, we'll take on the whole of Kindred. There are only four of us."

Joseph stood and picked his staff up. "I think you'll find, when the time comes, that there will be many more than four of you."

Lexi met his eyes. "I hope so."

He patted her on the shoulder. "Before you go, you should take a ride on the *Creole Queen* paddlewheel boat. Try the gumbo and listen to a jazz band play on the Mississippi."

"Maybe we'll do that." She frowned when she realized he had taken Delphine's ring out and held it in his hand. "Will it be complicated? Drawing the spirit out?"

"No. I have everything I need. I could do it here. Scott, would you like to help?"

"Sure." The young sorcerer was always excited by new magic.

"Can you clear a space over there?" Joseph pulled a pouch from his pocket.

Scott moved a table to the side of the room and the other man told him to cup his hands. "We need a circle—big enough for the ring, is all."

The young man watched the particles pour into his hand from the pouch. "What is that? Sand?"

"It's cornmeal."

He allowed the cornmeal to pour slowly out of his hand in the vague shape of a circle but didn't look happy with the result. "It's not a very good circle. Would you like me to do it again?"

Joseph chuckled. "No, it will suffice." He passed the ring to Scott, who placed it inside the circle and sat on the floor beside it, not wanting to miss a thing.

The other man chanted and twisted his staff so the bones on strings clattered against it. The sorcerer's gaze on the ring was almost hypnotic and his face moved closer until his nose was barely outside the circle.

The chanting ceased and there was silence for two seconds before the staff pounded onto the ring and shattered it.

Scott's entire body left the floor as he hurtled away. "Jesus!"

Joseph chuckled. "The ring merely needed to be destroyed."

"So, what was all the ritual stuff for?" The sorcerer had his hand over his chest.

The old man beamed. "Fun."

Lexi exhaled a sharp breath. "Well, I could have destroyed it."

The old voodoo priest's eyes glittered. "Where's the fun in that?"

She grinned as Scott scraped the metal and stone up.

"Joseph, you are a funny, funny man." He held the pieces of the ring out, but the other man was nowhere to be seen.

He shrugged, stood, and threw the pieces of jewelry into the trash before he headed to the door.

Lexi folded her arms. "Where are you going?"

"To watch the movie." He pointed at the door.

"And the cornmeal you sprinkled all over the floor will clean itself up, will it?"

Scott looked at the mess and then at her. "Yes." He clicked his fingers and it was gone.

"Smartass."

CHAPTER FIFTY-FIVE

"So you won't do anything about the doppelgänger?" Dick's eyebrow was raised in surprise.

"What's the point? It's not like she's stolen my life. She's wearing my face, yes, but that wasn't her doing—or, most likely, the person she was before. Why even tell her what she is? She has her life and I have mine. I think it's best if I simply leave. We still have Caleb to deal with." Lexi, Scott, and Dick looked out from the deck of the Creole Queen. A long drive awaited them but for now, she felt they deserved a few hours R and R.

The paddle began to turn, the jazz band struck up, and the boat glided through the water.

A handful of people stood on the shore and waved but mostly, they continued with their day.

Scott turned to Dick. "What about you? Do you regret day-walking now? It's all anyone's talking about."

He raised a finger in the air. "But they're all talking about a witch and a spell pouch. You're off the hook. I think it's worked out rather well."

Lexi turned and leaned her back against the rail. "I wonder if things will settle here now that New Orleans is two vampire clans lighter."

The vampire raised an eyebrow. "Pfft! Almost half of the Quarter is up for grabs. I think it's a good time to get out of town." He pointed along the boat. "Unless I'm very much mistaken, I think the bar's this way." He wandered in that direction.

She turned to look at the shore again.

Scott did the same. "When is Dolores expecting us in Charlotte?"

"Not for another—" She froze as she found herself looking into what seemed to be her own eyes. It was Alice. Her hair was the same color and her build identical. The only differences were the angry scars raked across her face. The doppelgänger stared at her with wide, horror-filled eyes.

Scott spun quickly. "I'll speak to her." He materialized beside the woman and opened his mouth to speak.

The next moments for Lexi were like watching herself but it all happened much faster.

Before her friend seemed to have managed a single word, Alice acted defensively. She swept her hand across her thigh, exactly where Lexi's dimensional pocket was located. A glint in her hand preceded a swipe. The woman looked quickly at her before she raced away and left Scott alone. His mouth shaped into an O and his eyes were wide as a bloom of red appeared on the chest of his white t-shirt. He stumbled and his gaze sought hers as he fell. She opened her mouth to scream but nothing emerged.

Pain and fear surged through the empathetic link and she looked around. The boat, the shore, and the distance all seemed impossible.

I have to be there.

In the next moment, she was. She wobbled to her knees and vomited. Lexi stumbled to her feet a few feet away from him, his agony intense through the empathetic link of their blood bond.

Lexi dropped to her knees and tears streamed down her face as bubbles of blood came from his mouth. A hand caught hers and she looked at Dick, who had appeared beside her. He was soaking wet from the waist down. She realized he wasn't holding her hand.

Instead, he held her arm out, his expression compelling. She looked at the scar and recognized the presence of the white magic. She still had magic? Shit!

Quickly, she put her hand over her friend's chest. Sensing the hole in his heart, she poured out her desire for it to be healed.

The vampire eased her back by her shoulders. "His heart's beating. I think he'll be okay."

She stood and glowered in the direction in which Alice had disappeared. "Make sure I don't lose him," she told Dick coldly.

"How am I supposed to—"

"You know what I'm saying. I will not lose him."

He nodded once and prepared to bite into his own wrist.

Lexi ran after the doppelgänger. She'd intended to leave her alone but now, she would crush her. Fury fueled her pace but the area was deserted. She couldn't know if her quarry had continued in the same direction or turned off so she chose the direction that made the most sense to her.

As she ran past a building near the tracks, the woman lurched out with a knife in her hand. She had half-expected it as it was what she'd have done. Unfortunately, that was where the similarities ended. She mostly managed to dodge the knife, but it sliced her arm before she kicked it from the assailant's hand. The girl swept a hand across her vest and another one appeared. Lexi did the same.

Her adversary blurred as she moved quickly to attack again. The speed was shocking. It was like fighting a vampire except they always tried to bite when they fought and were predictable. Alice wasn't. Without warning, she flicked the blade at her. She ducked her head and felt the sharp sting along the edge of her ear. The woman had cut her twice now.

Alice didn't retrieve another blade but somehow looked more dangerous, crouched as she was like a shifter about to turn. She flicked a shuriken and it bit into Lexi's shoulder as she twisted to avoid it. Before she could regain her balance, her opponent picked her up and hurled her through a window in the side of the building. She landed in what looked like an abandoned workshop.

The woman stood outside and glared at her where she lay dazed. "Why would anyone make such a weak doppelgänger of me? What's the point?" She vaulted through the window but stopped and shook her head as though dizzy, then continued toward Lexi and dragged her onto her knees by the hair. The familiar sound of the button being pulled from the vest indicated the release of the garroting wire. She tensed, then froze as she heard the unmistakable squeal as the wire coiled in again. Alice had released it and stumbled into the back of her.

"What have you…done to me?" She sounded suddenly exhausted, which made no sense at all. She hadn't done anything to the girl…yet.

Lexi felt suddenly powerful. "Scott only wanted to talk to you, Alice. You almost killed him."

"It's Alicia."

Acting on pure adrenaline, she grabbed the woman and flung her the length of the room. She bulldozed into a row of cupboard doors and splintered them.

Alicia scrambled behind a row of desks, her breathing labored.

Lexi drew her katana and scraped it along the worktops as she walked along chanting, "Alicia, Alicia, not gonna miss ya."

Where did that come from?

"What?"

Lexi leapt over the desk and swung her fist into the woman's head to leave her dazed. She elbowed her in the face and was amazed to see her slide across the floor and impact the wall behind with extreme force. Driven by cold anger, she grasped the girl by the vest and punched her repeatedly in the face. The more she did it, the stronger she felt. She was starting to enjoy this and hadn't felt this strong since — A vision of herself holding Lorenzo by the throat came to her. She stopped, let go of Alicia's vest, and grimaced when the girl fell.

Breathing hard, she drew herself tall and looked at the doppelgänger. The face so eerily her own was slick with blood.

How many times did I hit her?

As she dropped to her knees, she drew the katana from her pocket. It was time to simply finish this and get the job done. "I intended to simply leave town. You brought this on yourself." She wasn't even sure the girl was conscious as she spoke to her.

With the blade held above her head, she felt power pulse through her.

She was ready to strike when the door flew open.

"Lexi, stop. She's not a doppelgänger. She's your sister."

Something in the tone penetrated and she froze and stared at the bloody girl with her face. She put the sword down and looked at Scott. He wasn't alone. Dick was there and so was someone else. She looked into the face of the man beside Scott.

He was older. Of course he was—he'd been fifteen when she'd last seen him. Before she'd been made to forget him, made to forget he'd been bitten by a shifter, made to forget being dragged out of the room, and made to forget she'd heard the shot.

"Bryan?"

Being distracted, Lexi didn't see the powerful right hook from the girl on the floor.

The lights went out.

CHAPTER FIFTY-SIX

"*Alexa, Alexa, I hope a witch'll hex ya.*"

"*Alicia, Alicia, I'm not gonna miss ya.*"

"*Will you two knock it off? Don't make me come up there.*"

Lexi's eyes snapped open. The world spun and her vision was blurred. She closed her eyes again for a few seconds, then opened them slowly and blinked to try to clear them. An unfamiliar room slipped in and out of focus. She stretched on a couch and a face loomed above her, but it was too blurry to identify.

"She's waking up."

That voice. I should know it.

As she shook her head slightly, the face began to clear. The dark hair and olive skin were familiar, as were his brown eyes. The stubble was new, though, and her hand moved as if of its own volition to touch it. "Bryan?"

"Hi, Lexi-Loo." He smiled at her but moved beyond her reach.

She startled when she heard the nickname he used to call her and withdrew her hand. A few moments later, her surroundings settled and her vision cleared.

Briefly, she wondered if she was in a dream, but common sense told her she couldn't invent this adult version of his face. "You were bitten by a shifter. They shot you."

He nodded. "With a dart gun. I remember."

When she tried to sit, the dizziness returned, so she gave up the effort and stared at him.

Dick's voice spoke from behind them. "You must have been what, fifteen? I didn't think they let mages out to chase shifters at that age."

Bryan turned to speak over the couch she lay on. "I wasn't supposed to be there. The family had been called out while I was with them. I think we were on the way back from a restaurant."

Lexi closed her eyes again. "It was Maggie's birthday." She smiled as a memory came to her. "Isaac hung a birthday banner across the living room, but he attached it using his little cross-bolt gun and fired it into the corners of the room. Dad went nuts and the dinner was almost canceled." She remembered the restaurant. Her Kindred sister, Maggie, had blown out seventeen candles on her cake.

Her Kindred brother chuckled. "I'd forgotten about that. Lexi had only just started going out on jobs with the family. I was supposed to stay in the car, but I was bored and fifteen and thought I'd be able to watch the action from a safe distance. While they were looking for the shifter, he had escaped from a window and surprised me. I couldn't make an energy ball yet, but I managed to shock him enough to make him run off.

"The family didn't realize I'd been bitten. I'd healed the wound before they returned to the car because I was more afraid of being grounded than dying. Within hours, I had a fever and started hallucinating. I remembered events I swore had happened but no one else seemed to recall them."

She opened her eyes to look at him again. "When they realized you'd been bitten, I was forbidden to go near you, but they couldn't keep us apart. We did everything together. I'd climbed in the window and found you covered in sweat and shivering. Then, after a few days of you raving, a Kindred unit came from another city. Some cold-faced bitch pulled me out of the room, and I heard shouting.

"Braxton argued with them, then I heard the shot. I thought it was from a silenced weapon. I tried to break away from the woman, but she counseled me. She took the memories away—not only of that event, but it was as though you had never existed until Barry the vampire tried to turn me. I tasted vampire blood and the memories tumbled back." Still gazing at him, she asked. "Have you always remembered?"

He paused for a moment before he responded. "Yes."

Still befuddled, she tried to process it. Her memories of him had only returned a year before and she had thought he was dead. But he had always known he'd left her behind. It hurt that he'd never made contact.

Her eyes stung at the thought and she dragged her gaze away from him. The blinds were closed and she couldn't get a sense of where they were. "How long have I been out? Where are we?"

"You've been out a few hours. We're in North Carolina." Dolores appeared from behind the couch. She put a cup of coffee on the table in front of her before she walked out of sight again. Lexi looked at the cup. It was one she had bought Dolores and said *I'm Tired Of Adulting. Let's Be Fairies.*

The others seemed to be giving her and Bryan a little space, but she could feel a swell of emotions from Scott. They were all hopelessly entwined with her feelings and she wasn't sure who felt what or even that she had the energy to sift through them.

She looked at Bryan. "Where is she?" She didn't have to say who she meant. Everyone would know she was talking about the sister she'd only recently discovered existed.

He frowned and scraped his mop of dark hair away from his face. "Back in New Orleans, at Dad's place."

"Dad?" Her heart raced. Had Alicia been living with their parents?

Bryan seemed to know where her thoughts had jumped to. "Our Kindred unit leader—Kevin Rand, the police chief. Not her real dad."

"The chief's your dad? The man who gave Lorenzo the go-ahead to murder all those people? How are you okay with that?" Lexi was shocked.

"I'm not okay with it. Dad wouldn't be either. Not that it matters. He had one of his weird phone calls from Caleb. I've seen him when it happens. The man calls and starts speaking, his face goes blank, and there are things he doesn't remember. It's different than counseling. I don't know how Caleb does it." Bryan shrugged. "As far as Kevin knows, Lorenzo went crazy. I told him she'd fought him and killed him."

"Kindred saves us all again, woohoo!" Dick's voice, still from behind, dripped with sarcasm.

Bryan looked up, presumably at the vampire, and shrugged apologetically. "She collapsed after your fight. I counseled her before she woke up again. Dad's not happy about that and it's against Kindred procedures. I don't like counseling her but it's the only way I could think to cover your trail and give me space in which to get answers. I already suspected you were involved as the hotel staff in Cabo were adamant that Ali had been there for over a week."

Dolores spoke from where she presumably waited with Dick. "Didn't they counsel you?"

"Not yet, but the memories always come back anyway. They don't know that."

Lexi nodded. "Because of the shifter bite."

His brows drew together in puzzlement. "No."

"No?" She frowned at him in confusion. "But I thought that was why they shot you—because the counseling stopped working and you remembered things they were trying to hide."

Bryan nodded his understanding. "You're kind of right. If we're tainted by a sting, bite, or the blood of a supernatural, counseling might not work for a while until we're fully healed. Then, usually, everything goes back to normal."

"I didn't know," she responded, still a little confused. "It was one of the reasons I ran from them. I thought they might realize I'd been tainted by the vampire blood and call someone in to kill me."

"Tainted? Excuse me, I'm right here." Dick sounded offended.

Bryan looked up. "Sorry, that's a Kindred term."

"Quelle Surprise," the vampire muttered.

She watched her once-brother while he spoke. He'd grown into a handsome man. She twisted her mother's wedding ring.

He looked at the ring and smiled. "You still have that."

Lexi smiled when she looked at the band. "It's always meant a lot to me but I never knew why. When they took the memory of you, I also lost the memory I would have had if I'd found out it had belonged to my mother."

Bryan returned his gaze to her face. "Dolores told me about the vamp trying to turn you. Is that when you started to remember me?" He waited for her to confirm with a nod, then tilted his head with a curious expression. "But that's only one of the reasons why you ran. You thought they'd murdered me. What else?"

"We'd been on a job. A kid had been kidnapped by a vampire—the one who tried to turn me. We rescued the boy and he was supposed to go back to his parents. They counseled us the next morning after I'd submitted my report but it didn't work on me. I was scared so I didn't tell anyone. Later, they counseled us again and implanted the existence of a little brother called Bobby. It almost worked and for a brief moment, I totally believed it. When he walked in, though, I recognized him instantly as the kid who'd been kidnapped. They hadn't taken him to his parents. He had mage potential so they kept him." She shook her head. "His poor parents."

"It sounds like the taint—uh, the vampire blood was wearing off and counseling was starting to work again. But then they introduced the kid who was already in your memory. The moment you saw him, it caused a conflict. Your brain rejected the new information."

Lexi felt confused by it all. "So they don't kill people who have been tainted—I mean…uh, contaminated. Sorry, Dick, that's not any better, is it?"

The vampire sighed dramatically.

Bryan shook his head. "You mean the horror stories we heard growing up? Sometimes. If that vampire had succeeded in turning you, they would have eliminated you."

She nodded. "Or if the shifter had turned you back then."

"Exactly."

That triggered her recall of something she'd been curious about. "That reminds me, what attacked Alicia? Those marks on her face."

He paused and gnawed his lip before he answered. "Yes, that was a werewolf."

After a niggle of guilt, she chastised herself mentally for being so blunt. "I'm sorry. Did you kill it?"

"I tried." He looked away.

Lexi narrowed her eyes. "It was you, wasn't it?"

His mouth opened but he didn't say anything.

While she knew he knew what she meant, she said it anyway. "In the street, when we were with Thomas and Lorenzo attacked us. It was you who saved us."

"Er… Yes. Joseph had told me about you."

"I wish he'd done me the same courtesy." She lowered her head carefully. "So, I have a sister and I almost killed her."

Bryan put his hand on her arm. "She won't remember it."

For a moment, at his touch, memories and feelings flowed through her like a tidal wave, followed immediately by a feeling of jealousy and hurt that came from Scott.

She did her best to push Scott's feelings away, not because she didn't care but because it was all too much. "But I remember it. I don't know what got into me."

"It was probably something residual from the ring," Dolores said, still out of sight. Bryan looked up and Lexi had a feeling they shared some unspoken concern.

Without thought, she rubbed her face where Alicia had punched her. It didn't hurt, obviously. Scott would have seen to that.

Bryan looked at her again. "Do you remember anything about Alicia? Have any old memories resurfaced?"

"No." She thought about the dream she'd had—two little girls teasing each other—but it had been fleeting and was already drifting away. "I didn't know I had a sister until you came into that room and stopped me from taking her head off."

He raised an eyebrow. "Well, thank you for stopping. Look, I'll tell you what I know, but it's not much."

"I think I need to sit for this." Lexi swung her legs to the floor and pushed into a seated position. She caught a glimpse of Scott, Dick, and Dolores at a table behind the couch. Scott was the only one who didn't return her gaze. He stared resolutely ahead.

God knows what must be going through his mind.

Bryan continued. "I only know what I've overheard and it's not much. When you were six, a decision was made to separate you and you were taken to different Kindred families."

"What about our real parents? Were they Kindred? Or were we kidnapped like Bobby?"

"I don't know about that. I'm sorry, but Ali is unusual. She's the strongest and fastest legacy I've ever seen."

His words hurt although she knew he hadn't intended that. He would remember that she was almost a complete dud. She covered her discomfort by rubbing her jaw again. "I noticed that."

She thought about the fight with her sister and how she'd seemed stronger than might have been believed, and how at the end, she had sagged. "Right now, I feel weaker than I've ever felt in my life."

Dick cleared his throat. "It's understandable. She slapped you into next week."

Lexi twisted in her seat and leveled a gaze at him. He sat at the table facing her and shrugged. "Well, she did."

She turned to Bryan. "Can I meet her?"

"Rematch?" the vampire muttered.

"Are you for real?" Her glare didn't seem to have much effect.

Dick raised an eyebrow. "What? You broke my neck. I can't experience a little schadenfreude?"

Bryan spoke quickly. "I don't want to put her in danger. Also, it would be awkward because she doesn't know I remember things. I've told her things before, but she didn't take it well and I had to counsel her. I hate doing that."

Lexi knew she had to ask her next question as dispassionately as possible, but she couldn't do it looking into his eyes. She picked the mug of coffee up and stared into it. "She's your wife, isn't she?"

"Yes." His voice was soft

While she tried to remain nonchalant and managed to swallow the lump in her throat, it seemed loud as though it were a rock. She grimaced, sure the whole room had heard it. Again, a swell of pity came through the empathetic link.

She silently tested the question she wanted to ask but couldn't because it was stupid and pointless. *Why did they take you away from me and give you to her?*

Lexi felt like she was fifteen again and the pain of losing Bryan was still raw from her core to her fingertips.

With a slow, deliberate movement, she put the mug down. It was time to regain control of herself. "Is Broullard okay? The chief and Caleb were going to—"

Bryan shook his head. "He's fine. I counseled him before I came here and he won't remember any of you."

Dick sighed. "Charles won't remember me? That makes me sad."

Lexi understood how he felt. She liked Broullard too.

"I told the chief I'd done it," Bryan continued. "They'll leave him alone—"

"You can't assume that," Lexi interrupted. "Caleb wanted him dead and he has a very long arm."

"He's safe for now. I don't know what else I can do." He shrugged as though helping the detective was truly beyond him.

She stood. "Counsel him again. Tell him to retire on medical grounds. Send him on a cruise. Get him out of there."

He put his hands on her arms. "You're right. I'll do what I can."

The move shocked her. For a fraction of a second, she thought of either kissing him or head-butting him.

Bryan seemed to sense the conflict and stepped back.

Lexi sat again. "I assume you know all about Caleb now."

"We told him," Scott said.

Her Kindred brother picked a glass of water up and took a sip. "I've had suspicions about him for a while. I've met him a few times, but they always counsel me after, thinking they can make me forget him. Still, there isn't much I can tell you. It sounds like you all know a hell of a lot more about him than I've gleaned.

"I've overheard Dad talk about him having business interests in South Africa. But more recently, he purchased a business on behalf of Kindred in Maine. I don't know the details, only that it was some kind of hostile takeover and he's in the process of changing the management team. There isn't much I can do to help you without putting Alicia in danger."

She was annoyed and felt the situation deserved to be taken more seriously. "Why not? Surely Caleb's a risk to everyone. I assume they've told you he's trying to bring a particularly powerful high-level demon into our world."

"I don't know who else is involved. If we show our hand now and discover the whole council is conspiring with him, we're dead. I know for a fact he's been practicing outlawed magic."

"I know that. I killed his doppelgänger, remember? That ritual takes thirteen members—or proxies like your dad. Yes, we noticed your dad's lost twenty percent of his fingers."

"Precisely. The council is thirteen. What if it's all of them? I might be able to get some information out of Kevin, although it wouldn't surprise me if Caleb counsels him each time they go to meetings together. That happens at least once a month."

Lexi straightened. "That works perfectly. We could find out where they meet and stick something pointy between his ribs."

Bryan looked doubtfully at her. "You don't look like you could poke him in the ribs with a finger. Maybe you need to get your strength back. I'll keep my eyes and ears open and let you know anything I learn, but I'm not sure this is even your problem, is it? You left Kindred."

She raked her fingers through her hair. "Like I said, this is everyone's problem. If I thought I could trust Kindred to deal with their own mess, I would because honestly, I think this will be the death of us."

He moved her mug and sat on the wooden table in front of her. "Lexi, I have to ask this. Did you do anything to Alicia? Anything magical?"

The memory of the fight resurfaced and she put her hands over her face and shook her head. "I almost pulverized her but no, nothing magical. Why?"

"We're keeping her sedated because she had aggression issues. When she initially woke, she threw her mom across the room so hard, it would have killed a normal person. Luckily, her mom was able to translocate out. Then, she punched her way through a metal door. She was feral. When I scanned her body, the density of her bones had doubled. That can't suddenly happen by itself."

Lexi felt the accusation in the air. She leveled her gaze at him. "I said I didn't do anything like that. Scott and I have only been matched for a few months. I'm still learning."

Bryan held a hand up. "That's fine, I believe you. I merely need to look harder for an answer, that's all." He sighed and looked at her. "I didn't think I'd ever see you again, Lexi-Loo."

She looked away, feeling awkward. "I thought *you* were dead so I doubt you're as surprised as I am." She looked back at him. "Why did they take you away?"

He shrugged. "New Orleans is a melting pot of supernaturals. It's a huge community." He made a gun with his fingers and pretended to blow smoke off the imaginary barrel. "I guess they needed their best man." He gave her a lop-sided grin.

And their best woman.

Bryan stood. "I need to get back. Scott knows how to contact me if you need me." He vanished.

Lexi looked up and scowled at the others, who all seemed to watch her with pity in their eyes. She hated it. "So, what's next for us? I can't sit around waiting to hear from him."

"A break, then. A real one this time." Dolores patted her on the shoulder.

She shook her head. "I'd rather get back to work if it's all the same."

The woman sighed and it appeared that was the response she'd expected. "As you wish. I've had a job come in and I was going to give it to someone local to the area but honestly, there aren't many supernaturals near this one. It's in Las Vegas. A lucky talisman has been stolen."

Dick spun in his seat. "Stolen? Magical items are protected in Las Vegas. The only way to steal them would be with magic, which is impossible with the wards in place."

Dolores nodded her agreement. "I don't understand it either. Many magical items are in Las Vegas for that precise reason."

Lexi drained her mug and stood. "Surely it would have been taken out of town immediately. Even if it were somehow stolen, I can't imagine how it could be used in Vegas."

Her boss took the mug from her. "I think you're right. If it really is gone, I hope Scott can follow it."

Dick asked the question she had intended to ask next. "Why haven't they called the local Kindred unit in for this?"

"One of the staff members at the museum is a supe," the fae explained. "An old friend who works as a historian. He did call Kindred yesterday morning when it was found to be missing, and they told him to keep looking for it. They think it's more likely someone at the museum has mislaid it. He knows that's not the case, freaked out, and called me."

Scott's brow wrinkled. "Why would a supe work somewhere they can't use all their abilities?"

Dolores continued to speak as she put the mugs and glasses into the kitchen. "He likes the dry heat."

Lexi had the feeling that wasn't the real reason, but it was none of their business. She watched as Marcel woke, yawned and stretched, and padded to Dick.

The vampire scratched the puppy's head absently. "Are Kindred sure the wards are all still in place?"

Dolores returned to the room. "They insist that no magic has been or could be performed in Las Vegas except by license."

Lexi turned to the fae. "Why is there even a Kindred unit in Las Vegas if it's so locked down?"

The woman laughed. "Because they perform twice a night on the Strip, dear."

"That figures." She stood. "At least I'll know who the local Kindred mages are. It'll be fairly easy to avoid people whose faces are plastered all over the billboards."

"So we're going. Marvelous! I wonder if Celine's performing. I'll give her a call while I walk Marcel." Dick stood and took the lead from the table. "Marcel, walkies."

He attached the lead while the puppy wagged his stumpy tail. When he opened the door, the sudden loud cacophony of traffic sounds made Lexi jump. He turned to them. "Toodle-pip." Marcel scrambled to get through the door and Dick followed before he closed it behind them.

The room returned to silence. After a moment, she flopped like a sullen teen and rolled her eyes. "Does he have to come?"

Dolores's eyebrows raised in surprise. "Don't you want him on the team?"

Lexi tutted. "No… Yes… He's so annoying."

The fae patted her cheek. "You can be annoying too, dear."

She exhaled sharply. "That's what he says. Okay, fine, but only because I've grown attached to Marcel."

CHAPTER FIFTY-SEVEN

Lexi sat at the table next to Scott. He'd barely said a word and she placed her hand palm-up on the table beside his. He continued to stare ahead with worry lines across his forehead. After a moment, he stood and walked through the French doors at the back of the room and onto a porch.

Dolores stood behind the girl's chair and put her hands on her shoulders. "Give him time. He knows Bryan was your intended blood match and whatever feelings you have for him, Scott can feel that. He's confused."

"I know." She walked to the window and opened the blinds. It was dark but she could see a row of lights from homes dotted along the shores of a lake. The gleam from an almost full but waning moon reflected on the water. Scott walked along a small boardwalk. "I don't know what to tell him. He's not the only one who's confused, but it's not like we're a couple or anything."

"He probably wonders if you regret being matched with him now you know Bryan's still alive."

"Bryan's still alive and apparently, he's my brother-in-law. I don't think Scott has anything to worry about." She studied their surroundings curiously. "Where exactly are we?"

"Here and there." Dolores joined her at the window and pointed. "That's Lake Norman. It's about thirty miles from Charlotte."

They watched together as the sorcerer walked to the end of the boardwalk and sat with his legs crossed. Lexi glanced at her companion. "Maybe I should talk to him and apologize."

The fae remained focused on Scott. "You have nothing to apologize for. I've always felt the blood match is more curse than anything. They make you all want it so much—like you won't be complete without the never-ending agony of an unhealing scar and the weight of someone else's emotional crap for the rest of your life."

She smirked. "Well, when you put it like that..." She looked at the still water and quiet woods. "How far to the nearest coffee shop?"

"If you go out that way? About five miles. Leave by the front door instead. It opens into the middle of Charlotte and there's a Starbucks across the street."

Lexi crossed the room and opened the front door to look out. The city sounds blasted again. It was late in the evening and the traffic was still quite heavy, but she located the Starbucks sign across the street. She turned to her companion. "Okay, so what would happen if I stepped out of here and climbed over the roof? Where would I be?"

Dolores smiled. "Good luck with that."

With a grin, she strolled out. On the street, she turned and looked at the door she'd left through. Her gaze traced up the building from there and she had to crane her neck to follow its lines to the top. It was a skyscraper. Chuckling, she turned and headed across the street.

Fae magic is so cool.

She returned ten minutes later with an iced caramel latte for herself and an iced peppermint white chocolate mocha for Scott. He was still out near the water in the dark and she wandered out to join him. As soon as she opened the door, insects buzzed in the otherwise silent world.

As she approached, she noticed that he held a little energy ball in his palm. "That's nice."

He glanced at her as she settled beside him. "This will be your next lesson. No more exploding voodoo stones for you."

Lexi recalled the liquified gore that had dripped from his hair after she'd used the voodoo stone in New Orleans a few days before. It was inappropriate but she couldn't stifle a giggle.

Scott looked sharply at her before he chuckled too. "God, that was awful."

They both laughed.

She put the cupholder between them, pulled her latte out, and looked onto the water. "If it weren't for those houses over there, it would be almost completely black out here." She looked at the apartment. It was an abandoned fishing shack from the outside.

He threw the energy ball and they watched as it skipped over the water like a stone and left a trail of light before it flickered and disappeared. He picked his drink up and took a long sip of it. "So, what's it like to have a twin sister?"

Lexi thought about it, then sighed. "I think I was happier when I thought I had a doppelgänger."

The sorcerer turned to her. "You were looking for answers—"

"She's not an answer. She's a thousand more questions."

"I'm sorry for how I reacted." He returned his focus to the water. "It's confusing, feeling all those emotions coming from you."

She wasn't sure what those emotions were herself but did know he felt insecure. Talking about it seemed unfair so she decided to divert the conversation. "That goes both ways, you know."

"What do you mean?" He looked genuinely puzzled.

"You've been pining for your new fairy girlfriend since you got back from Fae." She smirked.

Scott put his drink down. "That's not fair. She's not my girlfriend. She attacked me. I have to ride it out until her compulsion wears off."

Lexi elbowed him lightly. "You mean *we* have to ride it out."

He sighed, then barked a laugh. "We're not exactly the poster kids for life after Kindred, are we?"

In response, she held her cup up. "Dude, I think we're the only examples. To the ex-Kindred fuck-up society."

"I think we do some good, though, don't you?" He bumped his cup against hers.

"No. I think we do a ton of good. I think we do great." Lexi adjusted her position so she faced him. "We're on the run from the largest supernatural organization on the planet. Are we hiding?"

Scott gave her a lop-sided grin. "A little."

"Well, okay, but we still kick ass." She held her cup up and they bumped again.

Dolores opened the door of the shack. "If you two have finished congratulating yourselves, Dick's back. Let's get to work."

They walked inside to find the vampire pulling cartons of Chinese food out of a bag. "I didn't know what you all eat so I bought a selection."

The fae looked at Lexi with her eyebrows raised in silent admonishment for her suggestion that he shouldn't be on the team.

She smiled in response and nodded as she put her coffee cup on the table. "I'm going to wash up."

Dolores pointed. "It's past the kitchen."

After the kitchen, one more door was visible along the hallway. She stepped in and washed her hands. When she joined the others at the table, she opened the box in front of her. "Orange chicken, perfect." She looked at Dick. "Thank you."

After dinner, Dolores cleared the cartons into the trash. "Okay, you guys, I need the table for work. Go out and get some exercise."

Scott turned to Lexi and Dick. "Do you want to explore the town?"

The vampire looked out onto the water. "I'll have a little quiet time at the lake. I might catch up later."

The two young people left via the front door and walked along quiet streets for a while.

"We don't seem to be in the middle of the action, do we?" the sorcerer said when he finally stopped. He didn't wait for an answer but scrolled through his cell phone. "Right, let's move this along." He caught hold of his companion and teleported.

Lexi looked around and after a few moments, realized that they stood on the street outside a large gate. She read the sign. "Hey, a theme park."

Scott grinned. "I've always wanted to visit a theme park."

"You've never been to one?"

"Not as far as I know, but you know what it's like. I could have been to ten theme parks and they might have taken it all away. I can't believe I ever thought counseling was justified." He looked through the iron bars of the gate before he extended his arm to her. "One more hop."

She took his arm and he teleported them into the entertainment venue.

They walked along stalls which were all closed but which carried signs for popcorn, cotton candy, hook-a-duck, and hotdogs.

Finally, they stopped in front of a huge rollercoaster.

He gazed longingly at it. "Look at the size of it."

Lexi pulled him. "Let's sit in it."

They climbed easily over the gate and up to the first car, then sat in the front and clicked the safety belts.

She shook her head. "I can't believe you haven't been to a theme park. That's a tragedy. We should go to one."

Scott put his hand on the car. His lips moved and it moved a few inches, then stopped. He looked at her. "What do you think?"

"What's keeping you?" She grinned. "Fire this baby up."

The car climbed the track slowly. When it reached the top, he took his hand away and it stopped.

He looked around into the distance. "We can see for miles."

They both laughed, then fell silent. He turned to her. "I know you're thinking about him. You can talk about him. I don't mind."

Lexi thought he probably did mind, but a memory had come to her in those moments and she wanted to share it. "When Bryan was with us, we must have been around twelve. We used to climb out of the attic window and sit on the roof. While we were up there, we'd play a game called What Would You Do?"

"What's that?"

"Okay, let's give it a go. What would you do if a shifter suddenly appeared in front of you?"

Scott's brows drew down in thought. "It depends. Might it be Edward or Agatha?"

They knew shifters, so the game wouldn't be as easy as it had been when they were kids. She sighed. "Say it wasn't. For the purposes of the game, it's a bad shifter."

He grinned. "You're my legacy. I'd call you."

Lexi looked at him, her expression deadpan. "I've been knocked unconscious."

"Oh, right. I'd paralyze him until you woke up. Then you could deal with him."

She rolled her eyes. "Now you ask me one."

The sorcerer thought for a moment. "What would you do if a dark fae suddenly appeared in front of you…with malicious intent?"

Lexi nodded. "Easy. I'd take my katana out and chop her head off."

"Her?"

"You're thinking of the one who attacked you, aren't you?"

He exhaled huffily. "I guess. Although I think I could have guessed that answer."

"My turn. What would you do if Azatoth appeared in front of you?"

Immediately, he gave her a lop-sided grin. "Run like fuck."

What could she do but laugh? "Come on, then. You ask. Try to make it a hard one."

Scott chewed his lip as he thought hard. "What would you do if Dick suddenly appeared in front of you and…uh, and kissed you. With tongues."

Lexi thumped his arm and laughed. "Oh, gross. I'd break his nose."

"You wouldn't be that lucky." Dick's voice startled them.

"Christ almighty, you almost gave me a heart attack." Her hand clutched her chest.

"Don't blame me. I was on the other side of town and I suddenly appeared here as though I had been conjured."

She twisted in her seat to look at him "You're kidding!" She glanced at Scott, about to ask if he'd done it.

"Of course I'm kidding. I heard you two from half a mile away. Does this go?" Dick settled into the seat behind them and clicked the safety belt. "Safety first. Actually, I did once get my nose broken for kissing a woman. I'll tell you about it sometime."

Scott put a hand on the front of the car and it accelerated along the rails.

As the car came in toward the rear of the others, she noticed the beam from a flashlight.

"Who's there?" a gravelly voice demanded in the darkness.

Scott grabbed Lexi and Dick and teleported to the apartment.

Seconds later, they stood outside the building. The sorcerer seemed surprised and he looked around with a frown. "I aimed for the inside."

They stepped into Dolores's apartment to find she'd left a note on the table for them. *I've turned in. Bedrooms have been prepared for you. Please lock the doors before you go to bed.*

Scott turned and locked the door as instructed.

Lexi looked around, "Where are we supposed to sleep? I didn't see any bedrooms." She looked down the hallway. It was longer than she remembered and there were now two doors she would swear she hadn't seen before beyond the bathroom. She opened the first to find it had two beds and the second had one bed and a dog basket. Marcel was already asleep on the floor next to the basket.

She returned to the others. "There are now two bedrooms that weren't here before." She shook her head and chuckled.

Dick paused at the French doors. "What are you laughing at?"

"I've been around magic my whole life, but it was mostly only used to hurt or control people. Since I've worked with Dolores, I've seen the good things it can do—and the fun things."

The vampire opened the French doors. "Lexi Braxton, I do believe you've gone native. Welcome to the dark side." He wiggled his eyebrows and stepped out.

Lexi yawned. "I'm heading to bed."

Scott looked at the lake. "I'll be along soon. I'll sit with Dick for a few minutes."

She went to sleep listening to the low murmurs of the men talking.

The sorcerer was leaving the bathroom when Lexi stumbled out of the room. "Morning, sleepyhead. It's ten-thirty."

Lexi attempted to say, "Morning," through a yawn.

She stepped into the shower, still half-asleep. As she washed her hair, she wondered about the magic apartment. Her eyes widened.

If the front is in Charlotte and the back is a shack on the edge of a lake, what are the water pipes and electrical cables connected to?

Suspiciously, she peered at the shower and shook her head. "Well, that woke me. It's best not to think about stuff like this."

"Sorry, dear?" Dolores was outside the bathroom.

"Nothing, only…thinking out loud." She scrubbed her face.

Back in the room and dressed, she waited while Scott laced his high-tops and walked to the door.

Lexi cocked an eyebrow. "Where are you going?"

"Dolores has made bacon and pancakes." He turned to her with a grin.

"What about making your bed?"

He frowned. "This room will disappear when we've finished with it."

"That's no excuse. Show some respect."

His shoulders sagged but he rolled his eyes and returned to make the bed. He finished by plumping the pillow. "Happy?"

"Yep." Lexi walked to the door.

Scott looked at her unmade bed. "Hey, how about yours?"

She smirked. "There's no point. This room will disappear when we've finished with it."

"Very funny," he muttered.

With him on her heels, she wandered through to find coffee, piles of bacon, and pancakes waiting for them.

"You won't get it if you don't sit." The vampire held a piece of bacon up and Marcel jumped to try to reach it. "Now sit."

The puppy's butt hit the floor and Dick gave him the bacon. "Good boy."

They ate and prepared to leave. As Lexi stood at the door, she noticed that Dick's bedroom door had disappeared but hers was still there. Curious, she walked down the hallway and glanced at the two beds. Hers was still untidy. She stepped in and made it quickly, then looked around to see if Scott had left his beanie or she'd left a blade somewhere.

Nothing was obvious so she stepped out of the room and walked past the bathroom. She turned to see if she'd left anything in there and grimaced when she faced only a wall. The bedrooms and bathroom were gone.

Dolores stood beside the front door to the little apartment.

"Call me if you need anything." She opened the door and the others filed through. They immediately stood in a cozy diner.

A young woman smiled at them. "Welcome to Southwest Diner."

Lexi glanced over her shoulder. The door to the fae's living room had closed and was now a glass entrance door from the street.

Scott glanced at the specials board on the wall and didn't miss a beat. "Cherry pie, please."

She stared at him in disbelief. "You've just had breakfast."

Dick raised an eyebrow. "He is a growing boy."

The woman laughed. "Let me show you to your table."

They sat at one with a pink check tablecloth next to the window and ordered coffees, one cherry pie, one Bloody Mary, and a bowl of water. Lexi glanced around the room. She noticed a guy who looked like a truck driver staring at the vampire with a perplexed expression from across the room. He saw her looking and returned his gaze to his newspaper.

Scott whirled his finger in a helicopter gesture, which indicated that no one could listen in on their conversation.

"Will your magic work when we get into Vegas?" she asked.

He shrugged. "Probably not all of it. That'll be inconvenient, I guess."

She looked out of the window. "I assume there are no casinos in Boulder, then."

Dick waited for the server to put the drinks down and leave before he spoke. "There are casinos here but they have individual protections on them, the same way many banks and high-end stores do everywhere else. The problem with Vegas is that there are so many casinos, the protection spells clashed. It was a mess. That's why they decided to set up the wards over the whole city." He picked his drink up and looked at it. "It's a mason jar. How quaint." He stirred it with the celery stick, tapped it on the side, and took a large sip.

They talked as they ate and drank, then the vampire pointed when a large white SUV parked outside. "Here's our ride."

Lexi gazed at the shining monster. "Holy smoke! Did Dolores order that?"

"Pfft! Dolores ordered a car. I upgraded it." He leaned forward conspiratorially. "I know for a fact that some of her clients are really rich. I know that because, before I worked for her, I hired her. I don't know why she's so stingy with expenses."

Scott shrugged. "She prefers us to be inconspicuous."

Dick stood and dropped a twenty-dollar tip on the table. "Well, there's being inconspicuous and then there's catching nasty diseases from the motels she puts you in."

The young man narrowed his eyes. "Aren't you staying with us?"

He laughed. "Heavens, no. I have my own place."

Lexi made a mental eye-roll. "Of course you do. Come on, then. Let's go see what palace she's lined up for us today."

CHAPTER FIFTY-EIGHT

Dick pulled his car into the forecourt of the Vegas motel. Lexi remained silent and studied the building as he parked. They climbed out and the vampire leaned on his car door. "Dear God, it's déjà vu all over again."

Scott squinted with his hand above his eyes. "It looks better than the motel in Palm Springs. This one has a pool."

She looked quickly at Dick. "Oh! You're still here."

He frowned in response. "Sorry?"

"I wondered, with this no magic rule in Vegas, if you'd go whoosh in the sunlight."

His jaw dropped. "Jesus Christ! That didn't even occur to me. Wait, you didn't mention it until now?"

With a shrug, she stepped out and went to pull her small case from the trunk.

The vampire stared open-mouthed from her to Scott, who chuckled.

"She's kidding. Dude, I changed your physiology on a molecular level."

Dick glanced at Lexi as he walked Marcel to a flowerbed filled with weeds to relieve himself. "Are you sure she knows that?"

The sorcerer nodded. "Of course she does. You knew that, didn't you, Lexi? We know that now."

"Hmm?" She looked up as though she hadn't been listening.

Dick raised an eyebrow. "What do you mean by now?"

"I'll be honest. That morning in Cabo after I'd done the spell and the sun was rising, my heart was in my mouth."

"You were one hundred percent certain I was safe. You said so."

"I was—pretty much." Scott pulled his bag onto his shoulder.

Marcel sniffed the weeds, yelped, then ran to the car and peed on a tire.

Dick rolled his eyes and turned to the younger man. "I was about to ask if you'd rather stay in the guest room at my condo."

Lexi took a few steps toward the office, then turned. "No, we'll be fine. We'll see you at the Mob Museum in the morning."

"I wasn't asking, I was rescinding the offer I hadn't made." The vampire stuck his tongue out at her and climbed into the car with Marcel.

The two friends continued to the motel office.

"We're booked in." Lexi took a credit card from her pocket.

"You're in room fifteen. Ground level." The receptionist placed a keycard on the desk.

Scott looked at her, surprised when she took the card. "You never want ground level."

"I don't mind. I'm still tired so I'd sleep right here standing up." She wasn't kidding and wondered when she would get her strength back.

They left the registration office and walked around the pool to room fifteen. She left Scott outside to hold the bags and gaze at the pool while she went in to check the room. The first thing she noticed was the sticky carpet and the Velcro-like sound and resistance when she lifted her feet to step. The walls were dirty, and the bed cover was decidedly threadbare.

She called him in. "It's clean. Well…not clean. I mean it's safe." She added quietly, "On a non-microbial level."

He entered and dropped his bag onto the innermost bed, then approached the bathroom door and pushed it open hesitantly. She retrieved her toiletry bag and shorts from her case when his shoulders relaxed. He stepped out, picked his bag up, and entered the bathroom.

A few minutes later, he emerged with a towel over his shoulder, wearing swimming shorts and a big smile. "I'm going for a quick swim."

"Is your beanie waterproof?" She smirked when he clapped his hand on his head.

"Oh. Ha!" Scott pulled the hat off and threw it on his bed.

When he opened the door, two boys of about ten years old stood at the balconies above, one on either side of the pool, and began a shouted conversation from one side of the motel to the other.

"Hey, Jaden."

"Yeah?"

"It looks like they fished the body out. You wanna go swimming?"

"My mom says I gotta wait until they clean the pool but Mr. Casey says they ain't gonna do that 'til October."

Scott took a hasty step back and flicked the door. It swung shut. He stared at it for a moment before he returned to the bathroom.

When he had dressed and entered the room again, Lexi waited for him with her case in one hand and his beanie in the other. He looked around, confused. "What?"

"This place is a hard no for me. We're not doing it. Let's find somewhere else." She shoved his hat into his hand and marched out of the door and past the other rooms.

He followed hurriedly. "Where will we go, then?"

"We'll get a cab to the Strip. I can't promise the nicest hotel but we'll go somewhere with a halfway decent pool." She rounded the corner to the parking lot and came to a halt so suddenly that he bumped into her.

Dick stood with his sunglasses on, sunning his face as he leaned against the car. Marcel lay in the scant shade at his feet.

Scott backed away and walked around Lexi to the car. "What are you doing here?"

"I'll be honest, it took longer than I expected." The vampire looked at his watch. He opened the passenger door and Marcel jumped in and scrambled into the back of the car. "I contacted a friend who owns the condo next door to mine. We bought them at the same time. It's free for a few days."

They hesitated and Scott said, "Er…we were going—"

Dick put a hand up to stop him. "There are two pools and three hot tubs in the complex."

The young man took several steps forward and wrapped him in a huge hug. "I love you, man." He jumped into the back seat next to Marcel, clicked the seatbelt into place, and grinned.

The vampire looked into the car while he smoothed an eyebrow. "And just like that, the chase is over, the battle won, and the spoils laid at my feet."

Lexi chuckled. "Sorry, Romeo. I think you have a way to go before you can mount that prize…on your wall." She climbed into the car. "So, where are we going?"

He clicked his seatbelt and started the engine. "The complex lies a couple of blocks from the Strip. I've never actually been there."

Scott leaned forward. "I thought you said you owned a condo."

"I do, but I rent it out through an agency. It was a business purchase, but I'm interested to see how they've maintained it."

They arrived at the complex and he ran into the office. When he came out, he dropped a key into Lexi's hand. They walked through the gardens and finally, he pointed as they reached the buildings. "That one's yours." He returned to the car for his case.

Scott stood at the door while she walked around the condo. "What's it like?"

She popped her head around the door. "I feel like I should have taken my boots off. Everything's white."

He followed her through the hallway into the plush living room with its white rugs, white walls, and white furniture. His jaw dropped. "This place is *nice*."

"Good grief!" Dick's voice reverberated through the wall.

Lexi ran out with Scott at her back and they burst into Dick's condo.

She had her katana in hand the moment she was through the door.

The vampire stood in the middle of the living room. It wasn't as nice as theirs but nice enough. "What's wrong?" Her gaze darted around in search of potential problems.

His face was a mask of horror. "I paid for top quality furnishings. It looks like Ikea stumbled in drunk and threw up everywhere."

Scott looked around the room. "It looks okay."

The vampire gazed incredulously at the furniture. "Pfft! Okay— okay for you."

Lexi stared at him, amazed that he seemed completely unaware that he was being rude. "Gosh, no. It's not okay for us. Ours is much nicer. Come on, Scott. Let's get those swimming shorts on you." She marched out as she slid her katana into the pocket.

He followed. "All right, but I think I can manage that myself."

Half an hour later, he was in the pool and floated on a giant, triangular, inflatable pizza slice. Lexi lay on a sunbed in her leather pants and linen vest. Dick joined them in his Versace swimming briefs and held a tray of margaritas.

She squinted at him. "It's good to see you've calmed somewhat."

"I've spoken to the management company."

"We heard." She chuckled. "The walls are thin."

"They'll see if they can fix it before I can contact my lawyer on Monday. It's like a race."

"Yes, we heard. Who do you think will win?"

"Them if they have any sense." He handed her a drink and walked to the pool, where Scott sat on the inflatable and paddled to the edge to take a glass. The two men clinked glasses and signaled a toast to Lexi, who reciprocated.

Dick settled himself on the sunbed beside hers. "I've been thinking about this case. Does it ever make you wonder…"

Lexi waited.

He took a sip of his drink before he continued, "Why do they insist on keeping magical objects in museums? This is our second in as many weeks, and that last one certainly wasn't my first."

"Delphine's ring wasn't magical until that boy cast a spell with it."

"Ah, yes. Poor Jamal. But there must be thousands—maybe

millions—of objects in museums that belonged to people who don't need to be brought back. All it takes is someone to get hold of Hitler's jockstrap and we're all in trouble."

Lexi coughed as her drink went down the wrong way.

"Are you all right?"

She took another sip. "I'm fine. You're not wrong. That's a thought to give anyone nightmares for all kinds of reasons."

Dick tilted his head, his brow wrinkled. "*Are* you all right? You look tired—weary even."

"The last few days took it out of me," she admitted.

He rolled onto his side to face her. "What was it like wearing the possessed ring?"

"I felt incredibly powerful, but she didn't take over and I didn't feel a compulsion to do her bidding like Lorenzo did. She did talk too much, though. In the few minutes I wore it, she wouldn't shut up. It was so annoying."

He took another sip of his cocktail. "So, snapping Lorenzo's neck like that was all you?"

Lexi recalled how easy it had been to break the vampire's neck with a flick of her wrist. She smirked. "Do you think I should have done it with my thighs?"

"Well, that does seem to be your signature move. It surprised me, though. It all seemed so…casual."

"In my defense, I didn't know it would kill him—like, properly. I guess the zombie bite stopped him from healing. *And* he was about to die anyway. *And* if I hadn't done it that way, I'd probably have done it another way."

"Okay, calm yourself. I'm only saying that the ring must have had some kind of effect. Your eyes went completely black. That didn't happen to Amy, Betsy, or Lorenzo."

Scott walked up to them. "I still need to research the black eyes."

Dick looked at the sorcerer. "Did you see it? I almost ran away after she threw me across the room."

"I didn't mean to do that. I didn't know how strong I was and you were crowding me. I only meant for you to give me some space."

Lexi pulled the stiletto knife from her dimensional pocket and flicked a slice of lime from her drink onto the tray.

The vampire pointed. "Hey, how are you still able to access that pocket? It's magic isn't it?"

Scott sat in a chair next to them. "Some things are acceptable for mages and legacies. Not everything, though. I can't translocate, which is annoying. We can't portal into or out of Vegas and we can't use objects with magical properties. Dolores has had to give us real paperwork for the job. I know it's all so people can't simply stroll in and magic the money out of casinos, but I feel like I have one hand tied behind my back." He looked at Lexi. "Getting back to the black eyes. I'm sure I've read about it happening before. I'll have to look into it." He smiled but it looked forced. "Do you want a top-up?"

She knocked the rest of her cocktail back and held it out to him, and Dick did the same.

He looked at them both. "I meant a magical top-up, but I'll do the drinks too."

Lexi turned her arm to show him. "Look, I'm still full. I'm not leaking unused magic. It must be something to do with the restrictions in place."

Scott smiled. "Cool." He balanced the empty glasses and headed to the bar. She followed him with her gaze. When he was concerned, so was she, and she had felt his concern through their link. She wondered what he wasn't saying.

Dick lay back to enjoy the sun. "Where do you want to eat dinner? Or would you prefer to explore Vegas by yourselves?"

She sighed. "I thought I might turn in early. You two should go out, though, and bring Cheetos. That'll do. She closed her eyes and sighed, soaking in the warmth.

"It's up to you. I don't mind." Scott shrugged.

"I don't eat," Dick said for what seemed to be the fiftieth time, "so it's most definitely up to you."

Lexi lifted her sunglasses. "This has been going on for almost an hour. You're like a married couple. Dick, decide where to eat. Take Scott somewhere you think he'd like." She dropped the sunglasses onto her face.

"That works for me." The young man grinned.

"Great. I know a fabulous barbecue place off the Strip. Everyone raves about it, but I think we should go there when we're all out together. Lexi shouldn't miss Jessie Rae's. Scott, I'll take you to The Burger Bar at Mandalay Bay. Everyone I know—well, everyone I know who eats food—tells me they do the best burgers in town and apparently, their shakes are to die for."

She sat quickly. "Thank God that's agreed." She looked at Dick. "How are you doing for rations?"

"I'll eat later. I've ordered in." He didn't offer any further details and she didn't ask.

Instead, she turned to Scott. "Will you get ready?"

"One last swim." He headed to the pool and dropped in.

Dick watched with a somewhat bored expression. "What happened to his floating pizza?"

"The girl it belonged to came and snatched it while you were at the bar."

He raised an eyebrow. "The evil bitch. I hope he turned her into a mung bean."

"She was, like, six."

"And?"

Lexi rolled her eyes. She looked at the pool and smiled. "He's making the most of it. I'm glad we didn't stay at that shitty motel."

Dick stood. "Good for him. I'll start getting ready. I'll meet him out front in forty-five minutes."

Lexi woke in the middle of the night from a vision of flashing lights and the heavy vibration of bass. She lay in the dark and realized it hadn't been a dream. Sometimes, she had a sense of where Scott was when they were apart. It would appear that her two friends were in a club dancing to seventies disco music. She smiled and closed her eyes to sleep again.

A muted thump made her sit. It had come from Dick's condo. She was dressed within sixty seconds, opened the front door silently, and crept out. When she saw no one about, she scurried across to Dick's entrance. She tried it and the door wasn't locked. With a slow, careful movement, she turned the handle the rest of the way and opened the door silently.

Once again, the katana was in her hand. The house was in darkness, but she could hear someone moving in the living room. Sweat prickled her scalp as she took another silent step forward. The hyper-awareness brought a cold sheen along her arms followed by goosebumps. Suddenly her vision blurred, and her stomach lurched. She flailed in the darkness, found the stair rail, and leaned against it.

When she looked up, an eerie glow came from the area ahead. It cast enough light to enable her to see the hallway around her. She rounded the corner into the living room as a large billowing specter came toward her, and she struck out with the katana. A scream pierced the night.

When Lexi turned the light on, Dick's house boy from Palm Springs stood holding half a sheet in each hand. Jesús wore a strange glass pendant, which was the source of the bright yellow glow. Before she could say anything, he looked at her and fainted. She stared across the room and into a mirror on the wall. Her eyes were black.

What's happening to me?

She checked that he hadn't died of fright, then sat on the couch with her face in her hands.

"Lexi?" Jesús half-whispered, his voice trembling.

She raised her head from her hands to where he sat on the floor. He sighed with relief and put a hand on his chest. "I must have been seeing things."

"I'm so sorry." She somehow managed a smile for the shaken young man. "I almost killed you. I thought... I don't know what I thought."

"Mr. Levin asked me to bring some things for him." He held up the ripped sheet and shrugged.

Lexi face-palmed. "Please tell me they're not two-thousand-dollar sheets."

He started to fold them. "No, no, don't worry. They're only the six-hundred-dollar sheets. It's fine. I brought a few."

She couldn't tell if he was joking but suspected not. "Scott and I are staying next door. I heard a noise and came to investigate. What were you doing?"

"Luckily, I had a travel bag in the trunk. I used it to cover the window in the master bedroom, but I had to climb on the dresser to do it." Jesús rubbed his elbow. "I fell off."

"A travel bag?" For the life of her, she couldn't grasp what he meant.

"You know…" He crossed his hands over his chest like a corpse.

"Oh. A body bag. When did you last speak to Mr. Levin?"

"It's been a couple of weeks." The man put his hands on his hips. "Why would he stay here? I looked for a basement, but I couldn't find one so I started on the window. Do you think I did the right thing?"

"I guess you'll have to speak to him about that." She had no idea why Dick hadn't told him about the daywalking, but that was his business.

Jesús gazed around the room. "I thought I was in the wrong place. First the windows, then this furniture. It's horrible."

Lexi wanted to ask him why his pendant was glowing, but she'd had enough. "I'm going back to bed." She turned and left the room.

She wanted to tell Scott about her eyes but what could he do? It seemed he was already nervous about Bryan, which made it unfair to bother him further. She decided to let him enjoy his night out and pretended to be asleep when he came stumbling in at four am.

CHAPTER FIFTY-NINE

After lying awake for another couple of hours, Lexi got up at six am, made coffee, and sat at a table on the deck outside. She didn't know what to think so she didn't think at all. After an hour of simply blanking out, Dick joined her. "A penny for your thoughts?"

She opened her mouth to make a glib response but nothing emerged.

He tried again. "Well, you scared seven shades of shit out of Jesús last night."

"Sorry about that—and your sheet. I'll ask Scott if he can mend it."

"Don't worry about it." He slid his sunglasses on. "Jesús told me he thought he was hallucinating because your eyes seemed to have turned black."

All she could think to do was shrug because she was at a loss to explain it. She changed the subject. "What time should we head to the Mob Museum?"

The vampire raised an eyebrow at her diversion. "Dolores has arranged for us to meet her friend near the museum for a chat first."

"What the fuck?" Jesús screeched from the doorway. He gazed in horror at his boss, who languished very comfortably in the sunlight without catching fire.

Several people seated outside their apartments eating breakfast stared at him in alarm.

Dick waggled a finger in his ear as though he had deafened him. "Good morning, Jesús. Perhaps you'd like to put some clothes on."

The man leapt back through the door.

Lexi chuckled. "You didn't tell him?"

"I thought I'd surprise him," he said blandly, a small smirk at the corners of his mouth.

"I think that between us, we'll surprise him to death." The smile left her face as she recalled how close she'd been to gutting him. She sighed. "I can't feel Delphine there but what else could it be?"

"Perhaps Scott could…I don't know, have a poke around up there to see if he can find her."

"I don't want to distract him from the job. If we find the guy and get the talisman today, I can talk to him later." She picked her empty mug up and stood.

Dick fixed her with a stern look. "So you're asking me to say nothing to him?"

"I wouldn't ask that of you." She didn't need to and was fairly sure he knew what she expected.

He didn't seem happy about it but nodded and she took that as his agreement. The vampire turned to Jesús, who had put on a pair of shorts and resumed his bemused stare at his boss from the doorway. "We'll head out for the morning. Would you mind looking after Marcel?"

The man nodded. "Yes, Mr. Levin."

***

They sat at a table in one of the casino restaurants on Fremont and Lexi perused the menu.

Scott slouched like a grumpy teen. "Come on, I'm starving."

She handed the menu to the server. "Eggs over medium with bacon and coffee. Thank you."

The young woman looked at Dick with an expectant smile.

"I'll take a Breakfast Jack." He handed the menu to her without looking at it.

The waitress looked confused. "I'm not sure—"

Scott laughed. "Let me guess. It's a Jack Daniels served at breakfast time."

The vampire nodded and the girl left the table.

Coffee was provided and she listened as the two men chatted and laughed.

Oh, God, they've bonded. Her lip twitched but she said nothing.

Dick took his cell phone out and showed the screen to the other man. They both laughed.

Lexi raised an eyebrow. "If you two are showing each other dick pics, I'll happily move to another table—or restaurant."

"Lexi, please. My good name would never be associated with something so vulgar." He showed her the screen. "We found a restaurant called Chin Chin last night. Peter told me that Chin Chin is Japanese for penis, which is hilarious, so I took a selfie with the restaurant in the background and I'm sending it to him."

She remembered the young blood donor who had almost died after being drugged by Lorenzo in an effort to kill Dick. "How is he?"

The vampire put his cell phone away as the waitress arrived with the food. When she left, he answered, "He says he's taken himself out of the food chain but wants to keep in touch. And he's off the recreational drugs."

"That's probably a good idea. He was lucky he didn't die." Scott splashed ketchup over his impossibly large plate of food and looked at Lexi. "Hey, doesn't this remind you of that breakfast we had in LA that time?"

She stared at the red-covered plate. "No. It reminds me of Jamal's corpse."

"You're trying to put me off my food but it won't happen." He bit defiantly into a piece of bacon.

The two men continued to chat while she ate her breakfast, unable to stop thinking about how close she'd come to hurting Jesús. Scott looked at her occasionally with a concerned expression, which she pretended not to see.

Finally, he finished his food and focused his attention on her. "So, what happened last night? I felt your nerves ramp up. I tried to translocate because I was too drunk to remember I couldn't do that, then I sensed you calm."

Lexi shrugged. "I thought Dick's condo was being robbed. I went in but it was only Jesús, so I went back to bed." She avoided looking at the vampire.

Scott looked guilty. "I'm sorry I wasn't there. If I can't translocate, I shouldn't be so far or let myself get into that state."

She finished her coffee. "It was fine. You do deserve the occasional night off." She wiggled her eyebrows. "Strutting your stuff to 'Dancing Queen' and 'Blame it on the Boogie.'"

"Hey! No spying on the guys' night out." His cheeks went pink.

"A girl can't help what she dreams." She chuckled.

Dick knocked his bourbon back and glanced around the room.

He froze and some of the drink escaped his mouth and splashed onto his shirt. "Dick? Are you okay? You've dribbled half your drink down your shirt."

Dick gasped. "It's fine. The rest of it is in my lungs."

"You must be Dolores' friends. I'm Albin." Lexi looked into the face of a man who was, quite possibly, the most beautiful living being she had ever seen. He was tall and dressed professionally. His white shirt was stretched tight across his chest and arms, fighting to hold in the muscles beneath it. She put him in the late-thirties. His jaw was chiseled and his chin dimpled, while his eyes were the cornflower-blue that people talked about but, until now, she'd believed didn't exist. His lips turned up playfully at the corners.

Those lips.

She had never seen a specimen like him. Besides, she didn't usually have time for relationships or, God forbid, romance.

But all I want to do right now is grab hold of this man, throw him onto the table and—

"Lexi!" Scott's urgent but quiet warning made her jump. "Can you just…not?" His face was aflame.

"Oops!" She blushed as hotly when she realized that he would have felt her wandering daydream through their link.

"And you are?" Albin directed the full intensity of his heavenly gaze at the vampire.

"Dick," he managed in only a slightly squeakier tone than usual.

"Really? What a coincidence." A slight smile played on Albin's lips. "I've been looking for you." His eyebrow twitched a fraction of an inch and Dick groaned.

Scott turned in his seat to see what was going on. "Oh! Right, I see." He turned, took his cell phone out, placed it on the table, and opened his notes app. "Take a seat. I'm Scott and this is Lexi."

"Hi." The man complied.

Dick stood. "Can I offer you my chair?"

Albin smiled. "I'm fine, thank you. I'm sitting."

"Of course you are, yes." The vampire sat but immediately stood again. "Can I get you something? Coffee? Jewelry?"

"A coffee would be great, thank you."

Dick disappeared.

Albin followed him with his gaze. "He's interesting."

"No, he's not." Lexi couldn't believe she'd blurted that out. From the corner of her eye, she could see Scott staring at her.

The man turned to her. "He's a vampire out at eight am. That's interesting."

She dragged her attention away from the man's face and looked at Dick, who seemed to be fighting the waitress for the coffee jug.

"When did you notice the talisman missing?" Scott tapped his cell.

The vampire returned to the table with a mug and the coffee jug. The bewildered waitress stared at his back, a hundred-dollar bill clutched in her hand.

"Two days ago." Albin leaned back as Dick poured the coffee. His gaze remained glued to the historian's face. "That's enough, thank you."

Dick looked down to see the coffee had poured over the top of the mug. "Good heavens." He snatched the serviettes and mopped the spill.

Scott gave up. He retrieved the coffee jug and refilled his and Lexi's mugs, then waited for the vampire to return to his seat. Finally, he continued. "What do the security cameras show?"

Albin drank carefully from the overfilled mug. "A throng of people —more than usual—around the case. Then the camera went on the fritz. When the crowd cleared, the chip was gone. All the thief left was the little embroidered pouch the talisman had rested on."

Lexi looked at her coffee. It was easier to speak to the Adonis when she wasn't looking at him. "I don't understand why Kindred hasn't taken an interest. It sounds like it was, without doubt, stolen."

"I went to the Strip myself and spoke to the father of the local unit. I had stills from the security camera. Most of it was useless but I think it was clear from the footage before and after that it had been stolen. They looked at me like I was being hysterical."

Dick put his elbow on the table and his chin in his hand. "Those bastards. Would you like me to kill them for you? I could, you know."

"That's very kind of you, but I wouldn't like to start a war because my feelings are hurt."

"How thoughtful," Scott muttered. "Did you have any questions, Lexi?"

"Hmm?"

He put his cell phone away. "No? That's fine. Let's go over there."

Dick bolted out of his seat and held Albin's chair.

Lexi glanced at him and noticed that his fangs were showing. She stared hard at him. "We're out in public. Calm yourself."

The vampire smiled awkwardly. "Oopsie." He followed Albin to the exit.

She turned to face Scott. "What just happened?"

"I have no idea. Let's get out of here." He paid the check.

At the museum, they climbed the steps to the entrance of the building.

"Where are the papers Dolores gave us?" she asked Scott.

He pointed. "Dick has them."

Lexi grimaced when she saw Dick gazing at Albin while the historian removed his ID and lanyard from a pocket. The vampire was fanning himself with the paperwork.

She approached him and took the documents out of his hand "Get a grip."

His expression awed, he gazed at the other man from behind. "But *look* at that."

Unfortunately, she looked and had to agree. He wasn't wrong. Her gaze lingered on Albin's perfect form.

Scott snatched the documents out of her hand. "Get a grip."

The three of them followed their guide into a silent foyer and through another set of doors.

The sorcerer took a map of the exhibit from a display as they moved between the various artifacts.

Albin stopped at a door with a rope across it and a sign that stated the room was closed to the public. He swiped his ID across the pad on the door frame and it let them through. "I can show you what security footage there is," he said and pointed to the cabinet.

Dick tapped him on the shoulder. "I'll come and look at that."

"It's this way." He walked toward a door and the vampire raced ahead and rattled it loudly as he tried to open it for him. The historian held his ID up. "Careful, you'll have that off its hinges."

With an attempt at nonchalance, he smoothed his eyebrow as the other man stepped forward and swiped his ID. "Sorry, I don't know my own strength." He opened the door and followed their guide through.

Lexi stared after them. "Oh, my God. Dick's like a dog in heat."

Scott looked at her with an eyebrow raised and smirked.

"What?" She pointed at the glass display case. "Get on with it, then."

They stared into the cabinet at the label indicating where the lucky poker chip had been displayed before it was stolen.

She looked at him. "Anything?"

He closed his eyes and waved his hands around. "There's no dust and the wards won't let me create an energy ball to follow the magic."

He opened his eyes again and looked inside the glass display case. "That might help."

A shiny silver cigarette case lay inside. He opened his hand but nothing happened. "Damn it. I can't get it."

Lexi walked around the case. "I hope Albin's taking care of the security cameras." She dipped to the back of the case and slid her lock-picking tools out. Crouching close to the lock, she set to work. After a minute, she heard the satisfying click. "We're in."

She reached in and snatched the cigarette case as a door opened. In one fluid movement, she had closed the back door of the cabinet and stood next to Scott.

"What are you up to?" A man in a security uniform entered the room.

Scott held the papers out. "We've come to look at this display."

He ignored the documents, took them both by the arm, and led them to the door. "This room is supposed to be closed to the public. Out you get."

"We're not the public. We're here—" Lexi scowled when she realized she was speaking to a closed door and knocked peremptorily.

Scott looked at the security scanner beside it. "Is there any way you can break into this?"

Lexi glanced at it. "I could shoot it." She hammered on the door again with her fist.

"Would that open the door?"

"Probably not." She grasped the handle and rattled the door. "Open, you son of—" She felt a jolt of magical energy and the door opened.

The sorcerer looked at it. "That shouldn't have worked." He created a ball of energy in his palm. "The wards are down." He extinguished the orb and they raced into the room. There was no sign of the security man. They ran to the door Dick and Albin had used and along a hallway, looking into each room as they passed. Finally, they entered the security office.

It took a moment for Lexi to interpret what she saw. Albin stood with a hand over his neck and Dick was at the other end of the room with his shirt off and his fangs protruding.

"I'm so sorry. I don't know what came over me." The vampire looked horrified. His face was scarlet as he scrambled to replace his shirt.

"It's okay, honestly. It happens more often than you'd think." The historian removed his hand to reveal a scratch.

Dick pushed past Lexi and Scott and out of the office.

She stared at the screens, then turned to the other man. "I assume you didn't see what happened out there."

He sighed. "The wards went down again?" With a scowl, he went to a screen and rewound the footage. "It's the same as last time. Here you are, looking into the case. It goes blank, then the picture comes back—" Albin looked closely at the screen, then bolted from the room. They ran after him and the three of them gathered around the display case.

Albin tapped the glass. "Did you take anything out of here?"

Lexi showed him the cigarette case. "Yes, this. Scott can use it to help in the investigation."

"Of course, for the reflection." He nodded. "Good thinking. And the pouch?"

She looked into the display. The little embroidered pouch was also missing. "Could I have knocked it down?"

The historian retrieved a key and opened the back of the cabinet. He searched quickly but carefully for the missing item. "It's definitely gone. What happened?"

His frown deepened when she told him about the security man throwing them out of the room.

He shook his head. "Why would someone go to such lengths to take the pouch? It makes no sense."

Dick rejoined them. His shirt was on but his face was still pink and he didn't seem to be in a hurry to make eye-contact with anyone.

Lexi looked at him. "I didn't know vampires could blush."

Albin's lips twitched. "Blushing is simply what happens when all the blood rushes to one place in the body in response to emotional or physical stimuli."

The man waited for Dick to look at him, then winked at the blushing vampire. He turned to Scott. "Will your reflection spell work within the wards?"

Scott looked doubtful. "Probably not but we can try."

Lexi turned in surprise. "Why not? It seems like an innocent enough spell."

"Until you use it to spy on someone entering a safe combination." The sorcerer shrugged.

She raised an eyebrow. "Okay, I never thought of that."

They headed to the employee section and into Albin's office.

Scott took the cigarette case out. "If it works, it would be better with a mirror."

Her quick scan around the office didn't reveal one, but the historian took a lab coat off a hook on the wall to reveal a mirror beneath it. She looked at him, her expression curious.

"I hate mirrors," he explained simply.

Lexi shook her head. *If I looked like him, I'd walk around naked in a hall of mirrors all day long.*

Scott held the case up to it and muttered a few words but nothing happened. "Nope, it's not working."

"It was a long shot. I have to go and wipe you from the security cameras before the day shift starts." Their guide led them to the exit. "Perhaps we could meet later?"

The sorcerer nodded. "Beyond the wards? Then you can see the reflection yourself."

Albin handed Lexi a card with his address on it. "I don't go beyond the wards. You look at it and let me know. I'll see you at eight." He turned to Dick and handed him a card. "And I'll see *you* at six."

Scott looked at the card over Lexi's shoulder. "Park Towers— sounds nice."

The historian shrugged. "It's a roof over my head."

They said goodbye and returned to the car.

Lexi opened the passenger door. "How far out do the wards stop working?"

Dick climbed into the driver's seat. "I have no idea, but I don't want to stop every mile to check. Let's head to Boulder. Southwest Diner?"

Scott's head popped into the space between the seats. "Sure. It's almost an hour since I last ate."

After they had been driving for a couple of minutes, Lexi turned to the vampire. "What happened to you back there?"

He gave her a wide and slightly hysterical-looking grin. "Let's put music on, shall we?"

When they pulled up at the diner, they didn't leave the car.

Lexi looked into the eyes of the truck driver, who was seated at the same table as before. "Doesn't that guy have a home to go to?"

Scott looked out. "Who?"

She was about to point him out but he was no longer staring at them. "Never mind."

The sorcerer shuffled across the back seat and settled himself in the middle. He held the cigarette case up facing the rearview mirror and muttered his quiet words.

First, they could see little of interest. He rolled back and it showed them looking at the case before they left the museum. From there, he whirled back what the shiny case had reflected for the previous couple of days. Finally, he stopped it and allowed it to play forward. They watched as a man approached the cabinet.

Lexi pointed. "That's the douche who kicked us out."

The man gazed at the display for a few moments before he walked out of sight. A minute later, a hand appeared from the rear of the cabinet and picked up a golden poker chip. The stranger walked quickly out of view.

Dick pinched his bottom lip as he thought. "Can you put it back to the start and record it on a cell phone?"

Scott reversed the playback in the mirror and passed his cell phone to the vampire, who videoed the theft, then took close-ups of the security guard's face.

When he clicked the cell phone off, he turned to Lexi. "We don't need to bother going into the diner then."

The young man slumped in the seat. "I wanted to try the apple pie this time."

"What are you, twelve?" Dick looked at him in the rearview mirror. "Get a slice to take out, then."

Scott grinned and jumped out of the car.

Lexi opened the passenger door and shouted, "Scott...get two." She smirked at Dick. "I understand why you'd want to get back. You only have eight hours to prepare for your date."

He smoothed an eyebrow in his habitual tell. "Oh, I don't know that I'd call it a date." He giggled. "It's totally a date, though, right? And you're quite correct, looking this good doesn't happen by itself." He sighed. "This must be what it's like to go on a date with me. How thrilling."

She shook her head and chuckled.

CHAPTER SIXTY

Scott gazed sadly at his empty plate. "That was the best pie I've ever eaten. What's next?"

Lexi stood and dropped the empty boxes in the trash. "It seems like a waste of time to spend the whole day doing nothing. We should have gone straight to the museum to show Albin the picture. Did you get the impression he wanted us out of the way?"

"It was probably because of what happened with Dick," he shrugged. "We could spend the day by the pool."

She looked at the time. "Scott, do me a favor. Step outside for a moment, please."

He narrowed his eyes. "Okay..." He stepped out onto the deck. "Holy shit. How hot is that?"

"It's August in Las Vegas. I'm not sitting outside in the middle of the day."

"It wasn't this hot yesterday." He sounded sulky.

"It was almost sundown when we went to the pool yesterday."

Scott gazed mournfully at the water. "I wonder if I could run really fast and jump in. I miss translocation. I miss it so much." He closed the door and walked into the kitchen. "What's on tv?"

"I don't know." Lexi narrowed her eyes at him. "Not Star Wars."

"Barbarian!"

The door burst open and Dick flew in. "Jesus, it's hotter than hell out there."

The young man stared at him. "Are you wearing a t-shirt? Like regular people?"

"That's why I'm here. I have nothing to wear. We have to go to the Strip."

Lexi narrowed her eyes. "And *we* need to go with you because?"

"You're my compadres. I need help."

She raised an eyebrow. "You need someone to stand around and tell you you're stunning."

"That's what I said. I need help."

"Fine." She rolled her eyes. "We were only going to watch tv anyway."

Dick grinned. "I know. The walls are terribly thin."

Ten minutes later, they headed to the car. The vampire shouted instructions to Jesús. "Don't let Marcel outside. My poor baby will fry in this heat."

Once they'd left the car with valet parking, they entered the Crystals shopping mall. Lexi consulted the store map and started walking.

"Where are you going?" Dick called after her.

"Versace is this way." She pointed.

"I might not want to buy from Versace. Let's go up to Gucci." He marched ahead and they followed.

Where she stood behind him on the escalator, Lexi whispered to Scott. "He'll drag us around this whole place and I can guarantee you, he'll end up buying from Versace."

Dick didn't turn and merely called in a sing-song voice, "I can hear you."

"I know," she responded in the same tone.

Four hours later, Lexi and Scott waited for him to pay for his purchases in Versace.

He glanced at Lexi while he waited for the tags to be cut off. "Don't look at me like that. I can't simply buy the first thing I see. I need to be sure."

She smiled and was about to respond with "I told you so," when her cell rang. She looked at the display, then answered. "Hi, Dolores."

"Are you hard at work?"

"We're hard at work helping Dick choose a shirt for his date tonight."

"Well, now you're back to work. Someone has stolen a bag of money from a casino. I suspect it might be related to the talisman."

Lexi walked to a quiet corner to hear her better. "Why do you think that?"

"A security guard transporting money from the Bellagio to an armored vehicle tripped and dropped a bag of cash. A man approached, picked the bag up, and walked away with it. Two guards gave chase and somehow ran into each other and knocked themselves out, and a third tried to shoot the thief. His gun fell to pieces in his hand."

She frowned. "Wow! That was all very…unlucky."

"Or lucky, depending on whose perspective you're looking at it from. The bag has a tracker inside it and has been traced to one of the MGM Signature buildings. Be careful. Kindred has been alerted and they'll probably be in attendance."

"Okay, we're on it." She disconnected and hurried to Scott. "Where's Dick?" she asked and looked around.

"He's gone to change into his new clothes. He's due at Albin's in half an hour."

Lexi repeated what Dolores had told her. "We need to hustle. Let him know what's happening and tell him we'll see him at Albin's at eight."

He walked to the changing rooms and was back in seconds. "He'll come if we need him. I said we'd call. He says the hotel is across the street." As they walked, he retrieved his cell, opened the maps app, and directed them to the closest exit.

She turned to him as they approached the MGM Signature buildings. "We're right across the street from that mall. How did it take us a full half-hour to get here?"

"In retrospect, it would have been better to get Dick to drop us off." Scott looked at his watch. "He'll be at Albin's by now. I hope the new clothes have impressed him because my feet are killing me."

Lexi looked across the street at the building's security office. "How can we get past them with no magic?"

Scott pulled their documents out. "This should help."

They crossed the street and approached the security guard. She opened her mouth to speak when an ambulance screeched to a halt and turned in. The security guard ran to release the vehicle barrier. They took advantage of the distraction and walked through.

He gazed at the three golden high-rise buildings. "Do we know which one it is?"

She walked faster. "I have a bad feeling. I think we should follow the ambulance."

The commotion drew them to the correct building. They rounded the corner as the ambulance crew moved to cover a body that had clearly fallen from very high up.

Scott leaned close to her ear. "Was that our guy?"

Lexi stared at him. "Can you imagine how far he fell? I couldn't even tell if that was human."

A group of men leaving the building caught her attention. She grabbed her friend and pulled him around the corner. "I think that's the mage who performs on the Strip."

He snuck his head out and withdrew it quickly. "I've definitely seen him on billboards and tv."

They wandered to the back of a crowd of onlookers. Hidden behind them, they were able to amble around the corner to listen more closely to the men and what appeared to be the end of the conversation.

Someone—presumably the mage—asked, "Are you sure there was absolutely nothing on the body? Nothing in his pockets?"

"Like what?" another man asked.

The first voice answered impatiently. "A golden casino chip."

"No, nothing. That's strangely specific."

The mage sighed. "Forget I said anything about the chip."

"Like what?" The man repeated his question and sounded a little confused.

"Oh, I don't know. I thought maybe the tracker had stopped working because it shattered on impact."

"Oh, I see. That's good thinking, but no. There wasn't a cent in his pocket." The voices grew quieter, so Lexi and Scott moved behind the crowd again.

When the people saw the mage, they recognized him as the famous magician and turned their cameras from the corpse to him.

Unaffected by the attention, he continued. "If the security tracker in the bag was here one minute and gone the next, he must have deactivated it and stashed the bag before he threw himself off the balcony. Search for the bag. I'm on stage in an hour. If you haven't found it tonight, I'll see what I can do, but I can assure you that the wards are still in place."

Lexi was suddenly aware that the crowd around them had begun to disperse. She and her companion looked at each other, certain they were about to be revealed.

Scott said, "Eww—is that his guts in the grass over there?"

The crowd turned and huddled to stare in the direction of the covered corpse again. When the mage had moved out of sight, the two left the way they had entered.

Back on the Strip, Lexi called Dolores to tell her the thief was dead. She explained that the wards had stopped working at least twice that day.

"It sounds like Kindred knows the talisman has been stolen." She stood in the shade with the cell phone on speaker. "The mage asked about it and counseled someone in front of a crowd of people. Why do you think they've denied it's been stolen?"

Her boss was silent for a few moments. "Probably because it calls the wards into question."

After a little thought, she decided it made sense. "About the wards —who could bring them down?"

Dolores paused for a moment. "No single group can do it. It would require the Kindred council and the Fae Council of Elders."

Lexi looked at Scott as he released a frustrated breath. She knew he had the same thought as her—some kind of alliance between Caleb and the Elders. She turned to the cell. "We're going to see Albin in an hour to see if he recognizes the guard. I guess we should have returned to the museum earlier."

The fae tutted. "Oh, dear. You'll be lucky to find him. I expect Albin has sequestered himself somewhere."

The young people shared a puzzled expression. She asked, "Why would he do that?"

Dolores' voice sounded hesitant through the speaker. "He wouldn't want to be caught with someone while the wards are down." She waited for her boss to continue. "You did realize he's an incubus, didn't you? Good heavens, I hope he's alone. I pity anyone who's with him when the wards are down."

"I'll call you later." Lexi disconnected the call. She closed her eyes and sighed. "Of course. That explains it."

They hurried to a line of cabs. "I've heard of incubi," Scott muttered, "but I'm not certain what they do."

"It's a demon. They are irresistible and use that ability to gain control over their victims to plant their demonic seed." She clenched her fist. "Dammit! I knew he was too good to be true. We need to get there. Dick could be in real danger."

They reached the opulent high-rise apartment block twenty minutes later. The sorcerer stared at his phone. "I've tried Dick about fifty times. There's still no answer."

The elevator opened onto the floor and they found the right door. "It's almost seven. He's been in there an hour."

Lexi drew her katana. She raised her hand to knock on the door but Scott stopped her.

"Wait." He held his hand out, palm up.

"What are you doing?"

"I tried to do some magic I know would be restricted. We have no other way to know whether the wards are up or down right now. It looks like they're up."

She nodded, then knocked.

A few moments later, Albin opened the door wearing nothing but a towel around his hips. "You're early."

Lexi paused and stared at his sculpted face and muscled arms. Her gaze traced the muscles from his chest to his towel "Wow!" Her eyeballs sent signals to parts of her body she didn't need to think about in that moment.

"Lexi... Lexi," Scott muttered urgently. She slid her gaze to him. "Breathe."

With an impatient shake of her head, she pushed Albin back into the room. "What have you done with Dick?"

"Do you want to know everything?" His lip twitched. "Well, let me think."

"Is everything okay?" the vampire called from another room.

"It's Lexi and Scott. I think they've come to warn you I'm an incubus."

Dick walked into the room with wet hair, wearing a hotel robe and with a cut crystal glass in his hand. He looked at Lexi. "Oh, I know that, silly." He took a sip of the drink. "Did you find the talisman?"

She shook her head. "It appears the thief threw himself from the balcony of the hotel."

He raised an eyebrow. "Appears? Do you think he might have had a little help?"

"I'd bet money on it." She folded her arms.

The historian gestured expansively. "Well, you're in the right town."

Scott turned to Dick. "Were you here on time?"

Albin snorted.

The vampire looked offended. "I would have been on time, but I stumbled into Tiffany on my way to the car."

Lexi looked at their host. "Where were you this afternoon?"

He walked to the bar and held his hand out for Dick's glass. "I was concerned about the wards so I came straight home to be alone. I almost canceled our meetings this evening."

She nodded. "It's a good thing you came home. The wards have definitely come down twice today. Once to steal the pouch and once to steal the money from the casino. I suspect it might have happened again at around six pm."

Scott turned to her, surprised. "When the guy went off the balcony?"

"It sounds like the money's gone." She nodded. "It would only take a few seconds for a mage to translocate in, throw the guy off the balcony, and disappear with the cash."

Dick raised his hand "Excuse me, but doesn't that constitute the exact opposite of lucky?"

Albin released a relieved breath. "Thank goodness I was alone and you were late."

"Dick was saved by his tardiness." Lexi pulled out the silver cigarette case and handed it to the man.

The vampire chuckled. "I wasn't tardy, I was fashionably late. Anyway, I'm not the one who would have been in trouble. Albin would have been incredibly irresistible. I would have become…bitey."

"Oh. Sorry." She was embarrassed that she'd made sweeping assumptions.

He shrugged and patted her on the shoulder. "Don't worry, I'm quite flattered that you came to save me. I'll get dressed and you can show Albin the video."

The historian looked at his towel and blushed. "Yes, of course. Help yourselves to drinks. I'll make myself more presentable.

Lexi watched him disappear through the door and felt a little disappointed that he would get dressed.

The moment he closed the door, Scott turned to her. "It's a roof over his head."

She studied the huge apartment with its high ceilings, curved windows, grand piano, and lavish furnishings. "I bet Dick's in heaven with this furniture."

"And you'd win that bet," the vampire called.

Albin returned in jeans and a polo shirt. She looked at him and sighed.

"How do incubi get on if they don't live in a warded city?" the sorcerer asked. "It can't be very practical walking down the street and having humans diving onto them in a frenzy."

"We're supposed to be able to turn it on and off. I was cursed, so I have to stay within wards, be protected by some other magic means, or put a bag over my head."

Scott took the cell phone from his pocket. "Who cursed you?"

"My father. He cursed me and disowned me."

Lexi sighed. "I thought our families were bad."

"The whole point of an incubus is to impregnate women. That was supposed to be my job."

The young man scrolled through the cell phone and glanced at him. "You didn't want to do that?"

"It may have escaped your notice, but I don't like girls in that way."

Dammit!

"Praise the Lord," Dick responded from the bedroom.

Scott shook his head and started the video. Lexi pointed to the screen. "That's the guy who threw us out of the room at the museum."

He watched as the thief walked out of sight. The hand came through from the back of the case and grasped the gold poker chip.

When the video ended, he gave Scott his email address and he sent the video file to him.

That done, the sorcerer put his cell into his pocket. "There you go. The guard did it."

Albin raised an eyebrow. "Except that I've never seen that guy before. He didn't work at the museum."

Scott looked crestfallen.

Dick entered the room wearing his new black shirt with the Barocco printed collar. "Was the jumper definitely the guy from the museum?"

Lexi wiggled her head from side to side noncommittally. "Honestly? It's difficult to say. His head looked like spaghetti and meatballs."

The vampire rolled his eyes. "Charming."

CHAPTER SIXTY-ONE

Lexi woke to the sound of her cell phone ringing. She answered it with her usual early-morning disapproval. "Urgh! Oh! Hi, Dolores. Another one?" She continued to listen as she sat and yanked one of the rolled socks out of her boot and threw it at Scott's head. "Wake up." It hit his face and landed next to his nose.

"Gross." He threw the sock at her and they both stared as it burst into flames mid-flight. She batted it away. His eyes went wild as he leapt to pick her boot up and pounded it until the flames were out.

She returned to the phone. "Let me guess, the wards are down again." Lexi walked into the bathroom still with the phone at her ear.

Scott thumped the wall between their and Dick's condo and shouted, "We're up."

"I know. Dolores called me first." The vampire stood in the doorway with two cups of coffee. "I was able to warn Albin about the wards." He passed a cup to Scott.

"Did you reach him in time?" Lexi called from the bathroom.

"Barely. He was heading to the door but he's called in sick." Dick took a sip of coffee absent-mindedly and spluttered. He stared at the cup in his hand as though it were an alien, then began to heave.

Lexi walked into the room and took it from him. "Thanks." She watched him retch and slapped him on the back. "Are you okay?"

He pointed at the mug in her hand.

"It amazes me that you vamps can tolerate alcohol at all. I think coffee might be a step too far." She took a gulp and rummaged through her dimensional pocket for another pair of socks.

Dick recovered and shook his head. "With alcohol, the higher proof, the better. The margaritas are pure, dogged determination. I don't know what I was thinking, drinking coffee. Perhaps the daywalking has gone to my head. I'll order McRibs next. Then I'll know I'm ready for the final death."

Scott looked up. "I love McRibs."

The vampire shuddered.

Scott looked from one to the other. "So, what's happened? Why are the wards down?"

She put her hand into her dimensional pocket and thought, *clean panties.* When she pulled a pair from her pocket, she gave them a sniff. *Just to be sure.*

"Dear God." Dick turned away from her to Scott. "I'll tell you outside."

As the two men exited, he began the story she'd been told by Dolores. "Someone had a very lucky win at one of the casinos last night."

They stood at the security desk in New York, New York while Lexi showed the Security officer the forms Dolores had given them. "We merely need to look at the video feed of your lucky customer from last night."

The man gazed at the papers, nodded, and turned away to speak into his radio.

Dick leaned forward and tried to read the documents. "What does it say?" he whispered.

Scott shrugged. "I don't know. I haven't read it. Lexi?"

She responded with a mirrored shrug.

The vampire rolled his eyes. "The lack of professionalism in this team disturbs me. We'll probably get arrested."

The man turned to them. "This way."

Dick appeared disappointed that they hadn't been challenged.

They followed their guide to a control room with banks of screens and people watching them. He led them to a workstation at the back of the room where a young Asian man sat in front of several screens.

The security officer tapped him on the shoulder. "Okay, Mo, go ahead."

They watched the recording in silence. Mo pressed pause, then zoomed in on the man's face. "This is him. He's not in our database." He pressed play again.

No one spoke as the feed showed an average man in his fifties—wearing a Hawaiian shirt and carrying a large cocktail—won on the roulette table a few times in succession. He moved to the craps table and repeated the process. A large crowd gathered around him.

After a few minutes, Lexi asked, "How long does this go on for?"

Mo paused it and spun in his chair. "About an hour and a half. He cashed out at one-point-four million."

Dick whistled. "So who is he?"

The man checked his paperwork. "Melvyn Dunk from Idaho."

She frowned at the paused screen. "Any idea where he might be now?"

He looked at his notes, which was a list headed *Time and Activity*. "Still in his suite."

Scott looked openly surprised. "He's here?"

"Of course. We comped him a suite and we're taking his 'wife' shopping today." He very deliberately added air-quotes around the word "wife."

Dick nodded. "While he'll be in the casino giving you the chance to win your money back."

"That's what it's all about." Mo spun to face the screen. "But we can't work out how he did it."

The sorcerer frowned. "There's no chance he won fairly? Surely it must be statistically possible."

In response, the security officer chuckled. "Melvyn left the world of believable statistics a long time before his run ended. He also shot straight through the land of outlandish possibilities and out the other side of dumb luck. Nope. Melvyn cheated and finding out how is more important to us than getting the money back."

"Leave that to us," Lexi answered. "Are you sure he's still in his suite?"

"Yes. The wife left half an hour ago for her free treatments in our spa. I mean, the 'wife.'" He did the air quotes again with a smirk on his face.

"Yes, I get it. He's with a hooker." She made a mental eye-roll. "Which room?"

Mo looked at a screen and read a suite number out. She noticed that conveniently, one of the security cameras was in the hallway directly outside that room.

She smiled. "I'd like to meet Mr. Dunk. Give me a bunch of flowers and a bottle of champagne."

The security guy's eyes traveled down her body and seemed to take in the leather jacket and tight leather pants. "You don't exactly look like a representative of this hotel." He studied the three of them. "In fact, he's the only one who does."

Dick's face lit up. "Why, thank you."

Lexi stared at the man and continued to do so when she didn't receive the response she expected.

"Right, well…I'll get that sorted for you." He swallowed a little nervously and turned to his radio.

Once he nodded confirmation that arrangements had been made, the team headed to the elevators where a young man waited with the champagne and flowers.

She entered the elevator while Scott took the flowers. Dick held the champagne and sneered when he looked at the label. The hotel employee entered the elevator behind them, and they continued to the room in silence.

When Lexi knocked on the door, there was no answer.

"Mr. Dunk?" She knocked again as she called through the door. "I have gifts from the hotel management."

Once again, no answer was forthcoming.

After a few moments, she stepped aside and gestured to their escort to use the keycard. He opened the door and stood in the doorway. A little of the room was visible behind the security officer—a huge spa bath along the left wall. She had to peek around the man to see why he appeared to have frozen on the spot. Melvyn Dunk lay on the bed at the far end of the room with his throat cut.

"Mr. Dunk appears to have run out of luck," Dick muttered.

Lexi put her hand into her pocket to retrieve a weapon.

"Security cameras," the vampire reminded her softly.

The young man uttered a strangled cry, shook himself, and bolted out and down the hallway. She stepped out after him, turned to face the camera and looked into it. "We need to see the"—she held her fingers in little air quotes—"wife."

She lowered her hands and returned to the room, which was partially sectioned off midway down on the right by what looked like a large, floor-to-ceiling closet. It gave the large space the feel of a suite of rooms and partially blocked the view of half the room. A case lay on the bed and she suspected it either held or had held the money. She wanted a peek.

Lexi turned toward the unexplored section and gestured for the men to keep an eye on the grisly scene. "Stay here." She stepped into the room and was only a few steps in, having reached the spa bath, when a man darted from the hidden side of the room. It was the security guard from the museum, now in jeans and a baseball cap. As he snatched the case, he noticed her, shock on his face. He bolted behind the closet and out of view.

With a yell, she broke into a run, raced after him around the corner of the cupboard, and expected to see he had entered from a connecting room. Before she could stop herself, though, she raced through a fae door.

Shocked, she stopped and realized she was in a forest not at all like the one surrounding the glade Scott had described to her. This one smelled unhealthy, stagnant, and decaying. The man sprinted through the woods in front of her. She spun but the fae door was gone.

"Oh, shit."

With no way to go back, she gave chase. She tried to tie his laces, but it didn't slow him. It occurred to her that he probably didn't wear any. She gained ground slowly and thought about the energy ball Scott had created. It was time for a little on-the-job learning. She touched the scar.

I'll have one of those energy balls, please.

The ball appeared on cue but didn't grow in her hand the way her friend's had. It was simply there and about the size of a basketball. She wished she'd taken the time to let Scott teach her how to create them properly because this seemed large. Unfortunately, she didn't know what size it should be for this purpose, nor was she sure how best to throw it.

How hard can it be? I'm a perfect shot with a blade.

She simply lobbed it as best she could. As she did so, a root seemed to rise and trip her and she tumbled awkwardly. She scrambled to her feet as the ball hit a tree.

The trunk exploded

Oops!

Lexi landed hard again and the man was thrown sideways. His hat came off and she could make out pointed ears. It wasn't a surprise.

Quickly, she conjured another ball but visualized one half the size. The ball appeared and seemed better proportioned than her previous one. She hurled it as he created another fae door and disappeared. Her projectile flew past the portal and damaged another tree.

"Oh no, you don't." She increased her speed. When she was almost at the door, something on the ground drew her attention and she immediately recognized the little silk pouch. She stooped, scooped it up, and launched herself through the portal before it could close.

A loud crack heralded her impact with hard concrete. She swore and hugged her arm, sure from the immense pain that she'd broken it. It was a shock because she'd never broken a bone in her life. An extra-strong bone structure was one of the benefits of being a legacy that she did enjoy.

She didn't recognize the building she was in but a quick scan revealed it to be the entrance of a parking garage. In search of her quarry, she ran out to the street and searched the throngs of people who bustled past. Her hasty scrutiny revealed nothing, though, and she glanced into the garage in bewilderment. He stood a few feet from where she'd landed.

The fae door she'd arrived through had vanished and another lay behind it. The criminal lurked on the other side of it, stared directly at her, and grinned.

"You sneaky fucker." She tried to make another energy ball, but she was out of magic. His grin widened before he disappeared.

Lexi stumbled into the street, hugged her arm across her chest, and joined the crowds.

When she reached the intersection, she looked around in bemusement. "Holy shit, I'm in Times Square."

A woman glanced disapprovingly in her direction but not directly at her, then strode on.

Completely disoriented, she leaned against a wall. Her arm throbbed from the pain and she felt queasy. She reached for her dimensional pocket, but her fingertips met her leather pants. Bewildered, she tried a few times with the same result.

What the fuck?

She looked at her scar and gasped when she saw it was gone. All that was visible was the fine silver line that ran along the inside of her arm, which was how people with no magic saw the unhealing scar. Her heart began to race. "Where's my magic?"

"Honey, all the magic's gone from this world. Sadness is all there is."

Lexi looked at a homeless woman bundled in blankets in the doorway beside her. She made another attempt to access her pocket with her good arm, with the same result.

The impossibilities crowded in and she couldn't think. "I need to get off the street."

"So do I, baby, so do I."

She stumbled past the woman, along the street, and into a coffee shop.

The barista stared at her as she staggered in as though he expected her to be trouble. She wondered if he thought she was drunk or on drugs.

Distracted by everything and a little panicked, she spoke to the barista while she scanned for an empty table. "I…was mugged. I need to call my mage."

"Your what?"

Lexi grimaced and turned to him. "My…friend."

He sneered at her. "You have to buy something if you want to sit."

"Jesus, man." A guy spoke from a table near the counter. She turned to see he was seated with a young woman. They both looked at her with concern. "She's been mugged, it looks like she's hurt, and you want to throw her out? I'll buy her a coffee, okay?"

She was embarrassed but fortunately, remembered her emergency cash. "Wait, I have money, thanks. I have money."

Quickly, she turned to the barista and slipped two fingers into her vest. His eyebrows raised but she noticed that he didn't look away. "A triple-shot extra-large latte."

It was awkward because the little seam in the vest where she kept a rolled-up twenty-dollar note was more naturally approached with the other hand. Still, she managed to access it and dropped it onto the counter.

He looked at it and rolled his eyes as he flattened it. Seriously, he had begun to get on her nerves. He rang up the sale and gave her the change. "What name?"

She smirked, then grimaced as her arm jostled a little. "I'll spell it. E-Y-M-A-D." She paused. "I-C".

The idiot frowned but wrote on the cup. "That's unusual."

"It's Dutch." She nodded to the couple and moved to a table in the corner next to the window.

Lexi looked at the pouch. It was empty. She stuffed it into a back pocket and tried to make sense of what had happened.

I can't see my scar. I have to assume I've used all Scott's magic. Maybe I've never exhausted this much magic before. It could have been the energy balls.

She closed her eyes and reached out for her friend but they snapped open when she couldn't feel him. Now, she began to truly panic and wondered what had happened to him.

Were there more fae but I didn't see them? Is he dead?

She couldn't ever not feel him. He was always there and with his absence came real fear.

"I'm a dick. I'm a dick," shouted the Barista.

"I know you are, but what am I?" The young man and his companion both laughed.

"I'm—" the Barista closed his mouth and looked at the name he was reading out. He glared at Lexi, put the cup on the end of the counter, and walked away to serve a young couple who had walked in.

With a smirk, she collected it and decided she felt a little better. After levering the lid off with her teeth and pouring a mountain of sugar into her latte, she returned to the table and her thoughts. She'd have to call Scott.

"Damn it. My phone's in that goddamn pocket."

A man working on his laptop glanced at her. She returned to her thoughts.

The couple at the counter walked to the table next to hers and sat. She looked at them and met the eyes of the young woman, who was thin and pale and looked like a timid, quivering mouse. Lexi glanced quickly at the young man. He didn't seem to look at her but she felt somehow that he was very aware of her. She knew she must look a sight. Her arm was swelling and wasn't the color it usually was.

She wondered if she could find a pay phone or borrow a cell to call Dolores. That immediately raised the next problem and she facepalmed. *I don't know anyone's number. God, could this get any worse?*

To calm herself, she drank more coffee, closed her eyes, and took stock of her situation. *No money, no cell phone, and barely any weapons.* She rocked her head to the left, then the right, and cracked her neck.

Lexi's eyes snapped open. *If I'm no longer connected to Scott or have access to his magic, do I still have his shield? Or can I now be traced by Kindred?*

She glanced at the girl again and their eyes met.

She's Kindred. The idea seemed to come from nowhere, but she knew it to the very core of her. Not only that, she had a good idea who the girl and her partner might be.

Her senses picked up a thrumming excitement in the young man's body—the telltale sign of anticipation.

He's here to kill me, but I'm not in any condition to fight. She sighed. *There's one number I know by heart.*

Lexi stood, picked her coffee up, and made her way to the couple seated near the counter. She pulled a chair closer with her good arm and sat. "I'm sorry to bother you. I wonder if I could borrow your cell to make a call to my…family?"

If they even remember me. It hadn't even occurred to her until that moment that her family could have been counseled. She might have been erased from their minds in the same way Bryan had been erased from hers.

"Of course." The guy put his password in and passed it to her.

She typed the number in, held the cell phone to her ear, and waited for a few seconds.

"Hello?" Hearing the woman's voice almost made her cry. "Hi, Maggie. Remember me?"

"Lexi? Oh, my God. Lexi? Are you okay? Where are you?" Maggie *was* crying.

Lexi swallowed. "Can you come and get me?"

"We haven't been able to find you. Where are you?"

"You'll be able to find me now." Lexi closed her eyes. She disconnected and handed the cell to the young man. "Thank you."

"Do you need money?" the woman asked.

"No, I don't. They're not far. They'll be here soon."

The buzzer on the door sounded and Lexi looked in as a man entered and made eye contact with the Kindred couple. One of his eyes was white. *Eric.* Another man entered behind him and remained at the door.

She hoped her old unit would arrive in time to help her. Then again, maybe they would help their fellow Kindreds instead.

"Thanks for your help. You've been really kind." She glanced around the room and wondered how many patrons might be injured in the fight that was about to break out. That made it an easy decision to take it away from the couple who had helped her.

Lexi stood and headed to the ladies' bathroom. Cradling her arm, she turned and bumped the door open with her butt. Inside, she glanced in a mirror and grimaced. She'd never seen herself so pale. Wearily, she walked to the end of the stalls and entered the last one, closed the door behind her, and locked it.

In the few minutes she had, she took stock. She was down to what was in her vest and pants and what she could use. The garotte was out as she didn't have the mobility to use it. She had two shurikens on her vest, one outside and one inside, and various little blades hidden in seams.

The outer door to the bathroom opened and someone walked in. Her senses told her it was the Kindred girl.

Casually, she unlocked the stall door and stepped out. She looked at the gaunt figure. "I'm sorry. Dolores told me your name but I can't remember it."

"Lucy."

"That's right, and Warren?" she asked.

Lucy nodded.

Lexi remembered her boss appearing from her dimensional pocket after being attacked by Warren, Scott's insane Kindred brother. Scott had been intended as the blood match for him but preferred to go on the run on account of Warren being a total psycho.

She smirked. "I bet Warren was furious when Dolores escaped."

The girl lifted her hand to her cheek. "Yes. He was."

The smirk faded from her face. *She must be going through all kinds of hell.*

"Can I ask you a question?" She had no idea how long Maggie would take. If she planned a quick bath before coming to get her, she'd likely find her dead.

Lucy didn't say anything but she waited.

Lexi turned her arm slowly. "Why can't I see my scar anymore?"

The girl narrowed her eyes, perhaps suspicious of a trick. "I don't know. I can't see anything either."

"And I can't feel him." She heard her voice tremble.

"The link is broken. Maybe—" The door opened again and interrupted her.

"I told you not to talk to her. I told you to simply get it done."

Lucy jumped in fright at Warren's voice. "But she said—"

He pushed her back toward the door. "Get out. I'll do it."

The girl ran out. Warren thrust his arm at Lexi and she darted to the side and into the cubicle after she released a shuriken which had been hidden between her fingers. The hand dryer exploded off the wall behind where she had stood.

She stuck her head out cautiously, half expecting it to be blown off. Warren pulled the shuriken from his neck. Blood pumped out as he dropped the spiky metal throwing star on the tiled floor, where it landed with a ping. He held his hand up to his neck and stared directly at her as the blood leaking through his fingers stopped.

Slowly and with an exaggerated motion, he drew a sword from his dimensional pocket. Lexi imagined that the long scimitar was supposed to intimidate her, but the sword was so long that drawing it out took several seconds longer than it should have and seemed almost comical.

"That's a long one." She chuckled. "Are you compensating?"

Warren's face settled into a cold mask. "I planned to do this quickly but now, I'll take my time so I can tell Scott how you begged and cried."

"Oh, my God. What are you? A Bond villain? Do you get paid by the hour or what?" She tossed another shuriken but he was expecting it. The little star careened away and struck one of the mirrors on the wall beside him.

Her adversary took one step toward her but froze when a bolt drilled through his neck. He writhed as he made choking sounds.

"You still favor the pistol crossbow, then." Lexi watched as her

Kindred brother Isaac stepped out of a cubicle, followed by Maggie. "There's more of them outside. His name's—"

"We know who he is," he interrupted. "The mental fucker keeps turning up looking for you, saying you kidnapped his intended blood match."

Maggie stared at her. "Where the hell have you been?"

"I have so much to tell you. If it's worth it. It might not be and they'll probably simply counsel it out of your head again. I found things out about Kindred. Some really bad th—"

As she spoke, Isaac lifted his pistol crossbow and aimed it in her direction. Her words stuttered to a halt and she stared at it in disbelief.

He made a "come here" gesture with his other hand. "Lexi, move toward me. It's fine, but come to me."

"Hi." Scott's voice behind her made her shriek and turn.

Isaac loosed a bolt at the sorcerer, who flicked it away where he stood in a fae doorway. He stared at her. "I couldn't sense you. I thought you were dead." His voice trembled.

"I completely ran out of the good stuff." She raised her arm and winced in pain. "I couldn't sense you either. How did you find me if not through the blood match?"

"A common old locator spell with one of your socks."

"You're matched?" Maggie squeaked.

Lexi fixed her gaze on Scott. She'd never been so happy to see him. "This is Scott. Scott, Isaac and Maggie."

He waved awkwardly. "Hi."

"You're matched?" Maggie said again. "So *this* is Scott."

"Calm down. We're matched, not married. Listen, Zac, Mags. It looks like I don't need that lift now. But we do need to talk. I'll keep in touch. It was good seeing you." She caught Scott's hand, stepped through the fae door, and looked at them from the other side.

Maggie smiled at her, then looked at Warren. "Is he dead?"

Isaac checked him. "It looks like he's waking up, so he's not dead yet but could be soon."

He seemed to think about it before he fired a bolt into the bathroom door to alert those outside that things weren't going to plan. Then, he took Maggie's hand. The four of them looked at each other briefly before her Kindred siblings disappeared.

"I'd have let him die," Scott said bluntly and glowered at Warren, who opened his eyes. When he saw the sorcerer, the man flopped like a fish and stretched toward him.

Scott turned away. "Come on, let's go."

CHAPTER SIXTY-TWO

Scott and Lexi stepped out of the fae door into the garden of a little cottage.

Dolores was waiting for them. "Was that my old friend Warren?"

"Yes." Scott nodded. "Should I have killed him?"

"For the good of all mankind, probably." She patted his arm. "Don't worry about it for now."

Lexi looked around. "Where are we?"

"We're at my place and will return to Boulder City in a moment. We merely need to make sure you're safe when you're back in your world." Her boss turned to Scott. "Okay, do your thing."

"I'm trying. The magic's not going into her." He looked at Lexi's arm.

She looked at it too. "Can you still see the scar? I can't."

His gaze doubled its intensity as he stared at her arm. "I don't understand. It's not working."

Dolores nodded. "Okay. Shield her. We'll talk about it when we get back."

He put a hand on her head, then nodded.

Their boss opened her fae door.

Lexi looked over her shoulder before she stepped through. "Why don't we stay in your cottage?"

"The cleaner hasn't been in yet," the fae replied in a deadpan voice.

She narrowed her eyes. "That's not the real reason, is it?"

"No dear, it's not." The woman smiled, then sighed. "There's a limit to my protection. I already have Betsy and Todd in there."

"Aww! I'd have liked to have seen them." Scott frowned.

"You will, dear." She patted him on the back.

They walked through to a suburban garden.

Lexi gazed around at a soccer ball and a little pink bike lying outside the door. "Who lives here?"

Dolores opened the door and they entered. It was her little apartment, no longer a fishing shack near the lake.

They sat at the table and the girl retrieved the pouch from her pocket. "He dropped this."

"What is it?"

She handed the item to her boss. "It's the pouch the talisman was resting on in the museum. He went back to the museum for it. Should we leave it here for safety?"

The fae felt the material with her fingertips. She turned it inside-out and back, then handed it to her. "I think you should keep it with you and wait. If it's important enough that he came back for it once, he'll try again."

Lexi took it and winced.

Scott shook his head. "Let's fix your arm." He turned his chair to face her. She sat while he placed a hand gently on her arm and began to mutter unintelligibly.

After a minute, he looked at her. "You're all done."

She flexed her arm. It felt as good as new but when she looked into his face, she saw the concern there. "Yes?"

"Nothing."

"Say it." She was getting annoyed.

He frowned. "Your bone density is…different."

"Scott. I broke my fucking arm for the first time in my life. Do you think I haven't already figured that much out?"

"Sorry."

Lexi sighed. "No, I'm sorry. I'm not used to feeling so..." She wanted to say *scared* but chose not to. "Useless."

"Okay. Dick freaked out when you went missing. It's time to get back." Dolores went to the door. "We're back at the diner. I can't get us any closer with the wards."

She snorted. "Have you tried lately? We know for a fact that someone else is doing it."

Her boss grasped the handle and opened the door. "The wards are up now. I don't understand how it's happening. I'll have to look into it."

They walked through and Lexi looked around. She immediately noticed the truck driver again. He wore the same Raiders cap and plaid shirt and was seated at his table near the door, reading and drinking coffee. She was about to mention him but something more pressing was on her mind. "Is it my imagination or are we traveling an overly elaborate route?"

Dolores nodded. "Caleb knows you're both with me, so all of Kindred probably knows too. It's getting difficult to move around safely."

The fae turned to the man. "Thanks, Bill."

He looked up from his newspaper, smiled, and threw her a set of keys. "Take care, Dolores."

Lexi did a double-take. She was certain the guy had been there last time.

They left the diner, climbed into an old Honda, and headed to the condo.

The moment they entered, Dick leaped to his feet. "We thought you were dead."

Jesús walked into the room. "Mister Levin cried."

"I did not."

Jesús walked around the room, picking up glasses and tidying, but when he was behind his boss, he looked at Lexi and nodded his head as he mouthed, "He did."

Dick rolled his eyes. "I know what you're doing, Jesús."

"Yes, Mr. Levin." The man took the glasses into the kitchen.

"I wasn't crying. I'm allergic to the cheap fabrics in my condo. I'm allergic to so many cheap things—like that oxblood leatherette jacket you wear, Lexi."

She narrowed her eyes. "It's leather."

He looked pityingly at her. "I'm sure that's what they told you in the store."

"Fuck you."

"Fuck you too." The vampire put a hand on her shoulder. "Do you want coffee?"

Lexi nodded and patted his hand.

Dolores smiled. "It's so nice to see you two getting along."

A few minutes later, he was back with coffee. He put the mug in front of her.

She looked at him and nodded her thanks. Then she looked at Scott and extended her arm. "What's going on with me? Are we not matched anymore? Can that even happen?"

"I've never heard of this happening. I have no idea so I'll message Bryan." He took his cell out and began to tap it.

Lexi's stomach flipped. Her first thought was that she might see Bryan and she must be an awful sight. Then she remembered he was married to her sister and she sighed. "Great."

An hour later, he arrived and knocked on the frame of the open door. "Can I come in?"

Her heart lurched and she stomped on it mentally.

"Come in, Bryan." Scott shook his hand. "Anything?"

"I might have something. Well…it doesn't really explain why, but it might explain how…" He looked at them. "Here goes. As I said before, You and Ali were separated at a young age. The reason must have been because of what's happened now. When she's strong, you're weak, and when you're strong, she's weak. I think this gives us some good news too. I think this tells us you're a born legacy. You weren't made one by ritual. At least one parent must have been a legacy."

She frowned. "Why do you think that?"

Bryan crossed his arms and leaned back on the doorframe. "I think you're identical twins, so you started as a single cell with the legacy blood already in your DNA, then you divided into twins. That makes sense, right?"

Lexi looked away and mulled over what he'd said. "The fight with Alicia did leave me feeling ultimately weaker, but I hurled energy balls at the fae who killed Melvyn."

"You did?" Scott grinned.

"Yes. You're a crappy teacher. I blew a tree up."

The sorcerer gave her an incredulous look. "I haven't even taught you that yet."

"Exactly." She waited for a beat, then winked at him. When she turned to Bryan, he was frowning. "What?"

He grimaced. "That was probably residual magic. Whatever magic you had remaining in your system from Scott."

She clapped her hands and rubbed them together. "So, all we need to do is go to Alicia. I'll touch her for a few seconds and get my mojo back."

Bryan drew his brow down in a look of concern.

Lexi worried he would try to stop her. "I won't hurt her."

Quickly, he put a hand up to reassure her. "It's not that. I'm simply trying to work out the logistics. She's staying at the chief's house so there's always someone to look out for her." He thought for a moment. "Okay. I'll go back and I'll contact Scott when it's safe to come. You need to get out of Vegas so you can come immediately by fae door. We might only have seconds."

"Okay." She nodded. "We'll be ready."

Her gaze followed Bryan when he headed out the door and when she turned, the others were staring at her. Even Marcel was seated on his haunches with his head tilted and his gaze fixed on her.

"What?" It came out more aggressively than she'd intended.

Dick changed the subject. "So, what happened to the guy with the case?"

"I lost him, but he dropped this." She pulled the little pouch from her pocket.

"The talisman?" He looked delighted.

Lexi waved it. "It's empty."

The vampire slouched. "Oh. Never mind." He picked it up and examined it. She watched his face as he considered its relevance. "This is good, isn't it? Because he went back to the museum for it. If it's not important, why did he risk going back?"

She smiled. "That's the conclusion we came to."

"And he'd had the talisman for a couple of days before we arrived," he continued, "but he didn't start using it until he had the pouch. Oh… He needs this." He handed it to her with a grin on his face. "We don't need to find him. He'll come to us."

"Maybe it's not the talisman that's lucky at all. Maybe it's the pouch." She scrunched it in the palm of her hand.

With her fist closed around it, she wished with every hope inside her. "I wish I had my scar and legacy abilities back."

Lexi tried to create an energy ball. She looked at the others who stared pensively at her once again and shook her head.

Scott sat beside her. "After you disappeared, Dick went through the security footage of Mr. Dunk winning on the tables. He realized that the security guy from the museum stood in the background at every table Melvyn had played at. He held something in his hand but we couldn't see what."

She leaned down to stroke Marcel as he walked past. "Could it have been the talisman?"

"No, Melvyn had that." Dick picked Marcel up and kissed him on the head. "Jesús, would you take him out to do his business, please?"

Jesús took the puppy with a smile. "Come with me, little man."

"Melvyn took the chip out of his pocket a few times and kissed it," he continued. "In fact, every time he did that, Murder-Fae scowled."

"*Murder-Fae.* That's what we're calling him, is it? Well, it fits." She smirked.

Lexi scratched Marcel behind the ears as Jesús carried him past. "So Melvyn never was the lucky guy and you don't have to hold it to be the one winning. Interesting."

Dolores asked, "Where did the fae door lead to?"

"The first one led to a forest. Man, it stank like stagnant death."

Her boss sighed. "You shouldn't have chased him."

"I thought he'd been in a connected room. I flew around the corner and was through it before I knew what had happened. I chased him, threw the energy ball that blew the tree up, and when he escaped through another door, I launched myself through it behind him but he got away. That's how I broke my arm. God, that hurt."

Dick put a hand up. "May I ask a question?"

Everyone looked at him.

"What if that energy ball had killed him? How would you have gotten back?"

"Well… Oh!" Lexi shrugged. She hadn't considered that.

Scott was hesitant but asked, "What was it like seeing your f…unit again?"

She paused before answering. "I've spent the last year demonizing them all in my head, but Maggie and Isaac were simply Maggie and Isaac. She was thrilled that we were matched and happy for me. What was it like seeing Warren?"

He ran a hand through his shaggy, blond waves. "I couldn't believe his face. God, what a mess. That poor mage. I regret not taking the time to kill him. I hope they didn't get to him in time. It would save lives in the long run."

"His face?" She frowned in confusion.

"Oh, you wouldn't have seen it." The sorcerer sighed. He opened his mouth, then closed it again.

Lexi could see he was struggling. "We don't have to talk about it if you don't want to."

"Do you mind if we don't? Honestly, I feel sick thinking about it."

They stood and headed to the cars.

She turned to him. "I'll need your help with something else. I can't get into my dimensional pocket. Everything's there—my money, cell phone, weapons...well, the good ones. I haven't lost it all, have I?"

"No, it's still there. I'll get your stuff out through mine." He sat on the back seat of Dick's car and hauled her gear out of his bag. She took a few items and rolled another twenty to hide in her vest.

Dick followed Dolores' vehicle out of town to the diner. They parked and entered, and she handed the keys to Bill, who remained at the same table.

The man didn't speak and instead, stared from the vampire to the clock on his wall. "My supe-dar says vamp but my clock says something else."

"Pleased to meet you. I'm Vamp Two-point-oh." Dick nodded at the man. "It's a little upgrade we're trialing."

Lexi rolled her eyes. "Could we have three coffees and whatever Mister Two-point-oh's having, please."

They sat with their drinks and waited to hear from Bryan.

"Maybe something's gone wrong. Should we call?" she asked when impatience finally won her internal battle.

"I'm not sure that's—" Scott was interrupted by a text message on his cell and he glanced at it. "We're up."

She rolled her arm and bent her elbow to ensure it wouldn't give her any more trouble. "How do you know where he is?"

"He gave us something to channel." The sorcerer opened his hand. A small pin with a police badge on it lay in his palm. He held it while Dolores put her hand on his arm.

The fae door opened into a bedroom with a single bed. Lexi looked around before she stepped through. They surmised this had been Alicia's bedroom growing up.

Scott was openly curious. "Huh. She has eclectic taste."

She glanced at him. "What?"

"The posters. She likes Linkin Park, The Black-Eyed Peas, and Leonard Cohen."

"That's weird," she commented as she studied the posters. They were the same as those she'd had on her walls.

The woman with her face lay asleep in the bed. Bryan stood over her and looked nervously from Alicia to the bedroom door.

Dolores put her hand on Lexi's arm. "I can't leave the door there. If there's another mage in the house, they might sense it. Call me and I'll come get you."

They stepped through and the portal vanished.

Bryan stepped back. "Let's get this done fast. The chief's just told me Caleb's coming over."

Lexi's face brightened. "That's useful. I could simply kill him now."

A voice came from outside the room. "Bryan? Is she awake?"

The man's face was a vision of shock.

His hand jerked out toward them when the handle on the bedroom door turned. Suddenly, the two friends stood somewhere else.

She spun in confusion. "Where are we?"

Scott ran a finger across a row of coat hangers. "I'd say we're in a closet."

Fortunately, it was a fairly spacious walk-in closet and they were surrounded by clothes, tools, weapons, and books. She stretched to open a drawer and a full-length mirror at the end of the little room clicked and swung open. They exchanged a glance and walked through onto a platform that overlooked what resembled a convention hall. The space was arranged in row upon row of booths.

"It looks like comic-con with no people," Scott said.

"I thought I heard you speaking."

Lexi jumped. Several large screens around the hall all displayed Chief Rand. He looked directly at the camera.

"She's not awake. I was talking to her anyway," Bryan replied. The view switched to the sleeping girl.

The sorcerer raised his eyebrows. "We're in his dimensional pocket."

"What? But it's huge. Mine's like a cupboard." She descended the stairs and he followed.

"It can look like anything you want it to. But I'll admit, I've never heard of anything like this." He looked as perplexed as he sounded. "Look at the signs. The booths are organized by year. Why would he do this?"

They walked past booths with pictures and screens on the walls while the conversation between Bryan and the chief continued. Lexi was drawn to one with pictures of a little girl. She recognized Braxton, the father of her unit, but he was far younger. Several pictures of a girl of about six playing with a doll caught her attention and she touched a screen on the wall. It immediately sprang to life.

The little girl was crying loudly and screamed, "I want Alicia."

Braxton stood nearby talking to a woman she didn't recognize. "This is horrible."

The woman stroked his arm. "It'll be okay. You know that sometimes, it can take a few counseling sessions to shift some memories. It's for the best."

The camera moved closer to the little girl and Lexi realized this was Bryan walking toward her. "Hi, Alexa. I'm Bryan. Look, here's Alicia." He placed a doll into the little girl's arms and she hugged it. Slowly, he sat on the floor beside her and showed her a toy truck.

Lexi wiped the dampness on her cheeks.

"Ah, Bryan." Caleb's voice boomed over the speakers and she went rigid at the sight of him grinning on the screens above.

Bryan nodded briefly and turned to Alicia.

"I'm sorry," Caleb continued. "I can't remember—have we met?"

Bryan took Alicia's hand and raised it to his face. "No... Well..." He suddenly appeared in the hall and stood at a noticeboard at the end of a row of booths. He was there for two seconds, at most, while at the same time, he tucked his wife's arm under the covers. Calmly, he stood, turned to the visitor, and proffered his hand. "Kind of. We've spoken on the phone."

In the dimensional pocket, the two friends walked to the board with *Caleb* written at the top. Beneath were two columns for the things Bryan should and shouldn't know about the sorcerer. Lexi had the distinct impression that the man had tried to catch him out.

Caleb winced, then smiled. "Of course. Yes. How's our little superstar?"

"Did you see that?" Scott pointed at the screen. "Caleb's face? I bet that demon's still driving him crazy."

Chief Rand leaned closer. "We're keeping her in a magic-induced coma until we can find out what's going on."

The visitor continued to address Bryan. "Could you bring her out? I have some questions I'd like to ask her."

The young man paused before he answered. "Do you really need to? If it's about Cabo, we've completed our reports. But if you need anything about her fight with Lorenzo, I'm afraid I already counseled her."

Caleb smiled at him but his frustration could be sensed behind it. "Before she was debriefed? And why did you do that?"

"She was out of control and violent. I've never seen such ferocity and I assumed it must have been something Lorenzo did. I thought if she forgot it—I mean, that's why we have counseling isn't it? To protect us? But while it did remove the memories, it didn't work on her other issues."

"You were both told to stay away from Lorenzo."

"I didn't know she planned to do it but perhaps I should have guessed. She was upset when she heard about what he'd done to Thomas."

The sorcerer frowned. "Thomas?"

Chief Rand grimaced. "The vampire priest."

"Ah yes. That was most regrettable." Caleb sighed.

He leaned over Alicia's unconscious form and swept his hand above her. "Her bone density is almost double any legacy I've seen. And her legacy ability readings are off the chart." He grimaced and pinched the bridge of his nose, then turned to Chief Rand. "Kevin, may I use the bathroom?"

"Of course, you know where it is."

With a curt nod, he left the room

CHAPTER SIXTY-THREE

Caleb stood over the washbasin and his hands clutched the sides. Blood dripped from his nose onto the white porcelain.

What is the result of the experiment with the demon? Azatoth's voice was so loud in his mind that his eyes rolled back in their sockets and blood pulsed at his temples.

He had anticipated the question and attempted to lead with the good news. "The demon has fulfilled our primary purpose. It tried to escape by drawing a thinner from the demon realms, as we knew it would. We captured the thinner."

Azatoth hissed annoyance. *I know that. And the experiment?*

The sorcerer glanced into the bowl at the cascade of blood that now gushed from his nose. "As suspected, its body was strong but the mind is useless. It would not withstand your presence."

The demon paused before he issued his command. *Bring the girl. She will contain me. She will withstand my presence.*

Caleb pulled toilet tissue from the roll. "What about the sister? She's obviously been here. Bryan may know something."

Find out what the boy knows but let him live. I can combine my power with his air magic through their blood match. You are pathetic. You house a mere fraction of my mind within you and you crumble. Look at the mess you are.

He forced his gaze to focus on the mirror as Azatoth stripped the glamor he projected and he saw his true self. Most of his body was almost entirely riddled with broken capillaries in his skin. His eyes were bloodshot and his head was almost completely bald now. He had lost weight and jowls hung from his face. More than ever, he resembled a cadaver. It disgusted him and he looked away.

"The meteor storm is almost upon us. The conditions are favorable." Caleb's comment was met with silence. He looked unwillingly at himself in the mirror before he closed his eyes and drew a few deep breaths.

And clean yourself up. You're disgusting. His eyes flicked open as Azatoth's voice rattled through his mind. The demon laughed.

His movements slow and weary, he washed the blood from the sink and wiped it from his face with the toilet tissue, then flushed it. He took several more breaths to settle himself before he recreated his glamor. Soon it would be over, one way or another. He would either be rid of Azatoth or dead. By that point, he wondered if he cared which.

CHAPTER SIXTY-FOUR

Caleb returned to the bedroom. He looked at Bryan and smiled again but this time, somehow looked more dangerous. "Have you heard from Alexa recently?"

"Who?" The young man's vision flicked from him to Rand.

"Surely you know who Alexa is," the sorcerer pressed.

"I'm sorry. I haven't a clue." He didn't need to visit the hall for that one. It was obvious he shouldn't know who she was.

"Alicia's sister." He stared intently at Bryan and his face filled the screen.

"Her what?" Chief Rand interrupted. "I'm sorry, you're mistaken. She doesn't have a sister."

"Actually, Kevin, she has a twin, and coming into contact with her is the only way Alicia's abilities could have increased like this. It also means the other girl is now very weak. The council has kept them apart to stop this from happening." He looked at the sleeping woman.

In the pocket, the two friends glanced at each other. Lexi felt relieved to have their theory confirmed.

"So if we get the other girl back here, it might fix this?" Kevin sounded hopeful.

"Sadly, not at the moment. Alexa is a problem. She absconded from Kindred a year ago."

The chief's eyebrows reached his hairline. "She left? I've never heard of such a thing."

"It gets worse," Caleb continued. "She then seduced a young mage away from his family and from his intended blood match, a young man who is beside himself with worry."

Scott snorted.

"Now, she seems to be on a vendetta against the organization. We think she opened the portal in Palm Springs and attempted to murder me in Cabo."

Bryan looked from one man to the other. "But what about Ali? How can we help her? Can't we track this woman?"

"Clearly, the sister's after her. Perhaps she was in collusion with Lorenzo. She might have encouraged him to go on this evil, murderous rampage." Caleb shook his head as though he were genuinely sad. "We must keep Alicia safe. There's a place—you may have heard of it—Emmersley House. It's kind of a spa. She'll be protected there."

"You're taking her away?" Her husband sounded nervous.

A whirring noise started in the dimensional pocket. Lexi jumped and whirled. Her hand fumbled instinctively for her katana but she dug herself in the hip. "I really miss that pocket."

"You'll have it back soon," Scott assured her.

They stepped to a printer and watched a document print out of Emmersley House and Spa, followed by a picture of Caleb with his hand in Alicia's hair. They looked at the screens to see that it mirrored what happened in real life.

"Gross." Lexi shuddered and turned away. She stepped into an aisle and studied the booths on either side.

Scott stepped beside her and did a double-take "You're right. You did have the same posters."

She looked at the pictures of her old bedroom. Sure enough, it displayed the identical pictures.

He scratched his chin thoughtfully. "Maybe you're psychically linked with her."

"Maybe." She didn't think so, however.

They continued to walk.

Her companion looked into a booth while she wandered up an aisle. She came to the end of the row and a black, metal door with a sign that read *Bad Stuff.* Lexi put her ear to it, sure she could hear something on the other side. She moved her hand cautiously to the handle.

Chief Rand's voice drew her attention to the screens. "Maybe you should get out for a while. Have a walk around the Quarter. Sitting in here isn't doing either of you any good and you know they like to see us out there doing our job."

Bryan guffawed. "Are you sure about that? I've had very strange looks from the witches and shifters I've seen, and I mean more strange than usual. They want to know why we left them without support when Lorenzo went crazy."

Kevin patted his shoulder. "There was nothing you could have done about it. It was chaos in Palm Springs and your investigation in Cabo was important. For God's sake, someone tried to kill the head of the Kindred counsel."

Bryan turned to the sorcerer. "I'll come with her though, right?"

The man smiled his insincere smile. "Of course. I'll get her settled and we'll arrange a replacement unit to cover you here. You'll follow within a couple of days. I promise." He clapped his hands together briskly. "That's agreed then."

The young man looked at him, his expression wary. "I don't understand why she has to leave. If Ali's even stronger now than she was before and that means the sister's weaker, surely she can't be in danger from a powerless ex-legacy. It doesn't make any sense."

"Let's get a picture of that address." Scott started to retrace his steps and Lexi turned hesitantly away from the curious black door. They reached the printer and he picked up the sheets of paper lying in the tray. His cell phone appeared instantly in his hand and he took a picture of the details.

Caleb shook his head. "Bryan, you're a clever young man."

His tone drew their attention and they walked closer to a screen.

"That's a very good point," the Kindred leader continued. "I should have thought of it myself." He stretched his hands to the other two men at the same time and placed one on one each of theirs.

A slam drew the attention of the young hideaways. It was the door they'd entered through on the platform above. Alarmed, they looked at each other and hurried to the stairs. They both slapped their hands over their ears as hundreds of shutters descended over all the booths. One clunked over the printer as they moved past it. The screens changed to a black background with a red digital five-minute countdown.

Lexi lowered her hands as the sounds echoed and faded around them. "What the hell is going on?"

"I think Caleb's counseling him. I don't understand why the shutters—" As Scott spoke, the image and words vanished from the sheets of paper in his hand. "Oh."

They reached the top of the stairs. The door to the walk-in closet was clear glass from their side. Lexi was about to push on it when their adversary appeared in the room on the other side and they froze.

He looked around and poked through a couple of drawers before he pulled a copy of *Playboy* out, flicked through it, and shoved it back. With a smirk, he flicked a glance at the mirror door, half-turned, then looked again, directly into her face. Her heart hammered in her chest as he walked toward it.

She clenched her fist, ready to punch through the glass.

The sorcerer stopped about a foot from the glass and straightened his tie. With an inward sigh of relief, she realized he saw only himself in the mirror. He tapped at the floppy fat under his chin, turned, and disappeared.

Breath exploded from Scott in a panicked exhalation. "I didn't know it was possible to gain access to another mage's dimensional pocket without their permission."

Lexi was confused. "Dolores got into mine."

"She has permission because she puts things in there for us and I trust her—and I don't stash Playboy magazines in there."

"Really?" She smirked. "Where *do* you stash them?"

He rolled his eyes and led the way into the large area once more.

She looked around the hall and her gaze settled on the blank papers in his hand. "I don't understand this. I've never heard of objects vanishing from a dimensional pocket because someone's been counseled."

Scott raised an eyebrow. "How would they know?" He slid the blank sheets into the printer tray.

Startled by the question, she stopped and gaped at him. "Oh. Fair point."

He smiled. "I think you're right, though. We only use ours as storage."

"Yes...for teddy bears," she teased.

"And candy wrappers," he retorted. "Bryan seems to have this connected to his memory. Honestly, it's genius. The paper is an object but what's stored on it is a memory."

They stood and watched the screen as it counted down. At one minute to zero, the counter turned green and the shutters began to rise. Lexi wandered to a booth and pointed to a photograph of a book. "Hey, this is my favorite series—*The Belgariad* by David Eddings."

She touched the screen and it sprang to life. Alicia threw the book, which hurtled toward Bryan and he caught it. "Look, I'll take it back. I only thought you might like it."

Alicia, who looked about eighteen, pointed at him. "I feel like you're trying to turn me into someone I'm not. I don't even like fantasy and who the fuck is Leonard Cohen? Stop putting posters on my walls."

"I don't want to look at this stuff anymore." She stopped the screen and led them to the printer again. "It's supposed to be private." The truth was, she didn't know what to make of it.

The countdown reached zero and a beep sounded. Bryan appeared in the hall on the platform at the top of the stairs where a huge button had appeared on the wall with *stop alarm* written on it. He pressed the button, then froze when he noticed the two of them. Scott stepped in front of Lexi and she rolled her eyes.

The other man shook his head before he walked down the stairs. "Sorry. It takes a few seconds for things to come back."

Lexi looked at the screen. He was also in the bedroom, staring at the empty doorway.

When he reached the bottom of the stairs, he went directly to the printer. "Why was I counseled? That memory hasn't come back." He picked the blank sheets up.

"Caleb told you he's taking Alicia to recover at a spa," Scott explained.

Bryan flicked through the papers. "Caleb was here? I don't see the printout."

"Sorry. I saw it before the shutters came down, though."

"Shutters?" The other man looked around the hall.

"All the booths and the printer were sealed behind roller shutters."

"Ah! That makes sense. I've never been in here when it happened. That's interesting." He looked around. "I apologize if you've seen anything embarrassing. I panicked and didn't know what else to do." His gaze shifted to the door which read *Bad Stuff*.

Lexi wished she'd had time to open it. "We watched a video of me ugly-crying my eyes out. You gave me a doll."

"That was the day you joined us." Bryan turned to Scott. "Do you remember the details about where Caleb wants to take Ali?"

"I took a picture of it." The sorcerer took the phone from his pocket and showed the other man the photograph.

Bryan looked at it and the printer whirred to life again. A photo spewed from it of Scott's screen with the details from the note. He picked it up and they followed him to what appeared to be the most chronologically recent row of booths. He stopped at the noticeboard marked *Caleb* and he pinned the picture to the wall. The board was sparse. "As you can see, there's barely anything here, yet."

She raised an eyebrow. "I have a whole stack of information for you about him. When I get my abilities back, maybe I could set something like this up and send it over."

He narrowed his eyes as though he wondered how that might work. She suspected she'd given him a new project to work on.

"Did you know Caleb was in here?" Scott asked.

The other man froze. "In *here?*"

"Well, in the walk-in closet up there." He pointed.

Bryan exhaled sharply. "That's what it's there for. I've suspected for a while that the more powerful mages might be capable of peeking in our private spaces, so I keep weapons and spare clothes there and a few things that make it look like it's where I keep my secrets. The idea is that they hopefully won't look any further."

Lexi smirked. "Yes, he saw that too."

He blushed.

They walked along the row to the entrance. She tried not to look at the booths—it felt even ruder because Bryan was there with her—but she drew to a halt when she saw a picture of herself perched over Alicia with her katana. She gazed at it in horror before she looked away quickly.

It made her think about why she had attacked the girl so violently. "Why did she stab Scott?"

"When I got her home, she was raving about a doppelgänger and a sorcerer trying to kill her. She thought she was acting in self-defense and it was purely instinct. Let's get your legacy abilities back. Maybe Caleb won't take her away if I can convince him this extra strength has simply worn off."

Lexi looked at the two mages. "Will it disturb her when my magic leaves her?"

Bryan shrugged. "No, she'll stay asleep until I wake her." He turned and she realized with some surprise that they had returned to the bedroom. The two friends stood in front of the bed and Bryan was seated exactly where he had been during Caleb's visit.

"Where is she?" He stood.

They all stared at the empty bed.

"He's taken her already?" Lexi turned to Scott.

The other man looked at the wall. "The posters have gone. Everything's gone. He doesn't plan to bring her back." Bryan's face had turned white. "When I first came into the hall, I wasn't thinking about her at all. He'd taken her out of my mind completely. Now, I have to pretend I don't remember her. Oh, God, not again."

She looked at him, surprised. He seemed more annoyed than anguished.

Scott typed rapidly on his cell. "I'm messaging Dolores. We'll get on this immediately and will find her."

Lexi could think of nothing to say. She found the disappointment overwhelming. When the fae door appeared, she pushed to her feet and hurried to it.

"We'll let you know as soon as we know something," was the last thing she heard Scott say before she stepped through.

In the diner, Dick took one look at her face. "Shit!"

She tapped her hip nervously where her dimensional pocket should have been. "Caleb arrived and took Alicia. He said he would take her to somewhere called Emmersley House."

The vampire tilted his head and he frowned. "Emmersley..." he said as though the name resonated.

Scott stepped through and heard her explanation. "Should we go after him in your current condition?"

She turned to him. "He has my sister. It's very clear from what he said to Bryan that the excuse he gave for taking her was a lie. I can still wield a sword and fire a gun. I'll be fine. Of course, I'm not happy about feeling so weak. Maybe I should start on the vamp blood again."

Dick stepped away hastily. "Don't look at me. My contribution was involuntary."

Dolores waved a hand and her fae door vanished. "It wouldn't work anyway. Without access to your legacy abilities, you're essentially a regular human. They don't get superpowers from vamp blood." She slapped Scott's arm. "Are you looking for pie again? Everywhere you go, it's pie, pie, pie."

He dragged his gaze away from the menu. "Sorry, but they make amazing pie here."

"If you want amazing pie, I'll take you to Phil's Cornerdown

Kitchen sometime. Or maybe not. We don't want you to die of longing."

Scott fixed his gaze on her and smiled. "Die of longing? Where is this place?"

"It's in a corner dimension of its own. People have been known to sit and die because they didn't want to eat anywhere else."

"What does he make?"

"Meatballs in Can't-Feel-My-Face sauce, Wings with Fuckno dip. The usual."

The sorcerer's eyes glazed over. "I have to try it, Dolores. You need to make that happen."

She checked the time. "Right, focus. You head to Vegas and get packed. I'll look into the fae who killed Melvyn."

"Can we help?" Lexi wondered if she would ultimately be squeezed out of the team. She knew that shouldn't be her first concern, but she couldn't help the feeling that she was losing who she was, piece by piece.

Dolores sighed. "I'll look for answers in Fae. You head to Emmersley House. I'll prepare your background and arrange your flights."

She stared at her. "We don't even know where it is."

Dick's brow wrinkled in puzzlement. "That name sounds so familiar."

The fae stared at him. "It's in Maine."

Scott nodded to her. "You know it? Cool."

She looked at him with an odd expression. "I'm surprised you don't."

He grinned at Lexi. "This place must be famous. I wonder if we'll meet any celebrities."

They left the diner and climbed into the SUV. The sorcerer sighed. "When we get there, I want a last dip in the pool."

Dick turned in his seat to look at him. "You have something important to do, remember?"

"Oh, right. Well, after that, I'll jump in the pool."

Lexi massaged her temples. "I'm going to lie down." She wasn't even curious about whatever they were talking about.

Jesús came to meet them when they approached the condos. "Mr. Levin, the furniture has arrived. They asked what to do with what they were removing. I told them to pile it at the management company's offices."

Dick grinned. "You did the right thing. Wait, did you tell them to set it ablaze?"

"No. But I let Marcel pee on that nasty couch."

"We shouldn't teach Marcel bad habits but I think you're heading for a bonus this year, Jesús."

The man jumped up and down and clapped enthusiastically.

The vampire turned to Lexi and Scott. "Come and look at my new furniture. I can't wait to see what Jesús went with. He's so close to that bonus."

Jesús looked sideways at him and led them in. "This way." He sounded nervous.

The entrance hall now had a large brass gong hung vertically in a wooden frame with a mallet on a bracket at the top.

Dick looked at it. "Bold. Very bold."

Scott's gaze fell on it. "That's perfect."

"You think?" The vampire's face brightened. "Onward, then."

They moved into the living room. His eyes narrowed slightly as he looked around.

"I chose to go with mostly Florence Knoll Bassett," Jesús explained hastily. "Her lines are clean and understated. The corner sofa is a statement piece. White would have been preferable, but this is a rental, after all, and you can't always guarantee quality guests. This and the credenza work together beautifully. The Rennie Mackintosh Italian Ash dining table and chairs, while matching well with the colors, contrast playfully with the Knoll in style." He took a deep breath.

Scott put his hands on his hips. "You're very knowledgeable, Jesús."

The man grinned with pride. "Mr. Levin has been paying for my college degree in design."

"He can't be a house boy forever, and he has a keen eye." Dick nodded as he looked around the room.

"One thing, though." Scott pointed at the gong. "Can I borrow that?"

The vampire looked both wary and confused. "Erm…sure."

Scott picked the gong up in its frame and took it through the front door.

Dick and Jesús looked at Lexi.

"Don't ask me." She shrugged and followed. When she reached him in the kitchen, he'd put her weapons on the kitchen counter but there was no sign of the gong. "Where is it?"

"It's in my dimensional pocket. I have some work to do on it." He sat and closed his eyes.

She retrieved her weapons and trudged up the stairs. Standing in the doorway of their room, she looked at the two beds, hers closest to the door and window to protect Scott. She sneered and wondered if she could even protect him now or if he might have to risk his life to protect her. The thought made her cringe inwardly.

Lexi walked into the master bedroom and dropped onto the bed. Her mind revolved through everything she didn't want to think about —all the unanswered questions. Seeing Mags and Zac had confused her. Bryan had confused her. Her stomach had done flips from the moment she knew he was alive, but it looked like he might have tried to turn Alicia into her? Now the possibility that he might want her existed, she realized she didn't want him at all. Not that it mattered.

What use am I to anyone?

Irritated, she straightened and realized she needed to keep busy. She closed the door, took her jacket and vest off, and hunted for more places to hide weapons. After an hour or so, she dropped the blades she'd been unable to fit in the clothes onto the bed. She threw the garment onto the pile, stretched beside it, and drifted off.

CHAPTER SIXTY-FIVE

Lexi woke to "Mr. Blue Sky" from Dick's cell downstairs.

He answered in moments. "Hello, Dolores... Upstairs resting, I think. Would you like me to check? Tomorrow? Excellent."

She listened to silence for a while.

"Good heavens, no," he continued. "Don't book *me* into cattle-class. Book me first-class and invoice my accountant. Oh, yes. I'd forgotten I need to choose a surname. I'll mull on it for an hour or so. It's an important decision, you know. I've had the same name for a hundred years... Yes, I'll let you know tonight. Do the others need new identities? Let me choose Lexi's, please. How about Mary-Beth, or Mary-Jane? Something with a hyphen... Oh, very well. I'll update Scott." After a moment he added, "Marcel, walkies."

Just when she thought Dick was a decent guy, he'd start being a dick again. She rolled her eyes. He was mostly a nice guy and he would give you the monogrammed shirt off his back but sometimes, he could be utterly thoughtless. She turned over and lay quietly for a few minutes before she opened her eyes and sighed. Moping was pointless. She decided to get ready for dinner.

At that moment, the ruckus broke out.

The sound of a crashing cymbal echoed around her. The air shimmered in the room and Murder-Fae appeared with a nasty grin on his face. He held an evil-looking curved knife but didn't approach her with it. Her gaze shifted from the knife to his face and she scowled belligerently. She'd fallen asleep without her vest on and the moron now stared at her breasts.

Scott teleported into the room. He raised his hands, no doubt to perform a spell, when he also noticed that she was bare-chested and froze momentarily. The fae tapped the mage's forehead and he was suddenly nowhere to be seen.

Lexi looked at the intruder in horror. "What have you done?"

He glanced at the floor and moved his foot. She edged slowly onto her knees and looked over the end of the bed to where a tiny Scott waved at her from the floor.

The fae hovered his foot above him. "Give me the pouch or your boyfriend's floor jello."

She put her hands up, clasped them around the back of her head, and simultaneously arched her back a little. "Please don't hurt him. I'll do…anything." She noted that the creep's gaze darted between her face and breasts.

"Just…just give me the pouch." He continued to look, though.

"It's in my vest. Do you want me to take it out?"

"No! Pass the vest over slowly." He seemed to sense that she was up to something.

"Fine, okay. Look, I won't try anything." She leaned sideways with her one hand still at her neck and the other stretched to reach the vest.

He sneered at her. "I know you won't try anything. The word's out that you're a total dud—no abilities, no nothing."

How in the hell would he know that?

Her face flamed with the shame of his words but she picked the vest up with a finger and thumb so he could see she only intended to pass it to him. She kept it far away from her body and swept it in a slow arc, hoping Scott had the sense to run from under the guy's foot.

"Take it. And here I thought there was nothing to learn from those Vegas magicians."

His gaze flicked to her face and inevitably, to her breasts. "What does that—"

She acted as fast as her half-naked, total-dud body could move.

"What does that mean? Let me answer that for you. Misdirection. It means that while you gaped at my girls here, I was able to slip a blade from under my vest with my toes. And while you stared over there at the vest and here at my breasts, I passed that blade to my hand and was able to stab you through the head with it."

"Lexi." Dick stood in the doorway. "Why are you talking to the dead fae?"

"We were having a conversation. I see no reason to end it simply because he died while I still had a point to make."

A hurried glance at the floor revealed Scott coming out from under the bed. She picked him up gently and placed him on her hand.

"Get Dolores," the tiny sorcerer yelled.

Lexi put her ear closer to him. "What?"

He tried again. "Call Dolores. Do-lor-es."

Dick knelt beside the fae's body and began to search through his pockets. "He's asking you to call Dolores."

"Oh, I know. I can hear him perfectly well." She smiled at Scott. "But he's so adorable this size. Can't I keep him like this? I've heard the teacup human line before, but it's never been this literal."

The vampire looked at Scott, who was seated in her hand with his head in his hands. "I suppose you could get a little cage with a wheel so he could exercise and a Barbie to talk to."

He scowled at Dick and made a rude gesture.

Lexi straightened on the bed. "Oh, my God, that's so *cute*. Did you see? He flipped you a teeny-weeny bird."

Dick chuckled, then held up the golden poker chip "Tadaaa!" He threw it on the bed.

She gave him a thumbs-up and focused on her friend again. "Now, Scott. We need to talk. It's about breasts. These are breasts, see?" She held him at breast height. "They are not a reason to lose focus and get yourself killed—or shrunken. Do I have to walk around topless until you get used to them?"

He put his hands over his eyes and shouted, "Put them away. They're really big and it's freaking me out."

The vampire leaned against the wall and raised his hand. "Excuse me. I'm impervious. May I be excused from class?"

Lexi nodded. "Yes, would you mind calling Dolores?"

"Roger that." He nodded and walked away.

She returned her gaze to Scott. "I'd also like to point out that while Dick had his strength and speed—"

"I was walking the dog," he interjected from downstairs.

With a sigh, she continued. "And you had all your powers to hand, I was the dud with no legacy abilities but I was still the kickass bitch. I *am* still the kickass bitch and I will always be in this team." She thought for a moment. "Unless you count my breasts as a superpower. And to be honest, I do lean in that direction."

Gently, she placed Scott on the bed and pulled her vest on.

She glanced at the talisman. "Hey, see if you can use that to regain your regular size."

He crawled across the bed to the chip. When he was almost there, she moved it six inches further away. He stopped and stared daggers at her and she giggled.

The sorcerer reached it and sat on it. He scrunched his eyes closed for a moment, then opened them. "Nope. Are you sure this is the right one?"

Lexi considered the question. "Maybe it's because I'm holding the pouch and I'll be honest, I'm not one hundred percent invested in your request. Try asking for a pitcher of margarita to appear on the dresser."

Scott scowled at her.

She picked him and the talisman up as Dick appeared at the door

He stepped into the room and closed it behind him. When he opened it again, Dolores stood there in her apartment. "You're lucky.

I've been out of cell range and I was about to head out again. I happened to turn back for something when my phone rang."

Lexi raised an eyebrow. "Hmm. That *was* lucky."

Dolores went to the French doors on the opposite side of her room and opened them. "Quickly." She gestured urgently to Dick.

He yanked Lexi's blade from Murder-Fae's brain, picked the corpse up, and ran through the apartment at vamp speed and up the boardwalk. With little compunction, he threw the fae's body into the lake.

Lexi carried Scott to Dolores and looked through to the lake beyond the doors. "I hope no one discovers that body any time soon."

A series of splashes drew their attention and the vampire looked over the edge and grimaced. He hurried to the portal. "Alligators."

Dolores raised her eyebrows. "Really? I've never seen alligators there before." She turned to Scott and tapped his tiny head gently. He outgrew Lexi's hand and she dropped him but before he had the chance to fall, his growth had covered the distance. He stood with an angry look on his face. "Thank you, Dolores." He turned to Lexi and shouted, "Yes, I know you have breasts," before he stormed to the bed and sat with his arms folded to stare straight ahead.

The fae looked from one young person to the other and shook her head. "I won't ask. I need to go before they put the wards up again." Dick stepped out and she pulled the bedroom door closed.

Two seconds later, the vampire opened the door again with a flourish to confirm that Dolores' apartment had vanished, and he bowed dramatically.

Lexi clapped.

Scott put his hand out to Lexi. "Talisman and pouch, please."

He dropped the talisman into the little bag. "A pitcher of margarita," he said acidly.

Dick looked around. "That's disappointing."

The sorcerer put a shielding spell on the items and handed them to Lexi. "No one will be able to track this now. I suppose you want me to get rid of the blood."

She looked at the floor. "If you don't mind."

He stood over the blood with his hands outstretched.

The gong sounded and the blood remained where it was.

Dick raised an eyebrow. "Whoever's messing with the wards must have realized he's not coming back." He wandered out of the room.

Lexi glanced at her friend, then at the floor. "You did offer."

"Fine." Scott stormed into the bathroom and returned with a scrubbing brush and a bucket of hot water. She blocked his path at the door and took them from him. "Go for a swim. You deserve it."

After she'd scrubbed for a few minutes, Dick appeared at the door. "What on earth are you doing?"

"Getting the blood up."

"Stand aside, sister. I'm an expert in all things blood." He took the bucket and brush into the bathroom and returned with the bucket refilled and a bottle of hand wash in his other hand. "This needs cold water." He rolled his sleeves up, squirted the hand wash onto the floor, and scrubbed with the cold water. She went to the bathroom and retrieved a towel. When she started to kneel, he stopped her.

He put his hand on her shoulder. "I've got this. You empty the bucket."

Lexi tipped the bucket to empty the contents down the sink, refilled it, and squirted bleach in.

I miss the zombie twins.

She paused at the sound of singing and returned to the room to find Dick standing barefoot on the towel while he shimmied across the floor.

"Blame it on the Bossa Nova." He looked up. "Oh, Lexi. I learned this technique from Jesús. He's a little genius."

Scott shouted, "Lexi, Dick," from downstairs as they finished. She went into the bathroom and squashed the towel, pink with blood, into the bleach.

They headed downstairs to where the sorcerer stood in the hallway with a pitcher of margarita. "Look at what I won at the pool bar."

Lexi pushed her plate away. "If I die today, it'll be with a happy stomach." She looked at Scott who appeared to be seated in front of an elephant graveyard. Huge, stripped white bones piled on the two plates he'd cleared in Jessie Rae's.

He put his hands on his stomach. "It's with great sadness I have to announce that as much as I'd like to, I cannot possibly manage a third plate."

Dick raised an eyebrow. "I'm sure the local cattle wranglers were holding their breath."

She grinned and passed the talisman to Albin. "What will you do with this?"

The man held the little pouch in his hand. "I can't thank you all enough for this. I can't put it on display yet. It will probably simply get stolen again."

Scott put his hand out. "Keep it somewhere safe. It's shielded so they shouldn't be able to find it, even with the wards down. If you decide it's too hot to handle, call Dolores. I'm sure she'll be able to put it somewhere safe."

Albin shook his hand. "I'm about to see Dolores anyway. She has asked me to help her with something. Then, I'll work out where to keep it."

Lexi stood and, although she intended to shake his hand, she somehow hugged him instead. He kissed her cheek and she sat again, a little dazed.

She smirked when Dick stumbled awkwardly to his feet.

The historian turned to him, took his face in his hands, and kissed him for a full minute.

Unable to help herself, she leaned forward and stared, her elbows on the table and her face in her hands. "I wish I was Dick's lips." She grimaced. "Did I say that out loud?"

Albin broke away. "And I'll see *you* when you're next in town."

The vampire swayed on his feet. "I'm not leaving. I live here now."

"Call me." Albin chuckled and turned and walked away.

Dick took his cell phone out and fumbled with it.

Lexi leaned across and took it out of his hands. "Not now. Show some restraint. Call him tomorrow."

He frowned. "Are you sure? I mean, have you ever actually dated anyone."

She stared at him. *I am a calm pool of tranquility.*

"Yes, you're right." He put both palms on the table. "I'll play it cool."

To refocus herself, she checked on Marcel who was asleep under the table with his paws around a stripped beef bone that was roughly the same length as his body. She took the cell phone out of the satchel she was now forced to carry and snapped a picture of him to send to her boss. "I'm texting Dolores. Any messages?"

Dick straightened. "Oh, yes. Tell her "Bond." She'll know what it means."

Lexi had forgotten about his new name. "Bond, as in James?"

"Precisely." He smiled and she thought he looked quite smug.

She shrugged. "Okay." She began to tap the screen.

A few minutes later, her phone chirped. "She says our flights are booked for twelve pm tomorrow. Tickets and extra documentation will be in a sealed envelope at the information desk."

The vampire smiled. "Perfect."

Lexi refused to allow an evil little giggle to escape her lips.

Scott straightened abruptly. "Something's wrong."

They focused on him and waited as he rifled through his bag.

He withdrew a sheet of paper and stared at it.

She waited a whole two seconds before she asked, "What's that?"

Dick peered around the sheet. "Is that a fax? How retro."

"Yes. I asked Dolores to put the machine into my dimensional pocket. It's a message from Bryan."

Lexi took it and read it aloud. "To: Scott, From: Bryan, Subject: Urgent. Message Reads: Caleb has returned, I think—" She flipped it but it was blank on the other side. "Where's the rest of it?"

Scott had his cell in his hand again. "I'm messaging Dolores. We need to get to New Orleans. It'll take too long to do it in jumps."

Jesús stood on the sidewalk, waiting for them. They pulled up and Dick passed the sleeping puppy to him before they accelerated away.

Twenty minutes later, they were at the diner outside the city and Dolores was waiting for them. "I don't have long. It's taken me this long to secure a meeting with the elders."

They hurried through the fae door and stopped outside Chief Rand's house.

She looked at her watch. "I'll be back in a minute."

"I'll look around back and see if I can peek through any windows." Dick stepped to the side of the house and made his way toward the rear.

Scott turned to Lexi. "Can you stand out of view of the door? Your face might complicate things."

Lexi nodded when she realized he might be right. She stood at the side of the house while he knocked on the door.

It opened and a man spoke. "What do you want?" He was abrupt and sounded hostile.

The sorcerer responded in his best polite tone. "May I speak to Bryan, please?"

"Bryan? There's no Bryan here. You have the wrong house. Get out of here." The door slammed.

He tried knocking again.

The door flew open and the chief shouted in his face. "What?"

"I'm sorry. You might remember me—I was helping Alicia with her car."

"I told you, you have the wrong place. I don't know any Alicia. I'm busy and I have to get this done. Leave me alone." The door slammed again.

Scott wandered to where she waited at the corner of the house. "Well, that was weird. Caleb must have counseled him to forget Alicia and Bryan. I'd say it looks like he doesn't plan for either of them to return. The chief was really angry."

Lexi turned to him, her expression grim. "As angry as Mayor Todd was when Caleb sent him to burn Dick's house down?"

They stared at each other.

Dick appeared. "The kitchen window was open. The house stinks of gasoline and a woman is simply sitting there, staring into space."

"Shit!" the two friends said in unison.

"Get him out of there." She turned to Dick. "The wife."

Scott disappeared and a moment later, a loud whomp made her freeze in concern.

Dick vanished in the next moment.

Dolores's door arrived at the end of the yard a second before Scott appeared with Chief Rand unconscious in his arms.

Lexi looked around as the front window exploded. "Was Bryan in there? And where's Dick?"

The sorcerer disappeared again and returned with Mrs. Rand and Dick. Without a word, he was gone again.

Dick spun and hurriedly extinguished a few flames on his jacket. "I thought I was a goner. I tried to get her out, but she put some mage whammy on me and I couldn't move."

A few seconds later, Scott returned. He coughed and shook his head. "He's not there."

They stared at the blazing house for a moment before Dolores called her door. "We need to get them out of here." She frowned. "Where to?"

Lexi thought for a moment. "Joseph's bar."

Scott lifted the chief in his arms and Dick threw the man's wife over his shoulder. The fae put her hand on Scott for directions as she called the door. They stepped through into the courtyard at Joseph's bar.

He walked out to them. "Is that the chief of police?"

"Hello again, old friend." Dick put the chief's wife on a table. "It is."

The sorcerer laid Kevin on the next table and stood with his hand on their heads. "I've counseled both of them. They shouldn't remember anything, but they may still have the compulsion to kill themselves. I don't know enough about the magic that caused this."

Lexi turned to Joseph. "I'm sorry to dump this on you. Bryan and Alicia have been taken."

The man nodded. "Go. We've got these two." He looked at the unconscious form of Chief Rand. "The War of the Blood has begun."

She stared at him, both confused and alarmed. His words resonated in a way she couldn't quite grasp.

Dolores turned to her and opened her fae door. "I need to return to the Hall of the Elders. You get to Vegas and prepare for your flight. I'll try to keep you updated."

Lexi faced her. "What aren't you telling us? Why do you keep swapping how you travel? And why are we flying tomorrow?"

The fae sighed. "I think I'm being tracked by the Elders. Something's not right."

Dick was at her side in a moment. "What can I do? Do you want me to stay with you?"

She shook her head. "You can't come to fae."

The vampire rolled his eyes. "Bigots." He looked around. "Scott, then. Or what about Joseph? You'd go, wouldn't you Joseph?"

Dolores put her hands onto his chest. "I'm fine. Calm down. You have to go. Look after each other."

They returned through the door and walked to the car. As Lexi climbed into the passenger seat, she considered everything that had happened. "What's changed?"

Dick glanced at her but didn't respond. He and Scott waited.

"Caleb's known the chief for years—and presumably, Bryan and Alicia." She looked at the two of them. "Why is he burning his bridges now?"

The sorcerer looked out of the window as the car began to move. "It feels like something is coming."

At the condos, they reached the door as Jesús stepped out to walk Marcel. Dick took the lead from him. "Don't worry about that. I'll walk him."

He released it and watched as Dick strode along the sidewalk with Marcel bounding along beside him. "He's changed."

The comment so eerily echoed her question in the car that she did a double-take. "How so?"

"For a man with many years to fill. He seemed so empty before.

He's always been kind to others." Jesús chuckled. "In his own way. But I think now, he's starting to be kind to himself."

Lexi looked at the young Mexican man. "Goodnight, Jesús."

She thought about what he had said. There was no denying it. Dick was a complicated man. She suddenly winced as she remembered the childish trick she was playing on him and realized she had begun to regret it.

I hope he's feeling kind tomorrow.

CHAPTER SIXTY-SIX

E rika stood in line at her local convenience store.

The woman ahead of her was flustered. She turned and apologized for about the ninth time. "I'm so sorry. I know my wallet is here somewhere."

She smiled kindly. "There's no need to hurry, I'm fine."

As she watched, more of the woman's hair slipped out of the knot on her head and made her appear bedraggled. It was clear her head wasn't in the game. She had started by asking for a scratch card, then put her groceries through, then asked for a scratch card again.

"Here it is." The woman yanked her purse out and paid for her groceries. She put her change away, then looked at the two tickets. "Oh. I didn't mean to buy two." She turned to Erika. "I'm sorry I kept you waiting. Here." She thrust one of the tickets into her hand. "Good luck."

The shopper moved to the end of the counter to start scratching her card.

Erika paid for her sandwich and moved to the end of the counter. "Any luck?"

She shrugged. "Not today. How about you?"

It made sense that she might as well scratch the card before she left

531

the store. If she was lucky enough to win ten dollars, she'd have to come back to cash it in.

When she felt in her pocket for a coin, the woman handed her what appeared to be a poker chip.

With a smile, she took it. "Who should I thank if I win a million?"

"I'm Dolores," the woman responded with a smile.

Erika scratched the silver coating from the boxes. Ten dollars, four million dollars, two dollars, ten dollars, four million dollars, two dollars, five dollars, one dollar. She looked at the last box. She could win ten dollars, but most likely two dollars, if anything. After an inward shrug, she scratched.

"Erika? Are you all right?" Dolores stared at her. She held her hand out and the girl wondered if she wanted the ticket back.

Instead, the woman plucked the chip from her fingers. "It's my lucky chip."

"Am I— Sorry, what?" *Did I tell her my name? I guess I must have.* She looked at the card and counted, then counted again. Finally, she checked the instructions. It was the same figure three times. Four million dollars, three times.

When she looked up, Dolores had gone. After a moment, she refocused on the ticket, then stuffed it into her bra. She left her lunch on the counter. While she loved her job and loved the people at Emmersley, she decided not to work today.

CHAPTER SIXTY-SEVEN

Lexi turned away from the information desk with a large envelope in her hand.

Scott looked at the time. "We'll have to run to make this flight." He stared at Dick.

The vampire rolled his eyes. "I said sorry."

"Seriously, dude. How could you forget you had a dog?"

"He's my first dog ever. I didn't know I couldn't pop him under my arm and bring him along. I'm sure I've seen the Kardashians do it."

"The guy said it depends on the airline," she explained. "Some allow pets in the cabin. Unfortunately, we're traveling with an airline that wants to throw dogs into the cargo hold."

He was outraged. "Over my dead body."

She snorted. "So much is wrong with what you said."

Scott shook his head. "Poor Jesús was halfway back to Palm Springs when you called him to collect Marcel. What did he say when you called the second time and said not to bother?"

Dick grimaced. "He'd already arrived at the condo. I told him to stay there and drive back the next day. Do you think Marcel's okay?"

They walked quickly as they spoke. "He's fine. He was asleep on the couch in front of the tv last time I checked."

Lexi raised an eyebrow. "It sounds like you've expanded your dimensional pocket."

"I put Marcel's basket in there and stuff to keep him amused. Dolores put a few things in there for me this morning."

They approached the check-in desk, which had two lines. One had a long line of customers and the other was empty with a *Business and First-Class* sign.

"Well, this is me. See you at the other end." Dick walked ahead and down the left side to the counter.

Scott turned around, "Where's he going?"

She rolled her eyes. "He booked himself into first class."

"I suppose if you can afford it." He shrugged.

Lexi folded her arms and looked at him. "Would you do it?"

He appeared to give the question serious thought before responding. "No. Not if my companions couldn't afford it."

"Exactly." She shook her head. "Keep watching. This will be fun." *I hope.*

"Oh no." He looked sideways at her, his expression horrified. "What have you done?"

Dick removed his passport and boarding pass from the envelope and handed them over. The woman on the check-in desk gazed at the passport, then showed it to her colleague who glanced at him. Her lip twitched.

The vampire stiffened a little and adjusted his shoulders. He was obviously uncomfortable.

"Thank you, Mr. Pick. Have a nice flight."

"Mist— Thank you." He took the documents and stepped away from the desk. His face unamused, he opened the passport and flicked his gaze to Lexi before he strode through the gate.

She guffawed.

Scott gaped. "Mr. Pick?"

A smirk settled on her face as she waited.

Her companion's jaw dropped. "Oh, my God! Dick Pick—you changed his name to *dick pic?*"

They moved forward in the line while she almost cried with laughter. "I needed that."

He frowned, slid his passport out of his envelope, and paused nervously before he checked it. "Shaun Green. That seems normal." He exhaled sharply with relief.

Lexi checked hers and showed it to him. "Lena Hearne."

They boarded the plane, where an unhappy cabin crew waited for them. They apologized and moved to their seats.

Scott grinned as they hurried through the aircraft. "On the bright side, everyone's already seated so we don't need to wait to get to our seats."

"Yes, but look—they also hate us because they should have taken off ten minutes ago."

He looked at the faces of the people they passed. "Oops."

A young uniformed man stood at their seats to help stow their gear. "You're lucky you were traveling with a first-class passenger. Otherwise, they would have simply left."

They sat hastily and buckled in.

The sorcerer looked out of the window and then at the screen in front of him and pressed a few buttons.

Lexi stared at him. "Can you calm down?"

He grinned. "I've never been on a plane before."

She nodded. The excitement was one she could identify with as she'd only been on a plane once, just before she met him.

"I need to check on Marcel." Scott closed his eyes.

Idly, she wondered if Marcel was in his dimensional pocket peeing on the chihuahuas. She had a thought and poked her companion. His eyes flew open. "Don't let him anywhere near my swords or knives. If he loses an eye, Dick will probably try to kill us."

He nodded and closed his eyes again.

The cabin crew completed their safety routine and the plane taxied to the runway and took off.

Scott had seemed to be in a trance but the moment the seatbelt light went off, he bolted out of his seat. "I need to go to the bathroom."

They walked to the back of the plane and Lexi stood outside the bathroom. At a sudden bark, one of the cabin crew looked suspiciously at the door. After two more barks, she hurried away.

Lexi kicked the door. "Keep the noise down in there."

When Scott emerged two minutes later, three crew members waited. They looked into the cubicle as he left.

"Is there a problem?" he asked.

One of the women was still suspicious. "What was that barking sound?"

He smiled broadly at her. "Oh, the alarm on my phone went off. It sounds like a dog barking. It's hilarious isn't it?"

She gave him a withering look and marched away.

Lexi slid into the cubicle. "You'd better have cleaned up if you had a dog peeing in here."

One of the crew laughed and she smiled before she locked the door. The smile dropped from her face and she began to examine the seat.

When she returned to their seats, Scott had settled into the window seat again. "Did you manage to get him to go?"

"Yes. But I had to conjure a little patch of grass. He was a very good boy but he's lonely in there, so I'll have to sneak off for a while. Can I have the chicken and a bottle of water when they come to take orders?" He waited for her to nod, buckled in, and closed his eyes.

A few minutes later, the phone under her screen rang. She picked it up. "Hello?"

"That wasn't very funny," Dick said.

"Really? And Mary-Jane is?"

"Oh. You heard that." He coughed. "How's Marcel?"

"He's okay. Scott took him to the bathroom and no, don't ask. He's gone in with him now. They're probably playing fetch. What about you? Are you stretched out and drinking champagne?"

"As a matter of fact—" The vampire sounded brighter.

Lexi scowled and hung up.

Two flights and seven hours later, they arrived at Portland airport in Maine and met in baggage claim.

Dick's case had been the first one through and the others had only carry-on luggage, so they headed out quickly.

She looked at his suitcase. "At least you're not traveling with that ridiculous trunk."

"Of course I am. Scott's carrying it." He turned to the sorcerer. "How's my baby?"

"Snoozing. I gave him the chicken from my meal on the flight."

When they stopped at the first gas station, Scott took Marcel out of his dimensional pocket.

Dick opened his arms and the dog leapt into them. "The poor little guy looks traumatized."

"You know how animals usually travel," Lexi muttered. "He had it good."

After the puppy's walk, they climbed into the car.

She stretched on the back seat. "Has Dolores sent you any further information about this facility?"

Scott turned in his seat. "Only the location. All we know is it's called Emmersley House and Caleb said it's some kind of spa."

"Emmersley House. That still sounds so familiar. Perhaps it's a world-class spa—that would explain why I've heard of it. I could use a good massage."

"Dolores will text us our cover stories," the sorcerer continued. "She's already told me I'll work as a physiotherapist."

Lexi thought about that. "Maybe we should stop somewhere for dinner and go over the details before we get there."

Dick swerved the car. "Nope. That's a no. You're not to even look at it. We won't go in as staff members. I absolutely will not give foot massages to people with questionable hygiene. We'll go in as guests and that's the end of it. Scott, I'll buy you a back, sack, and crack. And Lexi, I'll buy you a facial." He looked sideways at her. "For both your faces."

Scott looked from one to the other. "We can still stop for dinner, though, right?"

They drove slowly through the town and drew into the parking lot of a bar called The Red Lion, which was styled on an English pub. The building was white with black beams, a nod to the British Tudor style. It was the only establishment they could see on the main street that appeared to still be open and serving food. They entered and the only other customers they could see were several elderly people seated together at a table. The locals stopped speaking and looked at them suspiciously before they returned to their drinks.

Lexi chose a table at the back and they sat and took the menus from the center of the table. She ran her fingers down the options. "I don't even recognize half of this stuff."

Dick raised an eyebrow. "It's British-themed so I assume this is British food." He glanced at the options. "Good heavens. They have faggots on the menu." He leaned back, folded his arms, and stared at her.

She looked up. "What?"

"I'm waiting for you to tell me to run for my life."

"Don't be silly." She shook her head.

He smirked at her thinly veiled disappointment.

Scott glanced at the vampire between picking condiments up and studying them. "Have you ever been to England? The real one?"

"Yes, a few times. I entertained the troops during the war. Bing and Bob went to the South Pacific and I went to South Birmingham. I've been a few times post-life too, but I've always flown cargo in a crate. You think standard-class is bad. At least you can watch movies and drink bourbon."

Lexi felt a twinge of guilt for the trick she'd played on him and for the way she'd judged him for traveling first class.

The sorcerer tapped her arm with the menu. "Do you know what you'll have?"

She glanced at the menu again. "I think they've taken this English-themed food a little too far. I'll play it safe…chicken pie maybe."

The waitress came to the table.

Scott looked up enthusiastically. "I'll have faggots, chips, and mushy peas, please."

Dick looked at Lexi. "The gauntlet has been thrown down."

She looked at the menu again.

The vampire took the opportunity to place his order. "I'll have two double bourbons, no ice."

"I'll have…" She lifted her head. "Toad in the hole with bubble and squeak." She placed her menu down like a winning poker hand. She and her friend looked at each other, neither sure who had won.

The waitress didn't look at all fazed by their strange requests.

After she had left, Dick looked at them. "Do either of you know what to expect on your plates?"

Scott grinned. "Not a clue."

Lexi shrugged.

The drinks arrived. Dick took one bourbon and tipped it into the other.

One of the people at the other table stood. He looked the worse for wear and stumbled around chairs and tables as he headed toward the *Bathroom* sign.

When the food arrived, they looked doubtfully at their plates, then swapped.

They had finished eating when the door banged open. The waitress had been setting cutlery out on the tables and jumped with fright.

A heavy-set, angry-looking woman with a silver whistle on a chain around her neck entered and looked around the room. The people at the other table immediately fell silent.

She delivered a stare at the elderly people, so frosty that it made Lexi uncomfortable. "I might have known," the woman snapped.

The two ladies at the table slumped and groaned. The man gave the angry newcomer a drunken wave. "Hi, Nila. Come and have a drink." He slapped his knees as though offering her a place on his lap.

"If I don't see you in the back of my car in ten seconds—" She spoke coldly and gritted her teeth.

"You'll what?" asked the drunken man. "Y'old sourpuss."

The woman glanced at the waitress but didn't seem to notice the others at the table at the back of the room. "We'll talk about that later."

Lexi was shocked by the menace in her voice.

The two ladies stood immediately, although it seemed to be a struggle. One of them negotiated a somewhat shaky path to the door with two walking sticks and the other shuffled along behind her. The man stood and finished his drink. She suspected he was being deliberately slow. He joined the others at the door and the three elderly patrons filed out in silence. As they exited, the woman took her whistle and blew hard, and the lady with the sticks wobbled in fright.

Instinctively, she grasped Scott's hand. They didn't have the link anymore but she knew him well enough to know that he was about to jump to his feet. The door closed. His face was outraged.

Dick shook his head. "Well, she's a piece of work."

The waitress who had stood nearby returned to collect their plates. "She scares the crap out of me. What a dragon."

The vampire smiled. "I think that comparison might be unfair to dragons."

She giggled and blushed under the gaze of his topaz eyes.

Lexi made a mental eye-roll. *What is it with him and waitresses?*

The bathroom door opened and the man who had gone in there about a half-hour earlier stumbled out. He looked around the room when he realized his friends had left. He wove to the waitress. "Ahh, feck it. I fell asleep, Gina, and they abandoned me."

The old man's musical Irish accent was appealing.

Gina smiled at the old man. "You dodged a bullet there, Patrick. Nurse Ratched turned up."

He sighed. "Jeez, I'd best start walking then. Here's hoping my hip doesn't fail me before I get there."

The girl patted him on the shoulder. "I'd give you a lift to Emmersley but I have another two hours here."

Dick turned in his seat. "If it's Emmersley House you're going to, we're about to head there if you'd like a ride."

The man's face became guarded. "And who might you be?"

"We're weary travelers about to check in there." The vampire held his drink up encouragingly.

Patrick chuffed a laugh. "I can guarantee that you're nowhere near as weary as you'd need to be to get into there."

Dick pushed the fourth chair at the table out. "Would you like to join us for a drink? Patrick, is it?"

"Well, if you'll give me a lift, it would be rude not to." The man sat and proffered his hand. When he looked at him, his brow creased. "You look mighty familiar."

The vampire's face brightened immediately. "Well—"

Lexi kicked him under the table.

He shrugged and gave a tight-lipped smile. "I've been told I have one of those faces."

The newcomer leaned forward and looked at each of them. "So what will you be doing at Spandau prison?"

Lexi fixed him with a confused look. "Span what?"

"Kids!" The old man rolled his eyes.

"Spandau was a German prison," Dick explained. "It was famous for housing Nazi war criminals."

Patrick grinned. "An educated man. I like you already."

Scott mumbled, "This place sounds less and less like a spa."

The vampire turned to him with a disgruntled look on his face. "It might be time for you to check that message from Dolores."

After a quick nod, he scrolled through his phone, then held it out so Lexi could read the message with him. She sighed and deflated. "It's not a spa. It's a residential care facility for elderly and convalescing supernaturals."

Dick slapped his palm to his forehead. "Now I know why I recognize the name." His shoulders slumped.

Scott's jaw dropped. "No. No, it's a spa. Caleb said it's a spa."

She raised an eyebrow. "I believe his exact words were 'a kind of spa.'"

"But a residential home isn't any kind of spa." He looked utterly despondent. "Not even a little."

Patrick looked at them all in turn, his eyes narrowed. "Now that we've ascertained that you're not spa guests, who are you?"

The vampire sighed. "I don't even know what my cover is and it's already blown."

Lexi kicked him again.

He brushed his pant leg with his hand. "Would you please stop kicking me? This is a thousand-dollar suit."

The old man's eyes widened. "Cover? You're investigators? I'm confused. When that guy from Kindred visited, he said there was nothing to investigate and told Maisie to stop wasting your time."

Scott exchanged a look with her, then turned to Patrick. "We're not Kindred. I'm Shaun, this is Lena and Richard. Can you tell us why you called Kindred?"

He gestured to the waitress. "Gina, could we have a last round before we go—and one for yourself."

His voice lowered. "It was my friend Maisie who reported that two of our friends had disappeared. We were worried about reporting it to Kindred because they own the place now. But who else do we turn to? Something's not right there. Maisie said she could trust the Kindred team from her local town, so she made the call. Then she went missing too."

"When did the disappearances start?" Lexi asked.

"A month ago. The last one was…" His voice caught. "Maisie, a few days ago."

Scott took his cell phone out and tapped quickly. "And how many?"

"Three residents. But you're not here because of that?"

Lexi shook her head. "It's likely that your disappearances are connected to our investigation, though. Did they start happening after the change in ownership?"

Patrick nodded excitedly. 'Yes. About a month after. We had great hopes when we heard about the buy-out. The place has needed a few repairs for a while. Then we learned it was Kindred who took over, sticking their big nose in where it's not wanted again."

Scott paused his finger over his screen. "Can you give me details? What exactly happened?"

"A couple of my friends disappeared in the night—a week apart with no notice and no goodbyes. Just gone. Nurse Ratched—that's Nila, who you had the pleasure of seeing this evening—said they'd moved back with their families but neither of them had any family to speak of. Maisie was much more vocal about it than I was. She suddenly went to live with her son in Australia a few days ago but I know she doesn't have a son in Australia. She doesn't even have a son, period. I haven't said a word about it since I'm terrified. We all are."

They stopped speaking while Gina put the drinks on the table. Lexi took a sip of hers and decided to risk a question specific to their case. "Have they brought any new residents in over the last day or so?"

He paused, clearly thinking. "None that I'm aware of."

"And how about construction work?" Dick asked. "Is anything going on?"

Patrick shook his head. "But it's a bloody big building with large land around it."

"Have you seen any Kindred other than your local unit?" The last thing she wanted was to run into Caleb before she had her legacy abilities back.

"They've visited a few times, but I haven't seen any sign in the last few days. They might not be staying in the main house. There are a couple of lodges on the grounds."

She leaned forward. "I assume that while we carry out our investigation, we can rely upon your discretion, Patrick."

He responded with all sincerity, "Of course. But can I ask—who are you? I've never heard of Kindred being investigated by anyone. In my experience, they act with impunity and we simply suck it up."

Lexi and Scott flicked a glance at each other. She felt ashamed and she guessed he did too.

"I'm a sorcerer—"

"Let's get up to the house," she interrupted hastily. "It's getting late." She didn't want to hear how Scott would describe her—or worse, if he stumbled over his words or was unsure. If he said she was a legacy, she'd feel like a fraud, and God forbid he'd introduce her as a normal human. How humiliating. She shuddered inwardly.

Soon, I'll find Alicia and get my abilities back and I'll never complain again that I'm a dud.

Lexi wondered if getting her abilities back meant never seeing her sister after that. She shook the thought away. One problem at a time was more than enough to deal with.

CHAPTER SIXTY-EIGHT

The car eased between large iron gates and wound slowly around a tree-lined drive to the house. It was late and the only sound was the crunch of the tires on gravel. Scott gazed out of the window. "This place is huge."

Patrick nodded. "It sure is."

They parked at the side of the main building and walked toward the entrance.

The old man smiled. "Now, if you don't mind distracting young Stuart on the night desk for me, I'll sneak past."

Lexi chuckled. "You're a rascal. I'll have to watch you."

She entered through large glass doors with Scott and Dick. A small desk was situated on the side of the lobby and a young man was seated behind it. He tried to balance a pen on his forehead. When he noticed them, he fumbled to right himself and opened his mouth to speak, but his attention was drawn down the hallway. "Oh no. Not again."

When the clerk's attention was diverted, Lexi glanced over her shoulder to where Patrick darted from the door to duck behind the stair rail and start climbing.

Satisfied, she looked in the same direction as the clerk. A door at the end of the hallway burst open and an elderly, naked gentleman shuffled through, swinging a pair of underpants. It was the drunken man from the pub and he was singing. "Look for the bare necessities—"

Lexi looked down and smirked. "I think I found them."

The old man let the underpants fly and headed through the front door.

The clerk glanced at Lexi, then looked at Scott. "We cool?"

The sorcerer cleared his throat without looking at her. "Yeah, we're cool."

She stood in silence while he placed his pen down and stood. Her shoulders drooped. "We cool" was something supes said in front of humans to ascertain whether or not it was safe to reveal their supernatural nature in their presence.

Belatedly, she wondered if she should have tackled the old guy but a man in white and holding a robe pushed through the door and raced after him. He was followed a moment later by another man, also in white, who ran through the door, saw the three of them, and slowed to a walk.

The clerk pointed at the door. "They're fine. Just go."

He shifted—or, rather, his bottom half shifted. The man was a satyr and now raced away on his goat legs. He picked up speed and continued through the front door.

When the clerk stepped out from behind the desk to retrieve the underpants—now hanging from a large potted plant—it was evident that he too was a satyr.

Dick muttered, "I'm remembering more and more of the things I've heard about this place."

Lexi glanced at Scott, who picked up a brochure titled *Emmersley House Residential Care Home, Senior Living and Rehabilitation.* He flicked a final glance at the instructions from Dolores on his cell.

The clerk stepped behind the desk and returned his attention to the three of them. He smiled as though they'd only now walked through the door and nothing whatsoever had happened. "Hi, I'm Stuart. How can I help you this evening?" His gaze darted toward the door the absconding naked man had fled through and returned to the three of them.

Scott took the lead. "I'm Shaun Green and this is Lena Hearne. We're here with Mr. Richard Pick. You should be expecting us?"

"Hmm?" Dick glanced up from the brochures. He stepped to Lexi and asked with his voice lowered, "What exactly is our cover?"

She shushed him.

"Yes. Mr. Pick. I'm afraid we were only notified of your transfer earlier today. We're still organizing your room downstairs." He continued to read the notes, then looked at Scott. "Are you certain he's no longer a risk to himself or others?"

The vampire's whispers into her ear became more insistent. "What have you done now?"

"This is all Dolores," she responded quietly but impatiently. "I haven't a clue. You'll have to ask Scott when he's done." She glanced up the stairs to where Patrick lingered to listen to the conversation.

"Absolutely. He's only here to recuperate and is no longer delusional." Scott smiled at the guy, turned his smile to Dick, and tried to shrug discreetly.

At the word "delusional," the vampire's eye began to twitch.

Stuart looked from Scott to Lexi and passed two room keys to the sorcerer. "Your two rooms are ready. You'll be in the old servants' quarters on the top floor. The rooms there are quite small so I hope they're okay for you. Most of us are local so we only use a couple of the overnight rooms here for standby shifts. The top floor hardly gets used at all, so you'll have it almost to yourselves. It's unusual for a resident's personal staff to stay here, though. He must have some pull."

Dick smiled. "Oh, I couldn't survive without Shaun and Lena. You know, you could always give me a room upstairs too."

Scott turned and stared hard at him before he smiled at Stuart. "He's kidding."

The clerk looked dubious. "Are you sure he's cured?"

The sorcerer nodded confidently. "That's what they tell me." He turned to the vampire. "You don't think you can walk in the sun anymore, do you, Richard?"

Dick's jaw worked as he fought back the instinctive response. "The malaise has left me. I only need a little rest."

Lexi looked at Stuart, who studied the new patient with discomfort.

Stuart narrowed his eyes. "He's…erm, lowered his pointy parts."

She swung to face the vampire, who stared dead ahead with his fangs bared. Her first instinct was to pull her foot back to kick him but she stopped when he turned and stared at her. Dick could look quite dangerous sometimes and this was one of those times.

"He hasn't eaten," Scott said quickly as the vampire retracted his teeth.

The clerk raised an eyebrow. "There's a refrigerator in his room." He took two bracelets from a box, wrote on one, and passed it to Scott. "Put this on him, please. What are you—a mage?"

"No. I am a sorcerer, but I'm in Mr. Pick's employment, not Kindred."

He held the second wristband out. "You need to wear one too."

Scott passed the first band to Lexi, who held it out and stared at Dick. After a few moments, he sighed and extended his arm to allow her to close it with a click.

Lexi waited, then asked. "What about me?"

Stuart laughed. "Normals don't need one."

She blushed furiously.

Her thoughts clicked into focus after a second and she wondered why Scott would need to wear one. She opened her mouth to ask as he clicked the second bracelet onto himself.

Too late.

Stuart passed papers to him for signature. "What do you two do then?"

The sorcerer handed each sheet to the man as he signed it. "I'm Mr. Pick's physiotherapist."

Dick stepped closer to the desk. "Shaun is a gold-star masseur. I would absolutely die without my daily massage."

The front door opened and the two white-coated care assistants—

both had fully shifted and displayed goat legs and horns—entered with the elderly man, who wore the robe.

Stuart called out to one of the men. "Josh?"

The other man tightened his hold on the elderly man. "I've got him. Come on, Albert. If you're good, I'll get you some candy."

"I only went out to give my candy cane a little air." Albert cackled.

The assistant chuckled and shook his head as he led the elderly man through the lobby.

"Thanks, Raj," Josh called after them and headed to the desk. "Hey, Stuart. What do you need?"

Stuart waited until he was at the counter. "Is Mr. Pick's room ready yet?"

"Yes. We filled the refrigerator minutes before Albert made a run for it."

"He reeks of booze." He lowered his voice but Lexi could hear him quite well.

His colleague grimaced. "Yeah, Nila caught a few of them in a bar again."

Stuart drew in a sharp intake of breath.

The man rolled his eyes and mouthed, "I know."

The man focused on the computer, then looked at Scott. "Oh, you *are* a physiotherapist. Dude, your qualifications are great. What a weird coincidence. We lost our physio today. She called in to say she won the lottery and she's not coming back."

"Wow! That's lucky." The sorcerer's gaze cut to Lexi.

"Don't you try to poach my masseur. I'm very attached to him." Dick stepped forward and linked arms with Scott.

"I wouldn't do that, Mr. Pick," Stuart assured him hastily. "I expect the position will be filled from inside Kindred."

When the vampire wandered away to leaf through brochures, Stuart turned to Scott again. "I've never met an independent sorcerer before. In fact, every one I've ever heard of has either been a Kindred mage or was training to be a Kindred mage."

He shrugged and looked around. "I've never been much of a joiner.

We heard they'd taken over. To be honest, we half expected legacies to be everywhere."

"If they are, I'll turn around and get on the plane again," Dick interjected.

Stuart leaned closer and lowered his voice. "It was really quiet when they first took over but now, they're always visiting—well beyond the regulation weekly visits we've always had. They're a pain." He stood quickly as though he realized he'd said too much. "If you *are* a mage, I guess I'm in trouble now."

Scott smiled. "I've worked for Mr. Pick for several years and I have no intention to jump ship now."

He seemed satisfied. "Right." He looked at Lexi. "And what do you do?"

The sorcerer looked from Stuart to her and back again. "This is Lena she's his…nail technician."

The clerk stared at Lexi and she stared incredulously at Scott.

Dick stepped forward. "She's my donor. I prefer to be discreet on paper."

Stuart raised his eyebrows but nodded his understanding. "I see. You won't need the refrigerator, then."

Dick waved a hand. "Leave the refrigerator. I like a variety and sometimes, Lena's a little…sour."

She flushed and she had to bite back a caustic comment. "Right, let's get our stuff."

They stepped out and walked around the building. Back at the car, she thumped Scott's arm. "Nail technician?"

The vampire laughed and she spun and thumped his arm. "Donor? Really? And would you stop talking about your cover within earshot of strangers? Cover this, cover that. It's just as well you didn't get the name Bond. You're the worst spy in the history of spying."

He smoothed an eyebrow. "Well, after that dick pic stunt you pulled, if I'd thought faster, you'd have been my proctologist."

Scott chuckled as they retrieved their luggage from the car. Dick put Marcel on his lead and he jumped down.

When they returned to the lobby, Stuart looked at the puppy. "I'm sorry, we don't allow pets."

The vampire lifted his dog into his arms. "This isn't a pet. It's my therapy dog."

The clerk looked doubtfully at Marcel, who whined appealingly. "I'm afraid it's up to Nila. Don't get your hopes up, though."

"Stuart, why don't you leave that decision up to me?"

He scrunched his eyes closed for a moment.

Lexi turned to where Nila stood in the doorway with the silver whistle around her neck. The hairs on the back of her neck stood up and she had to force herself not to shudder. She didn't need her legacy abilities to tell her this woman was dangerous.

Nila approached with steady strides and Stuart took a step back. "Sorry, Nila. I was only—"

The woman spoke over him. "You must be Richard." Her voice softened. "I've been expecting you." She extended a hand to Dick.

Stuart's face showed shock at her changed demeanor. Almost instantly, he seemed to remember himself and set his face to neutral.

Lexi noticed immediately there was no "Mr. Pick." This woman considered herself his equal. It seemed at odds with her role as a service provider.

The vampire shook her hand. "Nila. What a pleasure to make your acquaintance. I see you run a tight ship here. Very impressive."

She watched his face. He knew instantly the woman was enamored. The playful twitch of his lip was masterful. There was nothing in his face that betrayed his true thoughts about this horrid woman and he looked, for want of a better word, entranced. She glanced at Nila and found her eyes disconcertingly icy, with pupils like tiny pinpricks. There was something overly shiny about her skin—something unhealthy.

"Is he house-trained?" the woman asked.

Lexi caught a whiff of her breath and had to clench her stomach muscles to stop herself from heaving.

"I'm sorry?" he replied like he'd forgotten there was a world beyond her face. "Oh, Marcel. Yes, most certainly. I run a tight ship myself."

Dick deserves an award for this. He is pure method.

The ghastly woman smiled. "Well, how about I show you and Marcel to your room?"

He followed her along the hallway. She stepped through a doorway and he glanced at Lexi before he continued.

Josh—who had leaned on the counter—straightened. "I'll show you to your rooms."

Stuart held a pen out to Lexi. "You need to sign in." She tried to take it but he tightened his hold on it. She fought a scowl when she saw his grin. He winked at her. "You know what they say—all the girls go satyr sooner or later."

She stared at him until he released the pen, then wrote her fake name in the register. Without a word, she dropped the pen on the counter and turned away.

The two friends climbed the stairs behind Josh. On the fourth floor, they turned down a myriad of hallways.

"Are we expected to find our way out of this place?" Lexi asked.

Their guide shrugged. "I know. Sorry. It'll probably take you a couple of days to find your way around."

Josh showed them to two oddly shaped rooms next to each other. They were small but clean. "These were the servant's rooms at the turn of the century. As you might guess from the circular outer walls, we're in one of the turrets now. You should find it peaceful. No one ever comes up here except to access the laundry closets and clean."

Scott looked out of the window into the darkness. "How old is this building?"

"There's been a structure on this property for hundreds of years. First, it was an old stone tower. That was about four hundred years ago. Over the years, the house replaced that, and new parts have been added by different owners ever since. It's kind of a warren now." He turned to Lexi. "I wonder if you shouldn't be in a room on the basement level with your boss." He laughed. "I know I like to be near the snack machine."

She stared at him and tried to keep her face blank.

These satyrs will be a pain in the ass.

Josh put his hands out in a gesture of surrender. "It was only a thought."

Scott looked at her. "You will not leave me here all alone. It's creepy."

The other man pointed out the small staff kitchen, lounge, and bathroom facilities. After they assured him they didn't need anything else, he left them without a backward glance.

Lexi threw her satchel and overnight bag onto the bed in her room and showered. She headed into the small kitchen and dining area. It didn't appear to see any use at all.

Ten minutes later, Scott wandered in with damp hair and looked around. "I don't like this place."

Dick appeared at the door, also with damp hair. "I am with you one hundred percent."

She scanned the hallway behind him.

The vampire walked into the room and looked relieved. "Don't worry. She left for the evening. I thought I would have to throw her out of my room."

"Her breath." She screwed her face up in disgust. "What is she?"

He shuddered. "I know. Thank God I don't have to breathe. I haven't a clue what she is. I've never come across anything so disconcerting before." He stepped to the door. "I'll go down to Marcel. I think she even spooked him."

Scott ran his fingers through his damp blond curls. "So, what *do* we know?"

Dick spoke from the hallway without turning back. "We know it's not a fucking spa."

CHAPTER SIXTY-NINE

Lexi ran through old abandoned rooms lined with rough stone. She reached a stone spiral stairway and started to climb.

"I sense you are near." The voice was raspy and seemingly everywhere.

The stairs seemed never-ending and the muscles in her legs burned. Someone or something behind her was gaining. She stumbled to the top of the staircase and a door that was locked. The rushing footsteps came closer. She put her hand out and averted her face, not wanting to see what was coming.

A scream made her turn. It was Scott. He stepped back, his face burned where her hand had touched it.

She bolted into a seated position in bed. Her body was slick with sweat and she shivered in the pre-dawn cool of her New England bedroom. She put her hand on her chest and breathed measured breaths in an effort to slow her heart rate before she slid out. Still a little on edge, she crept along the hallway toward the bathroom and past the servants' lounge. Movement caught her eye and she stopped, retraced a couple of steps, and looked in. Dick was seated at the window in the dark.

"When exactly do you sleep?" She yawned.

He turned to face her. "I only need a couple of hours these days, but I'll be in that basement all day. Did you have a nightmare? Your heart is racing like a charging rhino."

Lexi wondered if she should deny it. She hated to appear weak but she nodded. "Do you dream?"

"I used to dream every day that I was either playing tennis with Harv or lying next to him near a swimming pool in the sun. I haven't had that dream for a couple of weeks. I miss it." He sighed. "I would give up every future moment of this life for one last tennis game with Harv." He returned his gaze to the window and the darkness.

She stared into the blackness. "Can you see anything?"

The vampire shrugged. "I can see my reputation will be in tatters after this. Delusional indeed."

"Not *your* reputation. Richard Pick's, and he won't exist after we leave here." She coughed. "That was a stupid trick with the name. But under the circumstances, it might have worked out for the best."

"You could be right. And with regard to your original question, I can see everything but there's not much of interest to see." He settled into silence and she continued to the bathroom.

Outside her room, she hesitated and considered looking in on Scott but heard him snoring. She entered her room and switched the light on to orient herself.

Lexi noticed a strange mark on the bedsheet. She walked to the bed to examine it. On closer inspection, it wasn't a stain as she'd assumed but a burn mark in the shape of a hand. "What the hell?" She sat beside it, her mouth agape. The dream came to her and she placed her hand over the mark. It was a perfect fit. She pulled away quickly, pushed to her feet, and threw the covers off the bed to remake it with the burn tucked in at the bottom. Although she tried, she couldn't return to sleep.

Finally, she rose with the pre-dawn light. Dick had gone, presumably to the basement. She wandered through the hallways of the top floor, opened doors to rooms, and looked out of the windows for signs of construction activity on the grounds. The rooms along one wall had no windows other than a small skylight in the ceiling.

How depressing.

During her exploration through the rooms and hallways, she located a walk-in closet with paint cans, brushes, and dust sheets. She darted to her room, snatched the burned sheet, folded it, and shoved it at the bottom of the pile of dust sheets.

With that disposed of, she took another sheet from a laundry closet and remade the bed. She could hear Scott moving and by the time his head popped around the door, she was seated on her bed, sharpening a shuriken.

She glanced up. "Sleep well?"

He frowned. "I snored, didn't I?"

Lexi stood and glanced at the bed. She turned to face him. "I have no idea. I slept like a log." Lying to him wasn't usually an option but without the empathetic link, it was surprisingly easy.

They headed to the small staff kitchen and made coffee.

She sat at a table while he went through all the cupboards from one end to the other and inexplicably repeated the process.

As he opened and closed the doors, she questioned her actions. *Why didn't I tell Scott about the dream and the mark on my sheet?* She knew why. While she hated to admit it—even to herself—she was afraid of losing him or somehow being unworthy of his friendship.

Scott sniffed. "I've been through every cupboard in here. There isn't a crumb of food but I smell bacon. I suppose we'll have to go downstairs."

Her eyebrows raised. "You sound unusually reticent to get breakfast."

He took her mug. "I don't want to run into that Nila woman. She's really horrible." He shuddered to emphasize his point.

As though he'd invoked her, the penetrating sound of her whistle pierced the air from a lower floor. His eyes closed as he exhaled sharply and this time, it was Lexi who shuddered.

She moved toward the door. "We need to start looking through this facility. If Alicia and Bryan are here, they're probably in danger. The longer this takes, the worse their chances are. I've had a look around this level and there doesn't seem to be much up here."

They walked cautiously down the stairs and as they rounded the staircase into the lobby, Stuart replaced the receiver and looked at them. "Hey, good morning. Would you like the tour?"

Scott grinned. "Will it start with food?"

The clerk laughed. He stuck his head around the door to an office behind him. "Karen, I'm taking Shaun and Lena into the breakfast room. Can you keep an eye on the desk?" He walked ahead of them but was still within earshot.

Lexi turned to Scott. "You and your stomach. I was looking forward to a tour straight away." She stared intently at him.

He smiled. "I thought it might be nice to meet the other residents and find out what goes on here...for Richard."

Stuart glanced at them over his shoulder and they both smiled at him.

Their guide led them into a room that was set up for breakfast with residents seated at tables, eating and talking.

Patrick's voice bellowed across the room. "Well, if it isn't my new pals. Come on. I'll buy you breakfast."

They made their way across the room to his table.

Scott shook his hand. "Good morning. How's your head?"

The old man winced. "It'll be better when I've got this down me." He pointed at a plate filled with sausages, bacon, eggs, and pancakes.

The sorcerer's stomach gurgled.

Stuart grinned. "I'll order breakfast for you, then come back in a half-hour or so. We can do the tour before I finish my shift. Do you want the same breakfast?"

They both nodded enthusiastically and sat at the table.

Patrick looked up. "And here comes Phyllis."

A lady in a purple leisure suit moved slowly through the room with a walker and joined them. Lexi recognized her from the evening before in the bar where she'd used walking sticks.

A young man followed her, holding an enormous plate of sausages, bacon, and eggs. He placed it in front of her as she sat. She nodded her thanks to him and rubbed her hands enthusiastically. "I love breakfast. It's my favorite meal."

The old man grinned. "But what about dinner, Phyllis?"

With absolute sincerity, she replied, "I love dinner. It's my favorite meal."

He passed the pepper to her. "This is Shaun and Lena. They dropped me here last night. He's a sorcerer."

The woman didn't look at them. Instead, she muttered. "You're living here now, are you? You only came a couple of days ago. I haven't gnawed on it since then." She waved her arm to reveal an identity bracelet similar to Dick and Scott's.

Scott looked confused. "We arrived last night."

Phyllis scowled. "I mean your other Kindred pals—or brothers and sisters or whatever you call yourselves."

Lexi looked at Patrick to confirm that he wore a band on his wrist too. Her brow wrinkled in puzzlement as she shifted in her seat to look at the other residents. Everyone wore them. It dawned on her that these bracelets—and the one she had fastened onto Dick's wrist—were more substantial than the flimsy hospital bands she'd seen in the past. She glanced at Scott's arm.

Why is he wearing one?

She glanced at him. He gazed pointedly at Patrick's breakfast. She tutted and rolled her eyes.

The old man patted Phyllis's hand. "Calm down. They're nice people."

"Rubbish." She groaned dramatically. "I bet Nila called them in. We'll be in trouble for leaving the grounds last night."

Scott dragged his gaze away from the food and looked at them. "Huh?"

Patrick lowered his voice. "They're secret investigators and are looking into the disappearances. They're undercover."

Lexi dropped her face into her palm.

Dick, so help me!

Her gaze bored into the old man.

He frowned. "Was I not supposed to say that?"

She leaned back when the food arrived and coffee was poured. As soon as the server had left the table, she explained, "We're not with Kindred. We work for a different organization."

Scott leaned closer and looked from Patrick to Phyllis. "What we're doing is dangerous. If it gets back to Kindred, we could be killed. I don't want to have to counsel you."

The woman's eyes narrowed. "I thought you said you weren't Kindred."

"That doesn't mean he doesn't know how to do it," Lexi muttered.

Patrick looked down, chastened. He looked so pathetic that she actually felt bad.

The sorcerer frowned. "I'm sorry to be rude but I don't sense anything at all from you or any of the residents, and I didn't last night in the restaurant either."

"We're all muzzled." The old man waved his bracelet. "These inhibit our supe natures, so we can't sense you and you can't sense us. They come once a week to make sure we haven't messed with them."

"One of you could be a goddamn vampire and we'd never know it," Phyllis added.

"Oh, they have a vamp with them too—a very nice chap for a vamp." To Lexi, Patrick added. "I happened to hear you in the lobby when you signed in last night."

She smirked. "Happened to hear."

Scott looked across the table at the salt. He opened his hand, then frowned. His eyes narrowed as he stared at the little bottle but it remained where it was. "My telekinesis isn't working. It's this." He began to tug at the bracelet.

Phyllis leaned forward and put her hand over his. "I wouldn't do that if I were you. You'll wake a week from now, drooling like a baby and wondering what hit you."

Lexi raised an eyebrow. "I was surprised when you put it on last night without asking why."

He shrugged. "I was so worried they'd know we weren't who we said we were, I wasn't thinking." He looked at it, horrified, but released it. "Why did they do this?"

Patrick tapped his band. "Only the staff are allowed to use their abilities. I don't mind it so much. Phyllis and I both have a touch of the Alzheimers. It's why many of us are here. When shifters get bad with it, we can shift at very inadvisable times. It's for our safety and others. A small price to pay."

The sorcerer looked puzzled. "Don't they let you shift to stretch the kinks out occasionally?"

He shook his head. "Neither of us has shifted for a couple of years. We probably never will again. Eat your food, lad."

"I'm sorry. I didn't know." Scott looked at his plate but ate as though he'd lost his appetite.

Lexi glanced toward the door. "So, what's Nila then? Some kind of demon, Anti-Christ, or what?"

"Aye, you'd think it." Patrick paused and sighed. "No one knows. We think she's a shifter, though."

"Why?" Scott asked,

Phyllis looked toward the closed door as though the woman might walk through it at any moment. She leaned closer and lowered her voice. "Because she's a cow."

The sorcerer snorted.

"So, have you any idea why Kindred has suddenly bought this place?" Lexi asked.

Patrick swallowed his food and glanced around before he spoke. "Emmersley has always been independent, but it's had a fairly civil relationship with Kindred as long as I've been here. Suddenly, though, some deal has been done and Kindred are the new owners. They promised the staff would be able to stay on with no changes, but then Nila turned up with her damn whistle."

Phyllis put her hand on Lexi's. "By all that's holy, I'd like to shove that whistle up—"

"Now, Phyllis," the old man whispered. "Don't get yourself worked up." He smiled at her and continued. "On Friday, almost all the office staff were fired. The only people still here are the kitchen and cleaning staff and a few care assistants. Apparently, they're hiring from within Kindred."

Scott looked up from his screen. "Weren't the staff suspicious that people had disappeared?"

The woman shook her head. "The staff insisted there was nothing suspicious going on after Maisie contacted Kindred. A guy came a week later—not one of the usual ones who check on the bracelets. It was a loud-mouthed, rich-looking man called Caleb Deane. He didn't seem very interested in the disappearances at all. He went into her room and later, she'd completely changed her tune. She said we were wrong and shouldn't make trouble. He'd obviously given her one of those counseling things they do. And I'll tell you something else, that Caleb guy was definitely pals with Nila. They were as thick as thieves." The two residents nodded in mutual agreement.

Lexi and Scott shared a look.

"Is he the one you're investigating?" Patrick asked after a moment.

Lexi nodded once and turned to him. "Then what?"

He sighed. "When we woke up the next morning, Maisie was gone. I thought someone would probably come and wipe our memories, but no one turned up."

Their quiet conversation was interrupted by a lady seated at a nearby table. "Phyllis, I think you've had the hot patootie for long enough, dear. It's time to share."

The other ladies at the table followed the comment with a burst of giggles.

The two young people looked up to see three of them staring adoringly at Scott.

He straightened and grinned. "There's more than enough of me to go around, ladies."

Lexi resumed eating her breakfast.

Patrick shook his head as he looked at the woman who'd called out. "Honestly, you'd think *she* was the dog."

Phyllis looked offended. "Patrick!"

"It was only a joke." He gave her a crooked smile and she tutted.

She wiped her mouth with her napkin. "I'm going for my morning walk."

"Don't forget your frame." He pointed to the walker near the table. "You don't want to get halfway round and have to be rescued again."

The woman gave him a withering stare and struggled to her feet.

Scott was out of his seat and around the table in two seconds to help her to the frame. "Perhaps while I'm here, I could give you physio. I'll catch up with you when we're settled."

Phyllis smiled and patted his arm. "I've had physio, but there's not much hope for these old bones."

"But you haven't had *my* physio." He waved his fingers in a pseudo-magical gesture.

She raised an eyebrow. "I might take you up on that if you can get your muzzle off. Our regular physio, who we've just been told has quit, is a lovely girl but she relied on concoctions which are of no use at all and they stank to high heaven."

Once she'd left, they finished their food and Stuart returned to give them the tour.

As they walked through a hallway to a large sitting room, Scott dangled his bracelet in front of their guide. "Why do I have to wear this? I'm not a resident."

The man looked awkward. "Sorry. It's the rule for all supes who aren't staff members."

They continued through the building while he pointed out fire exits and other safety features. Their tour finally took them into the basement and they paused at the bottom of the stairs. They were in a brightly lit hallway and a painting of a serious-looking man faced them on the wall.

"This is Jonas Maybury. He was the original owner of Emmersley."

"Ahh! The New England Mayburys." Lexi smiled when she was reminded of Betsy.

He pointed to the left. "Mr. Pick's room is along that hallway, room S-Eight. That's sub-level Eight."

They followed him to the right and into a gymnasium with weights and treadmills that didn't look like they saw much use.

Stuart picked a weight up. "You can use the facilities. It's a perk of staying here."

Scott wandered around the room and stopped at a set of doors. He opened them to reveal a darkened room. "What's this?"

The clerk hurried to him. "We're not allowed in there. Health and Safety rules. It used to be the hydrotherapy room, but they didn't have the money to finish the repairs to the tiles in the swimming pool."

Lexi imagined her friend's disappointment at finding a pool he couldn't use, but when he turned, she was surprised to see a look of satisfaction on his face.

He's planning something.

They glanced into the changing rooms at the end of a small hallway. On the way back, Stuart opened an office door and entered. He sorted through a pile of mail he'd carried.

She noticed a list of names on a whiteboard. It indicated that all residents received at least ten minutes of exercise twice a week. Most of them were simply encouraged to move around a little, walk a short distance, or lift a very small weight. It didn't seem very engaging. Studying the chart on the whiteboard, she noted that several names had been wiped away but they had been written there for so long, the board was lightly stained with the names David, Florence, Martin, and Maisie.

The clerk dropped the mail into the tray.

Lexi stepped out of the way to allow him to step out. "Whose office is this?"

He shrugged. "We used to have our own training staff but now, someone comes from an agency once a week. Or did. Kindred canceled that too."

Scott leaned against the wall. "What will you do about your physio leaving?"

Stuart stopped beside him. "I don't know if there's anything we can do. Previously, when Erika went on holiday, we'd get an agency replacement. I'd bet Kindred will want to send their person."

The sorcerer shrugged. "I'd be happy to offer my services while I'm here. If you're interested, that is. If you're not, that's fine too."

"Would your boss be okay about that?"

"What I do while he's asleep all day is up to me. I'm not asking for a job, merely offering to help."

Lexi could see the opportunity interested Stuart. "Do you mean regular physio or enhanced?"

"I could do either," Scott said casually, "but obviously, the magic helps."

The clerk thought for a moment, then looked around before he spoke quietly. 'If you want to do that, it's best if you don't offer."

Scott frowned. "I don't understand."

"I'll make sure Nila sees your credentials. She always wants something for nothing. But if she thinks you want to do it, she'll happily say no and cut off her nose to spite her face."

He shook his head. "Good grief."

"Yeah, welcome to Emmersley." Stuart turned to Lexi. "And if you're qualified at anything, she'll probably try to get some work out of you too."

This wasn't good news for her as she needed to be free to look for Alicia and Bryan. "If I was qualified at something, do you think I'd work as a vampire's mobile buffet?"

The man looked awkwardly at his mail. "I need to finish dropping the rest of this."

He turned to Scott as they followed him through a hallway. "Nila told the residents that she would cover physio for now. I don't expect many would go. They'd rather suffer. If it gets out that you're qualified—" They turned the corner to find all six chairs outside the physio office were taken by ladies.

Lexi smirked. "I think the word is out."

Stuart held a hand up. "Ladies, I'm sorry, but Shaun is only visiting."

The women looked crushed.

Scott grinned. "I don't mind seeing what I can do for now."

The clerk thought about it and turned to the ladies. "Okay, but only this once. Do not breathe a word of this."

He headed upstairs and Lexi made her way to the gym. She looked into the hydrotherapy room but couldn't understand what her friend had seen to put that expression on his face. When she returned to the trainer's office, she looked around the desk, found the key to the filing cabinet in a drawer, opened it, and flipped through the resident files.

She found the file on David. It had *deceased* stamped on the front. "Hmm... No Florence, Maisie, or Martin."

A knock at the door made her jump.

"It's only us." Dick entered and waved Marcel's paw. He walked to the desk and sat opposite her. "We need to get this done and get out of here."

"What's wrong?"

"I'm bored. And look at poor Marcel. He's so sad."

She looked at the puppy, who didn't look sad in the slightest. "I'll take him for a walk shortly. Make sure you don't get caught out here. You're supposed to be asleep." Lexi closed and locked the drawers and stepped out of the room.

The vampire wandered off and she found a back staircase and made her way to the second floor. She crept along the quiet hallway and looked at each door. Most had nameplates but a few didn't. She tried the handle of one with no name assigned. It swung open to reveal a bedroom with a bare mattress and an empty closet. She stepped out, closed the door, and continued her exploration. A little farther along, she passed Phyllis's room and paused at an open doorway. Loud sounds emanated from within where a woman was seated in the chair next to her bed watching tv. Lexi shrugged and continued unnoticed.

The next door had no name—only an X on the nameplate and nothing more. Was it empty or not? Something about the door drew her to it, a warmth that somehow called to her.

Could it be Alicia? Some kind of twin connection?

Her heart thudded as she stepped closer and raised her hand toward the handle.

"What do you think you're doing?" Nila's acerbic voice grated the back of Lexi's neck.

She didn't react although inside, she thought she would have a heart attack. Instead, she turned slowly. "Hi. I'm looking for an empty room."

"You're Lena, Richard's...nail technician." The woman spoke the words like she was saying "blood whore."

"Yes, that's me." She abandoned the door reluctantly, approached Nila, and proffered her hand.

The woman glanced at her hand, then looked at her face. "Why are you looking for an empty room? Is the room you've been provided insufficient?"

"Oh, it's very nice." Lexi lowered her hand, relieved that she wouldn't have to touch the greasy woman. She enthused over the pokey little room on the top floor. "It's a lovely room, but there's no tv up there. The residents are already watching a quiz show downstairs and I usually watch something at this time. I thought an empty room would have an unused tv."

Nila looked at her with her pinprick eyes. "What do you like to watch?"

"I love those vacation home shows. I'm addicted." Lexi grinned as disarmingly as she could.

The woman stared at her like she thought it would make her break.

"The X means 'do not enter.' The previous inhabitant had a bad infection and the room has to be disinfected." She continued to stare, her expression grim and cold.

Lexi made a point of stepping away from the door and glanced at it with a grimace.

Finally, Nila said, "Follow me."

She walked along the hallway behind her unwanted guide and wondered if she might, with her reduced strength, be capable of snapping the horrible woman's neck and hiding her body in a closet. Regrettably, she discarded the idea. It did occur to her that she hadn't recognized her, so she clearly hadn't seen Alicia.

Nila stopped at an open door—the one with the woman inside watching tv. She walked in without knocking and Lexi followed.

"Anne?"

The little lady looked up and seemed positively terrified.

"This is Lena. She also likes those shows you love to watch. Would you mind if she joins you?" To Lexi, she said, "This is Anne Lown."

Anne looked at the girl and smiled. "You're late." She moved onto her bed and gestured to the chair she'd vacated. Lexi sat without a word.

Nila rolled her eyes. "Yes, of course. You would have expected her, wouldn't you?" Her tone was rude and sarcastic, which seemed to indicate that this career probably wasn't a vocation. She turned to Lexi. "Anne's a seer. Or she was when she still had all her marbles. I'll leave you to it." She gave her a smug smile and left.

Her jaw dropped. *What a way to talk about someone right in front of them.*

She turned to Anne, who looked hopefully at her and held a photo album out.

Where in the hell did that spring from?

The woman pointed at a photograph. "This is Leo. He was killed in the war."

Kill me now.

CHAPTER SEVENTY

When she could finally make her escape, Lexi wandered past the gym to the physio room. No more ladies were seated outside but a woman left the treatment room and wandered past her. "He has magic hands, for sure." She giggled.

She knocked on the door frame.

Scott was writing notes. "Hey! Where were you at lunchtime?"

Lexi entered the room and looked around the anatomy charts on the walls. "Not eating. I'm starving. Are you ready?"

They headed to the dining room, ordered Chilli Con Carne, and went to sit with Patrick and Phyllis.

She kept her voice pitched low when she voiced her question. "What do you know about the resident in the room with an X on the nameplate."

Phyllis shook her head. "There's no one in there. Apparently, they're disinfecting the room, but it's been like that for a couple of weeks."

"Have you seen it empty?"

The woman seemed to think for a moment. "Not personally. Nila told us to steer clear of it because they were doing a deep clean. I thought it was strange because there hasn't been anyone in that room since Hilary passed, and that was a good two months before Nila arrived."

Lexi waited until someone had walked past the table before she continued. "Have you seen anyone go in or come out?

They both shook their heads and Patrick added. "But I don't frequent the ladies' level."

Scott leaned in with a conspiratorial eyebrow wiggle. "How do you feel about distracting the staff while we take a look in there tonight."

The man's eyes lit up. "An operation? Sure. But you won't need to do much distracting. We have a nurse in the on-call room and she'll be asleep. Then there are only the night boys. They are satyrs so as soon as Nila leaves, they'll wander off to drink and smoke dope in the greenhouse."

Phyllis and Patrick's food came out and the woman smacked her lips. "I love dinner. It's my favorite meal."

Her friend laughed. "What about breakfast?"

She looked at him. "Why, I love breakfast, Patrick. It's my favorite meal."

Lexi smiled. This was obviously a little mealtime ritual they had. She thought it was cute.

Phyllis glanced away and the smile slid from her face as her gaze froze on something behind Lexi. She knew instantly who it was. More than ever, she missed her enhanced perception and hated that someone nasty like Nila could creep up behind her.

"Mr. Green." It *was* Nila. "I know you think you're here for a holiday but your employer and I both think your time would be better spent contributing to our community. I understand you're a qualified physiotherapist. There's an office you can work from in the basement near the gym. Stuart will remove your inhibitor bracelet and show you to the office bright and early tomorrow morning. Let's see if we can't keep you busy."

Scott frowned. He put his fork on his plate as though the food had soured in his mouth. With an admirable show of resignation, he sighed.

Lexi was relieved to note that Nila didn't seem aware he'd already started work in that office.

"Miss Hearne."

Nuts.

"Anne enjoyed the time you spent with her today. Richard and I would like you to devote your days to providing companionship to the residents."

Richard and I. She made a mental eye-roll.

The two young people both looked at Nila, who smiled. "That should keep you both busy. I have a meeting to attend."

Patrick stared hard at the door swinging closed behind the woman. "Look at her sweeping out like a tour de France."

Scott frowned. "Don't you mean tour de force?"

The old man grinned. "No, I mean she's an old bike." He laughed.

Dinner plates were placed in front of Lexi and Scott.

She looked at the food. "I think I've lost my appetite."

Her friend was already on his third mouthful. He swallowed and looked sideways at her. "Are you kidding? You've been told to visit all the residents. I'd take that as permission to see them in their rooms—and anywhere else you feel like poking your nose."

"I never thought of that." She smiled.

Scott filled his next forkful of food. "You should probably wait a couple of hours until they're in their rooms and go make as many new friends as possible."

Her smile widened into a cheeky grin. "This might work out. Can you do a house call? Apparently, Anne Lown doesn't get out of her room very often."

He nodded. "And is Anne's room by any chance near room X?"

Lexi wiggled her eyebrows. "Maybe."

"As Nila's about to be out of the way at her meeting, I'll find Stuart and see if I can get this band removed tonight. I'll stop by after." He waved his arm with the bracelet on it.

She hurried to Anne's room. The door was slightly ajar and as she approached, a loud shout came from within. It was Anne. "No, don't do it, please."

Instinctively, she slid a thin blade from the lining of her jacket, burst through the door, and went in low in case someone with a weapon might fire high. In a second, with the tip of the blade between her fingers ready to throw, she identified that no one other than Anne was in the room.

The woman looked at her where she crouched at her feet. "Hello, dear." She returned her eyes to the tv screen. "No, don't say yes to the dress. What's wrong with you? Turn and look at that back fat."

Lexi flopped onto the floor and groaned. She looked at Anne. "I feel like you did that on purpose."

"How would I possibly have known you were coming?" The resident's eyes glittered with mirth.

She scrambled to her feet and brushed herself down. "Hmph! I have my eye on you, madam." She cocked a half-grin. "Anne, I hope you don't mind but I've asked Shaun to come up and see you. He's a physio and I'd like to see if he can help you to move a little better."

Anne chuckled. "I don't think much will get these old bones moving again."

"Well, you never know. If you can get mobile, we can take you out of this room and go for a little walk."

"I'm happy to help if I can." The woman winked at her.

Lexi smiled. "We're the ones trying to help you."

Anne patted her hand. "Yes, dear."

Scott came around the corner and knocked on the door. "May I come in, ladies?"

"Oh, yes, of course." Anne looked at two young people. "What a beautiful couple you make."

"We're not a couple," Lexi quickly said. "We're only colleagues."

Again, the woman winked. "That's fine. Your secret is safe with me. But you can't fool a seer with matters of the heart."

Lexi looked at Scott's wrist. He no longer wore the bracelet. "I see Stuart obliged. How did he do it? Do satyrs have magic?"

He grinned with relief. "Not personally. He had a tuning fork and tapped the bracelet with it. It simply sprang open. Interesting little spell."

She chuckled. "You're such a spell nerd. I'll leave you to it, then." She hurried out.

As she closed the door, Scott said, "Good evening, Anne. My name's Shaun."

"If you say so, dear," Anne replied enigmatically.

Lexi hurried along the hall, intending to merely knock on as many doors as possible to get a look at the inhabitants. Twenty minutes later, she returned having only done two rooms. The residents both wanted company and she hadn't had the heart to leave them. She found Scott and Anne going through the photo album.

The resident pointed at the first photograph she'd shown Lexi earlier that day. "This is Wilfred. He died in the war."

"Leo," she corrected automatically.

"Pardon, dear?"

She pointed at the man in the picture. "You told me his name was Leo."

"Did I? Maybe it was." Anne flipped the book closed. "I don't know. It's not my album."

Her jaw dropped. "But what about all those pictures of you as a little girl?"

"I meant those pictures are representative of what I would have looked like as a young girl." The woman giggled when she shook her head.

Scott laughed. "You're a sneaky one."

Anne grimaced. "I'm sorry dears. I like the company and I don't get very much beyond the television."

A bark sounded from the hallway and the woman's eyes widened. "Did I hear a doggie?"

Marcel ran into the room, trailing his lead behind him.

A minute later, Dick arrived to find him on Anne's bed getting a tummy rub. "I'm so sorry. He ran off and this damn thing interfered with my speed." He waved his bracelet at them.

Lexi stared wide-eyed at him. "What are you doing up here at this time? Has anyone seen you?"

"I came up the back stairs. It's fine. No one saw me. Except for this lady, obviously."

Anne looked at him and blushed. "Oh, my! Well, this is embarrassing—to have all three of you here at once. I don't want any fights to break out here."

She looked at the two men and focused on Anne. "Why would we fight?"

"I saw the two of you kissing." The woman swiveled her pointing finger from Lexi to Dick.

The vampire shuddered.

Lexi shook her head quickly. "Yeah, no. That's not something that'll ever happen."

Anne put her hand to her cheek. "Oh, it hasn't happened yet? Oh, dear. I'm sorry. I do hate to give spoilers."

He smoothed an eyebrow. "Have they, by any chance, been giving you psychedelic drugs?"

"Oh, dear." she frowned. "Everything gets so mixed up these days. Well, out you all go. I'm tired and you have a busy night ahead of you." She passed Marcel to Lexi while Scott tucked her in.

The elderly lady smiled at him. "I feel so much better now. Thank you, dear. I think I might be well enough to take breakfast downstairs tomorrow."

He nodded. "That's great news. Good night, Anne."

"Good night, dear." She looked at Lexi. "I'm sorry she wasn't the right one."

She frowned in confusion. "What?"

Anne waved a hand nonchalantly. "Oh, that's only my silly brain again. Good night."

"So, has Nila definitely left for the evening?" she asked as she closed the door.

Dick glanced at his watch. "It's gone seven pm so I certainly hope so. Raj told me she's usually gone by six. The only reason she was there so late last night was because Patrick and his friends had gone AWOL."

Lexi nodded. "So how will we get Josh, Raj, and Stuart out of the way?"

The vampire grinned. "Patrick's already sent them looking for Marcel in the grounds after he ran off." He scratched the puppy behind the ears. "Didn't you, you naughty boy?"

She chuckled. "How long do you think they'll look for him?"

"Oh, they've already given up. According to Phyllis, they're in the greenhouse drinking and smoking pot."

Scott frowned. "Such dedication."

"As long as they're out of the way, I don't care what they're doing," she responded.

"I need to head to my room. I'll listen out and message you if it sounds like they're coming back into the building." Dick took a last speculative look at her and shuddered again.

She turned to her friend. "Can you take them downstairs? I don't want to risk them being seen."

He patted Marcel. "Sure. I'll be back in a second." He vanished with Dick and the puppy and reappeared alone.

The two of them walked in the direction of room X. They stood outside and checked the hallway once more before she tried the door. It was locked.

Scott muttered a word that was quickly followed by a satisfying click. "It's good to have that bracelet off."

Lexi opened the door. A dark lump on the bed confirmed the room was occupied. She breathed in and grimaced. "Good grief! What's that smell?" A woman lay handcuffed to the bed. Her head was turned away and her face was covered by her hair, the same color as hers.

"Alicia? Is that you?" She stepped in. Immediately, she felt dizzy and leaned against the wall. Her eyes were drawn to a strange yellow glow that issued from something on the dresser.

Scott stepped beside her. "Are you okay?"

She blinked and nodded. It was true. She *was* okay and felt better than she had in a long time, but she shook off the introspection. Still, she couldn't allow herself to become distracted by that or the horrible smell. She moved quickly to the bed.

"Alicia? It's okay. We're here to help you." She began to undo one of the wrist straps. Her fingers slipped in something greasy as she struggled with it.

Scott muttered. "You should make sure it's—"

With a wrist free, the woman whipped her arm and shoved her aside.

Lexi met the wall, slid to the floor, and tried to find her feet. The woman had the second strap untied in a moment and rose in a single unnatural movement to stand on the bed. She turned her face toward Lexi, who instantly saw the mistake she had made.

With her hair no longer swept across her face, it was obvious the woman wasn't her sister. She wasn't even certain it was a woman. There were no eyes, for one thing. The top half of the face was a blank canvas. A snout was positioned in the center and below that, a circular hole for a mouth with numerous tiny pointed teeth. Whatever it was turned its face to the source of the yellow light and threw itself toward it with its arms outstretched to snatch it.

Fortunately, it hadn't registered that its feet were still strapped to the bed. The creature landed face-first on the floor with its feet bound by the straps on the bed. While it had fallen several feet short of its goal, it had caught Scott by one foot and dragged him to the ground. It tried to get hold of him but the stinking, greasy substance frustrated its attempts.

Lexi panicked and forgot she was a mere human. She took one step closer and whipped her arm in the direction of the bed as she screamed, "Get back."

The creature arced onto its back on the bed. Scott looked at her in shock and she didn't have to ask. Her eyes were black again.

The creature appeared pinned to the bed by her command. She ignored her companion's stares and strapped one wrist, then walked around the bed with the intention to strap the other one. The closer she moved to the glowing object, the stronger she felt. Her head spun with the force of it. Excruciating pain flooded her arm and she looked at her scar. It had reappeared and was filled with a black substance as it had been in Lorenzo's apartment. She focused on the job at hand, continued around the bed, strapped up the creature's remaining wrist, and marched past Scott. In her hurry, she almost tripped over a black box on the floor with magical symbols drawn on it.

The sorcerer looked at it and frowned. "Should we—"

"Let's get out of here." Lexi was so freaked out by the demon, she only wanted to get out of the room.

He closed the door, locked it, and followed her to their rooms on the top floor.

Ten minutes later, she left the bathroom, having washed away the grease and changed her clothes. She stood at the wall mirror in her little room and stared at her eyes. They had returned to normal.

Scott knocked. "Can I come in?"

"Yes."

He looked uncertain as he studied her.

"What am I?" Lexi dropped onto her bed.

"You're still you." He sat beside her. "That's all that matters."

She was shaking. "I was so sure it would be her. What the hell was that?"

"A demon of some kind." He examined his leg where it had grabbed him. "Not a particularly high-level one, fortunately."

"Maybe there's some kind of monster inside me. Perhaps Delphine."

Scott sighed.

Dick appeared in the doorway. "Are you all right?"

Lexi rolled her eyes and looked at the sorcerer. "Did you call him up here?" She switched her gaze to Dick. "You still shouldn't be awake yet."

Instead of responding to her, the vampire looked at Scott. "I think you need to tell her."

She glanced from one to the other. "Tell me what?"

Her friend stared hard at Dick before he returned his gaze to her. "It's only a theory and not one that makes much sense at the moment." He paused but she remained focused on him and with a reluctant sigh, he continued, "You remember I said I'd read about people with black eyes?"

Lexi nodded.

"I found it again in a book about sorcerers. Specifically, dark sorcerers."

She wrinkled her brow in confusion. "There haven't been dark sorcerers for hundreds of years. I thought they all died out."

Dick leaned against the wall and folded his arms. "You and everyone else."

"Okay, so you said this doesn't make sense." She rubbed her forehead and scowled. "Do you mean because there *are* no dark sorcerers?"

Scott shifted a little uncomfortably beside her. "Well, that's certainly a factor but one I think I can explain. No, the problem lies in the magical source. You know that magical beings get their magic from different sources?"

Lexi nodded. "Yes, you source magic from the air and so does Dolores, and witches take theirs from the earth."

"Do you know where voodoo practitioners source theirs from?" he asked,

She sat for a moment in thought before she shook her head slowly. "Not a clue."

"They get their magic from the ancestor realms."

"So that's where dark sorcerers get theirs? The ancestor realms? It seems a tall order for me given that I don't know who my ancestors were."

He shook his head. "No, I'm merely introducing the concept of sourcing magic from other realms."

Lexi began to wonder if she would have to drag it out of him. "So, let's cut to the chase. I assume dark sorcerers would have taken their magic from the same place as dark fae."

"And you'd be wrong," Dick interjected.

Lexi stared at him. She wished her eyes hadn't returned to normal and—for now, at least—she was disappointed about that. In that moment, she'd have liked to scare the crap out of him. She looked at the scar, which remained half-filled with the black energy. Strangely, it gave her comfort.

Scott smirked. "He only knows that because he guessed wrong too."

She narrowed her eyes. "So you two have had conversations about this."

"Well—" Scott started.

"Yes," Dick finished.

Any number of smart retorts occurred to her, but she put her irritation aside. "So where *did* dark sorcerers draw their magic from?"

He drew a breath and held it for a moment before he answered. "From the demon realms."

Lexi thought about it. "We went through a portal that traversed a demon realm when we saved Dick from being cubed with a silver net. Could something have…latched on to me?" She shuddered.

"No. We'd have known. I think this has always been part of you but it was masked by your other legacy abilities."

She nodded slowly as the theory began to make sense to her. "And now, Alicia's got all the legacy abilities and because I used all your magic, this has somehow been activated?"

Scott nodded. "I think it's shown itself in tiny ways we haven't noticed. And Alicia doesn't have all the legacy abilities. I think that for the first time, she has hers and you have yours. In fact, it's likely that some of the dark sorcerer blood had been locked inside her until the two of you met."

Her analytical mind began to sift for holes in Scott's theory. "But no dark sorcerers were present when they first came together to make the legacies."

He gave her a crooked smile. "There may have been one."

Lexi could see exactly where he was going. "You're referring to that ridiculous myth about the one sorcerer who added his blood to the spell, aren't you?"

"It would explain this."

"I feel like you're making huge assumptions simply to fit your hypothesis. Anyway, this is all academic. I haven't been near any demon realms since Palm Springs. There wasn't one in New Orleans, or at the condo—oh!" She froze and remembered she hadn't told him about what had happened. She sighed. It was time to come clean. "This isn't the first time this has happened since New Orleans."

"The other night in Vegas?" he asked. "It's okay. Dick told me."

She stuck her tongue out at the vampire. "Traitor." She paused for a moment, then continued. "Something happened last night, too. I had a dream. I don't really remember it but when I woke up, I found a burn mark in the shape of my hand on the sheet."

"Why didn't you tell me?"

"It freaked me out. I didn't want to freak you out too. We have a job to do here."

"It's possible you might have come into contact with an object or substance that was somehow connected to the demon realms," Scott continued, although he frowned at her as though a little disappointed that she'd excluded him. "In New Orleans, that would have been Delphine's ring."

Lexi held a finger up. "But that magic was voodoo—ancestor realms. I have been listening, you know."

Dick picked an invisible thread from his jacket. "Do you remember I smelled sulfur at the scene of Jamal's murder? He was an amateur so he might have used something he shouldn't have in that ritual."

The sorcerer moved to the corner of her bed. "But that's where my theory stumbles. There doesn't seem to have been a demonic source in the condo or, as far as we can tell, in room X with the demon."

The vampire's eyes widened. "Are you kidding me? There was a demon in that room? Is that what the stink is? It's revolting. I tried not to say anything, though."

Scott stared at him. "You could have tried harder. Anyway. That smell is tallow, which is animal fat. The demon was covered in it."

Dick raised an eyebrow. "I wonder if it's anyone I know."

Lexi stared at him, then shook her head when he shrugged in response.

The younger man gestured impatiently. "It didn't appear to be up to your standard of conversation."

She found a towel and wiped her hands again, only too aware of the smell. "Couldn't the demon itself have connected me to the demon realms?"

He shook his head. "A demon that's stranded on this plane is about as connected to its realm as we are. I don't think it can act as a conduit to the demon realm. It can have its own power and lend it like Azatoth seems to do with Caleb. Anyway, I can't think of anything that you would have been able to draw on in Dick's condo."

"What about the eerie yellow light?" She put the towel aside. "What was that?"

Scott looked at Dick and then at her. "What yellow light? Where?"

"Coming from something on the dresser. It illuminated that demon's bedroom. You can't have missed it."

"The demon's bedroom was dark until I turned the light on. I didn't see any yellow light."

Lexi turned to the vampire. "Jesús wore a pendant that glowed with that same strange yellow light that night at the condo."

Dick's brow wrinkled as he pinched his lower lip in thought. "Pendant? A little glass tube?"

She nodded quickly. "Yes, I think it was a tube."

He stroked his chin absently. "Interesting. That's brimstone. He's a superstitious little soul and says it protects him from evil spirits."

The reality of the discussion struck her. She sighed. "So, just like that, I'm an evil sorcerer now."

"Do you feel evil?" Dick asked.

Lexi sighed. "I don't know what I feel."

Scott stood. "The glowing object was on the dresser?"

She nodded and he vanished.

He reappeared moments later. "We have a problem."

CHAPTER SEVENTY-ONE

Lexi, Scott, and Dick appeared in the small, windowless bedroom.

"We really should do that more often. It's so expedient." The vampire looked around and shuddered. "Eugh! That stench."

She stared at the bed, which was unoccupied. "Oh!" Her gaze slid immediately to the strange little box to find it was now open and also empty. She wondered what had been in it.

Scott examined one of the greasy straps. It didn't look broken and he focused his gaze on her. "How tightly did you redo the straps?"

Her face flushed. "I didn't want to hurt it."

Dick raised an eyebrow. "Yes. You are clearly an evil sorcerer. Exhibiting that much empathy was a totally evil sorcerer thing to do."

A squeal made them jump and Lexi raced to the other side of the bed. The demon crouched, grasped a small creature with bat-like ears in its fist, and held it against the wall. The little thing was almost crushed and beat its tiny arm against its captor's hand.

The demon seemed to try to squeeze through a small hole in the wall. It had managed to get its head through, but the aperture wasn't big enough for the rest of it to follow. Its captive squealed again. She had no idea what it was, but it was clearly suffering.

Scott inspected the barrier. "Look how the wall's wavering around this little monster. I think the demon's somehow using it to create a portal."

Dick squinted at it. "Could it be a thinner?"

Lexi retrieved a shuriken and threw it at the demon's hand, which sprang open and allowed the little creature to scuttle away.

The moment the demon lost contact, the hole in the wall disappeared. Unfortunately for the demon, its head was already on the other side of it. It's body, from the neck down, fell clumsily.

The vampire grimaced. "Oops."

When she looked at the dresser, the object was gone but a slight glow came from the wall where the portal had been. She could make out a rough yellow circle, not much bigger than the demon's head, drawn on the surface. Curious, she crouched to where the little creature attempted to hide under the bed while its hand softly glowed in the dark. "What's a thinner?"

"I've heard of them," Scott answered. "It's a kind of demon that can be used to make the veil between dimensions—"

"Thinner," she finished. "So this is one?"

He looked at Dick and the vampire crouched to look under the bed. He straightened after a moment. "I don't know, honestly. I've never seen one. But if I had to make an educated guess…"

It crept toward her. Instinctively, she skittered away from the wall until her head hit the side of the dresser. "Ow! Shit."

The small, black, scaled creature had huge, amber eyes and its wide bat-like ears twitched. It held itself in apparent pain and whimpered before it flopped onto the floor.

Lexi moved closer to it. "I wonder how it got here." She was aware of Scott shuffling closer. "Be careful. Don't touch it. For all we know, it could be poisonous."

Slowly, she extended her hand to the being, which shrank away from her as best it could and made a frightened, trilling sound. "Hey, little guy, it's okay. I'm only going to try to help you."

"*Little guy?*" Dick whispered. "Even if it's not a thinner, it is some kind of demon. It'll probably elongate its jaw and bite your arm off. I can't watch."

She flicked a glance at him and smirked when she saw he watched from between his fingers. When she looked at Scott, he'd pulled his face back so far he'd given himself a double-chin. She rolled her eyes at the two of them. When her hand was close enough that she'd still be able to pull it away quickly, she held it still and simply waited to see what the demon would do. It moved forward tentatively and sniffed her. The pupils in its giant eyes became huge, and its arm reached toward her almost in slow motion before it grasped her hand with long spindly fingers.

Two sharply drawn breaths behind her made her smile.

The moment they touched, the glow from the creature's hand brightened and she felt her unhealing scar tickle. It scampered up her arm and hugged against her shoulder.

Dick covered his eyes. "Dear God, it'll bite her head off."

A quick glance confirmed that he had covered his eyes with his hands. "Hey, Prince of Darkness. Look, it's fine." She shook her head, completely at a loss to explain why she trusted it.

She could see that while the hole was gone, the wall still appeared to be in a state of flux. "Hey, little guy, do you need the portal to get home?" She lifted the creature away from her shoulder and held it closer to the wall. "You should be able to get back to wherever you came from now."

He tightened his hold on her hand and refused to let go.

Lexi turned to her companions. "Should I shove it through?"

It squawked and raced up her arm again.

The sorcerer sighed. "I think this little...uh, whatever it is—"

"Demon, Scott," Dick supplied. "It's a demon."

He shrugged. "Okay, this little demon doesn't seem to want to go in there. Maybe all the big demons pick on it."

"No personification of the monster. I absolutely forbid it." The vampire stepped closer to Lexi and attempted to take the creature. "Fine, I'll take it outside and crush it with a rock." He leapt back and cradled his hand. "The little bastard bit me."

"Well, now you know what it's like." Scott smirked.

"I already know what it's like. How do you think I became a vampire? Osmosis?" Dick retreated. "I'll simply let the little fucker cling to you like a limpet, but if he tries to eat Marcel, all bets are off."

"Fine. What will we do about this?" Lexi pointed at the corpse.

Scott stooped and took an arm. "Let's get it on the bed, strap it, and leave it how we found it."

She moved to grab its feet. "It's a start."

Dick raised an eyebrow at her. "Someone will notice it doesn't have a head. It won't look good that you were seen snooping here and the next time someone checks, the demon has no head."

The two men took an arm each and they swung it onto the bed and retied the straps at its wrists and ankles.

The little creature scrambled off Lexi's shoulder and scampered to the wall.

The vampire glanced at it. "At least your little limpet's going back to wherever it came from. That's one less problem."

Scott looked at the headless corpse on the bed. "Maybe we could burn it."

He pinched the bridge of his nose. "Great idea. Let's leave a packet of cigarettes. Perhaps Nila will think it was smoking in bed."

Lexi rounded on him. "You're not being very constructive."

"Erm… Guys." Scott stared at the wall and they turned as one.

The little creature had pushed its arms through the undulating surface and now pulled at something. It tugged a few times, placed its little black feet on either side of the hole, and yanked harder. After a loud popping sound, it sprawled on the floor with two fingers up the nostrils of the demon's snout and one in its mouth like a bowling ball. It squealed, dropped the head, and studied a finger that had caught on one of the pointy teeth. Strange chattering noises followed as it kicked the head and rolled it to Lexi's feet. It climbed her leg, then her arm, and settled onto her shoulder.

Dick turned to Scott. "So, how exactly does this counseling work? Could I hire you to eradicate the last few minutes?"

She picked the head up by the hair and plopped it onto the corpse.

"There, perfect." It immediately rolled across the pillow. Speculatively, she looked at the black energy running through her scar.

Why not?

Before she could change her mind, she put the head in position, slapped her hand over the scar, and pointed a finger at the demon. "Stay put."

The three of them stared as the head sealed itself to the neck. She was delighted. "I have my mojo back."

Dick shook his head. "That's definitely not the mojo you had before."

Ignoring him, she turned excitedly to Scott but he simply frowned. "What?"

"*Stay put?* Mutter it, at least. You'll give sorcerers a bad name."

Lexi pointed at the demon. "But look what I did."

The little black creature on Lexi's shoulder made an "Ooooooooh!" sound.

The vampire raised an eyebrow. "You impressed the little demon."

She shrugged. "I'll take what I can get."

He leaned close to the corpse's neck. "God, this thing stinks. But I can't even see the join. You did a good job."

The demon's eyes snapped open and a high-pitched howl issued from its mouth.

Dick screamed and leapt back several feet.

Scott's jaw dropped.

Lexi stepped forward as it began to sit and punched it in the head, and it flopped unconscious.

The three of them stood and simply stared, not quite willing to believe the evidence of their own eyes.

She opened her mouth to say, "Let's get out of here," when a key rattled in the lock. Scott caught their hands and muttered softly. A moment later, they were in her room.

Scott frowned. "How the fuck did you do that? You reanimated it."

"I don't know what that means." She picked a towel up.

"You brought it back to life." He gestured wildly with his hands to punctuate his words.

Lexi shrugged as she wiped her arms. "I don't know how demons work. Its head is on and I thought that was what we wanted." She was being intentionally obtuse and was well aware of what had happened. It terrified her and excited her in equal parts. "I wonder who was going into the room."

He narrowed his eyes. "I'll take a quick look."

"Wait. Be careful and stay invisible."

The sorcerer rolled his eyes and vanished.

Dick stared at the little creature on her shoulder. "I can't believe you brought that with you. They'll know someone was in there when they see it's gone."

"Or when they see the demon's blood on the wall and floor from its temporary beheading." She shrugged and sat on her bed. They both remained silent for a minute.

The vampire looked at his watch. "What's keeping him? Should we go down?"

Scott reappeared. His eyes were wild, and he looked slightly green. He sat heavily on the chair.

Lexi was instantly alert. "What happened?"

He focused on her. "It was Nila."

"Did she notice something different?" She stood anxiously. "Did she see the blood on the wall?"

He exhaled a slightly panicked breath and raised his eyebrows. "I don't think the blood on the wall will be an issue. She killed it."

Dick narrowed his eyes. "Scott, you've seen demons killed before. You've done it yourself. What has you so freaked out."

Scott shook his head. "It was so…visceral. That box you almost tripped over on the floor—she held it over the demon asking, 'Where is it?' I'd guess that's where your little friend was. The demon only made that whining noise. Nila lost it and pounded the box into its face. Then, she threw it aside and ripped its head off with her bare hands."

The vampire folded his arms and leaned against the wall. "It lost its head again? I'm not a fan of demons but that one had a seriously shitty day. I feel sorry for it."

Lexi bit her lip. "What the hell is Nila doing?"

The sorcerer shuddered. "Nothing good. What now?"

Dick stood and his face brightened. "Go down and put its head on again."

After a moment, both Lexi and Scott asked, "Why?"

He smirked. "To screw with Nila. Can you imagine her face?"

Scott shook his head. "What happened to you feeling sorry for the demon?"

He picked an invisible thread from his shirt cuff. "It comes and goes."

They stopped speaking at the sound of approaching footsteps.

"Hellooo. Hello?" Patrick's voice came through the door as he knocked.

Lexi looked urgently at Dick. "He might not be alone."

Scott disappeared with Dick and returned alone a moment later.

She spoke loudly. "Hi, Patrick. Come in."

"I'm sorry to disturb you. I wanted to check you were all okaaaaaa — Holy Mother of God. What the fuck is that?"

In her rush to get the vampire out of the room, she had somehow forgotten the creature. She turned and looked into the saucer-like eyes of the little being clinging to her shoulder and peeking out from behind her. "It's my…cat."

An awkward silence settled on the room. She looked at the two men in turn and their faces indicated that they had come to the same conclusion.

No way does this look like a cat.

"Monkey," she finished. "It's my cat monkey."

Remarkably, a silent consensus was reached by everyone in the room, and each person seemed prepared to go with it.

"Does your…uh, cat monkey have a name?" Patrick seemed to struggle to get "cat monkey" out of his mouth.

Lexi turned and looked at her shoulder. She was almost touching noses with the creature and its giant eyes stared unblinkingly into hers. "Limpet. His name's Limpet." She smiled confidently at the old man.

"All right." He looked directly at the strange, black, hairless demon. "Hello, Limpet." He stepped forward and extended a hand. "Is he friendly?"

She stepped back while Scott blocked his path.

"He's nervous around new people," she explained hastily.

"Very nervous." The sorcerer nodded furiously.

Limpet had disappeared behind her and she could feel him clinging to her hair. "You wanted to know about the operation. I'm afraid it was a bust."

"I'm sorry to hear that. So, whoever was in there wasn't who you were expecting?"

Scott clapped him on the back. "*Absolutely* not who or what we were expecting."

"That's a shame. What's plan B?" Patrick looked around the room. "There is a plan B, isn't there?"

Lexi had convinced herself that she had been about to find her sister. She hadn't thought past that room. "They might be in another building on the property. We'll need to explore the grounds."

The resident looked disappointed.

Scott put his hand on the man's shoulder. "We'll let you know how it goes."

Patrick left the room, still looking a little despondent, and she reached to the demon. He jumped onto her hand and she held him close to her face. "Hello, Limpet."

He scrunched his giant eyes closed and when he opened them, they were a quarter of the size and looked exactly like a cat's eyes.

She gaped. "Do you see this?" She didn't bother to turn to Scott and instead, put Limpet onto the bed and watched.

The little creature began to shake. He vibrated so fast, he actually blurred. Suddenly, a shock of black fur erupted all over his body. His hands still had little fingers, though, and he stretched his arms toward her. She could see something in his hands. He opened them to reveal a ring with a yellow crystal. The stone glowed and reflected eerily in Limpet's little golden eyes.

Lexi stared at the ring and realized that this was the source of the light she had caught glimpses of in the demon's room. "I wondered what the glow was."

Scott frowned in confusion. "What glow?"

She looked from Scott to the ring and back again. "You don't see a yellow glow coming from this stone?"

"Nope."

Her head tilted curiously, she studied Limpet. "Is that for me?"

He pushed the ring closer to her face. When she took it, his hands changed into paws. He purred, curled comfortably, and closed his eyes.

Lexi held the ring and studied it. The yellow light it gave off was entrancing. She held it over her finger.

Scott took a step forward. "Erm…maybe you shouldn't—"

Before he could finish, she slipped it onto her finger. Immediately, a warm feeling radiated from her hand. Her scar tickled, then ached, and the black energy seemed to come to life with sparkling specks of yellow.

She closed her eyes and felt the magic rise within her.

Every nerve-ending in her body and every pore in her skin came to life. It felt wonderful and she groaned with pleasure. Her eyes were black. Somehow, she knew that and kept them closed.

"Erm… Lexi?" Scott sounded a little strangled like he couldn't quite breathe properly. "Maybe I should wait outside. You seem to be having a…moment."

The magic surged through her veins and settled in her core. She felt her bones harden and her muscles tighten. When the wave had settled over her, she knew her eyes had returned to normal. She opened them and stared ahead.

"Oh, boy," Scott whispered. "You are definitely a dark sorcerer. But your eyes aren't black. That has to be good, right?"

Lexi looked at him. "We have work to do."

He frowned. "Work?"

She stood and put her hands on her hips. "I'm all charged up with no place to go."

In response, he simply stared at her with a bemused expression on his face.

A little impatient, she poked his arm. "What was your first lesson in sorcery?"

Scott exhaled slowly as he tried to remember. "I learned to meditate for a year or so."

Her face scrunched in distaste before she raised an eyebrow. "Yeah, we're gonna go ahead and skip that part."

Limpet stretched, curled again, and went to sleep.

The sorcerer took her arm and they translocated.

CHAPTER SEVENTY-TWO

The friends appeared in the cover of trees and a safe distance from the building.

Lexi looked around. "Why didn't we do this at the house?"

Scott shook his head. "We don't know what we're dealing with here. It's best if you don't blow the residents up."

She nodded. "That makes sense. So, what will we do, Obi-Wan?"

He froze and stared at her. "Lexi Braxton. You referenced Star Wars. You've only been a sorcerer for five minutes and you're already cooler."

"Calm down, nerd." She rolled her eyes. "It'll never happen again."

His grin was a little smug and he looked around. "We need to see what else might be happening here on the property, so we may as well make the first lesson how to use spellglass balls. Don't be worried if this doesn't work. Hold your hand out and picture a small glass sphere with a mirrored finish, about the size of a golf ball. Its purpose is to hurtle around and gather information that you will look at when it returns. Basically, it's the mirror spell I use." He held his hand out and a little mirrored ball appeared in his palm.

Lexi repeated his motions. She closed her eyes, opened them again, and frowned. Her hand was empty. "Where is it supposed to come from?"

He sighed. "This is why we meditate. Some concepts simply can't be explained in words."

"We don't have time for this." She fiddled in the lining of her vest, retrieved a shiny silver bullet, and held it between her finger and thumb. "Will this do?"

Scott looked at it a little cautiously. "I guess, but make sure you don't blow your hand off."

She put it into her palm, closed her hand around it, and recalled him making her pendant. When she opened her hand, it was a sphere but it had turned dark like hematite.

"Why did it come out like that?" She frowned. "Is it because of the dark sorcery?"

"I don't think so. My guess is that maybe, deep down, you're afraid of what you are, and it affects what you're doing—"

"I wouldn't say it's deep down," she muttered. "I'm fairly terrified on the surface."

"There's no reason why you shouldn't have been able to create a silver ball," he continued. "Never mind, it should work fine. Next, you want to levitate it and send it in a circle above us."

His ball rose slowly into the sky while hers rocketed from her hand.

Scott looked at her. "It's not a race."

She shrugged. "Okay. But if it was, I'd have won." She closed her eyes. "Oh!"

"What's up?"

"This is so cool." She grinned. "I didn't think it would work like this. I can see what the ball sees."

"You can?" His voice sounded higher-pitched than usual.

Lexi opened her eyes. "Is that wrong?"

"No. It simply never occurred to me to do that." Scott closed his eyes but immediately frowned. "It doesn't work for me. Maybe it's in how you created it in the first place." He sounded slightly annoyed.

"Okay, let's each take a half of the property. If you need to follow yours as it flies, I'll keep watch down here."

She closed her eyes again and focused as her ball moved to the edge of the property, through an orchard, around barns, and past several lodges. "Only one of the lodges looks lived in but it seems to be empty right now."

Her half of the property was covered in minutes so she sent the sphere to the other side and investigated a storage building and some beehives. Scott's floated along and she raced past it several times before she called hers back. "Well, there's no construction work going on here."

He shrugged. "We need to search the whole house from top to bottom. If we can't find your sister, maybe we could ask Dick to get information out of Nila tomorrow night. She seems quite fond of him, you know, when she's not ripping heads off."

Lexi smirked. "I somehow don't think the feeling's mutual. But you're right. He might at least be able to get her out of the way. Come on. It's almost time for him to be awake. You ask him about distracting Nila tomorrow night and I'll check on Limpet."

She entered the room to find the creature still asleep exactly where she'd left him. Intrigued, she watched him for a few moments while he slept. He looked exactly like a cat. When she attempted to stroke his ear, his giant, saucer-like eyes snapped open and he bolted off the opposite side of the bed. He struck the wall at speed. It wobbled and he vanished through it.

With a sigh, she straightened and stared at the wall. He'd gone and she couldn't help but feel a little disappointed. She turned to leave but heard a squeak behind her. When she turned, his face appeared from the wall. He gazed warily around the room before he pushed into it again. The little demon leapt onto the bed, screwed his eyes shut, and became a cat once more. He kneaded the covers and purred.

"I'm going for a walk. Do you want to come?" Lexi left the room and Limpet followed.

They headed toward the basement and she could hear an argument from halfway down the stairs.

"I absolutely and positively refuse." Dick was definitely upset about something.

"But we've looked almost everywhere," Scott replied.

She put her head around the door a little cautiously. Dick stood in front of Scott and they were nose to nose.

The vampire spoke as if through gritted teeth. "I don't care. I won't do it."

"I can hear you two halfway to the dining room. What's going on?" Lexi stepped into the room.

Dick turned to her. "I am as dedicated, professional, and loyal an employee as Dolores could ever hope for. I work ridiculous hours, I spend more on this job than I earn, and I'm even prepared to put up with you two lunatics. But this is simply too much."

She raised her palms in a placatory gesture. "Dick, calm down. What has Scott asked you to do?"

"He wants me to— Jesus, I can't even say the words." He put his palm to his forehead.

Lexi stood and waited while she wondered what Scott had said.

The vampire took a deep breath. "Scott has suggested I...take one for the team."

She almost laughed but instead, shook her head in apparent confusion. "Take one what?"

He put his hand on his chest. "He wants me to take Nila and—dear God, and *pump her*. I think I'll throw up."

"Oh, that." She smirked. "I asked him to ask you."

"Excuse me?"

"If we can't find out where Caleb has Ali and Bryan, I thought you could..." She winked and clicked her tongue a couple of times for effect. "You know, pillow talk and whatnot. She seems to have taken a shine to you."

"I'm calling Dolores." Dick took his cell phone out.

Lexi chuckled. "Put that away, for goodness sake. No one's asking for you to go that far. Scott was supposed to ask you to take her out for a drink tomorrow night and pump her for information so we can finish searching the place."

The vampire pointed accusingly at the other man. "That's not what he said."

She looked at Scott.

He grinned. "Sorry. You should have seen his face, though."

Dick wheeled to stare at him, his face red. "I'll feed you vampire blood, then kill you. And when you wake up, I'll keep breaking all your bones just for fun."

The sorcerer chuckled. "Would that make you my dad?"

"Fuck off." He stormed to the door and held it open. "Get out, the pair of you."

"What are you doing?" Lexi asked.

With a long-suffering sigh, he stopped in the doorway and turned. "Getting ready to invite Nila on a date. It'll take at least a day of meditation." He looked at Limpet. "Do you intend to keep that?"

She shrugged. "Sure, why not?"

He gaped at her. "You don't even know what it eats."

"I'll figure it out."

A *yip* drew their attention. She looked to where Limpet leaned into Marcel's food bowl.

"We might be about to find out now," Scott said.

The cat-demon picked a handful of dog food up, sniffed it, and fell on his butt as he rubbed his nose in disgust. Marcel approached cautiously and sat on his haunches with his head tilted to stare at the little creature.

Limpet, who still had a lump of dog food in his hand, held his arm out and the puppy licked it out of his hand. He giggled and Marcel yipped again and wagged his stumpy tail.

The demon took another lump of dog food and the process was repeated.

"Not dog food, apparently. You have another half-hour before you said you'd be awake. Come on, Limpet." Lexi walked out of Dick's room. Scott and Limpet followed.

She turned to her friend in the hallway. "What's next for you?"

He looked at the time. "I'm meeting Phyllis."

"Really? It's late for work."

"I wanted some quiet when I see her."

They headed through the gym toward the physio room. Limpet found a mirror and sat in front of it to study himself.

Phyllis waited outside the room.

Scott smiled. "Sorry to keep you waiting."

She leaned on her walker and stood. "I was early."

While he washed his hands, Lexi helped her step up to sit on the bed. Scott returned and looked at her bracelet. "This won't help." He muttered a spell and her bracelet jumped with a spark and stayed where it was.

"Ow!" She yanked her arm back.

"I need..." He looked around the little room, opened a glass-fronted cupboard, and pulled out a wide box. Without an explanation, he opened the box and selected a long piece of metal. He studied it for a moment, looked at Phyllis, and nodded.

The woman recoiled and stared at the long, curved, shiny piece of metal in his hand. "What is it?"

"It's a Graston tool. It's only a physio tool for rubbing over muscles."

Hesitantly, she held out her arm again and he tapped the metal against it. As it chimed, he muttered. Instead of fading, the tone went higher. When it reached the right note, the bracelet fell and the old woman rubbed her wrist and nodded her thanks.

"Oh!" She suddenly looked alarmed.

"What's wrong?" he asked.

Phyllis shook her head. "My senses came back. I can tell you're a sorcerer now. You smell of ozone."

He chuckled. "It's an occupational hazard."

She stared at Lexi. "I don't understand. I thought you were human."

"Let me guess—brimstone." She rolled her eyes. "We're still trying to confirm what I am."

The woman narrowed her eyes. "Really? You smell a little like a demon."

"I'll wait outside," she said with a sigh.

When she returned to the gym, Limpet remained motionless in front of the mirror. She spent a few minutes trying the weights, then decided to see how Dick was getting on. As she approached the hallway around the corner from his room, the sound of voices made her pause.

"I shouldn't make an exception but as you'll only be with us a short time and Marcel is so adorable, I've decided I'll let him stay. But your staff must be better behaved. I can't have them wandering around the building alone."

"I quite agree, Nila," he responded,

Lexi realized the voices were getting closer. She stood next to the painting of Jonas Maybury. A door stood on either side of the indented wall and she opened one. It was a cleaning closet and she stepped in quietly and closed the door.

She felt around in the dark and put her hand on what seemed to be a stick with a hard, cold handle. It was better than nothing, she decided and picked it up to hold it ready in case she was discovered.

Silently, she asked herself, *Am I prepared to bludgeon that woman to death if she opens this door?*

The answer was a resounding yes.

Moments later, the voices were directly outside the door.

"Well, I'm sure Lena will be along shortly," Dick said. "I'll speak to her." After a moment, he added a loud, high-pitched, "Oh! Erm. Righto."

Lexi heard him walk in the direction of his room and Nila take the stairs. She gave it a minute before she left and knocked on his door. She waited but he didn't respond.

After a few moments, she knocked again. "Dick?"

The door was yanked open and he pulled her in. "Thank God it's you."

"What's wrong?"

"That woman is disturbing. She was here a few minutes ago and walked in without even bothering to knock. I'd heard her shoes on the floor and wasn't ready to admit to being awake yet so I jumped into bed and pretended to be asleep. She simply stood there and stared at me for about five minutes. She didn't move a fraction of an inch. Then she—" Dick paused as though he didn't want to finish.

"She what?"

He shuddered. "She smelled me."

Lexi stared at him.

"She leaned right next to my face and sniffed. It was the creepiest thing that has ever happened to me in my life. Her breath was disgusting. And I felt so…exposed."

She guffawed. "Clearly, you've never been on the last MetroRail train. That shit happens all the time. You're standing there minding your own business when some creep starts sniffing your hair. I've ruptured so many balls that way." She smiled fondly at the memory, then blinked and looked at him. "Wait, if you were pretending to be asleep, how do you know she was staring at you?"

"What else is there to look at in here? And I felt her eyes on me." He shuddered again. "Finally, I had to fake waking up and she started to speak to me like everything was normal. I managed to start walking her along the hallway past where you were hiding in the closet at the bottom of the stairs. I thought *she* might hear your heart beating, never mind me."

"I almost walked into the two of you. I barely escaped."

"Speaking of escape, we need to get out of here. That woman looks like she won't leave me alone, and she won't keep her hands off my ass. I'm ready to report her to Human Resources."

Lexi shook her head and hid a grin. "There is no Human Resources department. They were all fired on Friday so Kindred can take their roles."

Dick sat in an armchair and pulled his shoes on. "Hardly surprising, I suppose."

"It's good for us. We have to find my sister and brother-in-law and the missing residents. When you two go out on your date, we'll search properly."

He sighed. "As she was still around, I asked her out for a drink tonight but she said no because she was heading out for a meeting with the new owner. It means Caleb's definitely around here somewhere. Here's hoping he can keep her interest for a couple of hours and we can get the job done. Then, I won't have to take her for a drink tomorrow night."

She thought for a minute. "Good. Let's go through this place from top to bottom."

Lexi returned to the physio room and waited for Scott to open the door.

Phyllis was seated and flexed this way and that. "I can't remember the last time I felt so good."

He moved to help her, but she hopped down herself. "I have another suggestion for you," he said. "Come with me."

The two left the physio room and walked past Lexi. She glanced at Phyllis's walker still in the room, smiled, and followed them to the big double-doors at the end of the gym.

The old woman looked at Scott with confusion on her face. "I think this used to be the swimming pool. They stopped using it before I arrived."

He opened the door and switched the light on as they entered. The room was empty except for a single chair and a few boxes of tiles. It looked like they'd given up halfway through the repairs. A long wooden plank went from the side into the three-foot shallow end of the empty pool. "I thought you might appreciate somewhere to work out the kinks. I think it could help with your arthritis."

A look of fright appeared on her face. "You want me to shift? I'm not sure."

Scott indicated their surroundings. "There's no one in here to hurt and I'm here if you need me. How about you sit here and think about it. See if it's something you'd like to do in a safe environment. I'll come back for you in around twenty minutes."

"I suppose I could think about it." The old woman walked to the chair and sat with her hands in her lap.

Lexi looked at her. She didn't think Phyllis would shift as she seemed so uncomfortable at the mere thought of it.

The two friends returned to the physio room and Scott sprayed sanitizer on the bed and wiped it.

He looked at the time. "Anne Lown is next."

She watched him work at this role that didn't involve hunting rogue supernaturals and thought it suited him. "I'll go upstairs and collect Anne." She turned. "Nila rejected Dick in favor of a date with Caleb tonight. We need to stay vigilant if he's around."

The sorcerer nodded.

As she hurried through the gym to the elevator, she glanced at where Limpet curled in sleep next to the mirror.

Anne was seated in a wheelchair beside her bed when she arrived. "You're right on time."

Lexi flicked the chair's brake off with her foot. "How are you feeling?"

The woman turned in the chair to stare at her. "I feel nervous. It's a big day."

She negotiated the doorway and pushed the chair toward the elevator. "It is? Is it your birthday?"

Anne laughed. "Not for me. It's a big day for you. No spoilers, though."

As she pushed the chair through the gym, she noticed that Limpet had moved off and wondered if she should have called him when she went up. She hoped he wasn't lost in the big house.

Lexi delivered Anne to Scott's office and closed the door behind her.

She returned to Dick's room.

"Is Limpet in here?"

The vampire looked at Marcel, who was snoozing alone on his bed. "No. We'll probably find him while we're searching the—" His face suddenly became alert. He turned to the door and tilted his head. "I thought Nila had left already. She's coming back." He looked wildly around the room and finally, his gaze landed on her. "Lexi, I'm truly sorry about this."

He put his arm around her waist and pulled her against him, clamped his other hand on the back of her neck, and kissed her.

Her first instinct was to knee him in the groin, but damn if Dick wasn't the best kisser by a mile that she'd ever experienced. She grasped his hips a second before the door opened.

"Disgusting!" Nila spun and marched away. Her heels echoed loudly along the hall.

The vampire released her. "You may rupture my balls now. If that woman leaves me alone, it was worth it."

Lexi stared incredulously at him. "You are really, *really* good at that."

He smoothed an eyebrow and preened. "Why, thank you. Years of training. Goodness, I haven't kissed a woman like that since Marilyn Monroe."

"Wait, you kissed Marilyn Monroe?"

Dick picked an invisible piece of fluff from his shirt. "Yes, for a dare."

"What was it like?"

"Painful." He rolled his eyes. "Her husband at the time, Joe DiMaggio, broke my nose. It was quite a scandal."

"Okay." She was impressed, there was no hiding it. After a moment, she looked around. "Where's Marcel?"

The vampire looked under the bed. "He must have gotten out when she opened the door."

CHAPTER SEVENTY-THREE

Nila pushed the bar on the fire exit and flung it open.

She stamped up the outside steps to ground level. Marcel struggled in her arm, but her hold tightened. She walked across the lawn to the copse of trees surrounding the house and shoved him into the branches of a tree. He slipped and regained his balance, looked doubtfully at the ground, then stared fearfully at her.

While she glowered at him, she took the silver whistle from around her neck and hung it in a branch of the same tree. She didn't move her gaze from his as she kicked her shoes off and began to change.

The puppy whined as spiky antlers pushed through her scalp and her nose and jaw elongated into a snout. Her shoulders broadened and her spine curved with immense cracking sounds. The clothes shredded as she transformed and she ripped them away with her hands as they turned into long, menacing claws. Nila growled and saliva slid through pointed teeth.

Marcel lost his balance and fell but was caught in the whistle's cord on the way down. He yelped as he landed and something cracked, and he tried to limp away.

He didn't manage more than a few feet, in pain and tangled in the whistle as he was. The woman had completed her change and stalked the injured puppy slowly, snorting and slavering.

Unable to walk on his injured hind leg, Marcel stumbled and fell. He scrambled a few more inches as her gaping mouth began to descend.

Nila howled when a brown and white Pitbull terrier landed on her back and bit savagely into her neck. With a growl of rage and pain, she reared and the dog slid off. Undeterred, it savaged her leg. She twisted, swept a huge, clawed hand at the dog, and hurled it several feet away.

She hadn't lost sight of her goal and shook herself, focused, and crept toward Marcel again. A small, black cat leapt over the quivering puppy, landed on her face, and scratched at her eyes. She howled again and tried to swipe it away, but it was too fast and scampered clear before she could reach it. Nila shook her head but before she could continue, the cat repeated its attack on her face and eyes with its claws. She snapped at it and tried to gore it with her antlers while she screamed in frustration.

Marcel squealed and continued to try to scramble away. The Pitbull ran around Nila and the cat and approached the puppy from the rear. She lifted him in her mouth by the scruff of his neck and raced toward the house. Without looking back, she ran down the emergency exit stairs and put the puppy down before she turned and scratched at the door.

⸻

The warmth from Scott's hand's radiated into Anne's knee and relieved the arthritic pain in the joint. "How does it feel?"

She flexed it. "That's wonderful. I wish you had time to do the other one."

He smiled. "We still have fifteen minutes. I can work on your wrists too."

"No, it's all right. I need to get out of the way before it all goes crazy down here. And you need to get that door."

Scott narrowed his eyes at her. He walked to the door, opened it, and peered into the hallway. "There's no one there."

"No, but it needed to be open or you wouldn't have heard the noise until it was too late." She smiled and patted his hand. "Thank you, young man. Don't forget to remove all the bracelets or it'll be a blood-bath around here."

He frowned and turned to the hallway again. "Can you hear that?" He stepped out, listened, and began to walk down the hallway, then paused at the intersection.

The old woman followed and turned toward the elevator. She pressed the call button and turned to him. "Chop, chop. And don't forget, curiosity killed the cat."

She stepped into the elevator, muttering, "Good heavens. You'd think they had all the time in the world."

Scott followed the sound of scratching. He moved more quickly when the howling started, pushed the bar, opened the fire door, and stared at the brown and white Pitbull. "Phyllis? You weren't supposed to go—"

Phyllis picked Marcel's drooping form up and raced inside as though something was chasing them.

He stood at the open doorway and wondered if he should take a look outside.

Curiosity killed the cat.

Quickly, he shut the door.

The sorcerer followed the dogs into the physio room and lifted Marcel onto the table. He untangled the cord with the whistle on it from the puppy's neck and feet, held the cord, and examined the whis-tle. It was easily recognizable as Nila's. He tried to touch it and it sparked. "Ow!" He dropped it.

When he glanced at Phyllis, she had shifted to human form. She had some bruising on her face and looked dazed. "Let me—"

"Fix the puppy. He's in a worse condition than me. I think his hind leg is broken."

Scott turned to Marcel, ran a hand over his hind leg, and muttered softly.

The dog whined.

"Marcel?" Dick called from the hallway.

"He's in here," he shouted in response.

The vampire appeared at the door. "I've been all over the place looking for him."

He looked grimly around the room and took everything in.

His eyes rested on Marcel and his face hardened. "What happened?"

"It was a wendigo," Phyllis answered. "I think it was Nila and I think she intended to eat him."

"I will kill her." His face was rigid and white with fury.

Marcel sat, whined, and barked at his voice and he stepped across to him, lifted the puppy, and let him lick his face. "Will Daddy kill the nasty wendigo, Marcel? Will he? Yes, he will." He looked at Scott. "That explains her breath."

The sorcerer frowned. "Why would she suddenly go nuts like that?"

"She caught me kissing Lexi and lost her—"

"Wait, what?"

"Keep up, Scott. Lexi and I are getting married and we want to adopt you."

"I thought you were Shaun," Phyllis interjected, her expression bewildered. "And who's Lexi?"

"I am. What's going on? She stood in the doorway.

Dick turned to her "Nila's a wendigo."

She stared at him, completely unsurprised. "That makes more sense than anything else in my life right now."

"It seems Nila was getting ready to eat Marcel but Phyllis saved him," Scott explained.

Dick inclined his head to Phyllis.

She waved him off. "I wouldn't have rescued him from her if it hadn't been for that cat."

After a momentary pause, the three of them asked, "Cat?"

"A black cat came from nowhere and attacked her face. It

distracted her long enough for us to get away. That poor cat. I hope its luck didn't run out. I saw it go flying a couple of times."

Lexi was about to race down the hallway, then hesitated and turned to the old woman. "Where? Can you show me?"

Dick gaped at her. "With a wendigo on the loose? There could be a bloodbath."

Scott froze and stared at him.

He froze too. "What?"

The young man stared at his bracelet. "That's what Anne said. Remove the bracelets or there'll be a bloodbath."

The vampire stuck his arm out. "Off, please."

The sorcerer flicked the box open, retrieved the Graston tool, and struck the band lightly. A moment later, it was off.

Phyllis stood. "Okay, I'll take you out there." She shifted and led her along the hall to the exit door.

Lexi opened the door and the Pitbull went through. They raced across the lawn and she waited impatiently while Phyllis sniffed the ground.

After a moment, the old woman shifted again. "It was here. I smell wendigo and look, Nila's shredded clothes are everywhere. But I can't smell a cat. I smell something demonic, other than you. There's wendigo blood here. The trail heads into the trees. Do you want me to follow it?"

She shook her head. "No. Let's get to the house in case she's doubled back. I don't want to spend the night out here if she's roaming the hallways."

The old woman sighed.

Lexi looked at her. "Are you okay?"

"We won't find my friends, will we? Wendigos eat human flesh and they eat once a week." Her eyes glittered with tears in the moonlight.

She hadn't put that together and was too startled to think about how to respond. Maisie and the others hadn't been moved out by Kindred. Nila had taken them. "I assumed Nila was Kindred because she arrived after the takeover. I bet she was placed here by Caleb."

They headed to the house in silence. Before they entered, she turned to Phyllis. "I know you prefer to keep your bracelet on but—"

"You can forget the bracelet. I have a houseful of friends to protect." The old woman strode in.

Lexi smiled and followed. She found Scott in the lobby and looked at the reception desk. "Where are the three amigos?"

"Still getting baked in the greenhouse."

She shook her head. "Let's go talk to them."

They headed to the greenhouse in the garden. She opened the door and waved a hand to clear the smoke from her face. "It's like a jazz club in here."

The three satyrs shushed each other repeatedly, the admonitions almost louder than their conversation.

When the two friends walked around a wall of moss, Stuart, Raj, and Josh sprawled on beanbags, frozen in the process of passing a bong, and looked at them with wide eyes.

Stuart flailed a hand as if in protest. "How did you find us?"

The sorcerer looked around. "You're not exactly well hidden."

Raj giggled.

Lexi made a mental eye-roll. "And we followed the smell."

The clerk's face went slack but brightened quickly. "We're looking for the dog."

Scott folded his arms. "How's that working out?"

"He hasn't come here yet, but we've set a trap." Stuart pointed to a sausage on the floor between them.

Lexi looked at Josh, who was poking himself in the cheek. "What's up with you?"

"I can't feel my face."

She shook her head. "Scott."

"On it. Sorry, boys." He muttered a few words and the satyrs blinked and shook their heads.

Raj looked at him. "Why did you do that, man?"

Josh pointed at Scott's arm. "Who removed your bracelet?"

Stuart slumped. "I did."

Raj looked at his colleague. "Why did you do that, man?"

Lexi had heard enough. "Okay, focus. Did any of you know that Nila's a wendigo?"

Stuart's face seemed expressive of an a-ha moment. "That makes so much sense."

Raj nodded. "Right?"

The three of them nodded at each other.

Lexi turned to her friend. "Are you sure you sobered them up completely?"

Scott shrugged. "I thought I had."

She looked at the three goat-legged men. "Okay, I'll try again. Nila's a wendigo and she's eaten three of the residents in the last month. She's loose on the grounds somewhere. Get your asses inside and protect the residents."

Stuart climbed off his beanbag. "Protect them? How? How do you even kill a wendigo?"

They stared at her.

"Fire." She turned to leave, then looked over her shoulder. "Or tear it to pieces."

She and Scott walked a few steps but stopped when they realized the satyrs weren't following.

Raj was picking up the beanbags and looking underneath. "Who's got the M&Ms?" He dipped a hand into a giant plant pot. "Never mind, I found them."

Lexi pinched the bridge of her nose while the satyrs filed out with their giant bag of peanut butter M&Ms.

Scott sent Raj to the third story of the building where the men's rooms were, and Josh sat on a chair in the hallway of the second story, the women's level. Stuart remained at his desk in the lobby but locked the doors. All three had armed themselves with a can of hairspray and a cigarette lighter.

They spent the night patrolling the building, checking windows and doors, and making sure Nila hadn't found her way back in.

Lexi walked into the staff kitchen. Her eyes were tired and gritty and she looked at Dick seated on a chair next to Marcel. "Shouldn't you be hiding in your room?"

He shrugged. "What's the point? Nila seems to have gone. I'm sorry if we kept you awake last night."

She laughed. "You mean after I went to bed two hours ago at five am? You didn't keep me awake. I didn't hear a thing."

"Really? Marcel howled in his sleep at one point. I would have thought someone on the other side of the wall would have heard him. The poor little thing."

With a frown, she looked at the wall. "I think the stairway's on the other side."

Dick raised an eyebrow. "No, that sweeps down the other way."

Mentally, she traced her steps through the house. "The hallway?"

He shook his head, bewildered. "It must be. This place is a labyrinth."

She rubbed her face. "I wonder where Limpet is."

The vampire looked a little sheepish. "I'm sorry I was horrible to him. If he hadn't attacked Nila, Marcel would be dead now."

Without meeting her gaze, he continued to stroke Marcel absently and focused on the wall. Suddenly, he stood.

Lexi narrowed her eyes at him. "What?"

"I only…" He walked out of the room.

She leaned over to stroke the puppy. Dick returned a few minutes later and jerked his head toward the hallway. "Come see."

Curious, she followed him out. They walked along the hallway.

"Where would you say the kitchen ends?"

Frowning in thought, she looked toward the door they'd just walked through. "Around here."

They looked in closets along the wall but none were particularly deep. Then, the hallway turned to the right. They passed a stairway, walked around a few corners and back in the direction they'd come, and passed the little hallway to hers and Scott's rooms in the turret.

When they reached the kitchen again, Scott was there trying to tempt Marcel with a chicken drumstick. He looked up. "I wondered where you'd gone."

Dick stared at him. "What are you doing?"

"I'm trying to cheer Marcel up. He looks sad."

The vampire looked at Marcel. "Scott. Come with us and bring Marcel. I don't want to leave him alone if he's awake. He might get frightened."

He followed them around the upper hallways. This time, they opened every single door and searched along every wall and in every cupboard.

Back in the kitchen, the sorcerer turned to the others. "So there's been a secret room on this floor, right under our noses all this time and we didn't realize it."

Dick looked ready to kick himself. "Because of the ridiculous design of the building."

"This explains why there are no windows in the rooms on this side of the hallway." Scott paused. "Just a minute." He left the room and Lexi followed him. He entered his bedroom, leaned out of the window, and sent one of his little mirror balls into the sky. Seconds later, it returned. Scott muttered a few words and the ball flattened to a wide disk. The two of them watched the journey the little sphere had taken over the roofs. A square section in stone blocks had been created in the middle of the tiled expanse, completely out of character with everything else.

"Let's go and take a look." He took her hand.

They appeared on the stone roof. It was roughly thirty feet in diameter.

Lexi looked for some way to enter the hidden room. "There's no roof access."

"I wonder what's in there." He apparated a little ball and dropped it, and it hovered for a few moments before it descended. It stopped on the roof and remained there.

She frowned at it. "What's it doing?"

"Nothing apparently." She looked irritated. "A magical field is keeping it out."

"Okay, let's get back to Dick." He took her hand again and they appeared in the kitchen.

The vampire looked up. "So what do you think the strange stone section is? It looks fairly old."

Scott narrowed his eyes. "How did you—"

Dick held his cell phone up. "Google Maps."

Lexi rolled her eyes. She was learning quickly how easy it was to rely on magic when other methods would suffice.

The sorcerer tried to direct his little ball through the wall. Initially, it sank through the stucco kitchen wall with no problem, but his frustrated face told her it hadn't breached the full wall.

He turned to Dick and put his hand out. "Can I look?"

The vampire held the phone out to him.

Scott looked for a few seconds, then handed it back. "Well, what your app couldn't tell you is that there doesn't seem to be any way to get into that room. We've been all the way around it and found nothing. It must be magically sealed."

Dick gazed at the wall. "How thick would you say the walls are?"

He shrugged. "One and a half to two feet all the way around."

"And you believe that thickness of stone and the stone roof is simply sitting on a regular floor?"

They stared at him.

"It has to be a tower," he continued, "so it goes all the way down and the entrance must be on a lower level. This whole place has been built and designed to hide the existence of the tower in the middle."

Dick picked Marcel up and they headed down the stairs.

Once they understood that the convoluted design of the hallways was to draw attention away from the giant section in the middle of the building, it made much more sense.

Lexi stood outside a resident's room on the men's floor of the building. She chewed her lip in thought. "We can't simply start searching people's rooms while they're in them."

The vampire hesitated before he nodded. "Surely they'll go down for breakfast shortly anyway."

"They don't all go downstairs for breakfast. We need to get all the residents in one place so we can keep them safe and keep looking for a way into that tower."

They heard the elevator and as one, turned as the doors opened and Anne Lown shuffled out.

Scott hurried to her and offered his arm. "Anne. What are you doing up here?"

"Don't worry. I'm heading down again." She stepped past him and drew her arm back to punch the fire alarm on the wall. The glass broke and she yanked the handle down. The siren began to wail.

"Ouch." Anne shook her hand out, turned to Dick, and put her arms out for Marcel. He paused for a moment, then passed the puppy to her. She shuffled into the elevator.

"You're not supposed to use the elevator during a fire emergency," he called.

She flipped the bird as the doors closed.

"I like her," Scott yelled over the alarm.

The vampire nodded. "And that will do nicely." He walked along the hallway shouting, "Proceed slowly and carefully to the Fire Test Assembly Point which is the entertainment lounge. If you need help, press your call light and someone will come to you."

A man wandered out in his pajamas. "What's going on?"

"Fire alarm test," Lexi explained glibly.

"At this hour? I was napping."

"You're always napping." Raj wandered along the hallway with Josh and Stuart behind him.

"What's happening now?" the clerk asked.

"We're getting everyone into one place so they're easier to protect," Dick told them.

Stuart's eyes widened when he saw the vampire. "Dude. What are you doing out of the basement?" He halted in total shock when he realized the vampire was bathed in the morning light coming through a window.

He smirked and smoothed an eyebrow. "I've had a relapse."

People filed out of the rooms and they continued to direct them down.

"I can't get down those stairs," someone shouted.

"It's a test," Stuart called in response. "We're allowed to use the elevators. Those of you who can use the stairs follow Raj to—" He looked at Lexi.

"The entertainment lounge."

"Did you hear that? The entertainment lounge. If you need to use the elevator, line up here."

Albert stepped out of his room. "Why is this happening?"

Dick sighed. "I'm sorry. Kindred told us to do it. You know what total bastards they are."

"Oh, don't talk to me about those shit-heads." A man in a dressing gown wandered past with a walking stick.

Lexi chuckled. *Blame Kindred, why not?*

Stuart tapped her on the shoulder. "Has anyone seen Nila?"

She shook her head and turned to Scott. "You help Stuart get people out of their rooms. How will I know if there's an entrance?"

He fumbled in the bag on his back and pulled her pendant out, held it for a moment and muttered, then passed it to her. "If you come across anything hidden by magic, this will glow."

"You come with me," she told Josh.

The two of them went to the women's level where Anne and Phyllis were helping ladies out of their rooms.

"If you can manage the stairs," Josh shouted, "follow me to the entertainment lounge."

Scott's voice blared throughout the building as though he had a megaphone. "Please make your way to the entertainment lounge in your most expedient manner."

Lexi began to go through the rooms. She waved the pendant along the walls of every room but couldn't find anything that seemed suspicious.

She returned into the hallway, where Anne sat in her wheelchair with Marcel in her hands. "Do you want help to get downstairs, Anne?"

"Yes, please." She went with her in the elevator.

Only ten minutes had passed but all residents were gathered in the entertainment lounge.

Stuart approached her. "There are no kitchen staff."

Lexi frowned. "What time do they usually arrive?"

"An hour ago. And none of the day staff have arrived."

"Is that unusual?"

"It's unheard of."

She stepped out and found Dick about to enter the room. "It looks like all the staff have been canceled for today. Why would that be?"

He narrowed his eyes. "I think whatever they have planned will happen today. You keep searching. I'll distract the residents."

The vampire entered the room where most were still agreeing that Kindred were bastards. Some who hadn't seen him were wide-eyed. "Yes, I walk in the daylight. It's a thing. Since we're all here, let's have a sing-song." He walked to the piano, cracked his knuckles, and began to play "I get no kick from champagne."

Lexi stopped at the door and listened for a moment before she chuckled and shook her head and returned to the ladies' floor to check rooms and closets. She opened a door to find a lady fast asleep —Delia, according to the name on the door.

Quietly, she stepped in and checked the back wall of the room and the closet for any sign of an entrance to the tower.

"What are you doing?"

When she turned, the woman was seated in the bed. "I'm so sorry to disturb you. This is a shake-down."

Delia put her glasses on. "A what?"

"Kindred have insisted we check for drugs and associated para-phernalia."

"But I keep my medications in this drawer." The woman patted the bedside cupboard.

Lexi shook her head. "I'm looking for illegal drugs. You know, bennies, coke, smack, crack, meth, mollies, oxies, purple...drank."

The woman shook her fist at her. "They're not taking my oxies. Kindred are bastards"

"That does seem to be the consensus. If you have a prescription for them, you're fine. Well, you're clean. There's a fire test going on. Everyone's in the lounge."

"Good." She lay down, muttering under her breath.

Relieved that it hadn't proved too much of a problem, she stepped into the hallway but wasn't sure what to do about the woman.

Scott leaned against the wall and grinned. "Purple drank? Where did you get all that?"

"Isaac used to listen to a ton of rap music. Have you finished upstairs already?"

He nodded. "Stuart and Raj helped with the residents."

"This woman doesn't want to budge. I don't want to leave her alone with a wendigo on the loose."

"A what?" Delia stepped out. "Did you say a wendigo?"

"Well—"

The woman scuttled down the hallway like she might once have been an Olympic sprinter.

Scott watched her with a grin. "That's solved that problem."

They finished searching the rest of the rooms on that level and continued while they listened to Dick belting out "My Kind of Town."

They found Delia in the lobby, trying to take her bracelet off with a pair of toenail clippers.

The sorcerer leaned over the front desk as they walked past and snaffled the tuning fork. "I'll sort that out for you."

Dick noticed them as they entered the room. "Okay, ladies and gentlemen. Let's have a little chat, shall we?"

The residents booed.

Patrick stepped onto the stage. "Hold up now. Something's been going on here that everyone needs to know. We've all been concerned about our friends going missing. Well, now I have answers." He drew a deep breath. "Nila is a wendigo."

Phyllis stood beside him. "I can confirm it. I saw her myself last night."

Someone shouted, "No one disbelieves you, Patrick."

"That explains her breath," another resident muttered.

Scott moved to the front. "I know some of you might be nervous about the idea of removing your bracelets—"

"Get these damn things off and let us protect ourselves," a man shouted.

Patrick leaned closer and added quietly. "Except Albert. He's crazy."

The sorcerer took the old man's arm and prepared to strike the bracelet with the tuning fork. The satyrs arranged themselves around Albert.

The moment he struck the band, it fell. Scott muttered and the note lingered and grew louder. The sound of bracelets falling jangled around the room.

Stuart caught Albert's bracelet in mid-air and snapped it onto him again. The crazy old man looked sadly at it.

"What now?" Patrick asked Lexi.

She frowned. "No day staff have arrived. You should get everyone into the kitchen and dining room and see if you can feed them."

He looked at all the people with their abilities returned. Some were shifting but others weren't. "They'd only not plan to feed us if they thought we wouldn't be here to need feeding."

"That was our thought. Barricade yourselves in." She turned to the satyrs. "Can you go in with them? Look after them?"

Stuart nodded.

When the residents had been herded into the dining room, Lexi, Scott, and Dick continued with their search.

They worked their way around the tower's walls but found nothing.

She wasn't to be deterred. "Okay. Basement."

CHAPTER SEVENTY-FOUR

They trudged down the stairs to the basement, checked all the rooms, and met at the bottom of the stairs again.

"Nothing. What's the point of leaving that tower in the middle of the building?" Lexi turned to the painting. "I don't suppose you'd care to give up your secrets, would you, Mr. Maybury?"

She froze as she remembered something. Her gaze slid to the closet she'd hidden in. "Oh, for God's sake." She went to the door, yanked it open, and found the wooden stick she'd picked up when she had hidden from Nila. Looking around, she found a small slot on the floor beside the wall. She put the stick into the hole, pulled, and looked around inside the closet. "Dammit. It must be something else."

"Er…Lexi." Dick called.

Hastily, she stepped out. The inset wall with the picture had swung upward to reveal a staircase leading down.

The sorcerer shook his head. "I've been all over this place feeling for some kind of magical spell. I can't believe it was a common hidden door."

Lexi moved toward the entrance.

"Wait," Scott whispered.

When she turned, he held her katana out. She took it and nodded.

They entered the old stone tower. The steps opened into a wide empty room, with a curved staircase leading up along the wall. They spread out. Although the space was dark, a flicker of light indicated that the room above was lit with torches. The only other light was from the doorway they had entered through.

Strange markings covered the walls but were most clearly visible where the light from the doorway bounced off the opposite wall. Lexi moved slowly toward it to see if she could work out what the symbols were. As she gazed at the markings, a shadow appeared across them in the shape of a head with antlers.

She spun and swung her katana into Nila's impossibly strong antlers. Vibrations reverberated along the blade to the handle but left not even a dent in her target.

"Good Lord, what a smell." Dick stood to the side and waved his hand in front of his face.

The wendigo turned to him and snarled. Drool dripped from her mouth and her claws dragged loudly along the stone.

"I'm sorry dearest," he continued. "It really would never have worked between us. And the fact that you're a stinking, drooling monster isn't even the number one reason."

Nila howled and stepped toward him. Lexi glanced at the stairs to the next floor but she didn't dare to take her focus off their adversary.

Dick noticed her indecision. "Off you go, you two. I'll keep her busy."

Her screech reverberated in the wide chamber as she attacked with her head lowered. Dick evaded easily at vamp speed and she was infuriated.

A sound from the doorway drew her attention. A pack of wolves, foxes, dogs, and bears crowded into the room. They snapped and snarled at Nila, led by a brown and white Pitbull who jerked her head at Lexi to tell her to move along.

She and Scott headed to the next level as the pack encircled the wendigo.

Ever cautious, she kept her back to the outer wall of the tower as they climbed the stairs into the next room. It was empty except for two shapes on the floor which were clearly bodies. She ran to one. It was Bryan.

Scott crouched beside him and checked his vitals. "He seems perfectly healthy but I don't see any brain function." He put his hand onto the man's head and closed his eyes. "There doesn't seem to be a reason for his condition but it's like his mind is empty."

Lexi approached the second body. It was an old lady who was very much alive but bound and shivering. "Are you Maisie?"

The woman nodded and she untied her. "Scott, blanket and water."

He retrieved both items from his bag and wrapped the blanket around the woman. She gulped the water thirstily.

"Don't leave me."

She put a finger to her lips and looked at Scott.

The sorcerer put a hand on the side of her head. "Sleep." The woman slipped into unconsciousness and he eased her down carefully and covered her.

They returned to Bryan and Lexi looked at him. "Could he have retreated into his dimensional pocket?"

Scott frowned in thought. "I suppose it's possible."

She nodded. "I'm going to see if I can get in there."

He shook his head. "I don't think that's a good idea. You might not be able to get in, and what if you do and can't get out again?"

"I have to try." Lexi put her hand onto Bryan's face, closed her eyes, and imagined where she wanted to be.

Once inside his closet, she stepped to the mirrored door and placed her hand on it. It swung open without a push and she walked to the edge of the platform over the big hall. The entire space was silent and nothing showed on the screens.

"Bryan?" There was no response so she took a deep breath and descended.

She went to the most recent booth and looked at the board with Caleb's name on it. There were no new updates but she touched the screen in the booth and it came to life.

The sorcerer stared out of the screen. "Calm down, Bryan. I won't kill you. Not your body, anyway. When Azatoth possesses Alicia, he will have his powers and he'll have access to her legacy abilities, which now include her sister's. With you alive, he'll also have your magic through the blood match. He will be the most powerful being in existence. I would have liked that to have been me, but it wasn't to be."

Aghast, she watched the scene play out.

Why isn't Bryan fighting this?

"I know," Caleb continued, "you're terrified that you'll be frozen inside your own body forever. But it won't be like that. I wouldn't do that to you. I'm not a monster. You won't be in there. You'll merely be a power source, nothing more."

The man stretched his hand to Bryan and the screen went blank.

Lexi looked around. She knew it was time to leave. He was gone. But still, she wondered why all this was still there if he had been erased.

She walked through the aisles to the black door with *Bad Stuff* written on it, put her hand on it, took a breath, and opened it.

This was a room with a few aisles. She saw pictures of herself from his perspective. One revealed the moment she was dragged away screaming before he was tranquilized and removed from the Braxton family at fifteen.

In the next booth, she found where he and Alicia had argued. He had shifted and clawed her face. She closed her eyes. What a burden to have to live with.

"Hello, Lexi-Loo."

Startled, she spun toward his voice. Bryan sat inside a cell. "Bryan! Did Caleb put you in here?"

He stood and walked to the bars. "No, I did."

Lexi walked closer. This Bryan seemed younger than the body he inhabited. "I don't understand."

"I've been in here since that happened." He indicated the video she'd just watched of when he'd slashed Alicia's face.

Her jaw dropped. "But that must have been five years ago."

"I separated the wolf from the rest of me and left it in here. I'm the part of me that did that. I'm the wolf."

"But you're not a wolf."

"I'm a were, not a shifter. We only change on a full moon, remember? Unless commanded by an alpha, which I don't have."

She was horrified. "You've been trapped inside a cell within your mind for this long?"

Bryan looked at her for a long moment, then lowered his gaze. "She's worth it. I love her and I had to keep her safe."

In that moment, she realized what had seemed wrong with him. He didn't have the warmth or the passion of the Bryan she'd known all those years ago. She had assumed he had grown out of those traits, but the truth was that he'd locked them away.

He looked at her now, his face puzzled. "Why are you here?"

"Caleb has taken Alicia and he's done something to you. You're not responsive. The rest of your awareness… I think it's gone for good."

"There's nothing I can do about that. I felt the other part had gone but being in here, I had no idea what had happened." He shrugged.

Lexi put her hands on the bars. "Your body is lying there. We have to get Alicia back so we need to get you out of here."

"Leave me here. I couldn't bear to hurt you too." He put a hand over hers. "You were my first love, do you know that?"

"Of course I do." She put a hand over his.

Bryan's face showed a whole range of emotions but mostly, he looked wretched. "You have to leave me here."

She yanked her hands away and looked for the door. There wasn't one. "The hell I do. You have to man up and get out of here. This body currently has no one at the wheel. You need to step up."

"But what if I hurt someone?"

"If you do nothing, you'll hurt many more people. Caleb and his demon pal will use your blood match with Alicia to hurt others. As you've already pointed out, you're a were. You change at the full moon and this is not a full moon. Alicia needs your help. You said you loved her. It's time to prove it."

Frustrated, she swung her katana against the cage but nothing happened beyond a loud ringing.

"That's the other problem. I was worried I'd weaken and escape. No known weapon or magic can release me." He shrugged.

"No known magic?" She stared at her katana and watched as the blade transformed to a dark hematite that glittered with flashes of yellow light.

She looked at him.

He stepped back in shock. "Your eyes—"

"Stand farther back. I'm not sure how this will work." She swung the blade at the bars and the cage burst open. In the next moment, she was in the tower with Scott.

Bryan lay motionless for a moment before he shook his head and groaned. He sat and looked at his hands, turning and flexing them in something close to wonder. "I forgot what a real body feels like." He looked at Scott with a puzzled expression, then shook his head as though to slough off a deep sleep. "That's so much to take in at once. Hi, Scott."

Lexi realized he must be receiving five years of updates from his dimensional pocket.

He stood and held a hand out, and an energy ball appeared and disappeared. He looked at her and nodded.

Dick appeared. "It's not going well down there. She's gored a dozen of the shifters." He looked at a gash across his chest that was healing as he spoke. "And me. She gored me and I don't even want to think about what this shirt cost."

Scott turned to him. "I'll come with you. You two keep going." He disappeared.

She didn't like being separated from him but he'd made the call and left. Rather than follow him, she nodded to Dick who disappeared at vamp speed.

Lexi and Bryan moved up to the next level.

Caleb stood with his back to them and Alicia lay on a wooden altar.

From her position on the stairs, she could see that her sister was shiny, no doubt covered in the stinking grease they'd used on the demon. She realized it must be needed for the ritual. What they now tried to do with Alicia, they'd probably already tried and failed with the demon.

The sorcerer was drawing a large rectangle like a doorway on the wall with a lump of brimstone. A squeak drew her attention to a box at his feet. It was Limpet, caged again, and he looked fearfully at her.

She glanced at Bryan, whose gaze was fixed on his wife. Calmly, she put a hand on his arm to get his attention. She signaled that he should get to Alicia and translocate them both away while she would deal with Caleb. He nodded. They stepped into the room and froze.

The man turned. He looked at Bryan, obviously shocked. "Well, I'm not sure how you achieved that, but kudos."

Lexi tried to open her mouth but couldn't manage it. A slight swivel of her eyes was all she could do.

"I'm afraid you've stumbled into my little safe space." He looked at Bryan. "You can't access your magic." His gaze shifted to her. "Or move. I certainly learned my lesson after our last encounter, although I understand you're not quite as formidable as you once were."

She tried to access her magic but found nothing.

Caleb finished drawing his portal and turned to her. "Are you surprised that I considered you a formidable opponent? I know you thought yourself defective, but you have a keen mind and excellent skills. Many of your contemporaries are lazy. They rely on the legacy enhancements or the magic from their mage. But you, Miss Braxton, are the product of your own will and determination. You've been mentioned in the council several times over the years."

There was a tiny part of her that couldn't stop herself from feeling proud. Her pride annoyed her, though.

"I wanted to experiment with the two of you," their adversary continued, "but your mother would never allow it."

Had Lexi not already been frozen, his casual mention of her mother would have chilled her to the bone. She wanted to rip the truth from him, but all she could do was listen.

"I wonder if it would have made any difference had you gained all the legacy abilities and become Azatoth's host. Well, it's too late to change plans at this late stage. Your sister is ready."

Caleb walked to the woman who lay unconscious on the altar. He picked a knife up and held it over her. "I'm afraid all you've been able to achieve is a ringside seat. Still, I'm sure it'll be quite a show." He cut Alicia's arm and allowed her blood to run into a bowl.

Lexi's eyes couldn't even widen.

Carefully, he ran a finger over the cut and healed it. "I mustn't damage the goods." He placed her arm down and stood staring at her. After a long moment, he reached a finger to her face and brushed it softly across her lips. Looking at Lexi, he smiled and licked his lips.

She wondered what would happen if she vomited in this paralyzed state.

He walked to the wall, dipped his fingers into the bowl, and drew an intricate design on the wall in the blood. That done, he crouched beside the box at his feet, unlatched it, and took Limpet out. "Azatoth is ready now." He looked at Lexi again. "This is all your fault, you know. If you hadn't interfered with him coming through the true portal in his own body, we wouldn't have to thin the veil and allow his essence to assume control of poor Alicia. It is such a shame. And if you'd stayed away from Alicia, you wouldn't have made her a viable host for him. You did that. I suppose we should thank you. I'm sure Azatoth will find a way. He is so creative."

A guttural scream issued from a lower level of the tower and Caleb sighed. "Poor Nila. She was very loyal. Azatoth liked her. He'll be vexed."

Scott and Dick appeared beside her and were instantly frozen.

"Ah, if it isn't my old friend William Levin. I do hope we have some time to chat later. I appear to be unable to find Betsy and Todd. I think you might be able to help with that." The evil sorcerer turned and tightened his grasp on Limpet. The little demon howled but he held the creature against the wall, which began to undulate.

Lexi stared helplessly as the barrier began to fade when the veil thinned.

The shape of a huge creature became visible. It wasn't as clear as the portal in Palm Springs but she could see Azatoth's outline.

Terror crept into her frozen bones. She was aware that Alicia stirred. This monster would kill them all, probably in the body of her sister, and she was powerless to prevent it.

Limpet struggled in his captor's hand. He freed an arm, plunged it into the wall, and almost made a tiny hole in the veil.

Caleb tightened his grip. "You're going nowhere."

The little demon relaxed in his hand as the veil thinned. Lexi noticed that Limpet pushed his arm slowly deeper into the wall.

She knew the exact moment when the veil was breached, even though the hole was no thicker than Limpet's skinny little arm. She felt the source of her power as it flooded the room and crept into her body, infused her bones, and released her from the paralysis. Her brimstone ring began to glow, and her unhealing scar tickled as energy surged through it. She closed her eyes and when she opened them again, they were black.

Caleb's gaze remained fixed on the Azatoth's silhouette, which became slightly more defined as the veil continued to thin.

Lexi turned to Scott as she moved silently past him. She allowed herself a tiny smile at Dick.

Her adversary must have sensed when she was directly behind him. He spun with a look of shock on his face. "How—"

He began to bring his arm away from the wall but she twisted it back so violently, a bone in his arm snapped. He screamed and fell to his knees. She put her hand onto Limpet to ensure that the wall remained in a state of flux. When she kicked Caleb in the temple, he went out like a light. Azatoth moved closer to the veil. His great arms came up and pounded against it.

She dropped her katana and it stuck into the floorboard and wobbled at her side. Her expression grim, she turned to the massive demon, made a fist, and punched her arm through the veil. It was like driving a blow through ballistics gel. She struck his rib cage and when her fist breached it, she grasped his heart and ripped it from his chest.

The faded figure of the large demon crumpled. Lexi yanked her arm away. Her hand was covered in dark-red, almost black blood. She crushed the heart and dropped the sticky mess onto the floor. Limpet withdrew from the wall and she allowed him to run up her arm and scamper to the floor.

When she turned, the others were still frozen.

Caleb began to stir. He opened his eyes and squinted as she retrieved her katana.

He cradled his broken arm and touched his head. "He's gone. He's finally gone." He was sobbing. "You've freed me. Thank you."

Lexi stared at him, unmoved. "You're welcome."

"He's been controlling me." The man looked down and flinched when Limpet jumped onto his knee and scuttled up his arm and onto his shoulder. He turned to her. "All these years, I thought there was no escape." He clutched his arm and winced.

She raised an eyebrow. "I know you've already healed it."

He paused and seemed to weigh his options. "Ah! I see. Then you should probably look at your friends. I can squeeze the life out of them from here so you might want to say goodbye."

While he spoke, Limpet sat on his shoulders. He dropped his head back to allow it to grow and his mouth to widen.

"Who would you like me to kill first? Your sister? You don't even know her. Or William—he's had a hundred years already. I could get rid of Scott for you and you could be with Bryan like you were always meant to be."

Limpet brought his head forward at incredible speed, and the sorcerer's entire skull was engulfed by his mouth. One loud crunch later, the headless body sagged and remained unmoving.

When Caleb's hold over the others broke, Bryan rushed to Alicia, Scott ran to Lexi's side, and Dick simply stood and stared at Lexi while he pointed at Limpet. "I told you. I fucking told you."

EPILOGUE

Lexi crept through the darkened hallway and tiptoed past ladders and dust sheets. The smell of fresh paint was evident but it wasn't unpleasant. Silently, she opened the door and approached the bed. She extended her hand tentatively to touch the sleeper's shoulder but the woman's eyes jerked open and looked directly at her.

"How are we doing?" she whispered

Anne Lown pushed her covers aside to reveal that she was fully dressed. She gave her a thumbs-up. "On track."

She helped the old lady out of bed. The woman retrieved her purse and walked past her wheelchair. She hadn't needed it since Scott had given her a full physio session.

Quickly, she headed into the room opposite hers and Lexi went to Phyllis' room. The door opened as she approached it and Phyllis walked out with Patrick behind her.

"Phyllis!" She smirked. "I'm sure that's against the rules."

"A little anarchy never hurt anyone." The old woman winked, and Patrick blushed.

"What's going on?" A loud voice made her jump.

Lexi turned as Stuart walked toward her on his goat legs. His eyes were so wide they looked like Limpet's.

He's baked again.

"This is a break-out," she explained,

His jaw dropped. "But you can't. I'll have to call Erika."

After the former physio had recently come into some money, she bought Emmersley for a steal at two million dollars and was putting additional funds into smartening it up.

She smirked. "Yes, you should do that. I think she should know that you three are getting high in the greenhouse every night."

Stuart froze. His gaze darted around for a few seconds. "You're bringing everyone back though, right?"

"Sure. We're only taking them for a night out."

He chewed his lip. "Where are you all going?"

"Vegas."

His face brightened. "Oh, wow! Can I come?"

An object hurtled seemingly out of nowhere and caught him between the eyes. It burst and he fell and immediately started snoring.

Lexi turned to the ladies, who had all exited their rooms and were waiting, dressed and ready for their adventure. "Who was that?"

"Sorry," said a little voice from the back of the hallway.

She grinned. "Nice shot. I need to check on the guys." She translocated and appeared next to Scott.

He jumped. "Jesus, can you not do that? Announce yourself."

Her chuckle drew one in response. She looked along the hallway filled with elderly men and turned to him. "Good to go?"

A grumpy voice down the hall shouted, "Just hurry up. I need to pee."

Scott's cell appeared in his hand and he sent a text.

The fae door appeared and Dolores walked through.

"Are you sure this will work?" Lexi whispered.

Her boss opened her hand to reveal the talisman." This will get us into Vegas but the wards are up again. Dick's rented a bus to take us out of town for the journey back." She turned to the men. "Okay, let's move."

As they filed through the fae door, Lexi vanished and returned to the ladies. "All right, girls, our ride's coming."

Dolores appeared with the door and the women chattered excitedly as they walked through.

Lexi looked at Stuart who was still asleep on the floor but now, he was covered in grass and daisies. It was very pretty. She and Dolores walked through the portal to New York, New York in Las Vegas. The vampire and Marcel waited for them beside Albin. Dick cut his gaze to the historian and back to her and wiggled his eyebrows. He looked like the cat that got the cream.

"Where's Scott?" she asked.

He glanced around. "I don't know. He came through. I saw him."

She wandered around the casino floor for a while and smiled at Albert, who had filled his pockets with quarters. "Keep your pants on, Albert, or you'll lose your money."

When she couldn't locate her friend visually, she took her silver teardrop pendant out and held it tightly in her hand. "Come on, where is he?"

Its gentle pull guided her through the building and the Big Apple Arcade to where Scott waited in a line for the rollercoaster.

He grinned. "Great! Are you all coming on?"

Lexi turned. She seemed to have unwittingly led the whole group to the arcade. "Not me." She held her hands up. "Maybe later." She pulled her cell out and sent a text.

Phyllis, Anne, and Patrick joined the line behind him while the others crowded around the arcade games.

When his turn finally came, Scott scrambled excitedly into the car and secured himself. He seemed barely able to move an inch.

Anne Lown, seated beside him, frowned. "I'm sorry. This will end badly for you."

Patrick turned in the seat in front. "Don't be such a Debbie Downer." He was spun and wrenched into his seat by a young woman who secured him. "I'm beginning to regret this myself."

"Don't be scared, Patrick. I'll protect you." Phyllis squeezed his knee.

A whistle blew and Lexi chuckled at the barrier as they all flinched visibly at the sound. The car jerked to a start on the roller coaster and the moment was forgotten. Scott's dimple-popping grin appeared. *He still looks like a twelve-year-old.* She smiled.

She sensed rather than saw the woman approach.

Alicia leaned on the barrier next to her. "Bryan will be disappointed to have missed this."

"Oh?" She raised an eyebrow. "Where is he?"

"It's the first night of the full moon. He's in the bayou with Geraldine's pack. They're looking after him as he hasn't physically shifted for five years."

She looked at her sister's face. "You've hidden your scars."

Alicia touched her cheek. "They're gone now. I let him take them away."

Lexi pushed away from the barrier "Why did you wait so long to do that?"

"I was punishing him." The woman shrugged.

She raised an eyebrow. "For five years?"

"I was angry."

"For five years?" She raised both eyebrows.

Alicia laughed, then frowned. "I could feel his emotions through the link. He didn't seem bothered by what he'd done. I could have forgiven him for doing it but not for not caring. Of course, I know now that he'd imprisoned the wolf and his emotions along with it."

Lexi nodded. "How are you coping with the enhanced legacy abilities?"

"I feel fine now. Everything seems to have settled, but that's why I wanted to see you. If you want to try to take some of it back, you're welcome to." She held her hand out.

"I don't need to." She shook her head firmly. "I'm dealing with more than enough right now learning how to use and control this new ability."

Alicia bit her lip, then took a deep breath. "I'd feel happier if you tried. You're my sister and I want to know if it's safe to hug you."

She nodded, held her hand above her companion's, then lowered it and took her sister's hand. They looked pensively into each other's eyes.

"Anything?" Lexi asked.

Her twin drew the corners of her mouth down and shook her head. "Nope, you?"

With a small smile, she shook her head. "Not a thing."

Alicia laughed. "I guess that's it, then. You have what you were supposed to have, and I have what I was supposed to have." She narrowed her eyes. "It's so weird sensing the dark sorcery within you. It's similar to sensing a demon but not quite. I've never known anything like it."

"None of us have. Scott says there hasn't been a dark sorcerer for hundreds of years."

The woman slowly twirled a display carousel of Las Vegas magnets and keyrings. "Do you think you'll come back? To Kindred?"

She shook her head. "I don't think so. I still have too many unanswered questions."

"Bryan told me about the little boy, the sorcerer who was placed with your family."

Lexi sighed. She turned and they looked at the rollercoaster. "There's that, but there are other things. Someone's been taking the wards down here in Vegas to commit crimes. Dolores says they're kept in place by joint spells between Kindred and the Fae Elders. Neither one can bring them down without the knowledge and support of the other. I guess it could have been Caleb's doing as head of the council, but he performed forbidden magic in a cabal of thirteen. That could have been the Kindred council themselves."

Alicia shrugged. "The Kindred council has denied any knowledge of his activities. They couldn't distance themselves from Emmersley fast enough. And they've started an investigation into some of the aliases he used. How will you know what's going on in Kindred if you avoid us?"

"And finally, there's our parents—our real parents." Lexi turned to her sister. "I want to know who they were or are. Do you know anything about them?"

"My earliest memories are of New Orleans. I don't remember having any other parents. I've been in Bryan's dimensional pocket.

That's something else. He's shown me how to protect and conceal my memories."

Lexi felt embarrassed, knowing there were memories of her in there. She wondered if Alicia would have seen the memories she had seen, the posters and the books, but decided she wouldn't ask. It wasn't her business what he shared with his wife.

"Thank you for what you did for us. You saved our lives. So, I'll give you that hug now. I'm merely a Kindred-legacy-killing-machine sharing a hug with her ex-Kindred-legacy-killing-machine-turned-dark-sorcerer sister. There's nothing weird about that."

Her laugh was spontaneous. "When you put it like that, it all seems perfectly normal."

They hugged and while it did feel weird, it was a good weird.

When they drew apart, they stood side by side while she searched the screens for Scott's face on the roller coaster. As her eyes searched each frame, she continued the conversation. "I'm in touch with my unit now. They tell me Warren, Scott's rejected blood match, is still harassing them. He tried to force them to submit to Eric for a memory extraction so he could find out what they know. He seems to have found a soulmate in Eric and he's moved to Colorado to join his unit."

Alicia's jaw dropped. "I hope the council said no to that request."

"For now. But Caleb's gone and Eric's ambitious. There's an opening on the council and apparently, he's trying to slide into it."

Lexi smiled as her eyes found a hilarious photograph of Scott. *There he is.*

She stepped up to the counter and paid for the picture.

The door opened and he walked through, dripping wet and covered in a pink substance from his neck to his shoes. "Who takes a milkshake onto a rollercoaster? Seriously, who? And why does this always happen to me?"

Anne walked past. "I tried to warn you."

Lexi and Alicia laughed.

Dick and Albin walked Marcel along Las Vegas Boulevard. They watched the fountains at the Bellagio for a while, then continued to walk until they turned off the Strip to walk the few blocks to the condo.

The historian smiled. "So you're going to be staying for a while."

"Kindred will be all over Palm Springs for some time. I think it's best I stay out of the way. And I have the place here so why not?"

"Why not indeed."

"I won't be here all the time," he continued. "We'll still go wherever the work takes us, but it'll be nice to have a base here."

They stepped aside to allow a group of young men walking a rottweiler to pass.

One of them pointed at Marcel and laughed. "Titus could eat that little rat. Couldn't you, Titus?"

His friends began to mutter encouragement. "Sic him."

Albin raised an eyebrow. "I wouldn't threaten Marcel in front of him."

They looked at Dick. "What will you do about it?"

The vampire smoothed an eyebrow. "He's not talking about me. He means *him*."

A black cat with impossibly large, amber, saucer-like eyes slunk out from the shadows and meowed. Its mouth seemed disquietingly wide with teeth that looked much too long. It strode forward in a not very cat-like fashion, stood between Marcel and Titus, and hissed. The large dog squealed and bolted down the street, dragging his owner behind him. The others followed.

Dick grinned. "Good boy, Limpet. Who's going to get a nice raw steak?"

<hr>

The next morning, Lexi and Scott sat outside their condo. She gazed, mesmerized, into the sparkling depths of her unhealing scar. When she felt him looking at her, she glanced at him and smiled.

"Do you still need me as a partner?" he asked,

She had guessed the question would come. "Do you still need me? I don't know if I'm even a legacy anymore. Aren't I a sorcerer now?"

He shrugged. "If your sorcerer abilities did come through the legacy bloodline, then you're a legacy who favors that ability."

"But I thought sorcery wasn't genetic." She took a sip of her coffee.

"So did I. Maybe dark sorcery is different."

"Maybe I should go back to Kindred and train to be a mage."

Scott frowned. "I've thought about that."

"I was kidding."

"No, not about going back to Kindred. I've thought about what might happen if they find out what you are. I've read the history books. I don't think the dark sorcerers died off. They were killed off."

"Are you saying I'll have a price on my head?"

He shrugged and looked away, his expression uncertain. "Where does this leave us?

Lexi turned toward him. "I don't know whether we're still matched or not, but unless you have somewhere else you need to be, I hope you won't leave. I mean…I understand if you've decided—"

"No, I haven't. I want us to keep working together. You need to learn how to use your magic now." Scott dug in his bag and retrieved her pendant.

She narrowed her eyes. "How do you always get that back?"

He held the silver teardrop in his hand.

"Are you going to make me jewelry again? I'll be honest, I don't mind when you do that."

"I'm not. We are."

After a moment, she opened her hand and he dropped the teardrop into her palm. He held his hand over hers and closed his eyes. She felt his intention immediately. Her eyes snapped open. "Is our link back?"

Scott turned his mouth down. "No, this is how I learned to do some of my spells. A teacher and pupil aren't matched but there is a connection, a flow of understanding between them.

Lexi grinned. She'd missed her connection with Scott and this alternative might be enough. Pleased, she closed her eyes again. He showed her how to change the form of the metal and she decided on a shape. Her palm tickled as the metal shifted within it. He removed his hand and she looked at the metal that had darkened again to look like a shiny, dark metal oval-shaped hoop.

He picked it up. "Nice work." He stepped behind her and clicked the clasp closed.

Dick walked outside to where they sat drinking coffee.

"Good morning," he said cheerfully and sat.

She took a sip of coffee then turned her face to him. "We know. Thin walls remember?"

"Oops." Albin stepped out and stood behind the chair. He kissed the vampire on top of his head and sat beside him. "Did your friends get home safely?"

Scott nodded. "All present and correct."

Dick picked an envelope up and turned it in his hands. "This looks interesting."

Lexi slid her gaze to the side and smirked.

He opened the large envelope with *Dick* written on the front and pulled out a sheet of paper and a smaller envelope. "Oh, it's from Dolores." He unfolded the sheet and read the short note.

"Dear Dick, please find enclosed your new ID and associated documents." He looked at Albin. "How odd. I haven't decided on a new name yet." He looked at the note and continued. "The documents contain your new name as chosen by *Lexi*." He stared at her with a look of pure horror on his face. "Oh, dear God, not again. What now?"

Scott looked at her. "You didn't."

Her lip twitched.

The vampire tore the smaller envelope and retrieved the passport. "Dick Erwin." He looked at her. "I don't get it." He tried it slowly "Dick-Er-win." Then, still puzzled, he tried it fast. "Dickerwin."

Albin picked the new driving license up. "I think that's a German name."

Dick grabbed his cell phone and began to type furiously, then read out loud, "Eric, Ernst...here we are, Erwin in German means..." He looked at Lexi, who studied her nails.

Scott leaned forward. "Well?"

He swallowed. "Erwin…honored or trusted friend."

The sorcerer blew a sharp breath of relief. He looked at him. "Are you crying?"

"No. I'm allergic to…to… Oh, come here." The vampire hauled her out of her seat and hugged her.

She patted his back. "Stop that. You'll ruin my reputation as a kickass dark sorcerer."

THE FUGITIVE LEGACY

Sign up for E.G. Bateman's email list and receive your free copy of *The Fugitive Legacy*, the exciting prequel to the Legacy of the Shadow's Blood series.

With faulty powers and a vampire attack, can Lexi do what's right?

Lexi has worked extra hard to compensate for her faulty paranormal abilities and prove she deserves her place among the supernatural protectors, Kindred.

The aftermath of a vampire attack leaves her questioning her loyalties.

Can she hide her secret? Or will she be forced to flee from the only family she has ever known?

But Kindred don't just let you leave...

<u>Get your free copy here.</u>

Once upon a time, I went to Bali. And that's where my life began.

There were many reasons to go; the awesome people, the incredible conference sessions, and *holy shit, it's Bali!* But I went there with a ridiculous, overly ambitious, presumptive goal. And the day I pushed a few chapters of a manuscript into Michael Anderle's hand, that goal was achieved. It could have gone horribly wrong. I knew he didn't usually accept unsolicited manuscripts at big conferences like Vegas, but Bali was an intimate gathering. I hoped the fact I'd thrown my life savings into an event that had been designed for authors who were *way* more successful than I was, would show I was serious. It was a massive gamble.

The whole experience was mortifying. After a conference session, I found him and Ell Leigh Clarke talking. I stood there with the chapters shaking a little in my hand. People were filing out of the room and I kind of assumed these two would stop talking and move like everyone else. Nope. Pretty soon, there were three people in the room. Two of them were (it was now abundantly clear) having a MEETING, and me. I stood 2ft away, watching like it was Centre Court at Wimbledon. Then, just when I thought it couldn't get any worse, they started ranting at each other.

Oh, dear God. They're having an argument.

I know what you're thinking. *Elaine, why didn't you just turn and leave?* I know, I was being all kinds of rude. But there comes a point when turning and walking away (through the large, echoing room) looks as weird as staying put. Also, I might never get the nerve to do it again. Also, I don't think my feet would move.

So, there I stood, thinking, *come on Michael, just flick your eyes in my direction and I'll shove these pages at you and run.*

Nope!

After I finally realized that ranting, wailing and gesticulating wildly was in fact their preferred method of communication, the meeting was over and Michael addressed the elephant in the room, me. I was surprised he didn't call me out for being so rude. But he was very kind, he took the sheets, and I bolted.

I was mortified by the barefaced cheek I'd shown. For the next day or so, I actively *hid* from Michael, to the point that I actually waded, fully clothed through the swimming pool to avoid passing him on a walkway. Okay, the water was only up to my knees, but still. Then, I got a grip of myself. I knew he wasn't going to read it until after Bali, so I stopped hiding and enjoyed the conference, the socializing, and the sun.

After two weeks of fearing I'd just blown the bank on a pipe dream, I got the call.

Forming the characters and bouncing dialogue around with Michael has been a hoot. I fell in love with Lexi the moment I visualised her clinically decapitating a vampire with her thighs (*sorry, Dick*). I love them all, and hope that you will come to love them too.

Elaine.

AUTHOR NOTES - MICHAEL ANDERLE

APRIL 13, 2020

THANK YOU for reading our story!

We have a few of these planned, but we don't know if we should continue writing and publishing without your input.

Options include leaving a review, reaching out on Facebook to let us know, and smoke signals.

Frankly, smoke signals might get misconstrued as low-hanging clouds, so you might want to nix that idea...

SERIOUSLY?

I don't remember the part of Elaine's story in Bali nearly like she did. Also, I thought I DID read what you gave me to read (your other story) while in Bali, and you were right.

I read it because you spent that much effort to get the stuff into my hands.

I don't do Vegas like that because it is MEANT to be an all-inclusive event that just about anyone can get to (or as close as we can make it.)

So, feeling a bit of guilt that she did all she could to make her dream happen, of course I would read it.

And yes, Ellie and I argue like that because we are friends and she has problems. I'm the normal one, *I promise.*

Me normal, her not. Not her, me.

Her problems start and end with "she's British," and there are a whole lot of funny other reasons in the middle of that British sandwich explanation.

But, this isn't about ELC. This is about Elaine.

One thing that hit me in the gut with Elaine was her super funny dialogue. Her challenge was fitting that dialogue into a story.

Bali was something like January 4th, 2019.

Elaine and I started discussing a collaboration and just having conversations on writing in general on January 16th, 2019. (I had stayed over on that side of the world for extra days. I don't think we hit the shores of the US again until about the very end of January.)

Then, Elaine went "all-in" and took time off work to finish her trilogy. I warned her that writing as your only occupation is very hard for those not accustomed to having no rules.

Elaine didn't believe me.

Here are a few snippets from our conversations. Note the dates.

February 4th, 2019

> **Elaine** 10:55 AM
> Cool, me too. Maybe catch up there. (*London Book Fair – Mike.*)
> 10:59
> You were dead right about people not working not being efficient writers. I'm on kind of a sabbatical. Today was the first writing day. Anyhoo, turns out The Marvelous Mrs. Maisel is really good.
> **michael** 1:37 PM
> HAHAHAHAHAH

February 5th, 2019

> **Elaine** 6:17 PM
> No Netflix today. Netflix is the work of Satan.
> **michael** 11:53 PM
> Yeah, better figure this stuff out!

February 6th, 2019

Elaine 4:12 AM

You're not wrong! Yesterday went better without the Netflix! I've been in organizing mode. I've finally listed out my characters (which I should have done from the beginning) and found a couple I'd forgotten that I can add to the current book. I'm surprised by how many I've killed. It's like SIMS all over again.

Thanks to the advice of Grace Snoke I've now got a wiki to list the characters for the readers (and me!). I'm glad I've taken the time to work on this.

This series has plot twists so I don't want to disappoint the readers who will be expecting to be surprised in the last book. But while books with twists are great to read, they're a time-consuming pain in the arse to write.

michael 8:41 AM

THIS !! >>>> "But while books with twists are great to read, they're a time-consuming, pain in the arse to write."

Pain or not, Elaine worked hard, and I hope you enjoyed the fruits of her talent & labor!

Remind me next time to plug in the parts that started THIS book. ;-)

Mike's Diary: "Sometimes life just *is*."

So, my company is testing new software to allow us a virtual experience while we work. As of now (4/13/2020), it is performing better than I could have hoped in bringing those who collaborate with LMBPN together, no matter the location or time of day (or night.)

This same software, I hope, will allow us to create virtual meetings with fans, and (I'm trying, but I'm not sure the company behind the software will make it affordable) I want to create a place for fans to get together and create all sorts of fun stuff with LMBPN.

And frankly just have a place to hang a while.

If you would like to know more (and are on Facebook) join us on the Kurtherian Gambit Facebook Group For Fans and Authors

Link: https://www.facebook.com/profile.php?id=127989844503323&ref=br_rs

I hope to have something up to start testing this in the next week or two. We will start with small groups, and possibly move up from there.

Clean is the New Dream

My office isn't messy… exactly. It is lived-in *chic*.

Honestly, a whole *lot* of the lived-in part. (If you add chic to the end of any descriptor, you immediately sound artsy. No, really, try it.

"That's ugly."

"No, that's ugly-*chic*."

"That man-cave crap has got to go."

"No, that's man-cave *chic*. It stays."

"That's hideous."

"No, that's hideous—"

"If you end that with 'chic,' I will shove my cottony house slippers so far up your ass you will be burping tiny clouds."

"Right. So, what now? I lost my train of thought with that visual."

(You thought 'Hideous *chic*, and that would have worked, #AmIRight?)

I will have to take another set of boxes to the storage room tomorrow after our meetings, and maybe then I'll have a bit of "clean" in my office. Judith cleaned the living room and Kitchen (both places she works from) yesterday, and believe it or not, I am a bit #Jealous of her clean areas.

(Don't worry, I'm having trouble believing it too.)

I'm So Going to Regret This.

So, I have the new 2020 iPad (#SupportApple and #ItsGoodTo-HaveAppleEmployeesWithDiscountsAsFriends along with #Support-FriendsByBuyingApple), but I don't like using it just as it is.

I want either a Smart Keyboard Folio or the new More Magic Keyboard for the iPad, or maybe something clamshell (but won't that effectively make it a Mac?).

Have I mentioned I'm seriously impatient? I work six often seven days a week (#ThankGodILoveWhatIDo), and when it comes to my technology, I splurge on myself. It's the one thing I can point to my wife and say 'it's a write-off' and 'Don't harsh my (writing) buzz, woman.'

(Actually, only one of those responses works on Judith. #ThankGodAppleDoesn'tRefreshOften and #IReallyDoWait2YearsBetweeniPhonesNow.)

I swear Apple better not upgrade their keyboard on the larger MacBooks in 2021, or I might have to try therapy to hold-back on an upgrade (yes, I have the 2016 MacBook 16".) If therapy is more expensive than my purchase, doesn't that make it smarter just to purchase the product?

I think it does.

Are you paying attention, Steve? (#StephenCampbellNeedsaNewMacbook13Pro)

Anyway. My iPad is sitting in its box unopened because I don't have a keyboard for it. I can't get the Magic Keyboard until May at this point, or maybe later. Since I suffer from #ImpatienceIsAThing, I am looking to see if anything cool is out for my iPad that includes a touchpad for mousing around.

You know, if—and this is for the benefit of my fans who might wish to know—I buy a clamshell with touchpad and report that information back here in a future *Author Note*, that's research and something I can write off on taxes, right?

So, I might sacrifice a larger credit card bill on the altar of #DoingItForTheFans.

If you happen to write a review for any of our books, maybe drop a line in the review "I Support Mike and his Magic Keyboard!" (Or, if you hate Apple products, feel free to suggest I buy other technology. Especially really *REALLY* expensive hardware that I can point to and show my wife how frugal' I was with the purchases I have already made or might <snicker> make soon.

Ad Aeternitatem,

Michael Anderle

CONNECT WITH THE AUTHORS

Connect with E.G. Bateman

Website: www.egbatemanwrites.com

Facebook: https://www.facebook.com/egbatemanwrites/

Instagram: https://www.instagram.com/egbatemanwrites/

Twitter: https://twitter.com/EGBateman

Sign up for E.G. Bateman's newsletter and receive The Fugitive Legacy!

Connect with Michael Anderle

Website: http://www.lmbpn.com

Email List: http://lmbpn.com/email/

Facebook
https://www.facebook.com/LMBPNPublishing/